BEND WITH THE WIND

PETER RIMMER

ABOUT PETER RIMMER

Peter Rimmer was born in London, England, and grew up in the south of the city where he went to school. After the Second World War, and aged 18, he joined the Royal Air Force, reaching the rank of Pilot Officer before age 19. At the end of his National Service, he sailed for Africa to grow tobacco in what was then Rhodesia, now Zimbabwe.

The years went by and Peter found himself in Johannesburg where he established an insurance brokering company. Over 2% of the companies listed on the Johannesburg Stock Exchange were clients of Rimmer Associates. He opened branches in the United States of America, Australia and Hong Kong and travelled extensively between them.

Peter now lives a reclusive life on his South African smallholding, writing his books.

For more information:

www.peterrimmer.com
books@peterrimmer.com

ALSO BY PETER RIMMER

"Cry of the Fish Eagle"

"Vultures in the Wind"

"Bend with the Wind"

"Just the Memory of Love"

The Brigandshaw Chronicles

"Echoes from the Past (Book 1)"

"Elephant Walk (Book 2)"

"Mad Dogs and Englishmen (Book 3)"

First published in Great Britain in October 2015 by

KAMBA PUBLISHING, United Kingdom

10 9 8 7 6 5 4 3 2 1

Cover Design *Hakim Julizar*

PROLOGUE

For eight hundred and seventy years the Beaumonts have enjoyed the privileges of wealth and position. The first of the family stormed ashore brandishing a sword and a leather shield with which he protected himself from the arcing flights of English arrows. One knocked off his helmet and as he bent to retrieve it, William, Duke of Normandy, collided with him for a moment in history. While the duke fell ignobly into the surf, the man immediately behind him was shafted by three arrows. So it was that Henri became the duke's talisman.

Henri's share of the spoils of war was six thousand acres of farmland on the banks of the River Mole, a gentle, meandering tributary to the larger Thames. Having seen his dream of conquest become a permanent reality, one of William's last acts as King was to make Henri a knight of his realm, to have for himself and his seed in perpetuity. Henri's life brimmed over with everything a man could wish for including a Saxon wife and seven sons.

In the autumn years of his contentment, Henri built a church from granite blocks which he had had quarried, cut and hauled for him from Box Hill. The Norman church still stands at Ashtead and many a rubbing has been taken from the tomb of Sir Henri and his good wife Clare. It is one of the rare tombs in England where 'Sir Knight' does not wear his helmet.

So THE CENTURIES BEGAN.

THE BEAUMONTS WERE content to be nothing more than farmers and through the centuries kept themselves apart from the intrigues of politics. When their King called for them they went to war and those who returned to the Hall did so rejoicing. And so it was that the Hall took its name. Burnt down twice, sacked by Oliver Cromwell, rebuilt and added to but still a Merry Hall of England.

Generation after generation found a direct male heir to inherit the baronetcy. Mostly it was father to elder son. Sometimes a war killed off the main branch of the family and the title and land passed to a cousin. A family bible kept track of all male members of the family.

THE TWENTIETH CENTURY dawned and found the current baronet astride a splendid thoroughbred he had brought with him from Merry Hall. He was talking to a member of Sir Redvers Buller's staff outside the small Natal town of Ladysmith. One of the few pieces of Boer artillery lobbed a shell in the general direction of the British and blew Sir Philimore Beaumont and his horse to small, fleshy pieces.

The result of this casual shell saw a cousin, Thomas Beaumont, step out of the Colonial Service in India and make his way by boat to Southampton from where he caught a train to Epsom. Sir Philimore's estate manager met the new Sir Thomas at the station and a horse and buggy took them onto Merry Hall.

By the time he arrived at the large, studded, oak-front door of Merry Hall the Beaumont family was down to two thousand acres. Worse, Sir Thomas knew nothing about farming and neither, so it seemed, did the manager. Sir Thomas had an urge to return to the railway station, Southampton and the first boat back to India and his butterfly collection, but a long history cannot be allowed to die on a November afternoon in 1901.

Translated from the Latin, the family motto reads: 'Where there is a will there is a way.'

Sir Thomas set about returning the estate to profitability. He fired the manager and did the work himself. By August of 1914 the situation was well in hand when war broke out in Europe. When it was over Sir Thomas and his four young sons were the only male descendants left of Sir Henri Beaumont. The trenches and Gallipoli had claimed eleven members of the family.

BOOK 1

1

JUNE 1933

On Saturday June 6 1933, Geoffrey Beaumont, the youngest of the four sons, arrived at Merry Hall on a weekend pass from Sandhurst. On the south side of the house, which caught most of the sun, two sets of French windows led onto a wide terrace with a balustrade broken by wide steps leading down to the lawns and rose beds. Then came the tennis court with tall netting at both ends. Under a walnut tree were long tables covered with tablecloths and gleaming silver, and tall, Venetian glasses. Some of the deckchairs were occupied and a mixed four was in progress. A murmur of conversation drifted to Geoffrey but the overplay was the 'thunk' of the tennis ball and occasional shouts of 'well played'. Racket in hand he sauntered down the steps to join the tennis party.

His brother Reggie was on the court partnering a pretty, dark haired girl Geoffrey had not seen before. Reggie was being charming as usual. His eldest brother, Henry, was sprawled in a deckchair talking to his mother and father but there was no sign of Tug. He recognised most of the other faces. One he did not, caught his eye and remembering how Reggie would do it, he made straight for the blonde with a turned up nose and long, surprisingly dark eyelashes.

"IT'S LOVELY to see the young enjoying themselves," said Lady Beaumont.

"Henry seems smitten with the de La Rivière girl," said Sir Thomas. "Who's the one partnering Geoffrey?"

"Georgina."

"Funny name for a girl,"

"Hensbrook only had daughters. Georgina was the last chance."

"I don't like the look of those clouds building up behind the elms."

"Never trust the weather."

"Geoffrey's doing well at Sandhurst."

"Keeps him out of mischief. Has Hensbrook any money?" said Sir Thomas.

"I didn't ask."

"Better tell Henry to marry money. You know those de La Rivière girls are damned pretty. Ah, the match is over. What's for lunch?"

"Salmon."

"Well played you lot. Have a Pimm's Geoffrey, we'll be partners after lunch so don't eat too much."

"DOWN HERE," said Geoffrey to Georgina after the game with his father was over. They had changed after tennis and were strolling away from the house. "It's where I go to read in peace."

"What do you read?" asked Georgina.

"Oh… mostly everything. History. I like to think of the family having been part of it all. And travel. I want to get a posting abroad. I've put my name down for the Singapore garrison. Tug's the same. He chose the Colonial Service. Poor old Henry's going to get bored. He's got to run Merry Hall."

"There are compensations," said Georgina.

"Yes," agreed Geoffrey. "It's beautiful. Not as much as there used to be but then England's shrinking."

"I love the soft smell of a summer's afternoon. We haven't had an estate since before the Boer War. Grandfather gambled it away, or so they say. Sounds better than getting into debt through bad farming. We still have the house."

"Here we are," said Geoffrey. "Come and sit down on the bench. The rhododendrons go back a long way. There's a clearing in the centre. Tug and I, he's the brother nearest my age, built a hut in the glade. Once Tug turned thirteen he was too big to crawl under the bushes. Maybe the next generation will find it. You see that path over there. It leads down to the river. They won't serve supper for a couple of hours. Where do you live?"

"We all live with Grandmother. Father was wounded in the war. Shot across the spine, so Mummy says. I never want to go through a war."

"It was the war to end all wars," said Geoffrey. "My father was lucky. Came through it without a scratch. The swallows are flying high. The weather will be good tomorrow."

"Look," she said. "Primroses. There are more over there."

"We can sit on the log and listen to the river," said Geoffrey taking her by the hand.

ON THE OTHER side of the river, Bert Brigley was looking for two of his cows that had not come in for milking. He had stopped and taken off his well stained cloth-cap to scratch his head when he saw movement and colour and saw them seated on the old willow tree that had done for a seat for more years than he could remember. A straw boater was perched on the back of her blonde hair almost translucent in the dappled sunlight filtering through the willows and a blue and yellow band around her hat tasselled at the back to the nape of her long neck and her shoulders were bare to the summer warmth. A blue dress cascaded around her perch upon the willow tree. 'Young Geoffrey,' he thought. Making no sound, he turned and made his way back the way he had come.

"Young Geoffrey's courting," said Bert ten minutes later stooping to enter the front door of his cottage.

"The older you get the quicker the time goes," said Martha.

"What's for tea?"

"Kippers. Don't know where Lilly is. Ain't seen her all day."

"Growing up, too. When's tea ready?"

"Nearly. Find them cows?"

"Found 'em but left 'em. They was near young Geoffrey and his girl. Right pretty she was. Wouldn't mind if I was thirty years younger."

"Girls like that don't look at Bert Brigley."

"I'm going to tie the climbing roses. Wonder where Lilly got all day? Soon they turn seventeen you don't know where they are. Maybe she's courting."

"You were courting me when I was fifteen."

"That was different," he said, going out.

"Was it Bert Brigley?"

Outside the old cottage he smelt a mix of the grass he'd cut that morning and the honeysuckle from the hedge. Lovingly, he tied back new shoots from the rose bush with raffia string. It didn't need doing but it gave him pleasure. He stood back to view the roses which climbed over half the house and nudged the thick thatch that had been combed and re-thatched so many times it was two feet thick.

"Your garden looks lovely, dad."

"Hello, Terry. I didn't hear you. Betsy, come and talk to your dad. That's what I like about dogs. They can't talk back. Cows milked?"

Terry nodded. "I'm off for my tea," he said.

"Have you seen our Lilly?"

"No."

"Must be courting. Been gone all day."

"Be getting married soon."

"Love to Flo and the kids. Ma and I'll come and see 'em Sunday. How do you like my asters?"

"Beautiful."

"Come here Betsy. We're going rabbiting."

"Look at that tail. That bit of rain didn't come," said Terry.

"They haven't put out supper," said Geoffrey.

"And where have you two been?" said Henry.

"Down to the river. I was showing Georgina the garden."

"I'll bet you were," said Reggie.

"Don't take any notice of them," said Sir Thomas. "Have a Pimm's."

"Pavy will serve supper in an hour," said Lady Beaumont and she took the girl's arm and walked with her through the French windows.

"I'll have a pink gin," said Tug coming out of the house in a blazer and flannels.

"And where the hell have you been all day?" asked Reggie.

"Minding my own business," said Tug. "Sorry about the tennis."

"You look very cheerful," said Sir Thomas. "Help yourself."

"Thanks. Good evening, Geoffrey. How was your day? The river pleasant?"

"Too many prying eyes," said Geoffrey.

"I only asked a question," said Tug.

"Where were you?" said Geoffrey.

"How is Sandhurst treating you?" answered Tug.

"It has a certain moral fibre."

"Here's to everyone," said Reggie lifting his drink. "Charming young lady. Just my type."

"Reggie," said Geoffrey, "she is not your type."

"Any woman," said Tug, "is Reggie's type."

LILLY BRIGLEY SAT on her old horse, Stanchion, the bridle loose over the horse's neck. She was in love. The horse turned its head slowly and blinked at her, all eyelash and brown eyes. A smile spread over Lilly's face with its unflawed skin. In her mind's eye, she saw guests in the old Norman church smiling their goodwill and sharing her happiness.

The summer evening was touched by a gentle breeze that caressed the oak leaves and bore with it a distant laughter from the terrace of Merry Hall. Lilly smiled, brought back to reality.

"Do you want to go home?" she said to the horse. "All those lovely oats and Betsy to keep you company."

They clip-clopped along the bridle path between the hawthorn hedges and old man's beard and the red berries of last year's juniper flowers. Bracken tangled with the hedgerows and a blackbird pecked at a juniper berry, fooled by its redness. A shot rang out and echoed with the evening, wrapping itself around the elms and the oaks. She hummed the opening bars of *Greensleeves*, suiting her mood. A lark trilled from a great height in the sky, almost too small to see.

"Hello, little bird," she called but the blackbird flew away leaving the juniper berry swinging on its stem.

The horse ambled into the farmyard and sent a scurry of chickens and ducks across the cobbles. Lilly dismounted and led Stanchion to his stable. Hobnailed boots echoed on the cobbles.

"Hi, dad. That looks a big one. Where'd you get him?"

"This end of the Thirty Acre. Where've you been all day?"

"With Tug. We followed the Mole for miles."

"You must be hungry."

"Cook made sandwiches."

"I'm sure Doris Breed has better things to do."

"She'll do anything for Tug."

"Too much charm, that one. Nice day for riding. When you've fed Stanchion, come and have your tea. What do you know?" he said, over his shoulder as he reached the cottage, "Terry and me thought you was courting."

"But I was," said Lilly.

"Not with Tug Beaumont, you wasn't."

'Parents,' thought Lilly. She took the horse's saddle inside and hung it on its peg. The horse raised its tail and added to the manure in the farmyard.

"Why do you always wait till we get home?" said Lilly, pouring oats into his trough.

"Your kippers ready, Lil'," called her mother.

"Coming, mum."

"Betsy!" her father said sharply. "Come here. Come here, you damn dog."

The labrador pushed itself over the half door into the yard and loped across towards Lilly.

"Alright, Betsy," she said. "You want a pat? You're slobbering. Behave yourself. How can I get my tea with a dog slobbering all over me? Go and say hello to Stanchion. Didn't dad let you chase enough rabbits?"

"You coming, Lilly?"

"Yes, mum. Call the dog."

"Bert," said Martha as the dog climbed back over the half door. "Why' do you leave the top of the door open?"

"Those kippers look good," said Lilly, coming into the kitchen.

"What do you want?" said Martha, "Toast or bread and butter?"

"Either's as good."

"Make up your mind."

"Bread and butter. Want me to pour the tea?"

"Thanks, luv. Riding with Tug?"

"No good in that," said her father. "Yer ma's family been tenant farmers for hundreds of years. Same as us. Now sit down and eat yer kipper."

"I've known Tug all my life."

"'Bout time you two realised you was grown up. Sit! Damn dog takes no notice of me."

"Yer too soft with him," said Martha. "And don't you get no fancy ideas about Tug, Lilly."

"It's what happens when girls win scholarships to grammar schools," said Bert. "You finish that Higher School Certificate and get yourself a job."

"We've been through that, dad. I'm going to get a scholarship to university. I don't have to be a tenant farmer's wife."

"What's wrong with that?" said her mother.

"Mum, please. What you like, what's a good life for you, may not be what I want out of life. Things are changing. The lower classes are getting a chance. Tug'll be overseas most of his life. We've discussed it."

"We have, have we?" said her father. "You be careful my girl."

"Oh, dad, I love you but don't be so old fashioned."

"Nothing wrong with being old fashioned. Beaumonts and Brigleys don't go together except as squire and tenant. Never have done. You change the order of things and happiness what lasts won't come your way. Listen to your dad. I may not be that educated but I knows a thing or two. Take this depression. Small farmers like us don't worry about such. Grow our own food. Sells a bit to pay the rent to Sir Thomas and that's it. Never had to want here, have you?"

"No, dad. Look. I can see what's good. I'll make a lot of mistakes. There's a big world and I want to see it. All of it. And I want to see it with Tug."

"Eat your kipper, Lilly," said her mother. "Lady Beaumont'll soon put a stop to that little game. More tea, Bert?"

"Thanks, Martha. Can't beat a good cup of tea. Mind if I smoke my pipe?"

"Dad, that stuff smells like burnt tyres," giggled Lilly.

"Shag. Best tobacco I know. Been smoking it all my life."

"Doesn't stop it smelling like burnt tyres," said Martha.

"That's my girl," said Bert contentedly tamping and drawing on his pipe. "Now look at that," he said, looking through the small, leaden window. "Freda and Spot. Typical females. Late for milking."

"Oh, dad."

"You want to milk them for me?"

"After she's had her tea," said Martha.

"You don't think I'm going to let this kipper get cold," said Lilly. "Dad, when are you going to buy mum an electric cooker?"

"What's wrong with the Aga?"

"Too much work, cleaning out the ash."

"How did I get to be living with two women?" said Bert, good naturedly. "Next thing you two'll want to change this scrubbed table for one of those fancy polished ones."

"They mark too easily," said Martha.

"Thank goodness for small mercies," said Bert. "Take that Aga out and this place'll be as cold as charity in winter."

"Then we put in an electric heater," said Lilly.

"Won't heat up the stone floor like the Aga. You'll get chilblains."

"The war's over, dad."

"Yes. Let's hope the Huns keep it that way."

"No one can be stupid enough to start another," said Martha.

"Hope you're right. Human nature likes a fight. Done it all down the centuries. Don't like the sound of this Hitler bloke." He stretched out for the butter. "The likes of us can't change anything."

"Here he comes," said Lilly excitedly jumping up from the table. "Come on, mum. He'll be past. Betsy, get out of the way."

"That boy'll kill himself," said Bert, hurrying out into the yard and craning his neck at the sky.

"There he is," shouted Lilly, over the roar of the Merlin engine.

"He's going to crash," said Martha.

"Flying low on purpose," said Bert.

"He's got Tug in the passenger seat," said Lilly, waving.

"How can you see?"

"Can't. Tug said Reggie'd bring him over the house. Just look at that."

The small biplane with the red nose cone roared away sending Betsy scampering into Stanchion's stable. "He's going to do a loop," shouted Lilly, hands on her hips, eyes burning with excitement.

"His engine's cutting," said Bert.

"Dad," screamed Lilly, gripping her father's arm as the plane finished the loop and wobbled over the trees in silence.

"He's going to crash in the Thirty Acre," said Bert, running out of the yard and down the farm lane. Skirts flying, Lilly overtook him while Martha kept up the rear. The biplane glided over the trees and disappeared.

"Bloody fuel line's blocked," shouted Reggie, pushing up his goggles so he could see better. Turning, he shouted to his brother in the cockpit behind, "Just as well she didn't cut half way up that loop."

"Try starting her," shouted Tug, "You got an air lock when you looped."

"Think so?"

"Shut up and get this thing over those trees."

"Don't call Mathilda a thing."

"You're going to make it."

"Of course I'm going to make it. You don't think I can afford another of these?"

"The Thirty Acre but mind the cows."

"Why does Bert always put his bloody cows where I want to bloody land? Here we go, brother, we'll bounce so hold on."

"You're enjoying this, you bastard."

"Beats playing tennis."

"Get her on the ground, you bloody maniac."

"Woops… woops… it's like a big dipper."

"Mind that cow."

"My pleasure," and Reggie brought the biplane to a stop in front of a spotted brown cow that hadn't stopped chewing.

"You made it, you bloody beauty," shouted Tug climbing out of the cockpit.

"Acting Pilot Officer Beaumont, London Auxiliary Air Squadron, at your service. Look at that for a sight. Lilly, Bert and I do believe it's Martha hauling up the rear."

Tug ran to Lilly, laughing all the way.

"Thank God," said Lilly, clinging to him.

"Why are you trembling?"

'I see,' said Reggie to himself, dark eyebrow raised. 'Young brother has not been wasting his time after all. . . Never thought of Lilly.'

"You two finished your Romeo and Juliet act?" said Reggie as everyone came together around the clinging couple. "Hello, Bert. Martha. Did I give you a fright?"

"Gave yerself one, I'd say," said Bert.

"Fuel pipes," agreed Reggie. "Aviation's in its infancy. I'll fix her tomorrow. Help me push her under that tree. Be alright for the night."

"Given a few others a fright," said Martha, pointing.

"Now there's brotherly love," said Reggie, waving. "That Bentley'll fall apart if he drives it over fields. The only thing that holds it together is the leather strap."

The Bentley stopped under the oak alongside the biplane.

"And he didn't even damage the damn thing," said Henry, surveying the tableau as he climbed out of the passenger seat.

"Missed the trees by a mile," said Reggie.

"You'd better move the twigs from your undercarriage," said Henry.

"Hey, Tug," said Reggie. "Look at that. We hit the top of the tree after all."

"Reggie," said Tug, "they should put you away."

"You wanted to come up for a flip. Wasn't it exciting?"

"Excitement like that, I can do without," said Tug. "I'll walk back to the Hall. I don't think my nerves could take Geoffrey's driving. You want to come for a walk, Lilly? Here, Reggie, put the goggles in the cockpit. Oh, and thanks," he said, shaking hands with his brother. "A bad pilot and we'd have crashed. I'll have to check those fuel pipes."

Lilly, still holding Tug's hand, was led away towards the footpath that wound its way among the oak trees.

"Half an hour, Lilly," called Martha.

"Okay, mum."

"What's going on there?" said Henry, watching his brother and Lilly walk into the woods.

"I don't know," said Bert, standing next to him, "but you'd better have a word with Lady Beaumont."

"Tug's being posted to Kuching. That's in Sarawak. Heard in the club last week. Three-year tour."

"Should be enough," said Bert.

"You think they're serious?"

"Until that forced landing, I didn't know."

"They'll get over it," said Henry. "I'll get the posting brought forward. Come on, Geoffrey. Get Reggie into the dicky seat. You should think of other people before you go off on your hare-brained schemes, Reggie. Mother's in a state."

"It was an accident."

"One of these days… How are the rest of your family, Martha?"

"All well, Mr Henry."

"Keep the cows off Mathilda, Bert," called Reggie from the dicky seat.

"Come on Geoffrey. Home James and don't spare the horses."

The three men waved and Geoffrey took off fast over the tufts and bumps of the Thirty Acre field.

"Calm down, Alice," said Sir Thomas. "We didn't hear a crash or see any smoke. Reggie is a very good pilot. If you worry about the boys every time they climb a tree… Well you should know. The only one who isn't wild is Henry."

"Thomas, you must have a word with Reggie. And Geoffrey. He drives that Bentley too fast. And Tug encourages them."

"Now what did I say. Here comes the Bentley and that's Reggie in the dicky seat. You can tell Pavy to put out the supper. I'll drink a Hock with my lobster."

"Where's Tug?" said Lady Beaumont, when the car stopped.

"Walking," said Reggie, unfolding himself from the dicky seat. "Nerves a bit shot."

"What happened?"

"Don't worry, mother, nothing happened."

"Well, where's your aeroplane?"

"I left her in the Thirty Acre talking to a spotted brown cow of Brigley's. Perfectly safe."

Georgina had made her way to the driver's side, while the others were talking. "How fast can she go?" asked Georgina.

"About eighty-four miles an hour," said Geoffrey, "but that's only when Tug's tuned her properly and there's a lot of straight road. Mostly I run out of straight road."

"Thank goodness you don't do these things," said Isabel, taking Henry's arm.

For the second time that day, Reggie's eyebrow rose a fraction. He went across and kissed his mother on the cheek.

"Reggie," she said, "you're incorrigible but please be careful."

"Yes, mother." He squeezed her shoulder before turning to Geoffrey.

"Put on the gramophone. Let's have some music." He waved to the guests on the terrace. "Everything under control, father?"

"Of course, my boy. Pavy's been circulating with those new-fangled American cocktails. When you driving back to town?"

"After lunch tomorrow. Can't make money without work."

"Never did understand that reinsurance stuff of yours. Seems to make you money."

"Actually, rather a lot," said Reggie, smugly, looking around. "This party's going well. Look at those lobsters. Doris Breed competing with the Café de Paris. I'll go and talk to her," he said, and walked away into the house.

Dusk came slowly. Candles guttered in the Georgian silver candelabra on the supper tables as Tug slipped around the house intending to join the party through the French doors.

"Enjoy your walk?" said Reggie sidling up to him from the kitchen.

Tug gave him a look and then smiled.

"We'll pick up Mathilda in the morning," said Reggie. "Come and have a cocktail. After supper, I've some new ragtime to put on the gramophone. Can't let Merry Hall forget its name… What a beautiful evening!"

They walked back into the party.

"What happened to the little dark one?" asked Tug.

"Plenty of time my boy," said Reggie.

LILLY STOOD UNDER AN OAK TREE, deep in shadow and watched the bright points of the candles and the reflection on silver and glass. The girls, dressed in summer frocks held her attention. Merry Hall, the whole size of it, beckoned to her. She watched the guests sit down to supper and Pavy pouring the wines. She watched the meal and then turned to retrace her steps. The sound of ragtime followed her as she walked deeper into the darkness of the woods.

Before Lilly reached home, the guests were doing the Charleston, knees flapping with the beads from their dresses. Reggie was a little drunk though not as drunk as he pretended to be. Once again he noticed Isabel looking at him with disapproval and gave her a lewd wink which only heightened her disdain. Henry, who was also watching carefully, decided she would make an ideal hostess for Merry Hall. Reggie looked around the party and caught the eye of his earlier tennis partner. A quick penetration of purpose and her eyes dropped to the glass in her hand. She slowly lifted the glass and drank, catching Reggie's eye for the second time.

'Two silent bites,' thought Reggie, and began to make his way purposefully between the dancing couples.

Isabel had caught both exchanges. A mixture of jealousy and frustration made her drink quickly from her own glass which she found to be empty.

Sir Thomas and Alice reclined on a sofa that Henry had brought out for them onto the terrace. Sir Thomas sipped a whisky and soda and felt content with himself. He finished his whisky and put down the glass.

"Better make a move," he said to Alice.

"My eyes are barely open."

"We'll slip away. Can't possibly say goodnight to everyone. Never used to leave a party early. Sign of old age, my dear."

"It does have its compensations. Clever of Henry to put the sofa next to the French doors."

"Very considerate, that boy."

"Your parents give you a lot of freedom," said Georgina as they watched them leave.

"Mother works on the principle that if people are going to misbehave they'll do so anyway. With Reggie around, she prefers not to watch… Would you like a glass of wine?"

"It'll make me tipsy."

"That doesn't matter."

"You'll have to look after me."

Geoffrey poured the glass of wine and turned to the family butler. "Better let the servants go, Pavy. Father's retired for the night."

"Very good, Mr Geoffrey."

"This is a happy house," said Georgina.

"Yes. It always has been."

"Which regiment are they posting you to? Your mother told me you pass-out from Sandhurst next month."

"I've put down for cavalry regiments."

"Do they still ride horses?" she said, laughing.

"No. Tanks. If there's going to be a war, tanks will decide a land battle."

"Do you think there'll be a war?"

"There'll always be a war. The only question is how far apart they're spaced."

"Feel like a nightcap my dear?" said Sir Thomas. "The walk along those old corridors wakes me up. Gives me the creeps, actually."

"Just a small one then," said Alice.

Sir Thomas walked across their bedroom to the mantelpiece where Pavy had left a silver drinks tray. Light reflected from the cut crystal of the water jug. He poured a good shot of whisky into both glasses and splashed soda from the syphon.

"I've been thinking," he said as he handed one of the glasses to his wife. "Chin chin," and touched her glass with his own. "Henry's capable of running the estate on his own. I don't understand some of his scientific methods but they work. Results count. Only damn thing that does in this world. We've come a long way with Merry Hall. Think we deserve a holiday. A long holiday. Always wanted to show you India. Funny thing to collect butterflies. Started at school but some of the best moments of my life were up in the foothills of the Punjab with a big net and a bottle of chloroform. Collectors. We're all collectors of one sort or the other. Henry collects new ideas for the farm. Tug collects paintings when he can afford them and Geoffrey collects every damn book on tank warfare. Anyway, it's India I want to show you before the Germans blow the world up again."

"What does Reggie collect?" asked Alice.

"Women, I suppose. Thinks I don't hear about his escapades. Comes of having too much money too young."

"Made it himself."

"Doesn't change the point. Those three friends led him astray. Never trust a Frenchman or a German. Don't know about the Danes. Here in the club they call themselves the Freebooters. Bunch of pirates except there aren't any pirates. The four of them have more money than sense." He sat down on the window seat. "Glad the party's on the other side. Can't hear a thing. One advantage of a big old house. Holiday, that's what we need. Six months. None of this shilly-shallying. Boat out of Southampton. Take a look at Italy and Capri. Across to Alexandria and then through Egypt overland to Cairo. Take a boat down the Nile and then back into the Holy Land. After that, it's Ceylon and India. Had a letter from Bertie Featherstone. He's now a big wig in the administration. Show us around. If I know Bertie, he'll give us a good time. Weather won't be so hot in the winter."

"You've thought about this Thomas?"

"Booked the passage. Whole damn itinerary. We'll be back in the spring of thirty-four."

Alice smiled and sat down next to him. Her mind toyed with the long journey and finally came back to Merry Hall.

"Henry's serious about Isabel."

"There's a cool one. Not much fire there. Probably suit Henry. Never been one for the girls. Better find out if Hensbrook has any money."

"She is rather cold." Alice looked out of the window. "What a lovely evening. Moons coming up... So much history."

"And if old Henri Beaumont hadn't had his hat knocked off we wouldn't be here. How do you like the sound of our cruise?"

"Wonderful, Thomas. Now pour me another of those small whiskies and I'll sleep right through the night."

"Reggie gave me a fright," said Thomas.

"You weren't concerned at the time."

"Can't show feelings in a crisis. Cheers, again. Good party. Geoffrey's been asked to play for the army at Lord's. Army v Navy. Three-day match. We'll stay at the Savoy."

"Wonderful."

"Scoring a lot of runs for Sandhurst. When does Tug leave?"

"Next week. Henry tells me he's fallen for Lilly Brigley."

"Bert's daughter? She's a tomboy."

"Not anymore. Henry described her as quite something. He made a phone call this afternoon to have Tug's passage brought forward. Three years will change their minds."

"You know how to handle these things, Alice."

"Henry's proposing to Isabel tonight."

"Is he? He's twenty-eight. Good time to get married. About time those boys gave you grandchildren. He'd better have the wedding before we go. You can talk to Hensbrook. Reception at the Hall, of course. Ashtead church. Old Henri must be proud of all his offspring getting married and buried in his church. Tug'll miss the wedding."

"The holiday sounds wonderful. I've always wanted to go to the Holy Land and India."

An owl dropped like a stone from an oak tree deep in the silent wood. The vicious clutch of the outstretched talons killed the field mouse instantly. Ponderously, the owl flapped its way back up to its perch. Round eyed and staring, it checked the silent wood before tearing at the mouse. The fox at the foot of the oak stood motionless. Even the owl hadn't seen him. A dog barked from Merry Hall and the fox crouched in the bracken. After some minutes, when the owl had eaten the mouse, the fox continued his way to the Thirty Acre field and the rabbit warrens behind the haystacks. He was fat for a fox.

Five minutes later, Tug walked under the oak but didn't see the owl whose eyes were shut in the pleasant contentment of digesting the mouse. In the Thirty Acre, the fox killed a buck rabbit. Tug made a lot of noise as he couldn't see the path properly and forced the owl to open his eyes and watch him stumble along in the dark. Tug broke out of the wood and stood for a moment to look at the biplane, nose up, tail down and chunky in the moonlight. Bert's cows were humps under the trees where they crouched, legs tucked under their bellies. The brown spotted cow was still chewing the cud next to the aeroplane. Tug walked out across the field with a spring that belied the flutters in his stomach. He had waited till two in the morning for everyone to be asleep at Merry Hall.

When he reached the last trees before Bert Brigley's cottage, he cupped his hands over his mouth and imitated the sound of an owl. The owl back in the wood wasn't fooled as he'd heard the imitation many times before. On the fifth of the two shorts and a long, who-o-o, who-o-o, the small window in the dormer window hidden by thatch opened wider and Tug's call was answered. He waited ten minutes before Lilly joined him at the edge of the wood. Silently, and hand in hand, they walked across the Thirty Acre, passed the aeroplane and into the wood to sit on the same patch of bracken used by the fox. Only then did they kiss. Slowly and gently at first. Then pushing, thrusting at each other. Tug's hands searched her body. He was almost ready to climax in his pants when she undid his fly buttons and pulled at his underpants. His penis sprang into her hand as with her other hand and the help of her foot, she got off her pants. The whole of her pubic was wet and sticky and she tried to lift up and get his penis into the craving between her legs. "Please, Tug. Please. It's safe. My cycle's just finished. Please give it me."

The owl, being able to see in the dark, watched with a startled expression as Lilly cried out in pain as she lost her virginity. For some time the wood was silent again and then they sat up with their backs to the huge trunk of the oak. The owl craned forward to see what had happened and then lost interest and closed his eyes.

Tug and Lilly, having made love a second time, had dazed off when the owl opened his eyes. He shifted slightly on his perch and stretched his feet in turn. A small sharp movement below showed him the brother of the mouse that was half digested in his stomach. Not being hungry he watched the mouse climb up and around the tall grass and bracken. It was two feet away from Lilly and Tug when it sat up on its haunches. An inherent instinct in the owl made him drop like a stone from his perch and his great wings flashed open and brushed Lilly's bare behind.

Waking to the touch, she looked behind and saw the monster owl, talons stretched and wings flapping for upward movement.

"It's only an owl," said Tug, holding her trembling body. "He's buzzed me a few times before."

"Thought it was the wrath of God," said Lilly.

"Just as well he woke us. My watch says half past three and dawn will be breaking."

"Maybe that owl has a sense of humour," and they began laughing until the tears came to their eyes.

Closer by many years, they walked back arm in arm. The fox was on his way back from the Thirty Acre with the half-eaten rabbit hanging loosely from his mouth. He stopped and watched them for a moment before trotting away into the wood.

"When you come back in three years," said Lilly, "I'll be almost finished with my degree. Lilly Brigley with a cap and gown will look a lot different to your family than Bert Brigley's daughter out of school. I'll make you a better wife. Children learn a lot from their mothers. That's why women's education's important."

"I want you to come with me now," pleaded Tug.

"I must get my degree. Only then will I feel equal to your family. Anyway, dad wouldn't let me go. With you in the Colonial Service, we can't just run away."

"I suppose not."

"Three years, Tug. It'll go in a flash. We have tonight to remember."

"I suppose so," said Tug, miserably.

"Come on. We'd better walk faster. There's a tinge of colour in the sky over there."

REGGIE OPENED the bedroom door and looked to the right and left down the old corridor before walking barefoot back to his own bedroom. The dark haired girl in the bedroom he'd just left heard the door close and began to play with herself until she climaxed for the fourth time that night. Satisfied, she turned over and went to sleep.

Henry Beaumont slept on his back, snoring gently, having fallen asleep the moment his head hit the pillow. Isabel had been another step in his well-ordered life. That and his new idea for racehorses.

Isabel de La Rivière, third daughter of the seventh Baron Hensbrook was unable to sleep. She had accepted Henry's proposal as she knew she would. She was twenty-two and conscious of having reached her peak in looks. Reggie had never shown any interest and if he had she thought it difficult to bring him to a marriage. And Henry was the future baronet and heir to Merry Hall. The only problem was she couldn't imagine making love to him.

Geoffrey woke with the full sun of day on his face. He never drew bedroom curtains. He got up immediately and rummaged for an old pair of grey flannels. With a shirt, white socks and a dirty pair of plimsolls, he was ready for his morning run through the woods. A peacock was screeching from the lawn near the tennis court.

2

JUNE 1936

*T*hree years later, on Thursday June 4 1936, Reggie Beaumont, dressed in a pinstriped suit with a rolled umbrella and black bowler hat, got out of the taxi that had brought him from his flat at 63 Whitehall Court in the West End of London. The pinstripes made him look taller than his five feet eleven inches. He paid the taxi driver and walked confidently into the foyer of the block where he maintained a suite of offices on the second floor. The liftman pulled back the door to the lift cage.

"Morning, Mr Beaumont."

"Morning, Charlie."

"Did you win on the Derby, Sir?"

"Henry's horses never win."

"Made a good start, I believe."

"It's the finish that counts."

The lift rose slowly and rattled to a stop at the second floor.

"Have a good morning."

"Thank you, Charlie. I've a feeling I will." He was expecting his overseas partners. Reggie opened the door marked Beaumont Ltd. His secretary was seated behind a long, mahogany desk.

"Morning, Mr Beaumont."

"Morning, Thelma."

"Monsieur Deauville is sitting in your office. Sitting behind your desk, to be exact."

Reggie opened the door and hung his bowler and umbrella on the hat stand. "François, you're early."

"Reggie, you're late." They both laughed.

"Well, just a few minutes. Gunter and Carl are never on time and I want to talk to you all at the same time."

"What's it about?"

"Money. If we can put this one together, the financial returns are enormous. What would you say to an annual income equal to five percent of the premiums of half the insurance companies in Europe, America and the Far East?"

"I'm listening."

"Let's wait for the others. That damn horse of Henry's didn't even get a place. Lovely day at Epsom. Maybe Henry'll win the Oaks with Lilliput."

"You know, Reggie," said François, getting up from behind the antique desk and looking at the paintings on the wall, "Tug has picked three beautiful Gauguins. How is he enjoying Sarawak?"

"Only time he writes is to send me pictures to store. But you're right. That hobby could make him rich."

"Money is knowledge and dedication."

"He's due back on leave in three months. Have some coffee. Thelma put the coffee over there where we can sit," and indicated the bay window with its leather settee and heavy chairs surrounding a coffee table.

"When do we have time for the pleasures of London?" asked François.

"Not today anyway." Reggie sat on the leather settee and spooned two sugars into his coffee. "How was the boat?"

"Stable for a change. Gunter was on the train from Dover."

"Where's he staying?"

"Savoy, though I didn't see him at breakfast."

"Carl's at Browns. Came over last week. How's the facultative reinsurance business?"

"Good but nothing special. And you?"

"Same. It's getting to bore me."

"Lucrative but repetitive."

Thelma opened the door for Carl Priesler and Gunter von Ribbeck.

"What's it all about, Reggie?" asked Carl, a large, good-looking Dane with a permanent smile.

Thelma couldn't make up her mind which one she preferred. She sighed inwardly and closed the door. Maybe the Frenchman, she thought erotically as she sat at her typewriter.

"Best looking girl in London," said François when the door had closed. "Where do you find them?"

"She is very efficient," said Reggie, leading them back to the bay window with the green foliage of a plane tree outside. "Have some coffee and sit down. Read this summary and then we can talk. I've spent eight months on the project."

Reggie settled back on the settee and watched them read. Gunter read fast and after ten minutes he started again at the beginning. François looked up first and pursed his lips. Carl put a hand inside his shirt and scratched.

"Where do we find an American and a Jap we can trust?" asked Gunter.

"Carl's lived in America. I have someone in Singapore to cover the Far East."

"How can we visit a hundred and sixty-three insurance companies in forty-three cities without the whole world knowing?" asked Carl.

"Speed," said Reggie. "We don't have to tell them what we're calling about till we get there. We are all pilots. We're going to fly. We need eighty insurance company signatures on that treaty. I'm sure of the Royal, the Royal Exchange, the

Guardian and the Alliance. Gunter must bring in the Munich Re, the Gerling Global and the Munster. Carl the Salamanda and the Swiss Re. François knows all the French companies I've listed. On large risks each insurer will then share one eightieth of the premium and risk of the others. The insurance companies will double their profits without spending a cent."

"You estimate the treaty will generate one hundred million pounds of premium in the first year," said François. "At five percent brokerage, that gives us five million pounds. Even split six ways, it's nearly a million pounds each."

"Yes," said Reggie.

"Isn't the treaty open to abuse?" asked François.

"I don't think so," said Reggie. "Companies of that standing don't have to accept bad risks at low rates. We will have created an insurance cartel. Certain known bad risks have been excluded from the treaty and the profit-sharing clause will prevent the underwriting company from playing games. I've had a team of lawyers on the wording. The biggest protection from a rogue underwriter is the cancellation clause. After three years of bad performance the others can take him off the treaty. I want each of you to write a report criticising what I've prepared. Thelma will give you a copy of my full report. I want us to meet here tomorrow at six pm. Tomorrow, I'll take you all out to dinner. Monday we start placing the treaty in Europe. The following Monday, Carl and François are booked on the *Queen Mary* for New York and Gunter and I are going on a charter Sunderland flying boat across the top of Africa to the Far East. I have further planes chartered for us in New York and Singapore. The flight plans are filed in the main report."

"I know just the man in New York," said Carl.

"Good," said Reggie. "Ask Charlie to flag down two taxis," he said to Thelma. "We'll leapfrog companies giving problems. We can go back if necessary. We need a fifty percent acceptance to fill the slip. I'll see you down to the taxis."

Five minutes later, Reggie returned to his office and closed the door. Thoughtfully, he poured himself another cup of coffee and got up to drink it in front of the painting Tug had sent. The South Sea islanders were strange but real. There was a knock at his door.

"Come in."

"Lord Migroyd to see you."

"Is it eleven-thirty already?" said Reggie coming to the door. "Come in, sir. Can we have some fresh coffee, Thelma?"

"Win on the Derby?" asked Migroyd, hanging up his umbrella and bowler. "Lost a few quid myself. Never could work out the horses. Sport of kings. Never treated me like one. How's your father?"

"Well, thank you."

"Doesn't look anything like Philimore."

"They were only cousins."

"Knew Philimore in South Africa."

"I believe so. Come sit down by the window. How are our plans coming along?"

"Your plans," said Migroyd, a florid man in his late sixties. "I just do what you tell me. Not much alternative. If Goldfields take over Union Mining I'm as good as sunk. They'll have me off the chair the next morning. Said as much in their bid. They want to replace all the directors. When are you going to have the money to put in your counter bid?"

Thelma put the fresh pot of coffee on the table.

"Thelma, would you like to pour Lord Migroyd's coffee. Do you like Tug's new paintings?" he said, turning back to Migroyd. "Gauguin. We think they'll be worth a lot of money in a few years' time."

Migroyd's protruding and bloodshot eyes followed Thelma across the room. She smiled at him before closing the door.

"Damn fine girl," said Migroyd.

"Yes, she is rather fine," said Reggie. "Three months to answer your question. But I must have fifty one percent of the shares. I'm looking ahead. A stock market quotation makes a company vulnerable."

"Hensbrook really appreciates your favour. Directors fees from Union are his major income."

"The directors have always paid themselves well."

"We have to watch the business."

"Of course. Have all the directors agreed to the ten-year clause?"

"Had to talk them into it. They're giving up a life income for only ten years. Well, that's how they want to look at it."

"If Goldfields succeed with their proxy fight, that lifelong income will cease. Half a million pounds is better than a slap in the belly with a wet fish."

"Yes, well," and he coughed discreetly. "Beaumont's always had a sense of humour. Goldfields have circulated shareholders with their offer even though the board turned it down. There are thousands of small shareholders and no one controls more than two percent. The small shareholder is loyal to his directors. Now your offer, when we tell them to sell, that'll be different. You're offering cash instead of the Goldfields' share swop. There aren't many people with three million pounds in cash. Amazes me how you made it. Philimore didn't have any money. Damn near broke. But that's your business. When can we announce the offer to the press?"

"You can tell them you've received a cash offer of five pounds ten shillings a share and that the formal offer will be mailed to shareholders."

"What are you going to do with Union?"

"A lot more than Goldfields. The shareholders that don't sell won't be sorry. I'm a builder, not an asset stripper. Union Mining will be my vehicle for straddling the globe. You'll be offered a dozen more directorships."

"Well, I'll be off. Get the press cracking. You think Lilliput will win the Oaks this afternoon?"

"Henry's confident."

"Made a lot of money out of his bloodstock."

"Merry Hall needs plenty of money. I've drafted a press release. Thelma has it on her desk."

"Damn thoughtful, my boy. When will you be in that club again?"

"I'll let you know. Did you enjoy yourself?"

"Best looking girls I've ever seen. Your owner friend will make a lot of money."

"I'm sure he will. Will you excuse me if I don't come down in the lift?"

By the time Reggie sat back at his desk, Migroyd's whole attention was concentrated on Thelma. Reggie smiled to himself and finished his coffee.

"You said you were taking your partners to Bretts tomorrow," said Thelma, coming back into his office.

"Yes, they'll enjoy it."

"I want to go."

"Plenty of competition."

"I can handle it."

"Migroyd's hooked." Reggie got up and looked out at the plane tree. "All we need is that treaty signed and I can borrow the three million pounds."

"And the premature press release?"

"If I haven't got the cash to make an offer then Migroyd's in the crap. But he's in it anyway. Should have been in it years ago. In fifteen years that board of directors have done nothing." The phone rang in the outer office. "That'll be one of the lads with a query," said Reggie.

Thelma picked up the phone, spoke for a moment and put the call through to Reggie. "Yes, Carl?... You're bloody right. Why the hell didn't I think of that?... I'll send Thelma over to type up your clause."

HENRY BEAUMONT ADJUSTED his grey top hat and climbed the inside stairs of the double decker bus he had hired for his racing party. Pavy was discreetly dispensing the food and beverage with the assistance of a valet from Merry Hall. Henry looked at his watch for the umpteenth time in five minutes and felt his stomach sink. He had convinced himself he was going to win the Oaks with Lilliput.

"Better have another glass of champagne," said Geoffrey who had joined him at the front of the top decker. Geoffrey was in civvies and had grown a semi-blond moustache to go with his military career. Behind him, Georgina smiled encouragement at her brother-in-law. She was a little uncomfortable in the sixth month of her third pregnancy. Her children, Lorna and Beau, were at the Hall under strict supervision of their nurse. At twenty-one, Georgina was a veteran army officer's wife having taken passionately to the diplomatic procedures of ensuring her husband's advancement. She realised there was a long way to go in a peacetime army. Discreetly, she took his hand and squeezed. They turned to each other and smiled.

Up from the finishing post, a line of double decker buses faced the railing which kept back the crowd from the turf. The bus drivers would have to climb along the rail to get back into their cabs, so close were they parked together. The tumultuous sound of people came at the Beaumont party from every direction. In front, the gaping mouth of the grandstand was gaggled by a mass of people getting up and moving down to bet, to look at the horses parading in the enclosure and to gawk at the well-known faces of royalty and power that strolled the lawns of their private enclosures. Jockeys in the ring leant down from the high saddles to talk to trainers. Tick-tack men waved from their boxes to signal betting across the Downs. The odds rose and fell as the bookies laid off their bets, leather bags on one hip and betting boards to the other. An immensely tall tipster, claiming relationship to a Red Indian chief, trailed the feathers from his head dress shouting, "I've got a horse." An accessional hat of a British bobby rose above the crowd but pickpockets were smaller and quicker and plied a profitable trade. Smells of stale beer from the big tents, trampled grass, dust and people flattened all smell of the horses.

Rising behind the finishing straight, which arrowed down from the sweep of Tottenham Corner, were parked cars with flap boots down and acting as tables for bulging picnic hampers and green labelled bottles of beer. Behind again, the hill rose and the crowds thronged for an all-round binocular view of the start and the finish. It was Englishmen of all classes enjoying themselves together, betting from a bob each way to a thousand pounds for a win. Sweaty shirts and dove-grey morning dress looked across at each other without an iota of animosity.

Isabel Beaumont, Henry's wife of three years, was thoroughly irritated that Reggie had stayed away from the last day of the races. Even if she couldn't take him to bed she liked to feel his presence. It gave her the imagination to endure the stolid and sexless love-making of her husband. She looked around the guests but with the best of wills she couldn't imagine any of them as lovers. The army officers were far too frightened of their wives and reputations and Henry's friends were in love with their horses. She would think up a shopping excuse to go up to town. If Reggie stayed away from today's racing there was a good business reason. She speculated on whether his partners had come into town.

Isabel watched, mildly interested, as the horses were led out of the paddock to begin their loping gallop to the starting gate, the long way around behind the hill.

"There she goes," said Sir Thomas. "Best of luck, Henry. Bit skittish but she'll settle down. What did you tell the jockey?"

"Good luck," answered Henry nervously as he followed his horse through binoculars as it galloped away to the left-turn, round the back course on its way to the start. The odd piece of turf flew from its hooves but the going was hard. He smiled at his colours of green and gold with a Norman helmet imprinted on the back. He ran the glasses round to the saddling enclosure and his trainer came into focus looking across at the bus. He gave Henry the thumbs up and walked away into the crowd. Henry picked out several of his racing friends and the tension was unbearable. He wanted to walk, move around, do something. Scanning across to the royal enclosure he had a good but brief view of the new king. Back again, the last horse had moved out of the saddling enclosure and was on its way to the start. The loudspeakers bellowed a multitude of messages but the crowds were burrowing into their race cards, checking the colours and numbers of the horses. There was a tangible excitement right across the Epsom Downs.

"They're under starter's orders," bellowed the huge loudspeakers and this time the crowd looked up.

"I do wish the race were over," said Lady Beaumont. "I get so excited at a horse race. Oh, Henry, I do hope you win."

The binoculars on the hill were turned in the opposite direction towards the start and the surge of sound built up to a final shout.

"They're off," said the loudspeaker, and the 1936 Oaks was on its way around the course.

Bookmakers had closed their bags and for the few minutes of the race stood idly and hoped the favourite would not win. They had quoted Lilliput down to six to one, fourth favourite. Everyone on top of the bus was standing and looking up the long stretch towards Tottenham Corner. Isabel had forgotten men and along with the others, was looking through her binoculars at the empty course waiting for the horses to appear. The progress of the horses could be measured by the moving buzz from the crowd.

"Here they come," shouted Geoffrey. "Can't see who's in front from this angle."

"Lilliput is on the inside rail," said Henry, suddenly calm and resigned to his fate.

"He isn't using the whip," said Sir Thomas.

"Good," said Henry.

The noise of the crowd was rushing towards them down the straight as everyone in the grandstand stood up.

"He's still there," shouted Geoffrey in his excitement.

"Must sit down," said Lady Beaumont, right hand to her breast.

"Come on, Lilliput," screamed Georgina, in a most unladylike fashion but drowned by the shouts of everyone else on the bus.

"He's ahead," shouted Geoffrey.

"He is," said Henry.

"He's going to win the bloody thing," said Sir Thomas. "My God, he's won it," as Lilliput streaked past the post.

Pandemonium broke loose on the bus as everyone hugged and kissed each other. Even Pavy stood, drinks tray in hand, with a broad grin on his face.

Henry turned to his wife and in her excitement Isabel hugged him back.

"Come on," he said. "We've got to get across the course."

"You lead her in, Henry."

"We're joint owners. It's the wife's job. You'll be on the front page of every newspaper. Not often the owner's wife is twenty-five and as pretty as you. We'll have to get the race steward to open the gate. They're going into the unsaddling enclosure."

Clutching Isabel's hand, they made for the back of the bus amidst the raised champagne glasses.

"I can't believe it," said Lady Beaumont as she accepted a glass of champagne from Pavy.

Henry helped Isabel off the bus and began to make his way through the seething crowds, some tearing tickets and others holding them up to the rows of bookmakers for payment. They reached the locked gate and Henry tried to pull it open.

"Can't go that way, sir," said a policeman.

"But I've got to get across. The King's going to present my wife with the cup."

"My good man," tried Isabel. "I am Mrs Beaumont, the owner of Lilliput."

"Can't go across the course unless you're officials. That's me orders." Henry waved to his trainer who was coming across with the course steward.

"Superstition," shouted Henry to the steward. "If I go that side I never win."

"Don't worry, Henry," said the steward. "We'll have you across in time. Congratulations. Had ten quid on her myself."

The gate was opened and the tall figure of Isabel in a broad brimmed white hat and long, pale blue dress strode across into the open, her beautiful legs touching the soft silk of her dress and showing the shape of her strong thighs. She was thoroughly enjoying herself as the cameras clicked all the way to where Lilliput was waiting. She patted the horse's muzzle in a way that pushed her right breast hard into her dress for the photographers before leading the horse into the King's presence to receive the cup.

REGGIE BEAUMONT DID a small gig around his office as the radio commentator described the scene in the winner's enclosure. The commentator was as much enthused with Isabel as he was with the winning horse.

"Thelma, tell Carl, François and Gunter that I'll be at Merry Hall tonight and tomorrow morning. What a family celebration. My brother's just won the Oaks."

AT SEVEN O'CLOCK THAT EVENING, the eldest and youngest of the Beaumont brothers were walking together through the woods on their way to the Thirty Acre field which had been set aside for the horses. Both were wearing grey flannels and blazers, Geoffrey's showing the British Army cricket badge and Henry's the Brasenose College rowing badge. The heavy bulk of Henry contrasted to the tall, thinner boned Geoffrey. Henry carried a gnarled walking stick that he used to point out parts of his domain.

"Do you really think there will be another war with Germany?" asked Henry.

"Yes," said Geoffrey. "The Versailles Treaty took away Germany's pride. Punitive to the extreme. A nation cannot live without its pride. Hitler is an excuse. He is re-arming them despite the treaty. They'll want their revenge."

"How long will it be?"

"A few years, probably. We must prepare but we're not. The army is lethargic. Some of the old goats would like to fight on horseback."

"Have you got any further with your flying columns?"

"Even among the old goats, there are some who see clearly. The colonel is right behind me. The next war is going to be a lot more fluid than the last. Aircraft. Tanks. Armoured cars. Trench warfare won't come into it. Armoured cars in independent flying units behind enemy lines would create havoc far greater than the size of the unit. The Boers did it in the South African war. Small commandos on horseback, free of the need for supply columns. You never knew where they were going to hit you next."

"I hate the thought of war," said Henry. "I don't think our way of life could survive another one."

"There'll always be a way if you think. Look what you've done with the stud. Merry Hall hasn't made as much money this century. The Hall wouldn't have lasted in our hands if we hadn't been adaptable."

"Pity Reggie missed the race. He'll miss the roast goose tonight. Mother says Doris Breed's gone berserk with excitement. How that woman turns out so much food for so many people at such short notice is beyond me."

They walked in silence with the centuries-old oaks on either side of them. The woods were at peace in the hot summer air, small sounds from the bent brown bracken and rustling leaves and sparrows chirping and a cabbage white butterfly gliding through the trees.

"How are you enjoying married life?" asked Henry.

"Love it. I haven't had a bad moment from the day I met Georgina. Lorna has reached the stage where she wants to ask questions. Beau keeps knocking things over. He wants to get up and go already. And you?"

"I love Isabel. Our wives are so different. Isabel wants things to happen all the time. She can never sit down and just enjoy Merry Hall. I thought she would be suited to farming life, but I was wrong. Holding that trophy up for the photographers was more her cup of tea. I have never seen her more animated. I wish she would fall pregnant. She needs something to occupy her mind." They walked on in silence. "How's the cricket going?"

"Fine. I've got a game for Surrey at the end of the month."

"That's terrific. Have you told father?"

"Not yet."

"He'll be thrilled."

"You must be thrilled with the race."

"Next year, I'm going to win the Derby."

They came out of the wood to the Thirty Acre field which had been surrounded by a heavy white-poled fence. Henry put a foot up on the crossbar and looked across at the three horses grazing, one of which was Lilliput.

"Isn't she a beauty?"

"Yes," agreed Geoffrey.

GEORGINA AND ISABEL sat in the same arbour that Georgina had been taken to by Geoffrey on her visit to Merry Hall three years earlier. The sisters had their heads together and they were worried.

"If father loses that directorship," said Isabel, "I don't know what they are going to do for money. I can't very well ask Henry for money though I expect he'd ask them to stay at the Hall. Parents and parents-in-law under the same roof would be disastrous."

"Geoffrey only has his lieutenant's pay," said Georgina, "and a small allowance from Sir Thomas."

"Can't Lord Migroyd do anything about it?" asked Isabel.

"Father says he's tried but with Goldfields going over their heads, there doesn't seem much hope. Not having money's terrible, especially when father can't do anything."

"I should have married Reggie," said Isabel. "He's got plenty of money."

"He'll be a bachelor for the rest of his life. Have you met his partners?"

"One of them," said Isabel.

"Terrible, aren't they?"

"Depends how you look at it. They're just four bachelors enjoying themselves. Wish I'd been born a man."

"Do you really? I like being a woman. When are you going to have a baby?"

"I can't make up my mind."

"What do you mean?"

"I've been taking precautions."

"Why?"

"I'm not like you Georgie. I want some excitement in my life. I get bored."

"With a couple of kids you won't get bored."

Isabel picked a flower from the rhododendron.

"I'm going to town tomorrow," she said, "to do some shopping. I'll take in a show."

"Is Henry going?"

"He doesn't like the city. I'll get Reggie to escort his sister-in-law."

"Be careful, Isabel."

"Don't worry. Reggie wouldn't touch me with a bargepole. I'm royal game as far as he's concerned. Do you like being married?"

"Yes. More than anything in the world."

"There are Henry and Geoffrey," said Isabel, looking down the walk between the herbaceous border.

"Hello," called Georgina. "Did you enjoy your walk?"

"Yes," said Geoffrey.

"Did you miss me?" asked Georgina.

"Every step of the way," said Geoffrey and took his wife's hand. "Are the children in bed?"

"In bed but not asleep. You'll have to kiss them goodnight."

"Little monkeys," said Geoffrey and frowned as Isabel deliberately walked next to her sister instead of his brother.

"Wait till we add the third one," said Georgina.

THE FOLLOWING EVENING, Reggie Beaumont was shown into the exquisitely decorated and furnished private office of Tony Venturas, the part owner and Managing Director of Bretts. Being friends since the day Reggie first flew, they didn't shake hands but smiled at each other. The blonde-haired beauty who had shown him in withdrew.

"New?" said Reggie, thumbing the closed door.

"Six new ones this week and she's the ugliest."

"Impossible."

"True. Whisky and soda?"

"Thanks, Tony."

"How's Mathilda?"

"We've cured her of stalling on a loop."

"Took long enough."

"Not really. I didn't try for a couple of years. I enjoyed the challenge of bringing her down with a dead engine. How's the club?"

"Want to see the books?"

"That's your job. If we aren't straight with each other all the accountants in the city won't help. I've three guests tonight. My partners."

"The Freebooters," said Tony, raising one eyebrow. "How are they?"

"I hate that name."

"The press like it."

"And they can be useful," agreed Reggie as he accepted his drink and sat down. "Migroyd was satisfied with the service. I may need to give certain insurance company personnel the treatment, but I'll let you know. As it turned out, Migroyd, needed me more than I needed him but it made him easier to talk to."

"Amazing how everyone's heads are ruled by their cocks," said Tony, crudely.

"You'd be out of business if they weren't."

"We all service a need," said Tony, sipping his drink. "Henry must be thrilled?"

"I don't know who was more excited, Henry or my parents. What a party! Doris Breed is the finest cook in the world."

"She is rather good. How's the deal going?"

"We'll win even if I have to use pressure."

"Come in," said Tony.

"Two gentlemen asking for Mr Beaumont. Foreigners," said the club manager.

"Bring them in," said Reggie.

"Will that be alright, Mr Venturas?"

"That'll be fine," said Tony, maintaining the facade that he was the sole proprietor of the club. "What do they drink these days?" he said to Reggie.

"Pernod and an ice cold German beer."

"No problem," said Tony, turning to his private bar.

"It's worse than breaking out of jail," said François, coming into the office. "Why the strict security? Hi, Tony. How are the aeroplanes?"

"Members and guests only," said Reggie. "Tony's my partner in Bretts."

"Long time no see," said Tony. "How are you Gunter? Have a drink. Pernod and beer?"

"Thanks," said François. "Who was that amazing looking lady that was standing by the door?"

"Sally Bollas," said Tony.

"Can I meet her?"

"First have a look around."

"There are more?"

"Tony tells me Sally is the ugliest in a batch of six new hostesses," said Reggie.

"There are forty in the club," said Tony.

The door opened again to Carl, ushered in by a different girl.

"I don't believe it," said François.

"I was invited," said Carl, sarcastically as the door closed behind him.

"That one was prettier than the one at the door," said François.

"What are you drinking you old bugger?" asked Tony.

"Tuborg," said Carl shaking hands with Tony.

"In a tall glass?"

"What a question."

"Tony is the only other person who knows about the treaty. We may need his help if some of the key insurance companies won't go along with us. It's the reason Tony and I linked up as partners in this club."

"Come in," said Tony sharply and Thelma was shown into the room.

"I asked Thelma to join us," said Reggie, smiling at François who was closely watching Thelma walk across the room in a long, apple-green dress that showed off her high, firm breasts to best advantage. Her auburn hair was combed and clasped to one side. She radiated an animal sex appeal. "You all know each other," said Reggie and waved his hand to indicate everyone in the room.

"Hello, Tony," said Thelma, and the voice was throaty and very different to that of the efficient secretary.

"As I was saying," said Reggie as Tony moved back to the bar and poured a glass of dry sherry for Thelma, "insurance companies are run by managers who answer to a board of directors who wouldn't know one end of an insurance policy from the other. They are all very comfortable, managers and directors, and they dislike rocking the ship or doing anything that will jeopardise their position. It is the epitome of the old boy network and as new boys we are watched with suspicion. Facultative reinsurance is part of their daily routine. We have all made friends with certain managers who pass us business. I give Carl's friend business and Carl gives my friend business. Very cosy. Very profitable. The new system will eliminate the work but it will also cut across a lot of cosy deals. Even our pet managers don't give us all their business and there is more than one manager per company. As we know and do, the managers who give out business are wined and dined and bribed with acceptable gifts. Cufflinks, champagne at Christmas, tickets to Wimbledon, etc. But all these he can buy himself, and what's more he's probably not even interested in tennis. This club is what they want, gentlemen. It's what they can't find themselves and even if they could they'd be too frightened to go out on their own. A toast to the treaty and to the enjoyment of certain insurance managers who see business our way."

"Hear, hear," said Carl and they drank the toast in formal silence.

"Your table is ready if you'd care to follow me into the club," said Tony.

"We have a Latin-American group this evening but they will play anything you ask. I'll first show you the table and then you can go through to the bar."

With Reggie bringing up the rear, they followed Tony to a table in its own private alcove that looked onto a small, softly-lit dance floor. The furnishings were rich and expensive in soft red material with gleaming silver and pure white linen.

"The bar is through there," said Tony. "If you require another view. There is a button under your table to call for service."

"After you," said Gunter, overplaying his bow to suggest that François went first into the bar.

François said nothing but his eyes swivelled around the room and continued to lust as he was led into the better lit bar with seats around the wall where only women in daring evening dress sat drinking cocktails. There were every variety, race and colour from the continents of Europe and Asia.

"I thought you might like our view," said Tony. "Everyone has a degree or is in the process of reading for one. Reggie and I have spent considerable time in our search for the perfect hostesses. They are extremely well paid."

"What do you charge for a drink?" asked François, as he started his face by face inspection down the right hand side of the room.

"If you have to ask such a question," said Tony, laughing, "you can't afford to be here."

"It is a pleasure to be Reginald's guest," said Gunter and accepted his beer in a tall, fluted glass that frothed perfectly at the top. François threw back his Pernod. "I don't believe it," he said. "This is the answer to every male sex maniac's most hopeful dream. They're perfect, Reggie. I have never seen so much sex appeal in one room in my life."

Thelma smiled to herself.

"They do turn you on a bit," agreed Reggie, sipping his whisky and soda.

"The man who controls this roomful of women can control any man," said Gunter. "This makes the clubs in Hamburg look like cheap whorehouses. Do you have a large membership?"

"One hundred members only," said Reggie. "When one resigns we accept another but not otherwise."

"A closed shop."

"Yes. Our members are all in business. Usually they accompany their guests. Not always," he went on, sweeping his hand around the girls in the room. "The club is full most evenings. When you sit at the bar, the girls will drift across in twos and threes for a chat. Just remember the name of the lady you would wish to dine with and she will join you at your table. And don't try on your male chauvinism as they will probably have more knowledge of many subjects than you. If they like you, who knows? In Bretts, you have to charm the girls like anywhere else. It makes for the challenge which is more exciting, don't you agree?"

"I'd agree with anything looking at this lot," said François, accepting another drink. "One day he's trying to give me millions and the next he drops me into this. Reggie, am I glad I went into business with you."

"We still have to complete the Treaty."

"We will, if it's only to let me back in here again."

"Enjoy your evening," said Tony.

Reggie smiled at Thelma and took a sip of his drink. Above the wall, seats around the room, were small downward directed lights which displayed the girls without destroying the candle-lit atmosphere of sensuality. The bar itself was well lit and decorated by a row of three chandeliers which tinkled light onto the marble bar top and its accoutrement of cocktail shakers, mixing jugs, cut fruit, condiments and huge onyx ashtrays that were cleaned after each use. At the other end of the bar were two elderly men in immaculately tailored evening dress, being discreetly chatted up by two of the hostesses in evening gowns. Reggie nodded to the one who was the member and was turning back to talk to Gunter when he quickly looked back at the group at the end of the bar. Staring, he became even more surprised when the lady smiled warmly in recognition and said something to her escort before walking serenely across to Reggie.

"Good evening, Reggie," said Lilly Brigley. "This is a surprise to find you in a night club. Tug always told me you had more girls than you can handle."

"What are you doing here?" said Reggie, moving her out of the others' hearing.

"Earning a living like everyone else. Even students at London University have to eat and buy clothes. And you?"

"Speak to Tony before you leave this evening and don't make an appointment."

"Is that an invitation, Reggie?"

"No, it's an instruction. Tony will explain. You'd better go back to your client," and he turned back abruptly to his friends.

Lilly looked perturbed and then annoyed before walking back to her end of the bar. "Excuse me for being rude," she said to her client. "I thought I knew that man."

"Reggie Beaumont?"

"Is that his name? Now, where were we?"

"Excuse me a moment," said Reggie. "Thelma, can you look after them for me?"

"My pleasure."

"And mine," said Gunter with a small, mock bow as his heels came together. Reggie made straight for Tony's office, knocked quickly and opened the door to stare for the second time in five minutes.

"Hello Reggie," said Isabel. "Your man said you'd be here."

"He's no right…"

"Don't blame him, Reggie. I said your mother was very sick and he knows how fond you are of your mother. Mr Venturas was about to send one of the charming young girls to call you but you have saved her the chore. I told you yesterday I was coming up to town and wished to be taken to a show."

"And I told you, Isabel, that I was otherwise engaged."

"Yes, it wasn't a very brotherly gesture."

"It wasn't meant to be. You are married to my brother. Where is Henry?"

"Probably sleeping with Lilliput but don't let's argue. I get bored at Merry Hall. As a good brother-in-law, you should think it better to be keeping an eye on me."

"Where are you staying?"

"In the family flat, of course."

"There's nobody there. The servants are at Merry Hall for the races."

"I don't need a nursemaid, you know. And how is François and your other continental friends? Oh, don't be silly, Reggie. I peeped round the corner into the bar and there you all were snuggled up together. Even Thelma looks a little different out of her office tweeds. Come on! Take me to your friends and we'll have a positively spiffing evening. But first the cloakroom and then I'll be ready."

"You can use the private suite off this office," said Reggie.

"How convenient," said Isabel, walking gracefully across to the door that was opened for her by Tony. She sailed past in her tasselled and glittering evening gown. Discreetly, he closed the door.

"Wow," said Tony.

"She's after François if she hasn't had him already. Where did you find Lilly Brigley?"

"Who?"

"One of your new girls."

"Oh, Lilly. Friend of Sally Bollas. London University students. Room together. Pretty, isn't she?"

"Very. The last I knew she was Tug's girlfriend."

"Isn't Tug still in Sarawak?"

"Yes."

"Long way away."

"When she asks what I want, tell her to wait in here when she wishes to leave. I'll wait for her to finish with Max."

"What's the problem?"

"I've too much respect for her father to turn her into a whore. He's one of our tenants. The Brigleys and the Beaumonts have lived on the same estate for hundreds of years."

The cloakroom door opened.

"Does that look better?" said Isabel.

"Just as perfect as before," said Tony, diplomatically.

"You are going to ask me for a drink?" said Isabel.

"Of course," replied Reggie.

"I've some business to talk as well," said Isabel. "About father. You're the only one I know who may be able to help."

"Has your father spoken to you?" asked Reggie, quickly.

"No. Why?"

"No reason. You can tell me over dinner. Thanks, Tony."

"There's more to running a club than adding up figures," said Tony, smiling at Reggie.

"Seems so. After you, Isabel. Just follow through to the bar."

Perplexed he followed his sister-in-law into the club.

"Hello, François," said Isabel.

"What a pleasant surprise," said François, turning from talking to Thelma.

"AND THELMA," said Isabel. "How nice to meet you out of the office. Now, let me guess. You must be Gunter and you must be Carl. I'm Isabel, Reggie's sister-in-law," and they all moved aside to let her sit on the bar stool.

Isabel made herself comfortable and looked around the room.

"My. But you men do make yourselves comfortable when you're away from home. Reggie, isn't that Lilly Brigley?"

"Yes."

"You'd better not tell Bert."

"Neither had you."

"Shall we all keep this evening a secret," she said sweetly. "I'd like a champagne cocktail," she said to the barman. "Now, don't let me interrupt your conversations," and she smiled straight at Lilly and nodded her recognition.

Carl couldn't take his eyes off Isabel. To help him, she smiled encouragement.

"Would you care for a cigarette," said Carl, offering her his gold cigarette case.

"Yes. Why not?" said Isabel and Carl snapped a gold lighter as she delicately put the cigarette to her lips. She leant slightly forward to take the light and took his hand to bring the flame up to the tip of her cigarette. She smiled at Carl and took up her cocktail.

"Cheers, everybody. I always think that people should be born with at least two champagne cocktails in their stomachs. It makes them so much friendlier."

"Congratulations on winning the Oaks," said Gunter.

"It was fun."

"Your husband must be thrilled," said Thelma.

"Ecstatic."

The band began to play in the dining room and the club filled up as the members arrived with their guests. The girls began to circulate and the party at the bar became less conspicuous.

At a little after two fifteen in the morning, Reggie climbed into a taxi beside Lilly.

"Where to, Governor?" said the driver.

"Sixty-three Whitehall Court."

"Nice evening," and he closed the sliding glass partition.

"I hope this isn't a seduction trip," said Lilly, tartly. "I presume that address is your flat."

"Yes. We can't talk in Bretts."

"Depends what you want to talk about. I understand it's ideal for certain subjects."

"Do you know what that place is?" asked Reggie, angrily.

"Yes."

"Then why are you there?"

"Because I need the money. My flatmate explained the rules. The worst that I have to put up with is an old man dribbling down the front of my dress. And as I found out tonight, they don't. Far too much the gentleman."

"And if they make a proposition?"

"I turn it down."

"Let's say it was one of my partners and he offered you five thousand pounds?"

"Then I'd have to think again. They're very attractive."

"Then you'd be a whore."

"Reggie, men are naive and women are hypocrites. Did Isabel pay for her supper tonight?"

"No, of course not."

"She probably will and with pleasure the way she was playing that Nordic giant. Poor man's balls were cracking."

"That's crude."

"It was meant to be."

They lapsed into silence as the taxi drove along the Embankment for five minutes and finally drew up at the kerb. Reggie opened the door for Lilly, then gave the driver a pound note.

"Keep the change."

"Good luck, Governor."

"Why do taxi drivers always suspect the worst?" asked Reggie.

Upstairs in his flat with the view over the Thames to the Houses of Parliament, Reggie put a Glen Miller on the gramophone and walked over to the bar where his man had put out the ice in a silver ice-bucket alongside a crystal jug of water.

"Drink?"

"Why not? Whisky soda. Not lady like but I think I'm about to get a lecture. But before you tell me how shocked my parents would be to find me in Bretts, what's your involvement in the club?"

"I own sixty percent of the shares."

"Oh, that's classic. You're going to lecture me and you own a knock shop. Lady bloody Beaumont would be really pleased to hear that one. What made you go into the business?"

"Such a place is necessary when entertaining clients. Using uncontrolled clubs can create problems."

"You mean the carrot and stick game is more difficult to play."

"That's well put," he said, handing her the drink. "People don't readily change their business patterns. The club is a persuader. You don't think I made my money by being a better reinsurance broker than the others. I place business in the same way that everyone else does. The secret is to get the business to place. Initially, Merry Hall, father's title, the old school tie and Oxford got me a few accounts but even they had to be serviced and the only service I could give them was better entertainment. That kind of insurance manager has crept up so many asses on his way to the top that he never had time to enjoy himself. And now he's almost too old. I give him a reminder of what he missed and the chance to do business with me and not miss out any longer. I wouldn't have the edge if my competitors could bring clients into Bretts. It's also cheaper on my expense account."

"How far do you want to go, Reggie?"

"In business?"

"Yes."

"As far as it will take me. I don't intend to be an insurance broker for the rest of my life, pimping for business. What's happened to you and Tug?"

"I haven't had a letter for over a year," she said and abruptly turned to look out of the window. "The view's very pretty."

"I'm sorry."

"So am I. Damned sorry. So damn men. Why shouldn't I use them?"

She turned to Reggie and buried her head in his shoulder. Reggie put an arm round her and let her cry.

"Just stopped writing," she said after a while.

"He hasn't written much to the family. Mother told me yesterday she'd had a letter saying he's postponed his leave."

"He's due back next month."

"Not coming 'til next year."

"Dad told me it wouldn't work. Why are parents always right? Three years, they said. In three years you'll both have forgotten each other. Well I damn well haven't and it's hurt, Reggie. I've been hurting something awful for three years."

"I'd better take you home."

"Can I stay? Sally said she was taking Gunter back to the flat. She ditched the old boys at midnight. She needs the money. Putting two brothers through school. Parents think she's an actress in her spare time from varsity but they don't enquire too hard. Reggie, I'm so damn lonely."

"Have another whisky and then you can sleep in the spare room. I'm going out to the Far East, week after next. I'll find out for you. Then you can make up your mind what you want to do with the rest of your life."

"THE SAVOY," said François, letting Thelma in by the fire escape, "is a very fine hotel but their morals are too strict. They don't mind what happens as long as they don't know. Only married couples stay at the Savoy." Carefully, François inspected the length of the corridor and taking Thelma by the hand, led her into his room.

Before opening the fire escape door, which only opened from the inside, François had prepared his suite. Books had been placed on the two single, lounge chairs and a drinks tray was set out on the coffee table in front of the deep settee. The wireless was playing background music and the one standard lamp was burning in front of the heavily draped windows.

Thelma smiled to herself at the preparations and picked up the book from the chair on the other side of the coffee table, bending down to show him a good view of her breasts.

"What are you reading?" she asked sweetly as she sank into the chair with the book in her hand.

"It's in French," said François, trying to perch on the arm of her chair.

"Won't you be more comfortable on the settee?" asked Thelma.

"Why don't we both sit on the settee?"

"I'm quite comfortable. A small sherry would be fine unless you want to ask room service for coffee."

"Better not," said François, reluctantly settling on the settee and pouring drinks. "I think Carl is going to be raped," chuckled Thelma.

"Do you think he'll complain?"

"No," said Thelma crossing her legs in a way that showed her stockinged thigh. Her dress settled back into place but François' eyes were still riveted on the spot where it had been.

"Every time I see Isabel she's on heat. The only one she'll never catch is Reggie." She smiled sweetly at François, "Was she good, François?"

"How did you hear?"

"I didn't. A woman can sense when people have known each other intimately. You both gave it away in the club by smiling just a little too indulgently at each other. She's had 'im, I said."

"And your lovers?"

"I don't have lovers. Have you ever heard of anyone marrying their mistress?"

"FLATS," said Isabel, "are so much easier than hotels. The Beaumonts are a very organised family. They bought a ninety-nine year lease on this flat just before the war. A true Englishman should have his estate in the country and a home in the West End."

"Won't anyone arrive?" asked Carl, nervously.

"It adds to the excitement."

Isabel was seated comfortably on the couch with Carl, excited but nervous opposite her. His otherwise rigid scruples on married women had left him in the club when he lit her first cigarette. Languorously, Isabel got up and took his hand. Looking down at him she leant over and kissed him, putting her hand on his erection where it was straining at the cloth.

"I think you're ready," she said and pulled him up from the chair. "Come," and she put his hand that she was holding inside the top of her evening gown where her nipples were rigid with excitement. Briefly she rubbed her thigh across his erection and led him into the bedroom.

"Don't let him go down while I change," she said, and let herself into the bathroom. "Take off your clothes," she said from the bathroom. "Tell me when you're ready."

"I'm ready," said Carl huskily, taking off his clothes but still watching from the bathroom door which opened and drove him almost to his climax as Isabel came into the bedroom wearing soft kid leather panties that clung to her box and the tight cheeks of her arse. On top, the bra of the same leather clung to her breasts except for the holes in the centre where her nipples thrust out a quarter of an inch. She was wearing high heels and carried a leather slipper which she gave to Carl.

"I like to be beaten. The walls are thick so don't worry how much noise I make." Impatiently, she lay face down on the bed with the curves of her tightly swollen arse pointed at him.

"Beat me." Carl tapped her on the bottom cheek.

"Hard," she called. Harder he hit.

"Hard," she shouted. Harder he hit.

"Harder," she screamed and he hit with all his strength.

"Now," she said and turned over with her legs open and pulled up to her chin.

There was a hole in the underneath of her leather panties and the sticky goo was open and waiting. He thrust into her again and again until they climaxed together in single ecstasy.

3

LATE JUNE 1936

On the 29 June 1936, Tammany watched from the veranda as a gentle surf brushed the pure white sand that she knew from childhood would squeak when walked upon. Mango trees clutched at the beach and majestic palm trees curved up from the edge of the sands to the peaceful blue-purple of the sky. She was thoroughly content. Her two children, Adam, aged two and Tammany Junior, aged eleven months, played at the water's edge. The water was inches deep for a hundred yards out and the sea was calm. Her soft, brown eyes were smiling.

Tug Beaumont and Perry Marshbank were seated on the bottom curve of a palm that reached sixty feet to the sky above them. They were deep in conversation.

"Adam, Tammany," she called in English and her children ran back. The tinkle of childish laughter was crystal. She saw her husband look up and they waved at each other. She could smell the baked fish cooking.

She stood up and her height was accentuated by the length of her pitch black hair. The heavy curve of her hips, hugged by the red cloth, were perfect for her height of five feet ten inches and her large feet were in harmony with the rest of her full body. The smooth brown glow of her skin rose from the toes of her feet to the tip of her brow where the hair was parted to fall on both sides of her smooth face cut by a long nose which matched a strong, curving jawline. She walked down the three steps from the veranda to the grass that separated her garden from the beach and took from each of her children an upstretched hand and walked them back into the house. Half a mile out to sea, the sun reflected from a long, white disturbance where the coral reef protected the lagoon from the China Sea.

"Tug," said Perry Marshbank, "there is no way out. Brook has decreed that all D.O.'s will go to Kuching."

Tug said nothing and continued to watch the pure grace of his wife as she led his two children into their bungalow.

"You're a stubborn bastard," said Perry, the D.C. for Rejong district of Sarawak.

"It's not me who's stubborn. It's that bastard Gray. I will not attend functions in Kuching without Tammany. She speaks perfectly good English and knows how to behave. She will make those pale faced wives look gauche."

"That's part of the problem. They don't want their territory invaded. Rebecca Gray is a snob."

"Rebecca Gray is a shrivelled up, childless prune and the only satisfaction she can get out of life is tormenting other people."

"She is a little sour," he agreed.

"Frustrated old bag."

"You'll have to come, Tug. The instruction is that all District Officers and District Commissioners attend. You're employed by the Colonial Office on secondment to Rajah Brook. If he kicks you out what then?"

"Why isn't life easy?"

"Didn't you make it difficult?"

"I couldn't help it."

"You had a girl back in England."

"And then I saw Tammany. Perry, not only are you my boss but my best friend. You know how Tammany and I feel about each other. It was sheer power pulling us together. Wait 'til you fall in love…"

"And if Brook kicks you out? You've even postponed your leave. The Colonial Office won't post you anywhere else with a native wife any more than they'll let you bring her to a function in Kuching."

"I'll resign."

"And take her back to England? You haven't even told your family that you're married. And how can Tammany live in England. She'll be like a fish out of water. Dried up old prunes don't restrict themselves to the outposts of the British Empire."

"What do I do?"

"Many planters and the like have taken up with a local girl. They never move them away from their local roots. When they go home they leave them behind."

"And Adam? And little Tammany?"

"You gave them life. That is a great gift."

"Never."

"Kuching, Tug. Next Thursday. Put that amount of pride in your pocket."

"And get sniggered at?"

"They'll snigger at both of you if you bring Tammany. She's sensitive. Living out here she knows nothing of prejudice, envy, the pecking order of the Raj. She's only twenty. One big dinner. A toast to the new King and you can go home again. There's no pleasure without pain."

"Maybe you're right."

"Keep her perfect in her own setting. You'll come?"

"I'll come."

"Good. Now bring me up to date with your project. Are the locals going to eat better next year?"

"With careful instruction they're farming properly. I've got them ploughing twelve inches deep and using fertiliser. My area will be exporting food by November. If we spread this pilot scheme across Borneo there'll never be starvation again. That's what we're here for Perry. To make it better. We have the responsibility of knowledge."

"My spies tell me you're very popular."

"Flattery, Mr Peregrine Marshbank, will get you nowhere. Tammany's waving. The snapper must be cooked. The beer isn't cold but it's wet. Come on. You should get yourself a Tammany and live like a king."

"A king in this castle, you certainly are," said Perry following him. "This heat is building up to bad weather. The air's too still."

"Typhoon season."

"As a part-time painter, you're more prolific than a professional," said Perry, looking through the veranda window into the lounge.

"Do you think they'd sell?"

"Don't know anything about paintings."

"Pity. Here's your beer."

"Thanks. Cheers."

"Good health," said Tug. "No, Adam, you can't have it all. Just a sip. That one is going to be a drinker when he grows up. Tall like his mother." Tug put his arm round his wife, his hand between long hair and her soft, silky skin. "I'm going to Kuching with Perry, tomorrow, darling. Will you be alright with the children?"

"Of course."

"Malaria still in the village?" asked Perry.

"Fertiliser and deep ploughing is one thing. Medicine another. As long as there are swamps there'll be malaria in the village."

"How's Dr Grantham coping?" asked Perry.

"Fine when he's sober, which isn't often."

"Where does he get it from?"

"Any alcoholic will find a way. He's better than nothing, even when he's drunk."

"Been out here too long. Thirty-five years on his own. Maybe he enjoys it. Some people are solitary. Prefer their own company. There must be hundreds of Granthams in the jungles of Asia. Probably had good intentions when they started."

"Probably."

"You should take leave when it's due, Tug."

"There is no way I can leave Tammany and the children for six months. The administration won't recognise our marriage and pay her passage and the children's. On my kind of salary I can't afford to pay the fare myself. So we stay. Simple. Better, in fact. Come. Tammany's going to put the food out on the veranda. Best cook in the world. I've got a bottle of white wine that we've kept in the stream. The houseboy's gone to get it. A siesta after lunch and then we'll take out the boat. It wouldn't win any races at Cowes but it's fun."

"You live well, Tug."

"I can't live better."

THE FOLLOWING DAY, Edward Gray, O.B.E., sat motionless in his chair, fingers steepled in contemplation. He neither heard the punkah that was going round and round above him nor saw the limp Union Jack clinging to the white pole on the lawn. Involuntarily his right hand came up and stroked his bald head as if he was hoping to find a growth of hair. He was thinking about his youth, his days at school, the best years of his life. Everything was exciting. The great future. The accolades of playing for the school first teams at cricket and rugby. Everybody liked Eddie Gray when he was young. He'd even enjoyed the war in the trenches, the camaraderie, the being liked by his platoon and his senior officers. He'd done his bit in those days. Even his early days in the Colonial Service had been alright. And then it had gone sour. He felt his bald head again and his eyes came into focus. Through the windows of his study in Government House he could see the harbour of Kuching. Apart from native sailing craft, and there weren't many of them, the harbour was empty.

"What a bloody backwater," he said out loud and got up to pour himself a pink gin. He put a hand into his trouser pocket and scratched his dhobi's itch. "What a bloody climate," he said out loud again and sloshed gin into the glass. In the old days, he'd have put three drops of bitters into the glass first, and shaken them out. Not now. He upended the bitters bottle and too much came out. "Damn." He filled up the glass with tepid water. "Cheers, you old pirate," he said to the full-length portrait of Rajah Brook, the first Rajah of Sarawak, and drank greedily. It was half past ten in the morning as he drained his third pink gin and put down the glass. "You even got Queen Victoria to condone your piracy," he continued to the portrait. "British Protectorate with Brook as hereditary Rajah. Good luck to you," and this made him contemplate the luncheon the next day without any enthusiasm.

"Edward," his wife called from the next room and made him wince. Quickly, he sat back in his chair and steepled his fingers again.

"Yes, my dear?" he called.

"Has everyone acknowledged their invitations?" she said, coming into his study.

"Everyone but Beaumont."

"You must have him dismissed from the service. Can't have a man going native. Appearances, Edward. Either post him or have him dismissed. Conduct unbecoming a gentleman. Frightful scandal."

"His family have influence."

"Aren't you the First Officer?"

"Yes, dear."

"Then what?"

"He's doing a good job."

"Nonsense. He's brought us down to their level. Two children. Things like that didn't happen before the war."

"I expect they did," he said softly.

"What did you say, Edward?" she said sharply.

"Close the door, my dear. The servants will hear."

She closed the door firmly and glared across the room at him.

"Edward, dismiss him. This is my final warning."

"It's not that easy."

"Dismiss him."

"What about the children?"

"He made the bed. I don't care. The other wives are scandalised. If you don't dismiss him immediately, you'll lose respect. I'll lose respect."

"Marshbank has an appointment at eleven."

"Good. You can tell him. Disgrace. I don't know what this administration would do without me. There wouldn't be any standards."

"Brook wants the toast to the Rajah before that of the King tomorrow."

"There you are. No respect. I'll see you don't stand up to that toast. That finishes it. I want your assurance that Beaumont will be dismissed. Now. Tell Marshbank to tell him to pack and leave, with or without his concubine."

"They were married in church."

"Roman Catholic Church. Church of England wouldn't do it. Those priests are as bad as Beaumont. No wonder they encouraged him. Never liked a papist. Lady Brook barely speaks to me. Disgrace. Englishman. Old family. I wonder what his mother would say to all this. Sometimes I'm glad we didn't have any children. Edward, have you been drinking gin again? This glass has been used. Pink gin by the smell of it."

"Apart from Marshbank, I have nothing to do."

"Find something."

"I think I'll go down to the club for lunch. Dr Grantham has arrived for tomorrow."

"That man's a drunkard."

"He's still highly entertaining."

"At least he doesn't appear drunk in front of the servants."

"Damn fine doctor. Could have been a surgeon."

"Still could if he disciplined his life."

"Yes, my dear."

"Good. I'll have a word with Marshbank myself."

"Yes, my dear," said Edward, but the door had been opened and closed already. "What a first class bitch," he said out loud to himself. "How could such a pretty girl become a shrew?" For half an hour, he let his mind travel away from the Far East and when Perry Marshbank was shown into the study, Gray was smiling gently, stroking his bald pate.

TAMMANY WALKED barefoot along the beach, a yellow cloth around her waist and nothing else. Firm, proud breasts moved with the rhythm of her walk. She pirouetted on one foot and her long, black hair flew out at right angles to her shoulders. Fifty yards behind, Adam and Tammany Jnr squatted with their bare behinds just touching the warm sea water as they foraged in the sand for sea shells. Adam found what he was looking for and ran to show his mother, leaving his sister to toddle along behind. Tammany lifted him up to her hip and the small hands gripped her large breasts for support before poking the small shell up to her face. She kissed the shell and then her son as they walked back to Tammany. Even with Tug gone away with Perry to Kuching, her heart was light and happy. He would be back soon and they would love each other with that burning intensity that came from separation. She would read her English book and then give the children their food. For a moment, the breeze changed its direction and she smelt the wind.

"Typhoon," she said in Malay and involuntarily quickened her pace. Looking at the deep purple-blue of the sky she knew the big wind was a few days away. Probably it would blow into China and leave them alone. Tug's small sailing dinghy rocked at its sea anchor out in the lagoon and the mast tinkled in contact with the ropes.

Chattering to her children in Malay, she knew she had everything a woman could want. A home, a man she loved and who loved her, and two children. Her parrot, vivid red, green and yellow flew out of the veranda to greet her and the children, squawking its hello in English. She'd have a surprise for Tug. The parrot flew on to her shoulder, gripping her perfect skin with remarkable gentleness as it nuzzled her hair. She would give the children mussels cooked in coconut milk for their lunch.

"You won't regret it," said Rebecca Gray.

"I already have," said Edward.

"Duty comes first. Always."

"There must be more to life than duty."

"Before retiring to England, we require a title. With a title we will have position."

"You used to have a heart, Rebecca."

"Getting on in this world is all that matters. What, Edward, is that noise?"

They both walked to the open window and looked out over the harbour.

"It's an aeroplane," said Edward, "and a very big one at that."

"It's crashing into the bay," said Rebecca. "Sheets of water."

"A crashed aeroplane in Kuching harbour will give them something to talk about for years."

"It's gliding over the water throwing up a sheet of spray on either side."

"It's a flying boat," said Edward. "Now you can see the propellers. Beautiful. Quite beautiful."

"I hope it's British," said Rebecca.

"I don't think there's much doubt about that."

"There's one thing to say for it," said Tug, sitting at the bar. "I won't have to go to that damn function tomorrow."

"What are you going to do?" asked Perry.

"Do you know, it doesn't matter a damn so long as I have Tammany and the children. In three years as a D.O. I've learnt a lot about farming. Maybe one of the planters will need an assistant."

"If Mrs Gray will allow them to take you on. She wants you out, Tug, and she's a very determined and nasty woman."

"Don't worry, Perry. You don't have to live with her. That's poor Edward's problem. I'd rather be unemployed and penniless than have her as a relation. Have another drink. Why are night clubs night clubs when you can drink in them all day long? Let's make them doubles and celebrate. I'll go to Malaya. Anywhere. What's the difference?"

"England?"

"No. She'd be like a fish out of water in England. Your words."

"Aren't you going to tell your parents?"

"Have to. Father will understand but mother won't. Why do mothers always want so much for their children? Maybe I can become a painter or my Gauguins will fetch a fortune and I can set up in opposition to Brook. Rajah Beaumont. Has a ring to it, don't you think? Cheers, good friend, and thank you for trying."

"No wonder your family lasted so long. You don't give up."

"Today, Perry my friend, you and I are going to get plastered. We'll give Tammany another day without worry. Come over here and play the piano. After a few more drinks I'll give a concert. And that's another idea. I could become a professional singer."

"WHAT IS THAT FOUL NOISE," said Gunter, pushing his way through the string beads that hung down the front door.

"The sound of a drunk Beaumont. We've found him," said Reggie, squinting his eyes to see through the murk and smoke. "What a dive."

"Not quite like Bretts," said Gunter.

"Old school song. Must be well on his way. You can only sing it drunk," said Reggie and wound his way between empty tables to the piano where Tug was thumping and howling, helped along by Perry who didn't know the words. Reggie took up the song with the correct words and cut Tug in full flight. Tug turned from the piano stool and recognised his brother.

"Reggie," said Tug. "What are you doing in Kuching?"

"Visiting," said Reggie. "Good timing by all accounts."

"And Gunter," said Tug in drunken amazement.

"Hello Tug," said Gunter.

"This is Perry Marshbank. My brother Reggie and his partner, Gunter. Perry is the only man in Sarawak who talks to me. Let's get out of here. I've had just enough whisky to face the wrath of the Raj in the dining room of our best hotel. They have a refrigerator and you put ice in your whisky. How the hell did you get here?"

"Sunderland flying boat. Moored in the harbour. Gunter and I are on our way home from a successful business trip. I'll buy you dinner, seeing you're out of work."

"You've heard?"

"You are the main topic of conversation in Kuching, brother Tug. Tomorrow we'll fly up country so Gunter and I can meet my sister-in-law and my nephew and niece."

"You know Reggie, it's bloody good to see you," said Tug and leered at his brother.

AS THEY SAT down to dinner in the dining room of the hotel, there were more waiters situated around the room than guests. At the round table two away sat Rebecca and Edward Gray, neither of whom had acknowledged the nods from Perry or Tug. In evening dress, they studiously ignored the Beaumont table but briefly spoke to the new diners as they greeted the First Officer and his lady.

"Our plans have a major problem," said Reggie, chewing his steak. "Gunter thinks there's going to be a war and I'm inclined to agree."

"Pride," said Gunter, putting down his knife and fork, "is a very real thing in a man's or a country's life. To be a man, he cannot live without it. Don't be fooled by the mass rallies of Hitler, the hysteria, the frightening passions he invokes. National Socialism is not a product of Chancellor Hitler, it is the product of the people. We cannot live with the burden of the Versailles Treaty, emotionally or financially. The German people want revenge and they are looking to Herr Hitler to give it them. He has done a lot for Germany. There is full employment. The Mark does not deflate by one thousand percent in one day. We Germans must be led and he is the only leader we have found since the Kaiser. It is my opinion that whether Hitler likes it or not he will be swept along into war. All wars are a waste of time but they are also inevitable. Mankind likes to fight each other. Because of this, Reggie, myself, Carl and François have created a contingency plan."

"It always amazes me," said Tug, still drunk but coherent, interrupting, "how you speak English with so little accent. A year at Oxford seems a short time."

"We wouldn't take him drinking with us unless he spoke properly."

"Powerful blackmail," said Gunter, nodding to Reggie. "Let Reggie tell you what we have in mind to overcome the problem of war between Germany and Great Britain."

"Stop it before it starts," said Perry, earnestly.

"There is nothing the likes of you and I can do to influence nations," said Reggie. "All we can do is look after ourselves. Business requires foresight. The four of us have agreed that reinsurance is boring to say the least. We have almost completed the signing of a reinsurance treaty between eighty of the major insurance companies in the world. Our commissions run into millions of pounds a year. We have removed the big bone from the industry and wish to move on. And this, Tug is where you come into the picture. One of the reasons for coming to Kuching was to ask you to resign… Who is that man at the next table?"

"Brook's controller," said Tug looking round at a large, red faced man in his middle forties. "Runs Government House."

"I think a couple of his remarks are aimed at you, Tug."

"Probably for the benefit of Mrs Gray at the next table. He drinks a lot. Most people do. Not much else to do. Ignore him, Reggie. He doesn't worry me. I've been getting these remarks for three years. There isn't much to talk about in Kuching."

Reggie shrugged and turned back to his table and went on.

"Union Mining is up for grabs. We've put in a bid to gain control. By coincidence, Lord Hensbrook is on the board but he isn't important. We have the chairman, Lord Migroyd on our side. Some might say it's bribery. I think it's good business. Goldfields, who are also bidding, are big enough already and we need a multi-national vehicle. Union has mining and trading interests around the world. We're going to expand them beyond recognition and that brings us back to the looming war in Europe. As a businessman I must ask myself who is going to win. If I was sure, the decisions would be easy. Gunter tells me that the German Reich is more powerful than anyone knows. He also thinks Japan will side with Germany. At this stage, America doesn't have an army half the size of the French and the Americans haven't launched a major naval vessel since the last war. England has a navy and not much else and her government doesn't believe in rearmament. The outcome in our opinion, that's myself, Carl, François and Gunter is that the outcome, if war happens, is anyone's guess… your friend the controller, Tug, is drunk and making me very annoyed."

"Leave him alone," said Tug. "He's harmless sitting over there."

"What the four of us are going to do," went on Reggie, "is back both horses. If Gunter owns a share in Union when a war breaks out he's going to have his investment confiscated. Same would happen if I owned a share in a German company. The reinsurance side is simple as if the treaty is interrupted through hostilities, commissions will accrue to each country. It's written into the treaty as we are trying to transcend governments and changes of power. Our thinking has decided us to exclude Gunter from the acquisition of Union Mining, officially that is. Instead, Gunter will be looking for a suitable German vehicle when he returns to Berlin. What our respective governments will not know about is the consortium agreement which gives Gunter the right to twenty-five percent of our holding in Union Mining and it gives us seventy-five percent of Gunter's company. That way, financially, we don't give a damn who wins the war so long as we survive… and that man at the next table is becoming louder in his abuse and I am not enjoying the sniggers from other parts of the dining room. Rude bunch of bastards if you ask me… what we need, Tug, is a representative in the Far East. Kuching's as good a place as any. Singapore is close and so is Hong Kong. If governments want to play at killing each other, then we want to make a profit. We need a go-down in Kuching to fill with raw materials of war and out here that means rubber. What I suggest, Tug, is buying you the house you are living in at present where you can live in peace and use as your base for buying forays throughout Asia. Gunter will most likely be doing the same thing so you'll have competition… and that man's getting up from his chair and coming over."

"Thought you'd been kicked out, Beaumont," said the drunk controller. "Best thing for wog lovers."

"Excuse me," said Reggie in a voice that carried across the hushed dining room as he stood up to face the drunk. "There is one thing I cannot abide and that is a rude Englishman," and hit him. The controller reeled backwards between the tables, flaying for support which he couldn't find until he sat on Mrs Gray.

"Unlucky direction," said Perry.

"Not at all," said Reggie quietly. "Extremely accurate. I'm sorry, Perry, you're probably out of a job as well just by being at our table. Let's face it, there's a lot more money in commerce and you don't have to put up with that kind of shit to get on in life. Excuse me a moment," and he walked across to the destruction at the Grays' table.

"My apologies, Mrs Gray, but the gentleman at your feet was being rude about my sister-in-law. Allow me to replenish the wine that has been spilt. Mr Gray, my apologies. Reginald Beaumont," and he put out his hand with a winning smile.

"Your arrival created quite a stir, Mr Beaumont."

"A bottle of Chateaux-Moutin-Rothschild for Mr Gray and charge it to me.

"The gentleman at my feet requires transport to his home," Reggie smiled at Mrs Gray and walked back to his table.

"The old boy enjoyed every minute of it," said Reggie when he'd sat down. "I've never seen a bigger twinkle in a man's eye. If I was a betting man I'd say he doesn't like his wife any more than you do. So there you have it, Tug. Do you want to join us?"

Tug turned back from looking at the waiters helping the controller out of the room.

"What happens if you don't get control of Union Mining?"

"I think positive."

THE NEXT DAY Tammany picked up the sound of the flying boat's engines when it was ten miles out to sea and watched in awe as the great, four-engine aircraft thundered over the sea and set down in the lagoon amid a cascade of sea spray.

When the fat hull had stopped moving and the big propellers were still, the door in the belly opened and an inflatable dinghy was lowered into place and then four men stepped into the rubber boat and an engine putt-putted into life. The helm pointed towards the sandy beach and made for the shore, grounding a hundred yards from the water-line. Adam was the first to recognise his father. Tug waved as he waded ashore, with Gunter pulling the boat and Reggie looking around at the mountains.

Tammany, dressed in a full sarong ran down to meet Tug. They hugged each other on the shoreline with Adam plucking at his father's shorts and little Tammany screaming her frustration from the veranda.

"Reggie, Gunter. This is Tammany. Reggie's my brother."

"Hello," she said and a smile lit her face. "Hello, Perry. Did you enjoy the function?"

"Yes, in a way of speaking," said Perry as they let Tug and Tammany lead them up towards the bungalow.

"Gunter," said Reggie quietly. "That is the most beautiful woman I have ever seen."

"This lagoon is paradise."

"Except when a typhoon hits," said Reggie.

"The forecast says it's moving up the China Sea away from Singapore."

"They change direction. We'll put her on long anchor ropes from three sides."

"You smell the typhoon?" said Tammany turning back to them.

"No," said Reggie. "Wireless forecast."

"The lagoon is well protected," said Tug.

"We'll fly out tomorrow," said Reggie. "I still have to bring in the Royal Exchange and arrange a three million pound facility with my bankers."

"How are you going to raise it?" asked Tug.

"Shares in Beaumont Ltd, backed by the treaty and if successful, the shares of Union Mining. Carl and François will put in their companies as collateral."

"What's collateral?" asked Tammany.

"Seeing your husband is going to be a financial wizard," said Reggie, "I'll explain to you over a long drink on your veranda. Your English is very good."

"Thank you, Reggie," the lilt of her voice as pretty as the smile on her face.

"I'll be off," said Perry. "Some of us still work for the administration. There must be a lot of arguments to sort out having been away four days. Why do people always argue and then need an arbitrator?"

"If Mrs Gray starts on you," said Reggie. "My offer of a job stands. Seems you're Tug's only friend."

"Best man at the wedding," said Tug.

"And I had to give her away as well," said Perry. "Just hopped round the other side. There was prejudice from more than one side."

"Will that rattle trap of yours get you home?" asked Tug as he climbed the three steps to his veranda.

"Never let me down," said Perry. "I'll call for you on my way to Kuching next time and you can collect your rattle trap. Thanks for the lift, Reggie. Quite an experience. And I hope you're wrong about a war, Gunter," finished Perry as he shook hands.

"I hope so too."

"I will make food," said Tammany, picking up her daughter, "and Tug will get you drinks."

"I want to stretch my legs down that beach," said Gunter. "I'm sure you brothers have a lot of family talk."

"Can I come?" piped Adam.

"Of course. If you get tired you can climb on my shoulders."

"Can I climb now?"

"Here, I'll help," said Tug and picked up his blond-haired son with the brown eyes and put him on Gunter's shoulders. "Hold tight to Uncle Gunter."

"Ready, Adam," said Gunter. "Let's run the first bit."

"You'll enjoy your drink when you come back," called Tug.

The two brothers watched until Gunter splashed into the water and began to head off along the waterline.

"Nice guy," said Tug.

"More than that."

"How's mother?"

"Well. So's father. They send their love. Geoffrey's been made a Captain and Henry won the Oaks with Lilliput."

"Terrific. Hell, that's terrific. How's Geoffrey's cricket?"

"One game for Surrey so far but I think it's more his army commitments that keep him from playing. We had an RAF auxiliary weekend where he's stationed. Working hard on his long range unit. His children are the same age as yours."

"Tammany wants as many children as possible."

"Georgina would go on if they could afford it."

"What will you drink?"

"Pink gin."

"You catch on quickly."

"When in Rome do as the Romans do. Who's your new artist?" said Reggie going up to the paintings. "Must be local. Most are of Tammany."

"Me," said Tug, self-consciously.

"They're damn good."

"Thanks."

"You could make a living."

"Prefer the enjoyment."

"Why didn't you tell mother about your family?"

"This," said Tug, sweeping his arm around, "isn't easy to write down in a letter. You can see Tammany. There's Adam and the little one. Seeing's much easier to believe, to understand."

"Why didn't you tell Lilly?"

"I couldn't."

"She hasn't heard from you for a year."

"Is that your other reason for being here?"

"It's the main reason. Until I arrived, I didn't know you were out of a job. Sure, I intended asking you to be our agent but I didn't expect you to accept."

"It was puppy love."

"Not for. Lilly."

"You've seen her?"

"Yes, we met in a restaurant," lied Reggie. "She doesn't come down to the farm very much. University takes up a lot of her time."

"How's she getting on?"

"Nearly finished. It's been three years."

"Yes... how was she?"

"Very upset. She thought you were coming back to marry her."

"You'll have to explain for me."

"I'll try."

"Life isn't easy."

"Never was and never will be."

"How do you think mother will take the news?"

"Sadly. It's as well I came out. When we've made some money, you'll come back on leave. All of you."

"Yes."

"That's a promise!"

"It's a promise... Reggie."

"Now I'll have that gin you still haven't poured."

"I'm sorry. My mind was elsewhere."

"The third reason for being here is to get you to time the Sunderland's engines. Mathilda misses you."

"Cured the fuel cut-out?"

"Yes, but only last year. I'm very good at landing aircraft that have run out of power."

"Don't know whether I'll understand those big engines. Cheers."

"Cheers. I'll take the big one with me," said Reggie, pointing to the life sized painting of Tammany over the mantelpiece. "You've captured her power, Tug. It'll be easier to explain what captivated you to Tammany. It's a lovely name. Do you mind losing your job?"

"I felt I was doing something our kind of family don't understand. Food. We take it for granted. If the crops fail at Merry Hall we go and buy food. Here, they starve. It's so primitive. Water buffalo to plough. Muscle power. I put a two hundred pound sack on the plough to make it go deeper but they need an extra ox. The soil's fertile alright, Plenty of rain. We need a small cheap tractor that every subsistence farmer can afford and then everyone would eat. Asia's very poor."

"I'll talk to Gunter. The Germans are better at that type of invention. Or the Americans."

"That's what colonialism should be all about. Giving people a better way of life. Passing on knowledge," Tug looked at his brother. "I think we could buy this house from the government. Keep Tammany near her family."

"If they'll sell, buy."

"Tammany," called Tug, "come and join us."

"Damn," said Edward Gray, running his hand over his bald head, "I thought it was going to miss us. Post the first alert."

"They don't think we'll get the full force, Sir," said his male secretary.

"When is it expected to hit?"

"Tonight, unless it changes course again. They've given it a name. Typhoon Sarah."

"Keep me informed, Fryer. All we can do is prepare, wait and clean the mess up afterwards. No wonder there are so few native craft in harbour. They know more than all our modern technology. Just as well the flying boat got away."

"The controller is waiting to see you," said his secretary.

"What does he want?"

"Said it was personal."

"Better send him in," sighed Edward.

"Very good, Sir."

Edward got up from behind his desk and looked out of the window of his study that served as his official office. 'They're right,' he thought, looking at the deeper purple, almost magenta, that reached up from the horizon towards the paling blue of the late afternoon sky. And in the south he could see the beginning of the black cloud base.

"Edward'," said his wife, coming in with the controller, "I agree with Miles."

"What do you agree with, Rebecca?"

"That man must be got out of Asia."

"If you're referring to Beaumont, I can ask him to resign from the Colonial Office as I have but I can't throw him out of Sarawak, let alone the East. From what I heard this morning from Soames, I think Mr Beaumont is going to be here a long time."

"What did you hear from Soames?" said Rebecca as she exchanged glances with the controller.

"Our esteemed manager of the Hong Kong and Shanghai Bank says the brother moved rather quickly this morning. In a matter of four hours he purchased the old Swire and McLean go-down that has been on the market for seven years and opened a line of credit for his brother in the amount of two hundred thousand pounds."

"Good God," said the controller. "That's a fearful lot of money."

"A bank account in the name of Beaumont Ltd," went on Edward ignoring the controller, "has been opened at Soames branch. Copies of the memorandum and articles of the company are in Soames' hands. It's one of those companies that allows it to do just about anything anywhere in the world."

"I'll bet he doesn't have two hundred thousand pounds," said Rebecca.

"Oh, but he does. Being a conservative and mistrusting banker, Soames did a check on Mr Reginald Beaumont and his Beaumont Ltd. The answer came back from London that he's good for a half a million pounds."

"What does this mean?" said Rebecca.

"Mr Edgar Beaumont, known as Tug, has been appointed the sole representative of Beaumont Ltd in Asia with full signing powers."

"Up to two hundred thousand pounds?" said the controller.

"Yes... now what was it you came to see me about?"

"I think..."

"I think," said Edward, turning to his wife, "that it would be best if you left us alone, my dear."

Edward waited for the door to close before turning back to the controller.

"If you ever behave again like you did last night I shall make it my business to see that Brook discharges you dishonourably."

"The man hit me."

"Yes. And the pity is he didn't hit you a damn sight harder... there's a typhoon warning so go and do some constructive work for once."

Edward got up without waiting for a reply and resumed his stance at the window. He didn't see anything or hear the door close. He was about to do something he should have done twenty-five years ago. He heard the door open but didn't turn round.

"I think it better for you to sit down for what I have to say," he said to his wife.

"Edward, we cannot have Beaumont making a fool of the English. Appearances are everything."

"It would be better for both of us if you returned to England."

"Whatever for?"

"How long have we been married?"

"Twenty-nine years but you know that as well as I do."

"What do you enjoy about life?"

"Edward. What are all these ridiculous questions?"

"Did you marry me then for any other reason than to climb the social ladder?"

"I don't know what you are talking about."

"I think you do. It was my fault. Men are too easily taken in by a good figure and a pleasant smile. And I was lonely. A bachelor's life in the East isn't much. I also had ambition in those days and though I was tempted, I didn't dare do what young Beaumont has done. There was a week left of my leave and I took you on your face value but then I wanted your face value to be the answer to my loneliness. I knew within a month of getting to Singapore that I was wrong but it couldn't be changed... For better for worse."

"What are you trying to tell me, Edward?"

"That I want a divorce. Your handling of this Beaumont affair has been the last straw. It has shown me what I knew but what I avoided facing. No. It's probably better not to say. We haven't said anything to each other for twenty-nine years so why should I start now? What a waste of a life. Two lives, though I can't see how you would have enjoyed yours more. No, I'm probably wrong. A different man would have handled you better and not given in to your whims. I just didn't care."

"I'm not leaving."

"I thought you'd say that."

"You can't force me."

"No... I can't but at least there won't be any pretence anymore. For the rest of our lives, Rebecca, I shall consider that you don't exist. If you wish to live under the same roof, then so be it. I don't even intend pretending to the community anymore. Once they know you don't have influence over me, they will turn away from you like you have turned away from many others. It's just a pity that I can't start my life all over again but even if you went back to England, I'm not much for starting anything at sixty-one. From now on, all I crave is a little peace and quiet."

"Have you finished, Edward?"

"Yes. Completely."

THE FIRST GUST of Typhoon Sarah, travelling at seventy miles per hour, hit the Sunderland at one-fifteen that morning. Reggie, Gunter and Tug had done everything to give her maximum protection. Ten minutes later a second gust of wind tore across the lagoon at one hundred and ten miles an hour and plucked out the sea anchor.

"She's coming straight for us," shouted Reggie over the storm and watched in wonder as the big aircraft, free of its snapped ropes, came hurtling across the lagoon as if she was ready to take to the air. The lightning flashes picked her out clearly, the four big propellers turning but visible and then she was on the shore and stuck and lurching onto her nose, helpless and hurt.

AT ONE FORTY-SEVEN Typhoon Sarah hit Kuching at one hundred and twenty miles an hour and imploded the front windows of Edward Gray's official residence sending shards of lethal glass across the room to shatter into the wall. No-one was hurt as they were all in the back rooms away from the direction of the wind. Three small craft in the harbour were plucked out of the water and shattered on the quay. Rain brought visibility down to ten yards. The banshee noise was terrifying.

At one forty-nine while Edward was starting a list to be implemented when the storm had blown itself out, Typhoon Sarah removed the roof of the old Swire and McLean go-down and deposited it in the mangrove swamps half a mile away and the flagpole on the front lawn snapped and hit the house like a lance with such force that three feet of the shaft stuck through the wall into the lounge. The lounge was in chaos, with its furniture shattered against the back wall. The wind kept up for four hours before gradually blowing itself out to sea. The silence was ominous. Edward ventured out onto his lawn and surveyed the ruins in the town and harbour.

"We've got a lot of work to do," he said to one of his staff.

REGGIE LOOKED at his beached flying boat and was pleasantly surprised by the way the Sunderland had withstood the force of the wind. The main damage was a hole in the hull, caused by the impact with the sand. Wings and engines were undamaged.

"Now what do we do?" said Gunter. "That'll take weeks to repair and we must have the treaty in Europe next week."

"We will," said Reggie. "First we must fix that aerial and then I will call up the reserves. I have had a back-up Sunderland waiting at Colombo throughout our journey."

"Why didn't you tell me?" asked Gunter.

"I was thinking of mechanical breakdown at the time but I couldn't admit to a German that anything could go wrong with a British aeroplane."

"You think of everything," said Tug, sarcastically.

"We'll get them to fly into Kuching. I don't want them looking for this lagoon and getting lost."

"Alright, smart guy," said Gunter laughing, "And how do you order a taxi to get us from here to Kuching? Tug's car's in Kuching."

"We can walk. It's only thirty miles. By the time the flying boat arrives, we'll be there. It'll be good for us."

"Perry's got a radio. He'll be called to Kuching for an emergency meeting of D.O.s and D.C.s. Some of the locals will be in bad shape after that wind. We can go in with him."

"Edward, I want a word with you," said Rebecca.

"Not now, dear," he said, using the last word from force of habit. "As you may imagine, I have my hands full at the moment."

"I've had word that my mother's very sick and I must go back to England immediately."

"Excuse me," he said to his secretary and took his wife to one side of the devastated lounge and said quietly. "What's all this, Rebecca? Your mother died ten years ago."

"Appearances, Edward. No-one in Kuching knows that she's dead. At all times we must keep up appearances."

"Well," said Reggie, surveying his go-down. "We didn't own that roof for very long."

"It'll be expensive to replace," said Tug.

"Won't cost us a penny. I'm not in the insurance business for nothing. The policy has reinstatement conditions. New for old. You'll get a brand new roof on your warehouse that won't leak a drop of water. Pity the wind didn't knock down the walls."

At five o'clock the following evening, Reggie watched with satisfaction as the replacement Sunderland made a perfect landing in Kuching Harbour, having made three stops on its way from Ceylon.

"One last job," said Reggie. "Back to Tug's house to pick up the fuel from our Sunderland and to load the portrait of Tammany. We should be in Europe by Wednesday. Let's go and pay our respects to Mr Gray and then we'll leave. Did you have a good journey?" he shouted up to the pilot whose cockpit window was open.

"Ready to go when you are, Mr Beaumont. Bad luck with that typhoon."

"Stretch your legs for half an hour and then we'll leave. You can load her now," he said, turning to the ship's chandler he had asked to supply fresh food for the journey.

"So you're back again, Mr Beaumont?" said Edward.

"To say goodbye."

"Could I ask you a favour?"

"By all means."

"My wife's mother has been taken seriously ill in England. Rebecca wishes to return home as soon as possible. Are you returning to England?"

"In half an hour. Should Mrs Gray wish to join us there is more than enough room in the Sunderland. Our main weight is aviation fuel."

"I would be in your debt."

"After my display the other evening it would give me pleasure to do something for your good wife," said Reggie, thinking the opposite. "We will be in England on Wednesday, three days from now."

"I hope to meet you again."

"I'm sure you will, Mr Gray."

4

CHRISTMAS 1936

On the morning of the 24 December 1936, Henry Beaumont stood with his back to the fireplace, his hands behind him spreading the bum- flaps of his Harris tweed jacket in order to air his knowledge at the fire. He was thoroughly content with life. The thought of an heir to Merry Hall and the baronetcy was the fulfilment of his thirty-one years. Pavy came into the morning room carrying a folded copy of *The Times of London* on a silver tray.

"Going to be a white Christmas, sir," said Pavy.

"Falling steadily," agreed Henry walking to the long, sash windows that reached up from the window seat. "Settling too. Has everyone arrived?"

"All the guest rooms are prepared. The fires have been lit for three days to drive out the damp. Rather large house party, if I may say."

"It's been a good year for all of us."

"Mr Reginald hasn't arrived. Neither have any of his party."

"Hope he's not going to fly Mathilda in this weather. It's cold away from the fire."

"Can I send you some coffee, sir?"

"Thank you, Pavy. You really do look after us."

"It's what I have always tried to do."

"Thank you, anyway," said Henry returning to his position in front of the fire with the morning newspaper. It was one of the pleasures in his day, reading *The Times*.

"Breakfast will be served in half an hour."

"Usual time, then?"

"Yes, sir. Nine o'clock.

"Anybody else down?"

"None I've seen, sir."

"Cold weather keeps them in bed. Any problems with the dining hall for tonight?"

"Exactly as Sir Thomas likes it. The long tables will be set for sixty guests. The vicar says he won't stay long as he has a midnight mass."

"Some of the party will want to go. I prefer the eleven o'clock morning service. Time after midnight should be spent sleeping. We'll open the presents after church tomorrow."

"I'll send in the coffee."

Henry hadn't heard the last sentence as he'd turned over the notices page of *The Times* and was reading the news headlines. 'War's just a question of time' he said to himself. 'Please Geoffrey. Always looking for an excuse to prove himself.' He hadn't heard the door open.

"Morning Henry," said Sir Thomas. "Anything in the paper?"

"They seem to think there's going to be a war."

"Nonsense. The Germans had enough last time. Think it'll be a white Christmas? Falling heavily now. Another couple of hours of this and everything will be white. Reginald arrived?"

"Pavy said not."

"Bringing a big party with him."

"He can bring an army having paid for a new roof."

"Yes, that was good of him. Isabel all right?"

"Sick as a dog, poor girl," said Henry.

"Gets some of them, quite natural. Family's growing. Tug's got two."

"Doesn't worry you?"

"That long in India. Your mother can't adjust. Takes time. Why I had that painting put up in the dining hall. Get her used to it. Be different when she sees the grandchildren. Damn pretty girl."

"Maybe Lilly would have been better."

"What's done is done. Ah, coffee," he said turning to the housemaid. "Bring another cup, will you, Conway. In fact bring two. My wife is up early this morning."

"Oh, and happy birthday, father."

"Thank you, my boy. Don't feel sixty-one. Don't feel fifty. Can you stand a bit away from that fire? Always been the problem with the Hall. Unless you stand on top of the fire, you freeze. Never seen so many presents under a Christmas tree. Those new lights work perfectly."

"Morning, Henry," said Lady Beaumont coming into the room. "We're going to have a white Christmas. Is the foal going to be warm enough?"

"I put a paraffin heater in his stall where even his mother can't kick it over. Plenty of straw. He'll be alright. That one's going to win the Derby for me in 1940."

"Reggie not arrived?"

"Not yet."

"Thank you, Conway. A hot drink on a cold morning is always welcome. Coffee smells delicious."

"Did you sleep well, mother?"

"Perfectly. Nothing like a feather bed in the winter. If you two men can move aside, maybe I can get some of that fire. Who's Reggie bringing with him?"

"Carl, François, Gunter, Tony, Thelma his secretary and two lady friends of Tony's. Oh, and the American. Forget his name."

"What an assortment," said Lady Beaumont. "Everything from a German to a Lebanese."

"Reggie's business is international."

"Don't understand half of it," said Lady Beaumont. "Hope cook's done plenty of breakfast as everyone's going to be hungry on a morning like this. We need some more holly and mistletoe for the dining hall. We always think we've collected too much but it's never enough. Better send out some of the guests before the snow's too thick. Gives them something to do."

"I'll say one thing about Geoffrey," said Sir Thomas, peering out of the window into the swirling snow. "He doesn't intend getting soft. Heard him go out at seven this morning. Pitch dark. Look at him. Running in boots."

"Treats everything the same way," said Henry. "Either does it properly or not at all."

"Covered in snow," said Lady Beaumont. "Beats me how he doesn't catch pneumonia."

GEORGINA WAS STILL in the large, wood-carved double bed with the blankets pulled right up to her nose which was cold despite the roaring fire in the grate. On either side were small, warm bodies. The new baby was tucked up in its cot beside the big bed. Beau heard the clunk of his father's heavy boots and two, very blue eyes appeared from under the blanket. On the other side Lorna wriggled nearer her mother for warmth. A cold blast of air greeted them as the door opened and closed and forced mother and son right under the blankets.

"You lot still in bed?" said Geoffrey. He looked into the cot at his second son, Raoul. "He's wet his pants. I can smell it."

There was neither reply nor movement from the bed as Geoffrey took off the heavy wool-lined jacket and put it on the stand by the fire where it began to steam. He stripped completely and rubbed himself down before dressing in civilian clothes. Very carefully, he undid the bottom of the bed and sneaked a very cold hand up towards his daughter and caused her to shriek and shoot out of the top of the bed clothes.

"Time to get up," he said. "Breakfast in twenty minutes."

"Can you put my clothes by the fire to warm, daddy?" said Lorna, getting back under the blankets.

"Mine. too," said Beau, showing his face.

Geoffrey pulled back the bed clothes and presented his wife with a moustache still covered in snow.

"It's going to be a white Christmas," he said and kissed her full on the mouth.

Georgina gasped and wriggled away from the cold mouth.

"Can you put my clothes in front of the fire as well," she said and smiled up at him crookedly.

ISABEL WAS sick into the large bowl that stood on the wooden table alongside a five gallon jug of cold water. It was the third time she'd been sick that morning. She felt cold and miserable. When the retching subsided she washed out her mouth and pulled her heavy dressing-gown closer before huddling up to the fire that a servant had banked up before daybreak. She looked out of the window through watery eyes. It was snowing heavily. She shivered, despite the heat from the fire. She knew that Carl wouldn't look at her pregnant but she didn't care anymore than she cared who'd fathered the baby.

"HERE WE ARE," said Reggie, turning the Austin shooting through the gates that separated the parkland of Merry Hall from the rest of the estate. The long, sweeping driveway up to the old house could only be recognised by the humped flower beds on either side. Everything was white, the grounds, the oak trees and the great house hunched on its mound and watching across the Beaumont lands to the River Mole.

"It's enormous," squealed one of the girls.

"How many bedrooms?" asked the other.

"Twenty-four," said Reggie, "if you don't count the servants' quarters which we don't. The first house on the site was built by the family nearly a thousand years ago."

"The house is very beautiful covered in snow," said François.

"There'll be a fire burning in every room."

"Magnificent," agreed Carl.

"We'll be in time for lunch," said Reggie, "but don't eat too much or you'll spoil your appetite for the birthday banquet tonight."

The long black car drew up to the brass-studded oak front door of Merry Hall and disgorged its passengers. Pavy opened the high gothic doors and revealed the thirty-two foot Christmas tree, fairy lights, tinsel, shining glass balls, candles and a fairy on the top. The whole floor under the fir tree was strewn with presents.

"That's no good," said Reggie surveying the scene as he got inside. "Where are we going to put all our presents?"

"Reggie," said Lady Beaumont, "get everyone inside so Pavy can close that door. It's as cold as charity."

"You know everyone, mother, except Penny and Clair and Chuck Everly. You'll remember Thelma, Gunter, Carl, François and Tony."

"Happy Christmas," everyone chorused.

"Has Pavy made a hot punch?" asked Reggie.

"Of course," said Lady Beaumont. "Your father's been keeping it hot in the morning room."

"We'll have some punch before we unpack," said Reggie. "Hang your hats and coats on those racks."

"THAT HIT THE SPOT," said Chuck Everly, putting down his empty silver stirrup cup. "I don't know what you English put in your hot punches but that was sure good after a drive through the snow."

"Father's Indian recipe," said Reggie and filled up the cup from the punch bowl that stood on the hearth close to the heat of the fire in the morning room. "In India they drink it cold."

"Nice of you to have me along for your festivities, Mr Beaumont or is it Lord Beaumont? Not too good at knowing these things, sir."

"Sir's right," said Sir Thomas, with a smile. "Hope you enjoy your stay in England. First time?"

"Yes, sir. Not been out of the U.S. of A. before this but I ain't going to make that mistake twice. From now on, it's every year."

Henry took the red hot poker out of the fire and dashed it into the punch, creating hissing steam and the full attention of the guests.

"Lunch is served," said Pavy from just inside the door and the lunch gong could be heard booming from the entrance hall.

"It must be rather like feeding an army," giggled Penny, the prettier of the two girls in Reggie's party.

"Except the food tastes a lot better," said Geoffrey.

"NOTHING like a good cigar and a glass of port away from all the noise," said Sir Thomas as he and Bertie Featherstone pushed Lord Hensbrook's wheelchair along the corridor. "Even Alice has never been in my den. A man must be private when he wants to be. Did it out soon after I came back from India, Bertie. It'll be as warm as toast as I had 'em put in a fireplace at both ends. Don't use it in summer. Here we are," and he opened the door with a large key and left Bertie to push the wheelchair into the den.

"Now, how do you like that?" he asked.

"Marvellous," said Hensbrook.

"Good lord, Thomas," said Bertie. "Your old butterfly collection. Don't they look splendid in those cases?"

"Had 'em shipped back after I knew I couldn't go back to India. You caught quite a few of those specimens yourself, Bertie."

"Beautifully laid out."

"That's what I like the look of," said Hensbrook, pointing to rows of dusty port and wine bottles.

"Have a cigar?" said Sir Thomas.

"Don't mind if I do," said Hensbrook.

"Marvellous aroma," said Bertie taking one out of the wooden box and sniffing. "Port or brandy?"

"Port," they both agreed.

"Everything I've collected over the years is here," said Sir Thomas. "Rowing hats from school. That pith hat with the hole in it was from the North West Frontier. Wearing the damn thing when it took the hole. Lucky the blighter didn't shoot an inch lower down. How are you getting on with those other two daughters, Hensbrook? Married any of 'em off?"

"Not easy when you don't have any money. If Reggie hadn't got control of Union Mining we'd have been out on the street. Kept me on the board for ten years though can't see why. Don't understand that side of business. Bunch of crooks, most of 'em. Looks as though my Isabel is going to give you an heir, Thomas."

"If it's a boy after all those girls you produced," said Sir Thomas. "Better introduce the other two to Reggie's partners. They're all rich. Reggie just paid six thousand pounds to re-roof Merry Hall and he didn't turn a hair. I couldn't raise six thousand pounds in ten years."

"Couldn't raise six hundred pounds with tax at seventeen shillings and sixpence in the pound," said Hensbrook.

"Better off out in India," said Bertie. "No expenses. House. Everything paid for by the government."

"That's a good life," sighed Sir Thomas.

"Doesn't Reggie want a wife?" said Hensbrook, hopefully.

"Says he hasn't got time."

"Union Mining will double their profits this year," said Hensbrook, puffing on his cigar and changing the subject.

"How does he do it?" asked Sir Thomas.

"Makes his assets work for him properly. The ones that don't work he sells. Most of the property in the company was shown at book value which was in many instances nil. We owned a hotel in the West End that had nothing to do with our real business. Reggie sold it for nine hundred thousand pounds. Didn't even appear in the accounts. I don't think Migroyd can read a balance sheet any more than I can. What did Reggie study at Oxford?"

"P.P.E.," said Sir Thomas. "Politics, philosophy and economics. The German, Dane and Frenchman were reading for their PhDs at the same time. They make a formidable combination. With this Everly man brought into the consortium, they straddle the globe. Tug's done wonders in the Far East, Reggie tells me."

"Lucky man," said Hensbrook.

"They were lucky not to get involved in a war," said Sir Thomas, sympathetically. "Help yourself to the port."

"Don't mind if I do."

"Bertie?"

"Thank you, Thomas. And when are we going to see you in India again?"

"Not next year," said Sir Thomas. "I was thinking of the end of 1939. There's a lot to be said for an English winter but there's a lot more to be said for getting out of it. Could you put up with us again?"

"We'll fill the other side of this den with some very rare specimens," said Bertie.

"So MY SON enjoys the East, Mrs Gray?" said Lady Beaumont.

"Loves it. Took to Kuching so well. We were so sorry that he wanted to leave the Colonial Service. Edward said in his last letter how much they all miss him. Our loss and Reginald's gain. It was so kind of you to invite me for Christmas."

"Can't have friends of Tug's on their own at such a time," said Lady Beaumont. "When are you returning to Sarawak?"

"Now that poor mother is dead, I should be able to sell up everything by the end of March."

"You don't have any children?"

"No. Edward and I didn't have any children, Lady Beaumont."

"Pity. Children are a great source of interest as we grow older. Don't you agree Mary? Now, who've we got on the list for those two younger daughters. No problem there as they're all pretty. Poor, ugly girls are the problem," finished Lady Beaumont, bluntly.

"If you'll excuse me, Lady Beaumont," said Mrs Gray. "I'll go up to my room to unpack."

"If you get lost, ask one of the servants. Easy to lose your way among the corridors."

Lady Hensbrook watched Mrs Gray leave the room and close the door.

"Who is that dreadful woman, Alice?"

"Reggie asked me to invite her. Business connection for Tug. Husband's the equivalent of Prime Minister of Sarawak but they call him First Officer for some unknown reason. She had the sense to leave us alone. She's probably quite the big wig in Kuching."

"Remind me never to go to Kuching," said Lady Hensbrook, lifting the tortoise-shell china tea cup to her lips. "Now, Reggie," began Lady Hensbrook.

"Don't think so. You've done well out of my family."

"On the contrary, Alice, your sons have found two most presentable wives. Why not Reggie?"

"Doesn't seem to want to marry."

"Has everything he needs?"

"Probably. He doesn't have time for a wife and children. I thought he might take a shine to your youngest, Pippa, but he treats her like a younger sister. She's easily the prettiest.

"Do you think so?" said Lady Hensbrook. "Gwenneth is so unusual."

"Too aloof. Frightens the men. Class is terribly important but there must be a little enthusiasm. How about one of Reggie's partners?"

"I wouldn't like them married to a foreigner," said Lady Hensbrook.

"Yes," said Lady Beaumont.

"ONE OF THE servants will be sending us black coffee," said Reggie, sitting at the head of the long table in the library. "With all of the partners together it's important to exchange views."

"Have these books been read?" said Chuck looking around the long room with its leather bound volumes from floor to ceiling.

"I certainly haven't read any of them," said Reggie. "Do you want to start, Chuck?"

"Sure. The States is fine. Once we had the Home Insurance Company out of New York, the rest came easy. The Fireman's out of Denver came to visit me in Kansas City last week. They haven't signed but they will. Some others will wait for the first year's underwriting results. Eleven companies so far. It'll only get better."

"Carl?" said Reggie.

"Nine Scandinavian companies. No change."

"Gunter?"

"Nineteen."

"François?"

"Fourteen."

"Seven in Japan and thirty-eight in England but then England has always been the home of insurance. We even brought the Royal Exchange in after a little persuasion. The man's besotted by Clair which is one of the reasons she's been invited for Christmas. Once the insurance companies have been at risk for a year the profits will speak for themselves. Ninety-eight companies in total. During this first year it's vital to keep close with your clients. Our reinsurance business does not present a problem. Union Mining does. The London Stock Exchange have finally agreed to our takeover as they were concerned that a British company might fall into foreign hands. After several assurances they now believe we have no intention of changing the company's nationality and despite tax benefits it will remain registered in London. The big problem is management. We need a professional firm of auditors who don't leave out of the accounts a large hotel. I am tempted to bring Tug back from the Far East but there are family problems. Anyway, he is more than valuable in Kuching. Our go-down after four months of buying is half full of raw rubber and the current CIF London is thirty percent up on purchase price. Anymore war rumours and the price will double."

"Agreed," said Gunter. "I have a go-down in Macoa filling up nicely. Rumours are that Portugal will remain neutral."

"You've no doubt about a war?" said Reggie.

"None, unless the world appeases Hitler until he is given what he wants. The man won't stop. The party is in control of Germany and everybody else is happy making money. They will not be so happy in the event of war but they do not see it that way. It is like childbirth. People forget the pain. It will be difficult for us but international business must transcend politics. If in the months or years to come our countries are fighting then we as individuals must not take it as fighting each other. It will be important to survive with honour... Reggie, back to management problems."

"I have appointed a new Managing Director for the reinsurance division," said Reggie. "I will take over as Chief Executive of Union Mining next month and visit our operations around the world. The three companies I looked into in London were in chaos. The hotel had broken even for eight years and the manager, on a salary of two thousand pounds a year, was a millionaire. He was fired and is being prosecuted for fraud. He will have a lot of friends with him in jail. From now on, Gunter, to safeguard our national interests and responsibilities, it is better to keep details from each other. No-one can then accuse us of aiding an enemy. What a bloody sad world we have come to again. Now, here is my outline for the group over the next five years. I have deleted any items that could embarrass Gunter or myself. After my report, the meeting will be open to general discussion. Ah, thank you, Conway. Could you put the coffee at the end of the table and we'll help ourselves." Forgetting the servant, he turned back to his partners. "In the group we have known deposits of gold in South Africa, chrome in Southern Rhodesia and nickel in Australia. Little of the mining side has been developed. After further surveys to confirm the depth of the deposits and the ore content, I propose we go to the Stock Exchange with a rights issue. We will then open three new mines with the money. I have had preliminary discussions with Barings Bank and they are prepared to underwrite the issue. The existing gold, copper and manganese mines will be investigated by a team of engineers. Their report will enable us to determine the future profitability of these mines. Now, turning to our present cash flow..." Thelma sat at the end of the table taking shorthand notes for the minutes of the meeting. She had only managed to catch François's eye on one occasion.

"Mɪɴᴅ ɪꜰ I ᴄᴏᴍᴇ ɪɴ?" said Tony Venturas, as the door to the girls' bedroom opened an inch. "Thought you'd be up here. The others are in a meeting which will last all afternoon. Reggie's either playing or working but he never sits still."

"We were wondering what to do with ourselves," said Clair.

"I've brought up a bottle of champagne from the car and the butler gave me glasses."

"Come and sit round the fire," said Penny. "They must own a coal mine to afford all the fires in this house."

"I believe Reggie does."

"What does he do?" asked Clair. "He's often in the club. Seems more than just a member."

"He's my closest friend. We fly in the Auxiliary Air Squadron."

"No, Tony, there's more to it than that," said Penny. "He's using us, isn't he?"

"Everyone's using someone."

"What's his racket?"

"He doesn't have one, but he does use the club's facilities, but not for himself. He finds his clients like him better for being brought to Bretts. The man from the Royal Exchange is an example. You handle him well inside the club, Clair, so I hope you are making good tips."

"Oh, we're doing alright, aren't we Penny?"

"I'll say, two hundred quid a night."

"We? I don't understand. He's Clair's client."

"The fat old bugger is kinky," said Penny. "He likes two or more at a time but he can't get it up. Hangs there like a two year old on Clacton beach. His favourite is a cocktail party in his flat, himself as the only male guest and all the female guests wearing high heels and a hat with a feather and nothing else. Likes them to go round chatting as if everything was normal, sipping fancy cocktails. Clair has to organise the other girls. For two hundred quid, I don't mind looking at the silly old bugger."

"Where does he get the money from? Reggie says he's only the reinsurance manager."

"He pinches it," said Clair. "When he's tipsy he likes to brag about it to the girls. Says he can give them as much money as they want provided they do what he wants. He likes being whipped when he's really drunk and then we have to steal the money that he's hidden in the room. We whip him, tie him up and then ransack the bloody room. Quite a giggle, everyone ripping the place to pieces and this fat old bugger roped up on the floor yelling at us to please rob him and whip him even harder."

"Who's he robbing?"

"The insurance company. Says the directors know nothing about insurance so he fiddles the books, writes out cheques to a company that doesn't exist except for a bank account. When he was really kinked up one night we found five thousand pounds in the copper vase right under the water and the daffodils."

"My goodness. I had no idea what you girls get up to."

"He is unusual."

"They'll catch him, sooner or later."

"Doubt it. Says he's been doing it for fifteen years. Despite everything else he doesn't lie. I wonder what his imagination is going to come up with next time."

"You must be careful, Clair. That type can get violent. I'll have a word with Reggie and keep him out of the club. If you've made good money without any trouble so far then it's time to stop. Out of the club is your business but we're also friends. If you get any more funnies, let me know."

"Thanks, Tony. And what does Reggie do apart from insurance broking?"

"Why don't you ask him? Quick, pass your glass. This stuff's fizzy when the cork pops."

Mrs Gray looked out of her bedroom window at the bleak cold of England and longed for the heat and view of Kuching harbour with the Chinese sailing boats and the dhows from Malaya. She was homesick but not for England. Here she was in a house with so many people but she was alone in the world. She knew the other ladies didn't want to talk to her. What had she to add to their conversation? To Lady Beaumont, Kuching only had a relevance through her son and she didn't want to hear about anything else. She, Rebecca, was a nobody in England and this infuriated her more than anything else. Even her dress for the evening was suited to the tropics. Anyway, she said to herself, she was lucky not to be spending Christmas on her own.

The Honourable Philippa de La Rivière, the youngest of the four sisters, glared at her sister, and stamped her foot on the bedroom floor.

"I don't care if he is a foreigner, he's rich. At school they say all Americans are rich."

"Don't be silly, Pippa," said Gwenneth. "He won't look at you, you're far too young. He must be all of thirty and you are seventeen."

"He looked at me twice at lunchtime," insisted Pippa.

"He looked at me as well," said Gwen, the second of the unmarried daughters, turning from the window. "He's probably married. I prefer Reggie."

"We all prefer Reggie," said Pippa, "but he wouldn't even look at Isabel before she was married, so we don't stand a chance."

"I wonder if he's sleeping with one of those girls he brought down? Maybe his secretary?"

"What do you know about such things?" said Pippa in surprise.

"Obviously more than you do," said Gwen. "And the secretary doesn't look like a secretary either. Secretaries wear two-piece suits and glasses."

"You have too vivid an imagination."

"What about the other three?" asked Gwen.

"They're foreign. Mother would never approve. You said so yourself."

"Father might. They're rich."

"I still like the American," said Pippa smugly, "and I'm going to make big eyes at him at the banquet tonight."

"The other guests aren't much," said Gwen. "Very horsy and no chins and only two of them aren't married."

"Worse," said Pippa, "they're as poor as church mice."

THE LONG CHAMBER had been the only part of the house that had not been destroyed by Cromwell as the old, oak roof-beams were hard as iron and had refused to burn. The structure went back to the time of Magna Carta and King John, a Beaumont having been one of the signatories at Runnymede. Two long dining tables with benches for seating ran the length of the room.

Sitting in the chair with the highest back at the centre of the table on the dais, Sir Thomas signalled Pavy that it was time for the baron of beef to be brought into the banquet. All around the chamber, with its thirty foot ceiling that guttering candles couldn't reach, stood the servants of Merry Hall dressed in traditional smocks with the facsimile of a Norman helmet stitched onto the front. It was the only time in the year that all the servants served at table.

"Why aren't you up at the top table?" asked Chuck, sitting next to Georgina at a long table.

"It's tradition. Men only on the top table. The incumbent baronet's birthday is the most important date in the Beaumont diary. The first baronet was concerned about a male heir always sitting in that seat with the tallest back. Most families die out, like ours, because no-one has kept proper records of all the, male descendants. The centre table on the dais is reserved for the immediate heirs of the baronet who are over the age of eighteen. The two tables on either side are reserved for other male descendants of Sir Henri Beaumont."

"But the tables are empty," said Chuck.

"There aren't any other males left," said Georgina. "The war. The Germans and the Turks killed eleven Beaumonts."

"How far back goes the family?"

"1066. Sir Thomas is the thirty-seventh baronet."

"There must be more male heirs after so many years. They just don't know about them."

"There aren't. There's a book in the vaults below us that is older than the Doomsday Book. Every time Merry Hall has been knocked to the ground, the vault has never been disturbed. I've not seen it and never will. I'm not a Beaumont by birth. My sons will be told where it is. In the book they've entered the birth of every male descendant. Every five years, or after a major war, the incumbent baronet is obliged to send out horsemen to visit the male members of the family and report back births and deaths. To prevent a man just disappearing without a forwarding address he has to register with his local parish priest. The church has been able to point the horsemen to where the man has gone."

"Aren't there any in America?"

"There were. The last of the American line was a colonel in the army who came across to France in 1917. He was killed in action. There was also an Australian branch. Two brothers. They both died on the same day at Gallipoli without reaching the beach."

"You can't use horsemen in today's world," smiled Chuck as the servants brought in the baron of beef on the oak shaft that had held it over the open hearth in the kitchen.

"No. Of course not. They use the post and tracing agents. It's easier now in some ways but more difficult in others. In the old days, a journey of twenty miles was a long way. Now the Beaumonts go all over the world. Look at Reggie. He flew to Japan and back in ten days."

"Why's there an empty chair beside Reggie?"

"That's Tug's. It will only be removed if he dies."

"It's medieval."

"Yes, it is."

"That's the biggest piece of beef I've ever seen," said Chuck.

"Now comes the fun. You men go and hack from the carcass what you want with that dagger beside your plate. The ladies hope the men will feed them. It's messy but fun. When we've eaten the carcass will go back to the kitchen for the village. Afterwards they will sing carols from that gallery above Sir Thomas. Drink and be merry. It's a family tradition."

"Who's that pretty girl down the table in the white dress?"

"My younger sister, Pippa. The Honourable Philippa de La Rivière."

"She's got a title?"

"Sure," said Georgina smiling and using one of Chuck's own words. She was enjoying his company.

"Why's she got a title?"

"Because father's the eighth Baron Hensbrook of Corfe Castle in the county of Dorset. He's also the last. We've run out of men."

"Then you must be an Honourable?"

"Yes. All daughters of Barons are given the courtesy title of Honourable."

"She's very pretty," said Chuck, catching Pippa's eye.

"And very young. Seventeen to be exact. Aren't you married?"

"If I was, do you think a wife would let me come to a do like this on my own? She'd have the skin off my back for letting that happen. American wives. Jealous, especially in the Midwest. That's Kansas City, Missouri, where I come from. How much of that beef can you eat, Georgina?"

"Lots. It's delicious and cook puts a crusty baste all over it."

"THE SECRET," said the vicar to Mrs Gray, "is to keep the juice on the plate and not in your lap." He fed another piece of rare beef into his mouth and chewed contentedly while cutting another piece with his dagger in preparation for the next mouthful.

"You're very clever," said Mrs Gray, who was covered in grease and gravy. "It keeps running down my arm and chin. But it is delicious."

"Use the napkin after each bite," said the Vicar. "I was as bad as you my first time but that was twenty-seven years ago. Ah, the vegetables," he said with satisfaction.

The servants placed large bowls of baked potatoes, Brussels sprouts, roast swedes, crushed sweet chestnuts in horse-radish and peeled root artichokes on the tables followed by troughs of gravy run off from Mrs Breed's basting that had soaked up orange and lemon juice, red wine, spices and herbs. The vicar ladled a spoonful of each vegetable onto his plate, alongside a large baked potato which he split with his dagger and filled with butter. Gravy went over his remaining hunk of meat and he smacked his lips, tested the various dishes for heat with his thumb and began putting it into his mouth using the first two fingers of his right hand.

"Help yourself," he said with a half full mouth, waving his left hand at the bowls. "Doris Breed's the best cook in the world."

"I think I would have liked living four hundred years ago," said Mrs Gray, and began helping herself from the bowls but with smaller spoonfuls.

"Don't know where he puts it all," said Reggie, nodding towards the vicar. Reggie helped himself to another spoonful of the chestnut and horseradish that was Doris Breed's speciality for the Beaumont night in the long chamber.

"You won't starve either," said Geoffrey leaning forward to talk past Henry and his father. "When you've finished hogging all the chestnut, you might pass some down here."

"Aren't they feeding you in the army?" asked Henry.

"In the seven years I've been at the top table, I've never been able to eat enough of Doris Breed's chestnut," said Geoffrey.

"And before that she was feeding it to you in the kitchen," said Sir Thomas dunking a half raw piece of beef in the gravy before putting it into his mouth.

"Leave some room for the Christmas pudding… Vicar's going to give one of his better sermons," said Reggie. "Conway keeps filling up his wine tankard."

"Anybody going from here will be asleep by then," said Henry. "Do you agree I breed the best beef in Surrey?" and he cut himself another cube of red-running beef with his dagger.

"Bloody uncivilised," said Sir Thomas. "I love it."

"Wish I had an extra stomach like a cow," said Geoffrey and got up to hack himself another piece of meat from the carcass.

"I always say," said Lady Beaumont "that it shows how close we all are to animals."

"Once a year," said Lady Hensbrook. "You must have cut down a holly bush to put so much around the walls. Do you know which is which among the portraits?"

"There is confusion over four of them as there is with some of the older shields. Sir Henri's must have been replaced with a copy many times. Anything before Cromwell is a replica. Ah, they're removing that hideous carcass. Looks more like a battlefield than a dining hall. Your husband appears to have enjoyed himself. He's covered with grease from ear to ear. They'll bring out bowls of hot water in a minute and then they can remove the worst. Savages, the lot of 'em and my sons are the worst. I've been watching Reggie. He's eaten a whole bowl of the chestnuts himself. He'll become portly in his old age. Your Pippa has her eye on the American. They say that one member of every generation ends up in America."

"She's far too young," said Lady Hensbrook.

"You never can tell. Married Thomas when I was nineteen. How old were you when you married Hensbrook?"

"Eighteen."

"There you are," said Lady Beaumont with satisfaction.

"I don't believe it," said François to Thelma who had been in charge of the seating arrangements for non-family members. "Christmas pudding on top of what I've eaten."

Four servants carried a six-foot long silver tray into the hall. The tray was covered in flaming Christmas puddings complete with a top of red berried holly. They walked around the room and presented the tray to Sir Thomas who put a spoonful on his plate.

"Now I know why he runs every morning," said Gunter watching Geoffrey pile his plate with Christmas pudding.

Servants put baskets of nuts, tangerines, dates, liqueur chocolates and bananas on the tables along with the nutcrackers.

"I thought the Germans knew how to make pigs of themselves at the table," said Gunter.

"Danes don't do badly," said Carl, studiously avoiding the glances from Isabel.

"Wow," said François, helping himself to a spoonful of Christmas pudding, "My stomach is going to burst."

"Have some more wine," said Thelma who had been keeping his tankard topped up all evening.

"If this is how the rich live," said Clair, "then I want to be rich."

"You'd end up round as a barrel," said Penny.

"Who cares, darling, when you're rich? Gunter, can you organise me some more of that cider? It's rough and gorgeous and I'm sure it will go with Christmas pudding."

"Did you see Reggie?" said Penny. "He's been eating more than any of you."

"And he still doesn't have an ounce of fat, so there," said Clair. "I'd also burn it up with mental energy. I'll tell you something too. They're telling dirty jokes on that top table. Reggie only guffaws that way when it's really filthy."

"You've a one track mind," said Penny.

Slowly the room hushed as the strains of *Holy Night* was heard from the inner courtyard of Merry Hall. The sound was strong and recognisable even if some of the villagers' voices were out of tune. The essence of Christmas flowed into the long chamber. The sound came nearer and then faded to grow again as the villagers and tenants, led by Bert Brigley, came out on the minstrels' gallery looking down on the upturned faces of the overfed guests. The strain of looking upwards caused the vicar to bulge red in the face and caused Lilly Brigley to break off a high note and giggle. During the third carol she saw the portrait of Tammany on the wall just below and to her left. Without being told she knew exactly who it was.

The villagers filed back into the courtyard and into the huge kitchen where they set to on the carcass and washed it down with beer and cider. Then came pies and Christmas pudding.

The vicar tried to get his feet out from under the table but had to be helped and with a wave and a lurch made his way out of the chamber.

"I laid on a driver," said Sir Thomas, watching with affection. "He really does enjoy himself. Pass the wine jug, Henry, one of your horsy friends is under the table."

"Probably asleep," said Reggie. "Wouldn't have the imagination to look up the ladies' skirts."

"Don't be rude about my friends," said Henry.

"Trying to be polite actually. Father, can you bang the table and tell everyone they can smoke and then we can join the ladies. I enjoy my brothers but they aren't very pretty."

"Your mother will take the older generation into the drawing room," said Sir Thomas doing what he was asked.

"Good," said Lady Beaumont, "now we can go and have a nice cup of tea and leave all this debauchery to the men."

"I think my girls will want to stay," said Lady Hensbrook.

"Let 'em. I'm glad that Mrs Gray went off with the Vicar. Poor man."

"He always rises to an occasion."

The two elderly ladies stood up and made their way out of the chamber, nodding to their friends to follow them.

Sir Thomas waved at his wife and she smiled.

"Have a cigar," said Sir Thomas offering the box to Lord Hensbrook and Bertie Featherstone. "I've sent Pavy for the port, or would you prefer a whisky and soda?"

"Port'll be fine," said Bertie cutting the end from his cigar and licking it all over. "Quite a feast."

"Some of the youngsters have gone to the library to dance," said Sir Thomas. "Reggie had the table taken out. Good floor for dancing. Must be cold outside. Don't envy the vicar. He'll never get the church warm on a night like this."

"How are you feeling?" asked Henry.

"Fine," said Isabel. "It's only in the mornings."

"Are you going to join us in the library or do you want to go upstairs?"

"Better be careful. Can't carry the heir to so much history without being careful. I'll see my way up. You go and enjoy yourself. After the baby, I'll be back to parties."

"Our guests will never survive tomorrow," said Henry.

"They will. The human body has a remarkable ability to recover when people want to enjoy themselves. Say good night to everyone for me. I'll go through the kitchen. I want to thank Doris Breed. Everyone said the food was perfect. How's the foal?"

"1940 Derby winner without a doubt. Sleep well."

Still smiling, but sick at heart, she left the guests, did her duty with the staff as Henry's wife and then made her way down the long, cold corridors to a lonely bedroom. She had not spoken a word to Carl.

"I'm glad you saw the painting," said Reggie, as he let her out through the French windows onto the snow-covered terrace. "She's not just a lady of colour."

"Let's change the subject, Reggie," said Lilly Brigley.

"Have you had your exam results?"

"Yes."

"Well?" asked Reggie who was dressed in fur-lined flying boots, a voluminous fox fur coat and a deer-stalker hat with flaps to keep his ears warm.

"Passed. Just. Took a third. I'd lost interest. People must have a reason to do things."

"You won't get cold walking back? I could have taken the car."

"It's beautiful out."

"Yes. It is," agreed Reggie, looking up at the cloudless night sky. "What are you going to do?"

"Try and find a husband, I suppose. It's what most girls of twenty are looking for. I just find it difficult to concentrate after Tug. We made love, you know. Under the great oak in the woods. Only one night. Then he was posted. Is the first one always so important?"

"Yes," said Reggie and fell uncharacteristically quiet as they started along the path between the herbaceous borders. There wasn't a sound in the night, the mantle of snow having softened everything to silence.

"Who was she, Reggie?"

"It's one subject I never talk about. We won't be seeing you in the club, then?"

"Until I find a job. A Bachelor of Arts degree in English isn't much commercial use."

"Where are you going to stay?"

"With Sally. She got a first and her brother's going up to Oxford next year. She said a little bit of whoring paid off."

"It's a strange world. And now everyone says there's going to be a war. I can't imagine Gunter and me in opposing air forces. Our trip to the East was a highlight of a long friendship."

"Sally's got a good job in a prep school near the flat so she won't be coming back to Bretts."

"Good. I'm glad for her. She's a very intelligent woman. She won't have any problem finding a husband. The combination of a 'First' and her good looks are unbeatable. I just hope her brother never finds out how she paid for his education."

"Especially when he becomes Prime Minister," giggled Lilly.

"You're not cold, are you?"

"Only my fingers and toes."

"Put one hand in my pocket. Then you can change sides. Can't think of anything to help the toes. Some of Doris Breed's chestnut keeps coming back on me. I ate too much."

"Looking down on the slumped bodies, you weren't the only one. This is the path Tug and I took so often."

"Better to start again, Lilly. You won't forget him but you've still got a lot of living to do."

"Am I going to see you in London if I don't go back to Bretts?"

"We'll have dinner together. Do you like Italian food?"

"Love it."

"Soho and a large bottle of Chianti."

"Can I change pockets?"

As they passed into the wood, the owl let out a hoot right above them and made them jump.

"When we get to the cottage, come in for cocoa. It's still cosy in the kitchen as dad wouldn't let me remove the Aga. You can ride Stanchion home if you like. He's a bit slow these days but he'll make it."

"Prefer to walk. Not enough exercise."

By two a.m., most of the lights in Merry Hall were out. The exception was the room shared by Clair and Penny. Clair crouched over François's open mouth while he gently tongued her clitoris and Penny ran his bulging cock in and out of her mouth. Carl got onto the double bed behind Penny and thrust into her from the back which made her suck François harder. Carl thrust five times and withdrew so that he wouldn't climax and made his way up the bed towards Clair who was facing away from him and watching François suck her almost to a climax. Each time she thought she was coming in his face, he stopped. Carl took hold of her thigh and pulled her over and away from François onto the other side of the bed and entered her bringing her quickly to a climax. Penny moved up and kissed François taking his cock deep inside her until he felt a barrier in her cunt and climaxed making her shudder with the feel of warm semen.

"I'm coming," said Penny. "I'm coming," which caused Carl to climax into Clair. Slowly they came back to the cold air and climbed under the blankets.

Clair curled up to the large frame of Carl and Penny locked together with François. They were warm and totally satisfied.

"Happy Christmas," said Penny into François's ear and fell asleep.

The chambermaid found them the next morning and discreetly came back with two extra cups for the tea. Outside it was snowing again and the landscape was totally white.

5

MAY TO OCTOBER 1937

Four months later, on the first Tuesday in May 1937, Geoffrey Beaumont watched the sun break through a bank of dark rain clouds that had deposited a shower of rain on the Middle Wallop runway. As he looked through his office window an Anson trainer trundled along the runway and took to the air.

"Come in," he said to the knock at his door. "Ah, Jim. Thanks for coming. Have you been to the Belgium Congo?"

"Don't be bloody silly. That's in the middle of Africa. Jungle. Disease. Gorillas. All that kind of thing."

"Well, we're going there. Amongst other places."

"Kenya's a better place for safaris," said Jim not understanding the implications. "Had a friend at school who went out with his father. Plenty of bearers and a white hunter to shoot things that get out of hand. Said the climate was very good especially during winter. The colonel will never give us leave. Anyway, I don't have any money."

"It's not going to be that kind of safari. A four month survival exercise to test our equipment and ourselves. We've perfected jumping out of aeroplanes and running around Salisbury Plain with the utmost efficiency but the terrain isn't tough. We think the new Vauxhall four-wheel drive is the best chassis we've turned into a fast long range armoured car but we don't know what it will do under extreme conditions. Our airborne drop on the Isle of Man was another good exercise but it didn't push us to the limit. What's the worst terrain you can think of?"

"The Arctic. The middle of Australia. Central Africa."

"Exactly. Deserts and Central Africa. We are going to make a journey from Cairo to Cape Town, overland. Start in Cairo and move through the desert into the Sudan. Then into the Congo, the Rhodesias and South Africa."

"Are you serious?"

"When it comes to the army, I never fool around."

"Are you saying you're going to take the whole unit on an exercise down the centre of Africa?"

"Na. Just you and me, Corporal Miller and Sparrow and Private Philpott and Kemp. We'll travel as a British Army unit under battle conditions in two vehicles. The R.A.F. will supply us from Aden, Nairobi and Gwelo in Rhodesia. Everyone will be asked to volunteer. Personally, I think it will be a lot of fun at the army's expense but if we can get ourselves and our equipment from Cairo to Cape Town then we will have proved the viability of the Long Range Unit. No-one will be able to say we can't survive on our own."

"What about the R.A.F.?"

"It's a good exercise for them. They'll have to be smart to find a couple of armoured cars in the middle of Africa. Most of the time we'll be living off the land. Our biggest problem is petrol."

"Did I have a choice?"

"Do you want one?"

"Not particularly."

"We'll write a survival manual for the others when we come back. The four men I want are strong. Miller did well finishing fourteenth in the Berlin Marathon. You'd better get them in one by one to see if they'll come. If they don't come they're off the unit."

"They'll come. The men like being elite but then who doesn't?"

"Don't tell Mary or Georgina until nearer the time."

"When are we going?"

"The C.O.'s given the okay for the 27 May, sailing from Southampton. We'll be in Cairo by the 2nd of June. Miss Wimbledon and the Derby but that's the army for you," he said sarcastically.

"What about your cricket?"

"There won't be any this season unless I can get a game in Cape Town. Their season's the reverse of ours. Vauxhall say the vehicles will be ready in time. I've collected as much information as is available about the terrain. There isn't much. A lot of the time we'll be driving by compass. We'll know what we've left behind when we need it.

"It is my pleasure," said Reggie Beaumont from where he stood on the small stand that had been erected next to the drilling shaft, "to turn the switch to begin shaft sinking at Union Mining's Kloof Mine. In two years' time it will give me more pleasure to witness the pouring of our first gold. May this be a safe mine, second to none on the Reef. It is my wish as chairman of the company to see that no funds are spared in pursuit of production with maximum safety. When, five months ago I set in motion the analysis to determine whether our exploration could be turned into a viable mine, I did not expect to be here so soon. It says a lot for the South African mining industry with which I am proud to be associated. I will now ask the Mayor of Johannesburg to say a few words."

Stepping back, Reggie looked out over the highveld autumn, over the rolling hills beyond Boksburg. He enjoyed the warm sun and the cool breeze that tugged at his wing collar. He stood in the vast open space of the veld with three hundred guests. Apart from the tall, fluffy brown grass that had grown well during the rainy season, nothing else moved until his eye caught the flash of sun on a lone windmill that the wind was whistling round to chug up the underground water from a borehole some half a mile away. Having made a decision to proceed with the new mine his mind was at rest with the project. Now they would find out how much gold lay under their feet. His thoughts turned to the nickel mine in Western Australia which needed a decision.

"The mayor's finished," said Thelma next to him, giving him a nudge and causing him to clap with the rest of them.

Reggie went round shaking hands with the senior staff who would work the mine and thanked the mayor and the regional manager of the Standard Bank for their co-operation. There was one thing Reggie had learnt in his brief years of business and that was not to allow one supplier or client to become too powerful. Barclays Bank would finance the nickel mine in conjunction with the ANZ Bank in Melbourne. Standard in South Africa.

"The company lies dormant for twenty years," said a man behind him in the crowd, "then this Beaumont man comes along and we're sinking new shafts."

"Ever since John Fox died no-one has done anything."

"He'll be another bloody Oppenheimer if he's not careful."

"Good luck to him, I say. Develops Johannesburg."

"Let's go," said Reggie quietly to Thelma. "If he knew how many sleepless nights I've had he wouldn't be so confident."

"Let's have supper together away from them all."

"You have some excellent ideas, Miss King… Dawson's it shall be. For two. Apart from waiting for the Cape Town train there's nothing more to do."

"WHY HAVE you never made a pass at me?" asked Thelma, toying with the glass of red Cape wine.

"You are worth more to me than a few nights in the sack."

"Commercially, you mean?"

"Come on, Thelma. This is an old chestnut. You know I never go out with staff. If you want to resign we'll have a rollicking affair all the way back on the boat but there'll be no more working for me."

"That's all it would be, wouldn't it?"

"Yes."

"At least you are honest."

"How are you getting on with François?"

"The 'don't touch, I'm a virgin' approach hasn't worked."

"Never thought it would but that was your business. Just drove him into the beds of other women. Men over twenty-three have to be ready for marriage then they fall in love seriously."

"What about men under twenty-three?"

"Then it is different. They are idealists. Believe the world is perfect or that it can be changed. They don't know the weight of responsibility or the sadness of rejection. I call it the happy period, eighteen to twenty-three. A perfect time to fall in love. There is so much future when you are eighteen," and he turned and caught the eye of the head waiter who hurried to their table. "Crepe suzette, Thelma?"

"Thank you."

"Two please," he said to the waiter, "but don't make them sweet."

"Do you think I have a chance with François?"

"He's thirty. French. Rich. A bachelor. Difficult to change. At that age the main reason a man marries is to have children. 1937 would not be my year for bringing children into the world. The Japs are pushing into China. Mussolini is strutting around creating an Italian Empire and Hitler is going berserk. Chamberlain smiles at him and says there will be no war in our time. We British are far too complacent. We'll pay for it."

"Have you been in love?"

Reggie toyed with his own wine glass, took a sip and put it down.

"Yes. Once."

"What happened?"

"Nothing."

"Sorry to pry. You don't want to talk about it?"

"It was a long time ago. Probably a dream. My first year up at Oxford before even François, Carl or Gunter came up. I went on a cycling holiday by myself. I had some idea of becoming a poet and the summer of 1926 was ripe for a young romantic. I'd stopped at a little pub in Godalming to have some lunch and had taken my half pint of beer and a large beef sandwich to eat on the bench outside when a group of cyclists pulled in for the same reason. What I didn't know was they were all from a Jewish youth club in Hampstead. Orthodox Jews. Do you know, I'd never met one before? Afra leant her bicycle against my bench which made me look up into green eyes with a depth of ages. We just went on looking into our souls until a friend pulled her away to where the men were laying out food they'd taken from their saddle bags. They were laying it out on the publican's long table. It was before twelve in the morning and I was his only customer but he came strutting out in high dudgeon and said they couldn't eat their food on his premises. I suppose he did have a point but his table was almost in the road. 'It won't hurt you I said,' standing up clutching my half-eaten sandwich.

'I have to make a living.'

'Let them be. Not everyone has a father who gives them an allowance. I bet yours didn't.'

'Of course not,' he said belligerently and went back into the pub.

"Afra smiled at me and we got talking, all of us in the end and I cycled off with them. Through Hampshire and Dorset, Devon and down to the tip of Cornwall. It was the happiest two weeks of my life. By the time I was back at Oxford I was in love and so was Afra. Ah, the crepe suzette, Can you bring me a Remy Martin and a Benedictine for the lady? You do still drink Benedictine with your coffee?" he said turning back to Thelma.

"What happened?"

"Nothing. There was nothing to happen as I discovered. Orthodox Jews don't allow their daughters to go out with Christians. I tried a few times and even met her father after sitting on his front doorstep for six hours. He was very nice but I was never allowed to see her again. They married her off in the autumn to the tailor's son. I met one of the men we cycled with last year. She has five children… How's your crepe?"

"Nice. Not too sweet… Now I understand you better, Reggie."

"You're the only person to hear that story. I've never had that emotion since. Until I do, I'll remain a bachelor."

ON THE OTHER side of the world Tug Beaumont put more crimson on the flower he was painting onto his canvas. It was the first afternoon he'd been able to relax by himself since he'd started his business trip from Kuching eight weeks earlier and he was missing Tammany and the children.

"Morning, Tug," said a British voice from over his shoulder.

"Morning, sir," said Tug without looking round.

"Didn't know you were a painter?" said Bertie Featherstone.

"I find it very relaxing. Take a seat on the bench. I won't be long. The light is fading."

"Did you see your man?"

"No. Not a word."

"Chinese are different. Not concerned with time. I made some enquiries for you. Indian Civil still has contacts in Malaya. Your Mr Ho is probably the richest man in these waters. Deals in anything worth buying or selling. Keeps out of sight. Above board… Had dinner with the Governor on Thursday. Your personal credentials and that of Union Mining will reach Mr Ho from Government House."

"There we are," said Tug looking up at the darkening sky. "That's exotic flower painting over for one day."

"We'll have a chotapeg at the swimming club," said Bertie. "Tommy was at school with me. Actually, he was my fag."

"Tommy?"

"The Governor."

"Oh," said Tug.

"Can I help you carry some of that stuff?"

"Thanks. I make two journeys by myself. My car's at the end of the path. Don't get paint on yourself."

"More humid than India," said Bertie. "Why is it that wherever the British colonise they put down a botanical garden and a statue of Queen Victoria."

"Something to do with Kew Gardens. Without Kew Gardens you wouldn't be buying raw rubber around here. The rubber trees originated in the Amazon forest of Brazil. The Brazilians had a monopoly until Kew Gardens sent in an expedition to steal seedlings. The Brazilians are still furious… Here. Put the easel in the back. Just made it. Either my watch is slow or the rain's early. Better wait in the car 'til it's over."

"Good idea," said Bertie.

"Spoke to mother on the phone this morning. I always phone on her birthday. Line was terrible. That younger brother of mine is in the middle of the Sudan on his way to Cape Town. Mother's worried stiff. Listen to the rain," shouted Tug as the downpour hit the roof of the car.

HENRY BEAUMONT WATCHED PROUDLY as the vicar sprinkled holy water over the brow of his daughter. He had timed the christening to coincide with the Epsom race meeting and many of his friends were watching the simple ceremony take place in the morning room of Merry Hall. Rosalyn had slept through most of the christening, draped in a long, lace shawl that had belonged to her grandmother. She wrinkled her month's old face at the water and looked at her mother. The eyes were pale blue and crystal clear. Reggie, as one godfather, looked distinguished in morning dress. Next to him, though very much lower down, Beau, two-years-old, asked his uncle if he could flick the baby.

"Not a good idea," said Reggie, taking his nephew's hand.

The morning room was a mass of cut flowers, arranged in vases and bowls. Bird song from the garden through the French windows was sharp. A strident screech from a peacock made the Vicar look up over the top of his reading glasses.

"I hereby christen you Rosalyn Alice Mary in the name of Jesus Christ," said the vicar and smiled broadly at the baby and then the parents in turn.

The guests began moving onto the terrace where Pavy had set up the food and drink and a central, round table for the thirty pound christening cake. The vicar was the first to take a Pimm's cup from one of the servants to propose a toast of long life to the latest Beaumont.

Isabel stood holding her child.

Georgina, watching her sister watch the child, looked around for Lorna through the swirl of people and winced as she saw her daughter bump into the legs of a waiter. A little Pimm's shot from two of the glasses before the waiter steadied himself.

"Tug sent a cable from Singapore," said Sir Thomas. "No word from Geoffrey."

"Don't imagine they have post offices," said Lady Beaumont.

"He'll be alright."

"That's what you always say."

"Well, they have been, haven't they?"

"Mother," said Reggie, "I'm going to change into something more comfortable," and disappeared inside the house.

"He's looking harassed," said Lady Beaumont.

"Ah," said Sir Thomas to his daughter-in-law. "They never look much at that age but she'll grow up as pretty as her mother. Look at that," said Sir Thomas, surveying the cold buffet. "Never lets us down. Best cook in the world. Where exactly is that husband of yours?" he said, turning to Georgina who had both her children by the hand.

"Since Cairo I've heard nothing."

"When's daddy coming home?" asked Beau. "I miss piggy back rides."

"I'll give you one," said Henry.

"Oh, good. Can we do it now?" said Beau, instantly turning away from his mother.

"Later, Beau," said Henry, bending down to his nephew's height. "Then I'll take you down to the river."

"Oh, goodie."

"They're easy to distract at that age," said Lady Beaumont.

"What's distract?" asked Lorna and was puzzled when the grown-ups laughed.

"I'll tell you when we get home," said Georgina.

"Ah, Alice, there you are," said Lady Hensbrook. "Which one is the bachelor?"

"I'm not sure," said Lady Beaumont.

"Gwenneth is twenty-two next week and not one proposal."

"She frightens them off."

"What do you suggest?"

"I'll have a word with Reggie. He normally has an answer for these things."

"When is he going to get married?"

"I've asked him. He laughs and says there's plenty of time."

"Not normal in a man of thirty."

"Why don't you tell him?" said Lady Beaumont as Reggie headed out of the house in their direction pushing Lord Hensbrook in his wheelchair.

"I'd like to."

"Reggie's been telling me all about the gold mine in South Africa," said Hensbrook.

"We're opening a nickel mine in Australia."

"One of these days I'm going to have a word with you, Reggie," said Lady Hensbrook.

"What about, Lady Hensbrook?" said Reggie. "Should I have stayed in tails? Once God left the dining room I thought he wouldn't mind if I changed. Who's going to win the Derby, Henry?"

"Not me. Nothing to race. Wait till 1940. Lilliput's foal is looking better every day."

"Wouldn't mind a game of tennis after lunch," said Reggie.

"Maybe Gwenneth and Philippa would like to play," said Henry.

"Singles, Henry," said Reggie. "Less complications."

"J FUCKING C," said Corporal Dusty Miller. "That's a fucking sea. We're not getting across there tonight."

"Nor tomorrow," said Private Wilf Kemp.

"That depends on the Captain," said Jim Forrester, in awe at the might and size of the Congo River.

"Wouldn't have minded seeing all that water when we was in the desert," said Dusty sitting in the front seat of the stationary armoured car as he looked in front of him at the fast flowing river with its flotsam of trees and grass.

"What the fuck's that," said Wilf, from where he was leaning forward to look between Jim and Dusty.

"An animal," said Jim. "Probably a cow. It's dead and bloated."

From the sandbank to their left, three crocodiles slid into the water and chased the carcass, hitting it at the same time.

"We don't go swimming there, mate," said Dusty.

"Nice cool breeze off the water," said Wilf.

"Wonder if there's any fish?"

"Must be," said Dusty. "That's where you get them Congo eels."

"Is that right?" said Wilf, impressed.

"No wonder you's a fucking private. No fucking brains. Don't know when your leg's being pulled."

"Got to be fish," said Wilf, ignoring the insult. "Wouldn't mind a bit of nice fish."

"Maybe they grow potatoes round here too," said Dusty.

"Got to be fish," said Wilf, ignoring him again. "The captain brought some fishing tackle."

"Well," said Jim. "We might as well get out. Miller's right. We're not crossing that river tonight."

"Big bloody river," shouted Geoffrey Beaumont heaving himself out of the second armoured car as it slid to a halt in the river sand that swept back fifty yards from the water. "We'll make camp high up the bank behind us. Hippo don't like running up hill and the river's full of them. I'm starving. We'll get the fire going and roast some antelope."

"Wouldn't mind a bit of fish," said Wilf to himself.

"I'm sure the captain will let you try," said Jim.

Using his four-wheel drive, Dusty crabbed the vehicle up the sand and onto the high ground. Geoffrey selected a campsite with creeper tangled trees towering above. Within a short time the required equipment was unloaded and the two tents erected. Camp beds were set up with their metal legs smeared in old engine oil to keep the crawling bugs from feeding on the sleepers during the night. Mosquito nets were hung from the cross-pole. Wood lying in crunched tangles underneath the trees was tinder dry when put on the fire. Water was set to boil for the day's drinking water. Wilf, having found a line and hook, went off to the water and a flat rock that broke out into the river's flow. He baited the hook with an old piece of bread they'd baked in an anthill two weeks earlier and lowered it into the murky water. Immediately the line was wrenched, cutting his fingers.

"I got one," he shouted at the top of his voice, which brought Dusty running from the campsite to see Wilf land a two pound river bream on the rock. "Full of bones," said Dusty.

"We'll see," said Wilf, extracting his hook, baiting it and throwing it back into the river. This time he was ready and the fish was hoiked out of the water without any ceremony.

"Better get the grill out," called Dusty up the hill. "Fish for supper."

"Excellent," called Geoffrey and came down himself in time to watch Wilf's third bream in as many minutes.

"That's fresh water bream," said Geoffrey. "The books say it's as good as trout with less bones."

"Told you so," said Wilf, tossing his line back. "Now you'd better go and find that field of potatoes, corporal, so we can make the chips."

"Got any ideas, Miller, as to how to get the carriers across?" said Geoffrey. "We won't find a ford in this one."

"We've got to float across, somehow."

"That's how I see it. A raft. Plenty of trees and we have plenty of rope, a Swedish saw with six blades and an axe in each vehicle."

"That's quite a job, sir."

"The problem will be keeping from running down river. We'll have to fashion a steering paddle that will tack us across by the force of the current. The light will be gone in half an hour so we can't do anything now. Should be possible. The front winches will pull the logs down to the water. You've caught another fish, Private Kemp."

"So I have, sir."

"Well pull the bloody thing in. Three more should do the trick. I'm sure Corporal Sparrow will eat two."

"The corporal's got worms," said Wilf.

"Just a big frame that needs protein," said Geoffrey. "What a magnificent spot. It's moments like this that make the trip a pleasure," and he walked back up the sand to the campsite.

"Won't be fun cutting fucking trees to float the fucking carriers," said Dusty and turned his attention back to the line which was again in the water. "Blimey. You've got another, Wilf. That fucking water must be teeming in fucking fish."

"They're not fucking at the moment, Dusty. They're eating my stale bread, bless 'em."

In silence, with a grin on his face, Wilf unhooked the fish and threw back his baited line.

"Can you hear thunder?" asked Dusty.

"You about to fart?" asked Wilf.

"No, you silly bugger. Listen. Winds changed slightly. Constant thunder."

"Can't be. No bleedin' clouds to knock together."

"This place's real wild," said Dusty, looking around the vastness of Africa. "Not a native hut. Nothing. It's like we're the only people what's left in the world."

"Nice thought," said Wilf. "Look at them hippos. Must be a dozen of 'em."

GEOFFREY STOOD AWAY from the campsite with Jim and looked across the grey coloured water. Three islands pushed river debris to either side as the constant flow of water surged on a journey of twelve hundred miles to the South Atlantic Ocean.

"One minute you can see and the next it's pitch black. No moon for three days. We'll keep the fire well banked. I heard lion earlier. Probably five miles."

"That constant roar is rapids or a waterfall," said Geoffrey. "We'll have to check the river in both directions before we cut trees. We need as much clear water as possible. Must be over a mile across."

"We've made good time," said Jim, looking around him. "This is our biggest obstacle."

"After this, there's only the Zambezi of any size."

"A pity we can't go for the bridges."

"Spoil the fun and the point of the exercise," said Geoffrey. "Henry's daughter is being christened today. Seems so far away. Difficult to contemplate a garden party. . . Getting across that water is going to test us to the limit."

"I wouldn't mind a bath and a cold beer."

"The fish smells delicious. We'll work something out for swimming in the river tomorrow. We got any scotch left?" asked Geoffrey.

"Half a bottle," said Jim.

"We'll share it round. We've come a long way. Those petrol bowsers have given us a range I never dreamed of. In enemy territory, we'll cache the bowsers and still have mobility."

"How many rafts are you going to make?"

"Two. How are your tsetse bites?"

"I counted a hundred and eighty-two last night. Thank God the light's gone and they've gone to bed. What about sleeping sickness?"

"Then we'll have to call in the R.A.F. The light goes quickly in Africa. One minute you can see and the next it's pitch black. No moon for three days. We'll keep the fire well banked. I heard a lion earlier. Probably five miles away but there'll be more than one pride in this open country. With so much tsetse even the natives can't live here. How's the cooking, Corporal Sparrow?"

"Smashing. I've just opened one up with me knife. Still pink by the bone. Another five minutes. How long will it take to get across, sir?"

"We'll find out when we try."

The camp closed in to the small area of firelight around the six men. The night sounds of Africa built up in the darkness and the distant thunder became a roar from millions of tons of crashing water. Crickets and Christmas beetles screeched from the long grass and the first touch of cold air came up from the river. There was no wind and the fire smoke rose straight up to the trees, rising sixty feet over the camp and leaning over towards the river.

"So many different sounds," said Jim.

"Can you make out the Southern Cross?" said Geoffrey and they all looked up at the universe.

"Seems you could pick them stars right out of the night," said Stew Philpott. "Won't forget this trip, long as I live. Friends never believe me. I couldn't describe it. Not even mosquitoes around the fire tonight."

"Will there be a war?" asked Harry Sparrow.

"Hitler wants one," said Geoffrey.

"Maybe we should stay here and let 'em get on with it," said Wilf.

"Wouldn't you miss England?" said Harry.

"'Course I would. Seems such a bleeding waste of time killing each other. My old man said the last one was horrible," and he got up to help himself to more coffee from the pot that was stewing next to the charcoaling fish. Keeping his face away from the heat of the coals Harry cut open another fish. "Get your plates ready. Done quicker than I thought. Wilf, bring the torch over 'ere so I can have a good look... Point the beam down on the fish, mate. You're throwing a shadow where I've opened her. Look at that, sir. Done to a bleedin' turn, never 'ad rations like this at Middle Wallop."

"Better taste, good," said Dusty, as the fish were taken off the fire and put onto their plates.

"You caught them, Kemp," said Geoffrey. "Better taste first."

Wilf carefully pulled back the skin to find pure white meat that exuded a gentle steam and a delicious flavour. He picked out a large piece of fish with his fork, blew on it and put it in his mouth.

"Marvellous. Fuckin' marvellous. No bones at all."

They all began to eat in silence.

"Could be in the Savoy Grill," said Jim.

"You's a bleedin' genius, Private Kemp," said Harry Sparrow as he took his second fish.

"Nothing better than eating what you caught yourself," said Wilf.

"Time for a scotch," said Geoffrey sitting back in his camp chair.

"I'll do the honours," said Jim and got up to fetch the bottle, six mugs and a water bottle.

"What's that bleedin' noise?" said Wilf jumping up and facing down towards the river.

"Hippo," said Geoffrey. "Coming out of the water to graze. They're grass eaters, not carnivorous."

"What's carnivorous?" asked Wilf.

"Means they won't want to eat you, mate," said Stew.

"Dangerous, though," said Geoffrey. "They can bite through a native canoe."

He got up when Jim came back with the scotch and poured each man a good tot into a tin mug before retiring to the other side of the fire.

"Not much privacy for them," he said quietly to Jim as they resettled their camp chairs. "Cheers. Here's to crossing the river. Never made a raft in my life before."

"Missing the cricket season?" asked Jim.

"Missing Georgina and the kids even more."

"Pleasure of joining the army."

"They really trust us, don't they Jim? Bloody great river and they just ask you how long it'll take to get across. Better get Sparrow to fix those punctured spare tyres first thing in the morning. My engine's overheating. Either the radiator's sprung a leak or the water pump isn't working properly. Could have done with Tug on this journey. Wizard with an internal combustion engine. How was your run today?"

"Timing out slightly. I'll adjust the points. Maybe the plugs need changing as well. There's lion all round us."

"Can't be hungry. Amazing how quickly we've become accustomed to Africa. I'll come back again. Safari this time with all the comforts. What we want is a spot where the river bends and the current pushes across to the opposite bank. Link the two rafts with rope. Lucky it's the dry season. Can you imagine what the river must look like in the rains? We'll leave the men in camp at first light and make a reconnaissance up and down the river. Take the shotgun and get some guinea fowl for lunch. That bream was delicious. We'll bring in some more and dry them. Split them open and hang them in the sun like the natives. Last as long as you like. Can't eat red meat every day. I'm going to sleep well tonight with that cool breeze off the river. Who's on guard duty first?"

"Kemp," said Jim and yawned.

"Come on. Let's go to our tent. They'll sit up for an hour or so nattering. I'm enjoying *Vanity Fair* for the third time. Maybe we'll find some books when we reach Salisbury." Geoffrey got up and stretched. "Can you bring the scotch bottle, what's left of it?"

"I wonder what the news is from Europe," said Jim, following him. "Maybe war's broken out already."

"No," said Geoffrey. "I wrote a letter to Hitler asking him to wait until we got back."

"Considerate of you."

"We don't want to have gone through all this training for nothing. Are you still worrying about Mary?"

"Wouldn't you? Whatever she does, she's still my wife and mother of the two kids. What makes them have affairs, Geoff?"

"I don't know. I've only had one woman," said Geoffrey as he pulled back the tent flap. He bent over to enter and sat on his camp-bed to take off his puttees and boots.

"You mean Georgina was your first?" said Jim in surprise.

"Yes. So was I for Georgina. Probably the best thing. Sure, I've thought what it would be like with another woman but I wouldn't do it. I have a very good life. From what I see, you had your affair so Mary had hers."

"It's different for a man."

"Is it? A man can't do it without a woman and vice versa. This trip will probably solve your problem. She'll either go off with him or give him up. Often, so I've heard, when affairs are made easy they're not so spicy. Half the urge comes from forbidden fruit. The worst thing that can happen is a divorce."

"But I don't want a divorce."

"At least you've worked that one out. Can you pass that scotch bottle you're clutching?"

"Why did she have to pick an R.A.F. officer on the same station?"

"Married women don't meet men other than their husband's friends."

"I'M GOING to buy myself a boozer and spend all day drinking with the customers," said Stew, sitting back on his haunches and looking into the flames.

"Only take me another twenty years to save up from my army pay."

"They don't have privates over thirty, so you'd better get yourself a stripe," said Harry. "Wouldn't mind a boozer myself. Bit of spare comes in boozers and if you's the gaffer you get first choice seems to me."

"Wine, women and song," said Dusty leaning back in his camp chair with his hands cupping the back of his head. "Wouldn't mind a bit of crumpet right now. Haven't 'ad nothing for three months."

"Don't tell us you's getting something at Middle Wallop," said Harry disparagingly.

"No. On my weekend pass. Went up to London. Met her in a pub off the Charing Cross Road."

"What was she like?" asked Stew, totally interested.

"Big tits. Remember that bit."

"Did she charge?" asked Wilf.

"No. But there wasn't any money in my wallet when I woke up. Either she'd took it or I'd drunk it."

"Probably a bit of both," said Harry sagely. "Next time we'll go on weekend pass together and I can watch yer money for you. It's always better to hunt women in pairs."

"Hear that, Stew?" said Wilf. "Maybe we should try it."

"Nothin' ventured, nothin' gained," agreed Stew who spent three quarters of his day fantasising about the women he was going to have in his life.

"What the fuck's that?" said Wilf, jumping up to face down at the river again.

"Elephant," said Dusty. "We'll get used to 'em after a couple of weeks. Can't see us making rafts in shorter time."

"It's fuckin' dark down there," said Wilf. "I'm going to get my rifle and put a round up the spout. I'm on guard duty first anyway and I don't like some of them noises. Specially when I can't see what's makin' them."

"Put some more wood on the fire, Wilf. Captain says that's the best way to keep off the animals."

"Never thought I'd be sleeping in a tent with bleedin' lions, all round me," said Stew… "Mrs Philpott's little boy in the middle of darkest Africa."

"Oh fuck," shouted Wilf.

"What's the matter," said Dusty, getting up quickly.

"Knocked me fuckin' shin on the bowser bar."

"Is that all," said Dusty.

"Fuckin' hurt, it did. You come and try it."

Dusty sat back in his camp chair and pulled a packet of Woodbine out of his tunic pocket and lit a cigarette.

"I've never 'ad it," said Stew, despondently.

"What?" asked Harry.

"A woman. Never had one."

"Go on," said Dusty, kidding him.

"Privates get three bob a day. Women want to go to the pictures. Want to go dancing. They want pickin' up and takin' back again. Costs money. Privates can't afford it."

"Neither can lance-corporals."

"You had one, Harry?" asked Stew.

"Only a pro in Piccadilly. Saved up for two fuckin' months."

"Bet it was worth it," said Stew, leaning forward.

"'Course it was."

"What was?" asked Wilf, coming back into the firelight carrying his .303.

"A pro," said Stew. "You never 'ad it, Wilf."

"What?"

"A woman."

"No. Women don't go for Privates."

"What I said," said Stew.

"I'll bet the lieutenant and the captain get plenty," said Stew.

"They're married," said Dusty.

"Makes no fuckin' difference," said Harry. "There's things going on in the officers' mess what the officers don't know about. I 'eard the lieutenant's wife's 'aving it off with a flight lieutenant in C squadron."

"Better keep the rumours to yourself, Harry," said Dusty. "Never did no-one no good."

"You're right," agreed Harry.

"Tell you what, lads," said Dusty. "As I've 'eard it, Cape Town's the place. Big sea port. Plenty of sailors. Must be women where there's sailors. What say us four go out on the town? We'll 'ave four months basic pay, an' overseas allowance waiting for us. We'll make sure none of 'em get back to Middle Wallop without 'aving had it. How do you say, Harry?"

"Good idea, Dusty."

"Wouldn't mind a pint of bitter," said Wilf.

"Shut up," said. Stew. "I don't want to think about it."

"Wouldn't mind a pint or two myself," said Dusty. "I'm turning in. We've got a lot of work to do before we get across that river."

"WHY DO TSETSE FLY ALWAYS GO for you at dawn and dusk?" said Jim the next morning, swatting at a small arrow-shaped fly that stung like a red hot needle.

They had stopped the armoured car after driving upstream for ten minutes, having had to move out on the flank for half an hour before cutting back towards the river.

"We're still down river of the waterfall," said Geoffrey and restarted the engine, engaged four-wheel drive and made away from the river along the banks of a dried up tributary that had gouged a deep ravine across their path.

After a mile, they were able to drop down the bank onto the sandy river bed and crab their way across and up the other bank. The buzz of a swarm of following tsetse fly could be heard above the Vauxhall engine. Geoffrey wound around thorn thickets and fever trees before coming back to the river.

Here, the river dropped over five hundred yards of swirling, vicious, frothing rapids that spanned out in front of them, the vast width of the Congo River.

"Quite a sight," said Geoffrey in awe as they watched the might of the great river spread for a mile in front of them. "We'll have to cross somewhere east of here where there are plenty of trees with straight trunks." After half an hour and having wound backwards and forwards to the river, Geoffrey stopped at the top of the river bank. The great mass of the Congo River curved away to their left where a hill on the opposite side of the river had changed the natural course of the water. Geoffrey climbed half-out of the car with field glasses and studied the flow of trees and clumps of grass-holding weed that was floating down with the current. Jim did the same. After some time Geoffrey put down the field glasses and looked around for the right type of trees.

"It's pushing the debris across river?" asked Geoffrey.

"Very slightly," agreed Jim.

"A heavy rudder may do the trick. We'll test first. I'm not putting the carriers on the rafts until I'm sure I can steer them across."

"First we make a raft and then I'm going to take it across the river and back again. We couldn't hear rapids to the east from our campsite which gives us at least thirty miles of navigable water from where we are… Look at that… pass me the shot gun Jim. There's a flock of guinea fowl in the long grass. The place is teeming with game. We won't go hungry even if it takes a month to get across."

"The carriers weigh eight tons," said Jim.

"You think a wooden raft will hold them up with a half-full petrol bowser tied on the back?"

"I don't know but I'm going to try. The raft may sink just below water but it should be buoyant. I want a wall of logs two feet high to imprison the cars. How did the early settlers in South Arica get across the big rivers with their wagons?"

"Dismantled them and floated the parts across. They were made of wood."

"That's my point," said Geoffrey. "They floated across. Let's go and get the others after I've shot four of those birds."

Six weeks later in Singapore, Kim-Wok Ho puffed a cloud of white tobacco smoke from his long, thin white-clay pipe but continued to ponder the question put to him by his cousin, Ping-Lai Ho, who was reclining on the opposite, silk-covered couch in Kim-Wok Ho's penthouse overlooking Singapore harbour.

The tapestries in rich Chinese colours, the oriental carpets and the French-period furniture somehow blended in perfect harmony. Kim-Wok Ho had no idea how much he had paid for his furnishings any more than he could answer the question as to how much money he was worth.

"America," he said finally.

"You have contacts in America?" said Ping-Lai Ho, speaking in Mandarin.

"I will make them," answered his cousin in the same language. "It is bad I do not have them already. There is much money in guns."

"There is much money in guns," agreed Ping-Lai Ho and puffed contentedly on his own white-clay pipe in which he had only placed tobacco. It was too early in the day for opium and when doing business with his cousin, Kim-Wok Ho, it was better to be in possession of all his faculties.

He looked out of the window and watched a British light cruiser cut sleekly across the harbour on its way to the biggest naval dockyard in the East.

His mind came back to guns. He had found the client. It was now up to his cousin to find the source of supply. He knew from experience that his cousin did not like being interrupted so he kept on watching the bustle of Singapore harbour across to the new causeway that joined the island to the mainland and Malaya.

"Who wants the guns?" asked Kim-Wok Ho.

"That cousin is information best known only to me."

"Who are they going to kill?"

"Does it matter?"

"Probably not. If people want to kill each other they will always find a way."

"They always do," agreed his cousin.

"It is always the same," said Kim-Wok Ho after some time during which he had come to a conclusion. "If you have something you must have power to keep it. If you have nothing you must get a gun to get it. Unless you are very clever. It is better to be clever. It is like an animal to kill for your food."

He thought further, puffing his pipe and then spoke again.

"The Japanese attack China from Korea and all the Chinese do is fight each other, it's good to have boats like that one," he said nodding his head at the harbour. "The British won't supply us with guns neither will the Germans nor America," he said again and clapped his hands.

They both waited in silence as the ten thousand ton cruiser came up to the jetty and executed a perfect docking.

"Humph," said Kim-Wok Ho in appreciation and the door opened and his housekeeper came in with a tray of green tea which she poured expertly. She was twenty-three, nearly six foot tall and exquisitely blonde. After two years with Kim-Wok Ho she was also rich.

Both men lusted after her as she leant over to offer them their delicate cups and both men looked down the front of her dress. Kim-Wok Ho watched his cousin with particular satisfaction as he always liked having what another man wanted and couldn't have and especially his cousin.

"Thank you, Linda," he said in English and smiled his set of pure white teeth.

Apart from his girth he was a good looking man in his late forties. He had found after the age of thirty-six that Chinese girls didn't pep him up enough. He watched Ping-Lai Ho follow the swing of Linda's tight bottom as it swung across the room conscious of the two men watching it. The door opened and closed again. They sat back puffing at their long, white-clay pipes. Ping-Lai Ho was aware that he carried an erection that didn't want to go down.

The thing he most wanted to ask his cousin was where he could buy such a European woman with such excellent manners and body.

Kim-Wok Ho knew exactly what his cousin was thinking and smiled at him with satisfaction. Ping-Lai Ho looked away embarrassed. He would give Linda an extra one tonight on behalf of his cousin and he smiled again.

"More tea?" said Kim-Wok Ho and gestured at the tray.

"You will have your guns. As many as you want. They will be the best in the world. If people wish to kill each other we must give them the very best to do it with, don't you agree, cousin Ping-Lai Ho? Now, in return, I want you to enquire of your friends where we can purchase large quantities of raw rubber without upsetting our friends at Swire and McLean or Jardine Matheson."

"Everyone wants rubber," said Ping-Lai Ho.

"Then you must find it. The only reason I will go to the trouble of finding your guns is if you will find me rubber. Lots of it."

HALF AN HOUR later in the same city, Tug Beaumont, seated in the foyer of Raffles Hotel had finished reading the second page of a three-week old London *Daily Telegraph* in disgust. The paper had been flown in on the new airmail route through Colombo and had arrived that morning. Hitler had moved into the Rhineland and no-one had done anything about it. 'Appeasement at its best,' thought Tug and turned to the next page where he read that Chiang Kai-shek was winning the war against the Japanese which he didn't believe. It was completely contradictory to his own information which indicated that Chiang Kai-shek was more interested in beating Mao Tse-tung than the invading Japanese.

He put down the paper, caught the eye of a waiter standing by the entrance door and ordered himself a cold bottle of beer.

He was half way through the beer when Tammany dressed to perfection in European clothes, came into the hotel. Every man in the room watched her walking across the foyer to where Tug was standing, waiting, not wanting to move towards her but watch the perfect grace of her walk and the swing of her long, silk-touched legs.

"Hello, darling," he said and held out both his hands so he could get a better look. He had sent her to a beautician to show her the art of European make-up and the result was startlingly exciting, especially the deep gash of her large mouth.

"Do you like it?" she asked.

"It seems impossible but it makes you even more beautiful. What will you drink?"

"A gin and tonic with lots of ice. How was your day?"

"Nothing exciting," he said holding up his hand for a waiter, "Found another six tons of rubber but it's barely worth sending for. Jardine's are deliberately blocking my supplies. Perry's meeting us here and then we'll go into lunch. Gin and tonic," he said to the waiter and looked back at his wife. After four years there was no resemblance to the seventeen-year-old from a village in Sarawak.

Tammany smiled at him, pleased at the look which she understood. She wondered if he knew how much work had gone into her Westernisation. She hoped that he was almost ready to ask her to go to England and to meet his family.

The waiter came back with the drink and a note for Tug that had just been delivered to reception.

"Perry, I expect," said Tug, taking the note. "I asked Sam to bring me any messages. Most efficient hotel in the world," and he opened the message… "Well, I'll be blowed. It's from Ho. Wants to see me. I've been trying to see him for three months without success."

"The messenger is waiting for a reply," said the waiter.

"Tell him I'll phone Mr Ho after lunch," said Tug.

"Thank you, sir," said the waiter as Tug gave him a tip.

"Don't want Ho to think I'm too keen," said Tug. "Ah. There's Perry. Finish our drinks and we can go into lunch. I'm starving. Wonder what friend Ho wants with me? Hello, Perry what are you going to have to drink?"

"Hello, Tammany. Same as you, Tug. Humidity building up outside." His eyes turned back to Tammany and for a moment the pulse stopped in his heart as the big red mouth looked back at him.

NINE WEEKS later at eleven-thirty a.m. on the 26 September 1937, Reggie Beaumont, uncomfortable once again in his dove-grey tails with a large button-holed carnation, looked up at the vastness of the fluted ceiling above him that went on up into the great spire of Cologne Cathedral. The organist had been enjoying himself for twenty minutes playing Bach while the ushers, some in morning dress like Reggie but others in the various uniforms of the third Reich, showed the four hundred guests to their seats.

"Nervous?" he asked Gunter von Ribbeck, who was standing next to him in the full dress uniform of an oberleutnant of the Luftwaffe.

"Very."

"It's the biggest decision you'll ever make."

They both looked round nervously at the vast nave that stretched to a point three hundred feet behind them but there was no sign of the bride and her father. Reggie fingered the ring on his right hand and wondered what it must be like to be getting married. The finality terrified him. He gave Gunter a weak smile and they turned back to concentrate on the altar which stood in great splendour and holiness ten feet back from the top of the four, red carpeted steps in front of them.

In the pew to the left immediately behind Reggie, Carl Priesler wondered if it wasn't the time in his life when he should also get married. He had turned thirty the previous week and the change from his twenties to his thirties had come as a shock. The only problem was he'd never found a woman he wanted to marry. He looked at Gunter and wondered what he was feeling on such a day. Looking at both of them, Reggie was the more nervous of the two. The other matter that concerned him most forcibly was the improbability of having said anything more than pleasantries to the ice-cold epitome of English aristocracy that sat next to him, her husband on her other side, the Honourable Isabel Beaumont. He must have been dreaming that night after Bretts.

The sudden, increased volume of the organ high in its loft, brought his head round with the others and there in the arch of the gothic doors, small from Carl's distance, stood the bride and her father. To Mozart's *Wedding March*, the procession began its long, slow walk to the altar and the waiting backs of Gunter and Reggie. Everyone in the cathedral stood up.

Isabel withdrew her hand from Henry's as she remembered the same music from a much smaller organ that had helped them down the small aisle of Ashtead church. It was the fourth time in the church she had removed her hand. Even the touch caused her irritation.

Tony Venturas wore a small smile and wondered if his God would forgive him for the way in which he made a living. Then he looked around the cathedral and wondered how many of the men had used a similar service. This made him smile broadly. 'Hypocrite, Venturas,' he said to himself and wondered what the bride, now halfway down the aisle, would look like when she removed her veil. 'Cynic, Venturas,' he said again to himself, 'she is probably the most beautiful woman in the world.'

Thelma King could feel a state of tearfulness begin to well up from deep in her throat and she knew that by the time the ceremony was over she would be crying. The fact that François Deauville was standing next to her didn't make it easier. She wanted him more than she had done when they had first met in the office. The guilt of thinking about sex in a church stopped her from going back to her most urgent thoughts of whether it was time to give in to François.

François's mind was back at Oxford, to the day, nearly eleven years ago, when he had first met Gunter von Ribbeck. They had been the first of the four to make friends and had joined the University Air Squadron together. Being foreigners on a post-graduate course, they had found themselves apart from the English. 'We had less worries in those days,' he said to himself. He looked at his first flying instructor in the pew in front and wondered what he was smiling about. Tony's infectious grin made François smile and made Thelma look sharply from one to the other. The ceremony began and François' mind reverted back to the cathedral and everything it meant to Gunter and Birgitt.

By the end of the ceremony, Chuck Everly had been brought to tears despite the fact that he hadn't understood a word. Thelma passed him a lace handkerchief which he used while kneeling at his prayers. Everything in Europe was so old and full of history. 'I really am a sentimental fool,' he said to himself and stood up with the others to watch the bride and groom walk back down the cathedral and out into a world of their own.

Henry Beaumont thought it a splendid wedding and hoped that this would make Reggie think again. He reminded himself to have a word with his brother when they got back to England and this set his mind off worrying again about his younger brother, Geoffrey, who had last been heard of three months before.

Full of rice and confetti and standing outside the cathedral for the photographers, Gunter was happier than at any moment in his life.

The rows of cars, including the new Beaumont Rolls Royce, moved away from the cathedral, with the bride and groom's Mercedes taking the lead for the forty-mile drive to the family schloss of Birgitt's father, Baron Armand von Essen, and the reception.

"How are the guns coming along, Chuck?" asked Reggie during the reception. "We got to get export permits but so long as we certify the buyer as Chiang-Kai-shek there's no problem. The United States don't like the Japanese or the Commies. Do you want me to go visit Singapore?"

"Tug can handle it. The consignments will go into his Singapore go-down against payment to you from Union Mining in London. Tug can do the horse-trading when he has the goods. We can't have certified letters of credit in a barter deal."

"The first order is for two hundred thousand."

"There's no payment problem. If we are efficient with our delivery dates there will be plenty of business. I don't like selling arms any more than you do, Chuck, but rubber goes into tyres and tyres go on military vehicles, so what's the difference?"

"Sure, we didn't start the war. Have another glass of champagne. Oh, there's one condition on the guns," said Chuck as he took another glass of wine from the passing waiter. "That rubber comes to the U.S.A."

"But we need it in England," said Reggie.

"Sure. But the guns are American. We're building strategic stockpiles of all war materials. Rubber is high on the list. Only way I could get a definite export permit. Profit from the rubber stays in the same company, Union Mining."

"There's always an angle in any deal," said Reggie. "If that's the case, Tug will ship the rubber to you as an internal company transfer. Then you can start the horse-trading with U.S. government. I like this one. The Chinese want guns they can't get so we push up the price of the guns and push down the price of rubber from them. The Americans want a rubber stockpile and we have it so we push up the price. You didn't tell your government how much rubber we were expecting for our guns?"

"No, Reggie, but I want your word that any rubber obtained in the barter will be sent to me."

"You've got it," said Reggie finishing the subject.

"What a wedding. You Europeans sure know how to lay on a party. These German women are real good lookers and that Birgitt's a stunner."

"Herr Beaumont," said Baron von Essen. "Let me show you our formal gardens. I think them more beautiful than the house. Gunter tells me your family home is nine hundred years old."

"Not all of it, by any means," said Henry. "The house is built on the same site so the foundations will be those of my ancestors. Did you attend Oxford? Your English is excellent."

"Yes. It is a family tradition. You Anglo-Saxons in England have the same tastes. But then we are the same race. Have you ever realised how much the English and Germans look alike?"

"And yet we fight each other."

"That is the pity. It proves so little. I have already forgotten why the last war was started."

"And yet there is going to be another one?"

"Only if you start it."

"But Hitler will move into Czechoslovakia and Poland. We have mutual protection treaties. We will be forced into war."

"But why? Herr Hitler wishes to restore the traditional lands of the Germans. Will not those lands be better off? To live, a man needs order, discipline. This brings security and wealth. Are your colonies not better off under the Empire?"

"That is different."

"I don't think so. The ordinary man will always be controlled by someone. Why must Germany and England fight over who is to control them? Only a few hundred Englishmen have ever been to Czechoslovakia or Poland. It is none of your business. They are our neighbours not yours." The elderly, white-haired man turned away. "In the forest to your left are wild boar. Tomorrow we will hunt them. For me a wedding is an excuse for a good hunting party."

"We will look forward to entertaining you at Merry Hall," said Henry, embarrassed by the main subject.

"I shall look forward to it. Pheasant shooting. I nearly broke my neck at Oxford hunting fox. But that is the excitement."

"I hope Gunter and Birgitt will be happy."

"But of course they will. It was arranged. People with the same upbringing make successful marriages. Those two have been married to each other today for good reasons. If they are in love as well then that is a bonus. But when the love has run away the good reasons will still be there and so will their families."

"But they are in love."

"How wonderful. It is the most beautiful experience of life. So you like my schloss?" he said, turning back to look at the house.

"It is very beautiful."

"THEY DO LOOK SERIOUS," said Thelma to Isabel as they watched from the second layer courtyard that overlooked the main courtyard and the carp ponds, green with lilies and oxygen weed.

"They look as if the weight of the world is upon their shoulders," agreed Isabel as she watched her husband and Baron von Essen make their way over the stone paving towards the wide flight of stone steps which led up to the entrance where some of the guests were mingling to enjoy the autumn sun away from the reception."

"The Germans are so stiff," said François standing next to Thelma. "The only one I've ever known to unwind is Gunter and he only does that away from home."

"He's still a good looking man," said Thelma watching the Baron. "Must have given the fräuleins a real run when he was younger."

"Where are they going on honeymoon, Reggie?" asked Isabel.

"Herr Beaumont," said a man servant coming up to Reggie and speaking in German. "Your call to Johannesburg is waiting for you."

"Excuse me a moment," said Reggie and followed the manservant into the house and the small study that led off from the main hall.

"Beaumont," he said into the phone.

"Mr Beaumont. Van der Walt."

"Any news?"

"I'm afraid not," said Van der Walt above the static. "Our office in Salisbury has been in contact with the Rhodesian Air Force at Gwelo. They've made three runs over the Congo but they don't have the range to reach the river from where your brother last reported. It's a vast country, Mr Beaumont, and large tracks are uninhabited. There are no roads or railways. He chose some of the most inhospitable territory in the world to test his equipment. Without radio contact we have no means of finding him."

"How long should it have taken him to reach Salisbury?"

"Without the river crossings, about two weeks. I just don't see how he was going to get two armoured cars across the Congo River and the Zambezi. The Congo River's three miles wide in parts. He'll have to reach Salisbury within the next month as the rains break at the end of October and then he won't be able to travel five miles. He'd have enough trouble getting from Salisbury to Johannesburg on the strip roads during the rains."

"How's the mine shaft progressing?"

"Three weeks ahead of schedule. Shaft sinkers are the best in the world."

"Tell them thanks from me."

"Where are you, Mr Beaumont? The operator couldn't speak English."

"Cologne, in Germany."

"You certainly get around."

Van der Walt started to say something else but he was cut off and the line went dead. Reggie put the phone back on the hook and deep in thought went back to join the others.

"Any news?" said Henry, coming towards him.

"Nothing. Not a damn thing."

"You've got to do something for mother. Georgina's beside herself."

"I'm doing my best," said Reggie and rested his hand on his brother's shoulder.

"He'll come in. He had plenty of fuel. You can't take off on a venture like that without problems. You'd better go and phone mother and Georgina. Baron von Essen has some way of getting calls through in a hurry."

"It's my pleasure," said the Baron and led Henry back into the house.

"It's not good?" asked Tony.

"No. Not at all. In fact it's bloody bad. He's taken three months doing a journey that can be done in two weeks."

"Where did he try and cross?"

"Probably in the most difficult spot he could find. My younger brother has little regard for his own skin. He forgets other people are involved. When are you going back to Paris, François?"

"Tomorrow. Carl's flying with me and then taking the train to Kiel."

"Henry can stay for the boar hunt but I must get back tomorrow as well. Chuck and I will fly in Mathilda and the others will have to come on by train."

"Tony and I can travel together," said Thelma, wondering why François hadn't asked her to fly with him to Paris.

"Here comes the bride and groom," said Isabel, who could think of nothing more boring than pig sticking.

THE FOLLOWING AFTERNOON, François turned the key in the lock of his apartment on the Rue de Honoré and opened the door for Carl. A violent yapping broke out and a white fluffy dog with green ribbons and a pom-pom tail leapt into François's arms and licked him all over the face.

"Fifi is a little mad," explained François as he closed the door and led Carl inside. "A lady that was sharing my apartment some two years ago left in a huff when I refused to marry her leaving all her clothes and the poodle. She never came back and I didn't have the heart to throw the dog into the street. I gave the clothes to charity."

"Why didn't you marry her?" asked Carl, putting his travelling bag and flying jacket on the oriental carpet next to the Louis XIV chair.

"Marriage scares me to death. What if you make a mistake?"

"We'll all have to settle dawn one day. I've just turned thirty. We can't be bachelors forever."

"Let's keep going as long as we can. Tonight, I'll take you to my club and you will see the other side of François Deauville."

"In all the years we have known each other this is the first time I have been to your home. We always meet in your office. You have good taste."

"Not me. The owner of Fifi. She was an interior decorator. For me a double bed and a cocktail cabinet is all that is necessary. Fifi stop jumping up and down like a jack-in-the-box. He is mad. My dog is quite mad. I have an idea. Let us forget business. My office thinks I am coming back on Wednesday which gives us three nights. This year we have made enough money for a lifetime. First, we must change our clothes. Where we are going on the Left Bank they will throw us out looking like this. I will lend you some old clothes and a beret. When I have finished you will look like an artist. My friends in the Pigalle only know me as François. They think I am poor like they are, so you and I don't talk about reinsurance and mining houses. Nor aeroplanes. In fact anything you and I have talked about in the past, we do not talk about in the Pigalle. Do you like jazz?"

"I think so. Do you?"

"Of course."

"But at Oxford you played the violin in the orchestra."

"Wait. You will see. Today I will show you Paris."

"FRANÇOIS," said Carl as they walked away from the taxi that had brought them to the Left Bank. "My trousers are covered in paints."

"But of course. For three days you are going to be a painter and drink aniseed. First we will sit at my favourite side walk café, smoke Gauloise and drink aniseed. After that we will eat food with a lot of garlic. Then we will begin to smell right and we can go on and meet my friends."

"Why are you carrying your violin in a battered case?"

"No-one must think it cost me ten thousand francs. From now on, Carl, you must believe you are a Bohemian. Talk about Gauguin. You have seen three of them in Reggie's office. If you don't know the answer to a question, pretend you are drunk. Most of my friends are drunk. They cannot create without the aniseed. They cannot make love without the aniseed and they can only sleep when they are very drunk. Some of them do not have homes. It is unnecessary. They sleep where they drop?"

"Where do they get money?"

"Don't be so practical. I never ask them. They probably steal it but not from me. For their friends, they will do anything. For the rest. Pah! Nothing. They do not like the rest. The rest, they say, do not live. Maybe they are right. Here we are. Waiter. Two aniseed. Big ones. My friend and I are thirsty. And a big plate of your mussels and fresh bread. With the mussels a bottle of wine. Cheap wine."

Four hours later, a little drunk but totally happy, they walked down the streets of the Pigalle with the night and the Seine and the neon lights bright around them. The streets were teeming and the café tables vibrant with laughter. Movement everywhere. A warm autumn night with the trees shedding their leaves in a constant salute to another year that was history.

François turned into a doorway and Carl followed him down the stairs where the body heat from below hit them at the same time as the noise and music. François found some francs inside his dirty smock and gave them to a fat, red faced woman whom he kissed on both cheeks.

Inside François fought his way to the back of the long room with its scrubbed tables and benches. The place reeked of stale wine, garlic and sweating bodies. Candles hooked high on the wall gave a lie to the darkness and the walls were painted black. A lewd artist had painted his ideas of naked women over the blackness. They would have been erotic if anyone had taken any notice.

Seeing François, a small girl with long brown hair jumped up from her bench onto the table and ran its length, skirts flying missing the bottles and glasses before launching herself at François who caught her and swung her round with his violin case, knocking people who shouted their approval. A tumbler of wine appeared in Carl's hand and he drank and smiled with the others. The girl, her legs round François's waist, leant back to look at him, a delicious smile on her face. Looking at François, Carl saw a gentleness that he had never seen before. The girl jumped down to look up at Carl.

"I am Simone. François's girl. Are you his friend?"

"Yes," answered Carl, speaking in French.

"Why you not bring him here before?" Simone asked François.

"He is from Denmark," said François. "A famous painter from Copenhagen. Show him Paris."

"You like Paris, monsieur?"

"How can one not like Paris?"

"The maestro plays tonight," shouted one of Simone's friends over the noise. "Will you play with him?"

"Sidney Béchet?" asked François. "First a drink. How can I play good jazz on a violin unless I am drunk? Bring me six bottles of wine," he said to a waitress with big breasts. "Today I stole a lot of money. More money that I ever stole. Tonight I am rich."

Carl found himself on a bench with girls all round him. Chorus girls. Artists. Weird clothes. Big earrings on men. The cigarette smoke curled and the noise increased and there was no-one there who wanted to be anywhere else in the world.

The high note of a soprano saxophone brought the noise to a halt as sharply as of the closing of a door. A man that François could only just see through the cigarette smoke stomped his foot three times on the bandstand and the band, sax, piano, drums, double bass, trumpet and trombone, broke into the haunting jazz melody of *'Oh Didn't He Ramble'*. The slow build up burst into the fast beat of the main theme and all the feet under the tables began tapping the rhythm. Some jumped up to dance on the small floor in front of the band and others sank back into their minds to absorb the music. The jazz numbers moved from one to another without a pause and the musicians sweated in the rising body heat as they rolled their eyes. François was picked up and the crowd made way until he was put down on the bandstand. The violin case was passed over their heads. The regular trombone player shouted into Béchet's ear and the maestro nodded and beckoned to François. The number changed and a new sound, gentle at first, danced in and above the other instruments, so sweet it was painful. The jazz violin, the first Carl had ever heard.

"Good, isn't he, your friend?" shouted Simone.

"He is amazing," said Carl who couldn't believe it was François Deauville.

"They want him to play professionally. He won't take money for the gigs. He says he steals enough."

"He probably does," said Carl, smiling to himself.

"I am worried the 'flic' will catch him. One day they will lock him up. Always I tell him to get a job. But no. He wants to steal. By his accent, he is educated but he wants to steal. But I love him. What can I do?"

Carl looked across the sea of heads to his friend, red scarf tied to the side, blue smock doused in red wine stains, trousers that could walk on their own and felt a sudden chill of sadness at so much contradictory talent.

"Enjoy him until they catch him," he said. "The police are not very good. For François, they probably don't try very hard. How long have you known him?"

"Three years. Since I was fifteen. He is my only lover. One day he will marry me, you will see. Then I will get him a job."

Carl could imagine the young body under the white top, puffed at the sleeves, and rich-red skirt, being as perfect as her face, smooth, soft-skinned, deep brown eyes full of laughter, no make-up but lips, never quite closed, sensual, pulling, wanting to be touched and loved. Even her long brown hair was as soft as silk.

"MY FRIEND LIKES YOU," said Simone as they came out of the club into an early morning mist just up from the river. "She wants to see your paintings. She told me so."

"They are in Copenhagen," said Carl, half believing the lie after so much jazz and wine. 'I am drunk and mad and very happy,' he told himself and found his arm around Danielle's shoulder as François put his arm around Simone's.

"Coffee and croissants, said François. "We must have coffee and croissants. I am dying if I do not have croissants and coffee."

'A little mad too,' thought Carl and laughed instead as they romped the morning streets in step with everything.

"What a night," said Carl. "You are a genius, François. Your violin is also a genius."

"I want to see your paintings," said Danielle.

"Later," said Carl. "I will bring them to Paris. We will have a big show. For you, I will paint a special picture. It will be beautiful. Good morning," he shouted at the buildings but there was nothing in return for in the Pigalle, everyone shouts at the buildings, day and night.

"That cafe is open," pointed Simone.

"They are all open," said François, drunk on his own happiness. "Waiter. Coffee. Much coffee. Croissants. And yes, a bottle of wine."

"We will be drunk," said Carl, pushing a chair out for his girl.

"We are drunk. On wine. On life. Love. Does it matter? Wine. We will drink more wine and coffee and eat croissants."

"You are drunk," laughed Carl.

"Of course."

"Have we money?" asked Simone.

"Of course. If we haven't I will steal some more and if they won't let me steal it I will stand on that street corner and play my fiddle. They will give me money to go back to sleep. After this we will go to Simone's attic and have a party. We will tell all our friends. They will all come. My friend," he said to the waiter, "you are a genius. You bring the coffee even quicker than I think. And the croissants. And look, my Simone, he has the wine. A whole new bottle of wine."

"You are crazy, crazy," said Simone. "Of course."

"You say you love me, yet you won't let me make love," said Gunter, head buried in his hands where he sat in a chair facing the catastrophe of his marriage.

"But you did make love," said Birgitt.

"Not that. You turned your face away in revulsion. You hated me."

"For that only. Does it matter? The marriage was arranged. We will have children. That is enough."

"For your father. For him it was arranged. For me I would never have married you unless I loved you. You said you loved me."

"I do. But not like that. I cannot enjoy sex with a man, Gunter."

"I cannot have sex with a woman who does not want to. It is revolting. Like rape. Worse, worse than a whore. Your father tricked us."

"No. I tricked you, Gunter. Now I am safely married I can have my friends and no-one will even suspect. You will have the Von Essen millions, the prestige."

"What is money, Birgitt, without love? If you will excuse me, I am going for a walk."

"You will get used to it," said his wife.

"Never," and he walked out of the room, out of the hotel into the first light of a Swiss morning that overlooked the lake of Lausanne and he cried and Gunter von Ribbeck had never cried, even as a little boy. The nerves in his fingertips ached with the pain. "What have I done to deserve this?" he asked. "I have done nothing wrong."

At the end of September 1937, Kim-Wok Ho watched the outline of Linda's bottom as she walked away from him to look out of the window over Singapore harbour. Two British destroyers were making their way out of the harbour.

"Back to 'Blighty' to fight the Hun," said Linda without a great deal of interest. The potential war in Europe was too far away to affect her life. She stood with her back to the room, hands on hips and legs strongly apart. She enjoyed the feel of the green silk of her silk stockings and the knowledge that the strong light from the window would show a V up to her crotch for Kim-Wok Ho to look at. Kim-Wok Ho moved uncomfortably in his heavily embroidered armchair.

"My cousin fancies you," said Kim-Wok Ho.

"So what?" said Linda without turning round.

"Could you find him another English girl?"

"I could try but it would be very expensive. We would have to be very subtle. Just to say to a nice English girl, 'would you like to be the mistress of Ping-Lai Ho?' is not good enough. They must be brought to bed slowly. The way you so cleverly caught me."

"The opium, you mean?"

"Yes. That is one way. The money more. It doesn't matter now when my looks fade. I have enough money in Switzerland, thank you."

"You cost me too much."

"It's worth it. What are you going to do with all your money unless you can't enjoy it? You want me badly so you pay."

"Yes," said Kim-Wok Ho, and sighed. "Why are all men's heads controlled by their willies?"

"Maybe Beaumont likes dark, native girls. He's married to one. Any man after a few years becomes sexually less interested in his wife. Give him erotic girls. Englishmen are very staid but they have filthy imaginations. Give him three at a time in a haze of opium… Then you won't have any problems negotiating prices."

"What about Ping-Lai Ho?"

"If there is enough money, any woman can be bought."

"She must be well educated. A lady, as you call it."

"The best mistresses are always well educated. They have been taught the value of money and the ease with which it can be obtained without scrubbing the floors and cooking the food. The only difference between a wife and a mistress is that wives are badly paid until they get a divorce. For you, I am inexpensive. You pay while you want me at a known price and not when you wish to get rid of me at a huge price decided by a judge. If I can fix up Ping-Lai Ho and Tug Beaumont I want two and a half percent of the rubber and the guns."

"Humph," said Kim-Wok Ho as Linda turned her head to look at him and sensually lick her lips. "Humph," said Kim-Wok Ho again as the blood pumped into him. "Where is that cousin of mine?"

"His car drew up a minute ago."

"Why didn't you tell me?"

"You didn't ask. That rattle trap of a lift should be bringing him up. I'll go and get him for you. Maybe he does have enough money to make me an offer."

"You only stay because of the money?" asked Kim-Wok Ho a little hurt.

"Of course not. But business is business. I see myself in a nice mansion in Surrey with lots of servants and a title. The British aristocracy are not too fussy about where the money comes from. Now, if you'll excuse me," she said and walked provocatively to the door. Outside, she quickly took off her bra, shrugging it off and pulling it through her sleeve and hid it in the umbrella stand before opening the door to a beaming, gold-toothed Ping-Lai Ho. She gave him a delicious smile and walked in front of him to the reception room where Kim-Wok Ho was waiting. As she opened the door to Ping-Lai Ho she let one of the stiffly erect nipples slide along his back, his skin protected by a cotton duck suit in tropical, western style. Ping-Lai Ho audibly sucked in air from the touch having realised, halfway across, what was running across his back. Both cousins were speechless for a moment, until Linda walked ahead into the room and rang the bell in the kitchen for tea by pulling a tasselled rope that hung from the ceiling. Four eyes were still fixed on the nipples bulging from the inside of her dress, empty of her bra.

"You'll have some tea, Mr Ho?" she said in her formal, British upper class accent which she knew to be particularly erotic in the circumstances.

"Thank you," was all Ping-Lai Ho managed in a constricted voice.

When the tea arrived, Linda got up and bent away from him to do the pouring and the pert rounds of her bottom were only three feet from his face and his eyes could trace every line of her panties. He even imagined there was a darker patch in the middle and he was forced to cross his legs.

"Linda has a friend," said Kim-Wok Ho smiling silkily. "She is a little younger than Linda and from a better family."

"What is her name?" asked Ping-Lai Ho.

"You would like to meet her?" asked Kim-Wok Ho casually as he took a sip of his tea. "Delicious. There is nothing more fragrant than the tea grown in the hills of the Middle Kingdom." He was still enjoying the filthy look bestowed on him by Linda.

"Linda, my dear," he said turning to her with a smile, "would you be so kind as to call Mr Beaumont on our new telephone and ask him if it will be convenient for me to call upon him in half an hour as he will wish to know how much rubber my most cherished cousin has located. After three weeks you must have hundreds of tons, not so cousin?"

"Many hundreds of tons, cousin. But of the price?"

"Of course, cousin. What is your price?"

"What is Beaumont prepared to pay?"

"Not so. At what price are you selling?"

"It is better if we know what Beaumont will pay."

"But we don't," said Kim-Wok Ho slyly. "So you must tell me your price so that I know if a deal can be struck."

"What price are the guns?"

"They will arrive from America in two weeks' time. You said speed was essential. The price? You must tell me what Chiang-Kai Shek will pay."

"No, cousin Kim-Wok Ho. You must tell me what you will sell them for and then I will see if I can make a contract with my buyers. There are other gun merchants operating in this field."

"But they do not have their guns on the water."

"We don't know. Maybe they have."

The door behind them closed softly and they both looked across under hooded eyes.

"How much do you want for Linda?" asked Ping-Lai Ho, when they were both alone.

"She is not for sale."

"If I give you a fixed price on the rubber?"

"She is not for sale," but there was a slight pause that was picked up by Ping-Lai Ho and which caused the blood to rush back and caused him to cross his legs again.

"I will introduce you to Linda's friend if you fix the price of your rubber."

He was thinking how much he could then charge Tug Beaumont for the same rubber.

"She may not like me," said Ping-Lai Ho.

"She will. That will be part of the rubber price."

"There are plenty of Chinese and Malay girls," said Ping-Lai Ho, showing a little indifference.

"But they don't turn you on any more, do they, cousin? The past has been consumed. It is the future that you wish to buy. May I pour you more tea?"

"Thank you."

"How many tons?"

"Seven hundred and twelve have been despatched. Five thousand by the end of the year."

"That is good," said Kim-Wok Ho, sucking his wisdom tooth while he furiously calculated his maximum profit. "You think it will be a long war?"

"A very long war. Twenty thousand tons at a fixed price?" said Ping-Lai Ho.

"Fixed price," agreed Kim-Wok Ho as he was now going to increase the price of the guns.

Linda came back into the room to find the cousins drinking tea in peaceful silence. 'They both think they have scored,' she said to herself.

"Mr Beaumont will see you in twenty minutes," said Linda to Kim-Wok Ho who got up and forced his cousin to rise and walk with them to the door.

"So nice to see you again, Mr Ho," said Linda taking Ping-Lai Ho's hand in hers and looking at him. As he moved past to the door, Ping-Lai Ho tried to brush against her breasts but she skilfully kept them just out of range of his shoulder. Linda smiled to herself. She was always amazed at the power she held over men.

ON THE THIRD of October 1937, with the heat building up oppressively in anticipation of the main rains breaking at the end of the month, Sergeant Dusty Miller marched into the office of Major Gerald Escort, liaison officer for the Southern Rhodesian army and came to a pounding salute.

"At ease," said Major Escort. "We're not too formal at this time of the year. Too bloody hot. Leave the fancy drill to the Askaris. Sit down and have a gin."

"Thank you, sir," said Dusty formally, taken off guard having never been offered a drink by a major.

"Don't look so shocked. This is the colonial army. White men are considered differently out here. Anyway, you're a celebrity. Pink or tonic?"

"Pink thank you, sir."

"Please sit down. We've got a long morning together. The War Office requires an immediate report and as you are the only one still on his feet, it'll have to come from you. I've put plenty of ice in the gin. Funny thing drinking in the tropics. Never has much effect. Sweat it out too quickly. Bottoms up."

"How are the others, sir?"

"They'll be fine now they are in hospital. They thought Captain Beaumont was suffering from blackwater fever but it was only malaria. Recurrent type unfortunately. He'll have bouts of it in decreasing intensity for the rest of his life. Had it for twenty years myself. Have another gin."

"Haven't finished this one yet, sir."

"Always find the ice soaks up the first one. They taste better as you get into the glass, so to speak. Lieutenant Forrester's in the worst shape. The dysentery has cleaned his guts out. Excellent hospital, the Salisbury General. They'll get him right. Take a few weeks. Can't rush a gut problem. Had it myself. Gypo gut, we used to call it though the type out here's a bit more serious."

"How's Corporal Sparrow?"

"They've had to re-break his leg to set it properly. Next time you go on one of these jaunts, take a doctor with you."

"Captain Beaumont listed that one before we got to Khartoum. Harry, I mean Sparrow was unlucky. Put his foot in an ant bear hole when we was shooting warthog. Broke like a bleedin' pistol shot if you'll excuse my expression. All he said was 'fuck me. I've broken my bleedin' leg.' No complaints."

Major Escort's eyebrows rose slightly and he took a large sip of neat gin before continuing. "Private Kemp has malaria and Private Philpott has developed the worst case of internal piles ever seen in the Salisbury General."

"He drinks too much."

"The doctor thinks it was bouncing around on his seat in your armoured cars. A perfect breeding ground for piles, according to the doctor. You'd better have another gin."

"Thank you, sir."

"You can visit them this afternoon. Know the doctor. First rate. Drinks a bit but first rate. Now to business. The army say that they last had a wireless report three months ago and they want to know your problem."

"There was more than one," began Dusty, taking a swig from his second pink gin. "First the river. It was big and swift and there was no place to get across even as it was in the middle of the dry season. Captain Beaumont says he's going to have an inflatable skirt made for the future. One we can lock on round the armoured cars and blow 'em up. Says there's some way of fixin' a pump by connectin' up to the engine by takin' out a spark plug. He then wants a removable drive from the engine what will drive a propeller. If we'd had that lot we'd have been back in England by now. Just shows you can't see problems till you get out there. Cars are good. Didn't let us down badly. Batteries are useless. Two days after we reached the bank of the Congo they packed up. Even the spares, ones we hadn't even used was no good. Captain thinks it's rapid change of temperature between day and night in the desert. He's going to have the battery people put one in out of a refrigerator and find out why it loses its charge. It took us six weeks to get the armoured cars across that river. The first set of logs we cut for a raft weren't buoyant enough. They floated, but almost submerged and when we ran a car on top they sank. We found one type of tree that floated properly but there weren't many of them. In the end, we were hauling twenty miles from the raft site which took a lot of time.

"Getting across proved easier than we thought as the current swept us across and down river. We had a big paddle fitted at the back which helped. We was going to test a raft on its own, over and back but there wasn't time what with Harry's leg. Captain said worst what could happen would be endin' up down river on the same side. But we went across. They'd chosen a bend in the river where a lot of debris was landing up on the other side and nothin' on our side. We was givin' Harry morphine by that stage as his leg was hurting. Captain was worried about gangrene.

"We dropped one of the bowsers in the water unloading. We'd specially sealed the cap and the petrol wasn't contaminated. Just as well. By the time we found petrol on the Copper Belt there wasn't much left and they was all sick except me. That river did us. Those mosquitoes were the size of a penny. That's somethin' else we'll be looking into when we get home. We came across the bridge from Elizabethville but could have floated the Zambezi if they wasn't sick. The Captain's got a list as long as your arm of what he's going to change. If we hadn't been fit when we left England we'd be dead. Better for us to find out the problems than the whole unit."

"I see," said Major Escort, dropping two lumps of ice into Dusty's glass and half filling the tumbler with gin. "You can have a rest now. See a bit of the country. Farmers very hospitable. Don't see too many whites. Get yourself civilian clothes and you'll have a good time. War Office is impressed you brought them in those last thousand miles. Told me to look after you. We've got a small house on the edge of a lake. Bit isolated. Fridge works. You can stay there and use it as a base to get around. Mazoe Valley. How's your gin?"

"Tasting better, sir."

"Excellent. Had that been wartime they'd have given you a medal."

"How's the news in Europe, sir?"

"Bloody awful. Ah, well. If they didn't have wars there wouldn't be a regular army and we'd both be out of a job. Between wars and without driving down Africa it's a pleasant life. You can swim in the lake. Fish as well. Bass. Good eating." Dusty pulled a face. "Oh, I see. You ate a bit of fish on the way down. Never mind."

"How long will it be?"

"You'll not get out of here for a month. Probably after Christmas. I've booked phone calls through to those with families in England to give them a first-hand report. Now, if you can give me answers to these questions I've written down, I can get a report off to the War Office."

MEGAN STRONG, nee Escort, watched her father's small Austin turn off the dirt road and start the winding farm track up to the company house overlooking the Mazoe Dam. The dust and distance were too great for her to see the passenger. Elizabeth and George, two wild pigs that she had nursed from birth, their tails rigidly vertical, followed her back into the house until she shooed them off the veranda. An old, black Alsatian dog watched expertly with one eye which he only closed when the intruders withdrew. The bush encroached to the wire-meshed fly screen that served as a front door. Megan's only gesture to civilisation and the bush fire hazard had been cutting the grass between the Msasa trees and ringing the nearer ones with small flower beds. Megan, wearing her only dress, which more resembled a sack than a piece of female clothing, sank onto the low couch that had been propped under the inside veranda window for five years, ever since she had arrived at the Mazoe Citrus Estate. Pressed down by the October heat she managed to pick the lace, bead-hung cover from the boiled milk jug and slosh a little into her cup before addressing the heavier brown tea-pot which had been stewing for twenty minutes ever since the house boy had padded it barefoot onto the low table next to the couch. At six o'clock in the evening the heat was intolerable.

She heard the Austin change uncomfortably into first gear and grind up the one in three gradients towards the house. Even after the engine had stopped on the path outside her veranda she could hear the radiator hissing. The house-boy appeared from inside the house carrying a tray with a bucket of ice, a large bottle of Beefeater gin and, to Megan's surprise, two glasses.

"Baas has friend," he said.

Megan didn't bother to get up and brush her hair. She was used to her father's gin- swilling friends coming home for the weekend. They would lay another place for dinner and the old piece of goat the cook had been stewing for three days would be enough for as many as wanted it. 'Anyway,' she thought, 'it's too hot to eat and father prefers crunching the ice in his pink gin.' The only thing that struck her as Dusty clanged through the screen door followed by her father was that he was too young to start drinking with her father. Major Escort kissed his daughter lightly on the cheek before turning back to his guest.

"This is my daughter, Meg. Meet Mr Miller," he said and took the top off the ice-bucket, beautifully dewed from the humidity.

"Hello." she said without getting up.

"Sorry," said Major Escort, without turning from the drinks tray. "Don't know your first name."

"Dusty."

"You must have a proper one!" said Meg.

"Jonathan but no-one calls me that. Been Dusty since I went to school."

"I prefer Jonathan," said Megan as she watched her father pour the gin bottle over two large tumblers of ice.

"Jonathan has just driven down Africa in an armoured car," said Major Escort as he passed one of the gins to Dusty.

"I prefer being Dusty. I'd always be looking for someone else if they called me Jonathan."

"What made you drive down Africa in an armoured car?" asked Megan who could be surprised by very little. "Won't you sit down? That chair shouldn't collapse if you sit in it."

"Captain Beaumont."

"And where is the Captain?"

"Pretty sick," said her father. "Sergeant Miller is the only one of his party who reached Salisbury in good health. Bottoms up. Goes down well after that bloody dust road. How was your week?" he asked his daughter.

"The orange trees look even more dejected than usual," she said and turned to the seated Dusty. "We have a pilot scheme going to develop a large citrus estate. Anglo-American Corporation have an idea they'll make money out of it and provide employment. It'll take years. I've tried every variety known in the world. I'm now grafting onto lemon trees."

"How's the gin?" asked Major Escort.

"Fine, sir."

"Good. We won't run out."

"Do you know?" said Megan to change the subject. "In winter we have a big fire at night."

"Doesn't seem possible," said Dusty, smiling at her. She was the first woman he had seen in four months, even if her hair needed a good wash.

"Wish the rains would break," said Major Escort. "What's for supper?"

"Stewed goat."

"Sounds delicious after eating game for four months," said Dusty and wondered if he did have dysentery after all.

"The goat was killed," said Meg sympathetically as her father poured himself another gin on top of two drops of Angostura bitters and ice. "It didn't die of natural causes."

There was a silence as Dusty watched a large blowfly noisily drone around the veranda and buzz at the fly screen. He was the only one who took any notice.

"Lake's drying up," said Major Escort, back at the fly screen. "Wish the bloody rains would break."

"Will we have difficulty getting to Johannesburg if it's wet?" asked Dusty, sitting up. He had had enough of Africa.

"You may have to wait alongside a few low level bridges while the rivers go down. Strip road most of the way. You'll learn how to keep your wheels on the tarred strips. Nuanetsi may be a problem but there's a good pub if you get stuck. Lion and Elephant. Owner drinks like a fish but a good chap. Meg doesn't drink, more's the pity. Nothing else to do in this heat. Custin!" he bellowed into the house, "Ice!" and said turning back to his guest, "melts too quickly."

"What made Captain Beaumont drive down Africa?" said Meg to make polite conversation as she drank her tea.

"Testin' equipment for the Long Range Unit. He wants to have us dropped behind enemy lines if there's a war."

"Dangerous," said Megan and put down her cup.

"War's always dangerous," said Dusty. "Pardon me askin', sir, but what was you in the last war? Them ribbons tell me a bit but not much."

"Turks. We were in the desert."

"Lawrence?" said Dusty, looking at Major Escort with renewed interest.

"That sort of thing."

"Rather like what we're goin' to do."

"Could be. But you won't dress up as a bloody Arab," he said, passing Dusty his second tumbler of gin and ice as Custin padded back inside the house with the empty ice bucket.

"Bottoms up."

"Good health," said Dusty. "Haven't had a drink for months neither."

"What else haven't you had?" asked Megan and Dusty turned away as she looked straight at him.

"A bath," said Dusty, after a noticeable pause. "I just want a good soak to soothe the tsetse and mosquito bites," he went on recovering quickly as Megan moved slightly.

"I see," she said and smiled at him before pouring another cup of richly-stewed tea into which she spooned four lots of sugar. "Seeing we've plenty of time, you can tell me all about it during the weekend. I presume you are staying the weekend?"

"Maybe longer," said her father. "Depends how long the others take to get fit. You need company, Meg."

"Thank you, daddy. Very thoughtful of you. I'm sure Mr Miller will have a pleasant stay."

A blood-red sky hung between the silhouetted Msasa trees as the sun dipped and the dusk came down.

"Always surprises me," said Dusty getting up. "The night starts so quickly."

"That's Africa," said Megan pulling the Tilley lamp towards her and turning up the gas tap. It hissed loudly. She lit the gas inside the white mantle. First it glowed red and then burst white-hot to throw shadows across the veranda. The dog got up and shook himself before pushing open the screen door and going outside to bark.

Within ten minutes, Africa had closed in around them and left only the patch of light on the veranda. Major Escort filled up his glass and sat down on a cane chair. Nobody said anything. Custin padded back, laid the table at the end of the veranda and put a casserole dish in the middle before withdrawing for the night.

"Good night, Custin," said Meg but she didn't make any move to get up.

"Not hungry," said Major Escort picking up the half-full Beefeater bottle, the ice-bucket and the bitters. "See you in the morning. If you want another drink, Meg'll find it for you. Meg'll show you the spare room."

"Good night, dad."

Dusty got up and sat down again.

They watched the night turn black. The crickets in the long grass built up to a furious noise. From far out in the Mazoe hills came an animal howl lost in the night. The dog nosed its way back through the fly-screen door which clanged shut behind.

"Are you hungry?" asked Meg.

"Not really."

"Too hot," she agreed.

They sat in silence.

"How long have you been here?" asked Dusty.

"Five years."

"Don't you get lonely?"

"Sometimes."

"Have you always been on your own?"

"No."

"Sorry. Wasn't pryin'. Just seems funny for a young girl to live on 'er own in the bush. Can't 'ave many friends around here."

"No."

They again lapsed into silence and Dusty listened to the multitude of night sounds. The Tilley lamp hissed harshly in the background. From inside the house they heard her father's bedroom door slam shut.

"He'll finish the bottle," said Megan, matter-of-factly. "Doesn't like the house on his own. Doesn't like anything on his own, really. Poor daddy."

"Your mother…?"

"Yes."

The dog settled down next to the settee and farted but neither of them took any notice.

"That dog has rotten guts," said Megan after a while, the smell having hung. "He's getting old. We've had him for fourteen years. There's scotch in the cupboard in the lounge."

"You're right. Gin's heavy."

"The food won't get cold. Tastes better than it sounds. Cook's good. Daddy's had him for twenty-eight years. From when he was a bachelor. Before the army. They farmed up at Umvukwes. It's not bad here when the rains break. The winter months are beautiful. Clear blue skies. Doesn't rain for seven months and no humidity."

"Why don't you leave this place?"

"Because I don't want to."

"Don't you want to get married?"

"No. I don't think so. I couldn't take the pain again."

"You've been married?" said Dusty in surprise.

"Yes. And a mother."

"Divorced?" asked Dusty, puzzled, having seen no sign of children.

"No. Widowed. We were crossing the Ruia River. Further up, near grandfather's farm. Flash floods. The car went over the bollards and hit the rocks thirty feet below. Martin saw it coming and pushed me out with the baby. The car had stalled in the middle of the bridge. I clung to a bollard but the water was over my head. The baby just sucked in river water. Nothing I could do. I had to hang on. Raining. Pitch black. Like tonight and then the flash flood subsided and I slipped and staggered to the bank. An old African came out of the bush. They do that. You don't think there's anyone around but there is. Helped me to his hut but it was no good by then. Martin was dead and so was my baby."

Dusty took the Tilley lamp and went into the lounge to find the scotch bottle and two glasses. Without being asked he poured her one and came back.

"Here, drink this. Then we'll eat some food."

"I haven't talked about that night for three years."

"Here… take the drink."

"Thanks. Silly to always be looking back on life."

"Yes."

"They never found his body. That bloody river is full of crocodiles. We were on our way back here. Martin had been employed to start the Citrus Estate, not me. After he died, they let me stay on in the house. We took our degrees at the University of Cape Town together, so we both had the same knowledge. And then Anglo-American employed me to take his place. Mother died soon afterwards so father stays here at the weekends. He doesn't like drinking where he can be seen. Like now. He'd have made Colonel if mother had been alive. You won't believe it but he's only forty-four. Looks more like fifty. Gin and Africa don't mix."

"It must be a hard life."

"Not really. We make it hard. Maybe it's that kind of person who wants to live in the bush. Martin and I could have stayed here forever. There is a great sense of peace. And achievement. Doing something new. Creating. The plan is for twenty-eight thousand acres of citrus; oranges, lemons and grapefruit, all under irrigation. Cut out of the bush. The land round here has never grown a crop. The few Africans ran cattle and grew maize in the clearings. If the rains were kind to them and their cattle grew fat, the Zulus, under Lobengula, came up from Matabeleland and killed them off before stealing the grain and the cattle. They never had a chance to multiply until the Europeans arrived. Grandfather was part of the column that occupied Fort Salisbury. The farm at Umvukwes was his pay. At first, the Shona were thankful for the protection. People forget. Father was born in Rhodesia. One of the first. When he retires from the army, he'll go back to running the farm. Grandfather can't last forever but you would think so. Tough as old boots. There's more than enough land for father and his two brothers, not that they get on with each other. They'll have to sectionalise Rongwa and run it as separate farms. If there's a war, they'll make a fortune out of tobacco. That's how grandfather got on his feet in the last year. All soldiers smoke. Is that true?"

"There's a lot of boredom in soldiering."

"Have you always been in the army?"

"Went in as a boy soldier at fifteen."

"Why haven't you got married?"

"What! On a private's pay! Don't be daft."

"But father said you were a sergeant."

"They only made me a lance-corporal six months ago. I'm acting sergeant, seeing as the others was sick. Captain Beaumont made me a sergeant after we got across the river."

"How did you get across?"

"Floated the armoured cars on rafts we made of tree trunks. Took us weeks, what with Harry havin' broken his leg. Harry was worth three of us when it came to choppin' down trees. Harry Sparrow. With a name like that you'd expect him to be little but he ain't. Six foot four."

"How long are you going to stay in the army?"

"Don't know really. With this war they say what's comin' in Europe, it's difficult to tell. Captain wants me to study at night school and go for a commission but I can't see my accent fitting into the officer's mess."

"You can always improve your accent."

"I quite like the one I got, see."

"Depends what you want out of a life. If you want to make something of yourself, you have to change. It's the law of progress. Yesco!" she said sharply to the dog. "You've done it again." She got up and walked to the fly-screen. "The moon will be up in a little while. The stars and the moon reflect so well in the lake. The rains can't be far away. I haven't talked to anyone for months. I don't often go into Salisbury. If father doesn't come out over a weekend, I can go for weeks without saying a word in English."

"I feel a bit odd your dad havin' asked me to your place. I thought it was his. Won't the neighbours think it wrong, when your dad goes back and us two left on our own?"

"What neighbours? There are the servants. We live differently. Anyway, no-one would look at me in this dress and I don't have anything better to wear."

"Why don't we go into Salisbury next week and buy some clothes?" said Dusty, brightly. "I've got a few quid."

"You mean that, don't you?"

"Of course I do."

"Better stay here and leave it as it is. Let's eat the goat. That scotch has got rid of the 'maubs'." She got up and went to the table and took the lid off the casserole. "Cook's put in carrots and onions and a few other things I'd better ask him about. Chillies, too. Doesn't smell bad. Can you find a piece of wood to wedge under the table? The floor isn't quite level. Mud floors aren't the best but cement's too expensive. You sit on that side and I'll serve. No. First go back to the lounge cupboard. There's a bottle of Cape red wine. Bring two wine glasses. I don't often drink but then I don't often entertain. If I was really going overboard I'd put a comb through this damn hair of mine but that would be taking it too far, if you see what I mean."

Dusty wasn't quite sure what she did mean but went and fetched the bottle of wine and after scrabbling around in a drawer found a corkscrew and pulled out the cork.

"That sounds good," she said from the veranda.

Dusty came back and put the Tilley lamp on the table along with the wine and the glasses. The dog had moved under the table. Outside the fly-screen, the moon was a sharp, colourless reflection on the lake's surface. Dusty poured two glasses of wine and took one to Megan.

"Here's your plate," she said. "Fair exchange."

"Thanks."

"I'm saying funny things. Light-headed. I talk to myself all day. Not out loud, you must understand. Just in my head. But it's the same really. Do you know I haven't had a glass of wine since Martin drowned? Cheers. It's time I left that behind... I loved him very much," she said after a while.

"It must be nice to love somebody that much."

"Haven't you?"

"No."

They ate in silence and the old dog began to snore. Neither of them took any notice.

"I suppose your bags are still in the car?" she said.

"Yes."

"Have you got a bathing costume?"

"Not really but I have a pair of army shorts."

"When we've finished supper, why don't we take the rest of the wine out on the lake and have a swim? There isn't any bilharzia in the centre. That's a bug that gets into your bloodstream. Breeds in freshwater snails."

"What about crocodiles?"

"None in the man-made lakes. Part of the civilising process. How do you like the casserole?"

"Not bad at all."

"I told you so... You know, living here I sometimes get the feeling there aren't other people in the world. The Africans don't talk to you. Apart from the material things of life, there is no communication. Can I have a little more wine? You can row, can't you?"

"Yes," said Dusty, smiling. He was feeling pleasant. The scotch had got to the gin and the wine was getting to both of them. The Tilley lamp picked out the curves and woman shapes under the old dress and the unkempt hair was not so noticeable. Apart from the dog and the Tilley lamp the house was completely silent.

Wine, the darkness around them and Africa for thousands of miles outside. A pool of light on top of the table throwing shadows, deep and black. Nothing else but themselves.

"Have you finished your food, Dusty?" Her voice was tight.

"Yes." And then after a moment, "I think so."

"Good," she lifted her glass and drank it. "Let's get your bags."

She got up and he followed to the screen door.

"Stay there, Yesco," she said to the dog, the snoring having stopped as she pushed back her chair. "Father always leaves the keys in the car, otherwise he loses them. No-one around here knows how to drive, so it's perfectly safe."

Their feet crunched on the gravel and Dusty looked up at the cloudless night sky. He knew so little looking up.

"Are your bags in the boot?"

"Yes. There's only one. My kitbag."

"Here we are," she said and he picked the kitbag out of the car. The moonlight showed her face washed in the colourless light. Her hand brushed his arm as she shut the boot and the sexuality sucked at his groin.

"I'll show you to your room," she said.

"Thanks."

"The boat's moored at a little jetty." They crunched over the gravel and into the house.

Alone in his room with one candle, he found the shorts that came down to his knees and put them on, rolling them up to remove the bagginess. Blowing out the candle, he felt his way into the corridor and through the house, crunching on the gravel to stand next to the car and wait and look out down over the moon-smoothed water of the dam that stretched away into distant patches that would be trees, water lapping at their roots among the new weed of the water's edge. She was gone some time and she came down dressed as before.

"I've brought a torch," she said and shone it on the path and led him down to the water and the little rowing boat that sucked at the slight tide of the dam. They got in and he took up the oars and rowed easily to the middle and shipped the dripping wet oars, moon touched, into the boat. She carefully propped the wine bottle in the bottom of the boat and pulled the old dress over her head.

"I don't have a proper bathing costume either," she said. "You don't mind?"

"No," said Dusty as he watched the perfectly proportioned body with heavy breasts and strong hips, as it stood up and dived over the side clothed only in pants and bra. She surfaced and flicked the water from her now long, wet hair that moulded an oval face.

"Come on," she said and he dived over the side to join her.

"The water's perfect," he said and squirted water from his mouth that dropped perfectly on top of her head and ran down over the ears, protruding from the wetness of her clinging hair.

"That body looks like you should be an athlete," she said and he smiled again and swam towards her under the African moon.

"Put your legs around my waist." She was treading water. "Then we can float on our backs together. Now can you see the Southern Cross?"

"Yes, I've been following it since we crossed the Equator."

She felt for him and tugged at his trunks. They began to drift apart as his shorts came away from his body. She tossed them into the boat.

"Now me," and he swam back and felt for the elastic at the top of her knickers and she floated back, leaving them in his hands. He threw them into the boat and she followed them with her bra, leaving her heavy breasts to float independently, big nipples thrust at the heavens. He swam to her and felt the length of her body. She turned over and held onto the side of the rowing boat, her legs trailing behind wide open. Her inner wetness and the water combined to ease him into her as he gripped her large breasts. They coupled together with a building ecstasy that made her scream with the pleasure of orgasm.

6

OCTOBER 1937

*A*t seven-thirty in the morning, the following day, in the City of London, Reggie Beaumont parked his Lagonda outside 51 King William Street. It was barely light and a chill fog tugged at him from the River Thames. He moved quickly up the four steps from the pavement and passed between the tall pillars that gave way to the revolving doors. The wrap-around sign in three feet gold letters above the door was new and untarnished. Involuntarily, he looked up and smiled. Reggie liked the sound of it; Union Mining House. His companies were the only tenants and had acquired naming rights to the building. When he had lesser things to do with his cash he would buy the six-storey building. In the meantime everything was perfectly satisfactory. He pushed at a panel of the door and followed it round into the central heated reception hall with its domed roof and Charlie in early attendance.

"Morning Charlie," said Reggie.

"Morning Mr Beaumont. Glad to hear your brother's safe."

"You must have read this morning's paper. Only heard from mother last night."

"Big article in the *Telegraph*," he said and held open the lift door for Reggie. "Take a lot of Germans to kill Geoffrey if they do have a war," said Reggie as the new lift rose to the executive management's third floor.

"They won't go to war, sir. Talk, that's what it is."

"I don't know so much," disagreed Reggie. "Have a pleasant morning, Charlie."

The corridor was thickly carpeted and sparsely lined with modern paintings that stood out well against the white painted walls. Each painting was watched over by its own hooded light. The Gauguins were in his office behind his antique desk. He opened the door to his secretary's office which would take him through to his own. Thelma was already behind her desk.

"Damn fog," said Reggie unwinding his scarf and taking off his overcoat.

"Morning, Reggie. You've a full diary."

"I'll dictate first. We must buy those American recording machines. Any coffee?"

"Just made it."

"What would I do without you?"

"Find yourself another secretary. Shall I bring my book?"

"Please. And ask Chuck for half a dozen machines. Nobody will like them to begin with but that's progress."

Having hung his coat and scarf on the hat stand with his bowler hat he walked behind his desk and opened his diary. The second desk on his left was piled with four neat stacks of files along with two telephones. A third phone rested in its hook on the right of his desk.

"Was Tony annoyed?"

"Yes… The first two lots of files are diary notes brought forward. The rest are Friday's mail. I've answered as much as I can."

"How are you coping?"

"Just."

"Get an assistant."

"And after six months she'll do my job."

"Never. You ready?"

"Ready," said Thelma coming in and sitting on the chair in front of his desk. She propped the shorthand book on her knee.

"The first is a draft report on contingency plans for the group should war break out."

For an hour, Reggie dictated as fast as he could talk and Thelma's shorthand flew over the pages. By eight-thirty the coffee was cold, the twenty-page report was complete and the files had been seen to.

"How's your hand, love?"

"Fallen off."

"Those machines and an assistant."

"Thanks, Reggie."

"And some coffee and ask Lionel to come through."

Reggie picked up his phone and dialled the Royal Insurance Company. "Crabtree?" he asked.

"He's not in yet, sir."

"Ask him to call Beaumont," and put down the phone. "Doesn't anybody work in this bloody country?"

"Did you call me?" asked Thelma from her office.

"No. Where's Lionel?"

"Morning, Mr Beaumont," said Lionel, coming into the office with a sheaf of papers.

"You're late," said Reggie. "But sit down and try not to shake those papers. What's our cash position around the world and what are our commitments?"

"I gave you those figures last Monday."

"And you think the figures will be the same this Monday? Any figures more than seven days old are worthless. This business runs on facts. You must set up a situation where the banks phone you at the end of business on Fridays."

"In some countries the banks close after we do."

"So? You have a phone at home? Set up a system. All I want are accurate group figures at eight-thirty Monday morning."

"Yes, sir."

"Now. Have you got those casino figures for me? Mr Venturas is due in five minutes."

"Yes, sir," and handed Reggie the shaking sheaf of papers.

"Alcohol or nerves?" asked Reggie, smiling.

"Nerves."

"They always say the first six months are the worst. You either survive and enjoy yourself or you look for another job. If we wish to compete with the establishment we've got to be better than good. If I know my exact worth I can make deals when I see them. To grow rich there is a fine balance between assets and borrowing. Thelma," he called, "bring Lionel a cup of coffee and then more to himself, "and I'll see how much he learnt getting his C.A. albeit the youngest in the country."

After five minutes of careful analysis Reggie was smiling to himself and Lionel Bennett was able to drink the last of his coffee without rattling the saucer.

"It's interesting to have to work back to a price," said Reggie, putting down the sheaf of papers. "Where did you get your running cost?"

"A friend of mine does the Savoy audit. It's only the standing charges that gave me concern. The variables will rise and fall with turnover. Knowing the cost of sales of beverages and food, I have projected a turnover that will be required to make a profit. Included in the costs are amortisation of equipment, obsolescence, depreciation and finance costs. As I see it, the unit must have three hundred and sixty bedrooms and the island cost less than five hundred thousand pounds to make the proposition viable. Building costs in the Caribbean have been static at ten shillings and sixpence per square foot for five years. I've included a two percent escalation for contingencies. The specification will be as luxurious as money can buy. Out of interest, sir, where are you going to find your management to run the operation?"

"That is always the intangible."

TONY VENTURAS WAS AGGRESSIVELY ANNOYED as he pushed through the swing doors of Union Mining House.

"Can I help you, sir?" asked Charlie.

"Mr Beaumont?"

"Third floor."

"He's here already?"

"Certainly, sir. He arrived at seven-thirty. Always does when he's in London. Fog's bad this morning."

At the third floor, Tony got out of the lift and purposefully headed for Thelma's office.

"Well here I am," said Tony as Thelma looked up from her typewriter. "Where's Reggie?"

"In his office with our accountant. Give me your coat and I'll hang it up for you. Tea or coffee?"

"Coffee, with a slug of whisky in it. I haven't been up at this hour on a Monday since leaving school."

"You run a different kind of business."

"Always the same," grumbled Tony. "Let a partner into your business and they end up giving you shit."

"It's not that bad. This is the first time he's not called on you."

"Why not?"

"Because he's got a surprise."

"You mean it's got nothing to do with Bretts?"

"In a way, no. In a way, yes."

"Thelma King, do not be so obtuse or I'll put you over my knee and give you a spanking."

"Oh, please, I'd like that."

"Thought I recognised the squadron leader's voice," said Reggie opening his office door and grinning at the tableau. "Up to his usual tricks, Thelma? You'd think he'd get enough working with it all night long."

"And that's my point, Reggie. Do you know what time I left the club last night? This morning, I mean?"

"About four-thirty. You usually do. Come in and meet Lionel Bennett. We've got some figures to show you."

"What figures?"

"Exactly. And Thelma, bring him some coffee well laced with twenty-year-old scotch and we'll get the smile back on his face. Mr Bennett, Mr Venturas."

Tony walked across the large silk Persian carpet and shook hands wearily.

"What's this all about, Reggie?" said Tony.

"Amazing how many people start their new lives by asking that question."

"What new life? Do you want to sell your shares in Bretts?"

"How much are we making?"

"Two hundred thousand a year and it runs like clockwork."

"So why would I wish to sell?"

"Let's have it, Reggie."

"First take a seat. Have your coffee. Do you like the decor?"

"I'd have walnut panelled the walls instead of painting them duck green."

"Sea-sky green. And it's not paint but a very expensive wallpaper. Panelled walls make me feel I'm in my stockbroker's office. This is modern with the exception of my desk. Do you like the carpet? Had it made especially in Persia. It's unusual to have so much yellow in a Persian carpet. How's your coffee?"

"Strong."

"Good. Have another."

"Why?"

"How would you like to run a casino/hotel complex in the Caribbean? On our own private island?"

"You'd never get a gambling licence."

"I've got it."

"The 'hoods' will run you out."

"Not on our own, very well secured island. Private landing strip. That kind of thing."

"Casinos are a licence to print money."

"Exactly. Couple that with your ability to find the best looking women in the world and we have a sure-fire winner. We'll be able to get at the American market and that's where the future will lie."

"What do we do with Bretts?"

"Keep it. I need it for the reinsurance business. We can use it as a training ground. Mike can run it. He'll probably steal but I'll put in a system that will keep it within reason."

"How many shares do I get?"

"How much money have you got?"

"That would be telling, partner."

"Ten percent, Tony, payable up front or out of your share of the profits. Here are all the figures. Go through to Lionel's office and pick holes in the project. I asked Lilly Brigley to come in as well. She'll be here at nine o'clock. She has a good brain and is looking for a job. She'll be your assistant, Tony, backing up in technical education what you've forgotten."

"Your eyes in the Caribbean?" said Tony, getting up to follow Lionel.

"Something like that except she'll always help and not hinder. If she hinders, you fire. You'll only report to me, Tony."

"Our roles have changed."

"Not at all. I still call you sir when I'm in uniform."

"They've gazetted you a flight-lieutenant."

"With Geoffrey back from the dead and in every newspaper, they're sure to make him the army's youngest major. You'd better work on that thin ring to go between the two thick ones. Come back when Lionel's briefed you. Thelma," he called as they left his office. "Send Lilly through to Lionel's office when she arrives."

A phone rang on his desk and he picked up the receiver.

"Beaumont!"

"Crabtree, Mr Beaumont."

"Hello, old chap. Nice of you to phone back. Terrible weather for October."

"When are we going to have a bite of lunch together?"

"You name it, old boy."

"Let's say Thursday at my club. Royal Air Force Club, 127 Piccadilly. Food's excellent. Twelve-thirty, old chap. Ask for me at the desk."

"We can have a good chat."

"Could you do me a favour, old boy?" asked Reggie, wincing with the forced gush of his charm.

"What can I do, old boy?"

"Chivvy your accounts fellows. They still owe us last year's reinsurance brokerage."

"I'll bring a cheque with me to lunch."

"First class, old chap. I'll have my secretary phone yours on Thursday and the girls can chase the accountants."

"Toodle-loo."

"Cheerio, old chap," said Reggie and put down his receiver. 'The arse creeping I do for money,' he said under his breath and called his Thursday instructions for lunch through to Thelma.

Reggie picked up the minutes of the previous week's Monday morning reinsurance management meeting and began to read it through carefully. The unlisted phone rang. Reaching across to the other desk, still reading the minutes, he picked up the receiver and finished the paragraph before talking into the mouthpiece.

"Reggie Beaumont," he said.

"Hello darling. Thank you for a lovely weekend. I just love your piano playing."

"Glad you enjoyed it."

"What's that loud noise?"

"My other phone ringing. I'll call you during the week. Have you got up yet?"

"Of course not."

"Have a nice day."

Reggie put down the receiver took his foot off the button under his desk and the phone ringing stopped. He smiled briefly to himself and carried on reading the minutes. The right hand phone rang again and he glanced at his wrist watch. Two minutes to nine and the City of London was beginning to work.

"Take it for me," he called out to Thelma as he carried on reading with total concentration.

"Hello? Mr Beaumont's office. Hello, Mr Fleming. There was a pause as she looked at Reggie who shook his head once without interrupting his concentration.

"Sorry, Mr Beaumont won't be in today. I'll ask him to call you the moment he returns from Paris. Good morning, Mr Fleming."

"I could have been in the loo," said Reggie. "Why did it have to be Paris?"

"That man's a creep. All he wants to do is grope one of the girls at Bretts."

"He should have got the message by now. I'm surprised the Royal Exchange haven't found out and given him the boot. Are the others waiting?"

"Yes."

"Send them in."

"Come in, gentlemen," said Thelma and the management team of the reinsurance division filed into Reggie's office. Reggie raised one finger off the polished mahogany of his desk but didn't take his eyes from the minutes. They sat themselves at the board table at the other end of the room and shuffled papers. Reggie finished his reading and got up quickly to cross the room to sit at the head of the table. Thelma was seated to take the minutes.

"Crabtrees and Flemings. Can anyone tell me why insurance company managers sound and look alike? And those two are both as bald as coots. Good morning gentlemen. Let's have your reports around the table clockwise but first I want to know which of last week's problems haven't been solved. Yes, John?"

"The Royal still haven't paid."

"I'm collecting the cheque on Thursday. Yes, Anthony?"

"There's still the rumour in the market of a treaty being set up in competition."

"So far as our existing insurers are concerned, we don't have competition. They are locked into our treaty until they do something wrong. The legal document was a fine piece of drafting by our solicitors. For the rest we will launch a programme to see all insurers in England who have not signed our treaty. Have your people investigate the backgrounds of the men who could influence the business. Private, business and pleasure activities. Every man has his particular foible. The treaty figures should speak for themselves but that's not enough."

"Ralph Sender," said Mark Opperman.

"Haven't we cooked that man's goose once and for all?" said Reggie. "I'll take him to the club."

"I don't think that will work. He's very religious."

'What religion?"

"Mormon."

"No chance with the club then," agreed Reggie. "I'll have a chat with his chairman. Just because we make a lot of money out of a good deal for everyone why should he complain?"

"He says it's far in excess of our work involvement."

"He's just jealous he didn't think of it first. There are builders and destroyers in this world and Mr Sender is no builder. Leave him to me. Next? Okay? New problems?"

"Insurance company reconciliation of accounts is a nightmare," said Mark.

"There is no way of getting them to agree."

"You're talking facultative reinsurance?" asked Reggie.

"Yes."

"Pass the buck. Don't pay them till they reconcile our statement."

"I'll try it."

"Be diplomatic. Just tell them how much better at accounting they are… new business?"

"Another aviation company," said John. "Chartering from Glasgow to London. Three aircraft."

"Excellent. We must concentrate on the aviation and marine markets. You'll get fantastic growth. For next week I want a list of every account you handle with last year's brokerage listed against next year's projection. Every month I want those figures updated. Try and gauge the size of your accounts. A careful analysis by you will give an accurate average and enable me to judge next year's cash flow. I want each of you to set a target for next year's new business. Anything more? Thelma will have copies of the minutes to you by this afternoon. Amazing: The phone didn't ring. Thank you gentlemen. Don't forget if you have a problem during the week bring it in here. Keep up the good work and we'll all get our Christmas bonuses."

"Glad to read about your brother," said Mark.

"Yes," chorused the others.

"Thanks," said Reggie and walked back to his desk as the phone rang.

"Beaumont."

"Migroyd, old boy."

"Morning. What can I do for you on a foggy day?"

"Heard in the club that Malay Tin want to sell. Thought you'd be interested."

"Very. I'll have Tug do a check."

"London listing. Cash problems."

"Thanks, sir."

"Glad to hear about Geoffrey."

"Yes. Good news." Reggie pressed the button under his desk.

"What's that noise?" asked Migroyd.

"Other phone. Cheerio."

"Cheerio, Reggie."

Reggie put down the receiver took his foot off the button and picked up the week's commodity broking report.

"Works like a charm," he said out loud.

"What does?" said Thelma through the open door.

"Our false phone."

"You see I do have some good ideas."

'There's going to be a war,' he told himself. Every strategic material had gone up in price and rubber was out in front. Reggie flipped to the last page to read their stock position and smiled again. Tug's warehouses were almost full. After ten minutes he had assimilated the shipping and commodities situation as it affected Beaumonts. Thelma came in and put a two-page set of minutes on his desk.

"That's quick."

"Makes the others think."

"True," said Reggie, reading down the centre of the pages signing each copy. "Do you know that old bugger Migroyd's actually working for his director's fees. If he finds another takeover prospect I'll have to give him a raise."

"Lilly's with Lionel."

"She's always on time."

The phone rang.

"Shall I answer?" asked Thelma.

"I'll do it. It just means two people saying hello. Beaumont," he said into the receiver.

"This is the Air Ministry. Please hold on for Wing-Commander Swan."

"Thanks," said Reggie and cupped the phone. "Why can't he make his own damn phone calls?"

Thelma shrugged, not knowing who it was and went back to her typewriter.

"What was that Beaumont?" said Swan, coming on the line.

"People in my office," and he trod his foot hard on the button.

"What's that infernal noise?"

"Other phone, sir."

"Place sounds like a madhouse."

"Quite right, sir."

"We've made you a flight-lieutenant."

"Thank you, sir. Must go, sir. Cheerio," and put down the phone in the self-induced confusion. Reggie was laughing uncontrollably. "Poor old bugger must have been purple."

The phone rang again.

"Shit," said Reggie before picking it up.

"Beaumont."

"Gunter," said a flat voice.

"Gunter who?" asked Reggie, not understanding.

"Gunter von Ribbeck."

"Gunter," shouted Reggie. "Where the hell are you? We haven't heard a word in weeks. How's your wife?"

"That's the problem."

"What do you mean, that's the problem?"

"Reggie, I'm in London. I have to talk to someone."

"Has the business got problems?"

"No... My wife. She doesn't want to be a proper wife."

"Well we can't talk about that on a telephone," said Reggie. "Where are you staying?"

"I'm at Victoria Station."

"Go to my flat. The caretaker will let you in. Thelma will phone him. Help yourself to whatever. Have a bath. There's food and booze. I can't get away 'til six. Can you hold?"

"Sure, Reggie."

"This is serious, Gunter?"

"Yes."

"I've never heard you like this."

"No."

"Go to my flat and I'll get through as fast as I can. Oh. Don't wake the lady in the bedroom. Her name's Wanda. Dark. Big tits. Not your type at all."

"I never want to make love to a woman again."

"Gunter, I was joking."

"What do you do with a wife that turns out to be lesbian?"

"I've never come across that before."

"Neither have I," and his phone dropped back on the hook.

"Now that is serious," he said. "Thelma. You'd better come on in here and close the door. We've got a major problem."

After talking to Thelma for five minutes, having taken all the phones off their hooks, Reggie asked, "What makes a woman go like that?"

"Something to do with a hormone imbalance. They can't imagine making love to a man anymore than you can."

"She was so beautiful. What do I do for Gunter?"

"He'll have to file for a divorce."

"Not in that society. I wonder if the Baron knew the problem."

"Probably. It was his daughter."

"The Baron's staying at Merry Hall next week. Henry asked him over for the pheasant shooting. I'll go down. Maybe I can get to the bottom of it."

"You make better friends than we girls. You better put the phones on."

"What a terrible thing to happen."

Thelma walked across the new carpet and opened the door to find Chuck Everly standing beside her desk. When Reggie heard his greeting he looked at his watch. It was exactly nine-thirty. "Come in, you old bastard. Thelma, your coffee had better be extra special. These Americans won't put up with the rubbish we drink. Come and sit down, Chuck."

"Why was the door closed? Never is."

"Thelma and I were having a 'quicky' on the carpet. We're always randy on Monday mornings."

"I don't believe a word of it."

"Neither should you. How's the big deal going?"

"Very well if you count the dollars. My conscience isn't too good."

"If Hitler carries on," said Reggie, "everyone will be killing each other. On the insurance side, Thelma's made appointments for you with four companies today. The English don't work as fast as the Americans. You'll pick up plenty of facultative business. On the big risks, everyone is looking for capacity and if you can show them your underwriters are first class security, you'll do well. The secret of new business is going out and getting it. Have a good day. Tony will look after you in the club tonight. I've got myself a high powered date. Dinner for two."

"With Wanda."

"We're just old friends. Eat at the club. There's a new piano player from your part of the world. They say Earl Hines is the best of his kind in the world."

"Wild horses won't keep me away. Do you always have weather like this?"

"Mostly, in the winter."

"No wonder so many of them went Stateside."

The phone rang on Reggie's unlisted line.

"Reggie Beaumont!"

"Reggie, I've had a report from Salisbury saying Geoffrey is very sick."

"Mother, so have I but it is not blackwater fever. I spoke to a Major Escort from the flat this morning. Apart from the fact he sounded a bit drunk, he was very helpful. The line was terrible. One of Geoffrey's sergeants gave me the full rundown. They're sick but fully curable. Sergeant Miller will be visiting the hospital this afternoon and sending me a cabled report. Is Baron von Essen coming for the shooting this weekend?"

"Yes. Are you sure Geoffrey's alright?"

"Yes, mother. I'll ring you this evening. Goodbye mother and don't worry."

"I can't help it. Goodbye, Reggie."

Thelma was standing in front of him with Chuck's typed appointment list.

"Just as well she didn't have another four sons," said Thelma.

"Or four daughters," said Reggie and walked with Chuck to the lift.

"Have you finished placing my personal insurances?" asked Reggie.

"When I spoke to my office from the hotel, they'd covered eighty-five percent. They'll be no problem for us. Your problem is paying the premium. Effectively, you've insured eight lives for two hundred thousand pounds each including war risk."

"There had to be a way round death duties."

"There always is. Around any problem. I'll see you back here nine-thirty tomorrow. Same time, same place. Have a good day. I'm sure going to."

"Catch taxis, I mean cabs. Even if it's one street. I mean one block."

"Okay. I got you. But even though it's quaint, I sure can speak English. Have a jolly day, old chap."

"Certainly, old boy," said Reggie, copying the appalling English accent imitation and touching him lightly on the shoulder. The lift door was closing as Chuck turned round and smiled. He seemed very satisfied with his life and Reggie was pleased.

When he got back to his office all three phones were ringing and he looked at them with his hands on his hips and a rueful smile.

"Well do something, Reggie," said Thelma rushing into his office.

"Two hands I've got. But not three," and he picked up the unlisted phone and indicated the other two. "Reggie Beaumont."

"Sounds worse than usual," said his sister-in-law Isabel.

"It is a bit. To what do I owe this honour?"

"I'm bored."

"Darling Isabel. Fond of you, I am. I have two phone calls, waiting a man waiting outside from South Africa and you phone up for a chat."

"Don't be angry. I've behaved very well these last six months. Have lunch with me?"

"I can't. I'm having lunch with the bank manager."

"Tomorrow."

"Thelma's signalling frantically."

"Tomorrow I want to have a long chat."

"Alright. The Berkeley at twelve-thirty."

"I'm looking forward to it." The phone went dead and left Reggie again looking at the receiver.

"What the hell does she want?"

"She's always wanted your body," said Thelma sweetly and handed him another phone.

"Ask Mr van der Walt to come in. Hello," he said into the phone. "Beaumont, can I help you?"

"My name is Halmsbury of the Contingency insurance company. I wondered if we could talk about my company coming onto your treaty?"

"Certainly, Mr Halmsbury. When may I call? Would two-thirty this afternoon be convenient? I believe you are in Billiter Street."

"Yes. That will be excellent. Good day, sir."

"Good day," said Reggie and hung up.

"You've already an appointment at two-thirty," said Thelma holding out the other phone.

"Hello. Mr van der Walt," said Reggie standing up and leaning over his desk to shake hands and at the same time taking the phone from Thelma. "Please sit down. Who's the appointment with Thelma?"

"Swire and McLean's London manager."

"Put him off. Be polite. This one's important. Good morning," he said into the third phone. Beaumont speaking."

"My name is Barnes from International Business Machines out of New York. I'd like to make an appointment to come and visit with you. We've got some ideas that can help you with that reinsurance programme of yours. Help smooth out the accounting side, so to speak."

"Certainly Mr Barnes. Please speak to Miss King and she'll get you into my diary."

"You sound busy, Mr Beaumont."

"Yes. Very."

"You don't get rich unless you're busy. I'll like talking with Miss King and find a time to suit you."

Reggie handed Thelma the phone.

"This looks nearly as bad as commissioning a new gold mine," said Koos van der Walt.

"There is only one way," said Reggie, smiling and taking both unused phones off their hooks as Thelma made his appointment with IBM.

"You can leave that one off too, Miss King," said Reggie. "Mr Bell's invention was excellent but too many people can get at me at the same time."

"Certainly, Mr Beaumont," said Thelma and smiled at him. "It was never like this in the beginning."

"True," said Reggie and walked around his desk and took Koos across the room to the board table. "You'll need plenty of room for those maps," he said to the South African.

"Thelma, would it be asking too much to get Mr van der Walt a cup of coffee. Chuck, to use one of his expressions, 'didn't even get to first base'. And I could do with another myself. How's the mine progressing?" he said to Koos.

"Still ahead of schedule."

"Excellent. And thanks for your help with my brother."

"The Salisbury General is one of the best tropical disease hospitals in the world. Our Salisbury manager will be across there by now."

"How was your boat trip?"

"Excellent as far as Madeira but afterwards the weather changed. When we left Cape Town it was blowing a black South Easter and the cloth was hanging heavily over Table Mountain. Union Castle looked after us. Do you have some paper weights or books? Then we can hold down the corners of this map. It is topographical but drawn from aerial survey photographs. Now. Let me show you. The existing gold in South Africa is situated on the Witwatersrand. Here. The reef. The gold reef. We in Union Mining, South Africa, have had a theory for many years that the South African highveld as we call it, is a repository for many of the known minerals found by man. We also think the mineral reef extends as far south as the southern Free State and as far north as the Belgium Congo but with saturation points in the Transvaal and Southern Rhodesia. During the last ten years, the Union government have granted a number of companies rights to prospect for specified minerals. The Anglo-American Corporation and De Beers have been particularly active in this field. The agreement with the government is that a specified amount of money must be spent on aerial and ground surveys for the companies to retain their mineral rights to given areas. As a result, most companies only specify gold and diamonds. What I think we should do as well is prospect for manganese, chrome, platinum and copper, all of which are wartime strategic minerals. Now, looking at this map we have prepared, the shaded areas are those we consider prime prospects and for which the government are offering prospecting rights."

"How much will it cost?"

"Roughly, ten million pounds over five years."

"Shit," said Reggie. "Sorry, Koos. I mean what if we don't find anything?"

"We will have lost ten million pounds."

"Why the rush?"

"The best prospecting areas will have gone if we don't put in our bid at the tenders."

"This one's big, Koos. What are our chances?"

"Excellent but then I have been watching progress of mineral development in the Union for thirty years. We have certain residual rights and because of our history, the government will prefer our applications to some of the inexperienced companies. The government wants to earn tax from profits, for us to create foreign exchange and capital for further developments. We have a large black population that has to be found jobs. It made me excited when you took over the company. I hoped at last a younger man would have vision and do something."

"I've got a lot of vision, Koos. It' a question of whether I can raise ten million pounds. Have you any idea how much money that is?"

"The return will be beyond any man's dreams."

"Your dreams are fine. Mine have to go through the bank manager. You've done a full report?"

"Detailed. You've got six years at University of Cape Town and twenty-four in the bush behind these documents," he said, taking a large file out of his briefcase. "I will lay every penny of my limited personal fortune to back my beliefs."

"How much have you got?"

"One hundred and ten thousand pounds. Mainly in Union Mining stock which have quadrupled since you took over."

"That's a big fortune for one man to gamble. Now you have got me interested. That's my kind of language putting your own money where your mouth is. If you'll leave me, I'll read this report. Tell my secretary to cancel all pre-lunch appointments. I've got goose-bumps on this one."

"I'll wait outside in case you wish to ask any questions. The tender has to be in by the end of November."

"Ask Thelma to give you a copy of my casino report. Give you something to read. I always like to have opinions from people removed from the business."

Leaving the phones off the hook, and without hearing Koos close the door, Reggie began to read. Since becoming Chief Executive of Union Mining, Reggie had methodically read every mining journal and made an in-depth study of the mining industry around the world. The ownership of raw materials and the ability to pinpoint its users around the globe was a perfect link. So often the commodity division had buyers but no suppliers. The future pattern of Reggie's empire was clear in his mind. A broker by profession, he still wished to eliminate the middle man or better, make his profit twice. The problem was always money. He would never generate sufficient capital for his potential. By ten-thirty, Reggie had read the report. He put it down on the board table and looked across his office blankly. He could see the trap. If they tendered for small concession areas they would get nothing. The bigger the concession area, the lower the cost per square mile to prospect. The report itself was a brilliant, clinical analysis of his chances. The tax rebates on new mines were excellent. The incentives were all in the package. Carefully, he took up the file and began to read slowly from the beginning, committing to memory as many of the facts that he would need to repeat. By eleven-thirty in the morning he was determined to find the money and asked Koos to come back into his office.

"It doesn't say so here," he said, "but I presume if we stop prospecting the concession reverts to the government?"

"Together with all our survey reports."

"We are presently producing twenty-three thousand ounces of gold from the old Union mines, the profit from which is financing part of the new mine. Kloof will not be producing for two years. If we are successful with our search, we will require massive capital to develop new mines."

"A rich strike never runs short of risk capital," said Koos.

"Yes. That part is easier, more tangible. If this programme goes ahead, we will have to postpone the new nickel mine in Australia. Anyway we are having trouble with the Australian government already. Seems they are not keen on foreign capital developing their mining industry."

"The stuff isn't much good sitting in the ground."

"Leave it with me, Koos. I'll do my best. You must stay in London until we finalise. I'll need to talk to all my partners and we're lucky that Chuck and Gunter are here already. Thelma," he said to the outside office. "Can you come through and take down a cable for Carl and François and put the phones back on again. Why can't the telephone people work out a way of transferring calls from one phone to the other? Ask Chuck, Thelma, I expect the Americans will have worked it out. What do you think of our casino?" he said to Koos.

"It would seem a quick way to get rich but that kind of gamble, I don't understand."

"It's not a gamble if you own the casino. I will call you when I have any news of progress. Enjoy London while you are here. There is plenty to do. Thelma can help you with theatre tickets. We'll have lunch together on Wednesday."

Reggie shook hands and immediately turned to Thelma who had put back the phones and was waiting with her dictation book. By the time Koos had closed the door to the outer office the cables for France and Denmark had been completed and Reggie was moving round to the other side of his desk to answer his private line.

"Reggie Beaumont."

"Reggie! What's going on here? I've been trying to call you for over an hour."

"I left the phone off the hook."

"Why? I was trying to get hold of you," she was whining and Reggie winced. "Don't let's go into all the detail," he said.

"There's a strange man in the flat. I heard a noise. I can't go out and I have a modelling job in Kensington at three and you know how long it takes me to get ready. Reggie, you must do something. The man's drinking."

"Go and introduce yourself. His name is Gunter and he's my German partner. But whatever you do, don't start vamping him. He doesn't like women."

"Doesn't like women!" said Wanda in awe. "I don't think I'd know what to say to a man who doesn't like women."

"Try good morning and make him some coffee."

"Don't be silly, Reggie. You know perfectly well I can't make coffee."

"Just be nice to him."

"Well, I would if he liked women."

"Wanda, darling, have I ever told you that you have a one-track mind. If you don't get home soon that photographer boyfriend will kill you. When's he due back from Manchester?"

"Ten o'clock this morning. Reggie!" she screamed. "It's nearly twelve o'clock and he'll be home."

"Tell him you went out and came back again."

"Reggie you are so clever. I'd never have thought of that. But what if he sees I'm wearing the same clothes I went out in last night?"

"He won't. He wasn't there last night. Tell him you've been modelling evening shots. Tell him anything. He's so dumb. He's besotted by you. Just pout those big red lips and he won't be able to say anything."

"You are clever, Reggie. What's that noise?"

"My other phone. Goodbye, Wanda."

"Reggie…"

"Goodbye," and he put down the phone to pick up the other one.

"Beaumont!"

"One day, Reginald Beaumont," said Thelma sweetly, over her shoulder as she walked back to her office, "it'll drop off."

"Hang on a minute. What did you say Thelma?"

"You 'eard."

"What? Yes. Lionel? Yes, come on in."

"Reggie," called Thelma, "you've got forty minutes to get to your luncheon appointment and by the sounds of things you'd better be nice to your bank manager."

"How's my report?"

"Not fast under the circumstances. While you are swilling hock and eating roast grouse, I shall be doing some work."

"Thelma. You're a darling. I don't know what I'd do without you."

"About time you appreciated me."

"But sometimes, I'd rather," he said with a sweet smile.

"What?"

"Do without you. Come in, Tony. How do you like the venture?"

"This one's going to be fun. When do we start?"

"First, you and Lilly will fly around the Caribbean looking for a suitable island but it must be British. The British were the only ones to swallow my idea of a private club. Members only. That way we can do what we like."

"The rich will beat their brains out to get there."

"Was it worth getting up early in the morning? Lilly, how about you?"

"Why did you choose me?"

"Because you've got brains and good looks. We're not employing ugly staff for that island," Reggie was smiling broadly. "Well, those are some of the reasons."

"We'll need private villas. A yacht basin. Golf course. Everything," said Tony, "and girls, girls, girls."

"Something like that," said Reggie, and they all laughed.

"Well done, Lionel," said Reggie. "You've briefed them well. Anything any of you want from me?"

"I've got so many questions and yet I haven't," said Lilly.

"I'll just have to put Bretts into a holding position," said Tony. "When do we start?"

"How about now?" said Reggie and walked across to the hat stand to put on his overcoat.

"Talking of tropical islands won't change the weather outside," said Reggie cheerily putting on his coat. "Enjoy yourselves. We've all known each other long enough not to have to worry about trust. Lionel will release expense funds. I've got to go. Bank manager. He's going to get a lot of business today. If he wants it." He wound the scarf round his neck. "Hold the fort, Thelma. I'll go direct from lunch to the Contingency. Give me a copy of the treaty and I'll have Halmsbury sign it straight away. Don't make any appointments for Chuck before eleven tomorrow and leave a message at his hotel for him to come round here at nine. By then I'll have Gunter back in the land of the living."

Outside in the corridor, Reggie rang for the lift and waited. Two of his staff passed and he said good morning. Charlie opened the lift door and they went down in comfortable silence.

"Taking a car, sir?" asked Charlie as he opened the lift and Reggie walked out onto the polished marble of the large entrance hall.

"Walking," said Reggie. "It's quicker than taxis. I need the exercise."

"Some of the fog's lifted."

"Good," said Reggie.

It was twelve-fifteen as Reggie pushed through the swing doors and turned up the street. Five minutes later the head waiter of the Miramar opened the door for him and took his hat, coat and scarf.

"Nasty weather, Mr Beaumont."

"Yes," said Reggie. "I want a private booth. Mr Hudson will be joining me shortly. We'll have the set menu and a tomato cocktail for me."

"Certainly, sir."

Reggie followed him to the back of the room and seated himself in the booth with his briefcase. Some customers were seated for an early lunch but he didn't look around to see if he knew anyone. Unstrapping his briefcase, he took out copies of Lionel's casino report and Koos's analysis of Southern African prospecting. He read his notes again. By the time the bank manager was shown to his table, his mind was crystal clear. Reggie stood up and smiled, holding out his hand to the slightly overweight and balding man in the Savile Row suit with the gold watch-chain looped from one waistcoat pocket to the other. Mr Hudson had a ruddy complexion as if he either did a lot sailing on the weekends or drank too much. In fact it was sailing.

"Private Booth, Reggie? I thought this was social."

"It was but a couple of things have cropped up and I want to talk business. I've ordered the set menu which I know you like."

"Excellent. I never know what to order from large menus."

"What'll you drink?"

"Same as you," said Percy Hudson nodding to the tomato juice as he slid through on his side of the booth. The high sheen on the dark wooden bench was as smooth as glass but warmer.

"How's Constance?" asked Reggie.

"Couldn't be better. Billy leaves school in a couple of years or so."

"Time never stops."

"Glad to read about Geoffrey."

"Thanks. He had me worried this time."

"Do you think there will be a war?"

"Probably. I have made extensive plans for the company in that event. We are very strong in rubber, gold and base minerals. The reinsurance will suffer but the rest will compensate."

"You'll be called up in the R.A.F."

"I've thought of that. America doesn't wish to be involved, according to Chuck Everly and the newspapers. He's agreed to come over to England and run the companies, reporting to me daily. He's rather sweet on Pippa de la Riviera, so he's hoping the war will start tomorrow. We're in a good position whichever way it turns. How does Lloyds Bank view the situation?"

"There will be a tremendous demand for capital. Armament factories. Clothing. Chemicals. War is a great consumer."

"In these two documents," said Reggie, resting his hand on the papers in front of him, "are the most exciting business prospects of my life. Let me explain and then we'll ask them to bring lunch. A war and what it will bring in new technology will consume vast quantities of raw materials. Base minerals. Copper, chrome, manganese, iron, coal," Reggie paused to look at his bark manager. "I can have an option on the mineral rights of the greatest storehouse of raw materials in the world. Already it is the richest seam of gold in the world and I believe, as do my management team, that there is a great deal more to be found in the Central African reef. I have been fortunate to make money out of a single insurance idea that all my competitors are kicking themselves for not having thought of. I was fortunate to gain control of Union Mining. The first was luck and the second calculated. In international terms, we are a small mining house. This document," said Reggie, picking up Koos van der Walt's report, "is a highly confidential analysis of my chances of turning the company into a major mining house, making it a real benefit to this country in dividends and control of strategic raw minerals. Tax is the major problem for Beaumont Ltd which is why I intend creating a pyramid company that will take in all the profits and losses of my insurance and mining groups. This will allow me to offset insurance profits against mining development costs. In this way the government, unwittingly admittedly, will contribute forty percent of my working capital. We will have created a consolidated balance sheet and pay tax on the net result. I will then have the new company listed on the London and the New York stock exchanges, offering forty percent of the equity to the public."

"Where do we come into the picture, Reggie?"

"As bankers. The second project is a casino playground in the Caribbean. I have obtained a gambling licence for a private club that will be run by Tony Venturas. He is an artist at running people and giving them what they want."

"I've heard so," said Percy with a smile as he touched his nose with his index finger.

"On the island we will have a five-star hotel, casino, luxury chalets, golf course, airstrip, cabaret of top artists and the security to give our clients total peace of mind. Rich people require protecting. We will put the facility on our own private island with gunboats patrolling the coast. No-one will get on that island other than members and their invited guests. The profit potential and capital requirements are tabulated in this second document."

"What is this all going to cost, assuming you go ahead?"

"The casino. Four million pounds. Mining surveys, two million pounds a year for five years and then an unknown amount to develop the new mines. I also wish to continue with the nickel mine in Western Australia."

"Why do everything at once?"

"Because I only knew of our mining potential this morning. Tenders for prospecting rights have to be in by the end of next month. The other two were in the pipeline."

"How much will the pyramid company floatation create?"

"The after tax profit of Beaumont Ltd will be one million eight hundred thousand pounds this year. The dividends from our sixty percent holding in Union Mining will be six hundred thousand pounds. As in Union Mining we will distribute fifty percent of our taxed profits to shareholders with the retained profit financing our borrowings. As you know, it is how I financed the development of Kloof Mine. I borrowed ten million pounds at five percent so that the bank's interest was covered twice. Total after tax profit of Union is two million pounds. One million retained of which five hundred thousand pounds was paid to the Standard Bank and our six hundred thousand pounds coming from our sixty percent of the balance. Therefore with the new holding pyramid company, which I propose to call Union and Overseas, the accruing after-tax profit will be two million four hundred thousand pounds. Again we will retain fifty percent in the company so that a five percent return to shareholders will value the company at twenty-four million pounds. By selling forty percent of this to the public in England and America we will raise nine million six hundred thousand pounds. We would then wish to borrow the same sum from the banks. Your security will be the assets of the company which will include the cash injection of nine million six hundred thousand pounds."

"What about your trading company?"

"We have not shown a profit as yet so I can raise little on this asset. I will use it next time," said Reggie with a smile.

"How are you going to channel the money into Union Mining Ltd? You have outside shareholders."

"By a rights issue. The shares are standing at twenty-two pounds each at present. There are one million one hundred thousand issued shares in Union Mining for which we paid five pounds ten shillings for our seven hundred thousand shares. We will have a one for three rights issue at twenty-two pounds a share thereby issuing three hundred and thirty-three thousand new shares at twenty-two pounds each and increasing the company's capital by seven million three hundred and twenty-six thousand pounds. Union and Overseas will subscribe for their two hundred and thirty-three thousand, three hundred and thirty-three shares in full plus any of the rights not taken up by the minority shareholders. In the process I will increase our percentage shareholding in Union Mining. This will leave plus minus twelve million pounds in the holding company in capital or bank facilities. It will also be enough for the casino, the Australian nickel mine, if the Australians will let us go ahead, and leave a healthy cash balance."

"Effectively, you are selling forty percent of your reinsurance company and forty percent of your shares in Union Mining."

"For the moment. How does it sound, Percy?"

"We will have to analyse both projects and your existing balance sheet. You paid us back the three million pounds you borrowed to buy Union Mining well ahead of time. Do you wish us to be the issuing bank for the new company shares and the rights issue of Union Mining?"

"Of course. That is where you make your profits. We have a good track form. Shares rising from five pounds ten shillings to twenty-two pounds in two years. The 'Freebooters' have a name in the market place. The public like the sound of it as much as we don't but good press can often be turned into cash. The public will be told exactly where we are spending their money. We will have to win the tender before we go to press but this should not present a problem. Koos van der Walt says the South African government will view us favourably."

"We will need a five-year profit projection."

"So will we, Percy. Now. How about some lunch? The Bretton oysters are fresh and the poached turbot is always good. In principle, will you put it up to your board?"

"I've got a lot of faith in you, Reggie, and the profit to us is also interesting."

"A good deal must always be satisfactory to all parties. Bankers, controlling shareholders and minorities… How's *Wavedancer*?" said Reggie, catching the eye of the head waiter and nodding.

"Billy and I pulled her out of the water at the end of his summer holidays. I spend the weekends painting and polishing when the weather allows. I'm re-doing the engine myself. Gives me something to think about apart from other people's overdrafts. How's Mathilda?"

"Perfect. She's slow but fun. The Hurricane is a beautiful aeroplane but I haven't quite got used to her. They came on to the squadron last month. She's unbelievably fast and has eight cannons in the wings. Would you like a glass of wine with the meal?"

"I try not to drink at lunchtime but it's an insult to the Miramar's food not to eat with a bottle of wine. With all these war clouds, we might as well enjoy ourselves."

"Better drink a Liebfraumilch in that case."

Percy looked off into the distance for a moment.

"The navy had an easy time in the last war," he said. "Jutland was only a skirmish, really. Anyway, this time I'm too old. War is such a waste of time."

"Yes."

The waiter put down the plates of oysters.

"Now, these look good," said Percy. "I like the way they serve them on seaweed."

"Thank you," said Reggie to the waiter. "Could you bring me a bottle of '34 Liebfraumilch?"

"Certainly, sir."

"Eating in a good restaurant is so civilised," said Percy and they both took up their two pronged forks and lifted the oysters out of the shells. Reggie rolled his eyes in appreciation and went on eating.

"You know," said Reggie with the last oyster poised on the end of his fork, "I've just realised I didn't have breakfast."

"Serves you right. You need a wife."

"I never have time to be serious."

"Make it. You make time for business."

Reggie rolled a thin piece of brown bread and butter and put it into his mouth and dabbed with his serviette.

"No-one will have me," said Reggie, smiling at the waiter who was standing with the open wine bottle. He tasted the little the waiter had put in his glass. "Excellent. Just the right temperature." The glasses were filled.

"Even if it is foggy outside, white wine must be chilled. To your health, Percy. And thanks for your help."

"It's been a pleasure doing business. Who are you going to ask to complete the American listing?"

"Chuck. He'll know someone. Remarkable man. Doesn't matter what you want he always knows someone."

"Useful. Any problems with the treaty?"

"None at all, apart from a little competitive jealousy. The first year showed excellent profits for underwriters. You always have friends when you make them money. I'm signing up another company after lunch."

"Facultative business?"

"We got to know a lot of new friends through the treaty. The one-off business is excellent. I've joined a marine and aviation syndicate in the Room, so on a lot of the business we're doubling our profits. You will see the figures when I send round the five-year projection. Underwriting profits of my syndicate holdings are payable to Beaumont Ltd and are included in the pyramid company. Kloof Mine is ahead of schedule and the other mines are performing to budget. This year's killing will be made in commodities." Reggie looked up as the waiter placed in front of Percy a large plate of poached turbot with white sauce, small new potatoes coated in butter and parsley and fresh Brussels sprouts. Reggie leant back for the waiter to put a similar plate in front of him. "We are filling our fourth go-down with rubber."

"Where are you getting it from?"

"A Mr Kim-Wok Ho. He has access to rubber and we have access to American guns. Chiang Kai-shek. He's fighting the Japs and the communists."

"I know."

"Tug's turned into a superb trader. We have quantities of tin and copra."

"When are you going to sell?"

"Not until war is declared. We begin shipping rubber to a rented warehouse in New York next month. I want all of the stocks in a safe place near their buyers. I like a buyer to see what he's getting."

"Who's financing the stock?"

"Hong Kong and Shanghai Bank. They hold a lien on the cargo but it's already worth a lot more than we paid for it. The trick is not to watch the price going up but to get hold of the material. I've chartered two boats to bring the rubber into America and they will both be well insured, including the war risks.

"How's the fish?"

"Perfect."

"What's Billy going to do when he leaves school?"

"He doesn't know. The only thing he's certain about is not wishing to go into the bank. He still thinks we sit on high stools with quill pens."

"I'm looking for bright young men to train. He'd be welcome if he doesn't mind Uncle Reggie kicking his arse for six months."

"Thanks, Reggie. I'll tell him. He might go for that."

"He'd have to be prepared to travel."

"That won't be a problem. What are you going to do about Gunter?"

"We've made arrangements that can't be divulged. He's over here now. Companies last a lot longer than wars or governments. You can take the two reports with you now and I'll have the projections across by Friday. I want you to meet our South African general manager to see if you can find any flaws in his report.

"He's agreed to put his entire fortune into the project."

"What will you do if you don't get your loan?"

"Get it somewhere else, Percy," said Reggie, smiling.

At two-fifteen Reggie signed the bill and saw Percy Hudson into a taxi before starting his walk to Billiter Street. A thin drizzle added to the fog but he preferred to walk. Maybe he should offer shares in Union and Overseas to Mr Kim-Wok Ho. He could do no harm by offering. The brisk pace took him to the Contingency insurance company in ten minutes. The sluggishness of food and wine had gone. The receptionist took him straight into the general manager's office.

"I didn't expect you to come round yourself," said Halmsbury shaking hands.

"I am a reinsurance broker by profession. The rest came by the way."

"Flemming of the Royal Exchange was good enough to show me the figures. I would like a fifty thousand pound line. You'll wish to study our balance sheets. Our assets are not sufficient to take a larger line. You'll see we've grown quite fast in the last five years."

"It'll be a pleasure. I've already seen your balance sheets," said Reggie, smiling. "In fact I've seen the balance sheets of every suitable insurance company in England. Here's a copy of the treaty," said Reggie, taking it out of his briefcase. "The entry date will be the 1 January."

"I've already had our solicitors study the document. Where would you like me to sign?"

"Initial every page and sign the last. I can witness your signature and so can your secretary."

Five minutes later, the document was back in his briefcase and he was standing up to leave.

"Can you lunch with me next week Wednesday?" said Reggie putting on his coat and again winding the scarf around his neck. "Twelve-thirty at the Miramar?"

"I'll look forward to it Mr Beaumont."

"I look forward to a long association."

By the time Reggie hailed a taxi less than half an hour had transpired since he had finished lunch.

"Sixty-three Whitehall Court," he said to the driver as he climbed into the taxi and settled back in the seat. 'They don't come quicker than that,' he said to himself and began to whistle a snatch of *Swan Lake* and with the whistle a pleasant, expectant smile spread over this face. He pulled back the driver's hatch. "Can you stop at a chemist's on the way?"

"Right, guvnor. There's one down the road."

Reggie got out at the chemist shop.

"Hang on. Won't be two ticks." Inside Reggie bought a bottle of sleeping pills. Five minutes later he got out of the taxi in front of the door to his block of flats.

Gunter was sprawled in an armchair, chin sunk on his chest. He looked up slowly and tried to focus.

"What do I do?" said Gunter, drunkenly. "Doesn't like men. My wife. Doesn't like men." The crystal glass in Gunter's hand fell through his fingers and shattered alongside a pile of broken glass, sticky with whisky. "Even the glass doesn't want me anymore. What do I do, Reggie?"

"That's your last drink. By the look of it that was my last glass. What we are going to do is get you to bed in the spare room with a couple of pills and get you a long night's sleep."

"I haven't slept since I got married. She's a bloody lesbian, Reggie. Me, Gunter, one of the Freebooters married a bloody lesbian. I'll buy you some more glasses," he slurred.

"Tomorrow we can talk. We'll get this one sorted out."

"How, Reggie?" and tears welled down his face. Reggie looked away.

"A new day. There's always a new day. Come. Let's get you out of that chair. Wanda must have gone home."

"There was a woman. I don't like women anymore," he said and allowed Reggie to heave him up on to his feet. Reggie half dragged him into the bedroom.

"You're heavier than you used to be at Oxford," said Reggie and dropped him fully clothed onto the bed. Reggie took off his shoes and clothes and made him swallow three of the pills. Rolling him over and back again Reggie got him into the bed. As Reggie closed the bedroom door he heard Gunter say, "You're a good man, Reggie." Reggie smiled with a warm flush of close friendship. He looked back but Gunter was asleep.

By three-thirty Reggie was back at his desk, signing the mail he had dictated that morning in between answering his telephones. Thelma came in with the finished war contingency report.

"Should never have gone for direct lines onto my desk," he said without looking up. "The idea of being readily accessible is excellent but the result is impractical. Can you answer that one," he said waving at the phone, "and then get the Post Office to move all but the unlisted line out onto your desk."

"Well, that wins me my bet with Lionel," said Thelma, picking up the phone. "Mr Beaumont's office. No, He's not yet back from Paris, Mr Fleming. Of course I will. No, I'm afraid I can't sign you into Bretts. I believe they are very heavily booked with the increased membership. That may be difficult Mr Fleming. You require eight sponsors, four of whom you must have known for five years or more. I'll ask Mr Beaumont to call when he returns."

Thelma put down the phone, smiling.

"You should train for the bar," said Reggie, reading through the report. "Your inventions are excellent and your lies ring true."

"That man's a pig."

"There are plenty of those in the world but they all have their uses. Lechery, correctly channelled, is a very powerful and profitable force. Without the sex drive, the race would be extinct. When you consider the amount of thought, skill and money put into it for a few minutes pleasure."

"Love's not like that."

"I didn't say it was. I was talking about Fleming's kind of sex drive."

"Can I bring in the files with today's mail?"

"Yes. I'll dictate and then please ask Lionel to come through." The unlisted phone rang.

"Reggie Beaumont."

"Percy, Reggie. I've read the reports and so has my accountant. I'm confident we can raise the money but I want to bring Barings in as co-sponsoring bankers. An outside merchant bank will help me with my board."

"And also give you a second opinion."

"And you, Reggie. You're the one taking the risk."

"Will you handle Barings?"

"One of the partners has an appointment with me tomorrow at ten."

"Thanks, Percy."

"You did say it was urgent," he said, chuckling. "Will you ask Mr van der Walt to be here at ten?"

"Do you want me as well?"

"You work on the group profit projections."

"I'm starting in half an hour."

"Cheerio Reggie."

"Cheerio," said Reggie and put down the phone, keeping his hand on the receiver for a moment.

"He has a lot of trust in you," said Thelma.

"And he's cautious. Thorough. It's like having another top man in the company without having to pay him a salary. Right. Circulate this report as listed and let's get rid of the new bumpf. But get those phones off the hook."

"Would you like some coffee, first?"

"Good idea. Let's both have a three-minute break."

"How was lunch?"

"Excellent. How was yours?"

"I still haven't eaten the sandwiches. No matter, I'm putting on weight."

"That will be the day. Any reply from François or Carl."

"Why do you equate my figure with François?"

"Don't you?"

"You are impossible."

"I'll take you out to lunch next week."

"I'll keep you to that. We haven't eaten together alone since we left Johannesburg."

"Where's the coffee?"

"Coming, master."

By five o'clock the dictation was finished and Thelma had left the office to catch the tube to Holland Park, to her basement flat below a three-storey, Victorian house. Her aim was to climb into a hot bath and be ready, new and rejuvenated, to go out to dinner at seven o'clock. If François didn't want her, there were plenty who did.

Reggie sat on the couch opposite Lionel for half an hour working on the five-year projection.

"The secret," said Reggie, "is to update the projection every six months. Costs can be held within reason but income projections are difficult. The value of a five-year projection is more in giving us a goal. Making us clear in our own minds as to where we are going. I think you've earned a drink. The bank manager was impressed with your casino report. What will it be?"

"Scotch, please, sir."

"And you can drop the sir," said Reggie, opening his cocktail cabinet and pouring two Dimple Haigs.

"Water?"

"No thanks."

"It's how the Scots drink a good malt. Welcome to Beaumont Ltd. You can say you've proved yourself. In future you don't have to shake the papers in front of me," said Reggie, smiling. "An attack of nerves is only good up to a point. Your good health. It's been quite a day. Profitable, but quite a day."

"Good health. Do your days change very much?"

"The ingredients change. The pace, never. I like it. If I don't have too much to do I get lazy. We're building up a good team and that's what it's all about. If you leave now, you'll catch the six-fifteen from Waterloo."

"That'll keep me going in the fog," said Lionel, finishing his scotch.

"Tell Charlie he can lock up. I'll let myself out."

"Goodnight."

"Goodnight."

Reggie remained seated for five minutes sipping his drink and enjoying the total silence. He had heard the lift go down with Lionel and then not a sound. He made his entire body relax into the settee and stopped his mind thinking of business, making it drift beside the rhododendron bushes at Merry Hall and past the tall oaks and into the Thirty Acre. He even had a flash of Mathilda next to Bert Brigley's spotted brown cow. It seemed a very long time ago and he tried to remember when it was. The summer of '33. More than four years ago. Geoffrey and Henry had not even been married. He finished his scotch and pulled the pile of blue flimsies close and picked up the first copy, a letter written by Mark Opperman to Carl in Copenhagen. Taking a red pen he made two points and started another pile of corrected letters that Thelma would send back to the writers. An hour later he had read, noted and corrected copies of every letter that had been written in his organisation that day. Satisfied, he picked up the first mining journal and began to read. By seven o'clock he had two journals to read but had run out of time. He walked through from the side door in his office into the small bathroom and ran the taps. A dressing room led off to the left with a single bed which he used on very late nights. He again whistled some bars to *Swan Lake* and took his evening dress out of the closet and laid it carefully on the bed. Going back into his office, he poured himself a second scotch and took it into the bathroom that was now full of steam. He was still humming Tchaikovsky. By seven-thirty, he walked to the lift with his scarf wrapped loosely around a white tie and his overcoat hiding his tails but not the shining patent leather shoes. He was surprised to find Charlie still on duty.

"You didn't have to wait, Charlie."

"Not much to do since the missus died."

"How's the flat?"

"Just what I wanted, Mr Reggie. Suits an old man of sixty-five. Finish work and I just go up in the lift to the top and there I am. Real grateful to you for giving me that flat."

"It's been a long time, Charlie. Don't you get lonely up there on your own?"

"Not really. I'll go up and cook myself some bacon and eggs. I try not to break them. Then I'll read a bit and go to bed if I don't nod off in the chair."

"What about your children? Don't they come and visit?"

"Can't really. Joe's in America. Married with three kids. Done well for himself, our Joe. Gladys and I was right proud of him. Sal's married to an Italian living in Australia and little Betty's up north. Married to a bloke in the coal mines. She came down last year but it's a long way and expensive."

"Don't you go up and visit?"

"No, I'd be in the way. They've got their lives to live like as I had when I was young. Gladys and I had a fine old time. I've no complaints. Do you think she'll start in this cold weather?"

"I should have put her in the garage this morning. She'll be difficult. There's always a penalty to pay for everything. Do you drink, Charlie?"

"Bit of scotch, when I can afford it."

"I'll bring up a bottle tomorrow and I'll have a look at this flat of yours."

"You'll come up to my flat?" said Charlie, amazed.

"That's the idea."

"I'd better get up there quick," said Charlie, laughing. "It'll take me 'till tomorrow morning to get it tidy. You know what bachelors are, living on their own."

"Yes I do," said Reggie, pushing his way through the swing doors into the cold.

7

OCTOBER 1937

*T*he following day, Ping-Lai Ho, the cousin, rose at his usual time of six-fifteen and spent two hours in his study completing the day's paperwork with his attractive, Chinese secretary.

"The Japanese officer is due at nine o'clock," she said in Mandarin.

"Show him up here when he arrives. Don't offer him anything." And Ping-Lai Ho majestically walked across the marble floor in his Chinese robe, his hands folded into the long hanging sleeves that reached from his elbows to his knees. The next half hour would be the most pleasant in Ping-Lai Ho's day and he bowed slightly as his secretary opened the heavily carved, oak door that rose high above the floor, oak being one of the few woods that the Singapore ants were unable to chew. From behind and high up above, attached to the ornate ceiling by a stout arm, a six-foot fan swished at the humid air. There was one fan in every room in the mansion. The morning temperature was ninety-seven degrees Fahrenheit as Ping-Lai Ho walked out onto the landing that circled the inside of the house, bannistered in a light Mukwa wood from East Africa and open only to the great stairs that led round and down to the marbled and fountained inner courtyard of the great house. Palms, twenty feet high, grew around the tinkling waters. Flowers, Ping-Lai Ho's favourite decoration, grew in profusion around the rock-strewn centrepiece. The old rubber baron, from whom Ping-Lai Ho had bought the house for ten percent of its value in the depression, had known his business, or better, the architect he had brought out from England. The wooden stairs were carpeted in the centre and Ping-Lai Ho surveyed his domain, step by step, pleased with everything he saw.

He had been born in an open sampan in Hong Kong harbour soon after his father had fled the wrath of Kim-Wok Ho's father. He had been lucky to be born at all but the first five years of his life were spent in abject poverty and he still smelt rotten fish the moment he woke in the morning. Ping-Lai Ho's father had worked for John Swire and Sons for five years before they recognised he was highly educated and the possessor of excellent contacts on mainland China. The English company had made discreet enquiries and proved that the man they employed as a stevedore on the docks was indeed the nephew of an important warlord. The stevedore was quickly transformed into a trader and put to a greater use. The sampan was handed over to three other families and the start of the independent Hong Kong House of Ho had begun.

Ping-Lai Ho admired the flower arrangement on its plinth at the foot of the stairs and stood, hand on the wooden balled banister and studied the flowers. The pretty girl who had spent since sun-up cutting and arranging the flowers waited patiently.

"Beautiful," he said in Malay and gently brushed her soft cheek with the back of his equally soft hand. The girl smiled gratefully. Ping-Lai Ho's house was entirely run by women, none of them over the age of twenty-five and all seventeen of them pretty. Kim-Wok Ho called them Ping-Lai Ho's harem and there was some truth in the matter. The fact, however, that he was married to none of them prevented most of the fights. Outside, the army of gardeners and the two chauffeurs were men but they were not allowed in the house. To the left, facing an ornamental lake was the Chinese room and the furnishings were priceless and equally beautiful. From the Chinese room he walked through open glass doors into the aviary with its abundance of tropical trees and plants all chattering with a host of multi-coloured birds. Ping-Lai Ho stood for a few minutes watching them enjoying themselves free of snakes and monkeys and mongooses. He opened one of the double doors and let himself out onto the lawn without being followed by a colourful cloud of birds and stood admiring the organised jungle that made up five acres of his perfectly planned garden, lush green and splashed with colour.

When his father had died in Hong Kong he had sensibly split the House of Ho into two separate and independent parts that would do business together if they so wished but were otherwise independent. Ping-Lai Ho had chosen the South East Station, based on Singapore, as he loved the exotic and the heat. His only brother had remained in Hong Kong and without any rivalry for Tai-Pan they had done excellent business together. With Ping-Lai Ho's father's death, the rivalry in the warlord's family had ceased and Ping-Lai Ho had been introduced to his cousin, Kim-Wok Ho who had been sent out of China by his father to learn the ways of the other world.

The gardeners were watering furiously. He looked back at the huge, white-faced house bathed in the morning sun. Business was good.

From behind a tall bed of red topped cannas he saw the Japanese lieutenant's car arrive and looked at his watch. The man was as bad as the English. Five minutes early for an appointment and five minutes late for a party. Ping-Lai Ho walked away down a garden path to a clump of tall trees that cut out the rays of the sun. Ping-Lai Ho did not like the Japanese but guns, at the moment, were good business. Soon he would be richer than his cousin and this made him think of Linda. He began to slowly retrace his steps, thinking of how to seduce his cousin's mistress.

The little Japanese lieutenant Horoshini, was standing in the middle of his study having refused a seat.

"Ah," said Ping-Lai Ho.

"This is insult," said the Japanese, speaking in English which was their only common language.

'Arrogant little bastard', thought Ping-Lai Ho but showing the stretch of his gold teeth instead.

"How so?" asked Ping-Lai Ho politely, knowing the Japanese were always saying something similar.

"I represent our Emperor. You keep me late. You keep Emperor late."

"So sorry," said Ping-Lai Ho.

"The Emperor wishes to purchase the one million dollars' worth of guns."

"So?"

"How much?" said the Japanese.

"Not one million dollars. They cost me much more than that. For you, two and a half million pounds sterling. America will not sell to you so we had to promise them the guns were for Chiang-Kai-shek, which they were, but a better price is always welcome."

"I have been instructed tell you if Japan no get guns, House of Ho considered enemy Japan."

"Is that a threat?"

"Japan powerful. Soon more powerful. Better you sell us guns. No trouble."

"You go and find the money and then we see."

"Don't sell to nationalists or communists. Sell Japan."

"I have the guns. You get money."

"Where are guns?"

"Money first, lieutenant," said Ping-Lai Ho not knowing where they were. "Delivery, Singapore, forty-eight hours after money. You like tea?"

"No."

"Ah. My secretary will show you out."

'Nasty little bugger,' thought Ping-Lai Ho, as the door closed. He wondered where Beaumont had stored the guns. Through Kim-Wok Ho, who was agent for the seller, he had received an official Beaumont letter stating the guns were in South East Asia and could be delivered to an agreed South China port within forty-eight hours. Everyone who knew about the consignment, including Ping-Lai Ho, was trying to find out where the guns were stored.

'Arrogant little bugger,' he said again to himself and pressed a button for his breakfast to be sent up. 'Arrogant little bugger.'

TUG BEAUMONT DID NOT KNOW where he was. The hallucinations of his mind were complete. Great owls swooped from monster trees and he cringed from outstretched wings that brushed his flesh.

"Lilly," he called into the smoke and suffocation. He tried to move from the silken couch but the message from his brain was worthless. His hands clawed at the smoke but nothing touched and he floundered into the horrors of his mind. A great bird flew out of the typhoon, straight at him and he screamed but the old Chinaman standing in the corner of the den heard nothing. The Chinaman walked towards the ornate couch and placed another ball of opium in the fire bowl, lit it with loving care and saw bubbles rising in the water bowl and the white smoke drifting up inside the long stem. Gently, the old Chinaman took the mouthpiece and sucked. Satisfied, he held out the pipe.

"More opium, Mr Beaumont. It will bring you good dreams." Greedily, Tug reached for the mouthpiece and sucked in the drug. Slowly and gently, sweetness returned.

"A girl, Mr Beaumont?"

He smiled.

"Smoke a little more."

Tug lazily drew smoke from the pipe and left it in his lungs so that it would find his bloodstream and go to his brain. The beautiful colours of the wall drapes were close upon his eyes. Dragons rampant in fiery glory. Bamboo trees and peacocks, brilliant in their blue-fanned tails. The beautiful kist, brown wood and golden lacquered. Such pleasure to touch it with his mind. The old Chinaman parted the drapes from outside and the girl, bare from the waist up, stood for her inspection and when Tug beckoned her she smiled. Her family would eat for another month. She knelt beside him looking deep into the false happiness of his eyes.

PERRY MARSHBANK STALKED the beach three hundred yards from Tammany's house, the flying boat full of guns, vast and shimmering in the moon behind him. The pilots were asleep, gently rocked by the placid bay, the coral reef showing a break line out to sea. The need in his groin was so intense he stopped. The children would be in bed and Tammany in her native dress would burn up his hunger. It's the tropics, the heat, he told himself, hurrying.

TAMMANY WATCHED a small lizard work its way up the fly-screen that shut off the veranda, tiny feet clawing the closeness of the mesh. Two candles burnt in the lounge. Turning her head, she saw a brilliant moon on the sea surface and a figure walking along the beach towards her bungalow. A tall, thin figure, European by his gait and height. She watched carefully and with relief recognised Perry Marshbank. Puzzled, she wondered what he could want at midnight. Her only clothing was a loose sarong that hung over her heavy breasts and thighs but for talking to Perry this didn't matter. They were friends, the three of them and it was only a pity that Perry had not found a wife to make it four. She watched Perry climb the veranda steps, stop for a moment to look at her through the fly-screen and then push open the door. She smiled a big mouthed greeting and got up, unwittingly allowing a fold of her sarong to gape open and show Perry a large brown-nippled breast. She noticed him staring but then that was all men. If they weren't nice he wouldn't have looked and neither would Tug and she wouldn't have a husband and two children and all the love and luxury a woman could want. Admittedly, Tug had been strange but he worked late every night and once he'd had a proper rest in Sarawak by the lagoon he would come back to his old self and they would make love and the children would chase him down the beach and into the lagoon.

Perry hadn't spoken but stood with his back to the closed, mesh-covered door and she took a step towards him, still smiling.

"Is there anything wrong, Perry?"

"You are very beautiful tonight."

"Why, thank you. Isn't it rather late to come visiting? I thought you were sleeping on board."

"Not enough room for three. Hoped you'd be up. Have a gin?"

"Are you alright, Perry?"

"Perfectly. Bit nervous. Tropics. Gets the white men in the end. Look at Dr Grantham. Perfect soak. Have a gin?"

"Well. Just one. You are nervous. You'd better come and sit down while I pour the drinks. The new fridge makes everything nicer," she said from the other end of the room where Perry's eyes had followed her. He'd had a small pipe of opium and didn't care. The flash of her large breast had snapped his civilisation and the sarong was riding high on her thigh and he felt certain she was wearing nothing underneath.

"Why don't you sit, Perry?" said Tammany turning back with the drinks. "Your eyes are funny."

"Can I sleep in the bungalow?"

"Of course. You've done it enough."

"But not with Tug away."

"Don't be silly. What's the difference? You're the friend of the family."

"Am I, Tammany?"

"Of course. Have a drink and you'll feel better. All this talk of the tropics and white men cracking up is making me nervous."

"Why don't you take off that sarong?"

"Whatever for?"

"So I can look at you."

"You're looking at me."

"Clothed. I want to see you naked."

"Perry, you're talking to Tug's wife."

"I know that. Known it for five years. You're not wearing anything underneath."

The first tremor of fear dug at the pit of her stomach and with it a strange exhilaration. The frightening pulse from Perry was totally sexual and the animal part of her surged.

"He doesn't make love to you anymore."

"That's nothing to do with you."

"But it is," and he laughed a high, squeaky laugh that was almost soft. Watching her, he took a long, savouring drink from his glass and licked his lips. "He's on opium you know?"

"Tug? Don't be silly,"

"And very young girls. They excite him. Opium and very young girls. I know. I've watched him."

"You've been drinking."

"No. One small pipe. Enough to let me do what I want."

"What do you want?" she said quietly.

"You. I've dreamt for too long. Can't slake it anywhere. You'll satisfy me."

"Tug will kill you."

"He won't. Doesn't know himself anymore. I took him there. The first girl was only eleven. No pubic hair. Small mounds for tits. Tight little bum. Tug couldn't control himself. Didn't even get inside her the first time before he shot his bolt."

"Stop!"

"Why? It happened. Still happening. Once they're addicted that's it. Take off your sarong."

"No."

"I'll take it off for you," and he stepped towards her.

"I'll scream. The children will wake."

"Will you? What do you say? Perry raped you? The children don't want to see. People will believe me. She likes white men. Mrs Gray will love the story. There won't be any England. No marriage. They'll believe me. Tammany, after three months you must want it badly. I've seen you watching me. You'd let me if you weren't married to Tug. Let me before I force you. There's a war coming. Everything will change. Better to enjoy than make a fuss. How would Tug feel if you said I'd raped you? He'd blame you. I'd have to tell him. My story. Take off your sarong."

Tammany threw the glass at him but he ducked and only the gin splashed his face.

"I liked that. More exciting. Are you excited? I can smell your heat. Why don't you run? I'll catch you."

In two long steps he was in front of her, looking down from steel blue eyes into her. Fear. Triumph. Behind was something else. The primeval force of male dominating and woman wanting. He stripped off the sarong and smiled.

"You see. I was right. Nothing."

Slowly he undressed himself and stood in front of her, erect, proud, jerking with lust.

"Perry, don't. Please don't. There are other women."

"No, there aren't. You will satisfy me. You're wet, aren't you?"

"Yes."

"You see."

"That doesn't mean I want it."

"Oh, but it does," and with both hands he cupped her breasts.

"Don't rape me."

"Of course not. We'll make love."

"You're despicable."

"That's a big word for you to know," and he felt for the silky curls of her pubic and it was soaking wet. He picked her up and took her to the day couch.

"You're going to be my mistress, Tammany, and nobody is going to know," and he entered her swiftly and hard and her world shattered away into the tropical night.

ON THE TUESDAY evening at the beginning of October 1937 a short, well-built Chinese was ushered into a badly lit office at the rear of a ramshackle go-down at the back of Singapore docks. An overweight Chinese in western clothing rose to greet the communist emissary sent to him by Mao Tse-Tung from the war zone deep inside the Middle Kingdom. The two men bowed to each other and the escorts left the room closing the door behind them.

"How is the war?"

"No war is good. We will win. That is enough. The warlords fight each other and the nationalists. There is no cohesion. We will win."

They spoke in Cantonese and the emissary settled himself in the carved, wooden chair as comfortably as possible. He was weary and had eaten no food that day.

"You are hungry?" asked the fat Chinese.

"No," lied the emissary who had learnt never to show a need.

"It is an old custom to eat before talking. Some old customs are good." The smile was friendly. He clapped his hands and immediately the door opened and the escorts brought in two trays of steaming food and a pot of tea.

"When Chairman Mao wins," said the fat man, "all of China will eat like this," and he began to heap a large bowl for his guest. "Fried rice, chop-suey, spring rolls. Pickled vegetables. Sweet pork."

They ate in silence for five minutes until the emissary had finished his food, laid down his chopsticks and burped politely. The fat man poured a small cup of green tea and put it down on the other side of his desk. He poured himself a cup.

They looked up at each other and the older man nodded.

"It is our decision to seize or, failing this, destroy the guns."

"It is a good decision."

"We have no money. Where are the guns?"

"I have all manner of people searching. It is said that Beaumont will deliver within forty-eight hours of payment but the guns are not in Singapore, of that I am certain."

"Then a boat off shore?"

"We have looked. Nothing. Every boat within two hundred miles of Singapore has been checked."

"Hidden in the jungle?"

"How do they load and unload? The guns must be crated. Too many to handle individually."

"We must find those guns."

"There is a way."

The emissary looked at the fat man, motionless in his chair. Nothing of the man moved.

"Beaumont knows their whereabouts," he said.

"Of course."

"Go and see Beaumont and make him tell you."

"That is a way."

"There is a great hurry. The nationalists or Japanese will take possession. The English are easier to handle. He stays at Raffles, room 203."

"HAVE ANOTHER DRINK," said Linda. "We won't be disturbed. I was introduced to Kim-Wok Ho in that cubicle over there," she said pointing through the bamboo curtain.

"I can't see," said Sally Bollas.

"Doesn't matter. Point is, it's private. Be a dear and ring the bell. Only thing that brings them. I like your tan. A natural blonde with a good tan. You are a natural blonde?"

"Want to see?"

"You've rung the bell… Ah, waiter. Two gins and tonic and a dash of speed."

"Coming, missus," and the bamboo curtain opened and swung shut again.

"Cut your throat as soon as look at you," said Linda.

"Gives me the creeps," said Sally.

"See. You need a protector. That silly old faggot who runs the botanical gardens couldn't protect a fly. And as for his wife. Beats me how they produced a daughter."

"I wouldn't have a job."

"How much do they pay?"

"Five pounds a week and full board."

"That's choice. I'll tip the waiter more than that. Only reason he doesn't cut my throat."

"You serious?"

"'Course not. This is British Malaya. Very civilised. Rule of law and all that junk. Smoked opium?"

"What?"

"Have you ever tried smoking opium?"

"Good heavens, no."

"You're not a virgin are you?" said Linda, knowing perfectly well that she was not.

"No."

"Thank God for that… Ah, waiter. You used the dash of speed. Just put them down with the ice and we'll do the honours."

"Don't you pay him?" asked Sally when the bamboo curtain had settled again.

"At the end. Run a tab. Very civilised. Just like the club. I'd better tell you our meeting in the Singapore Swimming Club wasn't casual."

"Oh."

"I'd planned it."

"What for?"

"I have a proposition."

"They usually come from men."

"So does this one."

"You're a marriage broker? Oh good. He must be rich. In India, they call me part of the fishing fleet but here there isn't much to catch."

"The rich catch the rich. Good looks are temporary. Wealth lasts longer. You came out here eight months ago looking for an eligible husband. Preferably rich."

"Preferably rich," agreed Sally.

"And you haven't succeeded."

"No."

"There are other ways of getting rich. I'm twenty-three. Do you know how much money's in my Swiss Bank account?" Sally didn't speak. "One hundred and thirty-two thousand pounds."

"You stole something?"

"Earnt every penny. Honestly."

"How?"

"That's why I asked you here. I live with a Chinaman. Very rich. I'm his housekeeper, ha ha."

"A Chinaman?"

"They fuck the same." Sally blushed. "You look pretty when you blush. Cheers, Sally. Kim-Wok Ho has a cousin, Ping-Lai Ho. Very rich. He would set you up. Fifty thousand pounds into Switzerland initially and five thousand pounds a month. And don't look shocked. I did my homework. It's one of the blessings of having money. You can find anything. Bretts, Mayfair. The most exclusive knock shop in London."

"You didn't have to screw them," said Sally," but you did?"

"A few times."

"Once is enough."

"I tried to get out."

"Didn't work, did it?"

"No."

"When in Rome… Here it's Chinamen. They've got what we want and we've got what they can't have."

"I couldn't with a Chinaman."

"And if he offered you a million pounds for one night?"

"I'd have to think."

"Sure. Well think about fifty thousand quid and not a penny to the taxman. Let me tell you a story. My father's a vicar. Highly respected. Loved by everyone. Very poor. I'm his fifth and last daughter and in Shropshire I had two chances. Governess or marry the organist and work myself into an early grave.

"Fortunately I looked in the mirror but even that didn't help in England. The county people were getting poor and their only way of holding on to what they'd inherited was marrying money. Where it came from didn't matter. If you were pretty and rich you could take your pick of half a dozen country estates. Even ugly and rich had a better chance than me. So I came out here to make my fortune. Now. When I get back, it won't be those country squires. By the time I'm finished with Kim-Wok Ho it'll be an Earl if not a Marquis. And the family will have to be old. None of your nouveaux-riches."

"Men don't marry prostitutes."

"Who used that word? Kept. That we are. Isn't a wife? Alright, there is a difference. Back in England we cook up a story. Two of us will make it easier. You're my sister. Both blonde. Daughters of a rubber planter eaten by a tiger. Well, died anyway. Mother had malaria. We'll take some pictures of the estate. Head boy. All that type of guff."

"We don't have a rubber plantation."

"So? We photograph one. By the time the man finds out we've a quarter of a million quid in the bank his hormones will do the rest. A lot of people don't have any relatives. Oscar Wilde spent his life writing about them. The word heiress is the biggest aphrodisiac in any marriage."

"What do we have to do?"

"Sleep with them. Not, thank heaven, in the same bed all night. Stipulate that one from the beginning."

"What does he look like?"

"Big, fat. Probably kinky. They all are approaching fifty. They've tried everything and still want something else. Kim-Wok Ho turned to me after the sub-teens didn't make him want it. Chinese are very touchy about impotency. Terrible thing. They want to have it off when they're ninety. Nothing wrong with that. It's in the mind. Make them want it and never give them enough. While they're wanting they give you anything. Flash the panties and the nipples but only just. Tantalise and then say they can't have it 'till after supper and then make them wait. It's a subtle build up to sex that gets them going. Cool, British aloofness. They've had too many little Malay girls baring their arses too soon… Help them with their business deals. We've both been educated. Especially when they are dealing with Europeans. But charge them. Take a percentage. Bargain hard. They want to screw you physically for having screwed their pockets. Masochism, 'don't hit me, I like it.' Makes the male in them want to dominate. They'll want a double date with us. Fine. We charge them. Put it into the Swiss Bank accounts first. Let them think about it until their balls are cracking. Five thousand each for a gang bang. Oh, and opium. Don't draw it into your lungs. Practise with a cigarette drawing the smoke into your mouth and letting it out of your nose in a thin stream. You've got to make that look good as they're experts. Opium can mess it all up. It's addictive. Tug Beaumont's hooked and that's not good for Kim-Wok Ho or Beaumont Ltd. Haven't seen Kim-Wok Ho yet. Cost him though, as he can have Mr Tug Beaumont doing just what he wants. Silly bugger. Good family. Good brain and he fucks it up on opium. Kim-Wok Ho will know how to handle it."

"I'll have to meet the Chinaman first."

"Same for him. I'll give you a lot of lessons in how to drive a man up the wall."

"Bretts wasn't easy to get into."

"I know. I checked. In this game you've got to be good."

"There was a Beaumont at Bretts. Reggie Beaumont."

"Tug's brother. It's how I got onto you. Apart from your looks and a dead end job. We met at a cocktail party when you first arrived. Talked about England. You mentioned your boyfriend was Tony Venturas and he ran a club. Three weeks ago, Tug Beaumont mentioned his brother's partner, Tony Venturas. Laughingly said he thought his brother was involved in a knock shop. Made enquiries. It's how I found out you'd been on the game."

"Very selective. Tony never wanted to know. Said business was business and shouldn't enter a private relationship. My flat mate lived on the Beaumont estate. Lilly Brigley. Now there was a sexy girl. Only thing I could never understand was she never took money for it. If she found someone in the club she liked, she gave it away."

"Will you meet Ping-Lai Ho?"

"What can I lose?"

"Good. Have another gin and tell me all about yourself. Good chinwag. Haven't had a good chinwag with a soulmate since I arrived in Singapore."

ON THE WEDNESDAY MORNING, Lieutenant Lord Angus Montel (RNVR Fleet Air Arm) took the decoded message from his co-pilot and read it twice before handing the sheet to Perry Marshbank who read it in silence.

"How well do you know this coastline?" asked Angus.

"Well enough," answered Perry, looking out of the big Sunderland flying boat's window across the sand for three hundred yards to where Tammany was standing motionless, the sea water up to her knees. Even the children were quiet. The opium had left Perry empty and very alone. Neither of them had spoken that morning but it wasn't a dream and Perry Marshbank had not been satisfied.

Angus re-read Reggie Beaumont's decoded message.

'Rumblings at Colonial Office. Suggest more than one party interested in cargo. Keep moving and out of sight till delivery advised.'

"Reggie certainly thinks ahead," said Angus. "I'd have delivered by freighter and lost the lot. We've plenty of fuel. Perry, you'd better come with us and point out suitable coves. We'll move every eight hours. Should confuse the best of them. If the Royal Naval Reserve lose this bloody cargo, the Royal Air Force Reserve will never let us hear the bloody end of it. Perry, my boy, this is more like it. I was getting bored. Who else can be interested? The communists and probably the Japanese. Our friend Ping-Lai Ho's been playing games. War is serious. People get killed."

"While you're doing checks, I'll get my things from the house and say goodbye to Tammany."

"Should we tell Tug in Singapore?"

"No," said Perry, emphatically.

"Okay. You're paying the bills."

"Radio silence and keep moving until we deliver."

KIM-WOK HO SLIT open the brown envelope and slid out the cable that had been addressed to him personally. He was mildly surprised to read the name of the London sender but he had never been one to underestimate. A man did not build an empire such as Reggie Beaumont's without ability.

'Too many interested and dangerous parties. Close deal immediately original client. Cable me coded agreed delivery point. Am floating my companies on London and New York stock exchanges. Would you be interested preferential parcel of shares? Regards. Reginald Beaumont.'

Kim Wok Ho sat for some moments smiling. The British were trying to turn him into an honest investor and he liked the idea. He leant across and picked up the phone on the desk in his study and waited for the operator to answer.

"One to one."

"Hold on, sir." The line crackled.

"Ping-Lai Ho."

"We have problems," he said in Mandarin. "Accept nationalist offer immediately and obtain the Letter of Credit."

"But the other offer is better and we may still go higher."

"Don't argue or the deal's off. It's urgent, cousin Ping-Lai Ho."

"Of course, I'll attend."

"Good. Bring the L of C to my house."

"Where is the cargo?"

"I don't know or wish to know. Sufficient that it will be delivered on time."

"You sound confident."

"I am. It's two o'clock. I want the money by five."

"I'll try."

"They will want to move just as quickly as you. Our cargo has become common knowledge thanks to your horse trading."

"I was only trying to make us some money."

"Make yourself, more likely. Beaumont's will accept c.i.f. Singapore plus fifteen percent. The difference between this and the nationalist L of C will be split equally three ways."

"That's not the way we do business," said Ping-Lai Ho, hurriedly.

"It is from now on with Beaumonts."

"We'll be giving them half a million pounds."

"Good. It should encourage them to give us more business."

"The deal was mine originally."

"You couldn't supply without me and I couldn't supply without Beaumont. It will still be the biggest deal you and I have ever completed. Get on with it cousin."

"Yes, cousin."

He put the phone down pleased with himself. He had no idea the differential would give him half a million pounds sterling. For a moment, he speculated the size of the Japanese offer but deliberately pushed it from his mind. When Linda knocked on his study door, Kim Wok Ho was having a delightful time imagining how he could spend half a million pounds and reluctantly concluded that the windfall would be best placed in a Swiss Bank. The Swiss were clever and would never involve themselves in other people's wars.

"Tug Beaumont's got himself hooked on opium and young girls."

"What?" said Kim-Wok Ho, coming out of his happy reverie.

"He's been at Dragon's Teeth since Sunday. Totally gone."

"Why can't the English stay away from opium? Only the Chinese know how to use it properly. How long?"

"His partner, Perry Marshbank introduced him to it three months ago. Quickly became addicted."

"Three months. Not so bad. Is the car downstairs?"

"Do you want me?"

"Better alone. What a damn fool. What made Marshbank hook him on opium?"

"Rumour has it he fancies Tug's wife."

"So much for the Englishman's honour. Have you found Ping-Lai Ho a nice, tall blonde?"

"Yes, as a matter of fact. Exactly right. When can I introduce her?"

"This evening. We'll have a dinner party here. Tell the lady eight o'clock and have the cook do something special. We must show her that Chinese homes are very civilised. Not that we haven't been civilised for five thousand years."

Kim-Wok Ho drove straight to the Dragon's Teeth den and found Tug Beaumont asleep on a couch, curled up like a foetus. The old Chinaman was delighted to recognise Kim-Wok Ho and speculated how much profit he could make if Kim-Wok Ho became addicted.

"I wish to take my partner home, old man," said Kim-Wok Ho in Cantonese. "This money will make you forget he was here. Help me take him to my car."

Disappointed, the old Chinaman obliged and watched two sources of income drive away down the narrow street. He shrugged philosophically.

Kim-Wok Ho, with Tug still out cold on the back seat, drove out of Singapore and along the causeway towards Malaya proper, the mangrove swamps spread out on both sides. The causeway, itself a miracle of engineering, no longer made Singapore an island. He drove for an hour and turned off at the Catholic mission station and parked outside the Father's house. The black robed priest welcomed Kim-Wok Ho and peered into the car.

"English?"

"My business. partner. Three months. He must be cured, Father. I will pay."

"You have always been generous."

"Without you I would be poor."

"It is good not to forget. So many do. We will look after your friend."

"No-one knows he is here."

"It is better that way. We will know him only as Kim-Wok Ho's friend."

They carried Tug from the car into the house and put him to bed in a room with padded walls.

By a quarter to five, Kim-Wok Ho was back in his flat where Ping-Lai Ho was waiting with the Letter of Credit.

"How do we get paid?"

"In Switzerland. I will cable London with our terms and ask them to open an account in Zurich. There may be war. It is good to be cautious. To show you my good faith and appreciation of such a splendid deal, I have arranged for you to dine with me tonight."

"Oh," said Ping-Lai Ho without enthusiasm.

"There is a difference. Linda will be introducing you to your future mistress and I will not even ask for a fixed price on the rubber."

"You are better without one on a rising market."

"Possibly."

"What is she like?"

"Linda assures me she is perfect for you. Now I must visit my bank manager and lodge this credit. Once the nationalists have signed the delivery documents, Beaumont's will be able to collect. Eight o'clock. Can you wait 'til eight o'clock to meet a five-foot ten inch honey blonde with big tits, cousin?"

"INFORMATION IN LONDON suggests the cargo is in Sarawak," said Edward Gray to his Chief of Police. "It must be found and confiscated before it falls into Japanese or communist hands. Search all the ships in the harbour. Anything else to report?"

"The villagers say a flying boat is moored in the lagoon next to Tug Beaumont's."

"When?"

"Ten days ago."

"That's it."

"What?"

"The guns, you fool. London thinks Beaumont's bought the guns in America. Beaumont's brother used a flying boat when he came out here. He's a pilot. That's how they're going to deliver and why no-one has found the guns. Get a detachment up there and impound the bloody things."

"Yes, sir."

"Well get on with it."

"Yes, sir."

THE COMMUNIST EMISSARY had staked out Tug Beaumont's room at Raffles and his office in down town Singapore with oriental patience. Unknown to him, the emissary was being watched carefully by three members of the Imperial Japanese Army. The Tongs who had been watching the Japanese and the communists on behalf of the nationalists and Chiang Kai-shek had withdrawn. The watchers and the watched were thoroughly bored.

WHILE PING-LAI HO waited impatiently at five minutes to eight for the entrance of Sally Bollas which Linda had geared for eight forty five, a short signal was received by the co-pilot of Lord Angus's Sunderland flying boat on his short-wave radio. They were moored in the centre of a small lagoon, half an hour's flight from Tammany's house which was presently being visited by an inspector of police who was told the plane had left that morning.

"Let's go," said Angus, and set a flight plan for the small French enclave of Kwangchowwan on the mainland coast of China, north of the Gulf of Tonkin. The exchange would be conducted on neutral territory. The big flying boat lumbered across the lagoon and into the air heading on a wrong course until the land had been lost to sight. Lord Angus was a cautious man when it came to delivering other people's property.

"Not even one big blow on the weather forecast," said Lord Angus.

"Good," said Perry Marshbank who was still on board.

PING-LAI Ha had arrived at five minutes to eight, and been shown into Kim-Wok Ho's luxurious flat by the fourteen-year-old Malay maid. Dressed in his best gold and red gown, ornately dragon-fronted and majestically sweeping the floor, he was pleased with himself.

"A drink?" asked the girl.

"Whisky, soda."

She showed him into the lounge. Ping-Lai Ho looked out of the wide window and was reassured by the bustle and wealth of the port. The chink of ice into crystal was pleasantly surpassed by the hiss from the soda syphon. The lights in the room were sufficiently low to set the softness of the evening without preventing him from studying his quarry.

"Ah," and he took a big sip. The girl left the room and he turned back to the open window, the chug of diesel engines, the smell of tar and fish. He loved it and smiled, wrinkling his nose above the small, black, soft moustache. He remembered the time he had been living closer to the tar and the fish. The swish of the soda syphon made him turn. Kim-Wok Ho had poured himself a whisky and was smiling at his cousin.

"I didn't hear you come in," said Ping-Lai Ho in Mandarin.

"You weren't intended to. To a splendid evening," and Kim-Wok Ho raised his glass.

"Where are they?"

"They'll be late. Linda went off with the chauffeur at seven. Doesn't mean anything. Don't be impatient. The cargo's on its way; not too much thanks to you. Didn't you think they'd fight for it?"

"Yes. Got the price up."

"True."

"Nothing wrong with the Letter of Credit?"

"Signed. Bill of Lading will have it cashed in minutes. The money's there."

"Heard the Japs and the communists have staked out Beaumont's office and hotel room."

"Good. Keep them occupied."

"What about Beaumont?"

"Never find him. Drying out. Drove him myself. That fool Marshbank took him on a spree of the opium dens."

"Ah."

"We need Beaumont. Cabled a report to his brother."

"Half a million pounds."

"You'll be able to afford your luxuries."

"It's ten past eight."

Kim-Wok Ho smiled and sipped his whisky.

"How will she react?" said Ping-Lai Ho.

"Fine. The cook's put a little opium in the soup. Just enough to make them relax and want to be friendly."

"You think of everything."

"Not always."

"Do you think there'll be a war in the East?"

"There is already."

"England? America?"

"Probably."

"How will we stand?"

"Carefully. We'll drop back into the mass of the population and see what happens."

"Better make plans."

"I've made mine."

"And this?" said Ping-Lai Ho, sweeping his hand around the luxury in the room.

"The flat will be a shell. I don't own the flat."

"My house is different."

"Sell it."

"Maybe I will."

LINDA LOOKED at her watch and then at Sally with a smile. "We'd better go. There's a point where being too late loses its effect. You look marvellous."

"Thanks."

"That bugger Kim Wok Ho told the cook to sprinkle ground opium into the soup. Silly sod doesn't know I speak Malay. Told the cook I'd cut his balls off. This is a business deal and we need all our faculties."

"THERE'S THE CAR," said Ping-Lai Ho with satisfaction having stood by the window for three quarters of an hour.

"Have another whisky."

"Five foot ten, you say?" he said, holding out his glass.

"Yes."

"Ah."

"You'd look better without all those gold teeth."

"Don't be ridiculous."

Kim-Wok Ho smiled indulgently.

"It's all very well," said Ping-Lai Ho. "You've made your deal."

"Can't keep her if she doesn't want to stay."

The door was opened by the chauffeur and Ping-Lai Ho slopped his drink as he turned. There was a pause and Sally Bollas entered the room in a long evening dress of the palest, pastel green, her large cleavage open to her navel and a big, single ruby on a gold chain hanging between the ivory whiteness of her firm, separate breasts. Long, blonde hair hung over her left shoulder and matched a flawless skin. She smiled in the entrance and the large, brown eyes, in total contrast to the natural blonde hair, lit up and smoothed the room before her long legs, easily seen through the soft silk of her flowing dress, brought her onto the Chinese carpet and up to Kim-Wok Ho who was speechless.

"It was so nice of you to ask me," she said in a husky voice and held out her gloved hand to be kissed and not shaken. A bad pause was broken by Kim-Wok Ho's memory of an American film and he took the hand, now almost under his nose, and kissed it, keeping his eyes firmly on her cleavage.

"Ah," said Ping-Lai Ho and Linda coughed.

"My friend Sally Bollas," she said introducing. "We're friends from England."

Ping-Lai Ho stood rooted to the carpet while his hormones bounced on the ceiling.

"You must be Mr Ping-Lai Ho," said Sally, hand still outstretched to the bowed Kim-Wok Ho, as she turned to her mark, the very tip of her tongue just showing.

'Don't overdo it,' thought Linda with a wince.

"May I pour the drinks?" said Linda. "Sally?"

"G and T."

"Perfect for the tropics," agreed Linda. "All that quinine," and she poured two with a splash of gin in each and a piece of lime.

THE SOUP WAS SERVED and then the steamed fish. By the time they were halfway through their bowls of fragrant pork, half an hour had gone by and the cousins were watching for the effects of the opium. Linda smiled at them and they continued to play the role of well-bred Englishwomen. By the time the small cups of Chinese tea were served, both the cousins were puzzled and a little drunk from the wine. The ladies withdrew and the Chinese, having scraped themselves up from their chairs, were left standing at the table.

"Bloody cook left it out," said Kim-Wok Ho in English and then reverted to Mandarin. "They drink coffee in the lounge. The maid's put it out with the brandy... Hold on. If they ask, I've gone for a piss." Within two minutes he was back at the table. "Now we'll see," he said with satisfaction.

"Ah, the ladies," he said, breaking back into English and standing up for them.

"The maid has put your coffee in the lounge. Shall we withdraw? A little cognac with your coffee?"

"Just a little," said Linda sweetly.

After ten minutes of drinking her coffee, Sally was feeling at peace with the world. She had never been in better company. Her companions were witty and attractive and Linda was a darling if not downright attractive. Her loins had stirred to a sticky expectation and she just loved the furniture in the room.

Linda, having smoked opium before with Kim-Wok Ho recognised the symptoms

a short while after and was determined to remove Sally from the flat before she lost her bargaining power.

"Sally, it's late. We must get you home."

"Not now, darling, I'm enjoying myself," and the cousins sat back hiding their smugness.

Linda was furious. 'The coffee', she thought. 'Bastards.'

"Kim-Wok," she said, "you and Ping-Lai Ho must have some of this coffee. It's particularly delicious tonight."

"I prefer tea."

"I insist," she said, glaring at him and pouring two cups. "Coffee and cognac. Very British."

"No thank you."

"But you like coffee with a cognac."

"Yes, but…"

"What's the matter?"

"Nothing."

"Drink your coffee."

"Very well."

"And you, Ping-Lai Ho. That's right. Now have another cup."

"One's enough."

"As your hostess, I insist."

"If you insist."

"That's better."

Half an hour after Linda had fed four cups of black, opium-laced coffee into the cousins who were now only able to imagine the beauty of sex. Sitting back in their chairs, they were happy to think and do nothing.

"Silly buggers," said Linda, aside to Sally. "Laced the coffee with opium."

"Lovely."

"Don't touch it. Lethal. I'll wake the chauffeur. You can ask him anything you want in the morning," and she nodded her head back at a peacefully smiling Ping-Lai Ho, who along with his cousin was unable to rise when the ladies left to go home.

"She is quite a girl, my Linda," said Kim-Wok Ho before drifting back to the kaleidoscope of his dreams.

WHEN LINDA TOOK the contract to Ping-Lai Ho, the next day, Thursday, the opium had worn off and left him feeling hornier than the night before. The price was more than he could ever have imagined but he had the money and when Linda told him it was the same terms she herself had agreed to with Kim-Wok Ho, he had to sign the agreement and the first cheque. That evening Sally Bollas was appointed Ping-Lai Ho's housekeeper and started her Swiss Bank account. For the first time in her life she was rich.

LORD ANGUS MONTEL adjusted the throttle and brought the flying boat lower to have a better look at the bay.

"Bloody great junk. Like looking for a needle in a haystack."

"How's your navigation?" asked Perry.

"Not me, old boy. Fred the Bed here. That man!" and he pointed with a thumb as he leant forward to have a better look at what was down below. "Nothing in a skirt's safe. Chase, chase. Never stops. You don't think that heap could be a Japanese frigate in disguise?"

"Doubt it," said Fred. "Circle her again."

"Frightened shitless," agreed Angus coming in low end breaking into song.

"She'll be coming round the mountain when she comes," he bellowed. "I don't believe it," said Angus, breaking off the song, "third time lucky. Look at those beautiful Very lights. Green, now red and yes, the white one. Well take her down."

Fred went back to check for movement in the cargo and Angus began his landing checks. It was pitch dark, the only light coming from the stars. As Fred came back to his seat Angus switched on his landing beam light and prepared for a dummy run. A large log was enough to rip the flying boat's fluted belly. Angus completed four circuits before kissing the water a long way out from the darkened junk. A line of white spray shot out a hundred feet behind the Sunderland as the craft bit harder into the water. Finally, the huge floats under the wings came in contact with the smooth sea and completed the three lines of hurtling spray as the monster slowed in the water, the four propellers screaming in reverse pitch. Angus taxied up to the junk and both craft bobbed gently in the swell, the wing of the Sunderland ten feet from the junk. Angus opened the hatch, hands on hips, and surveyed the rendezvous.

"Bloody thing smells and we're down wind."

"They put their little yellow arses over the side and shit," ventured Fred. "Sometimes the wind changes and they have to do it again."

"Someone is alive," said Angus. "A rowing boat. And they're not going to win the boat race." They waited, the only light coming from the Sunderland's flight cabin.

The rowing boat bumped the protecting tyres below Angus's feet. He looked down at ten Chinese and gave them his best smile. One of them, he knew, was obliged to speak English.

"Which one of you can speak English?"

"Just a little," said the man up front and Angus winced at his pronunciation.

"You'd better come up here."

"Okay," and the Chinaman scrambled up the rope-ladder and through the big door into the cargo bay of the flying boat.

"Come with me and you can sign the delivery documents. It'll take some hours to off-load."

"Okay."

Angus looked at the little man and led the way to the pilot's cabin.

"Right," said Angus. "Here's the Airway Bill or you may say Bill of Lading."

"Airplanes, Airway Bill. Ships, Bill of landing. Okay," said the Chinaman.

"Certified invoice ex-New York."

"Okay."

"You sign here and here but first your letter of authority to sign and I will compare the signatures."

The Chinaman bowed but kept his hands tucked into the sleeves of his black robe.

"The letter," said Angus holding out his hand. Fred and Perry came alert at the tone of his voice.

"Okay," but again did nothing.

"Not okay. Letter."

The Chinaman smiled but did nothing.

"The others are getting on board," said Fred.

Angus quietly slid back into the pilot's seat and turned a warm smile on the Chinaman that he didn't feel. "No letter. No signature. No guns."

"No," said the Chinaman and turned to indicate two of his men who were standing in the doorway to the cabin pointing guns at the crew. The Chinaman drew a pistol from his sleeve and pointed it at Angus.

"You damned British ask too much," he said.

"You damned Chinese agreed to the price," said Angus cheerfully.

"If we not, Japanese buy."

"That's war and business. Now, do you want my guns?"

"We take guns. You try fly we shoot. Take plane too."

"You are a slit-eyed, shitty little runt, if you understand."

"I colonel in army."

"You are about to become mangled shit."

"We have guns."

"You think an Englishman would let a little, shit-eyed, slit-eyed runt like you get on his aeroplane, without taking precautions? How come all you Chinese fight each other and we rule half the world? I'll tell you why, Chinky. We think. Brains. We don't stick our bums over the sides of boats and shit like you, shitty little runt."

"You no call me that."

"Why? You sign papers and call you a lot of nice names but at the moment you're a shitty little Chink who's about to be blown higher than the mountain over there. Now, let me show you what is going to happen if you don't behave. We don't carry hand guns because there is no need. On board my flying boat has enough explosive to knock bits off that mountain and your junk is in between. This lever is connected to a plunger in the belly of my aeroplane which a shitty little Chinaman could never find. I have my hand on the lever in such a way that if I am shot I will push it down even if I'm dead. And then you slit-eyed piece of filth will go bang with your men, the guns and your shit-smelly, toilet of a junk."

"You die too."

"No-one will worry too much. I have three elder brothers but you and your glorious army will have no guns. Now, you be sensible, give me General Isimo's letter, sign these papers and the money that is already in Singapore will be released.

Now, when I am about to die, I like to do it quickly so you have thirty seconds. I am going to count. One, two, three, four,…"

The Chinaman looked back at his men and then signalled them to lower their guns.

"You English, velly clever."

"Thank you, colonel.'

"Here is the letter."

"Thank you, colonel."

"It okay?"

Angus passed it to Fred without taking his eyes off the colonel. They waited with the tension.

"The signatures match, Gus."

"Good. Give me the papers. Thank you. Here you are, colonel. Just sign. Thank you, colonel. Now you may unload. Please check the cases against the certified invoice. You will find everything in order. An Englishman's word is his bond, colonel. Oh. One more thing. You will notice that my wings are pointed at your junk. By pressing this button, here, four small hatches drop and your junk will see the barrels of four Vickers light machine guns that the very clever English have made to fire two thousand rounds of incendiary bullets per minute. Your junk is made of wood so it is better if you wave to us as we fly away. You may now unload your guns, colonel. Without the original unpleasantness I would have helped you but instead I must sit next to my plunger and my machine guns. If you start now, you should be finished before the sun comes up which will be better for both of us."

The Chinese withdrew from the cabin and they watched the Chinese bring up a line of rowing boats and place them side by side from the Sunderland's hatch to the side of the junk. Planks were set across the boats and a line of coolies began to unload the guns.

"Only thing they're good at," said Angus and broke into, 'She'll be flying round the mountain anytime…'

By two o'clock in the morning, Singapore time, Angus started the engines.

The planks were being dismantled. The flying boat pulled away from the junk with its engines in reverse until they were five hundred yards out in the bay wings still pointing at the junk. Angus brought the plane round and made his take-off run along the same line of water where he had landed. They were at three thousand feet before anyone spoke.

"I'll bet the little bugger didn't appreciate my insults," said Angus.

"I didn't know you'd wired the cargo," said Perry.

"I hadn't."

"So what's that lever?"

"Starts the windscreen wipers."

"Machine guns?"

"Can you imagine four bloody Vickers in my wings? Couldn't even get the Sunderland off the water."

"You bluffed him."

"Half the British Empire was built on bluff, old boy. Right, back to Sarawak. Pick up extra fuel. Singapore to cash the loot and back to dear old England and a bit of pheasant shooting," and he and Fred broke into song.

By the time Angus put the stick forward to commence their descent to Tug Beaumont's lagoon, the sun was two hours up from the South China Sea and they had flown for fourteen hours. Three times they had hand pumped petrol from the row of forty-four gallon drums into the wing tanks, alternating the feed lines to the engines. Angus feathered two balanced engines as he made his final approach. The flying boat sank gently onto the lagoon and tied up at their mooring under the lee of the mountain and two hundred yards from the shore.

"Who owns that truck?" asked Angus pointing to the beach.

"Police vehicle," said Perry Marshbank.

"We've nothing to hide,' said Angus. We'll stay 'til tomorrow. How about a weekend in Singapore, Fred? A couple of bars. Dancing girls... You flying back with us, Mr Marshbank?"

"Thank you."

"Let's inflate the dinghy and paddle ashore. There are three men standing by that truck looking at us. You know them, Mr Marshbank?"

"The tall one's the member in charge. Local Chief of Police..."

"You'll be staying at the house tonight?"

"Yes, I was best man at the wedding."

"You don't think she'd cook us a big, welcome home supper?" suggested Fred hopefully, who had only caught a glimpse of Tammany but had liked what he saw.

"I can ask," said Perry. "She's very shy. Born here, you know. Local. Very beautiful of course but a local. Caused a stink. Wouldn't have done it myself but you know what it is when a man wants a woman."

"Not really, old boy," said Angus, yawning, stretching himself as he unfolded his long body from the pilot's seat. "Wouldn't say no to a pint in the club at the moment. Bit of cold pheasant. That kind of thing."

Fifteen minutes later they were paddling ashore to be met by the uniformed policeman.

"You the captain?" asked the inspector rudely. He hadn't spoken to Perry since he had left the administration.

"Matter of fact, yes," said Angus.

"I have a warrant for your arrest, signed by Rajah Brook."

"Well you know what you can tell Rajah Brook, don't you?"

"This is a serious matter."

"Even more if you lay a finger on me."

"Who do you think you are?" said the inspector.

"Well, now. That could be interesting."

"You're carrying guns."

"Not anymore as it happens but if I was I would have a perfectly legal export permit from the American government from where they were collected, old boy."

"You're on British territory."

"Where on earth did you go to school, old boy? The main point about the British Empire is the right of the British to carry cargo where they like and when they like. Now a foreign flying boat might have been different but then a foreigner'd never have come up with the dear old Sunderland. Now old boy, if you'd mind leaving me alone I have fuel to load and I could do with some shut-eye."

"Mr Gray says..."

"And who, dear boy, is Mr Gray?"

"The First Officer of the Government of Sarawak."

"Well tell Mr Gray that Lord Angus Montel says he is not interested. Anymore of this nonsense and I'll have questions in the Lords. Impeding Britain's wartime trade. That kind of thing."

"The instruction came from the Colonial Office."

"The Colonial Office. My dear boy, do you know where the Colonial Office stands in the House of Lords? No. Well it doesn't stand very high so if the Colonial Office tries to arrest the son of the Duke of Surrey they won't enjoy it. No, dear boy, and neither will you, or Mr Gray. Do you imagine my father would allow me to go on a journey that was illegal? My dear boy, you obviously don't know my father. And please, keep away from my flying boat. Now…"

"I have a warrant."

"Tear it up or I'll make sure you're posted to a spot that will make this place look like civilisation. And as for Mr Gray, he'll stay Mr Gray right up to the time he pops off."

"But you've been carrying guns."

"I've agreed to that already," snapped Angus.

"I'd like to inspect the flying boat."

"If an inspection will make you happy just paddle on out and have a look."

"You're not coming?"

"My dear boy I've been trying to tell you ever so politely you're barking up the wrong tree but if you wish me to be rude I have a certain skill. Now off you go like the good old 'Duke of York' and paddle your men to my flying boat and then you can paddle them back again. Good day, sir and my compliments to Mr Gray. Now, Mr Marshbank," he said, turning to Perry. "Let us ask Mrs Beaumont if she would be kind enough to feed three weary travellers."

"Well, I don't know…"

"Then I'll ask her. Don't sink the boat," he called over his shoulder to the struggling police. "Bloody landlubbers," he said to Fred. "Give them blisters if nothing else."

Halfway up to the house, Perry asked, "Is it safe with them going on board?"

"The only thing of value they could pinch is in my pocket and for the moment I wish to find a little spot in Mrs Beaumont's house to hide the shipping documents. Police give up easily. They'll be off in a couple of hours. Poor chap wasn't too sure of himself."

"MRS BEAUMONT," said Angus at the house putting on the full extent of his charm. "We are weary, footsore and hungry and throw ourselves upon your mercy. Food, dear lady, could we have food," and he smiled a broad, expectant smile and kept it there 'til she smiled in return.

"Of course. Come in."

"A beer, dear lady would see me in your debt forever," and he laughed and they all laughed except for Perry who was nervous and wanted to get Tammany away on her own.

Angus took one look over his shoulder at the dinghy crabbing its way to the flying boat and rolled his eyes before stepping into the house.

"Who's the painter?" said Angus immediately.

"My husband."

"He's good. Very good. Can I buy one from you?"

"Well. It's not for me to say. Come and sit. I will tell cook. A cold beer? Since my husband left the Colonial Office we can afford a fridge."

Angus stretched himself in an armchair and sighed contentedly. "With the cheque from Reggie Beaumont I shall just be able to pay off my debts," he said to Freddy. "Now, if you were a policeman you wouldn't look for this envelope stuffed under an armchair? Too obvious. Anyway I'm too bloody tired to look any further."

Perry found Tammany in the kitchen.

"You must fly back with us to Singapore. I can look after you and the children."

"And what's wrong with my husband?"

"He's very sick."

"I don't believe you. He told me to stay here. I have lived alone for many months."

"It's not safe."

"Only when you are here."

"You enjoyed it."

"That evening is best forgotten. I will think that opium took your mind. From now I am carrying a small knife. My people use them. If you come within the length of my arm I will kill you. It is you who are sick, not Tug. Now, go away. I will bring the beers."

LINDA AND SALLY arrived at the swimming club twenty minutes after the four o'clock rains that had cooled the day by two degrees Fahrenheit which didn't make much of a difference. Taking a table on the long veranda with the French doors leading off into the clubhouse, they each ordered a gin and tonic from the club waiter and settled back in the rattan chairs.

"Too hot to swim," said Sally.

"Water's tepid," agreed Linda.

"Fans don't help."

"Ping-Lai Ho's put in air-conditioning."

"Very American."

"Bloody sensible."

Dressed in light, cotton frocks they wore large hats which they took off and hung on the fronts of their chairs.

"Wish I could put my feet up," said Linda.

"In the Singapore Swimming Club?" said Sally in mock horror. "Heaven forbid."

"Happy about the deal?"

"It's done."

"Not consummated."

"Paid for."

"Yes, it is a lot of money."

"Money is important. We try to say it isn't but in a material world you can't live without money. Why should we be poor?"

"Are you rationalising now you've agreed?"

"In some ways. But I believe you, don't give me that crap about money not buying happiness."

"Quiet darling, this is the club," admonished Linda in her best boarding school accent. "Don't forget you are preaching to someone who was converted years ago. My mother never enjoyed anything. One long drudgery from getting out of bed. Father could at least play the vicar."

"How do you play the vicar?"

"Don't ask me. Too hot. The drinks. That perfect chink of ice on expensive glass. I prefer the heat to the cold."

"Feel anything for him?"

"Funnily enough, yes." Linda knew she referred to Kim-Wok Ho and not her father. "More brains than most. Knows what he wants and gets it. What's physical anyway? The best of them wear off. Cheers. No, I'll sign," she said to Sally. "Thanks, waiter. Bring another two in five minutes. Stuff evaporates."

"It's pleasant to know I shall never be poor," said Sally. "Breeds confidence."

"The rich always look smug."

"There's a problem at that table," interrupted Sally. "The waiter refused them a drink."

"Are they drunk?" said Linda, turning to look.

"Don't make it obvious."

"Thin one wouldn't be bad looking with a bigger chin."

"Wonder why? Here comes the club secretary."

"You have to be a member, sir," said the club secretary pompously to the tall, thin man. "There is a waiting list. Three years I believe."

"What, mate?" said the thin one in a strong Cockney accent. "To 'ave a swim. Cor blimey."

"I'm sorry, sir."

"Can't no-one sign us in, like?"

"Only a member." The club secretary had decided the man's broad accent did not require a 'sir'. "I'll have to ask you to leave."

"Never been frown out of a bleeding swimming club, Fred, 'eve you."

"Not me, mate," said his friend.

"'Ow you goin' to frow us out? All physical like?"

"People usually leave," said the secretary who was red faced, embarrassed and aware that he was at the centre of an incident.

"'Ow about you signing us in," and the tall, thin man caught Linda's eye with a broad wink.

"I can't."

"Not a member, mate?"

"I am a club servant."

"Good. Let's have a couple of drinks."

"You don't understand. This is a private club."

The thin man looked again at Linda and then continued to outstare the standing club secretary.

"Raffles Hotel will serve you."

"But I'm not in Raffles, mate."

"This is a private club. Only a member can invite you into the club." It was obvious by the secretary's look around the veranda that no such thing would happen. Linda got up from her chair and went across. "You seem to be having a problem, Mr Bell. Allow me to sign them in as my guests."

"It is irregular."

"Not at all. I'm perfectly entitled to sign in two guests and Miss Bollas is already a member."

"Very good, madam," and he made a dignified exit.

"You'll have to come outside and sign the book," said Linda. "Can't break anymore rules, can we?"

The tall man stood up, towering over Linda, seemed to pat his friend on the head to stay where he was and followed Linda to the visitors' book, watched over by the club secretary.

"Names and addresses," said Linda, handing her guest a pen.

She signed against both entries and smiled at the club secretary and led the way back onto the veranda.

"You'd better join us," said Linda. "Come and meet Sally."

Fred also stood up to six foot three inches and was fighting to keep a straight face. The other members had gone back to their drinks, the 'incident' forgotten.

"I hate pompous asses," said Angus Montel in his old Harrovian accent, bringing up a chair.

Sally looked up in surprise at the change of accent.

"Angus Montel. Freddy Gore. Friends for years, right old boy?"

"I'm Linda and this is Sally. Can I get you a drink? Only members are allowed to buy."

"Oh, really," said Angus in surprise as if he didn't know perfectly well the rules of a club. "How nice of you," and he sat down rubbing his hands together. Freddy was a little slower in taking his seat. "Good old G and T will do just fine. You, Freddy?"

"Same, thank you." Freddy Gore was acutely embarrassed.

"You sound different," said Linda having ordered four gin and tonics, each with a slice of lime.

"Lime's important," said Angus, smiling at her happily. "Nice club. Heard about it."

"You don't have reciprocity?"

"Of course. Army and Navy. In and Out Club, you know. Carlton. Public schools."

"Why all the fuss?"

"How else could we have been sitting here?" Which was true in a way.

"You mean that was all for our benefit?"

"Of course. Wasn't it Freddy?"

"Yes, Angus."

"When you get back to London, I'll sign you into my club as my guest. Sort of even it out."

"Thank you," said Linda.

"Come over often?" asked Angus.

"No."

'Thank God for that,' thought Angus and Freddy simultaneously. "Why ever not?" managed Angus.

"I live in Singapore. So does Sally."

"Married?"

"We work for a living."

"Jolly good, old girl. Oh. You don't mind me calling you old girl?"

"Not at all. What do you do?"

"Not very much. The old pater likes to keep me out of England as long as he can," which was perfectly true. "Large allowance," which it was not. "I just flit around with Freddy. Go where I please. That sort of thing. Alright if you're rich. Do you have an important job?"

"Very," said Sally as the drinks arrived.

"Cheers," said Angus.

"Cheers," said Freddy.

The girls smiled into their second drinks.

"Rotten hot. Weather, I mean. Share a flat?"

"No," said Linda as she signed the chit. "Would you mind if we visited the powder room?"

"Not at all," said Angus getting up with Freddy.

"Won't be a tick," said Linda.

"Lovely," and they appreciatively watched the girls walk away.

"Good lookers," said Freddy. "Which one do you prefer?"

"Don't mind old son."

"You sure you know what you're doing?" said Freddy.

"Necessity, my dear Freddy, is the mother of invention. Reginald would never have allowed me to get my hands on any cash. He has known me since the age of six. We were at prep school. I was in debt, even at the age of six. The flying boat has provisions and fuel supplied by a chandelling house. The commission for this highly dangerous journey is being paid direct to my father by Reginald Beaumont except a measly five hundred pounds which will allow me to be drunk in style for only a week. Those Chinamen have given me some hope. Those guns they pointed were loaded. I'm going to ask Reggie for some danger money. There was nothing in the contract about people trying to shoot me. We'll have to build up the story."

"That was for real, Angus."

"Don't be silly. They were bluffing."

"You were."

"Of course I was. So were they. Just trying it on."

"No, Angus. If Reggie pays a bonus we'll deserve it."

"Do you have any money?"

"Not a penny. If I had anything I wouldn't have left England."

"How much do you owe?"

"Seven thousand pounds."

"Not in the same league, old boy. Twenty-two thousand. Father's furious."

"You have a title to trade on. As plain Freddy Gore I think I did well."

"I hate not having money."

"Don't we all? Here come our ladies."

"We might even get dinner," said Angus, hopefully, the thought of tinned food and beans rising in his gullet.

"Wonder who they are?"

"Shush…"

"Hello," and the two got up. Everybody settled and lifted their glasses.

"Cheers, cheers," said Freddy.

"Cheers."

"Now. Why don't you tell us what you are really up to?" said Linda, "and we can all join in the laugh."

"Not here," said Angus, working on the problem. "Why don't we find a little restaurant?"

"It's early for supper."

"We can always have a couple of drinks and then go on."

"Yes," said Linda as she watched the lights sparkle in Sally's eyes. They all smiled at each other and the thought of tinned food evaporated for both Angus and Freddy.

Angus's wits being the only things that fed him properly in times of need were all about him. 'Well,' he thought to himself, 'if we have a story, why shouldn't they, and all being so far from England.'

AT EIGHT-THIRTY THAT EVENING, the Friday night, Linda showed them into the cubicle where she had talked business to Sally Bollas earlier in the week and ordered an ice-cold bottle of Chablis. Angus had grown quieter as the gin and tonics progressed in the swimming club. At first he sensed danger and again when they were shown into the private booth in a Chinese-owned night club in what he correctly suspected to be the wrong end of Singapore. For three and a half hours he had been trying to come up with their angle without success and the only one who was now enjoying himself was Freddy Gore who relied on the skipper to get him out of trouble. Angus and Linda had been sparring all evening while Sally kept a satisfied expression on her face and her eyes on Freddy Gore. She was a little drunk and enjoying herself. Linda had apparently been drinking drink for drink with Angus, except she had told the waiter to put water on her ice and blessed the colour of gin as she had done in the past. Linda sipped the ice-cold Chablis and smiled at the slightly perplexed Angus.

"The best money can buy," she said.

"I'm glad you ordered it," said Angus and there was a slight emphasis on the you.

"Haven't you guessed who I am?"

"No. But you're not what you said at the beginning."

"Wrong. I am a working girl, I'm working now."

"We don't have any money."

"I know. On the last count you owed your father twenty-two thousand one hundred and twelve pounds sterling, your father having been kind enough to buy up your debts. Freddy here, owes a third of that figure," Linda paused... "You're not saying anything."

"There's either nothing to say or a lot," said Angus who had snapped the alcohol clear from his brain as the adrenaline pumped into his system.

"Seeing you in the swimming club was a coincidence. We don't see too many strange European faces in Singapore. I know most of the locals. Sally and I know all of the good looking males," and she smiled putting a slight, twisted smile onto Angus's face. Freddy, out of his depth, was sipping his Chablis. "Signing you in as a guest was not a coincidence, Lord Angus Montel, Lieutenant RNVR, Fleet Air

Arm." Angus Montel's adrenaline was again screaming and he looked for something to use as a weapon. He should not have been so sarcastic in Kwangchowwan.

"Who the hell are you?" snarled Angus,

"Kim-Wok Ho's mistress. Sally's Ping-Lai Ho's."

The tension broke and Angus laughed but not with his eyes.

"What do you want?" he asked.

"Apart from a pleasant evening in English company, it strikes me that each of us have something the other needs."

"There's only one thing I need and that's money," said Freddy who was getting drunk.

"Exactly. Let me tell you something of our lives. At the end of my story I'll ask you how you intend living the way you would wish to live, especially when your youth has gone?"

"Marrying it of course," said Angus.

"You haven't found an heiress so far and you are twenty-eight next Thursday."

"Reginald didn't trust me."

"He did. Just cautious. It's why he's very rich. That and his ability to choose the right people to work for him." And Linda told them their story.

"With percentages," said Angus, "you could reach half a million pounds in three years. But will you want to leave? Your information on me and Freddy shows you have power already."

"It will never be the kind that I want."

"How can I help?"

"When we return to England, we will give you ten percent of our fortunes for finding us the right husbands."

"I can't lose. You'll be killed in the rush."

"Yes, with your families' sponsorship. And now, as Sally and I discussed in the powder room, we're going to give you an evening you won't forget by way of a deposit on the deal… if you'll forgive my pun?"

KIM-WOK HO STOPPED his car below the father's veranda and turned off his engine and lights. Within a moment the sweat was pouring down the sides of his face and into his collar. The night jungle was right outside the open window, singing, humming, calling to him; insects, night birds, bull frogs, animals. Some he knew, most he didn't. He waited. It was ten-thirty at night and the father would have been asleep but at his age he didn't sleep heavily or for long. Probably putting on his cassock, smiled Kim-Wok Ho in anticipation and waited. The heat in the car was too great so he got out and leant on the bonnet, dirtying his linen suit but it didn't matter as no-one could see in the night and the father was going blind. 'His eyes not his mind,' thought Kim-Wok Ho. A rustle of cloth in the night and a torch shone through the gauze screen of the front door onto the car, searched and picked out Kim-Wok Ho against the bonnet.

"Oh, it's you," said the father happily.

"Did I wake you?"

"'Course you did. Come up. I'll get the bottle and the syphon."

"You don't mind?" smiled Kim-Wok Ho.

"Whenever did I miss a chance for a drink or to talk?"

"I brought the scotch."

"Then it's ice and soda from me. You brought a good one?"

"Dimple Haig."

"I'm glad to wake up."

Kim-Wok Ho settled himself into a cane chair while the father went inside. His eyes grew accustomed to the dark and he put the full bottle on the coffee table. The jungle sounded louder as the engine noise receded from his ears. The father came back, his long white beard visible in the dark and the pebble, rimless glasses perched on his nose. Kim-Wok Ho couldn't see but he knew the nose was red.

"You think we need light?" asked the father.

"No. Brings the mosquitoes. How's the patient?"

"Bad. Very bad."

"Raving?"

"Raving mad. Terrible withdrawal. Not seen the likes."

"Will he recover?"

"Not here. Not in Malaya. Listen to it. Add this to hallucinations. When did he last go home?"

"Never has. Came out in '33."

"Some Europeans can't take it. He's in the padded room. When the craving's strong, he runs his head at the walls. Can't control anything. Place stinks."

"Can I pour?"

"Whisky before ice."

"Of course… How's that?"

"A little more."

"Certainly, father," and he chuckled. Two short shots from the soda syphon sufficed with two blocks of ice. "Your health, father."

"And you, my boy. The blessing of God, may He always be with you."

"What do you suggest?"

"Back to England. Cold climate. Good doctors. Familiar surroundings. Away from Malaya. Stay there."

"He's married. Two children."

"Take them," said the father.

"She's from Sarawak. A native."

"I see."

"What you suggest?"

"She can't have him like he is. No-one can."

"There's a flying boat going back on Monday. I'll take him."

"You?"

"I want to meet his brother. Business. Someone will have to go with him."

"I'll give you sedatives for the journey. How long will it take?"

"Five days. Maybe four. The plane was chartered by Tug's brother. Imperial Airways wouldn't take him anyway."

"He can't get opium in England so he'll have to dry out."

"He's left his wife in Sarawak for long periods. I'll have my Kuching agent go and see her."

"How's your mistress? So sorry. Your housekeeper?"

"You know," said Kim-Wok Ho in surprise.

"Sooner or later," said the father vaguely. "Why haven't you married? Children? You're forty-seven."

"Forty-eight."

"Worse."

"Too much, too many times, too easily."

"Heard from your father?"

"Of him. He's changed sides."

"What?"

"Father. My brothers. The whole family. Good communists. Took his whole army to Mao Tse-Tung."

"I don't believe it. He's a war lord."

"Obviously thinks Mao's going to win. You know that old Chinese saying. 'Bend with the reeds'. After the wind stops, the reeds always come upright again."

"And you've sold the nationalist's guns!"

"I didn't tell you."

The father waved it away with his free hand.

Kim-Wok Ho thought for a moment. "I'll sell the communists the next shipment," he said. "Don't want father to think I've taken sides. Anyway, that old tiger is usually right. Survival. He's been a great survivor like his other ancestors."

"And you?"

"And me."

"This woman, do you love her?"

"I don't think I know what that means. Can I pour you a little whisky?"

"Of course."

"She gives me what I want."

"And her?"

"She gets paid. Trading. What everything's about? I have money. She has youth. We swop."

"And when she leaves?"

"I'll get another one."

"Very cynical."

"Too much of the rest doesn't work in practice."

"Very cynical."

"Some people need a support. I don't. Linda contributes to my business. If I had to employ a European brain as good as hers it would cost me more than what I have transferred to her Swiss Bank account. And she doesn't steal. Very loyal. Perfect deal. I've set up Ping-Lai Ho similarly. Girl has a degree. Good for the face."

"And the ladies?"

"They will return to England with a dowry and a good story... Will there be a war in the East? Britain? Japan?"

"Yes. There is always going to be a war. '39, '40 who knows when? But war, yes. The Japanese generals want to imitate Hitler. Japan is too small for her people. And now that America has stopped supplying them with strategic materials it is only time. The British are preparing. Airfields in Malaya; Singapore naval base. What a waste of time... Enemies become good friends and vice versa. Mostly expediency."

"Who will win?"

"Does it matter? Business will go on. A boatman asked William of Orange, as he rowed him back from the Battle of the Boyn. 'Who won?' he asked. 'It doesn't matter to you,' said William. 'You will still be rowing this boat tomorrow.' The end is always the same. Life goes on living."

"You'll live another fifty years."

"No, I have cancer. Terminal. I'm ready. A good life. Teaching. Helping. Seeing you growing from the little boy your father sent me to educate. You learnt well."

"You haven't got cancer… Will the British stay in Malaya?"

"Does it matter? Their influence will remain long after their empire has been lost. There will always be English and Chinese doing business."

"That is how I see it."

"And once the war is over they'll be doing business with the Japs as usual. That is the way of our world. You remember your Plato. Socrates discussed in the Republic the all good government and proved there could only be one. A philosopher king who would always act for right and not wrong. 'But such a man if he were found,' said Socrates 'would be intelligent enough not to take the job and if he did, the mob would vilify him and crucify him.' Sounds familiar? Written hundreds of years, before Christ. No, however much we preach they don't want to be good. War. Fornication. Robbery. Swindling. Take that and a few more sins away and they'd die of boredom."

"But a priest can't believe that?"

"It's not what I believe but what I know. Certainly it would be nice for everyone to be good but not very practical. They'll do what they want, anyway… the scotch is beautiful."

"You sound despondent."

"Not at all. I'll leave this world in the state I found it… have you taken war precautions?"

"Yes… How long, father?"

"A few months."

"I'm sorry."

"I'm not. It has to come to an end. I've enjoyed my life. Try to enjoy yours. Don't hurt people… But, I've told you all this for forty years. The mission will carry on."

"You've been a wonderful teacher."

"That's flattery."

"It's true, father. And I'm still learning. Will there ever be peace in the world?"

"No. It's not in their nature. Aggression is as much part of nature as love."

"Have another whisky and tell me about Ireland."

"Now if that isn't pampering to an old man. Each one of the stories you've heard a thousand times."

"I'm going there."

"Where?"

"To Ireland. To where you grew up. I'll recognise every part of it and I'll come back and tell you it's just the same."

"I've got a terrible pain, Kim-Wok. Terrible pain."

"Can I get something?"

"Only the whisky. They say it'll get in the bloodstream and that'll be it. I'll find out then if the Catholics are right. Too late if they're not. Have some children, Kim-Wok Ho. They are the future. They are your immortality."

"But God? You believe?"

"I believe what I want to hear and I've always wanted to hear the Roman

Catholic Church. It takes care of the pain in living. When there's very little, like there was in Ireland, the only thing you could have was a faith. So let us believe in it. No harm. There are many rights. A way of life. Good life. What a beautiful philosophy. Love, be kind, be good and always do unto others as you would they should do unto you. The Philosopher King. Son of God. Jesus Christ. The pain, Kim-Wok Ho. My pain. Give me whisky. Let me die drunk like a good Irishman. The doctors would give me morphine. Addictive. Where's the good in that?" and he laughed, cutting it off with a choke. "A hot night in Malaya and I'm dying. Whisky in hand, I'll mind you. My best pupil. What else can a world give to send you off on your own? Give my love to Ireland. Say goodbye for me." A dog barked from the compound, a lonely, alien sound. "Now," he said, bringing his white beard up from the shadow. "I'll tell you about Ireland. Come a little closer and pour out the whisky. There's no good of it in the bottle. Forty years is it that I've been telling you? That's a mighty long time to be listening. Now, County Cork as you know is on the south end of Ireland and I was born in Cork Harbour seventy-nine years ago tomorrow and seeing it's late and if I finish the story I'll have made it to my eightieth year."

The tears were running steadily down Kim-Wok Ho's face but he made no sound to interrupt the story and a little after twelve the old man collapsed forward in his chair and Kim-Wok Ho picked up the frail, almost empty body and took him through to his bedroom and laid him down. Through his tears, Kim-Wok Ho lit the Tilley lamp so he could see the face he had known all his life.

"You're the only person I have ever loved," he said to the inert body.

"I heard that Kim-Wok Ho," said the father.

"I DON'T BELIEVE IT," said Angus Montel, sitting up in bed in the dark, "they're at it again."

"Walls are thin," said Linda as the sounds of excitement reached their climax in the bedroom next door. "What are you waiting for? Doesn't that turn you on?"

"Yes."

Ten minutes later, Angus, lying naked on his back in the heat, began to chuckle.

"What an evening. The expression on the club secretary's face when I gave him one of father's visiting cards. 'Please give me a call when you're in London,' in my best Harrovian. Then he looked from the card to me in bewilderment. 'Little joke, mate,' I said in best Cockney. He still doesn't know which part is the joke. A Cockney with a ducal card or a Duke with a Cockney accent."

"You're a fraud, Angus Montel."

"No I'm not, matter of fact."

"I don't mean the title. You. But I love it. What an evening. What a night. Where did you learn to make love?"

"The ladies' court."

"Stop it," giggled Linda.

"I've got an idea."

"Be careful, it may get lonely."

"Don't be rude. I'm serious," said Angus.

"I'm still tipsy."

"Champagne."

"The last bottle on the beach."

"Chasing you."

"Being caught," said Linda.

"Marvellous."

"Every bit of it."

They were holding hands in bed, a companionable silence.

"Why don't you come back to England with me Linda?" She leant back to look at him. "There's plenty of room in the flying boat. We can have such fun. A small cottage, big feather bed, low ceilings with old black beams, rose garden of course. Honeysuckle. Cows lowing from the fields. In winter, a big log fire in the den. A bear rug next to it. Mulled wine full of herbs. Making love six times a day. Long walks in the woods. Wood pigeons and squirrels. Foxes watching from the bracken with just a smile on their whiskers. We will be so happy. I've never had a night like tonight. It can't just stop."

"Dawn's breaking, Angus."

"We can go skiing in Switzerland. Rent a villa in the South of France for a month in the summer. Charter a boat, why not? Sail the Aegean. I can sail, you know. Wouldn't need a crew. Catch our own fish. Dive for lobsters. Cook them on open fires on lonely islands made for lovers. The world our own. Fly back with me, Linda."

He got out of bed. Naked, he stood by the window looking at his dream. "There she is," he said finally focusing. "I didn't know your flat overlooked the Teluk Ayer Basin. My Sunderland. Come and look at her. Beautiful. Proud. Rides high in the water. Look at her, Linda. Ready to leap into the air. We can go. Plenty of fuel, food. Five days. Maybe four if the head winds are kind. London Bridge. The Pool of London. I love flying. Isn't she beautiful?"

She got out of bed and stood next to him, naked, proud breasts pointed and the curves of all her flesh, sculptured to her body.

"Yes," she said.

"Let's go out to her."

"Like this?" and she giggled.

"Put on some clothes. Don't need shoes. The dinghy's over there. I can see it. Look at the sun, poking above the swamps."

"Alright."

"Just a shirt and top'."

"No pants or bra?"

"No. I'll wear trousers."

"How modest," and they laughed and pulled on the clothes and ran to the door barefoot and giggling.

"Careful. Don't jump into the dinghy. They turn over. I'll get in first."

"Can you row?"

"Ha, ha. Come on. Grip my hand. Sit over there in the middle."

"What a beautiful morning. Only time that it is cool."

Watching her with every stroke, Angus rowed them out to the flying boat, leaving a perfect V spreading out a hundred yards on the still waters of the basin. Boats moored along the jetty but quiet in the first breath of morning. The swamp smell was strong, mingled with spices and tar and the smell of the sea. Angus tied up the dinghy, unlocked the main door and pulled out the stepladder.

"You go first," he said and as she climbed, she turned back and saw him wickedly looking up her skirt.

"You have a one-track mind," she said.

"Certainly," and he climbed up behind her and led her through to the flight deck.

"It's enormous," said Linda.

"Like her?"

"Beautiful."

"Bunks come down for sleeping. Just like home. Food's not bad," he lied. "You'd make it better."

"What would Freddy say?"

"Jolly good show," he imitated Freddy.

"You are incorrigible."

"Undoubtedly."

"What are we going to use for money?"

"Well."

"It wouldn't be a cottage and the Aegean. It'd be London. Night spots. Parties. Monte Carlo."

"Yes. But that's fun. Terrific fun."

"Expensive."

"Well."

"My money?"

"Some of it."

"All of it, Angus. You wouldn't make it last long. A year, maybe."

"But what a year. You must take happiness when it comes, Linda. You can't store it in a bank account and hope when you're ready to find Mr Right. I'm here. We're the same. Takers. What we can. Enjoyers. We enjoy life. Take it now, Linda. There's a war coming. The whole damn world may blow up but they won't be able to take away our memories. Youth. Looks. They go away. Times are so short."

"Would you marry me?"

"Well."

"Well?"

"No. That would kill the excitement. You know that. Lord Angus Montel's fiancée. That would be enough. Every door would open."

"And shut when the money ran out."

"We'd have a ball."

"Yes. We probably would."

"What are you waiting for?"

"Oh, Angus. There's more to life than burning the candle at both ends."

"For some, yes. Not for you and I. We're wild. Opportunists. So if the money runs out we make more. Take it as it comes. You've got brains. My dad's a duke. What can stop us?"

"The war for one."

"If it comes. If it does. Stacks of opportunity."

"I couldn't leave Kim-Wok Ho like that."

"He means something to you?" said Angus. She stood for a moment looking out of the pilot's window, seeing nothing.

"I hadn't thought of it seriously until now. But yes. He's been very good to me."

"Don't be ridiculous Linda. He's a Chinaman. Anyway, if you really felt anything you wouldn't have been with me last night. You wouldn't have enjoyed yourself."

"You don't understand, Angus. I can't end up poor again. I won't. You have your family to bail you out. I have Linda. Linda and her Swiss Bank account. Linda and Kim-Wok Ho for the moment. Sure, he's a Chinaman. But he's educated. Brilliant in some ways. Kinky as hell but who isn't and some of it, most of it in fact, I like. He's Eastern. Old. Well, not old but he isn't young anymore. But in a man does that matter? Kim-Wok Ho will always be successful whatever happens because he's proved it. He doesn't have to dream about creating his wealth. And if he loses what he's got he knows how to go out and make it again. But he won't lose it because he's too damn clever. He's Chinese but one hell of a man, Angus."

"And I'm not?"

"Of course you are. A young man. Yes, we'd have your ball but I couldn't take it when it came to an end."

"You won't come back with me?" The lap of water was loud in the silent cabin.

"No, Angus. Let's remember an evening. Memories don't change. Maybe, when I'm really rich, when the income would keep you in the style you crave, we can talk again. Let's go back. Sally will be up and wondering."

"You don't know what you're throwing away."

"Oh yes I do and for weeks I'll regret it."

"Change it."

"It's made. Row me back."

"Are you sure, Linda?"

"Yes."

"Is this goodbye, Linda?"

"Yes… Have a good life, Angus."

"You're crying?"

"Of course I am, you fool," and he rowed her back in silence and watched in silence as she climbed up the steps and walked out of his life.

8

SATURDAY 16 OCTOBER 1937

*A*t the end of that week, Reggie Beaumont woke at six-thirty on the Saturday morning. His teeth felt as if small socks had been placed over each of them and his throat was parched. He tried leaning up on one elbow but gently lowered his head onto the pillows and shut his eyes. He always woke at six-thirty and cursed his built-in alarm clock. There wasn't a sound in the room or from the City of London. Knowing more sleep to be useless, he threw back the blankets, rushed at the open window without which he couldn't sleep, shut it, and shivered his naked body to the shower room.

"You can do it," said Reggie out loud and turned off the hot tap to let ice-cold water close the pores of his skin. He was not sure if this daily purgatory instituted by his mother from the age of six, was medically sound but it did have the effect of waking him up. "One of these days I'll get eight hours' sleep," and he rubbed himself down vigorously with a large, fluffy bath towel, despatched to him by his mother from Merry Hall. Back in the small bedroom that led off from his office, he turned on a two-bar electric heater and began to dress in casual clothes, the tradition for Saturday mornings in the City. Outside it was still pitch dark and he turned on the bedside lamp. As usual the small red leather travelling clock read twenty to seven. Reggie boiled the kettle and made himself a cup of tea in a breakfast cup.

Putting on socks and shoes, he padded across the thick carpet and opened the door to his office, turning on the lights.

At ten minutes to seven, Reggie's working day had begun and with a second cup of tea he made across to his desk and sat down. Taking a sheet of paper from the top, right hand drawer of his desk he began to write down the tasks for the day. Halfway through he made a third cup of tea and scrubbed his teeth for the second time. Back in his office, he farted loudly and smiled to himself. "Obviously old enough to live by itself." Sitting down he finished his list, checked it, crossed out two items that weren't worth worrying about and felt better. The third cup of tea met his teeth direct and the grit was leaving his eyes. In front of his desk, and stretching out on the Persian carpet in his office, he managed thirty press-ups, collapsed on his hands and coughed. The smoke in the club had been bad. Pulling himself up, he settled in the corner of the sofa and began his daily read of financial and mining journals. At eight-thirty, Thelma King let herself into the office.

"Morning Reggie. How are you today?"

"Better than I was an hour ago."

"Where'd you go?"

"Bretts. Chuck. That American drinks like a fish."

"Late?"

"Don't know. Must have been. Didn't look at the time. All I could manage was getting my clothes off. Slept here. How was your evening?"

"So, so. Tonight's will be better. Here. There was a telegram under the door."

"Let's have a look. Make some coffee. The tea's rehydrated me, now I need a boost. Wow, Thelma, half a million quid. That's better than a slap in the belly with a wet fish. Singapore. Kim-Wok Ho. Those guns of Chucks have made us a fortune. And Ho wants shares in the company. I'm glad. What's this? I don't believe it. Man says Tug's become a drug addict. Opium. We'd better keep this one from mother and father until we get it right. They've put him on a mission station. Catholics. Mother won't like that either."

"Are you serious?"

"Read it yourself."

Reggie began pacing his office, the points on his pad forgotten.

"Why would he lie?" asked Thelma.

"No reason. Do you know anything about drug abuse?"

"Nothing."

"We'd better start finding out. First try the tropical diseases hospital. Tell them we have a member of our Chinese staff in Singapore hooked on opium. If you make enough calls you'll track down the experts. Got to be someone in England who knows what he's talking about. Poor old Tug. Not like him at all."

"That's probably why. Someone led him astray."

"Yes. Tug always follows easily. We'll have to leave at nine-thirty. The shoot starts at one and father hates being kept waiting."

"Some of those hospital people are going to laugh at me."

"Probably."

"Are you going dressed like that?"

"No. I'll change later."

At nine-thirty, Reggie appeared from the bedroom and Thelma burst out laughing. "Wait till you see the rest," said Reggie and produced a deerstalker hat from behind his back and put it on his head. "The good bit is the earflaps. Damned cold shooting pheasants in October."

"Reggie, those plus fours are marvellous."

"Oh, yes. How about this lot?" and he produced the shooting stick and the curled pipe.

"You don't smoke."

"Got to look the part," and they both laughed.

"The others will dress like that?" she said pointing at him.

"All of them. The Baron will be a picture. Come on. The Lagonda's outside if it'll start. You have an evening dress? Mother will insist you dress for dinner."

"Everything, Reggie. I'm looking forward to the weekend."

"Not the pheasant shooting."

"How is François getting to Merry Hall?"

"Taxi from Croydon airport. There's a perfect country pub near the Epsom race course. My timing is to have a pint by the fire at eleven-thirty. Pork pie. Pickles. That kind of thing. I'm always hungry on a hangover. What time did you get to bed last night?"

"That is none of your business."

"Which answers the question."

"I don't sleep with every man I go out with. Damn. The phone," said Thelma and picked it up.

"Beaumont Ltd."

"Reggie Beaumont?"

"A call for you."

"Hello."

"Morning, Reggie. Tony."

"Where are you?"

"Montserrat. Leeward Islands. I'm working up towards the Bahamas. Bit of news for you, old buddy."

"You've found an island?"

"Not yet. Got engaged. Your old thumping mate is getting spliced."

"Tony. You are drunk."

"On love. Want to talk to Lilly?"

"Reggie. Isn't it wonderful?" said Lilly. "We can run the casino as a husband and wife team."

"Congratulations," and he mouthed the news to Thelma who mouthed back to him.

"Thelma sends her best. You see what desert islands can do to people. I'm driving down to Merry Hall now."

"Bye, Reggie." Male and female laughter came across the line before it went dead and Reggie stared at the mouthpiece.

"That will be his seventh engagement if I can count right. Come on. We'll be late. Let's get out of here before it rings again."

Charlie was waiting for them at the swing doors.

"Much of that scotch left, Charlie?"

"Half an inch, sir. Have a good shoot."

"Thanks."

"The fog's gone completely."

"THERE YOU ARE," said Reggie, as he drove up the drive to the Hall. "Unbelievable."

"Just look at Carl," said Thelma. "A green hat with a red feather."

"Better park away from the dogs. Excited enough as it is. You thought I'd over dressed," said Reggie, turning off the ignition and reaching behind for his deerstalker hat.

"Please. Not the pipe. I'll laugh."

"The servants will take the suitcases."

"There you are," bellowed his father over the noise of dogs and people as Reggie got out of the Lagonda.

"Everything alright?" asked Reggie.

"Brigley says so. Plenty of game. Good breeding season."

"Hello, Henry," said Reggie. "Not too cold."

"East wind coming up. Have a stiff drink. Pavy's serving over there."

"Hello, mother. You remember Thelma, my secretary."

"You always say that, Reggie. Of course I do. Hello Thelma. Come in out of the cold. They'll be walking soon, now Reggie's arrived."

"Hello, François," said Reggie. "Flight alright?"

"Fine, Reggie. Fine day for shooting."

"Love that hat," said Thelma.

"Do you really? Not as good as Carl's. Gunter's got one with three feathers."

"Are all your guns broken and unloaded?" bellowed Sir Thomas Beaumont over the tumult. "Check you guns. No accidents. Never had one at Merry Hall. Off in five minutes. Have a warmer before you go. Anyone who hasn't filled his hip flask can ask my man Pavy. Keep those damn dogs apart. They're here to retrieve pheasants, not kill each other. Reggie, have you found your gun? It's in the hallway by the hat stand."

"Thanks father. How many this year?"

"Forty-seven guns. Brigley's got two hundred beaters."

"Hello, Chuck," said Reggie. "How's your hangover?"

"Could be worse, how I see it."

"Have you seen Pippa?"

"You bet your arse I have. Prettier than ever."

"We made a bundle on those guns in Singapore. Half a million sterling plus your fifteen percent."

"Now that's what I call a deal."

"Hello, Baron," said Reggie. "Glad to see you at Merry Hall."

"It is my pleasure."

"Gunter here?"

"Over there by the drinks."

"I see him. Have a good shoot. We'll expect the Germans to show us how it's done,"

"Of course, Reggie. It is good. There is no rain."

"Uncle. Reggie," screamed Beau, two years old, as he ran through the crowd.

"What did you bring me?"

"Later, young man. How's your dad?"

"Mummy says better," said his sister, Lorna.

"Hello, Percy," said Reggie to his bank manager. "Glad you could make it. And Billy. They give you a weekend exeat from Mill Hill?"

"Yes, sir."

"And how's that boat of yours?"

"Sweet as a nut, sir."

"We'll have a long chat tomorrow."

"I'm looking forward to it, sir."

"This your first big shoot?"

"Yes, sir, but I'm a member of the school Bisley team."

"That's the stuff. You can show your father how it's done. Mother with you?"

"She's talking to Lady Beaumont over there."

"Hello, Koos," said Reggie, making his way through the jostling crowd, breath steaming as they talked and drank, guns under the left arm, cartridge pouches over the right shoulders resting on the back hip. Some of the men were stamping their feet and clapping their hands. "Being a Boer, you'll be the number one shot?"

"Well, I was given my first gun, eh, when I was seven. Could only get the butt under my arm. But it worked, man. Any news?"

"Everyone's here including the bank manager. All they've got to do is make a decision. We'll have an answer before tomorrow afternoon. Carl and François were handed full reports at Croydon airport. How do you like Merry Hall?"

"Good, man. Very good but a little cold in the corridors."

"Never get used to it," said Reggie. "I hope you've had some fun in London."

"Well, yes. My fun. I've visited thirty-seven Protestant churches. I am a deacon in the Dutch Reformed Church."

"You must come with us tomorrow for morning service at Ashtead Church. It was built by one of my ancestors nine hundred years ago. I'll show you the family vault."

"That will be interesting."

"Our vicar's quite a character. That's the rather large man over there drinking from a silver mug. Enjoy the shoot. Cock pheasants only. They're the ones with the long tails and fancy colours. Leave the others alone. Father gets upset with anyone shooting his breeding stock."

"I'll remember."

"THEY ARE MOVING OFF," said Lady Beaumont from the bay window of the drawing room that looked out over the wide, gravel-covered driveway in front of Merry Hall. "Now we can all have a glass of sherry. There is nothing more pleasant than a good glass of sherry by the fire on a cold day. And it is bitterly cold. Ah, thank you, Pavy. Be kind enough to offer the ladies a sherry."

OUTSIDE, the lawns down to the tennis court were hard from the previous night's frost and the ground broke under their walking shoes. The men began to fan out on either side to create an arc of guns that would eventually converge on the beaters.

The old owl watched them from inside a rotten elm tree. They had woken him up, crashing through the brambles and crushed bracken and the crisp, brown leaves of last autumn. The owl shifted further inside the hollow tree and tried to go back to sleep.

The air in the woods was still and cold, broken by the hurried flight of wood pigeons and the lonely caw of the black crows. The grey sky and the grey clouds mingled coldly high above the spreading line of white-breathed men walking the winter landscape. The fox watched them from his winter lair but didn't move, the breath rising from the left side of his jaw. The vixen beside him snuggled up closer and the fox was glad of the warmth. By the time the line of men had passed out of the wood, the fox and the vixen had fallen into an untroubled sleep.

"SHALL we have another sherry before going into lunch?" asked Lady Beaumont and waved Pavy forward in his black morning-suit, the tray was balanced on one white-gloved hand, the free white index finger pointing out the sweet, the medium and the dry, from rich brown to a pale amber.

"Thank you, Pavy," said Lady Beaumont as he passed. "I'll have a brown sherry. I don't like the dry stuff," she said, turning back to Mrs Hudson, the bank manager's wife, "but my mother said it was not the thing to ask for a sweet sherry. Ask for a brown sherry, she told me, and they'll give you what you want without announcing to the world that you have the wrong kind of palate. Silly, really. Now how do you think that boy of yours is going to enjoy his first pheasant shoot?"

"Very much, Lady Beaumont. He was almost as excited as when he takes his boat out into the Solent. And how is Geoffrey? We were so relieved to read he'd been found."

"Reggie spoke to this man Escort in Salisbury yesterday. They want to send Geoffrey down on the train to Cape Town where the hospital facilities are better. The weather's better. October in Salisbury is very hot."

"When will he sail for home?"

"My goodness, they never tell me anything as important as that. After lunch, you must come and see my chrysanthemums. Bonner has excelled himself this year. We heat the greenhouses, you know. Fresh tomatoes even now. He's using something called liquid manure. Showed it to me. Terrible colour. Black. But it does the trick. But the peaches are no good at all. Not even one flower this year. I like visiting the greenhouses. The hothouse smell of growing plants and the humidity is such a change from an east wind in the English winter. Did you hear that? Something's happened. Brigley promised us a lot of birds this year. We don't have an official gamekeeper but he looks after things. Been a tradition for his family. Entitles them to shoot what they like on the estate. My word. They are blazing away. They do enjoy themselves when there's plenty to shoot at. Well, I suppose that is what it's all about. You know, there are quite a few of Henry's friends here that I don't know. Isabel, my dear, I think it's time you took me round for a chat to some of your friends."

"Yes, mother."

"Georgina, come and talk to Mrs Hudson while I do my rounds. I've been so lucky with my daughters-in-law. I just wish Reggie would hurry up and get married. It is not right for a man of thirty to be unmarried. Don't you agree Isabel?"

"Yes, mother."

"I think I'll have forty winks after luncheon."

"Yes, mother."

"I hear that one of Henry's foals is sick."

"He spent last night in the stables. I believe the foal is better this morning."

"He is so fond of his animals, dear Henry."

THE GUNFIRE HAD SPREAD in a wide arc as the slow, cumbersome birds took to their short wings in fear and were systematically shot out of the sky, the smaller hen birds only floating to cover behind the guns. Dogs barked happily as they ran

across fields and ploughed lands to delicately grip the mangled birds and
occasionally chase one that was only half dead, fluttering uselessly across the stone
hard earth, its neck trying to elongate away from the snapping dog. Proudly, the
dogs trotted back to their masters and dropped the birds dead or half dead to be
hung by their necks from the belts, dripping blood from gaping beaks. The guns
moved forward firing left and right as the number five shot flew into the feathers. A
hare bounded across the Thirty Acre, darting from side to side but left alone as the
guns could only fire above forty-five degrees for fear of hitting the beaters
thrashing the undergrowth and driving the pheasants into the greyness of the sky.
The air grew colder with the closing day and by three o'clock the guns were silent
and the hip flasks tipped and sucked, feet stamped, end arms thumped across the
well-padded chests and the red glow of healthy faces sparkled with the pleasure of
the shoot. Forty-seven guns had killed three hundred and eight pheasants of which
only two were hens, caught flying too close to the cocks. The shoot tramped back in
the growing dusk and came to the long slope that led up to Merry Hall on its
ancient hill. The east wind had stopped and into the crisp, afternoon air of October
drifted the smoke from sixty-three fire places inside the Hall, fingering up from the
tall chimney stacks, clasped in stacks of four, red stoned and old, above the new
roof. Lights glowed from windows tucked among the granite walls and beckoned
them out of the cold. As they converged on the sweep of gravel path in front of the
great, studded oak door that dominated the front centre of the house, it was calls of
'how many' and 'well done, old boy', and the constant stamp of cold feet on the
hard gravel and they went inside to the warmth of fires and butter-run crumpets,
chocolate cakes, fresh sandwiches by the tray, steaming cups of tea and the house's
famous, spice-rich punch, steaming on both sides of the big, log-filled fire in the
gun-room that led off from the great hall. Servants took the dead birds to the
underground cellar where they would hang till maggots appeared in their dead,
sightless eyes or their necks gave way and plummeted their ripe carcasses onto the
old stone floor that had felt a million feathered birds in its time. Casks of old,
maturing port looked on with approval watching across to rows of dusty bottles,
necks stuck out from their pigeon holes and ready for the opening. The roof was
low as the men who had built it were smaller than today, and Pavy supervising the
hanging, was stooped from his six foot height and cramped in his shoulders. The
two hens were left forlornly at the end of the line, heads bowed in the line of duty.

REGGIE BEAUMONT PLONKED his briefcase at the end of the long table in the library,
opened the clasp and pulled out three files.

"We've half an hour before the dinner gong. Should be enough. Thelma, please
pass round the attendance register for everyone to sign. So far as the Companies
Act is concerned, this is an important meeting. It changes the whole structure of
Beaumont Ltd. You've all read the minutes of our last meeting. May I sign them,
Thelma? Pass me the minute book when you are finished. I've asked Mr van der
Walt to join us by invitation. He will answer any questions should you have any.
After the last minutes, the second item on the agenda is the restructuring of
Beaumonts and its flotation in London and New York. We have basic approval from
the banks who consider we will be oversubscribed. Overdrafts against the
restructured company have been approved by the banks, headed by Lloyds.

Attached to your minutes is the bank's Letter of Intent. Seeing that it is now Saturday and I only asked them on Monday, it says something for Lloyds Bank and our companies. Are we all agreed on the new format?"

"Can we discuss item three first, Reggie?"

"Why, François?"

"Because the restructuring is only relevant if we approve this massive new expenditure on mineral exploration and island clubs."

"That's the whole idea," said Reggie, "It's the way to raise the money."

"My question is, do we wish to raise it?"

"Why ever not? Everything is in the report and if there are any technical points, Koos is here to answer them as he did to the banks."

"It's not technical, it's principle," said François and Carl nodded his head in agreement, a gesture that Reggie picked up immediately. "Why do we have to stick our necks out when we have a perfectly good business making more money that we can spend? Union Mining was a viable company in its own right with assets far in excess of the price we paid for its shares. There was no gamble, the only problem being bank-bridging finance. This whole report in front of me is conjecture. We don't know if we'll find any minerals and we don't know if the people will come to our club. Against this we are gambling our existing assets. Union Mining has enough cash flow problems bringing Kloof Mine into production. And with war coming up we're going to need our reserves. Gunter tells me war is inevitable and I agree with him. Reggie, the timing is wrong."

"Alright," said Reggie, "we may have to shelve the club if war breaks out but minerals will be at a strategic premium. If we find what we're looking for even the government will throw money at us to get the stuff out of the ground. Why do you think base minerals are rising every day? Look at rubber. We've made enough out of rubber."

"At no risk, Reggie. We bought in a rising market."

"I agree," said Carl. "Why must we chance what we've built to create money we can't spend? Why take the chance?"

"That's how we started," said Reggie. "Don't you remember four impecunious undergraduates?"

"Then," persisted Carl, "we had nothing to lose. Why are you trying to do it, Reggie?"

"I'll tell you why. If business isn't fun it isn't worth being in. We all agreed reinsurance had become boring so we went for a mining house. Now we own the damn thing we've got to do something with it. If we don't find anything, the way I've structured the new companies will mean the government will pay half the loss in tax rebates. You said we're too rich for normal needs so let's use our wealth and gut feeling to try for the top. A company left dormant only goes one way. Look at Union Mining before we got hold of it."

"Consolidation, Reggie," said François.

"`Balls," said Reggie. "Sorry, Thelma. This is not a gamble in terms of horses and roulette wheels. It is a calculated business proposition, the likes of which don't come up twice in a lifetime and we only have till the end of next month; that's six weeks, to submit our tenders to the South African government. The banks are going for it, why can't we?"

"That's my point," said François. "The banks have collateral. They never lend without it. We have a major cough in our cash flow and the bloody banks will own us. Ralph Sender can create problems. Legal documents, like our treaty, are all very well if all parties wish to honour them. Insurers are greedy. If they can see a way of stopping our commission they'll do it. Sure, we sue them but meanwhile the banks have taken over. We will be using that income to finance our prospecting, to pay dividends, to pay interest to the banks. Take it away and we don't exist, Reggie."

"There is an element of risk in anything."

"Well this one's too big for me," said François. "I'm sorry Reggie. I've gone with you every other time."

"And Carl agrees with you?"

"I'm afraid so Reggie."

"Well. We're partners. Directors. You have the same say as me and I'll tell you now, there's no way I would go ahead on such a project without unanimous support. Let's thrash it out. Gunter?"

"I don't think I can come into this one way or the other for obvious reasons. I can't even tell you what is happening with my business."

"Chuck?"

"I don't quite go along with François and Carl on this one but then I've had longer to look at it and get my gut feeling in place, to use Reggie's word. The thing I like is Koos here, putting all his money on the nail.

"That's what I call putting his money where his mouth is if you'll excuse me the expression. All mining companies put a good part of their earnings into exploration or else they'd go out of business."

"That's right, Chuck," said François, "but not all of it."

"Sometimes in life you've got to go for broke. It's the difference between those in life who win and those who don't. That's how we built the good old U.S. of A. But just let me say I'm the new boy in this outfit, but for my money I'll take the risk."

"What would you do if we went broke?" said François.

"Start again. I didn't have much at the beginning."

"But that's my point. We've got it. Why gamble?"

"The most difficult thing in business is holding on to what you've got," agreed Reggie. "If you don't go forward you lose everything anyway."

"I can't agree," said François.

"I'm sure as glad we gotten round a table," said Chuck.

"Do you want more time?" asked Reggie.

"I don't think so. It's the principle of throwing everything into one venture, casino or no casino."

"This one I didn't expect," said Reggie, smiling. "Who wants a drink?"

"I could use one," said Chuck.

"I'll get a bottle of scotch," said Reggie. "You can talk without me and I can think. There's got to be a way to please everyone," and Reggie left the room in silence and went to look for Pavy. No-one looked at each other after the door had been closed softly. François got up and went to the fire.

"It's just too fast," he said after a moment. "We don't have time to consolidate. To build up cash."

"We just made half a million sterling in Singapore," said Chuck, lightly.

"It's a percentage," said Carl, "but a small one when he wants to go off on this scale. This can break the partnership."

"That must never be allowed to happen," said Gunter, quietly. "Let's put that up now as the first priority. Are we agreed?"

"I certainly don't wish to break the partnership," said François.

"So it's a good old compromise we're looking for," said Chuck.

"That report is quite clear," said François. "We either tender big or not at all. If it was only half the size I would squash my qualms and go along with it."

"I don't understand," said Koos. "The exploration expenditure will have been raised from outside sources with the added incentive of being tax deductible against your surplus income."

"We are effectively selling half our shares," said François.

"Reggie's not asking you for money François," put in Chuck.

"He's mortgaging my shares," said François. "I'm perfectly happy with the way its been invested at present. We have a good spread in reinsurance, mining and trading. Why must we change?"

"It's the opportunity, how I see it," said Chuck. "I've made some enquiries. Anglo-American. De Beers. Rio-Tinto, Goldfields. They are all tendering big."

"They are mining houses," said François, obstinately.

"So is Union Mining," put in Koos, feeling the unaccustomed collar of his dinner jacket with its black bow-tie.

"Union Mining isn't big enough," said Carl.

"It has the reputation," said Koos. "We have the geologists, the experience. We just want money."

"And as for this island casino."

"I made enquiries," said Chuck, and Thelma let a small smile fleetingly cross her face.

"Yes. A gambling licence off the coast of Florida would be like printing money. Reggie can get a licence and Tony sure knows how to run one of those places. Yes, sir, he sure knows how to run it. Best looking broads I ever seen and he keeps the new ones coming, sure as hell he does. Put that on a little island just off America along with a battery of roulette wheels and we'll have ourselves a bunch of money. Can't fault that idea seeing Reggie can get us a licence."

"It's not what we started," said François. "We are reinsurance brokers."

"You want to stay there with the insurance business all your life?"

"Why not?"

"Because it is boring," said Gunter. "I am also diversifying. Very much. It will be to all your benefits spreading the risk. It is the principle of insurance."

"We are all equal partners," said François. "Reggie can't just push these things on us. In chancing his fortune he's also chancing ours."

"Well I don't see it like that," said Chuck, getting up from the table in his tuxedo. "But I'm the new boy. Were it not for Carl, here, and I wouldn't be saying anything, but before I came in with you fellows I made myself some enquiries." Chuck paused and turned back to them, again missing Thelma's smile. She looked at each of them in their evening clothes and then back at Chuck, the blue cloth of his tuxedo contrasting violently with the black of the European dinner jackets. She leant forward on purpose in her low cut evening dress and saw François snatch a glance down her cleavage.

"You make a lot of enquiries," said François.

"Sure, that's good business. What I found out was that all along its been Reggie Beaumont who put up the ideas. Continental reinsurance up at Oxford. Putting the Freebooters together. Good connections, all of you. And it worked. Made rich men out of you all in one hell of a fancy time. And then he comes up with that reinsurance treaty and wasn't that one hell of a good one. Then he gets out in front of Goldfields and buys Union Mining for half of its real value and Koos knows that better than I do. Gunter's up to things I don't even want to know about but what did you two guys put in the soup pot?"

"And you?" asked Carl.

"Well, one hell of a bunch of guns for starters."

"Partners can't evaluate who creates the most wealth," said François. "Without Carl and me the treaty could have flopped."

"Sure. And don't get mad at me. We play our parts but Reggie has always played the big one. Goddamn it, the company's called Beaumont Ltd."

"We are directors of the company," said François. "Looking after the best interest of the shareholders and staff. There are thousands of outside shareholders in Union Mining. We are also gambling with their money."

"Well, I as sure don't see it as a gamble," said Chuck. "Looks like plain good business to me. And Reginald must be distilling that whisky himself, the time it's taking him to get a bottle. Now there's another good idea while we're on the subject. Why don't we go on out and buy ourselves a whisky distillery?"

"Let's be serious, Chuck," said François.

"Oh, I'm sure as hell serious. Wars always make people thirsty. Why don't you take the report to bed tonight? Sleep on it. Then change your minds, 'cause if I know Reggie as I think I do, he's going to have his way. He's sure made up his mind."

"He'll never split the partners."

"Sure he won't. He'll just buy you out at three times earnings or haven't you read the Articles of Association recently. I made enquiries about them and it says if any partner disagrees with the chairman on a major issue and votes against him at a meeting of directors, then he's got to offer his shares to the said chairman who can pay him over five years. I couldn't see how Reggie kept control of the company with only twenty percent of the shares until I read that Article. Sort of makes Reggie's shares voting and yours only voting if you agree with him. Damn clever. Your shares earn say one pound so all he's got to pay you is three pounds spread over five years. That way he pays us out of after tax earnings or in simple terms, pays us with our own money. It's still a good deal for us if you work back that we wouldn't be making five percent of what we are on our own. The only way to make money by selling shares is if this deal goes through and we go public. There are sure no flies on Reginald Beaumont which is why my money stays on him. He just wants control of the money he's made us. Seems fair. Now, if anyone can find a real problem with those proposals, I'm sure as hell Reggie will look at them and that's the way we pay our way. Using our brains to stop any damn mistakes."

"He wouldn't force us to sell."

"Want a bet? And if you do, don't. The hill isn't worth the climb. Why don't we just postpone this board meeting and go and find the chairman. He should have found the scotch bottle. Isn't that the dinner gong? And Thelma, may I suggest everything we've said without Reggie is off the record and not for the minute book."

"I'll second that," said Gunter getting up from the library table. "Chuck and I have had more time to talk to Mr van der Walt, François. Why don't you use this weekend? The bank manager's here as well. I'm sure we'll have a unanimous decision as usual. Thelma, gentlemen, shall we join the ladies for dinner? As you know my wife, unfortunately, was unable to join us this weekend. Not well at all, poor Birgitt. Not well at all."

Thelma looked away and in getting up from the table, she gave François another quick glimpse of her cleavage.

"WE CAN'T TALK NOW," said Reggie, "that was the dinner gong."

"Which means," said Isabel, "that your father will be dispensing sherry in the drawing room for the next half hour. There's no-one in the morning room."

"I'm meant to be at a board meeting and it wasn't going very well. Mother collared me and wanted all my news about Geoffrey, and then we got talking about Tug and how it was about time he brought his wife and children to Merry Hall. I didn't even get them a scotch."

"They can make up with a sherry. You've had since Tuesday to come to a conclusion. The Berkeley was nice. We must lunch more often."

"Well, five minutes," said Reggie. "And we can't talk in the corridor. Have you put Pippa next to Chuck?"

"Of course. And Thelma next to François and you and Carl on the side of me. I've put all the horsey people at Henry's end of the table and they'll have a wonderful time. The table decorations are beautiful. Bonner produced some lovely hot-house flowers. Close the door, Reggie… Well, should I tell him?"

"No. I've thought a lot. Telling Henry he's not Rosalyn's father won't help anyone. The family, you, Henry, Rosalyn, Carl for that matter though I'm sure he'd be shocked to find he's a father. So long as Henry believes it's his daughter then the reality doesn't matter. He loves the child and provided no-one tells her she'll be none the wiser. The alternative is a disaster."

"And if I have a boy?"

"Fine. Henry will be lucky."

"And the title will go out of the family after nine hundred years."

"I don't understand."

"How would you have reacted if Rosalyn had been a boy? Heir to the baronetcy to Merry Hall. You've always been concerned about perpetuating the family and its ancestral home. The new roof, for instance."

"But Rosalyn is a girl and the girls don't inherit."

"The next one might be a boy."

"As I said. Good for Henry. I'll see he inherits enough money to keep up the Hall."

"You don't understand, Reggie. Your elder brother Henry can't have any children. He fires blanks, to put it crudely. Everything works in its fashion but it just doesn't lay any eggs."

"How do you know?"

"I'm married to him. Soon after Rosalyn was born I became broody. That was six months ago and nothing's happened. Before that we'd tried but without Carl I'd still be childless."

"Has he been tested?"

"Of course not. After Rosalyn there wasn't any point. As it stands, you are the heir to Merry Hall and the title. You and your children. But if I have a son the whole structure falls. And I'm going to have more children Reggie."

"You're going to take a lover?"

"Carl's here and horny. When I do the job properly they don't forget and when they do me properly I don't forger either. Your brother is two strokes and away and a woman needs time. Henry thinks of horses and heirs to Merry Hall. Provided he's shot his lot that's good enough. Quite proper in fact."

"There will be a scandal if you have affairs."

"Probably. The country people gossip far too much and most of the women know their husbands would like to put me on my back. No, there won't be any problem with takers."

"Not in this area," said Reggie, quickly. "Town possibly. A foreigner like Carl but you can't start screwing the local gentry."

"Well, I will, unless you agree to my plan and I think it answers everybody's problem, yours, mine and the family's."

"I don't have any problems. Well, apart from François and Carl being obstinate about our company developments."

"You don't want to get married?"

"I haven't met anyone suitable. But anyway…"

"How old are you?"

"Thirty. You know that."

"Not married by thirty indicates a happy bachelor life. Apart from the physical side you are happier to live on your own."

"Yes, but what's that…"

"… got to do with it? Nothing if your brother was able to have sons. As it is, it's your duty to have the sons and heirs."

"There is Beau and Adam."

"Would you really like Adam to inherit Merry Hall? And Tug's older than Geoffrey and you yourself said they were legally married under British law. So it's your children or Adam unless I have an illegitimate son that would be difficult to prove after Rosalyn. But there is a solution," said Isabel, smiling up to Reggie.

"What's that?" said Reggie, quickly.

"You and me, Reggie. It's perfect. I've always wanted you and if you once try it out you'll want me as well. On the surface I'm distant and cold but underneath I'm as kinky as hell and what an imagination. You get a son and heir. Merry Hall gets the right bloodline and I get a proper fuck every now and again."

"You can't be serious?"

"Perfectly, Reggie. I'm certainly not going through life with a twice weekly bing, bang, thank you ma'am. I've also got hormones, Reggie Beaumont. We don't have to make a regular thing of it. Just enough to keep me from going screaming mad. And I can see some theatre at the same time. Henry will find me much more chirpy. We can have two or three sons and really make sure of the line. You can take me to Bretts. That place really has atmosphere. Now, don't tell me you're thinking of marrying?"

"No, I'm not thinking of getting married."

"Well that's settled then. When are we going to start?"

"The whole idea is quite ridiculous."

"Is it, Reggie? You give it some thought. And when you do, remember I've already produced one child that doesn't have an ounce of blood from the old Norman, Sir Henri de Beaumont."

"It's bribery."

"Of course. But a lot of fun. Come on, now. You can take me into dinner. We can say we've been talking about father's directorship. You see, we do have a lot in common and once you become accustomed to the idea, you'll thoroughly enjoy yourself. Just watch how Carl looks at me at dinner tonight and you'll see what I mean. It's the best of both worlds."

ONE FRONT CORNER of Merry Hall, the opposite one to the tennis court, constituted the dining room and along its west wing ran a well heated conservatory that specialised in tropical plants and flowers. Orchids were the main speciality and the particular pride of Bonner, the head gardener. The long mahogany table, with its three extra leaves, held court in the centre of the Chinese-carpeted room and was flanked by twenty-eight high backed and gilded dining room chairs that had been in the Beaumont family since before the Napoleonic wars. At each place setting stood a card on which had been beautifully calligraphed the name of a guest. Beside each card that bore the name of a lady stood an orchid corsage made from the best blooms in the conservatory, the big doors to which were open to the dining room giving it an air of the tropics with hot, plant-tilled humidity, culminated by lush green ferns.

Pavy, the butler, in pin-striped morning dress and fresh white gloves, slowly paced behind the chairs, checking for discrepancies that were difficult to find in his well trained staff. Finally, he inspected the rows of wine bottles and decanters. The red wines had been decanted earlier in the afternoon. Satisfied with everything, he went to the large doors and opened them to the reception room. The hubbub of conversation almost ceased.

"My lords, ladies and gentlemen. Dinner is served," and Pavy turned back into the dining room and signalled the servants to serve the crocks of clear, game soup.

The ladies were shown into the dining room and seated by Pavy. Grace was said by Sir Thomas. Six waiters set down the crocks of soup after the ladies had pinned the orchids to their evening dresses. A clink of silver spoons on well glazed china broke into the general buzz of conversation made louder by the sherries. The soup was followed by well-hung game that had been gently roasted by Doris Breed and soaked in a mix of hot port wine, cream and spices.

Fifteen minutes later the door opened from the kitchen and three waiters in short, green jackets and black trousers followed each other into the room carrying long, silver trays on which in full splendour rested suckling pigs.

By half past nine the guests, bloated with food and wine, were given a half hour to rest with nuts and fruit and vintage claret. At ten o'clock, Doris Breeds's famous boiled, ginger pudding was shown into the room, so light and fluffy it resembled a soufflé, and despatched to the guests covered in a wine fruit sauce. With the pudding, a very dry, French champagne was served in the last, tall fluted glasses and by the time it was finished the guests were tipsy and happy as crickets. Lady Beaumont led the ladies to the powder room and left the well satisfied men to port, coffee and Havana cigars. Within minutes, the room was blue with rich, cigar tobacco smoke and the noise level of the conversation had risen considerably. At ten forty-five, Sir Thomas rose and suggested they join the ladies in the drawing room and led the way, cigar held firmly between his fingers and his left ear cocked to a story being told by one of his cronies.

A WHITE, hoar frost had already gripped the lawn and blades of grass broke under their feet like so many shards of glass. The colours from the full moon were black shadows to twisted grey, oak fingers against the star-filled sky. There were no clouds.

"Can you see?" asked Reggie, well wrapped up in a large, fur-lined coat.

"Don't need the torch," said Gunter, looking up at the clear night sky. "Perfect night for a bombing raid."

"Don't talk that way."

"Can you imagine, Reggie? How bloody stupid. Me up there dropping bombs on Merry Hall. It's unimaginable."

"What a sick world!"

"What can we do?"

"Nothing," said Reggie. "Live through it. Enjoy while we can what we can."

"Doris Breed's cooking," said Gunter, appreciatively.

"Marvellous, isn't it?"

"I'm positively bloated. A walk in the night air was what I wanted. There's nothing worse than sleeping on a belly full of food and red wine. Claret was delicious."

"Matures well in the cellar. Temperature constant throughout the year. A frost like this can never get at the heart of Merry Hall. How far do you want to walk?"

"As the mood takes us. You're not cold?"

"Only my feet. How is your side of the business?"

"Very good. Many government contacts. Some I don't like but if I don't supply someone else will."

"How I felt about guns."

Hands deep in their overcoat pockets, they crossed the lawn and took the path between the herbaceous borders with the silent, dark rhododendron bushes behind and backing up to the elm tree.

"Not even a mouse out tonight," said Reggie, stopping and listening. "Not a sound except the cold gripping harder. Chuck seems to be winning with Pippa. She was listening to his every word, wide-eyed."

"He's a good catch. Did you speak to my father-in-law?"

"Yes."

"And?"

"He knew. Had done since she was twelve. She had an affair with her house mistress at boarding school. Taught her all the tricks. Gave her an appetite. The Baron thought she would grow out of it. Being very pretty she was never short of companions. Her family background gave her a chance to corrupt a string of girls. You know what they'll do at school to be popular. Birgitt was always the pack leader and told the ones she fancied to take down their knickers or they'd be out of the crowd. Nearly broke the Baron's heart. Did it right there in his own schloss, servants or no servants and you know they miss nothing. When she was seventeen a man seduced her badly and that was the end of it. The first woman was terrific. The first man was crude, painful and only wanted to get himself off. They say that's how it goes, Gunter. Most women have some lesbian tendencies but it isn't a crime so you don't hear about them like the men. Look, I'm putting it like the Baron put it to me. It seemed more understandable. Apparently, her mother didn't like her either, which didn't help. As he put it to me he had to do something and you were the answer to his social prayers. Once she was married, everything would be forgotten and if she did get her hands into knickers again it wouldn't matter. No-one would ever believe it. The Baron's great hope was that you would convert her again. He saw how much you loved her. He knew you were straight so he didn't say anything. Just hoped. What would you have done as a father?"

"But why did she marry me if she hates men to touch her?"

"She saw the problem herself. As a single woman of twenty-two she was finding it difficult to circulate. Much easier to ask a pretty, innocent woman home if you're married. Her real excitement, according to her father, is seducing girls who have never had a woman. The Baron said that when you came along he was at the stage where she was uncontrollable and a full-scale scandal was inevitable. The Baron loves his daughter, Gunter. You know her good qualities. Apart from her sexual preference, she's perfect. We all have our flaws."

"Some flaw... What does he think I'll do?"

"He hopes you'll carry on. Enjoy her good qualities. Give her a child. She's said she'll do that. In fact she likes children. Make a good mother. The physical side of a marriage doesn't last very long."

"For me it would with her."

"Only time would have told. The Baron says you are rich enough to set up a mistress. Just keep up appearances. In years to come you'll grow to love each other for reasons other than sex. And it is a short part of the day. I know, it's a kick to your pride. Everyone's blind when in love."

"It was so perfect."

"Then maybe you should have seen there was something wrong. Nothing is perfect. You couldn't even handle the scandal of that kind of divorce. The dirty papers would keep it going for months and keep on looking for new stories afterwards. They would never let you alone. It's a horror Gunter for you and her father. Treat her with a lot of sympathy, care, understanding. Just to tell her you understand the problem will go a long way to solving it. Talk to your wife."

"Maybe it is better in life not to fall in love," said Gunter after a while as they crossed the formal gardens into the woods and the gnarled oaks of the centuries.

"Maybe. I don't know. Life's full of tricks. You'll come out of this one. Fact is, knowing you, you'll come out of it stronger."

"I'll have to think."

"Why don't you stay at Merry Hall for a week? I'll be down again next weekend. Think it out. Go for long walks. Ride the horses. Take up Mathilda if you like. She's parked in the new cowshed at the Thirty Acre. Get away."

"Thanks, Reggie. Maybe I feel a little better. You're right, a lot is pride. For God's sake, the source of a man is in his manhood."

They walked on into the wood and Reggie used his torch to see the way along the winding footpath. Gunter thumped his arms across his chest and stamped his feet to keep up the blood circulation.

"Glad to be out of the smoke," said Reggie. "Don't get enough exercise in London. Doris Breed's the best cook in the world. That ginger pudding was as light as a feather."

"And the pheasant sauce."

"Soup wasn't bad."

"Not bad at all." They walked on in companionable silence.

"The world's fucking crazy," said Gunter.

"And you chose the right word. Maybe we should both thank our lucky stars every morning we were born normal. What happened in the meeting while I was out?"

"François's going to give you problems."

"He'll come round. So will Carl. The figures speak for themselves. Bankers don't jump onto bad risks. They raised the money in two days."

"He's jealous, Reggie."

"What?"

"Jealous of you."

"Don't be ridiculous."

"He was alright in the reinsurance business. He could contribute. To some extent, he helped with the treaty. Union Mining was handed to him. A present. The Far East trading house. A present. And now one that will make the reinsurance side insignificant in five years."

"What's his worry? He's making money."

"Pride."

"I don't believe it. I sweat my guts out to do deals. Fight with bankers, opposition mining houses, the Ralph Senders of this world. Put it all together and find I've hurt my partner's feelings. Well maybe he should vote no and I'll buy him out if that's how bloody grateful he is. François, of all people."

"Splitting the partnership is not the answer. You'll need them, Carl and François, as you get bigger. The most difficult thing to find is management you can trust. And we all do trust each other. If anyone has a go at you, François is the first to defend. This one is like a family squabble. There's an easy way to put it right."

"How?"

"Give him something to do. Let him contribute. Chuck doesn't feel jealous as he put in the guns. I don't," said Gunter, smiling, "because I've got something going that's even bigger than yours. And that would be a damn sight easier if we had the clout of one company. Same with your exploration. No, you've got to find something special for Carl and François." They walked on in silence.

"Thanks, Gunter," said Reggie.

"It's what friends and partners are for."

"I hope to God we don't go to war."

"So do I. If the politicians would get out of the way of business we could turn this earth into a paradise. Of one thing I can say. We'll have a little tractor for your undeveloped countries that will sell for under thirty pounds. And it works. Fact is it's damn difficult to break which is what you want when they don't know maintenance. Put in diesel, press starter and off she ploughs."

"You serious?"

"Never more."

"That will make more money than all the gold in South Africa. That one you can eat."

"You were the one to give me the idea."

"Wrong. It was Tug."

"How is he?"

"Not really sure."

"You want to talk?"

"Not about this one. Not yet. We'd better get back. Feeling better about Birgitt now you know?"

"In a way."

"Did you hear that old owl?" said Reggie. "I think he knows me. There hasn't been a sound and now as we turn back he gives me a hoot."

"There are a lot of things we don't understand," said Gunter.

HENRY BEAUMONT TURNED the page of yesterday's copy of *The Times*, crumpling the flimsy pages so that he was forced to put down his half-eaten piece of toast. After a few moments of irritating straightening he was able to continue reading the report on page four.

"Bloody Huns," he said to the empty breakfast table and the clock on the mantelpiece strenuously chimed eight, sonorous notes. Henry looked at the clock until it had finished chiming, picked up his piece of toast and without looking at what he was doing, crunched a mouthful and left his teeth marks clearly in the butter. The fire crackled in the grate opposite the heavily laden sideboards with rows of covered dishes kept hot by mentholated spirit burners. Down the centre of the starched white tablecloth, laid for ten, clustered pots of marmalade, sugar bowls, butter dishes and jugs of freshly made tomato juice.

Henry put down the newspaper and got up to pour himself a third cup of tea. He dropped in one lump of sugar and sat back at the table, automatically adjusting his old school square. Henry Beaumont had a fetish about not sitting down to Sunday breakfast in his churchgoing clothes. He preferred to change later. Back in his newspaper and the last piece of his toast, he ignored the opening door.

"Morning, Henry."

"Oh," said Henry looking up. "Morning, Reggie. Bloody Huns are spoiling for a war."

"Yesterday's paper?"

"The devilled kidneys are delicious."

Reggie walked down the sideboard and lifted the covers. "Scrambled eggs," said Reggie.

"Ducks' eggs," said Henry without looking up.

"Ever tried ostrich?"

"No."

"Tea's stewed."

"Ring the bell. I like it, anyway. Drink coffee. You're up early."

"Built in alarm clock."

"Cold outside. Lawns as white as snow."

"Hoar frost. How's the bloodstock?"

"That foal of Lilliputs's is going to be a winner," said Henry putting away the paper now he had found a topic, that interested him. "After next season, Lilliput's going out to full-time stud. That's where the money lies. There's an auction next week. Merry Hall's putting up twelve yearlings. Should make money if the blighters aren't thinking about war. If there is one, you'll be in the R.A.F. Fast as that."

"Yes."

"What happens to your business?"

"Chuck's coming to run it. Roosevelt's keeping the Americans out of a European war. Why fight other people's wars?"

"Exactly. And why are we saying we'll fight Poland's?"

"Something about the balance of power."

"An air war will be bad for civilians. Article here says the German Air Force can bomb London to pieces in a week."

"Doubt it. They've got to get there. Our Hurricanes are first class and three of the squadrons are flying Spitfires. That's an aeroplane."

"Think we can stop them?"

"Of course, old boy," said Reggie sitting down with a full plate of scrambled eggs, kidneys, bacon, tomatoes and sausages. "Just because the R.A.F. behave a little mad doesn't mean we can't fly aeroplanes. Anyway, it'll be us knocking the holy shit out of Berlin. Our Lancasters and Blenheims are first rate. Berlin and back with a full bomb load."

"Crazy bloody world."

"I've taken some precautions for the family, Henry. A lot of old families were wiped out by death duties in the Great War. Three sons killed one after the other. That kind of thing. Three lots of death duties. Can you pass the toast?"

"You hungry?" said Henry passing the toast rack and noticing the pile of food on Reggie's plate.

"Famished. Always feed a hangover. What I've done is insure each of the male members of the family including the children, against what I calculate the family would have to pay in death duties."

"Who's paying the premium?"

"Me."

"That's very good of you," said Henry going back to his *Times.*

"We are up early," said Isabel, smiling confidently as Reggie looked up from his plate of food and tried not to catch her eye. She walked to the head of the table and kissed Henry on the cheek. "Good morning, darling. Did you sleep well?"

"Damn fool. Had to get up twice. Slept in my dressing room not to disturb you. How's Rosalyn? The devilled kidneys are delicious."

"Nanny's feeding her. Tea's stewed," said Isabel, ringing the bell for a servant.

"What I said?" said Reggie.

"I'm going up to London on Wednesday, Henry. I have a second fitting with the dressmaker. I'll stay at the flat. Take in a show. Wouldn't you like to take your sister-in-law to a show on Wednesday, Reggie?"

"Better than going on her own," said Henry still reading his paper. Reggie said nothing.

"I said, Reggie, will you take me to a show on Wednesday?"

"Wednesday? Let me see… very busy."

"Take her, Reggie. I'd go myself if it wasn't for the farm. Bad time of the year."

"Call me at the office," said Reggie.

"I'll come to your office at six. Ah, thank you Conway. Bring some fresh tea. Do you prefer the ballet or a musical?"

"Neither, really," said Reggie.

"How is business?"

"Well."

"He's just insured the whole bloody family against death duties," interrupted Henry, turning another page. "Bit morbid. How much am I insured for?"

"Two hundred thousand pounds."

"My, I'm worth more dead than alive."

"Not really. That will only cover death duties."

"Pass the toast."

"Certainly, old boy."

"Good Lord," said Henry, looking up. "It's all gone."

"You can ask Conway when she comes back," said Isabel.

"There were three pieces when I passed it over to you," said Henry, peevishly as his wife sat down next to him with a plate of breakfast. "You'll have to wait for toast. Newspaper's full of war."

"Have a piece of my toast," said Reggie as the door opened. "Morning, François, Carl," said Reggie looking over his shoulder. "Where's Thelma this morning?"

"She's had a tray sent up to her room," said François.

"Oh. Has she?" said Reggie, raising an eyebrow. "And how do you know?"

"Well, I was passing…"

"Help yourself," said Henry interrupting, having missed the innuendo. "Devilled kidneys are delicious."

"Morning everyone," said Carl and François.

"When you've got your food, come and sit next to me," said Isabel, smiling sweetly at Carl.

"I'm leaving for church at twenty to eleven," said Henry to his newspaper and then looked up sharply. "Ah, Conway. Can you bring more toast? Put the tea on the table next to my wife. My brother's eaten all the toast again."

"How many cups?" said Conway, not sure which job to do first.

Henry looked at her dithering and she quickly put down the tea tray and left for the toast. Wordlessly, Henry went back to his newspaper.

"We can walk up to the Leg of Mutton and Cauliflower," said Reggie. "Church always deserves a drink afterwards. Good exercise. Can you and Carl leave your offices for a couple of weeks?" said Reggie, looking at François.

"Why?"

"You were right yesterday. We can't afford to take a chance. Maybe I am looking at this one with blinkers on. What I have in mind is you and Carl going out to South Africa and looking at the whole thing again."

"Do you have to talk business at the breakfast table?" said Henry, giving his younger brother a look.

"Very briefly," said Reggie, smiling at his brother and then turning back to François as Koos van der Walt came in for breakfast. "You and Carl can make the final decision. We are equal partners so why should I put my head on the block every time?" he said with a laugh. "See all the right people... Morning, Koos. Did you sleep well?"

"Good, man. Very good."

"Help yourself to breakfast," said Reggie and paused for his brother to put in his bit about the devilled kidneys. Henry carried on reading without looking up. "Can you Koos, introduce Carl and François to the Minister of Finance, local general manager of the Standard Bank, Head of the Chamber of Mines?

"People like that."

"No problem."

"You can charter and fly yourselves around the country," said Reggie. "Get a gut feeling. I have something else in mind. Koos will have his hands full commissioning Kloof and watching the technical aspects of our prospecting. If we are going to spend all that money, I think we should have one, preferably two resident directors in the area. Give it some thought. As Henry says, we shouldn't talk business at breakfast. We can go into detail in the office tomorrow."

"How long are you staying, Carl?" asked Isabel as he began to fill a plate.

"A few days."

"I'm going to be in London on Wednesday. Do you like the theatre?"

"Reggie's taking you, dammit," said Henry.

"I was only thinking that if my brother-in-law is too..."

"I'll make the time," said Reggie.

"Well then," said Isabel.

"I'd be happy..." began Carl.

"Maybe Reggie's better. You know how people talk. It looks better being seen in public with my brother-in-law. Ah, Conway. Put the toast here. Is Lady Beaumont coming down to breakfast?"

"I took a tray up to them, madam."

"They're getting older," said Henry turning to the rugby page.

"I do hope the vicar doesn't give us a long sermon," said Isabel. "Do you want some toast, Reggie?"

"Thanks."

"How's my sister getting on with Chuck?" said Isabel as the door opened. "Talk of the devil. Have you seen Pippa this morning, Chuck?"

"Morning everyone. Not as I know," said Chuck to Isabel. "Can I have a go at flying Mathilda?" said Chuck to Reggie, as he took an empty plate from the sideboard.

"You can't fly," said François.

"Well, now, that just isn't true anymore. Couldn't have all my partners flying aeroplanes without taking lessons."

"How many hours solo?" asked Reggie.

"Two," said Chuck.

"I think you had better leave Mathilda alone a little longer," said Reggie and they all laughed except Henry who hadn't heard.

AT TEN MINUTES past eleven on the following Thursday morning, Thelma King was sitting at her typewriter, hands poised on the keys, eyes unfocused on her shorthand pad and her mind dreaming of her affair with François. She had seen him off at Croydon airport that morning at the start of his long journey to South Africa. She sighed contentedly and was answered by a cough which jerked her back to the offices of Union Mining. She looked up quickly and gasped, bringing the back of her hand to her mouth as she pushed back her typist's chair.

"I'm sorry. Did I startle you?" said the Chinaman.

"I didn't hear you come in."

'Weren't meant to,' thought Kim-Wok Ho and let the door close behind him. Thelma was still fearfully looking at the apparition standing in front of her in a floor-length, electric blue, red dragon patterned gown that buttoned up to his collar. The black skull hat, wispy black moustache and black, small eyes that were softly watching her consternation, made for her fright. His arms were folded into the sleeves of his gown allowing the 'pixied' ends to point at the ground. His feet were invisible, hidden.

"My name is Kim-Wok Ho. It would do me great honour if I could see Mr Beaumont."

"From Singapore?"

Kim-Wok Ho nodded.

"You didn't receive my cable?" he said.

"Nothing saying you were here. Arriving that is. Please take a seat."

"Thank you," and he gave her an encouraging smile showing his pure white teeth. "Is he in?"

"Yes. I think so. Well he was."

"Then he's in."

"Yes. Must be. Excuse me please. Please sit down."

"Thank you," and Kim-Wok Ho smiled again.

Thelma quickly let herself into Reggie's office, closing their inter-leading door behind her.

"Yes," said Reggie, looking up irritably.

"There's a Chinaman outside who says he's Kim-Wok Ho."

"What's the matter, Thelma?"

"He's dressed in a long robe covered in dragons."

"Quite possibly. You don't expect me to dress in his garb when I go to Singapore. I can think of nothing more ridiculous than an Englishman dressed in anything but a dark suit in England and barathea in the tropics. Show him in and let's have some coffee."

"Do you think he drinks it?"

"If he doesn't we'll have to make tea. Did you know that tea is a Chinese word?"

"No."

"Well you do now."

Reggie rose from his chair and came around his desk as Thelma let Kim-Wok Ho into the office. Reggie held out his hand.

"What a pleasant surprise," said Reggie. "We weren't expecting you in London. How is my brother?"

"I've brought him to England. You did not receive my cable?"

"Not about bringing Tug to England. Your last cable said he was on a Roman Catholic mission for which I thank you."

"Your brother is very bad, Mr Beaumont. He needs a good hospital, not a mission station. I bring him back in the flying boat with the pilots. He is still on board. Lord Angus is with him. We cleared customs and immigration and I caught a cab straight here from the Pool of London. You know a good doctor? Specialist?"

"Come and sit down," said Reggie, going to the door. "Thelma. What did you find out about a drug abuse specialist?"

"There's one in the Lake District. Has his own clinic. I have the address and phone number."

"Phone them and book in Tug. Mr Ho has brought him back to England." And turning back to Kim-Wok Ho said, "We can fly him up in the Sunderland. Let's go."

"No. If I may presume. It is better for you to see him when he has been dried out. Bad memories do not fade at night. It is the same as a bad illness but you will both be embarrassed. Let him get well and then he can tell you what he wants. Lord Angus can book him into the clinic."

"You think so?"

"I have seen opium. You have not. Your pilot did well with the delivery. Very dangerous."

"I'll pay him a bonus."

"Give it to him… Gauguin?" said Kim-Wok Ho walking behind Reggie's desk to inspect the paintings.

"Yes. They belong to Tug. Where is his wife?"

"At the bungalow with the children. I sent my," and he coughed politely, "housekeeper to explain. They know each other. My housekeeper will stay a while. Holiday." 'Also,' thought Kim-Wok Ho, 'it keeps her out of mischief while I am away.' "May I presume again?"

"Of course."

"Dismiss your Mr Marshbank."

"Whatever for?"

"My housekeeper tells me that Mr Marshbank deliberately took your brother to the opium dens to make him addicted and dependent upon Mr Marshbank. Mr Marshbank, according to my housekeeper, has an obsession about your sister-in-law."

"Your housekeeper seems to find out a great deal of information."

"I have checked her information. It is correct."

"I can't just fire him by cable."

"Then instruct him to fly to England. Once he is out of Singapore he will be unable to cause you harm. My people tell me there are two sides to Mr Marshbank. Bring him back by boat. By the time he arrives, Tug will be coherent and I will have received a letter from my housekeeper after she has spoken to Tammany. I find it difficult to understand why Mr Marshbank thought it necessary to go to the bungalow with the flying boat. I asked Lord Angus and he tells me that Mr Marshbank spent one night alone with Tammany in the bungalow."

"He has probably slept there many times."

"Lord Angus saw him smoking an opium pipe before he went to the bungalow. Did not behave normally the next day and when they returned after the delivery he was inclined not to ask Tammany to cook them a meal. My housekeeper will find out."

"Who on earth is your housekeeper?"

"An English girl, twenty-three-years-old. She is very pretty," smiled Kim-Wok Ho, tightening the slants to his eyes. "I have also found out she is very astute."

"She sounds a perfect gem," said Reggie, picking up his telephone. "New system. They call it a switchboard. She can talk to me and put calls through. American."

"Whatever will they think of next?"

"One wonders. Thelma?"

"Yes, Reggie?"

"We want to get Tug up there right away. Can you take a taxi to the flying boat's berth at the Pool with directions for Angus?"

"I'll type them out first."

"And book a passage for Mr P Marshbank on the P & O Line. Singapore, Southampton. First available berth and cable Mr Marshbank I want a meeting with him in London. Make it sound friendly and send him my best regards. Instruct P & O to tell us if he doesn't board the ship. And please stop calls."

"Do you want the coffee?" asked Thelma.

"Coffee, Mr Ho?" asked Reggie.

"Thank you," smiled Kim Wok Ho having settled himself comfortably into the sofa.

"It seems so out of character," said Reggie, putting down the receiver. "Public school. Colonial Service. The man was a District Officer. Tug's best friend. Only friend, once he became involved with Tammany."

"Maybe you should check his credentials. Sarawak is a long way from England. We've had a number of odd characters despatched to the East and when they arrive they tell a very different story to the truth."

"But the Colonial Service?"

"Influence. You can have anyone sent anywhere if you have enough."

"I'll write to Mrs Gray in Kuching and have her help Tammany. She's back with her husband. Somewhat contrite. She'll help.

"I'm glad you'd like to come into the public company. I have a detailed report on our future developments. But what else can we do together in Singapore? Guns are out for the moment."

"Medicines. There'll be a terrible shortage before long. My father is with Mao Tse-Tung."

"The Communist?"

"Father seems to think he will conquer China. If we can supply modern medicines to both armies we will grow rich and save lives."

"I like it better than guns."

"I have a list from my brother who is fighting with Mao Tse-Tung. He will pay us cost plus twenty percent. Cash against documents; delivery Shanghai. The drugs are light in weight and high in value."

"The flying boats."

"We are in full control until such time as we are paid."

"That should keep Angus out of debt. I wonder where the hell I'll buy all this lot from," he said looking through the list. "But we'll find out.

"Thanks, Thelma. Don't bother to pour the coffee. Just get on over to Angus. They'll be able to fly in daylight. Tell Angus to call in tomorrow for his money. Tell him the balance has been sent to his father… He hasn't gone forever."

"Are you teasing me?"

"Of course not. Do you think he will like South Africa?"

"I've no idea. I'll have one of the other girls handle the switchboard while I'm out."

"I'll be taking Mr Ho to the club for lunch."

"Fine," said Thelma, raising an eyebrow in a way that indicated that that would be fun for everyone. "Shall I book a table?"

"Thank you."

"My pleasure."

'FULL MARKS,' thought Reggie as he watched the club maître d'hôtel not bat an eyelid as Kim-Wok Ho was shown into the dining room of the City Carlton Club. A number of elderly members were trying hard to make it look as if they were not watching. Overall it was if the club entertained a Chinaman to lunch every day.

"Do you know?" said Kim-Wok Ho with a smile. "I cause more of a stir in Raffles when I lunched out in this. It belonged to my great-grandfather. The stitching took three years to complete. Too hot for Singapore. Northern China is very cold, you know."

"I didn't," said Reggie, politely as they were seated. "For a pre-lunch drink, I recommend half a pint of Slack Velvet. Very smooth for cold weather. A club speciality. They use a slightly off-sweet champagne with the Guinness. That's a dark stout. Served in a silver tankard. You do drink alcohol," said Reggie as an afterthought.

"Oh, yes," said Kim-Wok Ho, bowing slightly from the waist. "My housekeeper would have left me a long time ago."

Reggie smiled up at the maître d'hôtel in confirmation.

"What day is it?" asked Reggie.

"Thursday, sir."

"That'll be roast beef and Yorkshire pudding."

"Yes, sir."

"Best roast beef in London," said Reggie, turning back to Kim-Wok Ho. "Now. Do you think our Singapore staff can handle the rubber and tin exports without Tug and Marshbank?"

"You'll have to charter the ships but the documentation was always done by them."

"A close friend of my father's is about to go on pension from the Indian Civil Service. Sir Robert Featherstone. Knighted in the new King's birthday honours. Bachelor. Hasn't lived in England for forty years. Might prefer retiring to Singapore and acting as non-executive director. He was the one who brought you and Tug together indirectly. Went to school with the Governor. Give us a bit of authority and stability."

"He's also well connected," smiled Kim-Wok Ho.

"Yes. That'll help. I'll get father to write to him. Ah. Thank you, steward. Just below room temperature. Your good health, Mr Ho. I'm enjoying doing business with you."

"Cheers," said Kim-Wok Ho and took a long draught before lowering his silver tankard, leaving a good white froth on his black moustache. "Very good."

"A favourite of mine," said Reggie looking up at a man standing by their table.

"Morning, Reggie."

"Oh. Didn't see you come in. Mr Ho, our associate in Singapore. Lord Migroyd, a director of Union Mining."

"Sad about Hensbrook," said Migroyd sitting down and indicating something similar to the steward.

"What is?" said Reggie.

"Died, this morning. On the eight o'clock news. Poor bugger. Twenty-two years of suffering. Not even the war to end all wars."

"Two of my brothers are married to his daughters," explained Reggie, wondering if Isabel was aware that her father had died. 'They'd find her at the family flat,' he thought thankfully and realised once again that the right actions in life were usually the best.

"You'll go to the funeral?"

"Of course."

"It'll be in *The Times*. Ah, thank you steward. You don't mind me joining you for a drink. Lunching that Sender man you said was giving you problems. He was so impressed with the bloody title he could barely talk in his effort to accept the invitation. You can tell me when he arrives and I'll push off. Church orphanages, you said. How the blazes I'm expected to talk through lunch about church orphanages is beyond me.

"Are you enjoying London, Mr Ho?"

"I only arrived a few hours ago."

"Any news on Malay Tin?" There was a slight pause as they each looked at each other's surprise.

"Malay Tin is on the market," Reggie said to Kim-Wok Ho as a way of explanation. "We're putting in a bid. Lionel Bennett is working on it right now."

"Companies not worth a penny," said Kim-Wok Ho. "The mine's flooded and it's too deep to pump out. Some land to sell. Bits of machinery. Had a look myself."

"That's interesting," said Reggie, quietly. "Then you'd agree that if someone knew how to pump out the water and keep it pumped out they'd make money if they buy the shares for one and three."

"A lot of money. Before the flooding, the shares were standing at three pounds four shillings and that was well before the rise in the tin price."

"We know how to pump out the mine," said Reggie. "Our South African general manager has been in England and I showed him the problem. Thought I was a complete fool. Apparently some of the South African goldmines are over a mile deep and they pull water out and push oxygen down without any problems. They couldn't operate the mines without this know-how. Our Kloof Mine shaft is already half a mile below the surface and we're pumping out water twenty-four hours a day. Normal routine. None of Malay Tin is below four thousand feet. We're making an unconditional offer to all shareholders on Monday. It'll be in the financial press."

"There are a lot of tin mines with the same problem."

"Find them for me. We'll buy them together. Five percent of the Malay Tin shares will be registered in your name, Lord Migroyd. Our way of saying thank you for the introduction. There's your man coming in. The one who looks like he doesn't belong."

"I have the feeling you two will have a more interesting lunch. Enjoy the roast beef. Nice to meet you, Mr Ho. Reggie says we do good business together and I hope to meet you again."

Reggie lifted his tankard as Migroyd greeted Ralph Sender profusely and took him over to a corner table.

"Here's to tin mining," said Reggie. "We'll book you into the Savoy after lunch and you can catch up on some sleep. I have an interest in a rather splendid night club that I'd like to show you tonight. I'll call at nine-thirty. I'm sure you'll enjoy Bretts."

"I'm sure I will," said Kim-Wok Ho.

"Would you like another Black Velvet?"

"Why, thank you," said Kim-Wok Ho, warming to his host, the lunch, the prospect of profit and the prospect of Bretts and forty girls all of whom he hadn't seen before and all of whom by report were as attractive as Sally Bollas. Kim-Wok Ho felt good as he knew that Ping-Lai Ho would be thoroughly jealous when he told him. They both smiled at each other knowing exactly what was going through the other man's mind.

"Your housekeeper won't object?" asked Reggie.

"How can she?" said Kim-Wok Ho, lifting his tankard.

9

SEPTEMBER 1939

*R*eggie Beaumont's built-in alarm clock woke him at six-thirty in the morning on Saturday the 5 September 1939 and he didn't know where he was. It was pitch dark and soundless. Reggie put out his right hand and surprisingly found the edge of the bed. Puzzled, he tried his left hand with the same result. He was in a single bed, on his own. A cock, and then a second, crowed from Bert Brigley's farmyard, the clear sound carrying across open fields and woods to Reggie's bedroom in Merry Hall, the one he had occupied since the age of five. He smiled to himself in the dark. He remembered he was at home in his own bed. The sudden warmth of security was tangible. Slowly the dawn chorus began, a few birds chirping away outside and then the hedgerows and woods, the arbours and copses, the fields of freshly cut hay and wheat came into their own and the full song of an English country morning filled his room and made him happy to bursting and gave him a great desire to be out in the lanes and the woods, to walk among the fields that had belonged to his family for nigh on nine hundred years.

Throwing back the sheets and blankets, Reggie jack-knifed out of bed and strode across the room to his oak cupboard and found an old pair of green, corduroy trousers in the growing light and an old rugger shirt, black and white rings with the one long sleeve half pulled off. Old socks without holes proved to be a problem which he solved by discarding the need for a pair. He found an old pair of gym shoes under a half stringed and warped tennis racket, and they fitted perfectly. He was outside in the long corridor before he realised he was ravenously hungry.

Immediately, he knew exactly what he was going to do. Quietly, not to wake any family or guests, Reggie wound his way through the old corridors and down servants' stairs that led off from unlikely nooks, known in detail to a small boy and now remembered with excitement by the grown man. The inner core of connecting stairs and corridors took him to the heart of Merry Hall, the great, medieval kitchens that had never been destroyed, the undisputed domain of Doris Breed. Even Sir Thomas asked permission to enter his kitchens. Reggie peered along the dimly lit flagstone floor, past the massive white scrubbed table that dominated the centre of the kitchen. Beyond were the big store cupboards, doors leading into stone floored and stone- shelved larders with lead meshed meat safes that kept the flies from the cut, uncooked joints, the hams and home-made cottage cheeses and the sour milk in bowls making junket for the children to cover with sugar and fruit. Reggie made straight for the larder that used to hold the home-made pies and savoury tarts and grunted with approval as he confronted the same array of mouth-watering food that he had first uncovered at the age of seven. Putting a hand into the meat safe, he pulled out a half of pork pie and tiptoed it to the table and followed it out with cold pheasant, pickles, a sugar and clove-coated ham, bacon and egg pie, freshly scrubbed radishes and a full heart of young celery, crisp and tender-white. Hunting around he found a wicker basket and cut from his prizes what he considered was necessary for a hearty breakfast. Hunting again he found an old Tizer bottle and tipped in three spoons of tea, blended specially and sent to his mother monthly by Fortnum and Mason. The big, pewter kettle was hot on the still hot fire. Reggie made tea in the bottle, poured in half a jug of milk and six teaspoons of white sugar. The cork-screwed black stone stopper gripped the threaded glass and hugged the red washer watertight. Deftly tossing the hot bottle from hand to hand, Reggie wrapped it in two old copies of *The Times* he found in the basket next to the kindling wood. Three not so fresh but well-buttered rolls were wrapped in muslin and with his picnic basket ready to burst he was ready to go. It was twenty minutes to seven, five minutes before Conway got up to make the early morning tea. By the time she arrived to discover the mess, Reggie had let himself out of a back gate and had crossed the moss-strewn yard and let himself out of the back courtyard through a creaking, wrought iron gate that led into the Hall's herb garden that had first been laid out during the reign of Henry VIII. From the herb garden he was out into the paddock and then off across the fields with the morning dew wetting through the canvas of his gym shoes.

His mother, who was looking out over the estate from her bedroom window, smiled happily to herself as she watched Reggie making off into the woods with his swag. She could tell, almost exactly, what was tucked in the basket and she wondered what he had used this time for his tea. Doris Breed would give her a full account of the theft before lunch and she and Doris Breed would have a glass of brown sherry together at the kitchen table to remember their years of happiness.

Reggie walked through the woods sending the rabbits scampering in the glades, the big bucks thumping their hind legs on the ground to warn everyone into the warrens. A doe got up on her hind legs, nose and whiskers twitching, to see what it was all about, saw Reggie swinging his basket and ducked back behind her tuft of grass and high tailed it off to the warren. The old owl had become hard of hearing and carried on sleeping in the elm tree, green with leaves and rich in the scent of a good summer. The worries of management had left him completely and he didn't care whether Kloof Mine came into production or the price of tin went up or down. He was free for a morning and found a good perch on the old willow tree beside the slow running Mole and the minnows he could see swimming under the weeping branches, in and out of brown, dead, leaves, pushed and turned by the gentle eddy of the flow, twig stuck and soggy, against the old, waterlogged branches. A piece of bacon and egg pie went down first and then the pheasant breast and handful of small, crunchy, pickled onions. Inside the Tizer bottle, the brown, bloated tea leaves swirled in the milky brownness and he had to let them settle before he could pour into a plastic mug that he'd found on the sink. Having eaten too much, Reggie packed the debris in the basket and began the long walk to the Thirty Acre. The sun was warm when it came down the tunnels made by cumulus cloud riding stack upon stack up into the heavens leaving blue, peep eye holes all over the sky. The clouds were white and fluffy with no menace of rain. The heavens were void of wind and hung the layers of cloud down to twenty thousand feet above the green, patchwork of the English fields. Reggie whistled as he walked, a string of nursery rhymes tumbling in his mind with thoughts of rocking horses and wooden building blocks and a great, big, sunny nursery into which he'd been born and maybe it wasn't so far away. There were larks high up in the sky, trilling away.

The Thirty Acres was full of Bert Brigley's cows and Reggie stood at the edge of the field, hands on hips, breakfast basket at his feet and wondered how best to move them without affecting their milk. Across the field he opened the barn door and smiled at the snub nose redness of Mathilda, sitting hunched and ready to go. Goggles and leather helmet were hung on a hook next to Reggie's fur-lined, flying jacket that he would need at the higher altitudes with the big, thigh-length flying boots that stood to attention beneath the coat. There were tufts of white looking, sunless grass growing inside the windowless barn and Reggie went back to push open the main doors that swung open and gaped with Mathilda down the bumpy field dotted with grazing milk-cows, not a bull among them.

"Well, we'll see," said Reggie going in again to dress for flying but keeping the goggles up on his forehead. His flying gloves were under the seat inside the aeroplane as otherwise they fell off the hook and rotted on the ground that seeped water in winter. Reggie climbed onto the bottom wing of the biplane, and then into the front, open cockpit fitting himself comfortably into the seat before, making a thorough check of his instruments, testing fuel levels in both tanks, flaps, aeroloins, tail-flap and altimeter gauge. Ready, he pressed the starter button that turned the one propeller and coughed and belched black smoke from her carburettor, through the engine and out at the back. Having ejected the excess fuel in the carburettor she fired on the second attempt and ran down smoothly to a steady roar that shook the timbers of the wooden barn. The cows out in front began to move away and Reggie eased the biplane out into the field. In short bursts, he taxied Mathilda down the field and cleared himself a path for take-off. Turning back at the barn he gave full throttle and the little biplane bounced down the field, faster and faster until Reggie eased back the stick and took them off the ground and pointed her straight at a tunnel of light that pointed to heaven, pleased with the pureness of the engine.

"There never was another mechanic apart from Tug," he said to the wind and pulled his goggles down over his eyes and let his whole body float up in the flight to freedom into a perfect world of fluffy clouds and pure blue skies and passing the larks until Reggie was above them flying high and looping the plane, barrel rolling her, stalling her and fluttering down his tunnel in the sky and pulling her out and plucking higher at the air on his way up and up and only looking up at the tunnel and singing on the top of his voice that couldn't be heard over the wind and the roar from his single engine. For those moments he was free of the world, by himself in the heaven with all the power that he needed to do what he wanted and with no-one to tell him he couldn't. After ten minutes the fuel gauge brought him back to reality and with the sadness which comes from wanting more, he cut the engine, pushed down the nose and pointed her down at Merry Hall, alive now with little people, little horses, tiny cows, a toy car coming up the driveway and he came, down silently from the heaven leaving his tunnel of cloud. Two thousand feet above the Thirty Acre he cut in the engine which roared at him in triumph and took him down and roaring across the field to warn off the cows before he came back and dropped onto earth for a perfect, three-point landing.

"UNCLE, REGGIE, UNCLE REGGIE," shouted five-year-old Adam Beaumont as he dodged along the terrace avoiding the grown-ups' legs. "Was that you up in the aeroplane and what have you got in that basket and can I have a swing on your arm?"

Reggie right angled his arm and held it rigid for young Adam to hang onto by clasping his small hands over the arm and being swung off his feet, round and round like a maypole, his long, blond hair, the same colour as his father's, streaming out with the centrifugal force. Slowing the speed and thoroughly giddy, Reggie brought his nephew's feet back to the paving amid loud shouts of, 'more, more.'

"What is in that basket?" asked Lady Beaumont as she smiled knowingly at her second son who instantly looked contrite and then broke into a good chuckle.

"Mother, you saw me crossing the fields."

"Haven't I been catching you raiding the kitchen for twenty-five years? You'd better give me the remnants and I'll return them to Doris Breed myself. You didn't ask her, did you?"

"It was too early in the morning," said Reggie, sheepishly as he handed over the wicker basket.

"Sounded good to me," said Tug striding down the terrace and taking his son's hand to stop him jumping up at Reggie's arm. "She didn't misfire, once."

"Sweet as a nut," agreed Reggie. "But that comes of having Mathilda doctored by the best mechanic in Surrey."

"I was marking the tennis court and mending the hole in the net. Are you ready for a game?"

"How about a Beaumont men's four?" said Geoffrey.

"It'll have to be you boys," said Sir Thomas. "I'm far too old for serious tennis. Henry's been looking for a good game for weeks. Damned teapot's dry," he said to his wife.

"Conway," called Lady Beaumont. "Be a dear and make a fresh pot of China tea. And some more of those home-made biscuits. Tell Mrs Breed from me they are delicious. Before you play tennis, Reggie, you must call your office. Thelma sounded very excited and said it was urgent. She wouldn't leave a message."

"It's either very good or very bad news, knowing Thelma. We've probably had a cave-in at the mine."

"Can't you ever get away from your business? I'm worried about you. You're either flying here or there or having meetings until ten o'clock at night. You must relax, Reggie. I'm your mother and I know. The body just won't take it. I was talking to poor Lady Hensbrook and she agrees with me. What are you going to do with all that money anyway?"

"Expand my business. I'll call the office and then you and I, Geoffrey, will take on Tug and Henry. We haven't thrashed them for a long time. You lot get changed and I'll be out when I'm finished. Ah, there's Pavy. Pavy, will you get my office on the line while I'm changing. Morning, Tony. How did you sleep?"

"I feel fresh as a daisy," said Tony Venturas. "Lilly and I are going to walk over to her mum and dad. If we are not back by lunchtime don't worry. I believe my father-in-law, wants to explain in depth how to prune roses."

"Do they grow roses on tropical islands?" asked Reggie.

"Most certainly," said Lilly, looking up at Tony as she hung onto his arm.

Tug watched her for a moment and then looked across the terrace at Tammany chatting away to Georgina and Isabel. Reggie caught the glances and felt a deep sensation of pleasure. At least he had sorted out that problem for the better.

"YOUR CALL, MR REGGIE," said Pavy imperiously as he handed Reggie the cream receiver that stood on the half-moon table, in the hall.

"Thelma? Morning. Where's the disaster?"

"Don't be such a pessimist," said Thelma. "First, find a chair and sit down. The triangular one from Sarawak will do. I presume you are in the hall?"

"Yes. Get on with it. I have three brothers waiting for a game of tennis."

"François phoned from Johannesburg. He was very excitable."

"The French usually are," said Reggie, sarcastically. "Did he ask you to marry him?"

"Don't you want to hear the news? I'm so excited I could burst."

"Thelma King. What has happened?"

"We've found diamonds. Not gold, copper, manganese but diamonds. Van der Walt's team have proved a diamond pipe that rivals the Big Hole at Kimberley. The stones are seventy percent gemstones and many are blue-whites. De Beers have already offered to buy it from us for five million pounds but François says he wouldn't sell for ten million. So much for the cynical François. I think the pair of them were half drunk when they spoke to me on the phone. Reggie? Reggie? Are you there?"

"Well, I'll be blowed. Have De Beers had a look at the find?"

"Yes. They only made their offer afterwards. When François refused they asked if we would be selling through the Central Selling Organisation. They are frightened our pipe will crash the diamond price unless the gemstones are marketed properly. François and Carl are looking into that one. You don't sound very excited, Reggie."

"Flabbergasted. Flabbergasted, Thelma. Until this moment I didn't realise what a gamble I'd taken. My knees are as weak as a kitten's. Send out individual cables to everyone concerned. All the geologists who were involved. Ask each of them how they are going to spend a bonus equal to a year's salary. I'll ring François and Carl myself. Hell, Thelma, I wish I was in South Africa right now."

"Maybe you don't Reggie. I've got the wireless on. They've just read the eleven o'clock news. Hitler's invaded Poland. Blitzkrieg. Tanks. Aircraft. The works."

"The stupid bastard. That means war."

"Yes, Reggie. Unless he pulls out. The British government have given him an ultimatum to pull out within forty-eight hours or consider himself at war with Great Britain."

"So much for a peaceful weekend in the country. You'd better phone my squadron and tell them I'm at Merry Hall. We might just need those diamonds, Thelma. I'll be in the office on Monday if I'm not in uniform. Cable Chuck to fly over if he isn't on his way already. Is he going to marry you?"

"Chuck?" said Thelma in surprise.

"No. François, you nit."

"He did say something about having selected the first of our diamonds for an engagement ring. He was quite sentimental and is using gold from the first pouring from Kloof Mine."

"Congratulations."

"Well, it's a start."

"You'd better get on to those cables before the lines are jammed with war rumours."

HALF AN HOUR LATER, when Reggie walked onto the tennis court to join his brothers, having given up trying to obtain trunk calls, he realised that no-one at Merry Hall had listened to the eleven o'clock news. The women were still chattering domestically and were still drinking tea. Beau was chasing Adam across the lawn and having little success with the one-year age gap. Tammany junior and Lorna, four-and five-years- old respectively, were gravely inspecting the contents of Lorna's dolls' pram at the far end of the terrace, well away from the stupid grown-ups, while Raoul, three-years- old, was digging in the rose garden with his bare hands. His face was covered in mud and Reggie smiled to himself and wondered how long he would get away with it before his mother or grandmother descended on him with a flurry of petticoats and exclamations of horror. Tony and Lilly were nowhere to be seen. His father was talking to two of his cronies under the oak tree at the end of the terrace and then the three of them got up and moved into the house for a surreptitious whisky and soda in the den. Lady Beaumont pretended not to notice. The large, white and pastel shaded hats of the ladies were keeping a strong morning sun from their faces, which was dappling their skins.

"Come on," said Henry. "We've won the toss so I'm going to serve. Elder brother's privilege. Anyway, Geoffrey's playing like a drain. Can't even hit the knock-ups over the net. Best of three sets. We'll win in two so it'll be all over well before lunch."

"Don't be too sure," said Geoffrey, taking the right-hand court. Reggie was determined to enjoy the tennis without telling any of them what he'd heard from his office.

"WELL PLAYED," said Sir Thomas, standing again on the terrace as the men's four finished. "Geoffrey, you and Reggie were a disgrace. Could have played better myself. You'd better come up and have a drink to make up for it. You've time for one before the news and then we can all sit down to lunch. Not often we have the whole family. Now, Tug, where's that beautiful wife of yours gone?" he said looking around.

"They've gone for a walk," said Lady Beaumont. "The three of them. The children have been taken up to the nursery for lunch. Raoul's not being given any jelly."

"That should cause some fun," said Geoffrey as he propped his tennis racket against the wall. "Father, why don't you give the news a miss? We're enjoying ourselves. All these rumours put a damper on things."

"Do you know something I don't?" asked his father, quickly.

"Of course not, I'm just sick of rumours. I'll have a glass of that Pimms. Reggie, come and have a Pimms. Your game was worse than mine."

"I was a little side-tracked," and Reggie caught the quick look from his youngest brother and realised why the best tennis player in the family was playing so badly.

"Why?" asked Geoffrey.

"We've found diamonds in South Africa. Rather a lot of them, as a matter of fact. Like millions of pounds worth of them."

"My goodness," said Lady Beaumont. "That is a lot."

"The gamble came off?" said Tug coming forward to shake his brother's hand.

"Yes. It has."

"I'm looking forward to sailing on Monday," said Tug. "I haven't contributed much the last two years."

"The experience in London will help you in Singapore."

"I'm going to corner the entire tin and rubber market."

"That's the stuff," said Reggie. "Give old Bertie Featherstone something to do,"

"And Marshbank some competition," said Tug quietly, his eyes as clear as they had been on his tenth birthday. If Reggie was nervous about his brother's return to the Far East, he didn't show it. The doctor in the Lake District had assured him the craving had gone and Tammany was pining for the East.

"Yes," said Reggie, "I'll have some of that Pimms. What's for lunch?"

"Are you sure you need any?" asked his mother, quizzically.

"Now, mother. That was at seven this morning. Now I'm famished."

"Fresh Scotch salmon. New potatoes. Freshly picked peas and a trifle for dessert."

"My favourite," said Sir Thomas as he poured himself a second glass of Pimms.

"Here's to Reggie's diamonds. The family can always do with money. And next year Henry's going to win the Derby. Goes without saying. Trifle, you say, my dear? Lots of sherry? Splendid. Well, come along everyone and help yourself to a Pimms. Looks as though the rain's keeping off. Don't trust those clouds behind the elm trees. Plenty of swallows. Still some summer left.

"Always make the best of an English summer, I say. How's my friend Bertie Featherstone getting along in Singapore?"

"Very well," said Reggie. "The Civil Service's loss was our gain."

"Always was a good man. Ah, there's the salmon. Better eat it now. We can listen to the six o'clock news instead. Bring your drinks over to the table. I had Pavy put out some champagne, seeing I've all my sons together. Thirty-one. Best damn vintage there ever was. Six bottles."

"You'll all be sozzled," said Lady Beaumont with a maternal smile to all of them. "Someone had better go and call the girls. Down at the rose arbour, I should think. No. Don't worry. Here they come. Lunch is served," she called in a louder voice and Isabel waved she had heard.

PAVY LEANT FORWARD to where Sir Thomas was sitting at the head of the lunch "Excuse me, sir. There is a telephone call for Major Beaumont."

"Tell him to call back," said Sir Thomas looking up sharply at his butler. "We're in the middle of lunch."

"I told the caller that, sir. But he insisted I inform Major Beaumont."

"Well you'd better go and tell him then," he said, testily.

"Very good, sir," and Pavy walked down the length of the long table set out on the terrace under the prolific greenery of the great oak.

"Have another glass of champagne," said Sir Thomas, waving a half empty bottle at no-one in particular. "Can't stand my meals being interrupted." Reaching Geoffrey, Pavy leant forward again.

"A Lieutenant Miller on the phone for you, sir. He says he is the duty officer of the day and says he would like to speak to you urgently. He's waiting on the line."

Geoffrey put down his napkin beside his plate and said, "Excuse me," and scraped back his chair. Reggie watched him go thinking, 'He's the first,' and went back to eating the perfect pink flesh of his salmon, making sure to eat the small green peas from the top of his fork and not from the upside down position.

"Anything wrong, Reggie?" asked Henry next to him.

"Shouldn't think so. The bogs are probably blocked in the officers' mess."

"Reggie. Not at the table."

"Sorry, mother," and they all tried to smother a smile.

"That must be the same Miller that went with him to Africa," said Henry, chewing contentedly.

"Yes," agreed Reggie. "Geoffrey put him up for a commission. I've met him. Good man. Type I'd like to be with in a bad spot."

"Have some champagne, Reggie."

"Thank you father. It's superb."

"Should be at the price you pay for it these days."

Geoffrey came back and sat at the table, picking up his knife and fork without saying anything. For a moment they looked at him and then resumed their lunch. The telephone rang again from inside the big house and Sir Thomas looked up irritably.

"Who has the bad manners to call at meal times?" said Lady Beaumont, as a statement from which she expected no reply.

Pavy came back onto the terrace and stood beside Sir Thomas.

"Now what is it?" asked Sir Thomas.

"There's a call for Flight Lieutenant Beaumont, sir."

"Who?"

"Flight Lieutenant Beaumont."

"You mean Reggie?"

"Yes, sir. The gentleman also enquired if Squadron Leader Venturas was staying at Merry Hall. I said he was but he was out at present and took the liberty of giving the gentleman Mr Brigley's phone number."

"You did?" said Sir Thomas.

"Can't be a gentleman phoning at lunchtime," said Lady Beaumont. "Can't he wait?"

"He said 'no' my lady."

Reggie put down his napkin, looked briefly at Geoffrey, said, "Excuse me," scraped back his chair and went into the house.

"What the hell is going on?" said Sir Thomas.

"War," said Geoffrey and everybody stopped eating to look up at him. "The Hun's invaded Poland."

"There you are," said Sir Thomas. "I told you I should have listened to the one o'clock news."

"It was why I dissuaded you, dad. The Germans went in at first light this morning. I already knew. I'd hoped we'd be able to finish lunch before that phone call."

"And what's Reggie got to do with it?" asked Lady Beaumont who knew but didn't wish to understand, having turned as white as the double-damask tablecloth.

"Quite a flap," said Reggie, coming back to the lunch. "They don't even want me to finish my lunch. Some talk of Gerry launching a surprise air attack.

"Anyway," he said, sitting down and picking up his napkin. "I'm not leaving my salmon or the champagne. Cheers, everybody. Looks like England's going to be at war by Monday. They've given Hitler an ultimatum to get out of Poland. Can't see the bastard doing it. Ah, Pavy. Can you give Mr Venturas a ring for me? Tell him to meet me at the Thirty Acre. Lilly knows where it is, it'll be quicker to use Mathilda than the Lagonda."

"Very well, sir."

"And Tug," said Reggie, looking at his brother. "Don't get any ideas about volunteering for the Air Force. I've asked Chuck to come over from America. François and Carl can handle South Africa but we must have you in Singapore. An army can't eat without tin. You must get every ounce of tin out of those mines and back to England. Rubber's the same."

"When do you have to report?" asked Georgina talking to Geoffrey.

"As soon as I've finished this lunch."

"I'll collect the children."

"No, Georgina. The L.R.U. is not staying in England. We're being flown out to France this evening. It will be better for you to stay at Merry Hall if mother and father have no objection."

Reggie studiously forced himself to finish his lunch. Silence had fallen at the table they ate. Over from the terrace, the wind ruffled the bottom of the lonely tennis net. Muffled sounds reached them from inside the Hall and a dog began to bark from a long way off. Geoffrey cleared his throat. "I'd better be off," he said. "Bye old girl," he said to Georgina and kissed her quickly on the cheek. They were all watching him. "Look after the children," he said, putting down his napkin. He got up from the table and crossed to his mother. Georgina was silently crying.

"Bye mother," he said and kissed her wrinkled cheek, dusted with the same powder she had been using for twenty years.

"Don't you need a bag?" said Sir Thomas, gruffly.

"It's in the Bentley," said Geoffrey as his three brothers got up as he shook his father's hand. The four of them walked off the terrace and down to the parked, three- litre Bentley. They shook hands firmly and then watched Geoffrey move away down the drive in the car. Pavy came out onto the terrace and stood waiting. Reggie saw him and walked back up to the terrace.

"I contacted Mr Venturas, Mr Reggie. He's going straight to the Thirty Acre. I understand that Mr Brigley has lent him a horse."

"Thank you, Pavy. Could you have Conway collect my grip? The rest can stay," and he sat down to finish his lunch.

"I'll give you a lift," said Henry.

"Thanks,"

"I'll refuel Mathilda," said Tug.

"Thanks," said Reggie.

Isabel watched him quietly and as Reggie looked up from his empty plate their eyes met for a moment. Reggie leant across and pressed Georgina's arm. She was still crying. Lady Beaumont was looking firmly down the table but her jaw muscles were moving. "Have you time for coffee?" said Sir Thomas.

"I don't think so. Tony will be at the plane in a couple of minutes. Thank you, Conway. Put it in the Lagonda. Can you drive her up to Tangmere later?" he said to Tug. "We can talk business before you sail if there isn't a flap," and he put down his napkin, pushed back his chair and crossed to his mother. "I'll give you a ring," he said to his mother, kissing her cheek.

"Yes."

Reggie shook his father's hand.

"We'd better go," said Reggie to his brothers and their mother watched for the second time. Underneath the table, her hands were clasped so tight that the blood had stopped circulating.

BOOK 2

1

APRIL 1940

*A*t seven am on Tuesday 11 April 1940 the Union Jack flapped briskly on top of the fifteen-foot high white flagpole, overlooking the Aldershot parade ground. A contingent of soldiers marched onto the square in columns of three. Henry Beaumont kept abreast of the man on his left, swinging his right arm to the exact level of his webbing belt, his thumb forced in line with the precise stiffness of his arm. His left arm protruded at right angles to his body and his left hand familiarly stopped the butt of his .303 rifle, its sling taut from the clipped barrel to the clipped butt. The khaki blanco was fresh and perfectly applied. His webbing belt and gaiters were equally perfect and his army boots shone from half an hour's spit and polish. There was not a trace of dust in the barrel of his rifle. His black beret was pulled over to the level of his right eye, the flash on his shoulder said East Surreys and his cap badge was backed by a white disc.

"PARADE HALT," bellowed the R.S.M. and the one hundred and nineteen men came to a thunderous but simultaneous halt. "IN TO LINE. RIGHT TURN," and in unison they turned to face their regimental sergeant major. "ORDER ARMS."

Henry briskly said to himself 'one, two, three, one, two, three, one,' and slammed the butt of his rifle on the tarmac precisely beside his right foot.

"STAND AT EASE."

Henry's right hand shot forward to its limit, rifle angled in front of him.

"Stand easy," said the R.S.M. in a more conversational tone. "Right. Gentlemen," he said, so that his voice carried clearly across the parade ground to the open window of the colonel's office. "You know me but I don't know you. As officer cadets, I will call you sir. As the R.S.M. you will call me sir. THERE IS ONLY ONE DIFFERENCE. I don't mean it, BUT YOU DO," and he waited for his meaning to sink in. "Gentlemen. You have completed your basic training. Ten weeks in the army. And here you are. Selected as officer cadets. Now isn't that marvellous. BUT YOU'RE A SHOWER, A BLEEDIN' SHOWER. My job, gentlemen, for the next three months is to make your lives miserable. And, gentlemen, I am very good at my job. IN THREE BLEEDIN' MONTHS I'VE GOT TO TURN YOU LOT INTO BLEEDIN' OFFICERS. Gawd help the lot of us. PARADE!" And they all came stiffly alert. "A... TEN... SHUN," and they snapped into rigid, unmoving lines, not even blinking.

The R.S.M. stood rigidly to attention, his swagger stick gripped by his left hand at right angles to his arm pit, the visor of his cap stiffly above the eyes. For sixty seconds nothing moved but the flag. There wasn't a piece of paper to blow away with the breeze. Everything, at Aldershot, was in place.

"OPEN ORDER MARCH," bellowed the R.S.M. and the back and front rows moved two paces sharply in different directions. The R.S.M. marched quickly to the right hand front cadet and inspected him from top to bottom, disgusted that he could find nothing wrong. He moved down the row, looking each man in the eye.

"NAME?" he bellowed.

"2759464 Officer Cadet Beaumont."

"Too much eating and not enough hunting," he said, prodding Henry's thick waistline.

"Yes, Sir," said Henry.

"WELL GET RID OF IT."

"Yes sir," and the R.S.M.'s eyes left him for the man on his right. The inspection proceeded to the back row.

"NAME?" bellowed the R.S.M.

"2759862. Officer Cadet Bennett."

"When did you shave, sir?"

"This morning, sir."

"This morning, sir?"

"Yes, sir."

"WELL TOMORROW SIR, TAKE TWO PACES NEARER YOUR RAZOR BLADE, SIR."

"Yes, sir."

The R.S.M. finished his inspection and marched around to a point exactly in front of the cadets.

"CLOSE ORDER MARCH," and the back and front rows stepped to within an arm's length of the soldier behind or in front. "Today is weapon training. We will show you how to strip a Bren gun. Clear blockages. We will teach you so well you will be able to strip a Bren gun in your sleep... at night... with the lights off. Then field training. We will teach you to crawl across a field so you don't stick you arses in the air. Arses in the air in warfare are targets. Painful targets. Today there will be map reading. Regimental history. A route march. This time five miles with full pack and rifle. There will be more weapon training. There will be initiative training. We have the perfect obstacle course for that. From now on you will have four hours sleep a day. On duty you will run everywhere which means you will always run as you are always on duty. There will be no passes for this course. If you fail, as one out of four of you will, you will be sent back to your units as privates. For those of you that pass remember, THERE ARE NO SUCH THINGS AS BAD MEN. THERE ARE ONLY BAD OFFICERS."

In the silence that followed the drone of a twin-engine aeroplane could be heard, the particular sound familiar to none of them. No-one moved.

"That, gentlemen," said the R.S.M., not looking upward, "is a German aircraft. A twin-engine Dornier which I can tell by the sound of its engines. That is a reconnaissance aeroplane as it is on its own. Flying high it is taking photographs so as when it gets back to Herr Hitler he will split his sides. What I want is that if that aeroplane comes back in three months' time, Herr Hitler will not split his sides.

"SLOPE ARMS… IN TO LINE RIGHT TURN. QUICK MARCH. Left, right, left, right, left, right…"

FIFTEEN PILOTS SAT AROUND inside the crew room of the Nissen hut at the south end of the main runway at R.A.F. Tangmere dressed in full flying gear. Outside, fifteen Mark I Spitfires were lined up in two rows, A, B and C flights in front with D and E ready to fly immediately behind. The wind-sock showed a good breeze running diagonally across the runway which would make a pilot concentrate when he came in to land. Some of the pilots were reading well-thumbed books and most of them were smoking. Reggie Beaumont sat at a table at the far end of the hut, partly hidden from the door by the cast iron chimney pipe of the coal fire, enclosed in its cylindrical pattern work of cast iron. His briefcase was open and had been set at the corner of the table with neat stacks of paper, a stapling machine, inkwell and pen holder. Reggie was writing a report and his mind wasn't even in England. It was essential the points he was drawing to François's attention were clear. Even though François and Carl had the right to make on the spot directors' decisions they were not allowed to overrule a decision already made by Reggie. The mineral exploration carried out by Union Mining had been spectacularly successful and Reggie was determined to maintain the pressure and not allow the geologists to rest on their laurels. Koss van der Walt had been right. Once the wealth of a mineral deposit had been proved and certified by qualified persons, the capital had proved easy to find. Reggie smiled to himself as he wrote. The trick was to find the diamonds, gold and manganese in the first place. In his report, Reggie again emphasised the need to set aside twenty percent of their annual profits for research and prospecting. A successful development program was compounding and the bigger the spread the less the financial risk.

Beside him at another table, Tony Venturas was also writing a report that had nothing to do with the Royal Air Force. His mind was projecting the needs of an island development, down to the design of the crystal ashtrays that would be strapped to the arms of the big chairs in the side lounge of his casino. His imagination was so vivid that he could see the paintings on the wall and for a moment he stopped writing and thought about how he could buy from Tug the Gauguins now removed from the office wall at 51 King William Street and stored in the basement. They would be perfect for the reception. Tropical, colourful, eye-catching and above all the work of a genius. Maybe Reggie would have a word with his brother but for the moment, the architecture was more important than the interior design. His frustration at not being on site when the American builders started excavating in May was physical. He was concerned about the growing shortages of certain materials but he was determined to build and find a way around and have it ready so that when the world stopped killing each other they would again be ready to play. Tony Venturas and Reggie Beaumont were two rare businessmen who ignored the immediacy of the war and recognised that like all the others it would come to an end. To both of them, the war was an interruption, not an all-consuming permanence.

"Why the hell Thelma can't be allowed on to the station to take dictation is beyond me," said Reggie, resting his hand.

"Get one of Chuck's recording machines sent down."

"Good idea but where do I record?"

"In the bogs," suggested Tony.

Reggie looked up to see if he was serious and then laughed, saw the frown on the Squadron Commander's face and went back to his report and penned his agreement to the explosive workshops at Kloof Mine being turned over to the manufacture of explosives for shells, mines and torpedoes. It was patriotism and business together, something that Reggie liked. An airman knocked on the outside door to the hut and was told to come in by the Squadron Commander.

"Morning. Mail, Sir," he said and proceeded to empty the contents of his leather satchel onto the tables of Tony and Reggie, letter by letter. By the time he was finished, two of the other pilots had received a letter. Reggie and Tony immediately set to, to open the envelopes and stack the contents, oblivious to the looks of the other members of the squadron.

"Shit," said Reggie, when he had finished piling the letters, "I'll never get through this lot today. If I could only have a telephone put in here everyone wouldn't have to write to me." He picked up the first letter from the pile that he had created and read how Kim-Wok Ho had obtained options on two tin mines that needed pumping dry. Every tin mine in their possession was working to capacity. Reggie put out his hand for the phone to send a wire releasing money for the purchase price. "Fuck me," he said. "I can't run a business like this."

"You're not meant to be running it at all," said his Squadron Commander. "If you get into a fight and your head is full of figures, Gerry will have you for breakfast."

Reggie glared at the Squadron Commander as both of them knew this was not true of either Reggie or Tony. In the air they were airmen.

"Bretts' monthly figures," said Tony as if he had not heard the S.C. which he had not. "Broken even again. Lilly must be giving away booze and food to every man in uniform."

"So?" said Reggie, absently reading a gold assay report from the second level at Kloof Mine. "Hope she's not giving away anything else."

"You don't think…," said Tony, turning angrily.

"Don't be bloody silly. Don't you know when your leg's being pulled? Now they tell me," said Reggie, reading another letter. "Lionel Bennett's been in the army ten weeks. I don't even have an accountant."

"You'll have to draft in a flock of women as I've done."

"You may be right. I've got a couple of sisters-in-law who are not using their brains. They're running clothing pools for the poor at Merry Hall. Should be able to trust them. They both got an education."

"That's the kind of thing," said Tony absently as he studied the configuration of a one-armed bandit for which he wanted to place an order for seventy. He noted the percentage house or client take could be altered and made a note for a firm order.

The klaxon above Reggie's head went off and was followed by an urgent voice through the tannoy.

"A flight only. A flight only. Scramble. A flight."

"Shit," said Reggie, grabbing his parachute and oxygen mask simultaneously. "That's us. Come on!" and he headed the rush down the hut with his other two pilots coming on behind. They burst out onto the tarmac pulling over the straps to their parachutes so the chutes bumped on their bums as they ran for the Spitfires. Their mechanics had heard the same tannoy warning and had removed the wheel chocks from the three Spitfires. The pilots climbed up on the wings of their aeroplanes and climbed into the cockpits, starting the single Merlin, Rolls-Royce engine into life and pulling on their masks and plugging them into wireless and oxygen. As the planes moved forward each of the pilots gave a thumbs-up sign and the aircraft sped down the runway and into the air, the wheels tucking back into the wings immediately afterwards. The three aeroplanes circled the aerodrome to gain height and Reggie turned his wireless to the fighter controllers' frequency.

"A leader to ground control. We are airborne."

"Bandit, angels one nine approaching London from the coast," said a female voice. "Head south, south east and we will intercept."

"Roger," said Reggie, having climbed to ten thousand feet. He put the Spitfire into a gentle climb that would take him above the enemy aircraft and opened the throttle, checking a Spitfire at each wing tip.

"One bandit," said Reggie. "Please repeat one bandit."

"One bandit," repeated fighter control and Reggie could visualise Constance studying the VH unit as the target pulled the line of ripples up from the bottom of her screen. Now she would be seeing the aircraft from behind but it made no difference to the jagged line that was vibrating well above the normal static on the rest of her screen at. R.A.F. Poling.

"You are closing fast, A leader," said the calm voice that never changed. "Have you visual contact?"

"Not yet, ground control." Reggie scanned the sky all round him, the oxygen mask hanging loosely from his face as he spoke into the attached microphone. Then, away through high cloud, Reggie picked up a thin vapour trail.

"I have visual. Thank you ground control."

Swiftly the three fighters closed in on the aircraft that should have seen them but had not changed course.

'Bloody brave or a bloody fool,' thought Reggie as he made out the distinctive swastikas on the fuselage and wings.

"Dornier; recce," said his left hand wingman.

"Are they armed?" asked Reggie, knowing they weren't.

"No."

"Sitting duck," said the right wingman.

Reggie watched carefully for a few moments as they closed on the German aircraft.

"Watch for his friends," said Reggie.

"Can't see any."

"That's the time to be worried," and Reggie made a decision. "We're going to take him back to Tangmere," he said, firing a burst of tracer across the nose of the German. "Crew of two," he said as both masked faces looked at him out of their

windows. Reggie used his right hand to violently signal downwards as the right
wing man fired a burst over the German's tail and the left wingman fired tracer
over the pilots' cockpit. The Dornier began to lose height and was forced round by
a wingman to fly towards R.A.F. Tangmere, a Spitfire at each of his wing tips and
Reggie flying behind him searching the sky for enemy aircraft. 'Silly buggers, all on
their own,' he thought and hoped he was right. Five minutes later the runway came
into view and the four aircraft drifted down to earth in perfect formation, their
wheels bouncing on the tarmac almost simultaneously. They ran forward to the
dispersal unit where an R.A.F. regiment armoured car was swivelling a Vickers
machine gun at the Dornier as it stopped. Reggie watched with mild amusement as
men with rifles aggressively ringed the aeroplane. 'They are playing war in
earnest,' thought Reggie, pulling back the canopy over his head. He unplugged his
oxygen mask and pulled himself from the seat. By the time he reached the ground,
an officious regiment officer had the two young Germans out of their plane and on
the tarmac with their hands in the air while they were searched. Reggie shook his
head and slid his parachute harness off his shoulders and pulled the combined
helmet/oxygen mask from his face. The pilots of A flight, bareheaded and carrying
their parachutes, walked back to the crew room they had left ten minutes before.

Tony was still working when Reggie dropped his gear on the bench and sat
down at his table. He sat back on the bench and stared at the papers in front of him.

"You could have claimed a kill," said a D flight pilot and Reggie looked at him
sharply but didn't reply.

"What was the silly bugger doing stooging around at nineteen thousand feet?"
he said to no-one in particular as the other two members of A flight sat down and
carried on where they had left off.

"I wonder what they'll do with them," said another pilot, gazing through a
window across the tarmac to where the bustle of regiment and S.P.'s had not
diminished, a guard having been set up around the German aircraft as its aircrew
were raggedly marched away to the admin block to the left of the control tower.
No-one bothered to answer his question.

"Didn't take much persuasion to come down with you?" asked Tony, reading
the last of his pile of letters.

"No," said Reggie.

"Must have had something go wrong."

"Yes."

"Poor sods. Lucky to be alive."

"Yes."

"Here. Have some tea. There's still some in my flask."

"Thanks," said Reggie.

"Taking pictures. Getting ready to bomb the holy shit out of us."

"They can try."

"They will."

"Anything in your mail?"

"Usual."

"Can't be buggered to read mine."

"It gets you that way. Anti-climax. Another half an hour and we'll be
stood down."

"I'll buy you a drink."

An orderly opened the door. "Flight Lieutenant Beaumont, sir. C.O. would like to see you, sir, after stand-by."

"Very good, Corporal," said Reggie and turned to Tony. "When's the balloon going up?"

"Soon enough."

"The war makes property, business, money seem futile."

"It'll come to an end."

"Yes," said Reggie and continued to stare into nothing.

AT FIVE-THIRTY REGGIE walked into the C.O.'s office and saluted sloppily. "Don't you know how to salute, Reggie?"

"Not really, sir. No-one showed us in the auxiliaries. We just flew aeroplanes and enjoyed ourselves."

"Sit down. Hang your hat behind the door. There's a standing order somewhere about wearing ties when in uniform. Where did you get that canary-coloured scarf?"

"A friend of mine sent it over from Singapore. Pure silk," said Reggie taking it off and letting it loose. "There's a dragon in the middle. Some kind of good luck symbol."

"Those fellows had a fractured oxygen pipe. Couldn't climb above twenty thousand feet. The pilot wants to see you. Talks English. You broke another standing order by not shooting him down. One day they'll use planes like that as decoys."

"I was conscious of that, sir."

"Well, why didn't you shoot the bugger down?"

"He wasn't armed. Ground control said he was alone."

"You'd better go and see the Gerry. Don't go soft on us. This is going to be a long war. The R.A.F. are being shot out of the sky in France but Churchill refuses reinforcements. Saving us to defend the island. Makes sense, I suppose. See you in the mess for a drink."

"How are our liquor stocks?" asked Reggie.

"Not too good."

"I'll see what I can do."

"I'd have done the same thing."

"What?"

"Brought him in."

"Murder's not up my street."

"DO YOU KNOW A GUNTER VON RIBBECK?" asked Reggie. "My age. Don't know his rank."

"The German Air Force is large."

"Worth a try."

"Why?"

"He's my business partner."

"Is that why you didn't kill us?"

"Not really."

"I must thank you."

"My pleasure. Why did you want to see me?"

"To say thank you."

"Your war's over."

"Possibly but not as over as it might have been."

"Yes. I see what you mean."

"I hope you survive the war."

"So do I. There's still a lot of life to be lived."

"THANK YOU," said Lady Beaumont, taking the telegram from the silver tray, balanced on Pavy's white-gloved left hand and glanced at the addressee. She looked puzzled.

"It's why I brought it to you, milady," said Pavy.

"Major Sir Thomas Beaumont, Merry Hall, near Ashtead, Surrey," she read. "The only Major Beaumont is in France. Thank you Pavy. I'll phone the post office and tell them where to send it," and slipped the cable into the large pocket that made up the front of her gardening skirt. It joined the twine and a pair of secateurs. The morning sun had already made the conservatory hot and humidity was rising from the damp earth, black and well manured, that nurtured the orchids, the tropical ferns and seven peach trees that had just bloomed out of their rightful season, a fragrant pink and white flower that fluffed out the stiff long twigs of the leafless trees. Down the far end of the conservatory, Bonner was meticulously spraying the first of the peach blossoms against insects that would otherwise have grown with the fruit and eaten the ripened flesh. Lady Beaumont dug around the plants with a small trowel, letting in the air, her thick, gardening gloves protecting her hands.

"Morning Alice," said Sir Thomas from the dining room. "Think I'll take a walk. Beautiful day. Why don't you join me? Right round the estate. I can have a beer and a sandwich at the Wheatsheaf even if the beer's watered down. You can have a brown sherry if they have any left. Those shoes'll do for walking. You can do that gardening when it's raining."

"A telegram just arrived for Geoffrey."

"Nothing serious?"

"Didn't open it. Funny thing is it's addressed to Major Sir Thomas Beaumont."

"It's, probably for me," said Sir Thomas, holding out his hand for the wire. She took it out and gave it to him, watching as he read the address. "Yes, I was expecting this one."

"But you're not in the army," said Lady Beaumont.

"I am from now."

"Don't be ridiculous, Thomas. You're sixty-four. They're not even calling up Reservists over the age of forty."

"Let's take that walk and I'll explain," said Sir Thomas, putting the telegram in his pocket. "I'll be going up to London tomorrow morning first thing." He was smiling at her as she deliberately removed her gloves, emptied the pocket and left the secateurs and the twine on the potting table. Bonner was engrossed so she didn't interrupt his spraying but went with her husband out into the ten o'clock sun.

"Spring has definitely arrived," said Sir Thomas, smelling the air and looking around as if he had brought the spring along by himself. "Have to cut the lawns soon, if I can find enough petrol for the mower."

"Don't you need it for the tractor?"

"Can't have lawns overgrowing. Gerry may be winning the war in Europe but he isn't going to stop me cutting my grass. Even if I have to push the damn thing. Look at that. The tennis net's gone rotten. Meant to bring that in all winter. That was Geoffrey's job."

"What's in the telegram?" said Lady Beaumont, getting back to the subject.

"From Bertie Featherstone. He's now a Brigadier in Whitehall."

"Last I heard he was working for Reggie in Singapore," said Lady Beaumont.

"They called him back three months ago. Bertie specialised in a particular kind of anti-warfare. Made his name in India.

"We'll take the short cut through the woods over there. The anemones are out. I found some cowslips yesterday, as well. Bit of warm weather and the spring flowers are out all over the estate.

"Now, what Bertie did was analyse the motive, the individual motives of enemies of the crown. The political motives are often more obvious but he was sure motives were often personal and if one could find them out they could be used against the man. If the man was analysed, Bertie felt it would be possible to have some idea of his future moves. Better the chinks in the man's personality that could be exploited. A number of Indian potentates fell into his trap over the years and problems that could have grown out of proportion were tackled through the vulnerabilities of the leader."

"What, Thomas, has this to do with you?"

"Well, you see, it was my idea in the first place. Bertie was two years my junior in India and only took over my job when I inherited the title. He tried to get the British Army to listen to him in the Great War but they wouldn't. Apparently they've listened to him now. Shows what a title does. They've put him in charge of a department that will analyse all the German leaders and generals and feed the information back to our opposing field commanders. It is a small weapon but important. It may point the direction for an otherwise blind decision. Political decisions will also be made from the same information. Bertie wants me to help him. My commission came through with that telegram so I shall have to have my tailor run up a uniform tomorrow."

"Who's going to run the estate?" They were now out in the open and well away from Merry Hall.

"Bert Brigley. That's who we're going to see when we've walked the estate. You have a way of calming Martha which is why I hoped you'd come for the walk. See over there. Ploughed and ready. And there. All the stud pastures. The barns I'm turning into pigsties. More chickens. Ducks on the ponds. Geese. Food. The Ministry of Agriculture has asked us to go for maximum food production. The Merchant Navy's having a bad time. Far worse than the papers are allowed to report. An island depends on imports and we are losing thirty percent of our tonnage to U-boats and the navy can't find an answer. They are trying convoys but the U-boats are getting at the merchantmen just the same. Every arable piece of England must be used for food production. The very best of the stud we will keep. There won't be any horse racing for years."

"You think the war will last for years?" said Lady Beaumont in alarm.

"Yes. Everyone's got to put in maximum effort."

"Reggie has an idea for Merry Hall," said Lady Beaumont.

"He told me. Said he should write to you. The work will be yours and the girls."

"He mentioned the merchant seaman in particular. He thinks that unless they are given a chance to properly relax on leave their nerves will go before they receive a torpedo."

"I saw it in the last war. The North Atlantic is cold and inhospitable at the best of times. A man can survive for less than three minutes in the water. How many people could you talk to?"

"I've made a list. I'm going to invite all the wives to tea and put it to them."

"You agree we should throw open Merry Hall?"

"Yes. And I think the tenants' homes and the labourers' homes should be made available to the men. People want to relax with a family. Reggie says thousands of the seamen coming into London and Southampton for a few days are too far away from their homes. He says the worst thing for them is to be left on their own to brood. Some good home food and a walk through those woods is what they want. I'll bring it up with Martha."

"Won't they be bored?"

"Not with families and certainly not at Merry Hall if I let Reggie have his way."

"Oh," said Sir Thomas, stopping on the footpath that was leading them between the big oak trees of the wood.

"That club of Tony Venturas. Apparently they have a lot of girls working there and I don't even want to think what they're working at, my goodness. But this is a war and if it helps our boys. Well Thomas, what are you laughing at?"

"You mean he's going to ship some of those girls down here to look after the troops?"

"Not permanently. The girls would do it on shifts."

"I'll bet they would. I've had my suspicions for a long time and then I made enquiries in the City. That club of Tony's is a high class knock shop and our second son owns half of it."

"What is a knock shop, Thomas?"

"A sophisticated brothel."

"Thomas!" exclaimed Lady Beaumont.

"The best of it is they've put it together in such a way that it's legal. I even had the family solicitors have a very discreet look at it. When Reggie saw what I was doing he had quite a hoot. 'My dear, dad', he said. 'There are more ways than one of killing a goose.' That was a couple of years ago and we haven't mentioned it since."

"Tony told me it was a very exclusive night club."

"Oh, he's right there. Very exclusive. They also have up to fifty very pretty girls sitting around to talk to the patrons. According to the man sent in by our solicitors they are very pretty. But give Reggie his head and you'll be meeting some of them. Oh, and don't be worried about their education or accents. Ninety percent of them are university students paying their way through Varsity… Reggie thinks the club serves a lot of good causes."

"Reggie is quite impossible. I wouldn't put anything past him."

"Anyway. That's how he proposes to solve the boredom problem."

"And if the men are married?"

"Alice, don't think about it. Accept them as they are. Peacetime conventions are bent in a war. There'll be a lot of officers you'll meet who will be anything but gentlemen. I just find it a great shame that I will be spending most of my time in the London flat. All those girls."

"Really, Thomas."

"You are a picture of pompous indignation," he said, smiling. "Come along this path, here, and I'll show you a spot that both of us will remember."

"Thomas."

"That's, better. Now you're blushing m'dear. Come along. The cowslips are out where they used to be. I had a look yesterday. Why is it older people always try and forget they were young when they talk about their own children? The people don't change, Alice. If they did, life would never have been worth the living. Now, about here I saw you for the first time. You were hiding in the bracken over there and thought I hadn't seen you."

"I was only fifteen," said Alice in her defence as he took her by the hand and led her to the foot of an old oak, its roots growing out thickly and one of them making a seat for two."

"Do you remember the owl?" said Sir Thomas and Lady Beaumont looked up at the tall elm.

"He's still there," she said in startled surprise.

"I don't believe it," said Sir Thomas turning and looking up. "Well, there's a thing," he said and the old owl blinked back at them. "Can't be the same one. How long do owls live?"

"Don't know," said Lady Beaumont watching the owl perched high up in the rotten cleft of the elm, "I never thought of it. Maybe a long time. Maybe he's been looking after us for all these years. I do hope he carries on," and Sir Thomas squeezed her hand.

"Of course he will. They'll be alright. The Beaumonts have always been survivors." The owl closed his eyes firmly and went back to sleep.

"Father said the Beaumonts were finished and that you were the last impoverished member of the line. He said I could do far better."

"Of course you could have, Alice," and he patted her hand.

"I'm worried about Claud. He's taken out another mortgage on The Grange. He's such a bad farmer."

"Wouldn't listen."

"No. He was always like that. Someone will sell him up and I couldn't bear to think of someone else living at The Grange. What a pity he wouldn't listen to you or Henry. Henry's done so well with Merry Hall."

"There won't be a Derby this year or next. I'm going to breed Lilliput despite the war so that when it's over we'll be ready. The war effort can afford a few racehorses."

"I hope he'll be alright."

"Who?"

"Henry. I just can't picture Henry in the army taking orders."

"He'll get by. They always do."

"What was really wrong with Tug, Thomas?"

"I'll tell you while we walk. Reggie said it was a tropical disease. Contagious which is why we weren't allowed to see him in the sanatorium."

"That's my point. A sanatorium. Why not the tropical diseases hospital?"

"I don't know, Alice. But he's well again and that is all that matters. And we got to know Tammany and the children."

"She's very beautiful."

"Yes."

"She found it very difficult. Such different backgrounds. She never talked very much. I'm glad they are back in Singapore and far away from this terrible war."

"Everyone's commented on his paintings."

"Yes. I think Tug should have been a painter," said Lady Beaumont.

"He still has plenty of time. I'll have a word with Reggie and ask him to buy up the mortgages on The Grange. That way the estate will stay in the family, however badly it's farmed. It's a good proposition, farmed properly."

"Do you think he would?"

"He'll do anything for you, Alice. You know that. Let's walk up to the hill."

For ten minutes they walked in silence through the country spring, a warm sun on their backs. The path sloped up and they climbed, Alice on two occasions resting her one hand on her left knee to catch her breath. At the top they sat down on the bench that gave them a view over the estate of Merry Hall in all its directions, with the Norman spire of Ashtead church almost hidden by trees and the old, Tudor house, The Grange, where Alice had been born.

"It looks so peaceful," she said.

"And beautiful. Our families have been very lucky."

"If only Claud had had more sons."

"He's a fool. He should have married again instead of moping around. The navy is a lot safer than the army or air force."

"It's all so terrible."

"John will be alright. You'll see. Now, from here you can see how much of the land we've ploughed. It will quadruple our produce production, not counting the pigs."

"Why hasn't Reggie married?"

"I think he's been too busy."

"Is that because of Bretts really what you saying?"

"Exaggerating a little. No, I'm sure the girls are just good hostesses to give the businessmen some female conversation when they're away from home."

"I wouldn't put it past him," giggled Lady Beaumont.

"Who?"

"Reggie," and Sir Thomas looked at his wife queerly before deliberately turning back to the landscape.

"If we're going round the estate, we'd better get cracking," and as he stood up and held his hand out to help up his wife, the air-raid siren wailed at them from the direction of Ashtead Village and kept on incessantly. They turned to each other and Sir Thomas squeezed her hand.

"It would be an hour's walk back to the cellar," he said. "Not much point."

"I feel so vulnerable on top of the hill," said Lady Beaumont scanning the blue patches of sky and the banks of cloud.

"You'll feel safer under that clump of trees down the slope," and he led the way down to the small thicket that surrounded the trunk of a beech tree, green with its new shoots of spring. The hazel trees were green and decked with last year's old man's beard. Walking at a brisk pace, trying not to show fear to the other, they reached the leafy screen but the sirens were still wailing incessantly churning the fear and urgency in their stomachs. They drew into the clump where a fox had made a run. They could still see out clearly over the landscape and off to the distant sky of blue and cloud.

"I can see them," said Lady Beaumont, whose eyes were better than those of Sir Thomas. "Black specks. Thomas, there are so many of them. And there are more of them. And another formation has come out of that cloud. By God, there are hundreds of aeroplanes. Why doesn't the R.A.F. do something about it? I can hear their engines," and the menacing drone of multiple piston engines encroached over the open countryside and the throbbing power built up with the oncoming menace. Lady Beaumont drew back further and trod in a fresh cow pat. A pigeon flew out of the beech tree right above them startled by the increasing drone of aircraft.

"I can make them out now," said Sir Thomas. "Heinkels. Bombers. They'll have escort fighters above them. Going for London docks."

"In daylight?"

"Gerry's changed his tactics. Looks like they'll be coming at us around the clock." The main formation was clear of cloud, flying in a wide patch of blue sky, growing more distinct as the aircraft droned directly towards Merry Hall. "Here they come," said Sir Thomas with satisfaction. "Out of the sun. I saw the flash on wings. Now we'll see," and the rattle of distant machine gun fire floated down to them as a squadron of Hurricanes burst through the German formation and swarmed up again underneath to fire at the unprotected bellies. Three of the German planes had lost height and one of them exploded violently, scattering debris over the sky. The white mushrooms of parachutes suddenly appeared in the sky as the high pitched scream of the two falling aircraft came to them diving straight at the ground. The explosions were almost simultaneous. When the Hurricanes flew back through the bombers they were met by the Messerschmitts and individual dogfights broke out all over the sky. The undamaged bombers droned on as if nothing had happened. They had changed neither direction nor height. The bombers were less than a mile away from the Beaumonts when a squadron of Spitfires came at them out of the sun and more black smoke began to trail and gaps appeared in the formation as the Spitfires broke them up while the Hurricanes kept the German fighters away from protecting their bombers. The sky was constant machine gun and cannon fire and they could clearly see the cannons firing from the leading edges of the Spitfire wings, four cannons in each wing. Sir Thames watched a bomber lose height as it flew on straight towards them, smoke and fire visible in one wing where a fuel tank was burning. Bodies dropped out of the belly of the plane and Sir Thomas counted three parachutes. The plane came on down steadily till it was too low for the pilot to bail out.

"He's trying to land it," said Sir Thomas. "The Thirty Acre."

The fire was right down the port wing and they could now see the masked pilot at the controls as the Heinkel lost its steady decline and dipped a wing and hurled itself at the bottom of the slope, well short of the Thirty Acre, some four hundred yards below them. It cartwheeled onto its nose before exploding with a shattering noise as the full bomb load went up with the burning aircraft, spewing bits for half a mile over Merry Hall. Something rattled in the beech tree above them and they cowered back into the thicket for protection. Small pockets of flames could be seen on the slope. A piece of the tail plane had come to rest seventy yards down the slope in front of them. Above, the battle raged with the Spitfires being attacked by Messerschmitts. Sir Thomas watched the R.A.F. again attack the bombers. The battle flew past Merry Hall and was lost to them over the hill behind.

"I'd better take a look," said Sir Thomas. "You stay here Alice. The pilot might have been thrown clear. The Home Guard will pick up the others."

"Poor boy," said Lady Beaumont.

"They are the enemy."

"It could just as easily have been Reggie. Do you think he was up there?"

"Possible, Tangmere protects London and that's where the Germans were going."

"It's so terrible," she said.

"Yes. War is never nice. Will you be alright?"

"Yes. As right as I can ever be."

Sir Thomas broke cover and made his way down the slope. There was no-one in sight. A tuft of grass made him stumble and he cursed. The sounds of the air battle were faint behind him but the smell of burnt oil was acrid in his nostrils and the crackle of fire dominated the small piece of countryside at the bottom of the hill. He had passed the wing section and the only other sizable piece was the nose cone that was resting half in the stream that ran round the foot of the hill and joined up with the River Mole. One of the engines had ploughed in and only a small part of the propeller showed above ground. Sir Thomas approached the nose cone carefully, not sure if there was anything inside that could explode. A tree had been snapped off as the front of the aeroplane came to its final rest, the white new gash of the tree clearly visible. The wind was taking the smoke away from him and he climbed over stones and pulled himself up by a piece of protruding metal to look into the cockpit. The airman was slumped sideways away from the instrument panel as if he had been jolted back. Sir Thomas had to walk round the broken fuselage and climb into the cone through the gaping hole at the back. The navigator's table was torn from its socket in the fuselage. The perspex hood was shattered and something was swinging from a wire in the slight breeze that was blowing through the shattered windscreen. Picking his way through the wreckage, he reached the pilot, took hold of his right shoulder and pulled him over. The head lolled, supportless, snapped by the whiplash of impact.

"Poor bugger," said Sir Thomas out loud and let the body flop back onto the navigator's seat that had half come out of its mounting. The clock on the dashboard had stopped at twenty-seven minutes past two and Sir Thomas found himself wondering if that was London or Berlin time. Fortunately, with the oxygen mask still in place, he had been unable to see the pilot's face.

"We'll bury you right here on the hill," said Sir Thomas out loud as he released the identification bracelet he could see on the pilot's left hand.

Back at the thicket he took his wife's hand and they began the walk to the Wheatsheaf.

"He was dead…"

"I worry about them."

"So do I," and they both knew they were talking about their children.

GWEN de la Riviera was dressed in a sleek white sheath with a frontal frill that just failed to hide the strong protrusion of her nipples. Her smooth, round breasts were equally visible. She was not wearing a bra as with the firmness of her young breasts it wasn't necessary. The sheath reached to her ankles and silver slippers and from where the barman was standing ready to start the evening trade, there were two clearly visible, round and pert cheek bottoms with a faint outline of her panties. Despite having seen some of the best looking women in London, night after night, he found himself getting excited looking at the new girl and when she turned with her hand outstretched to shake Claire's hand and showed him the stiff length of her left nipple through the white cotton, he was instantly aroused. She looked up and caught him looking. He quickly picked up a champagne glass and began to polish and turned to look at another new girl who had let herself out into the cocktail area through the ornate door that led from the ladies' powder room. There were fifteen girls in the club and no customers but it was only eight-fifteen and the band had not yet started to play. The barman looked around carefully for Lilly Venturas or any of the management and took a bottle of black market scotch from his inside jacket pocket and put it with the other bottles in front of the mirror bracket at the back of the bar. He had paid eight pounds cash for the bottle but at one pound per tot he would sell it for twenty-two pounds and the profit would be his and the bar stock would still be correct.

Nobody would know and fourteen pounds a night was good money. By the end of the week he would be able to afford the new girl if he couldn't convince her he should have it for free. Pippa joined her sister at the low, cocktail table having felt the eyes of the barman follow her across the room. She had seen him pull a bottle of scotch from his pocket. A waitress came to their table dressed in a frilled black skirt that just covered her white panties when she was standing erect but as she bent to put down the drinks, she showed the barman an attractive bottom but he wasn't interested. He had had her before and she wasn't very good.

"Cheers," said Penny, lifting her cocktail glass. "I didn't expect to meet you two here. I thought your father was rich."

"Well he wasn't," answered Gwen. "Didn't leave mother a penny. What was left of the family money went on our education and doctors' bills."

"But it was a war wound, I understood," said Claire. "I asked when we were at Merry Hall for Christmas."

"It was," said Pippa, sitting down and the barman had an unrestricted view of two white unsupported breasts. "He was too proud to ask for charity."

"But Reggie Beaumont's brothers' are his sons-in-law," said Penny. "And he's stinking rich from what I hear."

"That's how we got this job," said Gwen, patting Claire on the arm. "He spoke to Tony. They're flying together."

"You've certainly got the looks," said Claire.

"Thank you," said the sisters.

"Can you handle it?"

"Just because we were born with titles doesn't mean we're different," said Gwen. "I'm going to enjoy it and the money's good."

"How far are you going to go?" asked Claire.

"We haven't decided," said Gwen. "Probably the whole way. How did you find it?"

"No problem."

"How much can we ask?"

"That depends. Better not to. Let them make you a present. I know one kinky old bastard who would pay a fortune for two titled sisters at once. Some of them have had so much in their lives it has to be a real mental turn-on to give them a proper thrill."

"Point us out to him."

"I will," said Claire. "The barman's the best one to negotiate."

"Is he in on the deal?" asked Pippa. "Lilly said that anything like that was strictly between us and the customer and nothing to do with Bretts."

"That's how it used to be," said Penny. "Fact is we're making more after giving him ten percent. He'll probably want to try you out himself but that's no problem. That one even taught me a couple of tricks."

"Why isn't he in the army?"

"Too old. He's forty-two."

"Doesn't look it."

"Probably isn't. Forged his birth certificate. My father said there were plenty of those in the last war."

"How long's he been working here?" asked Gwen.

"Five months," said Claire. "Took over from a man who went into the Merchant Navy. Ah a customer. Must be that air raid this afternoon. Bit of fear makes them all run to the bottle. Make the girls take their knickers off. Funny thing, there are plenty of amateurs but our business has never been better. There are plenty of navy types with six months' back pay in their pockets and if they have the right contacts, a man in uniform doesn't need to be a member. Suits me. All I hope is they don't bomb the bank where I've put it all."

"Spread it around," said Penny. "That's what I've done. Have another drink?" she said to Gwen and Pippa. "It's always best to have a few drinks the first time. He won't charge us," she said, nodding her head at the barman who smirked to himself as he turned to mix four dry martinis having decided the two new girls would be paying him instead of the other way round.

BY NINE-THIRTY THE club was filling up and Lilly checked with the doorman that no-one had been let into the premises who was not a member or who had not been given an introduction from Reggie or Tony. So many of the staff were new, she was constantly checking. By ten-thirty the club was packed, despite the air raid that afternoon and the band was playing at full swing to the enjoyment of everyone on the small dance floor. Most of the men were in uniform, one a brigadier-general that Lilly recognised from Merry Hall. Lilly shook her head and smiled. They were all the same, whether you knew them or not and why shouldn't a man in his sixties dance with a girl of nineteen? How much of morality was sour grapes! The doorman unlocked the front door and let in a R.A.F. officer who smiled at Lilly and came across to her.

"What are you doing here, George? Where's Tony?"

"We had a bit of bother."

"What do you mean? What's happened to Tony?"

"He's alright. It was Colin Heath."

"Colin?"

"We lost him. Tony's gone to see his mother in Ewell. His father's dead."

"Come into the office."

"There was a flap this afternoon," said George following her into Tony's office. "The Gerrys sent in a decoy hoping we'd scramble the whole squadron. Reggie went up and shot down the decoy and then the balloon went up. First time Gerrys tried to bomb London in daylight. We caught them over Dorking and fought them right the way through to the docks. There were seventy bombers and as many fighters but only a few reached the target. Colin was shot down by a 109. Did a flamer. I watched him. Tony got the 109 too late. Hell of a mess. Everyone for themselves. Individual fights all over the sky. We lost four planes and one pilot from Tangmere. Biggin Hill came up to help. It's those 109s. The pilots are good. Biggin Hill lost six and three pilots. We had the surprise. The 109s were waiting for the second attack."

"Tony's unhurt?"

"Oh, yes. You know Tony. Far too experienced." Lilly put a neat scotch down next to him and his hand shook as he brought the glass to his mouth.

"Bloody tough. Shit, it was bloody tough. You couldn't even see who was shooting at you."

"Sit down, George. Have you eaten?"

"No. Don't think I'd keep it down. Shot down a bomber. Pilot flamed on the ground. Just went in. Three of his crew bailed out. Poor sod."

"That's war."

"Yeah that's war, doesn't help that sod or Colin. That's the worst, Lilly, a flamer. I hope to Christ I don't buy it in a flamer."

Lilly poured him another scotch and waited for him to drink.

"Tony didn't want you to hear casualties on the news. Well, I'll be going. Thanks for the drink. We're sleeping in the crew room tonight."

"Thanks for coming."

"Isn't far in a taxi. Reggie gave me the money."

"Be careful," she said, going out to reception.

"How the bloody hell can you be…? Sorry… Not like me. And it's going to get worse Lilly, a lot worse." She opened the front door and he went out into the blackout, a curtain falling behind them to screen the entrance.

"Give Tony my love. And Reggie. Can you sleep in the crew room?"

"No. Some of the boys are taking sleeping pills to go to sleep and Dexedrine to wake them up. Not me. I'd prefer to have no sleep than be on drugs. Up there, you need all your wits about you… Thanks for waiting, Cabbie," he said getting into his taxi.

"We'll have you back on the station in twenty minutes, governor," said the taxi driver, "and then you can give Gerry another sock in the nose from me. Bombing London in broad daylight. Bloody cheek, I say," and he put the car into gear and shot off down the darkened road with only a faint gleam coming from his hooded headlights.

Lilly turned back to the door as another taxi drew up to the club. The passenger door opened to let Chuck Everly out onto the darkened pavement. He followed

Lilly into the club and the door and curtain closed behind them. The smoke and noise hit Chuck as he pushed through the crowded rooms to Tony's office that was now Lilly's.

"Want a drink?" said Lilly. "I wasn't expecting you tonight. How's Beaumonts and Union Mining?"

"Making money. And you?"

"Should be but we're not. They're stealing me blind, Chuck. Club's full every night but I can't make a profit."

"Business is difficult to handle. Want any help?"

"Not yet."

"Who was that going out?"

"Tony's wingman. They lost the other one today."

"I'm sorry. I told Reggie I was joining the Eagle Squadron and he nearly hit me."

"It is difficult to trust anyone but family and partners."

"You think Gunter came over today?" asked Chuck.

"I hope not. The best way to help Reggie and Tony is to stay at 51 King William Street. That way they have a business to come home to."

"We're making killings in rubber and tin and Kloof Mine's working at full capacity. The diamonds will be earning Britain dollars within the next two months. The reinsurance business isn't worth much. Diversification. Reggie was right. You think Gerry will come over tonight? Reggie thinks they'll start hitting the radar and fighter stations. I'm bushed. Good meal. Couple of shots. Then me for down. Never worked so damn hard in my life. Will you eat with me or have you?"

"No. Let's hope there's a table."

"Manager's privilege."

"Got to be something."

GWEN WATCHED the barman come back from the men's toilet and turn his back on the customers to look at the rows of bottles on the shelves in front of the mirrors. When he turned back to serve a customer she noticed there was an extra bottle of gin on the white-spirit shelf.

"May we join you ladies?" said a man in his twenties in R.A.F. uniform with the wings of a pilot on his left breast. "The barman said it will be okay," and he put his beer on the glass-topped table in front of Gwen and sat down, smiling at the four girls in turn. His friend sat down next to Pippa, rather more self-conscious than his friend.

"I'm Claire and this is Penny, Gwen and Philippa. Do you want to order a drink?"

"Sure, if that's how it goes."

"Oh, I'm fine," said Gwen and received a brief frown from Claire. "Well, maybe a glass of champagne, if you insist," she said, recovering herself.

"I'm Max. This is John. We fly together."

"Bombers or fighters?" put in Pippa brightly.

"Neither. Coastal command. We fly a Sunderland flying boat on air-sea rescue. We pull pilots out of the channel. The problem for the R.A.F. is not planes but trained pilots. That's where we score over Gerry. When he bails out we've got him.

Thank you," he said turning to the waiter. "Bring me a bottle of Heidsieck Dry Monopole, 1933."

"We have a lesser known champagne, sir. The war, you know. I'll bring the bottle."

"Make it two and six glasses."

"Four," said Penny standing up, having seen the airmen were interested in Gwen and Pippa.

"Oh," said Max, standing up with Claire and Penny and then smiling down at Gwen and Pippa. "The barman said we should eat here and then go on to your place."

"Well," said Pippa, "I don't know about my place but…"

"That's the deal," said Gwen and caught the same look from Claire. "That'll be fine," said Gwen and kicked her sister under the table. "We're only round the corner."

"That's expensive, isn't it?" said Max, questioning.

"Yes. But you know we…"

"Yes, I'm sure. After what the barman said. Doesn't matter. I don't have to live from my pay and you never know these days. Both Tangmere and Biggin Hill lost pilots today and a Sunderland can't fight back."

"Who was killed from Tangmere," asked Gwen, quickly.

"You know some of the pilots?"

"They come in," said Gwen.

"A pilot officer. Nineteen. Didn't catch his name. Look at that. A bottle of French champagne with a label I've never seen in my life."

"There's always a first time," smiled Pippa, sweetly.

"It's cold enough. Thanks. We'll try it. If it's no good I'll go back to beer."

The waiter took off the silver paper, unwired the cork and expertly manipulated it out with his thumbs, popping the cork high and hard up against the back of the bar. The barman smiled back and watched the waiter fill a glass for Pippa.

"Shall we dance," said Max turning to Gwen. "John, you dance with Pippa."

The moment he was on the dance floor, having led her through from the cocktail lounge into the dinner and dance area of the club, he pushed himself firmly against Gwen so she could feel the thickness of his erection through the barathea. He circled gently his hand firmly on her bottom pushing her against him and slowly the moisture wet the crotch of her pants.

"You like that, darling?" he said.

"Yes," said Gwen to her surprise and involuntarily returned the pressure.

"Come on," he said, after a moment. "Let's drink that champagne, have a meal and get out of here."

"There isn't any hurry," she said, looking up at him in surprise.

"For me there is. I haven't been this horny since the last time, and he led her back to their cocktail table catching the eye of the maître d'hôtel and signalling him a table for four and quick-quick. They sat down. The bubbles were still rising lazily from the bottom of their champagne glasses.

"Cheers."

"Cheers."

"Do you know, it's not bad. Even the old pater would drink it."

"Bretts is a very exclusive club," said Gwen.

"You can say that again," he said appraising her nipple straining at the white cotton of her sheath dress.

"You can say that again," and she was forced to look down into her champagne glass. Max leant across and put his hand on her knee and began to rub gently.

"There's something erotic about a dress sliding over silk stockings."

"I'm not wearing stockings."

"Even better."

CHUCK SAT with Lilly at a back table but with a good view over the dance floor that was occupied by couples swaying together on the same spots as there wasn't any room to do otherwise. Lilly acknowledged the wave of a guest and turned back to Chuck who was eating enthusiastically.

"Your chicken casserole's delicious. You just tell that to the chef from me. Real tasty. This rationing business is the bit that bites. Fact is I can put up with air raids so long as this stomach of mine gets properly fed. My mama said to me that no man should work without the proper food in his stomach and she knew what she was talking about. Tell me where you get the chickens? Maybe I can put in for a short order except I don't know cooking."

"After you've finished," said Lilly. "I'll give a full run in on the London black market."

"Tony sure knows how to pick the dolls," said Chuck looking around the dance floor as he chewed happily at his food. "That one over here," he said pointing with the fork in his right hand. "Tarty version of Pippa. If that dress was any lower she wouldn't have to wear anything. Same build as Pippa, too. Just shows there aren't that many types of women in the world. Pity, but tarty women are just not my type. Don't like it being shown in public, or at home for that matter. My mama told me there was a time and place for everything and she was most always right. I'm taking Pippa down to Merry Hall this weekend. Isabel invited us. Now there's one who takes it too far the other way. Just plain cold. As a woman, I mean. Nice lady, otherwise. Have to be to be Pippa's sister. Yes sir. That tart over there sure looks like Pippa."

"Haven't you taken out any of the girls?" said Lilly quickly.

"Been here with the boys a few times. Don't mind doing a bit of drinking and dancing with the girls but that's as far as I can take it. We're a bit conservative they say, us coming from Wisconsin and some ways that ain't all bad. You got to have a set of rules, I say. That's what I like about this place. The girls talk and dance and some men even like them looking like that one but Reggie said they don't expect you to take them off and pay them money. Reggie did say that what they did do out of his club was their business but I never wanted to try myself."

"Don't you like women?" asked Lilly.

"Now don't say that," said Chuck expansively and swallowed the last mouthful of his casserole. "That was good. Now tell me where you get your chickens."

"It wasn't chicken, Chuck. Rabbit. There's a war on."

"Oh," said Chuck after a long pause. "Well, I'm sure glad you didn't tell me that when I was eating. Fact is you'll just have to excuse me for a minute."

As Chuck made hurriedly for the toilet, he passed Pippa on the arm of her pilot without seeing her but the sight of Chuck turned Pippa pale. Hurriedly, she danced the airman towards the cocktail lounge and their champagne.

"I've ordered a table," said Max as they sat down. "Gwen's said I can take a bottle of champagne back to their place after we've eaten. Share the same flat. This one's going to be worth every penny, John, you mark my words. Isn't that right, old girl?" he said turning to Gwen who just smiled as her sister took up a glass of champagne and swallowed it down.

"That's the stuff," said Max, filling her glass as she put it down on the coffee table. "Live for today and to hell to tomorrow and John and I have a forty-eight hour pass. So let's us make the best of it. Cheers Gwen. Cheers John. Cheers Pippa. I'm in a mood to enjoy myself."

"You open the champagne," said Gwen inside the flat, "and we'll go and change."

"You won't be long."

"Of course not. Come along Pippa," and she led her sister into the bedroom, closing the door behind them.

"Wow," said John. "If they look like that now can you imagine what they're changing into? Quick. Open that bottle. We want to have everything ready."

"Angus was right. The place is expensive but worth every penny. That girl's nipples must stick out half an inch. Quite a flat. They must be making a fortune. Classy. Not stupid. There must be more in this game than we imagine if educated girls go for it. We'll stay here the night. Save us a hotel room. I wonder if they'll give us breakfast. Cheers John, my boy. To a memorable evening. We'll probably be able to have both of them together. Turn that light out over there. We only need the lamp. Atmosphere. Even with whores you need atmosphere."

They sat watching the bedroom door, and finally the girls came out but dressed in casual day clothes that revealed nothing of the promise underneath. Gwen had on a tweed two piece and Pippa a grey twin set. Both were wearing sensible shoes and their hair had been brought back to normal. Both men rose to their feet without speaking.

"Is this some kind of a kinky joke?" said Max at length.

"No," said Gwen. "First, we haven't been introduced. I only know your Christian name."

"I don't see what that has to do with it."

"Well, I'm afraid it does. My sister and I are not what you think we are. Fact is we are helping out friends."

"Look, I haven't got time. That barman…"

"That barman had no right."

"He's employed by the club."

"Certainly. To serve drinks."

"Gave him twenty pounds."

"What for, may I ask?"

"You should know."

"What? Two gentlemen," and she emphasised the word slightly, "came to our table and asked us for drinks, dinner and could they come back afterwards. Well, here we are. What's all this about the barman?"

"He said you would sleep with us for one hundred pounds each. If we liked it next time he would negotiate some variations."

"And you gave him twenty pounds."

"You know what I think this is?" said Max getting to his feet belligerently.

"I think this is a con and I'm going back to that club and ask the manager."

"It's a woman. Lilly Venturas. She will give back to you your twenty pounds and the price of our drinks and dinner."

"Come on John," said Max. "Let's take that place apart. If there's one thing I can't stand it's a prick teaser, professional or amateur. Thank you for nothing," and he pushed John out of the door and followed him slamming it shut behind him.

HALF AN HOUR later Lilly let herself into her flat.

"He was close to getting violent," said Lilly, "but it did the trick. Fortunately the club was still packed when they came back and I got them into my office without a fuss. The barman denied it, of course. Had the cheek to say he hadn't even served them. Max was in such a state of frustrated rage by then that he went for him round the office a couple of times until he admitted taking twenty pounds. I then explained to Max and John how the club operates and that as far as we are concerned the girls are hostesses and nothing else, there to dance, and look pretty and that we'd heard some of the staff were running rackets and that this was the only way we could obtain proof that wouldn't upset the staff who were working properly. When I told Max who you were he went rather quiet and by the time I'd returned his money he was apologising profusely. Said he didn't recognise you, Gwen, and that how many times had he been to Merry Hall and for goodness would we all forget the whole thing or he'd be the laughing stock of the county. Bit of over-reaction."

"Chuck didn't recognise me either," said Pippa and then told Lilly how the bar stocks were being cheated.

"I've fired him, of course. From now on I'm putting women behind the bar and girls who have never been in a bar before and don't know any tricks. All food and beverage deliveries are being checked by me from now on. After discreet enquiries, I found out the chef's running a Bentley. They think women are stupid. The club should be making double the pre-war profit the way it's packed. Your next job is in accounts. Check every chit and we'll put in a new system. They must be stealing thousands between the tills and the office. Control, control. We've got to put in proper controls. Now I need a drink. Do you know, the first time I took over the club, when Tony was called up, I thought it was going to be cushy."

"Actually, Lilly," said Pippa, "I don't think I'm cut out to whore."

"Thanks, anyway. Cheers, girls. We nailed the bastard."

"There was only one snag," said Gwen.

"What's that?" asked Lilly, sipping a glass of champagne.

"I'd have given it to him for nothing. That whole atmosphere is erotic. I've never felt as randy in my life."

"That dress you wore was something else," said Lilly.

"That's certainly what Max thought. I've never had a reaction from a man like that in my life before."

"THEY'VE BLEEDIN FORGOTTEN US," said Wilf Kemp from where he lay on his back looking up through the thin foliage. His head was propped up by his haversack and the grass was wet.

"Who?" said Stew Philpott. "Gerry?"

"No, mate, the British fuckin' army."

"We should be so lucky."

"We've been in this wood three days and nothin'. Only thing I've seen up there's a bleedin' hawk."

"Camouflage is good," said Stew looking around at the parked armoured cars, draped in camouflage netting and dotted among the trees. "Smells good. Put in chillies?"

"Course," said Wilf.

"Learnt some in Africa. I liked that trip."

"What! Don't be daft. Fuckin' nearly died we did. All them fuckin' mosquitoes."

"Learnt to put chillies in stews. Makes all the fuckin' difference. Dried chillies. Who'd have thought?"

"Liked Cape Town," said Wilf, smiling to himself.

"All them black tarts in the catacombs."

"Was different."

"So was the dose of pox."

"We was recuperating. Might as well recuperate from two fuckin' diseases at once."

"Lucky it didn't drop off."

"Yeah. Stir the stew, Philpott. I can't be fuckin' bothered to get up... Remember them fish I caught?"

"Course I do."

"Didn't even need bait. You think the Major was havin' it off with that bird."

"Which one?"

"The one with the big tits."

"Look here, Wilf. There are a lot of birds in this world with big tits. You got to be specific," and Stew went across to the mess tin that was balanced over a methylated spirits burner. "Bubbling nicely," he said.

"The one in Cape Town. Short, brown hair. Big tits."

"Oh, her... I don't know. Doubt it. Major's straight. Got a wife and three kids."

"Wife's havin' another, so I heard. Must 'ave given it to her before we left.
We've been in fuckin' France for six months, you know that?"

"This is Belgium."

"What's the fuckin' difference... He took her out enough. Winin' and dinin', they call it the Mount Nelson Hotel. Must 'ave cashed in a lot of Beaumont money as 'e couldn't 'ave afforded that lot on his army pay, major or no bleedin' major. Bit of all right, that one. Wouldn't 'ave minded givin' her a go myself."

"Only thing what would let you give 'em a go," said Stew, stirring the bubbling hash in the mess tin with a stick, "was them black tarts."

"Well. You didn't do no better."

"Didn't get the bleedin' pox."

"No wonder it took the Major so long to recover," said Wilf.

"You've just got a dirty mind. It was the cricket what kept him behind. I liked that Newlands ground. Under them oaks with a cold beer. That's my idea of recovering. Watch the C.O. playing cricket, being on me back with a cold beer."

"Played well."

"I liked it when he made that hundred," said Stew. "Had me standin' up and when 'e got that single I was clappin' with the best of 'em, Never watched cricket in me life before. You know I haven't 'ad a recurrence of malaria for almost a year."

"You can keep it. Harry was lucky not to lose 'is leg."

"Wouldn't be here if 'e 'ad. Gives me the creeps. We've been runnin' away from the Germans for weeks and then we stops still like this."

"Not our fault," said Wilf. "Every time the major tried to hit Gerry, the bleedin' French 'ad fallen back another ten miles. Real bloody leap frog."

"That meant to be a joke?" asked Stew.

"'Course it was."

"Well, ha bleedin' ha. You think Dusty likes being an officer?"

"'Course 'e does. Better pay. Better food."

"You don't think he gets lonely?"

"'Course not," said Wilf. "Why should 'e want to get lonely?"

"No-one to talk to. We talked a lot in Africa. Wouldn't mind livin' there. Dusty's real sweet on that Rhodesian girl. Writes every week."

"How do you know?"

"I 'ave to post 'is letters. While we're being at death's door 'e's doodlin' the fuckin' major's daughter. No fuckin' justice, I say. No fuckin' justice."

"You said that twice," said Wilf, cupping his hands behind his back. "She was nice, Megan."

"Didn't think she'd come to Cape Town with 'im. He was only a sergeant then."

"Think they'll get married?" asked Wilf, wistfully.

"I don't know. No-one tells me nothin'."

"Think it's ready?"

"You hungry?"

"Always eat, I say. In the bleedin' army you never know when you'll get another fuckin' meal. Think Gerry's goin' to chase us out of Europe?"

"Probably. Nothin' much we've got to stop 'im with. The fuckin' Frogs aven't been much good. It's them Panzer divisions. Too many fuckin' tanks for my liking. Can't do nothing to a tank with a fuckin' machine gun," he said, looking across sadly at Elizabeth and George, the armoured car named by Dusty Miller after Megan's wild pigs.

"Can't do a fuckin' thing," agreed Wilf, and got up to rummage in his haversack for a tin plate and a fork for his stew. "Hey, Harry," he said. "Want some stew?"

"Got them chillies in it?" asked Harry.

"'Course it 'as," said Wilf and turned a dollop of the brown mess onto his plate."

"The place is too quiet," said Harry Sparrow.

"That's what we says. Too bleedin' quiet for three days."

"Maybe the major was givin' us a rest. Maybe he knows. If we run back much further from 'ere we'll 'ave our backs to the sea."

"Then what?" says Wilf.

"I don't know," said Harry. "I leave things like that to the major. He always gets us out of the shit."

"Makes you sweat for it," said Stew.

"How you mean?" said Wilf.

"The way he runs us around," said Stew. "Do it right and you're okay. Do it wrong and the shit hits the fuckin' fan."

"He don't ask us to do nothing 'e don't do 'im self," said Harry. "Don't take all the fuckin' food mate," he said to Stew, holding out his plate.

"Who's that geezer?" said Wilf, pointing with his fork between the trees past Elizabeth and George. They all stopped eating to look.

"Not L.R.U.," said Harry as Wilf began to shovel the food into his mouth.

"You'll fuckin' choke yourself," said Stew. "What's the hurry?"

Unable to talk with his mouth full, Wilf again pointed with his fork and rolled his eyes and then forked the remains of his food into his mouth. Harry ate steadily and Stew picked up the urgency. The camp of the Long Range Unit was rapidly coming alive.

"Trouble," said Wilf through a mouth half full. "That geezer means trouble. We're pulling out."

"How do you know?" asked Stew.

"Don't talk mate. Finish your stew."

"Here comes the lieutenant," said Harry and all three of them briskly came to their feet, cramming their berets onto their heads and coming to attention.

"C.O. wants to talk to us," said Lieutenant Dusty Miller.

"Now?" said Wilf, bulging his eyes slightly.

"Now. And on the double. We're moving out."

"See," said Wilf. "Told you so."

The men and officers in the wood were converging on Geoffrey Beaumont, standing at ease in a small clearing, a black swagger stick tapping his right thigh. The corners of his mouth were tight and he hoped his men could not see the tension that had quickly built up in his stomach. Geoffrey waited for complete silence.

"The French army is in extreme trouble," said Geoffrey, "and so is the B.E.F. The British Expeditionary Force are pulling back to the coast with the hope that the Royal Navy will be able to take us off. The speed of advance of the German mechanised columns has been greater than expected to put it mildly. The 3rd Brigade of the Household Cavalry has been retreating steadily for ten days. The men are exhausted and unless we can give them a respite they will not reach the coast ahead of the Germans. The R.A.F. report a Panzer column approaching the River Maas, north of Namière. The Royal Engineers have blown all the bridges but R.A.F. aerial photographs indicate that the bridge south of Namière, is serviceable, a condition apparently known to the Germans. We are twenty-two miles south east of this bridge. Captain Eriksen has brought with him sufficient dynamite to blow the central arch. Our job is to hold the bridge until demolition is complete. We will then make our own run for the coast. We've done a lot of training. Let's see if it was worth it. Lieutenant Miller will lead the column. I will command from the centre with Captain Forrester bringing up the rear. Come on. We're in a hurry."

Geoffrey Beaumont strode to his armoured car and within sixty seconds, the engines of fifteen vehicles had been started and the lead cars were leaving the cover of the wood. Geoffrey had had the explosives strapped to the back of his own vehicle.

"Fifteen fuckin' armoured cars to stop a German Panzer column," said Wilf as he drove into the lead. "He must be joking. Them columns have tanks and howitzers."

"Which is why that bridge must come down," said Dusty. "It has six spans but the second span is the key to demolition according to the A.A.F. photographic interpreters. Then all his tanks are on the wrong side of the river. They may have tanks but we have speed."

"Let's hope the German Air Force don't hear about it."

"It would be better if they didn't," said Dusty mildly.

"Birgitt, I do not have a mistress, neither do I want one, nor do I have the time," said Gunter von Ribbeck in German. "We are fighting a war."

"You do not think of my reputation?" said his wife.

"I think you should have thought of that ten years ago. Now, if you please, Klaus wishes to see me and he has also come a long distance. Our arguments have become pointless."

"But you accuse me of having an affair with Ingrid."

"Only because you made it obvious. Your father phoned."

"Ingrid and I are friends."

"I must see Klaus."

"Your business always comes before me," she said glaring at him as she gripped the doorknob to the private suite of rooms he had taken at the edge of the advance airfield where he had been stationed for a week. He was dressed in full flying kit, ready to fly the Stuka that sat on the grass verge outside his window, the first in a line of nine planes, hunch winged and vicious.

He watched his wife cross the airfield to her car and then she drove off out of his view. He had not bothered to get up from behind his desk.

"Damn," he said in English under his breath and slapped his flying gloves, strong black leather, against the corner of his desk.

"Come in," he said in German and the Managing Director of his industrial complex came into the room and looked in the wrong direction before seeing Gunter at his desk in the alcove, a warm sun bathing his black leather flying jacket. 'At least I understand business,' he said to himself and indicated a chair for Klaus to make himself comfortable.

"Problems?" asked Klaus, sympathetically.

"She makes most of them for herself. I think her father should have spanked her very hard on the bottom when she was a little girl."

"The responsibilities of parenthood. It is too often difficult to know what to do… How long will you be here?"

"It's nearly over, Klaus, thank goodness. The blitzkrieg has worked again. Once we have encircled the B.E.F. the war will be over. England will sue for peace. There will be nothing else for them to do and then we can get back to doing good business. Now, what have you come to tell me that is so important that you could not write it down in a letter?"

"The German Army has accepted the field tests. We have received our first order for ten thousand tons. We have to extend our factory in the Ruhr. Build another. Convert our tractor factory. Buy more coalmines."

"You go too fast. Were the field tests conclusive?"

"Our synthetic rubber is better than latex, and cheaper."

"When will the patents be approved?"

"They will be passed."

"Can you imagine the export potential when this war is over? Chuck will have to put up factories in America."

"Capital?" said Klaus.

"The last letter I had from François says they have enough diamonds to finance the war on both sides. Reggie will raise the finance. We have some power ourselves in the money market. It will be the group's biggest expansion. I just wish this damn war was over. Don't touch the tractor factory. Expand the others. I'll speak to the Baron about finance. The government will help. Strategic commodity. An army can't run without rubber. Once the war is out of the way, we must stop Tug buying any more latex. If we are quick enough he will be able to offload his stocks. Those go-downs in Singapore are full of rubber. You are right, Klaus, we must keep our synthetic rubber a closely guarded secret for as long as possible. Shit, I wish I could talk to Chuck about the American market. They've been having trouble with the Brazilians for years. Now they can tell them to shove their rubber trees right up, if you'll excuse the expression," and Gunter got up to pace the room in his excitement, his flying boots flapping where they were unzipped. "How much do we need?"

"One thousand million marks?"

"A lot of money. A pity we can't borrow on the international market. This damn war creates more problems than it solves.

"Come in," he shouted at the loud knock on his door.

"Briefing, sir," called his batman. "Very urgent."

"Right," said Gunter. "Get yourself some lunch in the officers' mess," he said to Klaus. "We're going up again," and he strode to the door, gripping Klaus's shoulder briefly on the way in appreciation. "How's the oil from the coal process coming along?" he said over his shoulder.

"We still have problems."

"Keep them at it. That one has enough by products to sink a battleship."

"British, I hope," said Klaus, laughing.

"But of course."

GUNTER WAS last into the briefing room, rows of seated pilots with their backs to him looking up at the Station Commander standing with his feet splayed and his back to a large blackboard over which was draped a map of northern France and Belgium, hooked black arrows showing the purpose of the German Army. A billiard cue rested next to his foot which was tapping with annoyance, the only movement apart from Gunter sitting down.

"It is most kind of you to spare us the time, Captain von Ribbeck," said the station commander icily in German.

"Business," mumbled Gunter whose brain was still looking for finance to extend the factory.

"Either you apply to the High Command for military exemption or you perform full-time as one of my flight commanders. Which is it to be?"

"Flight commander," said Gunter trying not to smile, the colonel and he having been close friends for six years. They had both been born thirty-one years earlier.

The stiff backs of the younger pilots relaxed as the colonel turned his attention to the map.

"The war is almost over. Another few days. Then the German people can turn their attention to creating order in the world. A lasting peace. Prosperity. There will never again be hunger. Unemployment. Inflation that needed a barrow box of currency to buy a newspaper. Order, gentlemen. Every sane man requires order to go about his business and live at peace with his neighbours. Germany will give this to the world and the power of industry will give it wealth. Humanity's energy will be channelled correctly, to the benefit of all of us. The dark ages are over but it is up to us to finish the job. The German Army has destroyed the French and Belgium armies and chased the British Expeditionary Force north of the River Maas in this enclave here," and he pointed with the billiard cue to the map. "They are heading for the coast but before they reach here, the port of Dunkirk, they must be surrounded. Under no circumstances must the regular British Army be allowed to leave the Continent. With the surrender of this army, Churchill will be forced to resign and the British government will sue for peace. They are Anglo-Saxons. We have much in common. A good peace with England will ensure the stability of the world from the Far East, through Africa to Europe. America does not want war with Germany. They didn't want it last time. Roosevelt will trade with the New Order and give his people even greater prosperity... Four Panzer divisions are converging here," and again he pointed to the map. "The speed of our advance has outstripped our supplies, otherwise the British would be surrounded. When the British withdrew over the Maas they blew the rail and road bridges except for one, here, and it is our job to patrol that bridge until the tank spearhead is across and able to defend it from the ground. Today there will be seven strikes against the retreating British and your squadron commanders have already been briefed by me. A short war is soon forgotten. Enemies quickly learn to live with each other. A quick war ensures there has been no time to build up lasting animosity between people."

Gunter's mind was brought back into the room by an orderly opening the door behind him and walking through to the station commander where he handed him a note, interrupting the colonel's personal view of a better world. Gunter had been pleased to hear the war was nearly over but he still had to raise the money and the thought of peace had taken his mind down a number of paths that would strengthen his companies.

"Blue squadron will scramble immediately," said the station commander, interrupting his thoughts. "A reconnaissance photograph has positively identified a flying column of British armoured cars on this side of the Maas. It appears they also know the bridge is passable. They must be dive bombed, strafed and annihilated. Flight control will give you your bearings."

Eight pilots had pushed back their chairs and were headed back for the exit. "Captain von Ribbeck," said the station commander. "Blue Squadron and that includes you."

"Yes, sir," said Gunter jumping up to follow the others. 'Flying,' he said to himself. 'Flying. The R.A.F. are not yet out of France and will know the importance of that bridge as much as us.' Slinging his parachute over his shoulder he ran for his Stuka and by the time he reached his dive bomber he was the first strapped into the plane and taxiing out onto the runway, ready for take-off, the flight controller giving them instructions as they screamed away off down the grass strip.

"Alright. Let's finish this bloody war," he said to himself as the Stuka left the grass and headed for the late spring sky warmed with fluffed up clouds, tokens of a coming summer.

BILLY HUDSON never enjoyed the first run of the term and this one had been no exception but as house captain of athletics it was up to him to set an example. The Easter holidays had been over for three weeks and he had put off the house run for a week. He cursed himself again for having failed his French exam during the winter exams which had forced him to stay at school for two more terms as otherwise he would have been in the navy and on his way to obtaining a deck commission. After the Battle of the River Plate, his frustration had made him lose interest in school and to what he now saw as petty rules and regulations, Billy Hudson had outgrown his schooldays and with most of his friends in the services there was no-one to talk to at Mill Hill School. If he didn't pass exams this time he would leave school anyway. He wouldn't be going to university. He pushed open the door to the prefects' ablution to find his fag sitting on the edge of the concrete bum bath.

"Chumley. What are you doing here?"

"Headmaster wants to see you. Very urgent. I was told to wait here for you. Here's the note saying I can."

"I'll have a shower and change."

"The head prefect told me to tell you to go straight away. Not to change."

"What's so bloody urgent? Where's the head?"

"In his study. That's what they told me."

"Alright."

Billy began the long walk down the old corridors, taking a short-cut through the sixth form entrance. Hands in his trouser pockets, having pulled them on over his running shorts, he made as good a speed as possible without running. House prefects were allowed to put their hands in their pockets but they were certainly not allowed to run in the corridors. 'What the hell have I done this time,' he asked himself and went through all the misdemeanours that could have ended him on the mat in the headmaster's study. 'Bad French marks would not lead to the head. Even being a week late for the house run was not that serious. Anyway, it was the jurisdiction of the house master. His mother was sick again,' and the inside of his stomach dropped like lead. 'That was it, his mother. He walked as fast as he could across the quadrangle and up the eleven steps, through the passage and out of the old building to the freshly sprinkled gravel that led across to the double-storey headmaster's house that he had last been into for a talk about his confirmation. 'It has to be family rather than school,' he told himself and then he saw his father's car parked outside and the inevitability pressed on his eighteen years and he stopped. It was the office car and his father should have been at work on a Tuesday. There were only three of them in the family. From a distance came the chock of cricket bats in the nets, hidden by the great oak trees that wound down the road to the playing fields on the other side of the public road. Looking hard at the headmaster's white front door he forced himself across the last thirty yards of gravel, up the three steps and banged with the brass knocker. Almost immediately the door was opened by the headmaster's butler.

"Hudson. The…"

"Come this way. Your father is waiting for you in the headmaster's study."

"Thank you."

The mournful tone had confirmed what he already knew. His mother was dead. He turned the brass handle and pushed open the heavy door to find his father pacing the room but no sign of the headmaster.

"Mother?" queried Billy.

"She's fine," said Percy Hudson looking at his son with pride.

"What's the matter, dad?"

"The British Army's been caught at Dunkirk. The Admiralty has put out a request to all small boat owners to get across the channel and bring them back. I'm on my way but need a crew. The head said you can go. You and I are taking *Wavedancer* across to France tonight. The boys are being hit badly on the beaches. Friend at the Admiralty says they are standing in water up to their necks waiting for us. The navy can't get close enough. The German air force is machine gunning them in the water. If we can't get those boys out of the water, Hitler's going to win this bloody war."

"Where's the R.A.F.?"

"Doing what they can. Dowding's holding most of the squadrons on the ground. If Goering has any sense he'll go for the airfields and the R.A.F. has got to be there to protect them otherwise England's wide open to the bombers. We don't have enough trained pilots or soldiers."

"The diesel tanks are full."

"Good. That's how you always keep them."

"Won't the Germans go for us?" asked Billy.

"Probably."

GEOFFREY BEAUMONT'S armoured car squadron moved round the twisting country lanes at fifty miles an hour, thirty yards apart, the drivers straining to maintain their positions. In front, Dusty Miller, his field glasses hanging around his neck searched the countryside ahead and on either side of the speeding hedge, the top half of his body out of the open hatch. Empty. No-one was out and about.

At the back of the column, his driver having to sometimes race at sixty miles an hour to catch up, Jim Forrester searched the same countryside with his binoculars, his dislike of being tail-end Charlie lost in the urgency and precision of his search. His mind was emptied of all other concerns.

In the centre Geoffrey searched the heavens for enemy aircraft, constantly turning and turning back. He knew what it meant to have broken cover after five days of being lost to the enemy in the woods. Checking his watch, the speed down below him on the car's speedometer and the mileage already run, he estimated a further twelve and a half minutes to the bridge and the captain needed twenty minutes to set the charges effectively. They had been out of the wood an hour.

"All I need's a fuckin' cow round one of these bends," said Wilf Kemp, "and it'll be the end of Wilfy's war in one solid thunk."

"How about a tank?" suggested Harry Sparrow. He was watching in front of him but the speed and twists in the road made it impossible to make any sense of what was happening. For comfort, he kept his left hand on the butt of the swivel machine gun and wondered if the British had thought of mining the road before they crossed over the Maas. Harry Sparrow had an instinctive fear of landmines that he couldn't see. He glanced up at Dusty standing between himself and Wilf and drew comfort from the years they had spent together.

"Shit," shouted Wilf and veered round a pothole causing Dusty to hit his kidney hard against the side of the hatch.

"Mind where you're going Wilf."

"Sorry, sir, but if I'd hit that one we'd have lost you, sir. Popped right bleedin' out you would 'ave done."

Dusty signalled the pothole to the car behind to start a relay of the same message back down the column. Nervously, he looked up at the sky for aircraft.

"The fork's coming up round the next bend," he said looking back at the road and comparing it to the map he'd memorised. "Left fork, sharp. Reduce speed and again he signalled the driver behind to slow down for the turn.

"Fuck me," said Harry, as Wilf took the forty degree fork without dropping speed.

"No thanks, mate, you're not my bleedin' type."

"Enemy aircraft," said Dusty again signalling the column behind. "Dive bombers."

"Shit," said Wilf.

"Don't you dare," said Harry.

"Nasty target for the pilots," said Dusty.

"Now ain't that comforting."

"Nine aircraft," said Dusty as he watched them drop out of the sky. They could now hear the scream of the dive bombers above the engine noise.

"They must know the bloody bridge isn't down." Dusty watched the bombs drop and the aircraft immediately pull out of their dives. "Patterning the road," and he watched the bombs explode half a mile ahead. The planes came out of their dives turning back to the speeding column where Dusty was signalling to break away from the road and into the countryside before the Stuka's judged the winding road and flew it against them, strafing its length.

"Don't fire," he said to Harry. "Waste of time. Now!" he said to Wilf and they broke away from the road and through the hedgerow into a field as the snout of a low flying aircraft came at them from around the bend up front in the road. He gripped the hatch with both hands.

"I can see the bridge," and he again signalled behind him as the second car burst off the road, a line of tracer cutting the tarmac behind.

"Those pilots are good," said Dusty. "Get back on the road and then drive down under the bridge. They won't bomb us. Might knock out the bridge."

"You're not wearing a tin hat, sir," said Harry looking up from below and winking as much to reassure himself. "Mind the fuckin' ditch," he said to Wilf who had veered away from the hedgerow bouncing the armoured car back into the field and slamming Dusty's other kidney against the metal angles of the hatch.

"Sorry, sir," said Wilf fighting the wheel to bring the car back along the hedgerow but on the wrong side of the road.

"Left ten," shouted Dusty and Wilf pulled instantly, accelerating violently at the same time, jerking the vehicle out of the line of fire. "Right twenty," shouted Dusty as he saw the pilot skid back into range by touching his rudder bar. Again the Stuka turned to point his guns and a line of fire whined over Dusty's head making him involuntarily draw down into the hatch. And then the plane was over them and turning back for another attack.

"The ditch was too deep," shouted Wilf above the noise of the engine. "It's alright getting off the fuckin' road but not much good gettin' fuckin' back again. Ramp effect from the bleedin' road side."

"We'll get through that three bar gate," pointed Dusty, "but make it look as if we're trying the hedge again. Full speed."

"What the fuck do you think I'm doing, sir?" said Wilf, his foot flat on the board as they bucked over the tufts and hillocks of the field. Dusty saw black smoke billow from his left and then heard the explosion. From over the tree tops from a copse to his left came the snarl of the single engine and he waited as the plane came nearer, the pilot intent on raking them. Dusty saw the pilot was waiting for him to make the first move. "Curve her," he shouted. "Curve her round to hit that gate but brace yourselves. BRAKES," he bellowed as he saw the wing cannons flicker light and the armoured car stood on its nose before thumping back on the wet grass as bullets ploughed the ground ahead of them tearing out in small explosions as the cannon shells exploded. The plane overshot ten feet above Dusty's head and briefly showed in Harry's machine gun sights but as Harry fired the plane pulled up to turn and come back at them again. Wilf accelerated and swiftly moved up the gears racing for the gate and the bridge that was growing bigger. They hit the wooden gate at thirty miles an hour, Dusty having ducked back through the hatch to avoid the flying bits of rotten timber.

"Down the river bank," shouted Dusty when he got back up and saw the clear run to the river bed and the soaring arches of the bridge, thin and three hundred feet high, a row of them reaching from the top of the bank and dropping further into the ravine until the last pillar supported the great arch that curved up and out over the water to join the first pillar on the other side, the narrow roadway tucked up high in the sky making the crossing vulnerable from the high banks on either side of the river. As the armoured car dropped down the plane was forced to pull out of its attack and hard ruddered away to scream up almost flat to the bridge before tugging away and flying out of sight.

"Cut through the second arch," shouted Dusty and we'll take up position on the other side where the road moves onto the bridge. Sparrow position the anti-tank rifle and give me the machine gun. It'll be easier to hit that plane from a stationary platform." Another car had broken through to the river and Dusty signalled the driver to follow. By the time they drove between the massive concrete arch there were three cars following. Dusty heard two aircraft coming at them and signalled all cars to stop and mount guns for aerial retaliation. As the two Stukas flew at them from over the trees they were met by accurate tracer from four armoured cars and were forced to break quickly.

"Those pilots are going to take a lot of killing," said Dusty as he swivelled his gun to follow them.

"Right," he shouted to the other cars. "Let's get this show on the road. I want two cars on either side of the bridge and one man from each with the anti-tank gun alongside the roads. This bridge is a bloody sight more important than even I understand. Anti-tank men to dig in if they can but find some cover from the air."

Geoffrey Beaumont, the Long Range Unit's pennant flying from the side of his car, drove through the gate shattered earlier by Dusty. He waved at Dusty and gave a thumbs-up sign and his vehicle, packed with dynamite, drove down to the river bed and the second arch, Stew Philpott bringing the car to a halt next to the concrete pillar nearest the water. The engineer captain got out and carefully began his inspection as Geoffrey helped to unload the explosives for the demolition. Having unloaded, he sent the car up to defend the bridge, his corporal in command.

"You been on a demolition course?" asked the captain in surprise.

"Sure. Everything. The idea is to be self-sufficient. You place. I'll help. You're in command here."

"Gerry sure wants this bridge."

"Yes. We lost three cars."

"I'm sorry."

"War," but the engineer was placing his charges around the hundred and twenty foot girth of the pillar and was oblivious to his surroundings. Geoffrey watched, satisfied. The man was a professional. Regular army, been practising for years as hadn't they all, the planes were coming back again.

"They'll be after us, captain," said Geoffrey. "No-one's playing games today. Shit. The bastards are coming in from both sides to stop us ducking away from them," and then the machine guns from twelve armoured cars opened fire and the pilots were forced to jink.

"Those things are meant to be dive bombers but the pilots are flying them like fighters." There was no answer from the engineer who was carefully wiring the packages of high explosive that he had attached to strategic parts of the pillar.

Geoffrey pulled the radio set round from his back and turned it on. "Casualty report all cars." He listened carefully for each armoured car to report. Three cars destroyed but only four dead. Watching the engineer begin to run out wire away from the base of the pillar, he ordered eight of his cars across the bridge as the aircraft came back but only three of them. 'Fuel and ammunition,' thought Geoffrey, expecting ground fire from the Panzers at any moment.

"Ready," said the engineer captain and Geoffrey ordered the remaining cars to retreat across the bridge. "The river's sluggish," he said.

"Pretty wide," said the captain.

"Depends from what perspective you look at these things," said Geoffrey watching the approaching aircraft. They were flying with their fixed wheels almost in the water.

"Down, captain," and he dived onto the pebble-strewn slope as the three aircraft opened fire on them and then flew through the centre arch. He watched the last car cross the bridge and waited for the signal which came immediately afterwards. Two bursts from the last machine gun.

"You can drop the plunger, captain."

"FUCK ME," said Wilf. "The whole fuckin' things fallen in."

"That's what the captain meant it to do," said Harry watching Geoffrey swim strongly across the river pulling the severed wire from the demolition and pushing in front of him a floating package containing his uniform, boots and radio.

"That's when it pays to be fit," said Dusty as he watched the engineer captain being pulled swiftly across the river by Geoffrey standing on their side of the bank and pulling in the wire attached to the captain. "And you're right, Corporal Sparrow, Gerry isn't going to use that bridge this summer."

2

AUGUST 1940

*I*n the middle of August 1940, at seven on a Friday evening, Carl Priesler pushed himself back from the building plans laid out on his desk and answered the knock at his door.

"Come in," he said looking up as Koos van der Walt came into his office at 62 Fox Street in Johannesburg.

"François in his office?"

"Bang on the door. Time we had a snort. T.G.I.F. Thank goodness it's Friday," and he pushed himself and the swivel chair away from the ornately carved yellowwood desk that dominated the carpeted office. Around the walls were modern paintings, the whole watched over by a painting of a male lion standing over its kill. Rumours in Hollard Street likened the lion to Union Mining and Exploration, the Exploration having been added by Carl and François when they arrived in Africa two years earlier.

"I never realised running a business required me to locate the shithouses."

"What's the matter?" said François opening his inter-leading door.

"Time to stop work for the week," said Carl. "I've had enough."

"Pour me a scotch. I'll be back in a minute."

"The Frenchman drinks scotch," said Carl with a shrug as he got up to go to his liquor cabinet. "Lion Lager?" he asked Koos who nodded. He opened the yellowwood cabinet door and then the fridge behind to get at the ice and the cold beers.

"How are the plans developing?" asked François coming back with his jacket hung over his shoulder.

"It seemed much easier to say we'll have our own office block. Architects never tell you what you should have but ask you what you want. As if I know. Never built a shack in my life."

"The price of being boss. Silly twerp this morning asked me to approve the purchase of a hydraulic lift. Koos, what is a hydraulic lift?" and the three of them laughed together.

"How long have you got to listen?" asked Koos.

"Thanks. That's enough."

"People don't make final decisions," said Carl, handing François his scotch as Koos uncapped two bottles of beer and poured. "Thanks," said Carl to Koos and raised his already frosting glass. "Prost!"

"À votre santé."

"Cheers."

"Are you coming to the party?" François asked Koos.

"A middle-aged married man, deacon in the church? No, man. But thank you. Parties like that are for young bachelors. Keep temptation away, my father always said. It's good. Helena has people for dinner. Old friends. Every Friday. Set in our ways. What can you do?"

"Enjoy it," said François looking at his watch. "There's a lot to be said for an ordered life. Is Mafutha downstairs?" he asked Carl.

"Ready and waiting," said Carl, picking up his jacket from the back of his chair.

"Guests start arriving at eight o'clock."

"Time for a 'quicky'," said François lifting the scotch bottle and pouring himself a tot.

"You want another beer?" asked Carl.

"No. We have wine with our meal and a drop of brandy afterwards. That's enough for a fifty-seven year old liver."

"You'll live to be a hundred, won't he Carl?"

"One hundred and ten. Sink that scotch. We're late."

"There won't be any traffic," said François.

"So? You think I can have an S.S. and S. in half an hour?"

"What's an S.S. and S.?" asked Koos innocently.

"A shit, shave and shower."

"Well, then you'd better go," agreed Koos. "Have a good party."

"See you Monday," said Carl. "Have a nice weekend. My best to Helena."

MAFUTHA, dressed in dull scarlet livery with the peaked cap surrounded by the U.M. & E. band perched accurately on his black head opened the back door of the Buick as Carl and François emerged into the parking lot next to 62 Fox Street. His pride, his large Zulu belly, pushed at the well-polished buttons down the front of his tunic and prompted Carl to tap it encouragingly as he got into the car.

"Mafutha," he said, "you are too fat."

"Yes, my baas. But my wives like it that way."

"So you say. Timber Lane and we're in something of a hurry."

"Anything your side today?" François asked Carl as the doors shut and the glass partition cut them off from the driver.

"Usual shit. Admin."

"Got to be done. Without control we don't have a business."

"You sound like Reggie," said Carl.

"It's true."

"Sure. But there has to be an easier way."

"Not on that one."

"I'd like to think otherwise. We've brought her a long way in two years and to think we didn't want to fund the exploration. Reinsurance income wouldn't cover salaries."

"It was a gamble that paid off."

"Who are the newbies?" asked Carl changing the subject.

"You'll find out soon enough."

"Have you met them?"

"Some of them," said François.

"Our type?"

"What a question."

"I really feel like a good thrash tonight. Five days' hard work builds it up and makes it that much more enjoyable. Paul called and said his four will blow our brains out."

"John White's confident," said François.

"What a bloody system."

"It's the best way I know to pull women."

"And the women like being pulled."

"John wants to talk about mining through from Wit Extensions to Kloof. Saves us sinking a third shaft."

"Will he sell?"

"No. Wants a royalty split."

"We'll sink our own shaft."

"Maybe."

"There's one thing I've learnt is you don't need partners in the mining business unless they are shareholders who just collect dividends."

"His project looks good on paper."

"I'm very fond of John at a party, as a hunting partner, but for the rest he talks a lot of shit."

"His father's very rich."

"Bloody predator."

"Who?"

"The father. That's the one to watch. The established mining houses hate us, François. New boys growing faster than them. We don't even belong to the Rand Club. Keep John on side. That's fine. One day he'll help us open a lot of doors. I like him. It's just all that Harvard Business Course that he sprouts, gives me the shits."

"A lot of it makes sense."

"Still. Watch his father. What's it to have money without the business? By the way, Tug's made another killing in rubber. The Americans are getting jittery about the Japs."

"The Japanese have their hands full in China," said François. "We thought Hitler had plenty to do and now the Luftwaffe are fighting it out with the R.A.F. and I can't work out which one's winning. The only advantage the R.A.F. have is that when one of their pilots bails out he can get back into the fighting. Gerry goes in the bag. Reggie worries me."

"He must be a little bit worried himself," said François sarcastically.

"Not a word from him this month."

"The papers are calling it the Battle of Britain. He's got his hands full flying aeroplanes and keeping alive."

"You think Gunter's flying over England?"

"You do what you are told in the services."

"At least we've hedged our business bets. A German or Allied victory won't affect Union Mining."

"There's more to this than money," said François.

"Both Denmark and France are occupied. Nothing we can do except hope the war keeps away from Southern Africa."

"Very selfish."

"Life is very selfish. People don't give anything for nothing and when you've got something they want to take it away. It's a very short life as a lot of young people have recently found out. Wars are a waste of time as in the end everyone has to get back to doing business with each other. Want a scotch?" he said and leant forward to pull the small cocktail box out of the back of the front seat.

"Put it that way, why not? You didn't see it, did you?"

"What?" asked Carl handing him the cut crystal glass, the bottom sloshing with whisky.

"The letter from Chuck. I gave it to Jean to pass it on, addressed to both of us."

"I stopped mail and calls all afternoon."

"You'll find it in your tray on Monday. Percy Hudson was killed at Dunkirk. They've put him up for a posthumous George Cross. He and his son took *Wavedancer* across the channel eleven times. They were dive bombed out of the water with thirty plus soldiers hanging on, some in the engine room. The ones on deck jumped overboard but Percy went back three times to pull wounded out of the engine room. Fourth time *Wavedancer* blew up. Marine major saw it. Percy's son's in hospital. Third degree burns. He'll live. Lad tried to pull his father back the last time. Percy pushed him overboard and the major picked him up. Oh! And Geoffrey is missing with some of his unit. Didn't get off at Dunkirk. Officially posted missing but not presumed killed… Gunter has passed out word through Switzerland that our company holds a patent for a synthetic rubber that works. Good for us but not for the Allies. We'll have to be sure we're not holding stocks of natural rubber when the war finishes, whichever side wins. Says he's short of development capital and we're sitting on a mountain of cash and can't help. Chuck says a cheap synthetic rubber in the States will make so much money he won't be able to count."

"Anything else?" asked Carl who was now subdued.

"Chuck says London is being plastered and is thinking of moving head office out of the city but it would make it too far out for Reggie."

"He must be having a hell of a time," said Carl, quietly.

"Yes."

"Maybe we should be doing something else than making money and enjoying ourselves. The Germans told the Danes who were Jewish to wear armbands. The next day the King and every other Dane was wearing them."

"This is going to be our last party."

"Why?"

"You'll have to run U.M.E. on your own."

"Why?" said Carl turning to look at François who was watching the passing jacaranda trees that spanned the roadside.

"I'm going back to France. Some of my friends have formed a resistance movement against the Germans. Sabotage. Assassination. Anything to disrupt the German effort. We think that the British can still hold out until the Americans come into the war. The R.A.F. has held up well and the Royal Navy is still intact. Australia, New Zealand, India, South Africa, Rhodesia, they're all sending men and arms to help. There's still a lot of fat on the British Empire."

"Then I'll come with you."

"No, Carl. Like Chuck in England, someone has got to run the group out here. We'll have to suffice with one M.D."

"Koos can run it."

"He's damn good as a mining engineer but in the final count he has to be told what to do. He's a very good number two. He doesn't want more responsibility at fifty-seven."

"How are you getting into France?"

"From here to England and then a Lysander will take me over. Fly without any moon. They can take off from a field. Marvellous plane. Army liaison."

"Which of your friends, François?"

"Certainly not my business associates. They will be far too concerned with protecting their backs and making money on the black market."

"Is Danielle involved?" asked Carl.

"Of course not," lied François. 'Women are not allowed into the military, however underground. Pour me another scotch. Tonight we are going to throw the best party of the lot. Wine, women and plenty of song."

"When are you going?"

"Monday. Monday morning early. Seven o'clock train to Cape Town and then a British destroyer."

"How do you get a ride on a British destroyer?"

"They offered."

"Why, François? Have you been waiting for this all along? Was it why you didn't rush off and join the French Army when the Germans invaded?"

"I was already in it."

"Which branch?"

"Intelligence."

"What with old Bertie Featherstone and Sir Thomas Beaumont we'll all be in intelligence."

"They are in a different branch."

"Well, that says something for a lack of company collusion. So the syndicate comes down to five."

"You'll have to look around for a new recruit."

"If you need help get word to me. You know bloody well I speak French without an accent."

"It's the people. They don't know you. There's going to be a lot of trust. And anyway, Carl, the people I'll work with know me as The Thief and you as my artist friend from Copenhagen. You haven't forgotten?"

"Then Simone is involved."

"Maybe."

"You love that woman, don't you?"

"Yes, as a matter of fact."

"Why haven't you married her?"

"Because she would never survive in our kind of world."

"Why didn't you go on playing jazz?"

"Because I'm a mix of two parents. One side's a Bohemian and the other, even if I say it myself," he said laughing, "is quite a good businessman. A bit cautious at stages."

"Is she in trouble?"

"Not yet."

"Sorry… Too many questions. Shit, I'll miss you, you old bugger."

"Touché Monsieur Priesler. Now, off that. Let's get our mind back to setting the weekend on fire. Here's the driveway to Timber Lane. And please don't stand in the shower meditating for too long. From eight o'clock we've a lot of living to do."

MAFUTHA, dressed in a white, Arab kaftan in the role of Major Domo, struck the three foot diameter gong suspended between two head-high, ivory tusks and the resounding boom echoed around the mansion announcing the party was open for host and guests. He struck the hanging gong a second blow and the sound boomed out onto the stone-flagged terrace that jutted proudly from the house and looked imperiously down onto the next level of the ten acre garden where the seventy foot pool shimmered from arc lights above while below the surface, beams, struck into the walls of the pool like so many portholes in a luxury liner, revealed the crystal clarity of the water.

On the third gong, and in the tradition of the syndicate who had paid five thousand pounds for the gong and its tusks, François, host for the night, appeared at the top of the stairs from his east wing in the house in a dinner jacket and descended the stairs. Mafutha put down the leather-tipped gong stick and picked up the silver tray he had previously prepared and staring firmly at the last banister in the stairs held the tray on the flat of his hand and at an exact level between shoulder and elbow.

"Everything ready, baas," he said as François removed the crystal glass containing two tots of Chevas Regal and three large lumps of ice. Walking across the polished hallway, that had been de-carpeted to produce a dance floor the size of the swimming pool, he walked with Mafutha out of the fifteen-foot high open French windows to inspect the night's arrangements. Immediately his nostrils were assailed by the smell of roasting sheep, well spiced and tanged with citrus fruit. Beside each spit stood a black man dressed in the same kaftan but without the splendid red fez that topped the six feet one inch of Mafutha. The heavy metal handles of the spits were turned every half hour to allow the wood fires in the pits below to cook the shoulders and legs more than the thin belly of the carcass. Regularly, long handled ladles were used to baste the roasting meat from the cast iron pots that stood on three tall legs close to the fire to give the marinade heat and bubbling substance. The sheep had been cooking for three hours already. On a heavy wooden table next to each spit lay a long, curved knife that had been honed to razor sharpness that would split the meat like butter. François looked carefully to be sure that the insides of the legs were roasting properly, sipping his scotch as he went. The front line of tall trees in the park-like gardens had been rigged with spotlights which cunningly created strong patches of light and darkness.

François turned back to look at the floodlit, front of the house he jointly owned with Carl and enjoyed the sight and smell of hanging jasmine that cascaded with yellow morning-glory to the floor of the terrace and then spread out two feet from the walls.

Two bars had been set up in the garden serving anything the guests should call for. Bonfires, strategically placed, gave heat to the chill, highveld night to allow the ladies to wear their summer evening dresses with something warm for their shoulders. The fountain at the far end of the heated swimming pool gurgled up at the pattern of stars in the black heavens of night. There wasn't a trace of wind.

"Pretty bloody good," said François finishing his scotch and handing the glass to Mafutha who then turned the tray and offered a second ice-soaked scotch. They retraced their steps into the high ceilinged dining room where plate after plate of fresh, Knysna oysters rested on ice that would be changed twice before the guest gulped down the slippery delicacy. Arrangements of fruit and seventeen salads completed the table.

"They'll never eat it all," said François.

"But my friends will," said Mafutha, smiling in anticipation.

"True."

The front door bell rang and Mafutha excused himself to let in the twelve-piece band that was shown up to the gallery, halfway up the spiral staircase and looking over the dance floor and arriving guests. Mafutha pointed out to the band a well-stocked portable bar and told them to help themselves explaining further details of the evening to the bandleader. Carl appeared at the top of the stairs and Mafutha broke off and hurriedly went down to strike the gong. In a muddle of put down glasses and picked up instruments, the band managed a strangled version of the first verse of the *Eton Boating Song*, indicating that a syndicate member had joined the party. Carl waved imperiously and with all the theatre he could manage descended the stairs to receive his Lion Lager from Mafutha.

"Send it, baby," said François giving the thumbs-up to the band, and the harmonised power of Glen Miller burst from the gallery.

"Beautiful," said' Carl, "beautiful. Where the hell did you find the band, François?"

"America. Contact of Chucks."

"For one night?"

"Certainly."

"You are mad."

"Certainly. The whole idea of a syndicate member throwing a party is to outdo the other syndicate members."

"That you've done. And in wartime."

"America isn't at war. This is my last party. Maybe forever. Who knows? It's going to be memorable. You never know what the hell is going to happen to you next."

"Say that again," said Carl as the band broke into *Little Brown Jug*. Cars began to arrive, led in by three U.M.E. office vehicles that had been sent out with drivers to pick up the newbies organised by François. By eight thirty, the long driveway to Timber Lane was strewn with cars parked off on the lawns between the trees. The band, having slugged back sufficient booze, were enjoying themselves. Waiters scurried between the guests and the men watched as each new arrival was announced by Mafutha in an array of mispronunciation. There wasn't a woman over thirty-five and every one of them handpicked by the syndicate members, were head turners, from tall and slim to short with big breasts, from genuine redheads to a blonde whose hair hung freely to her waist. The first bar of the *Eton Boating Song* was played four more times and then the numbers were complete and François, host for the night, payer for this night, mingled with the guests and totally failed to decide which one of the girls he fancied. At nine o'clock the sheep were carved and the guests began to look less formal. The booze was getting to them.

MEGAN STRONG DETACHED herself from the party and walked away from the floodlit house and band-noise into the depths of the formal garden that had lost its bush-power to civilisation. She had heard that morning from a base camp friend of Dusty Miller's that he had been reported missing and had decided in future that she would not give a part of herself to anyone. She had yet to cry and wondered if she would or whether she had cried for all her future when her husband and child had drowned. She was not a party girl and wondered why she had come. The girls at Anglo-American had been very persuasive when the invitation arrived. None of them had been invited to a syndicate party and it was for her to find out what they were like and whether the wicked, exciting rumours were true. As she stood back by a clump of bamboo it looked like any other party with everyone getting drunk and nibbling at the food. She certainly hadn't been hungry. She sipped at her glass of straight Cape brandy and listened to the music. She was shadowed by a floodlight and the twelve feet shoots of sentinel bamboo that harboured water and a vociferous bullfrog. The frog made her think of Mazoe and without effort she was out in the boat with Dusty and the moon was up and shining on the water. Even her father wasn't there anymore, sent up to North Africa to join the Eighth army and pick up where he had left off in the last war. It will help his drinking, she thought, something she was sure was killing him… Another cable, another letter. They were going to start squeezing the oranges and make them into concentrates for the Allied armies. Even her little patch of Africa was being used to wage war. She sipped her drink and enjoyed the sensation of the burning liquor and decided she would get herself a little drunk for the evening. And she had been so sure they would farm Grandpa's farm together and create a line of farmers who would live from her land for generations and off into the future.

"Parties are not for being on your own," and she jumped, startled by a man she recognised as one of the syndicate members.

"Sorry," he said.

"Miles away."

"Good dreams?"

"No," and she stepped out of the shadow and an arc light caught the top of her head and illuminated the rich auburn of her hair. She turned her green eyes to him and summed up the perfect male predator. Well dressed. Tall, good looking. Charming. Stinking rich. After one thing only.

"Can I get you another drink? I'm Carl Priesler," and added after a moment when she did not reply. "This is my house, with the host, François Deauville. You met him."

"The Frenchman?"

"Yes."

"You must be the Dane."

"Yes. That's me… The drink?"

"Why not? It's what we're here for."

"Don't put it like that."

"How else should I put it?"

"To enjoy yourself. Take a few hours of pleasure. We try hard to make them work. François flew the band from America."

"Bully for him."

"He likes jazz."

"And plays the gramophone or a band when he can get one flown in."

"That was a bad dream."

"'Fraid so."

"War?"

"What else?"

"I'm sorry."

"Are you?"

"Yes," said Carl beginning to get annoyed. "I'll leave you to them."

"Just like that?"

"It's a very short life, whoever you are. Make the most of it. I've made it a principle and it works. You know where the bar is?"

She didn't answer and watched his back walk away to the party and through the French doors into the crowd. She thought she heard him laugh but couldn't be sure. She'd asked for that one and shrugged and took herself off to the nearer bar for a stiff one. He had been right. Moping and being rude wasn't going, to get her anywhere.

"WHO'S THE REDHEAD?" asked Carl.

"Which one?" said François looking around the dance floor.

"Outside. Been standing alone for half an hour."

"Megan. Megan something. One of the newbies. Heard of her through a friend at Anglo. Fabulous body. Why?"

"Snapped my head off."

"You mean Megan Strong," said John White lifting his glass. "Husband drowned. New fiancé reported missing in France."

"That explains," said Carl.

"Got a problem," said John looking around approvingly at the female talent." Good stock tonight… Can't throw the next party."

"What?" said François. "Can't you afford it?"

"Army. They're sending a South African brigade to North Africa. Cape Town Scottish. Van's going. Leaves four out of six."

"Three," said Carl. "François' going back to France."

"Whatever for?" said John turning to François. "The place is overrun by the Germans. What are you going to do?"

"I'll find something."

"Pussy. Something like that?"

"Something like that," agreed François. "See that one over there? Watching her all night. It's against the law of gravity they don't pop out."

"We'll put the syndicate on ice till after the war," said Carl.

"We'll be too old," said John. "It's not the parties that are exhausting, it's following up on the newbies afterwards. What a bloody system. Thirty new birds to choose from every month and not an ugly one in the room. Where did we find birds before we put the syndicate together? I had eleven phone calls this month from young ladies asking to be invited to a party and that kind of lady never turns out ugly."

"It does help when all the male guests are single, under thirty-five and earn in excess of one thousand pounds a month," said Carl, sarcastically.

"They don't come for our bright faces. Only our bright bank accounts."

"Who cares?" said Van, joining them, "so long as they come."

"Was that a pun?" asked John.

"Take it as you will."

"I'm going to be the only man left in Johannesburg," said Carl, drifting away from the crowd with François.

"You won't be complaining," said François.

"It won't be the same without friends. All this is a game," he said sweeping his arm round the dining room as they moved away. None of us are really in it for what we say we are. Sure, taking out good looking ladies is a pleasure but if we find one we really like we'll kick the system."

"We've had a good run. Maybe it's time to stop… This one's going well. What are you going to do if your staff join the army?"

"Koos is too old. So are some of the others. We'll make out like everyone else in this crazy world. Will you see Thelma in England?"

"What do you say to a really nice girl that has everything for you but you don't want other than a friend?"

"She's hung around a long time. Didn't you propose?"

"Said I'd give her a diamond. One of ours. Took it the way she wanted. I've told her."

"About Simone?"

"No. That's another life," said François.

"Every woman thinks she has a chance if there isn't anyone else around. Thelma knows from Reggie you're not serious about anyone. She's been out here, don't forget. Probably writing to one of the girls in the office. Women are very purposeful when they've made up their minds they want to marry someone."

"I'll write to Thelma."

"Talk to her. More difficult but better for the other person. There's Megan back in the party. Come over with me. Pretty enough."

"Certainly," said François, following. "There's one thing, being a syndicate member is better than being called a freebooter."

"Those were good days at Oxford."

"There are plenty of good days ahead of us."

"I hope so," said Carl as they reached Megan at the terrace bar. "I'm sorry about your fiancé," and Megan looked up sharply.

"Life doesn't seem worth all the effort."

"Don't be so damn silly," said Carl. "Take a good drink and I'll walk you down to the river."

"Are you trying to get into my pants?"

"Probably. On the other hand I might be offering a shoulder to cry on. Also, I think we both might be lonely."

"You!"

"In a sense. A lot of my best friends are at war or are going to war. It's sad to know people well who might be dead tomorrow. Selfish too. We live through our friends. Enjoy life with them. It's not easy having a party for one."

"DON'T PUT your foot in the water. The rivers here are full of bilharzia."

"How long have you been in Africa?" asked Megan.

"A couple of years," said Carl.

"I was born here."

"Johannesburg?"

'Rhodesia, to be exact."

"I'm teaching grandmother to suck eggs?"

"Something like that."

"I know nothing about you?"

"We only just met."

"This is the second time in half an hour. Makes the difference. What do you do?"

"Grow oranges. For Anglo. Mazoe citrus estate outside Salisbury. Dad's in the army. Mother's dead. So are my husband and my baby. Grandpa still runs the home farm at Umvukwes. Fiancé reported missing. Lovely life. And you?"

"Well, I run U.M.E. with François. Dane. Grew up in Copenhagen."

'Parents?"

"Sure. Father builds ships. Or did until the Germans arrived. Sailing ships for rich Danes and Swedes. Finns can't afford them. Three masted schooners. Doesn't make a lot of money but enjoys his life. Born five hundred years too late. Would have made a perfect Viking. Big beard and shaggy head. You know the type. I love him to bits. Oh, and so does my mother."

"Brothers, sisters?"

"Sister. Married. Three kids. Very respectable. Considers her brother a reprobate. Sensible sister."

"Brother-in-law?"

"Rich and boring. Enough said."

"Let's go back to the bar," said Megan. "I feel like a drink. You've sense after all and that's difficult to find in a man."

'Well, thank you ma'am."

"It's my pleasure. Why doesn't the band play jazz? They've been playing swing all night."

"I'll ask François."

"To play a record?"

"Or something," said Carl, his mind taking him back to the cellar in Paris.

"Can you boogie?"

"My nickname is Boogie Woogie Priesler."

"You made that up?"

"On the spot. Quick as a flash. Very original. Excuse me a moment. Come and meet Van. This is Megan, Van."

"What a party," said Van. "That meat was delicious. The outside crunchy bits. Even at this temperature we'll have them all in the pool by midnight. One hour to dunking. And that band, man. That band. Must have cost the Frenchman a fortune. Twelve of them. All the way from little old America… Where's he gone?" he said to Megan.

"To ask the Frenchman to play boogie."

"Now that's something. Boogie. I always boogie best when I'm a bit pissed and I'm a little bit more than a bit. 'Nother drink? Must drink. Can't have a party if they don't drink. Hey, John! We're going to boogie. Come and meet Megan. Isn't she gorgeous? Best damn figure in Johannesburg. The Big J. Best damn mining camp for miles."

"Van you won't last the night."

"Maybe not but I'll have a try… The music's stopped… All the way from America and they want a coffee break… Sock it to them, baby. Sock it to them… What's the bloody Frenchman doing up there, pardon my French? The bastard's waving a violin, excuse my French. HEY, FRANCOIS. YOU GOING TO CONDUCT?"

"Your attention, ladies and gentlemen," said François from the gallery. "As syndicate host for the evening, welcome."

"Our pleasure," shouted voices in unison. "For he's a jolly good fellow…"

"Thank you. I have been telling myself that for years… We've had some fun this last year but this is the ninth and last party for a while. Van and John will be in uniform next week and I am leaving for France. I knew this was going to be the last party when France fell. I knew we would want it to live with us for a very long time. You see, the war as they said it would be was not over by Christmas. They never are. But for the moment we have a party. One of the great loves of my life is music. Swing and especially jazz. In the band tonight we have one of America's best jazz trumpeters and as you see we've moved in a piano and a double bass."

"You going to play Beethoven's sonatas on that thing," yelled a voice from the floor below.

"Maybe," said François lifting the bow and violin ruefully. "Bacon and eggs at midnight. Anyone swimming is daft but that never stops us."

"He's going to shove it up his arse," shouted someone else.

"This one's a Sidney Béchet number," said François. "Fellow Frenchman. I think one of the greatest. And Wes is going to play soprano sax. The number from New Orleans. Traditional. Ladies and gentlemen, *'Didn't he ramble','*" and François stomped five times on the wooden floor of the gallery and the trumpet, piano and bass trio played in the slow start; mournful, beautiful, the funeral march from a Negro past. Then the beat began to change and the tempo rose bringing in the high notes of the soprano sax and the figures below began to sway with the music as Carl re-joined Megan.

"What's he going to do with a violin in a jazz band?" asked Megan.

"François likes posing. Looks good up there."

"He's about to do something."

"So he is."

At first, the sounds François drew from the violin blended so well with the other instruments that it was difficult to detect his playing.

"He's not making any sound," said Megan.

"Maybe," said Carl and then the violin sound became apparent as it wove rapidly in and out of the trumpet and sax, dancing merrily in among the strong notes as the music built and the dance floor burst into activity as François built and built and finally dominated the band and led them into impromptu variations they didn't know themselves.

"It's very good," said Megan, just heard by Carl over the music.

"Yes. I've told him a few times that he's wasting his time in the mining industry."

"Why doesn't he play more often?"

"He's sad tonight. Going somewhere else. His other life, I call it. There he plays. I heard him play with Sidney Béchet once and the master bowed to François Deauville. Never knew myself till that night. I wonder what happened to Danielle?"

"Who?"

"No-one you'd know. I'm rambling. It's finally hit home to me that an era has come to an end. Come on, Megan, we'd better boogie while we can… Look out, everyone. Here comes Boogie Woogie Priesler and his new star dancing partner… Plenty of room… We're dangerous."

MEGAN OPENED her eyes to strange curtains and couldn't remember where she was. The bed was large and the ceiling high with a strong ray of sun filtering through a gap in the curtains. She quickly sat up and checked if she was alone and then lay back on her pillow to suffer the hangover. Adjusting her head to ease some of the pain, she focused on a bottle of Enos, a glass of water and two white pills on the table next to her bed. Gratefully she groped towards them and administered the pills with half the water and then added the fizzy salts which effervesced into her eyes and made them cry. Sinking back into the bed she waited for something to happen and it was then that she remembered Dusty was missing. After half an hour she got up and tottered into the adjacent bathroom and had a shower, turning her face up to the water and letting it run down her body and cascade between her large, firm breasts and down into the tangle of her pubic hairs and then on down the strong thighs to the ground. Had she or hadn't she was the question she was unable to answer and her mind was unable to trace back the evening from the point she had fallen naked into the pool and found it surprisingly warm. The hot toddy that followed was the end of her and the from then on was blank. 'Well,' she thought with a sigh, 'if I have and I've got myself pregnant I sure won't know the name of the father.' Painfully, she traced the time of the month and thought it reasonably safe. 'What a waste! If it was good I can't even bloody well remember. Rich men's parties! They had it all their own way. THE DANE!' and she came out of the shower in a hurry and racked what was left of her brains. 'How embarrassing. I'll have to ask him. Like father like daughter. I shouldn't drink. It's Saturday or should be. No more head office meetings until Monday. Should feel better by then.'

Back in the bedroom, she pulled back the curtains and hurt her eyes badly with the glare. 'Oh, no. I'm dying,' and then she looked out to see normal people sitting round the pool in bathing costumes, sucking on straws in orange and tomato looking drinks. 'Booze! Ugh… I'll never, ever drink again.' A good looking girl dived into the pool and came up shaking the water out of her hair. Megan felt the pain from the shake and winced as the Frenchman called out 'Morning' loudly, as he came out onto the terrace in his trunks with a towel thrown over his shoulder. After a knock at her door, she tried twice to say come in before she made any noise. Mafutha, face inscrutable, bore in a breakfast tray and the smell of fried eggs and bacon almost made her heave.

"Morning, missy."

"Good morning… What time is it?"

"Eleven o'clock. Drinks are being served round the pool."

"Didn't they go home last night?"

"Some. Not many. Big house. When you eat you feel better. Bathing costume in wardrobe over there. Plenty sizes. Food. Swim. Bloody Mary. No problem. Mr Carl says come down when you are ready."

"He does, does he?"

"Yes."

"I'll try but please put that food right over there."

"Yes."

"And close the door quietly."

"Yes."

"Thank you."

"Yes," and Mafutha got out of the door before the grin spread over his face and he shook his head, patted his large stomach which was very full and wondered at his boss's stamina.

Mafutha, in his day uniform of long white trousers and loose fitting linen jacket, walked sedately down the eleven steps to the pool deck, the silver salver held imperiously at the correct height between shoulder and elbow and presented its contents to François, Carl still hiding in his bedroom.

"Just arrived, baas," and François frowned at the buff envelope. Cables not sent to the office were never good news. François turned the envelope over and looked at his name and Carl's through the cellophane window. The first relief of knowing it wasn't Simone turned to ice-cold fears for Reggie. His mouth dry, he turned the envelope again and slit the back open with his index finger, taking out the form and quickly reading Chuck's name at the bottom before looking at the message. Carl had seen Mafutha from his bedroom window and had run down the stairs but forced himself to walk across the terrace to the pool.

"Reggie," said François, looking up at his partner. "He's been shot down again. Twice. Twice in one day and he went up again."

They walked away from the guests, between the tall trees and the well cut lawns.

"That's the fourth time, François," and they looked at each other.

"Alright," said François. "His luck can't last."

"It can't. Shit, it must be tough. How many bloody missions are they flying a day?"

"Short of pilots. They're just landing to refuel and rearm."

"He's going to get killed. Christ! Tony's gone down twice."

"Tony's dead, Carl… That's what the cable was really about."

"Poor Lilly… Poor kid. She just doesn't have any luck with her men."

"It's war."

"You just be bloody careful, François. This damn war's getting too close to home for my comfort."

"Anything wrong," said Megan. "Can I help?"

"Thanks. No. One of our top blokes has been killed over Kent. Our senior partner's been shot down twice."

"Reggie?"

"Yes. Know him?"

"By name. My fiancé's in the same unit as his brother."

"Geoffrey's reported missing."

"So's Dusty. They're pretty close. Dusty was a private when he joined the L.R.U. and Geoffrey made him go for a commission."

"Geoffrey'll find a way round," said François. "His L.R.U. is well trained and the equipment's good. Well tested."

"That's how I met them. Testing equipment down Africa."

"Venturas," said Carl. "Remember that first night in Bretts? Didn't know Reggie had a share in the place. Good pilot."

"He taught us all to fly at Oxford," explained François and the memories came back to him. "What a waste of life! The best always go first. I'll put a call through to Chuck."

"Waste of time," said Carl. "They won't be using up telephone wire to pass condolences."

"You're probably right."

"And how do we hear if Gunter gets hurt?"

'We don't. Shit. Tony taught Gunter to fly."

"Poor Lilly."

"Yes."

3

THE MIDDLE KINGDOM 1940

*A*t the time François Deauville scrubbed up the cable and threw it into the Jukskei River at the bottom of his garden, Kim-Wok Ho shifted the burden from his shoulder blades and let the yoke he was carrying drop to the dusty roadside. Dressed in a dusty smock and no shoes with a conical hat for sun protection, he looked like a billion other Chinese fighting their way through survival. He had been on the road for ten weeks and was seven hundred miles into the Middle Kingdom having first taken the boat to Hong Kong from Singapore. His destination was a large cave in the mountains three miles south east of Yungting in Hunan Province and he had passed through Yungting half an hour earlier. To reach the spot where he sat down wearily at the side of the dirt road, he had used every form of transport that moved in the Middle Kingdom but for the last hundred miles, where the Japanese army was relentlessly perusing the peasant army of Mao Tse-Tung, he had been on foot so as not to attract attention. Even in business, Kim-Wok Ho had never underestimated the Japanese and he had been impressed by what he had seen of their army. Every bone and joint in his body ached and the stomach and fat of good living in Singapore had evaporated and he weighed little more than the peasant eyeing him from across the road, a road that would just let two donkey carts pass without tossing one of them into the ravine down below. To add to his discomfort he was parched and the water bottle underneath his smock was empty. Money he had in plenty in the money belt strapped next to his skin but the sight of gold would have warned the Japanese as quickly as if he had walked into their camp. In the last ten weeks, Kim-Wok Ho had found out what it was like to be poor and he didn't like the experience one bit.

To cool his brain and fool his thirst he thought of his air-conditioned flat and that brought him to thinking of Linda and that brought him to the realisation that his imperial penis had only been used for pissing for a very long time. He looked across at the equally dirty peasant opposite and wondered if any of his bodily needs were ever satisfactorily serviced. Worse, he wondered if they ever would be. Trying not to remember that when his task was over he would have to retrace the same seven hundred miles in the same way he had come, he forced himself to his bare feet that were bleeding and raw and hoisted up the yoke with the two balancing baskets and forced himself to move forward to his final destination. Twenty minutes later he branched off the track at the point he remembered from his childhood when as the son of the local warlord he had ridden on hunts in the hills and even up to the cave that he hoped he would still be able to find. Step by step he made across open country almost double from the weight of his baskets and the lack of water and nutrition. 'I'm too damned old for silly escapades,' he said to himself in English and then wearily forced himself to translate into the dialect of his youth that he had been dredging up from forty years ago all along the length of his journey. The bony hand that grabbed him could have as easily killed him for all he cared and he fell to his knees, the two baskets plopping down beside him and the yoke sliding down his back.

"Get up," said a voice in the Mandarin dialect of Hunan. He toppled round onto his bottom and looked up at his assailant but couldn't see a face with the sun right behind. "I said get up."

"I know," said Kim-Wok Ho in the same language. "I don't think I can at the moment."

"Why are your feet bleeding?"

"I have walked many miles."

"Peasants walk many miles but their feet don't bleed?"

"Possibly," agreed Kim-Wok Ho and he didn't care anymore.

"How far have you walked?"

"Forever… Well, not quite… Three weeks of walking."

"Why?"

"My father is dying… I had a message… I live far, far away… not always… over there… that rock. I was seven. A rabbit. I killed a rabbit with my shotgun… over there… there'll be bloodstains. I cut its throat and let the blood run out of its mouth… My father was very proud… I mean seven's a bit young to kill a rabbit," and Kim-Wok Ho had been speaking in English.

"Are you Kim-Wok Ho?" asked the man in the sun.

"I was… I still may be… I don't know… Do you have any water?"

"We've been waiting for you. Leave the baskets. Come. Lean on my shoulder. We'll have a doctor look at those feet. When your brother said you were going to come I laughed at him. He said you were fat."

"Portly… Saved me… I've been living off my own fat for the last few weeks… My housekeeper will never recognise me… How is my father?"

"He will be better for seeing his eldest son."

"How the hell am I going to walk back to Hong Kong?"

"We'll find a way."

"Don't walk so fast."

"We've only taken ten paces."

"That's a lot of paces, believe me."

"I'll believe you. Were you speaking English just now?"

"I expect so. I don't speak Chinese at home. English and Malay. It will come better after a rest… You don't have any water?"

"Not here. It's not far. Do you want me to carry you?"

"No," said Kim-Wok Ho loudly and forced his back up straight. "Thank you for the help, I'll be alright now."

THE FOOD, rice, plain rice, and the water, were the best that Kim-Wok Ho could ever remember tasting and he shovelled the food up into his mouth with two closed fingers until the bowl was empty and he put it down to drink another cup of water even though he was no longer thirsty and his feet were bandaged and his back was resting comfortably against a pile of sacking and the wood fire in the cave was hot and no longer smoking. Without being able to control his terrible tiredness, he put his head back and was sound asleep. For ten hours, he did not move or dream and when he woke it was to a day that he thought he could live through.

The old warlord turned communist was watching him, a humourless glint in the one good eye.

"You've got flabby, son," said his father in high Mandarin.

"Thanks for letting me sleep."

"We didn't let you."

"I see."

"Feeling better?"

"Much. You look well."

"I'm dying. Happens to all of us. Damn nuisance. Just when I was getting things done the way… Do you want food…? Rice…? Not what you're used to. Not used to it myself. Better than starving. Much better."

"Much better," agreed Kim-Wok Ho and smiled at his father.

"What's the matter with you?" he said.

"Old age. Everything falling apart at the same time. Lucky I can see and listen. They've had to carry me around for three years. Told them to leave me behind after the Long March but your brother wouldn't hear of it. Said he needed my advice. Lot of nonsense… How many children have you got?"

"None, father."

"Something the matter with you?"

"No."

"Why?"

"The lady I live with is English."

"I see. Find yourself a Chinese wife when you go back. Find one here. That's an instruction. Grandsons. I need more grandsons. I want to be an ancestor that lasts a very long time. None of this dying out on me. You understand?"

"Yes, father."

"You've been a good son. Always done what I asked of you. They say you're rich. Very rich. Richer than me those years ago."

"Not that rich, father."

"You flatter me."

"No. It is not all a question of degree. There are many men in Singapore richer than I. Around here, there was no-one richer than you."

"We've got to move again before winter."

"I know. I hurried."

"Your brother said you wouldn't make it. Bloated capitalist. I said you would."

"I am still Kim-Wok Ho."

"Yes. We are what we are however we call ourselves. We were wrong before… Those peasants must have a chance. Chairman Mao will give it to them. I believe it. For thousands of years the Chinese people have not had a chance… This must change and I want you to help me make this change."

"What do you want me to do?"

"When the Japanese have been defeated, we will chase Chiang Kai-shek and his nationalists out of China. Then we will spread the word of communism throughout Asia. I want you to lead us in Malaya."

"But I am a man of business. A capitalist."

"So was I. It is the way for our line to survive. It is the only way that I will become a very old ancestor."

"What must I do?"

"Your brother will tell you. He has changed his mind. He didn't think capitalists could walk so far. He says you will make a very good communist. Now, concerning your bank accounts in Switzerland. Your brother knows you have them but not how many. The Swiss are very clever. Close the small ones but keep hold of the big deposits in case this communism doesn't work."

"You haven't changed, father."

FOUR DAYS after Christmas at the end of 1940, Ping-Lai Ho lay back on the couch and luxuriated in the pleasures of his body. The surge was exquisitely sensual but he gently pulled the girl's head off his cock and the suction thwacked as his penis sprang out of her mouth. She looked up at him enquiringly and he smiled back at the shy, brown eyes and the small, roundly moulded mouth and the close-cropped hair that he'd ordered to give her the page-boy style he had seen in an American magazine. Her hands went on very gently massaging his balls which he enjoyed knowing it wouldn't make him climax. He pulled her round, brown bottom towards him and pushed wide her legs and felt up to the slit between.

"I don't believe it. Wet as all hell!"

"Put it in her then," said Perry Marshbank who was watching from a couch six feet away.

"I don't wish to climax yet. One magnificent flood is better than five small spurts… We need another consignment of ammunition," said Ping-Lai Ho. "The nationalists are using it up quicker than the guns and with little effect. May this war go on forever and may my esteemable, missing cousin stay out of the business forever."

"How can you talk about business?" said Perry as the girl pushed her hips into Ping-Lai Ho's searching fingers and showed him an opening deep between the pink lips of her pussy.

"Sex must be built up slowly. Very slowly. This is only the hors d'oeuvres."

"This thing's going to come on its own accord," said Perry as it twitched and jerked in anticipation.

"Put that one in your mouth," said Ping-Lai Ho to the girl in Malay, "but don't suck," as he brought the girl to her climax with his fingers, watching and feeling the shudders. "Do it very slowly," he said to her softly and took his hand from her very wet slit and felt the firm, tight roundness of her bottom, pushing her gently towards his partner in the business of gun running and taking business from Beaumont Ltd.

In a short time Perry Marshbank had grown rich and joined the privileged that deposited large sums of money in numbered accounts in Switzerland. Along with this privilege came invitations, rare but choice, to join Ping-Lai Ho in the orgy room that he had designed for the top room of his house. The walls, bar, opium bowl and thick piled carpet were black and the couches, four of them, were covered in soft, black leather. The low ceiling was set with a multitude of mirrors all at different angles so that everyone lying back on the couches could see what everyone else was doing and from every angle and without looking at Perry, Ping-Lai Ho watched the girl open her mouth as wide as possible and fit it over the swollen penis which she had taken hold of in both hands to stop it jerking. Perry let out a long 'pooh', expecting her to suck but instead she licked at the overflow at the top of his prick with her tongue. She pushed the gap as wide as it would go and caused Perry to arch up strongly, forcing as much of his prick into her mouth as would go and making her stand up over the couch to stop it choking her. Very slowly, she let the totally rigid penis slide over her stomach as she leant over it on her way to put her small, smooth mouth onto his hairy moustache. She paused with the prick in her belly button and then let it move on down and let it enter her, which made Perry thrust as deep as he could go and climaxed with the first thrust.

"Wow," said Ping-Lai Ho. His partner said nothing, relaxing back onto the soft, warm leather.

"Better than being called up in the army," said Ping-Lai Ho nastily and he enjoyed the dislike directed at him by Perry.

"Reserve occupation, old boy. Got to keep the tin and rubber flowing into Old Blighty."

"Wait till the Japs arrive in Singapore."

"Perfect fortress, old boy. Too many troops. That kind of thing. Can't have a yellow army invading the British. Never do it. Too damned scared. Don't blame them. Army doesn't need Perry Marshbank. Anyway, I'd make a lousy soldier. Mind if I have a drink?"

"My pleasure," said Ping-Lai Ho and pressed the button on the side of the couch. "Stinga?"

"Thanks. Still plenty of scotch so the war can't be going as badly as the papers make it out."

"Oh, I wouldn't believe that, old boy," said Ping-Lai Ho with an edge of sarcasm. "But don't worry. I have plenty of stocks. What's the point of millions in Switzerland if you don't have a case of scotch when you want it?"

"My sentiment entirely, old boy. Can she speak English?"

"Not a word."

"The one I really fancy is Tammany."

"I know. What you can't have is more exciting."

"Oh, I don't know," said Perry with a smirk.

"What do you mean?"

"Where there's a will there's a way. The Beaumont motto. They've always taken what they wanted."

"So you intend taking?"

"Maybe. I like doing anything that annoys the Beaumonts."

"Might get your fingers burnt."

Perry didn't answer but let his memory take him back to the house beside the lagoon and the big breasts he had squeezed so hard before forcing himself into her. In the silence his penis stirred and came up again and the girl took hold of it very lightly in one hand and holding the skin began to rub up and down in little jerks just a fraction of an inch until she had it jerking, wanting more. Gently, Perry felt for her breasts and stroked the smoothness, found the nipple and pinched hard making the girl flinch with pain.

"You like that, don't you," said Ping-Lai Ho.

"Of course… She's paid, isn't she?"

The padded black door with the brass studs opened slowly and a tall Malay girl carrying a Chinese lacquered tray stepped smoothly into the room and looked from one to the other naked body, the door swinging softly closed behind her, a smile of shy pleasure resting on Ping-Lai Ho while she avoided the licentious leer from Perry Marshbank from the other couch. A piece of white cheese cloth, tied round her neck, held up the large breasts of the tall girl and the size of them reminded Perry again of Tammany and he drew the girl's hand back onto his penis and encouraged her to rub as he took in the hard mound of the tall girl's pubic tightly held by full pants made of the same cheese cloth. There wasn't a blemish on the rest of her skin and with a small signal from Ping Lai-Ho she silently walked across to Perry and held out the tray, leaning down to him and sagging her young, heavy breasts into the cheese cloth. Perry ignored the drink on the tray and lazily stretched out his hand underneath and rubbed the texture of the cheese cloth over her pronounced sex and worked the cheese cloth up into her for a moment before taking the drink off the tray with his left hand. As she stood up from him he drank and lay back on the soft, black leather and looked at her face. The dislike he saw excited him immediately and he slowly came up from the couch again and felt for her a second time.

"She doesn't like you, Perry. I wonder why?" and Ping-Lai Ho signalled the girl to bring him his drink which he took and nodded at the door. The rhythmic movement of her heavy bottom was still in Perry's mind after the door swung closed with a gentle thud.

"Why not?" asked Perry.

"She's not a prostitute. One of my staff. Exotic, yes, but one of my staff. I've offered her money but she won't take it and I respect her wishes. Kim-Wok Ho found her for me at a time when we were doing good business together… Don't you worry. The main meal of the evening is some time away and you won't be disappointed. Would you like some more opium?"

"No, thank you. I'm just right as I am. A little high but feeling everything."

"Well then, a little business first," said Ping-Lai Ho getting up from his couch and putting on a Chinese dressing gown, pitch black in background but patterned with rich reds and orange, pictures of far off China in an era without turmoil. Drawing the silk sash around his middle he picked up the flimsy clothes the girl had worn for her entrance and handed them to her indicating the door. Reluctantly, Perry got up, finished his drink in one gulp and pulled on a similar gown.

"This door," said Ping-Lai Ho, opening the door behind him that led into a dimly lit dining room furnished with heavy, black and gold lacquered furniture, a small, carved dining table to match in the centre of the room and laid for two.

"You said we'd have company," said Perry, irritated.

"Time will tell, old boy," said Ping-Lai Ho, knowing the 'old boy's' irritated Perry and threw him off balance. "A man must eat... You'll need it," he said knowingly, smiling encouragement.

"Well, if that's the case it's all in a good cause."

Ping-Lai Ho rang the small hand bell and sat down at the table indicating the other chair to Perry. The door from the small adjacent kitchen opened and a young Chinese girl came in bearing a silver dish with a domed cover and put it down in front of Ping-Lai Ho. She took off the cover to let out a cloud of fragrant steam and withdrew.

"Now, that was pretty," said Perry.

"The steamed fish?" said Ping-Lai Ho deliberately misunderstanding.

"No, the girl."

"Oh. Yes... I have a rule in my household. I only employ women and they must all be pretty in their different ways, the more ways the better. I employ six nationalities, all from the East, except for one."

"And what nationality is she?" asked Perry as Ping-Lai Ho expertly sliced off a piece of the fish and put it on his plate.

"English, of course. I thought you knew," knowing perfectly well that he didn't.

"No."

"The fish is excellent. A little vegetables?" he said scooping up lightly steamed vegetables. "A piece of bread? I almost forgot. All Englishmen eat bread with their meal."

"No, thank you."

"You like the fish?"

"Very nice."

"It's very important to keep up your standards."

"You sound like Mrs Gray."

"Mrs Gray?"

"The head wallah's wife in Kuching... He used to be my boss."

"She always kept up her standards?"

"Very much. She didn't like Tug marrying a native."

"But I thought you wanted to marry her."

"Not marry her, old boy."

"More fish?" said Ping-Lai Ho, after a pause.

"Thank you. Very tasty."

"It is, isn't it?" said Ping-Lai Ho, congratulating himself silently on his English small talk, his tongue firmly in his cheek.

They ate in silence, the only light from a wall bracket behind Ping-Lai Ho that threw a grotesque human shadow across the table, showing him Perry's face but hiding his own. As he moved and ate, the shadow changed across the stark bones of the empty fish, the head laughing deadly at the diners.

"We've made a lot of money out of guns," said Ping-Lai Ho softly, his mouth half full of chewed fish.

"Yes."

Ping-Lai Ho let the silence drag before going on. "There's a lot of money in other people's suffering."

"What are you getting at?" said Perry, trying to see the face hidden in the light.

"I have some friends. Thailand. Not far away across the Gulf of Siam. Easy for a fishing boat. Farmers."

"There's no money in produce."

"There is in this one."

"What do they farm?"

"Poppies. Acres and acres of poppies. You know what comes out of poppies?"

"Opium?" asked Perry, putting down his knife and fork and pushing away his plate.

"Your friends in America?"

"Which ones?"

"The ones who supply you with guns without an export permit."

"What about them?" asked Perry.

"How would they like to buy good quality opium?"

"That's drugs… It does terrible things to white people."

"Any people, Perry."

"No. I couldn't deal in opium."

"You weren't so squeamish when you hooked Tug Beaumont. Had it not been for my esteemable missing cousin he would be dead by now. You did get him hooked deliberately?"

"Don't be silly old chap. We were good friends in those days."

"Were you? Should a good friend covet his best friend's wife? You were his best friend? Stood up at his wedding. You just told me the one you really fancy is Tammany and that all these little diversions are nothing if you could clean yourself on Tammany."

"That came later."

"No it didn't," said Ping-Lai Ho sharply. "You wanted that woman the moment you met her… But you didn't have Tug's guts. You were afraid of the Mrs Grays. And it's eaten away at you ever since. You tried to kill Tug Beaumont, didn't you Mr Marshbank?"

"Who the hell do you think you are talking to?"

"Oh!" said Ping-Lai Ho, sitting back in his carved chair, stroking the lacquered head of a carved serpent on his arm rest. "That is quite easy. I am talking to a man out of his depth who will do in future exactly what I tell him. You see, Mr Marshbank, you can't have these little things in life without paying the price. There is an old English expression which says there is no such thing as a free lunch and that also applies to steamed fish, my girls and bank accounts in Switzerland… Don't look so angry. It's a good life, one to which you are well suited and one which you can have for the rest of your life if you persuade your friends to buy my opium… And talking of girls, there are things even more exciting. Once you have agreed to co-operate, I will give you one tonight. With the food and a little opium you will be strong again shortly."

"The waitress," said Perry, his genitals stirring despite the fear that was goosing his flesh, even erotic itself, driving his sex to cover its meaning.

"Much more exciting."

"How do we get the stuff into America?"

"I can deliver in Cuba. From there they must take over. We Chinese are conspicuous in the United States. Were we not I wouldn't be needing you. I thought it nice if you took a sea voyage and have booked you a passage on a freighter leaving Singapore at six tomorrow morning. If you agree you will be taken straight from here to the boat."

"Tomorrow?"

"Six o'clock," and Ping-Lai Ho opened a small drawer in the dining room table and took out a brown envelope. "Here is your passport, correctly stamped with a multiple visa into the United States. A Letter of Credit for ten thousand pounds sterling. And your ticket. While you are there you can arrange ammunition."

"How much opium have you got?"

"As much as you want. Your friends already trade in narcotics. Being the purveyor of an impeccable source of supply they will welcome you. I have also registered a company in your name. You are the sole shareholder. Marshbank Far East Trading Company. We are going to put a lot of rubber and tin business through your company. In a few years' time you will be a pillar of British society, far bigger than Beaumont Ltd. Even my cousin, even if he is not already dead, will be unable to compete with opium money."

"I'd like to think about it."

"Why?… What else would you do with the rest of your life? Go back to England and settle down with a wife and rear children? Catch the seven forty-five to Waterloo, I think it's called! Don't be damned silly. You're hooked on this way of life far stronger than Tug was hooked on drugs. He had an alternative. You don't… See it as though you're very lucky that I need you or you'd end up like so many of the bums you see around the East. Your Dr Grantham for one. He wouldn't do what he was told to do some years ago and look at him. Hasn't been sober for twenty years. Lucky he started with a good liver or he'd be dead. Now, relax and have a cognac with some excellent coffee," and Ping-Lai Ho rang the small bell, picking it up and tinkling it into the silence.

Perry looked at the envelope and wished he hadn't been smoking opium earlier in the evening. He looked up slowly from the envelope as the door opened and the same waitress came into the room with coffee and two well filled brandy balloons. Again she bent down and the heavily laden cheese cloth swung towards him as she placed a brandy close to his right hand. Her large, tightly clad pussy was on a level with his eyes but this time he didn't have the inclination to stretch out and take it in his hand. But despite his fear he felt his erection raising his dressing gown and he moved his elbows onto the table to hide himself as she poured the coffee. Ping-Lai Ho watched him in silence. 'Even trash has its uses', he thought to himself and warmed the brandy balloon in both hands.

"What was Dr Grantham asked to do?" asked Perry when the door again shut.

"Poison the Sultan of Sarawak. Rajah Brook. The whole family in fact but Dr Grantham said it was against his Hippocratic oath."

"Why did they want to kill Rajah Brook?"

"That's easy. They wanted a local man back on the throne. People out here don't really like foreigners."

"How did they get at him in the first place?"

"He was seducing all the local young girls. Frowned on in those days. Your friend Mrs Gray, very vicious tongue, that lady."

"So why did he turn to drink?"

"They cut off his supply of little brown bodies."

"I see."

"I hope so."

'Do I see?' thought Perry. 'Maybe. A lot more, too. There's past as well as future.'

He stared sightlessly at the hidden face of Ping-Lai Ho and the smell of boiled cabbage, mingled with a damp, cold, musty basement flat, took him forcibly and for a moment he wondered if the kitchen door had opened. Then he smelt fried onions but it couldn't be that again as they were both dead and there weren't any brothers and sisters. He let the little opium he had smoked take him away from the room.

Perry Marshbank had just turned thirteen when they arrested his father and charged him with embezzlement, a word Perry didn't know at that time. He was in his last term at junior prep school and looking forward to being a success at work and sport when he would walk across the road to the big senior school, parts of which dated back for two hundred years. He lived in the village, near the bank his father had managed successfully for ten years on a salary that was little more than a joke. But Jim Marshbank was a pillar of the village and ranked with the local doctor and the vicar. He'd even eaten with the squire on a couple of occasions, taking Brenda with him, only a trifle embarrassed at the old dress she'd been forced to wear. She liked the squire's wife and everyone in Cranleigh village liked Jim and Brenda Marshbank and respected him for being a shrewd lender and collector of money. That branch of Midlands Bank was highly profitable and showed a better return on capital than many other county branches. Whenever the inspector came down from London, Jim Marshbank pleaded for a raise that never came. Educated at grammar schools, Jim and Brenda Marshbank were determined their son would be educated at a public school and push the family a rung higher in society. To this avail they had scrimped and saved from the day Peregrine had been born and even though he would be a day boy it was enough for their burning ambition.

But by the time he was ready for the more expensive senior school, the new uniforms and books at the prep school had eaten away most of the meagre nest egg but Jim Marshbank was not to be thwarted. He decided to borrow some money from his bank. But, as he rented his house three doors down the street, there wasn't any collateral to offer the bank so he knew better than anyone that head office would turn down his application for an overdraft. Banks only lend money if you have it already.

After Jim Marshbank went to jail, the headmaster of the senior school also determined that Jim's ambition should come true and put young Perry through a process that secured him a music and work scholarship and five free years of education as a boarder. The headmaster himself chipped in for the books and the uniform but not a penny went as far as the tuck shop. Perry was the poor man's boarder and his fellow pupils never let him forget it. Consistently they asked him when his old man was coming out of jail. His first term at senior school was spent fighting. By then his mother had moved into the basement flat in Wimbledon, two rooms and a scullery with an outside toilet shared with three other families. She took a job in the newsagent, behind the counter, something Perry successfully prevented his fellow pupils from finding out. 'Well,' he said to himself, 'if he couldn't join them he'd beat them,' and his mother was the proudest woman in all England when her only son came top of the class term after term, year after year. By the time he was seventeen there was talk of a state scholarship to Oxford but his father was still in jail and young Perry's own ambition, as much as he loved his mother and father, was to put as much distance as possible between himself and his antagonists. At the age of eighteen he wrote the Colonial Service examinations and passed with flying colours. The good years began and all would have been well in his life and his mother's, who was now getting a regular allowance from her son in Sarawak, if Mrs Gray had not made her usual enquiries and unearthed the fact that the new District Officer's father was in jail and had been for some time. From that moment Perry hated the class he had aspired to and the break into trading from Singapore had been as much a blessing to Perry as it had been to Tug.

When his father came out of Reading jail, having paid his debt to society, he tried to get a job, any job. Three weeks later, Perry smelt fried onions which surprised him as he was on his rounds by foot and there wasn't a settlement for miles around. He'd looked at his watch. Exactly one o'clock in the afternoon. Two months later, a passenger steamer had called at Kuching and the headmaster, who had held such high hopes for him, wrote and said his parents had died when the basement flat had been gutted by fire. The police had estimated the time of death and the start of the fire to be approximately six a.m. or one p.m. Sarawak time.

'Bugger the lot of them,' thought Perry and leant forward over the table, away from the light so he could see Ping-Lai Ho watching him. With an effort, he cleared his mind of the opium and began to stretch his mind around the problem.

"If we're going to smuggle opium into America," said Perry, "we'd better do it properly. Can we hold that boat for two days?"

"Yes."

"I know very little about opium apart from smoking. When I leave I want to know everything. Who's in the business. The risks. The purity. The prices. How we move it around with enough cut-off points to confuse an army. My gut tells me only the best professionals survive in that kind of business. For one, you can forget about selling it out of Cuba. Too bloody close and too bloody obvious."

"Do you know anything about chemistry?"

"I have a distinction in my school certificate. If I had gone to Oxford it would have been as a chemistry undergraduate."

"Could you set up a factory for converting opium into heroin?"

"Probably. But not one. Many of them. All over Asia. And what happens to our suppliers if the Japanese go to war in this part of the world?"

"The fields are very remote. Everything comes in and out on the backs of a donkey. No-one would have enough troops or the inclination to stop it."

"Now this is my part of the scheme of things. You and I will each own half of the factories. The factories will pay a fair market price for your opium."

"That profit is yours. My American company…"

"You don't have one," interrupted Ping-Lai Ho. "Unless I sign…"

"I will. My American company will buy from the factories at a fair price and sell the final product in America. That profit is mine. That way we both have a check on each other. I pay too little, the factories sell elsewhere. You charge too much and I'll find another source of supply. And if we're going to survive in this traffic we'd better learn to trust each other. Tonight, I'm going to have one last blow of opium. After that it's out and I suggest you keep out of it too. The stuff saps the brain. Terrible bloody stuff."

"And yet you want to peddle it?"

"No-one's peddled me any good in the past."

"Have you finished your coffee?"

"Yes."

"Good. We'll go into the other room and smoke a little and I'll see if I can demonstrate my part of the trust."

"My pleasure," said Perry enjoying his new sense of power.

"After you."

Half an hour later, ensconced on their soft leather couches, Ping-Lai Ho pressed the service button and waited. They had both been careful to take the right amount of opium and watched the door in anticipation. The tall Malay girl brought in fresh tumblers of whisky and both men felt themselves grow slowly but with intense pleasure. Dressed in loose fitting silk shorts that moved silkily over her smooth flesh she offered them their drinks and let her heavy, bare breasts sway in front of Perry bringing him to full erection. He smiled at her and this time she smiled back before withdrawing having adjusted the lights to bring the two empty couches into focus.

They sipped their new drinks and Ping-Lai Ho pressed the button again and two Malay boys, barefoot and naked except for silk pouches ensconcing their genitals with a hole through which surprisingly large penises hung in anticipation, came into the room. Each of the boys carried a phial of oil. Ping-Lai Ho directed them to the empty couches and again pressed the button. The tall Malay girl brought Linda and Sally into the room. They were both floating high on opium having been given it in their bedroom by the tall Malay girl who had gently rubbed oil onto their bodies so they shone and smelt of musk. The girl carried sticks of burning joss she put in containers around the room. Linda and Sally were unsure of where they were and when the girl was finished with the incense she took each by the hand and led them to the boys' couches. Perry watched with growing lust as the boys very softly rubbed oil over the English girls' white breasts, brown hands kneading the nipples till they were hard. Black leather pants covered the girls briefly and Ping-Lai Ho smiled with deep satisfaction as the one boy oiled Linda all over until he finally felt the piece that Ping-Lai Ho had wanted for himself. The boys' penises were now erect and Ping-Lai Ho signalled them over to stand in front of his couch. Perry watched as Ping-Lai Ho took two, thick rubber rings from the pocket of his discarded dressing gown and slid them over the tips of the boys' cocks to hold the semen but enhance the pleasure of the girls.

"Perry. Please do me a favour," said Ping-Lai Ho softly. "Take off Linda's pants and see if she's wet."

Sally watched, unable to respond to danger, as her friend's pants were removed from her body and her legs opened wide by gentle pressure by Perry on the soft inside of her thighs. 'It doesn't matter,' she said to herself as Perry felt Linda. 'Ten thousand pounds each is a lot of money,' and she smiled at the thought and kept on watching as Perry took Linda's hand and led it to the boy's balls and then to his erection. The boy sat on the couch, his erection stiff to his belly, and at a signal from Ping-Lai Ho leant back and supported his shoulders on the long rest before bringing Linda over on top of him so that Ping-Lai Ho could see the tip of the cock poised an inch from the large, silky and wet pussy just above. Linda tried to go down for it but the boy held her hips and waited for Ping-Lai Ho to get up and take hold of the hips from behind and slowly raise and lower her onto the rigid erection that was desperately trying to climax without success.

"Get the other one to give it to Sally," said Ping-Lai Ho huskily without taking his eyes off the brown prick slithering up and down wetly inside Linda. He let her climax before pulling her bottom a little higher than usual so the boy's prick sprang free and Ping-Lai Ho entered her and brought himself up to a climax he thought would never come to an end.

As Perry removed Sally's black panties, the tall Malay girl came back into the room completely naked but Perry was intent on putting the Malay boy's cock deep inside Sally Bollas. While he watched the prick sliding quickly in and out of Sally, a brown girl's hand took his penis and he felt the heavy, oiled breasts on his back. Gently, the tall girl pulled him back onto the couch next to Sally who was pumping as hard as the boy and came down on Perry and took the full length of the huge penis right up inside herself until she brought him through to a powerful climax that shuddered his big frame for thirty seconds until the last drops of semen had gone from him.

"Fooled you, didn't I?" said Ping-Lai Ho when Perry was resting back on his own couch, a languid hand still holding the larger of the two heavy breasts.

"You can say that again."

"Oh, we will. This is just the beginning of a very long and profitable partnership," and he took the still heavily drugged Linda and Sally by their hands and sat them either side of him on his couch. "Now, would anyone like a drink?" said Ping-Lai Ho.

ON THE AFTERNOON of the 16 September 1940, when R.A.F. Fighter Command had committed its last reserves of Spitfires and Hurricanes to the battle, Tug Beaumont looked up at the sails of his three-masted schooner and was glad to see that the wind was strong enough to take them into Kuching harbour. Walking across the well-scrubbed planks of the slim-lined deck he looked over the side at the blue-green water and estimated the *Windsong* was making a good three knots. With a following wind she was steady as she went and the soft splash of the slight swell as the bows dipped and came up again was as soothing to him as the sight of his wife teaching his six-year-old son, Adam, the rudiments of the alphabet. He smiled hearing once again that Adam persisted in getting's his b's and d's round the wrong way. The books she was using were the same as the ones she had used herself at the convent in Kuching. Three of Tammany's brothers were crewing for him and the forty-seven foot boat was easy to handle in the light wind and he wasn't needed. Tammany junior was chattering away to one of her uncles being more fluent in the local dialect than English. 'Plenty of time for her education,' Tug told himself and again wondered why Edward Gray had invited him to Kuching and by a handwritten note. Tug watched the looming entrance of Kuching harbour for another five minutes before turning back to the sails which were rigid, sailing as they were so close to the wind.

"Bring her about," he called in a loud voice. "One more tack should be enough." The big sails lost the wind and the *Windsong* almost came to a stop before they had her on the opposite tack and the boat slowly picked up speed to diagonally cut to the opposite side of the harbour.

"We'll start the diesel when we cross the entrance." Tammany looked up and smiled at him, the sun almost down into the China Sea and throwing the shadow of her long, black hair over her face. Five-year-old Tammany junior moved quickly round masts and ropes to take her father's hand. The helmsman was holding the schooner close to the wind again and bringing them well within the harbour entrance.

"I like sailing, daddy."

"Good. We'll do lots of sailing now we have *Windsong*."

"Goodie, goodie. Can I have a sweet?"

"When we're tied up to the quay."

"What's a quay, daddy?"

"You'll see in a minute."

"Do you think Adam's finished his lesson?"

"Not yet, little one. Can you see the seagulls?"

"There's lots of them," shrieked Tammany and jumped up and down on the deck in her bare feet.

Half an hour later, and to Tug's surprise seeing how they'd parted when he'd left the Colonial Service, Edward Gray, first officer of Sarawak under Rajah Brook, was standing on the quay as the *Windsong* edged sideways towards the waiting jetty, ropes being thrown from the schooner just before she touched. Edward Gray himself caught one of them and made it fast to the bollard, one of the brothers having leapt off the boat to secure the other one. When the boat was secure, Tug led Tammany and the children ashore leaving the brothers on board.

"Good of you to respond to my message. Difficult times. R.A.F. holding their own. B.B.C. reports they shot down one hundred and eighty-six enemy aircraft today for the loss of thirty-seven of our own. Only seventeen pilots," he added, remembering that Tug's brother was a Spitfire pilot at Tangmere.

"Wish I was there to help."

"Can't be in two places at once."

"Maybe. I'm the only brother not fighting. You've met my wife?" knowing perfectly well that he hadn't.

"My pleasure," said Edward Gray offering his hand.

"This is Adam and this one is Tammany junior."

"They're big."

"It's been a long time, Mr Gray."

"You'll come up to the house. My car is waiting. After we've had our little talk my wife has asked you and your wife to join us for dinner. We can put the children down in one of the spare bedrooms."

"I don't want to be put down," said Adam.

"I'll look after them," said Tammany as two small hands took hers.

"My wife specifically asked that you join us for dinner. We'll find lots of things to amuse the children if they don't want to sleep. I've a tame monkey that can go down to the shops in town and bring back the newspaper," said Edward Gray, bending down to Adam.

"Where?" said Adam, trying to look behind the grey-suited administrator of Sarawak.

"And I've got lots of sweets."

"Oh, goodie," said Tammany junior, stamping her bare feet, bringing their nakedness to Edward Gray's attention.

"Tammany," said Tug, catching the administrator's expression, "maybe we'd better make the children wear shoes."

"Do we have to?" said Adam.

"Yes."

"I'll go," said Tammany junior, turning back to the boat.

"Don't slip."

"I'm five, daddy," said his daughter, planting her hands firmly on her hips and looking at him defiantly.

"All right. But don't be long."

"We won't," shouted Adam and beat his sister back over the rail of *Windsong*.

WHEN THEY REACHED the administrator's house, the flag was being lowered down the white pole on the lawn as the rim of the sun finally slid into the sea and showered the heavens, indigo-blue, with shards of sunlight reflected on the dust of a Borneo volcano that had been erupting on and off for three months. Tug stood for a moment on the lawn, marvelling at the richness of colours and the beauty of nature.

"The East is very beautiful," he said to his wife and reluctantly turned back to the crazy paving path which led back from the flagless pole to the house, in front of them a servant carrying the furled Union Jack that would again be raised at sunrise. Mrs Gray was waiting for them in the high ceilinged reception room wearing a long evening dress.

"How nice to see you again, Mr Beaumont," she said, coming forward. "This must be your charming wife. The children are so beautiful. Shall we all have a glass of sherry together before we let the men get on with their men's business? You do like sherry, Mrs Beaumont?"

"Yes, thank you."

"Good. I so much enjoyed my sherry when I was staying at Merry Hall. And how is Lady Beaumont?"

"Very well."

"Good. I'm so glad to hear it. And Lady Hensbrook?"

"Well, thank you."

"I do hope Lord Hensbrook is getting about."

"He died, I'm afraid."

"How terrible. I'm so sorry to hear that. Have you visited Merry Hall, Mrs Beaumont?"

"Yes," said Tammany.

"And you enjoyed it?" asked Mrs Gray in a way that suggested she surely wouldn't have done so.

"Very much. Tug's mother was very kind to me. So were his brothers. Adam and Tammany played with the other children."

"How very fortunate," said Mrs Gray, nodding to a man servant to offer the sherry and biscuits.

"Your mother always served biscuits with sherry," said Mrs Gray.

'But only in the morning,' thought Tug, hard pressed not to smile. "The only way to drink a good sherry," agreed Tug, giving a glass to his wife and taking one for himself.

"And what would the children like?" asked Mrs Gray.

"Sweeties," said Tammany junior who was looking behind a sofa where she had found a Siamese cat.

"Of course," said Edward Gray and pulled a strategically placed bag of bulls' eyes from the pocket of his suit. "Always carry them," he said half smiling at his wife. "We don't have children."

"Bulls' eyes," shouted Adam with glee, filling both cheeks.

"You'll choke," said Tug to his children.

"Your good health," said Edward Gray, pocketing the bag of sweets and picking up his glass of sherry. "How is your brother?" he asked turning to Tug, forgetting himself.

"Rather busy, I'd think."

"Of course. Air force. Splendid job." He had too many things on his mind for small talk. "My dear, would you mind if Mr Beaumont and I went into the study?"

"Of course not, Edward. Mrs Beaumont and I have so much to talk about. Merry Hall is such a lovely country house. There was a Lord… Oh, dear, I've forgotten his name. Charming gentleman. I'm sure you know to whom I refer, Mr Beaumont."

"Migroyd," said Tug to help her.

"That was the man. Very distinguished."

"Very," said Tug, following Edward Gray into his study.

"Scotch?" said Edward Gray, his back to Tug as he opened a cupboard behind his writing desk.

"Thank you."

"Never could stand sherry. Ice and water?"

"Half, half."

"Must drink it with water in the tropics… Sun's gone down," he said, going to the window.

"Yes," said Tug.

"Cheers, old boy," said Edward Gray and quickly drank from his whisky tumbler.

"Cheers, sir," said Tug, allowing a faint pause between the words.

"How's business?"

"Very good. Sell anything we can supply."

"Everybody's stockpiling."

"Yes."

"You enjoy your work?"

"Yes."

"I'd better come to the point. Despite what the press say about the size of our Far East navy we're in trouble. Churchill is sending out two capital ships. But it's flag waving. Can't afford to send an aircraft carrier as well. How do you protect battleships from aircraft if you can't strike at the enemy's aircraft carrier?"

"I don't know, sir."

"Exactly. Churchill's more concerned with England than Kuching, Singapore and Hong Kong. Has to be." There was a pause while Edward Gray filled his glass without offering one to Tug. Tug could see deep furrows on the man's forehead. "Do you know what a Japanese victory could do to our face in the East?"

"Destroy it. But they are not in the war."

"I've been out here a long time, Tug. I can read the signs. Imperial Japan is very strong, is sweeping through China. They wish to be the overlords of Asia. They want the British, the Dutch, the Portuguese to get the hell out of here and from what I have been told, they have the power to make us do it for as long as Hitler is keeping us occupied at home. For a while they will sweep the British out of the East."

"You think England will fight to get them back?"

"Oh, yes. She never gives up anything without a fight. The Island feeds off her colonies. Without her commonwealth and colonies, England would be a third rate power. Where would she preferentially buy her raw materials and sell the product of her factories? The Japanese, and anyone with local knowledge, know they must neutralise America if they are to subdue Asia. America shares the Pacific with Japan. If America were to sit back and ignore Japan's aspirations then we don't have a future in the East. But if America's raw materials and trade are threatened she will fight Japan, and win. The power of American industry is beyond even my comprehension." He turned back to his window, sipping his scotch absentmindedly. "It won't be long," he said, pointing at the lights of Kuching Harbour with four cargo vessels standing out in the roads. "A couple of shells from a Japanese frigate and I'd be forced to pull down the Union Jack. But that, as I see it, is as far as it goes. And why I asked you to see me, Tug... I think it's time we reverted to Edward and Tug, since you are one of the wealthiest traders in these waters. You've come a long way since you left my employ," he said, and smiled ruefully.

"Thank you, sir."

"That schooner's certainly the largest private yacht I've seen out of Cowes. Must have cost you a fortune."

Tug didn't reply but waited.

"You still speak the local dialect?" asked Edward Gray.

"Fluently."

"Would you be prepared to go back to your old district for me?"

Startled Tug looked up from his empty glass. "You mean join the Colonial Service?"

"In a way. Oh, I'm sorry, old boy. Help yourself to another scotch. Rule in my private study. I pour the first drink. After that my friends pour their own. You think your wife will be alright?"

"She can hold her own. She managed to keep the 'county set' in Surrey on their toes. The Kuching convent provides a good education and all the teachers come from public schools in England."

"The children?"

"Very robust."

"I'm glad."

"It is important. What I have in mind is a guerrilla army fighting the Japanese occupation force. From the jungle."

"Why do you think the locals will fight?"

"They will hate the Japanese."

"Why? Most of them have never heard of the Japanese."

"We're going to promise them independence if they help us fight the Japanese."

"But if we're getting out why bother to fight?"

"We'll be getting out of administering the place but not trading with it. Our reward for helping them throw out the Japs, will be preferential trading agreements. Favoured nation treatment. The right of our trading houses to operate in the East. We are using the same argument in India, Burma, Malaya, Singapore. All except Hong Kong as there isn't a Chinese government worth talking to and if the communists win they are not going to allow capitalist trading houses to operate from the Chinese mainland."

"You now have my attention."

"I thought I would. Would Perry Marshbank consider…?"

"Not Marshbank, Mr Gray. I have every reason to believe the man is rotten, through and through. He hasn't been a member of my staff for some time."

"But he is English."

"There is a rotten one in every barrel. He's our resident rotten apple in Singapore. I wouldn't trust him with the time of day."

"You have reasons?"

"Many. He raped my wife, for one."

"Don't be silly, old man. He was best man at your wedding."

"He also tried to poison me with opium. I have a good Chinese friend. He got me out to England. If I was a little less civilised I would kill the man. Whatever your plans for England and Sarawak, he would turn it only to his own account."

"That bad?"

"Worse," said Tug, helping himself to another drink and dropping in three good cubes of ice. "What do I do with the family?"

"Evacuate the children to Australia."

"And Tammany?"

"I have a job for her."

"Doing what?"

"Reporting on Japanese naval forces off the coast by shortwave radio to one of our people in Australia."

"You will need a very powerful transmitter. Easy to trace."

"That is the point. Tammany, without her children can blend back into the local population. We will set up a system of constantly moving the transmitter. It will be very difficult for the Japanese to keep chasing it around the jungle."

"Why Tammany?"

"She's English, by marriage."

Tug just smiled and gave a brief laugh. "Well, there's a turn of fortune," he said. Edward Gray said nothing. "Why are you so sure the Japanese will invade?"

"They wouldn't be so foolish as to miss such an opportunity."

"No. I suppose they wouldn't. And my carrot is that Beaumont Limited will be one of the trading houses in Kuching and Singapore after the war, when the Japs have been kicked out."

"Exactly."

"You'll have to include Hong Kong."

"You only operate through Hong Kong on an agency basis."

"Give us time."

"I'll see what I can do."

"And Marshbank doesn't get to trade."

"That may be difficult. One of our men has gone to talk to him."

"After what I said?"

"We need every man who knows the jungle and can speak the language."

"British pragmatism."

"If you wish. He was a good District Commissioner. The carrot is the same."

"And it doesn't matter to the British how many trading companies remain?"

"Not really. The best businessmen will out. Free trade. We built the Eastern business empire on free trade."

"Oh, come off it, Mr Gray!"

"Well, maybe it was free trade for the British."

"That's better."

"It is our navy protecting the sea route."

"Was."

"Maybe."

"You don't leave me or my company with very much option."

"You have been trying to join up for over a year."

"Yes… Even Reggie will have to agree to this one."

"Maybe Mr Marshbank will be killed in the ensuing war."

"Doubt it."

"From the point of view of British prestige…" said Edward Gray.

"It's better if he isn't," finished Tug.

"Exactly."

"Where do we go from here?"

"You agree then?"

"Of course."

"A three-month period of jungle warfare training for yourself and a full briefing for your wife. You were in the cadet force at school?"

"Yes."

"You'll be gazetted a lieutenant on completion of the course."

"Marvellous. I won't outrank two brothers but at least I'll be on a par with Henry. When do we start?"

"Let's join the ladies for dinner first."

"By all means. You don't wish me to return to Singapore?"

"No. Let it be known you've returned to England to join the R.A.F. You do fly I believe?"

"I've only flown Mathilda."

"Mathilda?"

"My brother's biplane. Lot of fun."

"I'm sure it was. Let's have another scotch first. I find it helps when dining with Mrs Gray. She will, as you will find, dominate the conversation."

"A large one then."

"Pour it yourself. You know my rules."

"Yes."

4

PARIS 1940

𝒜t the time Tug Beaumont sat down to roast beef and Yorkshire pudding in clothes that had been brought up for him from *Windsong*, François Deauville was standing around a street corner on the Left Bank in Paris, a pleasant summer breeze ruffling the tatty, canvas canopy that still enabled the passer-by to read the word café and, with good perception, the Bizet. François was thoroughly dirty and a self-rolled cigarette stuck to his lower lip having gone out ten minutes earlier. A black beret, itself topped by a small pom-pom that hung to the hat by three, elongated threads, kept his unwashed hair mostly out of sight. He had not shaved for a week and the battered violin case was propped against his left foot. Two armed German soldiers patrolled the opposite side of the street, pushing their way through an evening crowd of strollers who were stretching their legs before curfew came along with the dusk. Everyone looked to ignore the Germans. François spat the fag-end into the gutter and picked up his violin. He had been back in Paris for just over an hour. He pushed open the door to the Café Bizet where Simone sometimes worked and the smell of garlic forcibly hit him in the face. He had been away a long time. He sat down at a table and hunched himself to look out on the street, seeing little of what he saw and wondering if he was in fact two people instead of one. Simone was not on duty and an old man came up to take his order.

"Simone still work here?" he asked in French.

"Sometimes."

"Today."

"Maybe."

"When?"

"Soon, if she is to beat the curfew."

"Of course. Coffee. Wine. Red wine. Cheap. You got any tobacco?"

"No."

"Coffee and wine."

He waited three hours and no-one he knew came into the café. The old man had sat down at his table. Custom was bad. The war. Life was hard.

"You ever play that thing?" asked the old man, the only question he had asked so far.

"Sometimes."

"Can't make much money playing a fiddle."

"No."

"You good?"

"Sometimes."

"What do you play?"

"Want a tune?"

"Why not? Anything to brighten this place. It is a good place full."

"Very bad empty."

"Classical or jazz?"

"You can play jazz on a fiddle? Never heard of that."

"I try," and François unsnapped the case and took out his violin. The other customer watched him and the old man sat back in his chair. Neither was particularly interested. François carefully tuned the violin and plucked a tune with his fingers.

"Sure you can play?"

"Sure," and François began to improvise, chasing any tune that came to his mind and flowing it down through the bow and out of the box through the strings. The other customer sat up and began to listen, tapping his foot in time to the music. The light had gone so there was no chance of customers. The old man had to stay all night as he couldn't walk home in the curfew.

"You play well," said the stranger who was even dirtier than François and smelt badly.

'I'll get used to it,' François told himself and ordered a cup of coffee. "Who's paying?" asked the old man.

"Make it three," said the stranger. "Have one yourself. I'll pay."

"First, your money." The stranger fiddled among his old, smelly clothes and produced a franc.

"There you are. Ah," he said with satisfaction and put another franc on the table. "Wine. Cheap. Red."

"Three glasses?" asked the old man, hopefully.

"Of course."

"You are too kind," said François who had stopped to greet the customer but now put his violin back under his chin and played a Béchet composition from beginning to end. The old man had stood with the glasses and bottle of wine, putting them on the table when François stopped.

"The master," said the customer.

"You know Béchet?" asked François.

"Hear him. Who hasn't on the Left Bank?"

"The master," agreed François and rested his violin in the case. "Later," he said, sipping his coffee. The old man filled the wine glasses. 'Wow,' thought François as he tasted the wine. 'Red, cheap. I bet they don't come much cheaper than that.'

"You like the wine?" asked the customer.

"Marvellous."

"You are The Thief?"

"Why?"

"I hear you play. Simone will be happy."

"Where is she?"

"Two years, I think she said. Only letters."

"I have been busy."

"Where?"

"Here and there. Who asks these days?"

"Where do you sleep?"

"I don't know."

"You have been away from Paris?"

"Maybe."

"France?"

"Maybe."

"There is a shed at the back. You can join me. They don't mind."

"Thank you," said François.

"We are looking for people," said the customer looking at him closely, "you have the reputation of being a good thief. Would you like to steal from the Germans?"

"It doesn't matter from whom I steal?"

"Let us enjoy the wine."

'I'll try,' thought François. "Who are you?" he said. "What is your name?"

"Geoffrey Beaumont, François," he said in English.

"Shit, you bastard. You've fooled me for three hours. Even your accent is perfect."

"Thank you," he said returning to French. "I couldn't have got into Paris if it wasn't. You look pretty good yourself."

"You stink."

"Certainly. And so would you if you'd dunked yourself in a sewer."

AT TEN MINUTES past eight the following morning, the door to the Café Bizet opened noisily and two Frenchmen came out into the street, coughed badly from cheap tobacco and spat into the street, two large gobs of grey-flecked phlegm that wobbled for a moment as they stuck hard to the pavement. A well-dressed Parisian who shouldn't have been on the Left Bank, stepped around the hobos who turned back to look at her, one whistling to show his approval. His teeth were black as he grinned at the tight little bottom trying not to wiggle its way away from him. François spat into the gutter again for good measure, having cleared his throat, noisily, and hands in his pants' pockets followed Geoffrey down the street that was filling up quickly. All the better class citizens gave them plenty of pavement but they sauntered along looking back at people who stared at them. The unlucky few who took a whiff of Geoffrey, turned their heads away in disgust. Half an hour later, having made certain no-one thought anything of them they disappeared into a building, from the back of which they could gain access to the Paris sewerage system. Wordlessly François followed underground into wet, dripping walls and pillars, dark scuttling going away from the beam of Geoffrey's torch that he had collected from the entrance.

"How the hell do you know so much about Paris?" asked François in French.

"A bit depends on where you live as a child. My mother had a brainwave and sent me to prep school in Paris. Damn nearly ruined my cricket. Spent hours teaching young 'Frogs', you'll pardon the expression, how to play cricket. Wasted my time. Played at home in the hols. There's a good club side at Ashtead. At twelve they had me batting the first team because dad was the local squire. I'm not sure who was more surprised when I scored some runs... Careful, there. All that bobbing stuff in the water is French shit and there's a lot of shit in Paris... No, the idea was that I'd come back in the hols and teach my elder brothers to speak French as Reggie was having trouble with a foreign language in his final year and if he didn't get his school certificate he wouldn't go to Oxford. You can possibly say that I'm the reason you two met each other. Anyway, his French improved and he passed. Still can't speak French as you know. Terrible at languages, so he says. Bone idle in fact. I should know."

"Why didn't you speak French to me at Merry Hall?"

"Never thought of it."

"Did you fall in the sewer purposefully to smell like that?"

"Stops a lot of questions when you stink. Can't smell it myself."

"You are lucky."

"You'll get used to it."

"Do the others stink?"

"No. They have proper covers. The Gestapo wouldn't take long to break down my story."

"Where does the shit flow to?"

"The Seine. Further down. By then it's decomposed through sewerage farms. Now they stink something lovely."

"How do you know where you are going?"

"I've memorised the map of the Paris sewerage system. You will have to do it as well. When the basic idea of the old builders is explained to you a logical pattern emerges."

"Who's there?" challenged a voice.

"The smelly one," said Geoffrey unnecessarily.

"They are waiting. Everyone has arrived."

"How long have you been in the sewers?" asked François.

"Three weeks. Prior to that we were giving the Germans a merry dance. I have four base camps with fuel and food supplies. We strike from one camp and hide up in another. The Germans are not sufficiently mobile to catch up with us. That is the theory."

"You went missing deliberately?"

"Yes. We had this operation planned before the war broke out. As professional soldiers it was our job to work out a plan for every contingency. Most of our arms and ammunition, explosives, even food, has been passed back into Paris to start the nucleus of a resistance movement. Further supplies will be dropped by air. The people waiting for us are going to be shown how the weapons work. How to look after them. How to use them to annoy the Germans."

"They will retaliate."

"So what do the French do? Sit back and enjoy the occupation?"

"Where do I fit in?"

"Without them knowing it, you're going to lead them, François. Many of your low- class friends are very brave and very nice people but they haven't trained their minds to plan and outwit the Germans. They will get hurt at first if they are not looked after. That's why I thought of you when we needed someone."

"How did you know about this side of my life?"

"Reggie told me."

"Reggie doesn't know."

"Never underestimate that brother of mine. He says that in business you have to know everything. He thinks you're very lucky to be able to drop out of the rat-race every now and again. He said it was to you like flying Mathilda was to him."

"Does he know about Simone?"

"Yes. And she's waiting for you. I said it was better for you to meet in the sewers than in the café. Not every Frenchman is a patriot. Pétain is even trying to do a deal with the Germans."

"So it wasn't Simone who asked me to come back to Paris but you?"

"She was very keen on the idea. If the British had asked, would you have come?"

"Probably. So that was why the Royal Navy offered me a free passage."

"We try and help."

"How much further?"

"Another ten minutes. When there is a big meeting, we have men posted throughout the sewerage system."

AT THE TIME the Romans dug a sewerage system for the Gauls, they created a central working platform from which they webbed underneath the houses of the old Paris. As successive generations of sewerage contractors took up the task, they retained the central cavern which was big enough to house a tennis court. Best of all it was dry and free from the sight of floating shit.

The cavern was now well lit and displayed an array of Allied and captured arms that two of Geoffrey's corporals were explaining to Frenchmen in sign language.

"François," shouted Simone as he and Geoffrey came out of the shadow of the tunnel into the light. She ran across the old brickwork and jumped up into his arms, her feet round his waist and her arms hugging him as hard as she was able.

"The Thief," said someone François couldn't see for Simone, and the word spread.

"Hello," shouted Danielle.

"Have you got your violin?" said someone and he held it up for everyone to see.

"Now we'll get good music despite the pigs."

François disentangled Simone and waved to them.

"Where have you been?" shouted someone.

"Two years. Why two years?"

"How much have you stolen?"

"Lots," answered François.

"Did you bring us some?"

"Plenty," said François.

"He always brings money."

"And music."

"Three cheers for The Thief."

"Do you know how to use a gun?"

"Show him, someone."

"Explosives?"

"Give him some wine."

"Not now," said François, getting up on an ammunition box and holding up his hands. "The English major has only a week to teach us."

"Are you going to learn as well?"

"We're going to learn together."

SIMONE DU BOIS let go of The Thief and watched him being mobbed by his old friends. A smile of pure contentment softened her brown eyes as she watched him shaking their hands and hugging and kissing on both cheeks. There were so many of them. She was ready to burst with joy. The English major broke away from the crowd to change out of his smelly disguise into uniform but Simone watched François, taller than most as he talked to everyone. Shadows from the burning lights flickered and the head and shoulders patterned on the wall and part of an ancient pillar and the beret became the top of a suit of armour and she saw him clearly as the knight, which he was. Simone's mother had died of syphilis when she was twelve and as her mother had no known relatives, Simone had none either. There had been talk of an elder brother but she had never seen her uncle and the story went that he was at sea, a rather large place to find the one and only, and probably mythical, relation. Simone hadn't bothered. There had been a little money in a jam jar to bury her mother and she had felt better when the job had been done properly and the Church had sent her mother to God where Simone prayed she would find a better life than the one she had found on earth. Simone's mother had been twenty-four-years-old when she died but even a very close look below the rouge and lipstick would have shown nothing of youth. The disease had something to do with it but it was mainly her way of life. She had gone on the waterfront at the age of eleven, unable to afford contraceptives, even if she had known what they were, she had fallen pregnant but being very young and very pretty she was able to save enough money to birth Simone before she was forced to stop work. Some of the sailors were kinky, anyway, so a pregnant sub-teen was something that turned them on. It was a little different. Three weeks after the birth she had been back in full swing, a twelve-year-old mother with a passion for satisfying large sailors, preferably black or Turkish. What her mother had about the Turks, Simone never found out. She often wondered if her father had been Turkish and when she was old enough to understand she had asked her mother about him.

"When you sleep with up to fifteen men in one night it is very difficult to decide who is the father, even if you know their names and what they look like."

There was one thing Simone was sure about her father. He was a sailor. In the years she was growing up in the one room, with the gas ring that served as cooker and heater, she only saw her mother bring home sailors. That is when she was home at night as mostly she dressed as a boy and roamed the waterfront picking up anything she could find of value which wasn't very much. She made many friends as she talked to everyone and many of them knew her story and why she was roaming the waterfront at night instead of being tucked up in a warm bed with a yellow teddy bear. The only thing they did not know was the 'boy' was a girl. Simone found out about reading and writing when she was nine. Even though the law said she should go to school she had never been as it had never crossed her mother's mind that people should be educated.

She had seen the old sailor sitting on a bollard, his thick boots resting on the wooden wharf with, down in front of him, the black, oily water of the seaport. Nothing untoward in an old sailor sitting by the sea except for the fact he was reading a newspaper and not using it to wipe his bum. The man was mouthing the words he read and Simone had sidled up to see if she could hear what he was saying. Suddenly, the old man shot out his hand and grabbed her.

"What do you want?"

"Nothing."

"Then why did you slide up behind me?"

"To see what you were doing?"

"Then you weren't doing nothing."

"In a way of speaking I wasn't."

"But you was… What's your name?"

"Simon."

"Simon who? Do I know your father?"

"Possibly."

"Well, what's his name?"

"I don't know."

"How come?" said the old man, putting her feet back on the wharf but still holding firmly to the front of her shirt.

"My mother's a prostitute."

The old man, being worldly wise, had said nothing but he had let go Simone's shirt front and put down his newspaper.

"Why aren't you in school?" he asked.

"I don't go to school."

"Why?"

"I don't know."

"There is only one way to live comfortably and that is to be educated. Without education we become nothing. They use us. I was a cabin boy when I went to sea. But with a difference. I could read. I couldn't write then but I could read. I was the only one on the ship apart from the captain and he couldn't read proper like. So the cabin boy in time became a sea captain. You must learn to read, boy."

"How do I learn?"

"Well, that's the secret," and the old man's rheumy eyes looked back on his life. "I've never been married," he said. "Too long away. See that ship over there? Steam. Coal in its belly. In my day we just had the sails and the wind and the strength in our arms and legs. I was away from home port a long time. Marseilles, that's it. My home port. I was at sea for sixty-three years and all together I only spent three of them in my home port. I knew a lot of people like your mother. Often good people. Kind to a lonely sailor… How else could they earn a living? I often wonder if out in that great big world there isn't a boy of mine. You go back and it's two, three years and you can't find them. Maybe you belong to all of us, boy. The son of all us lonely sailors. We also had to make a living. Didn't have no choice. You don't have any choice unless you are properly educated. Reading helps but it's only the start. The educated children know a lot more today than they did when I went to sea. Where do you live, boy?"

"In a room with my mother."

"Would she mind if you visited an old sailor, once in a while?"

"I don't know."

"I tell you what I'll do. You come and visit the old sailor and he'll teach you how to read this newspaper. My eyesight's going but it should last long enough for you to learn to read."

"Will you tell me stories about the sea?"

"Of course I will."

"My dad was a sailor."

'I'm sure he was,' said the old man to himself and felt a tight choking in his throat. "Come along then," he said getting up slowly. "I'll show you where I live."

"Can't we go and ask my mother first she's not working in the day."

"Yes. Of course we can."

"I'm sure she'll make you a cup of coffee."

"I'd like that, boy."

By the time syphilis had finally buried her mother the old man had gone totally blind but Simone could read and she read to him every day and he told her stories of Indo-China, Saigon, the big ports of America, the Pool of London, all the places in a sailor's world and she always urged him on, living his life through his memories. Fortunately, as by now the old sailor had found in Simone his own son, he couldn't see the curves and bumps of the girl, as pretty as paint. To help the charade, she kept her hair cut short even after she had moved into his two-roomed house to look after him. The old sailor liked to ruffle her hair and he was the second person she loved in her life. When he died, his pension stopped and the house was re-let to another old sailor to outlive his life. She was sad but happy for the old man who towards the end could do nothing for himself.

"I've enjoyed my life, boy… Some good times… But God really blessed me with these last few years of my life… When I'm gone I can leave you nothing of worldly goods."

"You don't have to, father. You've given me far, far more than money."

"You never called me father before."

A small suitcase had gone with her to Paris, the most brilliant place in the old man's memory. "The Left Bank. You should see the Left Bank," he had told her and at fifteen, with too many memories in Marseilles, she had taken a train to the capital. Sensibly she was still dressed as a boy. The old sailor had warned that much without knowing it and even said young boys were sought after but he hadn't told her why. She'd seen them, though. Seen them on the waterfront.

Her lonely odyssey led her finally to the Left Bank and the search for employment other than in her mother's profession. There wasn't any work in Paris during the depression but she learnt to go to the market after closing time and buy the leftover vegetables for a few sous and eked out the old sailor's small savings in an attic room that was big and good for painters but not for draughts and the cold and one side of the roof leaked when it rained which it did most regularly. She might have been poor but she loved every minute of her new life and forgot about the need for a regular job. As she had done in Marseilles, she talked to everyone and it wasn't long before her secret was out. Danielle had befriended her first having observed dryly, that she'd never seen a boy with tits before and after that Simone had grown her hair and admitted to being a woman.

"You don't need much to live here," said Danielle, moving into the room with two of her friends. "Big place," she said.

"Enormous," they all agreed and each week one or more of them found enough cash to pay for the rent, but the room was best suited to parties and became a regular meeting place for the out of work. After a month, Simone got a part-time job at the Café Bizet but they only sent round for her when the place was getting full and stopped paying her money when the customers left. The Café Bizet was not very profitable as the market it catered to was far too poor and it was only when Simone's friends had 'made a deal' that they could drink the coffee and the cheap red wine and then afterwards go on down to the cellar next door to listen to the jazz. Simone had heard of The Thief before she met him and for two reasons. His inordinate ability to play a jazz violin and his generosity to her friends. The first time she saw him was through a heavy haze of blue smoke, his black beret firmly on his head and the violin tucked under his chin. Afterwards, the thing that impressed her most was the fact he drank Pernod and not cheap red wine.

"I'm a good thief, you see," he'd told her and offered her a sip which she'd refused. Then he'd been taken back to the bandstand and she hadn't seen him again that evening or for another five weeks. Casually she had asked about him.

"Where does he live?"

"Nobody knows."

"Where does he get all the money?"

"He's a good thief."

"They'll catch him."

"Never," said her friends, "but why do you ask?"

Simone was curious. Apparently The Thief just arrived and disappeared. When he was there, everyone knew about it... Then nothing. "When he's not here, he's out somewhere stealing," Danielle had told her and she'd left it at that until he'd arrived at her attic for a party and spent a Saturday and Sunday in the attic full of boisterous and mostly drunk friends.

The wine and Pernod had been kept flowing all weekend. And then, when she turned and looked for him he had gone. Not a word.

"Funny fellow."

"Why worry? He paid for the wine. The thieving must have been good last week. I wonder how he does it."

"Very carefully," someone suggested and the party built up to new heights. He'd come round on the following Tuesday night to help clean up the room. They'd gone out to supper, the first time Simone had eaten in a restaurant as a paying guest. By three in the morning she was in love and by the way he looked at her the feeling was mutual. They became lovers that night, Danielle and her friends discreetly leaving them alone in the attic.

"There is just one thing," he had said. "Never ask me any questions."

Apart from their mutual Left Bank friends, the only stranger she had met through him had been the Danish artist. And when he was away they wrote through an address in the business centre of Paris which he'd told her never to visit. When the last separation had drawn to a year, she'd overcome her promise not to visit the address. When she did, she was even more puzzled. It wasn't a place to live in but an office. The Paris office of an English firm of merchants and insurance brokers. She'd gone away thinking François had a friend who was the janitor and acted as a postman for The Thief to fool the police. It was a big office, she remembered. What puzzled her most of all was if he wasn't coming back why did he write to her every week! And then the police had picked her up and taken her to the big police station in the centre of Paris and a little fat man had asked her questions. Despite the occupation, the French police still operated. Before the small fat man had spoken he had checked the door was locked and the windows closed despite the heat of summer. She was terrified and knew they were going to lock her up for something.

"What have I done?"

'Nothing."

"Why am I here?"

"You know The Thief," and immediately her heart had pumped painfully and she knew he was in danger.

"Who is The Thief?"

"François Deauville," and it was the first time she'd heard his last name. "We are forming an underground to fight the Bosch. Your friends know every inch of the Paris sewers. We want The Thief to lead them and you are the only one with his address or else you wouldn't be receiving letters from him every week."

"How do you know?"

"That is our business along with a lot else. I want you to write him a letter. Tell him you and your friends have started an underground to fight the Bosch. Tell him they want him to join them. I think it will bring him back to you and you want that don't you? Almost two years, isn't it?"

"If you know so much, why don't you arrest him?"

"We have our reasons. Now, here is the letter I have drafted for you to copy." Simone hesitated. "You do want to see him?"

"Yes," she said and took from him the sheet of typed foolscap.

"We will post your letter," he said.

The policeman had been right. It worked. He was here and there was nothing else in her world that mattered. The cavern had grown quieter and then individual pockets of conversation petered out and the sound of burning paraffin lights came back to them. The paraffin smell was strong and lines of black smoke curled up into darkness.

Geoffrey Beaumont stepped up onto a full box of ammunition, bearing no resemblance to the Parisian hobo who had come in with François. His Sam Browne was highly polished and even his battledress trousers had a stiff crease in them. The single crowns on his shoulder straps were dull, the only sign of age and battle weariness. Even in the worst conditions, the Sandhurst training in Geoffrey required him to be correctly dressed.

François checked the exact level of Geoffrey's peaked hat and smiled. It was regulation to a millimetre. Everyone in the cavern was aware they were looking at the epitome of a professional soldier. In formal educated French he began to tell them what they could do to defeat the Bosch and regain the glory of France. He gave them a lecture on their own history and reminded them that the cream of Napoleon's army was drawn from people just as themselves. He failed, however, to mention that the same people had been fighting the army he now represented. 'Time,' thought François, 'changes all sides' and it was only then that he realised a nightmare had begun and he wondered how many of them would still be smiling at the end of it. There was a war on. He was part of it. François, looking at Geoffrey, wondered if his own father had looked as confident before the Battle of Verdun.

He had been in the old nursery of the chateau that looked out at the vineyards spreading over the hills in all directions broken by clumps of trees that grew among rocks. A cheerful boy of nine, he didn't have a care in the world. An only child, he had received as his right the individual devotion of both his parents and none of it spoilt him. His Dutch governess had brought him the news and the thing that had impressed him most was the fact she was crying and this was most extraordinary. François's governess neither laughed nor cried. On rare occasions she smiled. Apparently his father had gone over the top once too often and been cut in half by a German machine gunner who couldn't see who he was shooting because it was dark. The governess said she was sure his father would receive a medal, another Croix de Guerre to go with the others. The perfect testimony to a professional soldier. Cavalry no less. But that was the last war. Everyone was only interested in the new one. François's father was 'yesterday's' hero. The monuments were stone. Unread. Accepted as part of the village history. Even twenty-four years later nobody knew what they had been fighting about. From that point the light had gone out of his life. His mother hadn't gone out of the house for five years and when she did, it was only to the shops and back. The estate had run itself. The vines grew, were pruned, bare fruit were sprayed, picked, crushed and turned into brandy. The brandy from ten years earlier was sold, paid the bills and sent the small François to schools that interested him no more than the lonely chateau. He passed his exams because that was part of his heritage but he had no idea why he was concerned with Pythagoras. François became a loner and disappeared all day into the vineyards when he was home on holiday. His only happiness was dressing like the peasants and joining them at their labours. He was good, even in the early days and not one of the workers ever guessed they were talking to the owner of the estate. Fishing was another pleasure. Anything to get out of the house and away from his mother's misery.

François had inherited the Deauville estate from his father but his mother was richer by far in her own right, a heritage François would take from her when she died. On both sides of his family he was the last in long lines of ancestors going back into the Middle Ages. In his paternal grandfather's will there was a snag. Whilst his mother lived she had sole discretion over her wealth. She could do with it as she wished. His grandfather had been worried about tying the family money into a trust. The world, he had said, was too volatile. As a result of this indiscretion his mother was a wealthy widow and the object of many an old penniless 'buck'.

François was playing a Mozart violin sonata to his music teacher, a little gnome of a man from the village, when they heard a commotion outside the Chateau and went to the window to investigate. Being high summer it was open and the scene down below in the courtyard was centred on a man in his thirties prostrate on an improvised stretcher and in obvious pain. Three of the estate workers that François knew rather better when he was working with them in the fields had made a stretcher out of the long sticks they hooked through the fruit baskets to carry grapes from the vineyard to the horse drawn trailers. They had tied hessian in between to carry the stranger up to the big house as he was obviously a gentleman.

"Probably fell off his horse," said François, going to the door.

"Is the lesson over?"

"Yes, maestro… Oh, how am I doing?"

"Technically very good. Your heart is not in Mozart."

"Or Bach?" said the fifteen year old François with a rueful smile.

"It makes your mother happy."

"And that is what is important," agreed François from outside the door on the landing. "Next week Tuesday," and he was off down the wide staircase to see what was going on.

At closer range the stranger was a strikingly good looking man in his early thirties with thick, swept back black hair, a strong jaw and a well-trimmed military moustache. His riding clothes were expensive, especially his boots. Out in the courtyard, a lame Arab stallion was favouring its right front leg.

"Mustn't shoot him. Best friend I ever had. Poor old fellow. A mole hole in the road. Good of you young men to carry me here. Ah," he said, seeing François coming down the stairs. "Sorry to intrude. Damn nuisance. Just telling these good fellows. Mole hole. All that beautiful horse and a mole you can't see turns him into nothing. Flew right over the top. Can I explain my predicament to the master of the house?"

"I am the owner of the chateau… My father is dead," he added as explanation.

"Your mother, maybe?"

"She seldom entertains."

"Well, young man," he said, giving the three farm workers each a coin that represented two weeks' wages, "can you phone a doctor? I may be talking alright but this pain is a little excruciating. From my days in the military, I'd say I've broken my hip. It's where I came down anyway and bruises never felt like this before."

"I'll call him myself… Probably out on his rounds."

"Leave a message."

"Can I not take you to hospital? It's fifteen miles away. The trap…"

"No, young man. The pain I have at the moment is quite enough."

THREE WEEKS later Jean-Pierre Agier was still at the chateau comfortably ensconced in the best spare bedroom with the servants dancing to his tune and laughing most of the time as they did so. The pain had gone but the doctor had forbidden movement, the hip having fractured in three places. By this stage it was obvious that his mother was fascinated by this man and if it hadn't been for certain anomalies, François would have been as happy as his mother. The man talked of meetings he was going to, rich, titled relations, friends who were generals in the army though he had never heard of François's father's army friends and the ones that had survived Verdun, the few of them, had done very well for themselves. But nobody came to see him. Not a soul. It was as if the horse had done him a favour, which as it turned out, it had. After four months, and having returned for the Christmas holidays from boarding school, François was convinced the man was a fraud but he was charming in the process and François's mother enjoyed his company and had come back to the living, something for which François would always be grateful to Jean-Pierre Agier even if he wasn't to be so grateful for some of the other happenings at the chateau. But did it really matter? It was the only life his mother was going to have and if this man made her happy so let it be. The following holidays he heard from his mother that Jean-Pierre was up and about but still living at the chateau and taking an interest in the viniculture. François took up the standing offer of a school friend to spend the spring in the South of France and he only went home for two days to see his mother pack some clothes. It was during those two days that he was told his mother was marrying again and with a smile and a kiss on her cheek he wished her well but declined to obtain a special exeat from school to attend the wedding. By then, François had checked up on the man. He had been a sergeant in the war, commissioned in the field when the French army was running out of junior officers. All his new manners had been copied from the officers' mess. The poor man couldn't get a job even if he wished. The army had thrown millions of soldiers onto the work market. 1923 was not a good year for ex-sergeants to find gainful employment. But as François told himself again, did it matter? Provided his mother believed him both of them were happy. The bride and groom, instead of moving to his paternal grandfather's estate which was being well run by a cousin, moved into the chateau and François felt uncomfortable in his own house. Taking the easy way, which is often the best, he kept out of the way in the holidays and when he went up to the Sorbonne to read ancient Greek, he took a flat in Paris and only visited the chateau to see his mother. It suited everybody as the man was perfectly content to live in luxury, entertain his new wife and leave the estate running to more practical hands. All he required was the accolade of being the owner's husband and he built up a pertinent series of questions to ask the hands and managers as he did his rounds on his stallion, fully recovered, and the only material asset he brought to the marriage. By the time François left university, it was obvious he wasn't going to be making his own brandy while his stepfather lived on the estate but by then François had turned his violin to jazz and the prospect didn't worry him at all. The problem was what to do with his life and when he saw the notice for exchange students to go to Oxford on a post-graduate course he thought it a good thing to brush up his English. He enjoyed being a student and didn't take his Greek very seriously. What he enjoyed most was the company he kept, having been starved of good companions.

Reggie had first tried out his appalling French, got nowhere and then asked François in English to join him in a pub outside Nuneham Park to try out Reggie's Bentley that he had subsequently given to his youngest brother when the latter had entered into the Royal Military Academy at Sandhurst.

Reggie had found the money for the car by introducing a buyer to the impecunious father of a fellow student, forced to sell four paintings out of the family trust, illegal but done if all members of the family agreed. If you wanted to buy or sell anything, François discovered, Reggie knew somebody.

"There's never any reason to be poor," he told François, Gunter and Carl one night over pints of mild and bitter in the Leg of Mutton and Cauliflower.

"There's always someone moving money around. All you've got to do is find a way of stopping it for a short while, diverting it and taking a reasonable percentage. The thing that talks loudest in this little world of ours is money. The aristocracy turn up their noses to trading but they'll all rue the day. There's always a system. Always a system," he had repeated. "Now look at that bird over there, the one that's just come in. Now how do we find out the right system for that one?"

"The French approach?" suggested François.

"Direct. Go up to her," put in Gunter.

"Just keep smiling and she's sure to come over under her own steam."

"Won't work Carl."

"What will?"

"The Bentley approach. Best little pussy catcher in the business. Women can resist you or me but never money. Combine money and the four of us and the combination is deadly. But first a reconnaissance," and Reggie got up from the round table to go to the John and walked across the room making a show of greeting one of his friends. When Reggie returned he sat down at the table a little smugly and picked up his half empty pint, taking a good swig before he was prepared to say anything.

"That was Tony Venturas," he said, putting the pint back on the dark wood of the table. "Comes up weekends. Flying instructor at the University Air Squadron. You fellows should join. Lot of fun. Even better, the R.A.F. pay for it if you're accepted. Eyes, heart. That kind of thing… I was right about the girl wearing stockings but not wearing a ring. Bored with the guy who brought her in. Perfect for a pitch. First, Gunter, please go out into the car park and remove the fan belt from the car. Take it off the same way we had to fit the new one last week. And let's have another round while we're setting this one up. Money in the kitty," and each of them pulled out a penny-halfpenny and put the coins on the table.

"I'll go," said Carl and picked up the empties and took them up to the bar. "Four more, please," he said as Gunter went outside.

"I prefer drinking wine," said François who had just turned twenty-one and was now in control of his own money.

"Mustn't embarrass the others," said Reggie. "When they too can afford wine we'll drink it. That girl is extremely pretty. It's usually the other way round. The closer you get the worse they get."

"What are we going to do?"

"First, wait 'til Gunter comes back and from now on we all keep our eyes off the lady. I've had two silent bites and that's quite enough. There's Carl," he said as Gunter returned to his seat and picked up one of the full pints and drank an inch off the top. "All fixed?" asked Reggie.

"No problem."

"We'll finish these drinks and then leave."

"What about the girl?" asked François.

Reggie said nothing and concentrated on his drink thinking he had just had enough alcohol to give him the boost to try the stunt.

"Nothing ventured, nothing gained," he said finally, finishing his pint. "Let's go fellows," and he waved again to Tony on their way out of the door. "You guys lounge around the car," he said when they were outside. He started the car with a shattering noise, stopped it, jacked up the bonnet and was then on his way back to the pub, the car parked close to the door where it couldn't be seen from where the girl and her male escort were sitting.

"I say, old chap," said Reggie so that they could hear outside. "My friend's got a frightful problem. Generator light not working on the Bentley. Had a look. Damn fan belt's broken. Brand new. You'd think they'd make them work for that kind of money. The Bentley, I mean old boy."

"How can I help?"

"Very decent of you. What I'm after is to borrow one of your girlfriend's stockings. The Count will get it back to her tomorrow. A new pair of course. Knowing the Count with all that damn money of his, he'll probably give her half a dozen pairs. He's French and they're made in Paris, the very best ones. They say a stocking tied firmly will turn the old fan belt."

"Well, I can't take it off here," she said before her escort could say anything. "Excuse me a moment."

"Terribly good of you," said Reggie.

"Entirely my pleasure," said the girl.

Five minutes later, with the girl's stocking valiantly flapping under the bonnet and keeping the generator light from coming on, with François at the wheel in his new role as a French Count and with the girl's address and phone number firmly in Reggie Beaumont's pocket, they were rattling off down the country lane back to their rooms.

"Tomorrow," said Reggie, "I will arrive with a new pair of stockings, a dozen long stemmed roses and François's thanks."

"How will you explain the same car?" said François having thought that he had seen a gap for himself.

"Twins. You and I buy two at a time."

"What was her name?" asked Carl.

"Let's have a look," said Reggie, taking out the piece of paper the girl had given him and started to read. "She doesn't say her name," said Reggie. "All she says is 'nice try but I'm about to become engaged. Enjoy the stocking. The boyfriend can afford it'," and all four joined in the raucous laughter that lasted them through to the centre of Oxford.

François smiled at the recollection and tried harder to listen to what Geoffrey was saying, knowing his life would depend on his knowledge. Apparently to hear better he moved around the circle of people to come behind Simone and put his arm strongly round her shoulder.

FOR A WEEK, Geoffrey and his corporals put them through an intensive training course. At the end of the week the cavern people were asked to elect a leader. Prompted by the major, the responsibility was handed over to The Thief. The initial group of seven that had been approached by French intelligence would act as the committee with two more members put forward by the crowd.

"It's the best I can do in the time," Geoffrey told François. "Experience can only be gained in the field. My remaining men have now regrouped in the sewers and it's time to get them back to England."

"How are you going?"

"Walking."

"It's a long way."

"Not if you're fit. We'll move at night and hole up during the day."

"There's a curfew."

"We'll kill anyone in the way, isn't that right Corporal Sparrow?"

"Yes, sir."

"Be a good chap and tell Lieutenant Miller to issue civilian clothes."

"When do we leave?"

"In ten minutes. And tell Private Kemp to eat something first. I can't stand his belly aching when he's hungry."

"He's packed extra rations for himself."

"Make sure he carries them himself."

"Are you going to dunk in the sewer?" asked François.

"Of course. Self-respecting German soldiers keep away from smelly Frenchmen."

"Good luck," said François.

"We'll both need it," said Geoffrey.

"Regards to Reggie."

"If he's still alive," said Geoffrey looking at the ceiling. "They've shot him down six times. Sorry about Tony. War's so damn personal."

THAT EVENING at the end of September 1940, François sank into the spring less sofa in the attic and asked Simone to make him coffee. They had been left alone in the room and Danielle said she had found somewhere else to sleep.

"Love is better left alone," she said and humped her one small suitcase down the stairs.

"Where were you?" asked Simone from the corner that housed their gas ring.

"In the sewer all day."

"I know that. Where were you for two years?"

"In and around."

"Why is the name on the door of your postal address the same as the major's?"

"Is it? There's a thing. I'll ask my friend who collects my mail."

"Will you?"

"If you want me to."

"You knew the major before, didn't you?"

"I told you, he was the contact resulting from your letter. You asked me to come back. Meet you at the Bizét. The major was there."

"I've asked you to come back in all my letters. A policeman frightens me to death so I copy a letter and the next minute you're back hob-nobbing with an English major as if you'd known him all your life."

"Are we having an argument?"

"Who are you, François?"

"Does it matter?"

"I want to know everything about you. Fill in the gaps when you weren't in my life. All I know about the man I've loved for five years is that he's François, The Thief, who keeps on popping up in my life to make me intensely happy and then disappearing to make me intensely miserable."

"I take you as you are. Isn't that enough? Must we bring into our feelings the things from outside?"

"You knew the major before?"

"Yes," he said, finally, "I've known Geoffrey Beaumont for eleven years… Be very careful. You and I love each other on these terms. I'm not sure whether it would survive in another climate. Isn't what we have good enough?"

"When you are here," she said, starting to cry. "Where were you for two years?"

"Away, Simone. If I could have come back before I would have. You don't want to know the sordid way I make my living?"

"Of course I do, silly. I want to know everything about you I want to get so close to you we stick together so we can't come apart."

"I've never asked for your background?"

"Why not?"

"Because it couldn't increase our happiness."

"My mother was a prostitute."

"So what?"

"She died of syphilis."

"So what? So did a lot of prominent people."

"My father was one of my mother's clients."

"Must have been a good man to be your father."

"He was a sailor."

"My father was a soldier."

"What kind of soldier?"

"Does it matter?"

"I want to know."

"He was a colonel in the cavalry. Died at Verdun. How do you like that for a good lie?"

"Oh, but it isn't. I believe it. What happened to the family estate?" she said, taking hold of his hand, enjoying the joke.

"Nothing."

"They don't exist," she asked, raising her one eyebrow wickedly.

"They exist."

"Where? In your head?"

"You don't believe me?"

"Of course I do."

"You won't believe the next bit."

"I will."

"Do you know how I make a living?"

"By thieving. You've told me that for five years."

"In a way, yes."

"How do you mean, in a way? You're either a thief or you aren't. Like my mother. There was no grey area there."

"I'm a mining magnate."

"What's that?" she said looking at him queerly.

"A Rand Baron. In South Africa?"

"Where's that?"

"At the bottom of Africa."

"You've been that far!"

"Yes. And I earn ten million francs every month for myself."

"Now that is ridiculous," said Simone laughing. "Here. Drink your coffee. No-one earns ten million francs a month," and she began to laugh happily to herself.

She sat down next to him on the sofa and put her arm over his shoulder and whispered in his ear. "You really are a thief," she said.

"Of course," he said, kissing her cheek softly. "And a very good one."

"I don't like people who aren't good at their jobs... How long do you think this stupid war will last?"

"A long time. Much longer than we think."

After ten minutes when he thought she had gone to sleep in the crook of his shoulder, she leant up quickly.

"You met him in the Cafe Bizet?"

"Who?" asked François.

"The major."

"Oh, him. 'Course I did. I told you that."

"I'm glad... Let's go to bed."

"That's the best suggestion you've made tonight."

5

THE BATTLE OF BRITAIN 1940

*R*eggie Beaumont stumbled from the crew room, focused on his Spitfire and started to run across the grass, his parachute bumping against his backside, strands of loose hair blowing in the slight wind, his helmet gripped in his right hand. Eleven other pilots ran in a gaggle alongside and then began to fight their ways into the open cockpits and slam the hoods shut over their heads as the Rolls-Royce Merlin engines cracked into life and the squadron was bumping over the grass, picking up airspeed and taking off three at a time into the evening. Reggie looked at his watch having plugged in his helmet to air traffic control.

"Not bad. One minute and thirty-two," he thought he had said to himself.

"What did you say, Green Leader," said a girl's voice through the earphones.

"That you?" asked Reggie.

"Who else? Climb to twenty thousand feet, South, South East. They're coming over The Wash. Bandits one seven. Estimated one hundred."

"Shit, there are only twelve of us."

"Biggin Hill have scrambled two squadrons."

"That's better," said Reggie popping two Dexedrine tablets into his mouth and squeezing his eyes to have them focus. He then began to meticulously scan the sky above, below and behind. Automatically, he pressed the firing button to test his guns and eight Vickers machine guns went off at the same time. Again Reggie squeezed his eyes but still found they were out of focus. Once the Dexedrine took effect the wool would get out of his way and he would be able to see and concentrate on what he was doing.

"You alright, Reggie?" said his port side wingman on the controller frequency.

"Sure," said Reggie, shaking his head and bringing his aircraft into line with his wingmen, the R.A.F. roundels clear on their fuselages, the sun just catching the whirr of their propellers and showing a faint shadow. It was the squadron's seventh sortie that day and Reggie wondered how the others were faring, especially the youngest gamely keeping up with Reggie's starboard wing tip. He turned his head to him and gave him the thumbs-up sign and the boy waved.

'Maybe,' thought Reggie, 'at thirty-two I'm getting too old for this caper,' and he told himself not to even think such thoughts. With tremendous effort he forced himself to concentrate.

Five minutes later Reggie said quietly into the intercom, "I have them, control. More like a hundred and thirty."

"Good luck."

"Tally-ho!" said Reggie to his other eleven pilots and peeled off out of the sun to come down on the German formation, the big bombers droning steadily in the summer evening with their terrier escorts of 103s and 110s circling above and below. Reggie had looked for the Biggin Hill squadrons without success. As he dived towards the enemy formation a combination of Dexedrine and adrenaline popped the wool out of his head and he was fully in control of the attacking squadron.

"Ignore the fighters," he said, knowing they couldn't and put his aircraft into a vertical dive, the Germans floating along two thousand feet below.

"They've seen us. Watch each other's tails. And concentrate. I want to hear it."

"Concentrate," came the gabble of different voices.

Reggie consciously extended his lateral vision for fighters and concentrated on the bomber he had selected for himself. "Don't fire too soon," he said to his other pilots for the seventh time that day and then they were past the fighters and into the bomber formation, tracer coming up at them from the bomber turrets and the fighters trying unsuccessfully to cut their dive.

Reggie drilled small holes along the bomber's fuselage and clearly saw the bomber's cockpit explode in bits of metal, smashed instruments and blood.

With no control on rudder and stick, the bomber flipped onto its back and went on down that way into the English countryside, finally exploding a long way from the aerial dogfights that had erupted five miles away, the German fighter pilots having drawn the Spitfires away from the bombers still droning on towards the London docks. The Biggin Hill Wing Commander had watched the Tangmere attack and once the 103s and 110s had been drawn off, he led his two squadrons of Hurricanes down at the unprotected bombers giving them time to cut down and up into the bombers before they were also engaged by the German fighters by which time the German bombers were no longer in formation but straggling all over the sky.

"Break, Johnny," shouted Reggie and was gratified by the immediate reflex of his starboard wingman who slid out from under an arcing line of tracer from a twin engine 110. "Hit the bombers," he said again into the intercom and turned violently inside to dislodge the 109 that was following. Individually they attacked the bombers and broke up the formations further.

"Shit, they're turning," said Reggie, still watching all round for fighters. "Try to draw the fighters back with us. This is Green Leader returning home." 'Shit,' said Reggie to himself as the German bombers that could still fly, lumbered round and tried to head back to Holland. Reggie counted twelve parachutes and hoped none were British and then he broke off the action, knowing his guns and fuel tanks were almost empty. Finally, away from the fighting in a patch of clear, blue, evening sky, Reggie began to count. There were ten of them. A leaden malaise took hold of his legs and forced him to try and concentrate on the rudder bar to keep in formation. The Dexedrine and adrenaline had left him as quickly as they had come and his vision clouded badly and with it came an urge to sleep. Instinctively he knew that his body had finally rejected his mind. Then he wondered if this time he was dead and the heavenly voices whispering into his ears were somewhere else and so was he and the fact that he was still in his cockpit was simply because he had always been there.

"Green Leader!" shouted Johnny, as Reggie's Spitfire yawed dangerously close. "Are you hit? GREEN LEADER. SQUADRON LEADER BEAUMONT," but he was much more comfortable settling back with his hands off the controls and going to sleep.

"REGGIE," shouted Suzanne from ground control, having seen the one flight of Spitfires dropping back and hearing the starboard wingman. "It's Suzanne. It's me. Are you hurt? REGGIE, ARE YOU HURT?"

Instinctively the plane righted itself, flying towards Tangmere but at only one hundred and ten miles an hour, the two wingmen doing everything to revive the slumped figure of Reggie they could clearly see sitting back in his seat, his oxygen mask pointing at the sky.

"WHERE THERE'S A WILL THERE'S A WAY," she shouted at him and it penetrated the one small part of his brain that was not completely asleep.

"Sorry," said Reggie, groggily. "Must have dozed off."

"Turn your oxygen to full."

"Good idea, lady. Why didn't I think of that myself?"

"Are you hurt?"

"No… Don't think so… Just monumentally tired… How long's this war been going on… my brother's missing… dunked him in the Mole when he was a kid… gone missing… poor old Geoffrey's missing… Tony's not missing… he's dead."

"Keep him talking," said someone, an older voice that Reggie vaguely thought was his station commander but he didn't care. The only thing he wanted to do was sleep.

"How wide's the Mole?" asked Suzanne, the girl having caught the urgency from Tangmere.

"Not very wide… Full of minnows."

"What's a minnow, Reggie?"

"Little fish… You can catch them on a bent pin… Well, not really."

"You must increase airspeed," said his port wingman.

"Why?" said Reggie.

"Because you owe me a drink."

"Why?"

"You lost at chess last night."

"Terrence Pike, you are lying… I have never lost to you at chess. Drinking, maybe, not chess."

"Have you turned up the oxygen?" he asked.

"Not yet. I forgot… How are we doing, Terry, my boy…? I'll tell you what. If you can get me out of this one I'll let you beat me at chess."

"That's a deal, Reggie," said Terry Pike. "NOW CONCENTRATE!"

Isabel Beaumont answered the phone, Pavy having given up the task as the staff at Merry Hall had dwindled with the war.

"Merry Hall."

"May I speak to Lady Beaumont?" said a male voice.

"Who's speaking?"

"Group Captain Bishop, R.A.F. Tangmere. I'm…"

"Reggie's C.O," said Isabel, catching her breath. "What's happened?"

"I'm not quite sure at the moment. Ten minutes ago, he parked his aeroplane on its nose in the hedge at the far end of my aerodrome. The M.O's had a look at him. Nothing physical. The Spitfire wasn't even hit on that sortie."

"What happened?"

"Squadron Leader Beaumont went to sleep at the controls. He's still asleep. M.O.'s had him moved to sickbay. I've grounded him for the moment. Could someone be sent up to take him home? The M.O. thinks it's battle fatigue. I had to send him up for the seventh time today. No experienced pilots. M.O. thinks a lot of sleep and rest will bring him right. Shouldn't be any lasting effects but we don't know. M.O. says no-one knows much about how far the body will go. I checked up, Reggie hadn't been sleeping even off duty."

"I'll drive up myself. Lady Beaumont has enough worries. Her youngest son is reported missing."

"I'm sorry."

"So are we all."

"Yes. Well. You'll come and get him. For the official record, he's on two weeks' leave."

"Thank you, Group Captain."

Slowly, Isabel put down the receiver, smiling to herself as Pavy came into the hall, drawn by the ringing phone.

"Pavy, is there sufficient petrol in the Bentley to drive up to town?"

"I'll ask the chauffeur?"

"He went into the army two weeks ago."

"Of course he did. Silly of me… I'll have a look."

"Don't worry. I'll syphon from the Morgan… Tell Lady Beaumont I've been urgently called to London. Another batch of Merchant officers. My sister can look after everything."

"Very well, Mrs Beaumont," he said to her back as she went on her way to the bedroom she normally shared with Henry and began to pack the sexiest clothes she could find in her wardrobe.

Reggie woke up at eleven o'clock the following morning to find his sister-in-law seated in the chair next to him in the sickbay. The sound of Merlin engines had woken him as three squadrons took off to intercept.

"Why didn't anyone wake me?" he said, swinging his feet out of bed. "What are you doing here?" he said rudely.

"Thank you for the compliment."

"Shit," said Reggie, remembering. "Did I mangle Alpha Fox Tango?"

"A little, so they say."

"There'll be a replacement. Its pilots we're short of, rather than planes," he said pulling on his shoes and looking around for his flying gear.

"The C.O.'s grounded you, to use his own words?"

"Why?"

"You need a rest, Reggie... There's only so much..."

"I remember bits of it... I must thank Terry... made me pull out my finger. Shit, Isabel, am I tired," he said and sank back onto the bed, closing his eyes.

"Where do you want to rest up? Merry Hall?"

"No. Mother has enough worries with Geoffrey. Anyway there are too many bloody people at the Hall."

"Your swearing has got worse."

"It's the war."

"Yes," said Isabel smiling, "we can blame a lot of things on the war. How about your flat? I've driven up in Geoffrey's Bentley."

"Yes that will do I can play the piano. How long's the C.O. put me off?"

"Two weeks."

"Should be long enough. We R.A.F. types are pretty tough," he said trying to laugh. "Well," he qualified, "some of us are... Any news of Henry?"

"He's in North Africa. It's all I know... The bombing's bad."

"The flat? I don't care... If they didn't get me today they won't be clever enough to drop a bomb on 63 Whitehall Court. And I can call in at the office."

"The C.O. said he'd court martial you if you went anywhere near the place."

"He did, did he?"

"Yes."

"Then I'll use the phone."

"It's disconnected," she said and then to herself, 'or it soon will be.'

"What... Didn't the bloody office pay?"

"Nothing like that. The M.O. says you must have rest."

"How am I meant to order food? Drink? I do suppose I'm allowed to drink?"

"In moderation. The M.O. was specific about that one. You can do what you like in the confines of your home, provided it's done in moderation. I'm going to look after you."

"Why you?"

"I'm your sister-in-law and you don't have a live-in-lover at the moment, do you?"

"You know perfectly well I have never lived with anyone."

"Well, whatever you call it. I've packed your grip. There's a pair of flannels on that chair and your old sports jacket."

"No uniform?"

"No."

"Drop me at the flat and you can get back to Merry Hall."

"We'll see about that later," she said, smiling at him. "I'll wait outside while you change."

"I don't trust you further than I can throw you."

"Tut, tut, Reggie Beaumont. That's not a very nice thing to say about your sister-in-law," and she went out through the door backwards throwing him a kiss on the way.

"This must be the first night for weeks they haven't bombed London," said Reggie the following evening, looking out over the Thames past the Houses of Parliament. Behind him the lights were out so as not to break the black-out.

"I think we're winning the war in the air."

"You should know," said Isabel from the sofa. "Please draw the curtain. It makes me nervous."

"I was just tired. Another night's sleep and I'll be back in the air."

"Two weeks, Reggie. You were gnashing your teeth and thrashing around in the bed much better last night."

"How do know?"

"I'm your nurse."

"Bullshit."

"Alright. I'm here to seduce you."

"Sounds more honest."

"We have a pact, don't forget."

"Don't be silly."

"But I'm not. If you knew how many offers I get a week from lonely, frustrated sailors you'd blush... You must look at it this way. I'm doing my bit for the war. There's nothing better than sex to make you sleep properly at night."

"You're not a very nice person, Isabel."

"Did I ever say I was, life is short... Even shorter these days. I believe in enjoying the little bits of life while I can. Why don't you play the piano?"

"What would you like to hear," said Reggie closing the window, glad the subject had been changed.

"Chopin. At least he wasn't German... What are you going to do with Bretts?"

"Lilly's fine... Gives her something to do. Gwen and Pippa are helping."

"Now that's something. My two little sisters working for a whorehouse."

"It's an exclusive men's club."

"Call it what you will."

"The casino island has been shelved."

"And Carl?"

"What about Carl?"

"Maybe I should write to him to tell him he's the father of a little girl."

"He's doing very well. Servicing half of Johannesburg. Probably all of it now François disappeared. Some cock and bull story about starting a French underground... I wonder if he'll finally face facts and marry Simone?"

"Who's she?"

"The only woman who's ever got to François."

"Maybe he loves her."

"Maybe you're right... I don't feel like playing. Pour me another scotch. I might as well wake up with a hangover. Pour one for yourself. I'm going to sleep tonight without a sleeping pill. It was Tony, you know. Ever since he was killed I haven't been able to keep it all together properly... He tried to bail out but the fire got to him first. Fried. It's the one thing we all fear most."

"Drink your scotch."

"Yes, ma'am."

"That's better. Cheers."

"Cheers. And thanks... I really do feel better... It was like the power being switched off. Everything just stopped at once. The frightening thing was I didn't want to fight it."

"You need a son and heir. That'll give you something to fight for."

"There you go. Twisting everything."

"I've got a steak. Black market. Absolute fortune. Your father won't let us eat our own cows. Sells it all to the government like a good boy. And a bottle of red wine."

"Alright. But there isn't going to be any hanky panky."

"What's hanky panky?... Anyway, even if I do know, what's wrong with it? A bloody bomb might come through that ceiling in ten minutes."

"Do you know something? I've just about had enough. For the next ten days I'm not going to think about the squadron or my business. For this once they'll both have to look after themselves."

"I'm wrong," said Reggie, pushing away his plate, picking up his red wine glass and taking it to the drawn curtain. "That was good steak. Mind if I turn off the lights?"

"What a lovely idea."

"No... Switch the light off... Can you hear?" he asked opening the curtain.

"What?"

"Aircraft... Dorniers... Hope the night boys are around. New aircraft. Defiant. Radar. Swivel gun turret but as blind as a bat from underneath. Won't take the Luftwaffe long to work out how to shoot that one down. Poor sods. Must be worse at night. You can't even see who's trying to kill you." The air raid siren blared urgently and Reggie let the curtain fall back, into place. "You can turn on the light."

"Hadn't we better go down to an air-raid shelter?"

"Probably. I thought they weren't coming tonight. We really clobbered them on Monday. Biggin Hill have the answer. Hit in strength. Came in two squadrons after we'd hit them first... We must attack as a wing. Three squadrons at once. Then the fighters can't be everywhere. We turned them back, on Monday. First time. Maybe they're cracking a few days before us. Bertie Featherstone's idea of telling Churchill to bomb Berlin worked. Bertie had studied Hitler. The little man's pride overcame his strategy. Another couple of weeks of hitting our fighter and radar stations would have been enough. Now Hitler's turned everything to bombing London and Manchester. My, this is a big raid," he said, going back to the window.

"Stay away from the window."

"Scared?"

"Of course I am. And so would you be if you had any sense. Let's go down."

"Too late. What's coming is on its way... Hear that whistling sound?"

"REGGIE!"

"They come a lot nearer than that before we duck under the dining room table," he said as a series of violent crumps shattered the night outside and instantly started fires. "Hitler must have heard that Beaumont needed sleep. You know," began Reggie as a battery of ack-ack guns started loosing off from behind the building.

"What the hell is that?" said Isabel, jumping up from the table.

"Ours. Waste of time unless you get one of them crossed by searchlights. The rest is farting against thunder... Turn out the lights."

"I'm scared."

"Just turn off the light... Thanks... Hey, come and look at this. I do believe the anti-aircraft boys are about to score. Come over here. I'll even hold your hand if that helps... See... Up there... Those long lights are searchlights and where they cross is a German bomber and every gun around here has got his range... See what I mean... That red glow is burning plane... Poor sods... Poor, fucking sods... Blow up, you bloody aeroplane, blow up," and then they heard the explosion and the searchlights went out. "Bombers are worse. It must be worse in a bomber... "That's the all clear... How's your drink?" said Reggie, after a while.

"How do you take it so calmly?"

"I'm punch drunk, Isabel. The C.O. was right. Every man has in him a certain number of sorties. Maybe I've reached my quota."

"Are you going to stop flying?"

"Not until they kill me. I've put in to join the Pathfinders. Mosquitoes. Twin engine. Made of wood. Don't show up well on radar. We're going to put flares around the targets. Stop the boys dropping their bombs in the fields... Should be fun."

"You said it was worse at night."

"Pour me another glass of wine... There are a lot of things in life that are instinctive... It's probably sheer conceit or damn stupidity but I have a terrible fear that if I'm not out there, up front, we're going to lose this war. Tony felt the same. I'm going to find a second wind if it kills me."

"Don't let it kill you, Reggie," and genuine tears were coming down her face.

"We do things we don't want to do and we don't do things we shouldn't do," he said finally letting the curtain fall back into place. "It's part of our heritage, right or wrong. I think it's right which is why I do it. I like to think my brothers are the same. My ancestors, most of them. I believe there has to be a right in this life or it isn't worth living."

"You're lecturing me?"

"Yes."

"I'll do it the other way."

"I don't think you will."

"I can't live a cold, frigid life."

"I'll take the chance."

"Why? He'd never know."

"But I would, Isabel, and so would you."

"I don't care."

"That's what is different. I do. Now, let's finally get off this subject. As family we have a lot of years living together ahead of us," and Reggie turned on the light to find Isabel crying uncontrollably. "Now what's the matter? If you intend to have an affair I can't stop you."

"You don't understand a bloody thing, you fool. I'm in love with you and I always damn well have been... If you'd only got married it wouldn't gnaw at me so much. . . Maybe... Why don't you get married?" she wailed and Reggie looked at his cool, calm and ice-cold sister-in-law, absolutely appalled with what he saw. The fires, the outside aftermath of fire engines and ambulances, A.R.P. wardens' whistles was all the sound that was left but the tears kept running down Isabel's cheeks. "Why?" she asked again.

"I never had time… No, maybe the inclination… No, it wasn't even that."

"What was it, Reggie?"

"A lady with the wrong religion."

"How long ago?"

"Thirteen years, four months and twenty-seven days. Now let's have the wine, clear away your tears, hear you laugh and we'll talk about your little girl. Who's looking after her at the moment?"

"Your mother. She adores Rosalyn."

"Good. Let's keep it that way."

"Yes," she said in a small voice.

"Promise."

"I promise, Reggie," she said in the same small voice. "Somehow it's better knowing why you wouldn't love me. I would have been a very good wife."

"In your way, you're being a very good wife for Henry. I learnt one thing in life. We can't have everything. The whole damn thing's a compromise."

CHUCK EVERLY HAD LEFT the company flat in Baker Street after the all-clear and was walking down Park Lane feeling pleased with himself. Had there been a taxi he would have taken one but he was enjoying the walk and constantly patted the small box in the right hand pocket of his English tailored suit. He had thought, when he checked it out in the mirror, that it made his large frame look slim and trim, the exact image he was hoping to project. He did not even look at a fire engine careering past with six tired and hopeless firemen clinging to the rails on their way to confront another fire at the docks that was too big for all of them. They had had no respite for seven months and they were in for another bad night and if they had looked up two minutes earlier they would have seen Reggie looking down at them through his curtain.

Four minutes later, Chuck turned off Hay Street and was let into the bright world of Bretts. Pippa de La Rivière greeted him at the entrance and hand in hand they went to the table she had selected for them a little away from the other diners but with a good view of the dance floor.

"How are the books?" he asked when they sat down. "That dress is really something. Have they still got any champagne in this joint? Hey, waiter, any chance of a real cold bottle of bubbly. I guess we're going to celebrate. You want a cocktail first?"

"No thanks, Chuck. Champagne will be lovely. You look very pleased with yourself, tonight?"

"Oh, but I am. The best looking woman in England and a company that's making more money than I ever heard of. I don't like war but it's sure as hell good for business. There isn't a factory in the U.S. of A. that isn't working at full capacity and they don't get the hell bombed out of them every night."

"You think the Americans will come into the war?"

"Sure. They came into the last one didn't they? And when that sure as hell happens there's going to be no Reggie Beaumont to keep me in a suit and tie. We Americans have also got an Air Force that needs pilots."

"When will they come in?"

"Who knows? I'm not a politician. Right now Roosevelt says he ain't comin' in but that don't mean nothing when it comes from a politician and a damn good one too."

"The books are fine."

"What…? Oh, hell yes. Good," and he leant across the table to Pippa. "How's Lilly?"

"Working. Trying not to think. The club is the one link she has with him."

"Let me know if there's anything I can do."

"Thanks, Chuck, I'll tell her."

"Who's that old geezer your sister, Gwen, is having supper with?"

"An old friend of the Beaumont family. A bachelor. Lonely. Lived in India where he has friends. Found the club through Lord Migroyd and comes in for a bit of company. Likes to talk and tell the girls about the good old days. He doesn't know Gwen's surname or that she doesn't work here. Just collared her one night and I think he reminds her of daddy. Doesn't talk about the war. Just about his beloved India. He's a knight as well as a brigadier."

"Bully for him… Waiter… Just take out the cork and start pouring. There's nothing more stupid than a bottle of champagne sitting in a bucket with its cork still in the neck… Pull it out… Now that sounds good," said Chuck waving to Gwen who had looked across the dance floor when the cork popped out. "Never thought I'd be able to afford the best champagne. Farming don't bring in the big bucks. Lived well as a kid. No doubt of that. Remember those woods up in Wisconsin where my pappy farms till the day I die. Only way to bring up a boy is in the country. Birds nesting. Shootin' rabbits with my old rifle and not wasting bullets. We were poor in cash, you see, but rich in everything else. Here's to you, Pippa. I'd have thrown a big party for you on your 21st but this damn war just wouldn't go that far so you as have to make me look like one whole bunch of people… I want you to meet my pappy. Still got that farm. Mixed farm. Probably doing a bit better what with the prices. Three hundred acres and all his own. Inherited it from his father and he took it down from his. Not big like Reggie's family but ours all the same and I guess the feeling's as strong.

"And your mother?" prompted Pippa who had never heard Chuck talk about his family before.

"She died when my little brother was two. I was ten. Jack runs the farm with my pappy. Made pappy leave it to him. I got no use for a farm except to go visiting. Maybe I'll buy Jack a bit more land. Keep the home farm and build up to five thousand acres. Made a study of farming. Purely financial side. Can't make no money 'cept with one big acreage. Then you're in a different ball park."

"What's a ball park, Chuck?"

"Well, there's a thing. You don't know a ball park. Why it's just a park where they play football. Have a good few thousand watching but that's the only difference. Why don't you have a look at the menu?"

"What for, Chuck?" she said smiling at him affectionately. "I made it up this morning."

"Well, I never. You and Lilly have certainly kept up the standards. I like all the flowers. A bit more of a woman's touch how I see it. Nothing wrong with that.

Anyway, what are you going to eat as I didn't even have time for a sandwich at lunchtime?"

"And who's going to run the business with you in the American Air Force?"

"We'll cross that bridge when we get to it, using one of your expressions. I'm going to have duck as even Lilly can't turn rabbit into duck. They fooled me once here with a chicken. You know," said Chuck sipping at the wine in his wide-brimmed champagne glass, "I must have been the luckiest guy in the world when I met Carl Priesler in New York. I want to show you New York. Now, there's a city and that place really goes. I was just a life insurance salesman when I met Carl. Didn't look as if he knew where to go so I slapped him on the back and asked him if he was new in town as if I'd grown up in New York all my life. Just so turned out we were a couple of lonely guys in a city bigger than both of us and then we found we was both in the insurance business and one drink led to another and then you had it, a Yankee from right up there on the Canadian border and a Dane all the way from Copenhagen and both as drunk as skunks. Drunk as he was he said he'd come out all the way from Copenhagen to get the Home Insurance Company out of New York to give him some reciprocal reinsurance and he couldn't even talk his way past the door so I said I'd give him a hand the next day which just as well for us was a Sunday but on the Monday morning we marched in there as if we owned the place. I'd done some work on the telephone before us marching in and just said I'd come to see the vice-president of marketing and gave the girl at the desk his name and my card I'd had printed in one of those quick print stores and Carl gave her his that looked even more impressive. The real impressive bit was listening to Carl talking about reinsurance and what he had to offer Mr Robertson and then I realised that all the letters he'd had put after his name in the quick print store were real and it was just all mine that were phonies… Here, have yourself another glass seeing as we're celebrating… anyway, Carl walked out of that visit with a bunch of American business to place in Europe and a line on each of his European accounts taken by the Home. And they're still our biggest company in America… So when Reggie's looking for an American partner Carl thinks of the dumb jerk who got him drunk in the bar but Carl still insists that if I hadn't known my way around the American system he'd never have done no business in the States… Would you like to live in New York?"

"I've never been to America," said Pippa.

"Well, look," said Chuck self-consciously as he moved in his seat to get his hand into his jacket pocket. "I've got a present," and gave her a small box that fitted on the palm of her hand with the name of Asprey clearly displayed on the top. "Just press that piece of metal and it flips open. I should know. Opened enough… Give it to me and I'll show you," and he pressed the stud and displayed a two and half carat pure white flawless diamond in a bed of velvet, lilac blue, that made it catch a million lights in the club… Pippa watched amazed as it sparkled until the implication of what she saw came to her and she couldn't take the ring out of the box. "It is your size," said Chuck taking the ring out of its box and reaching for Pippa's left hand which she withdrew under the table and hid it among the starched white table cloth that reached half way to the floor. "We've known each other four years," said Chuck watching her withdrawal. "Don't you want to marry me, Pippa?"

"I hadn't thought of it."

"You must have done."

"Well, sort of… Look, I'm only twenty-one."

"And I'm thirty-two."

"Yes."

"Does a few years matter?"

"I don't know. The war. Everything's changing. Daddy's dead."

"Even more reason. Look, I didn't choose tonight without thinking clearly first," and he took her right hand that was still on the table. "It's your 21st. That's a big day. "Let's put it on your right hand, I'm stubborn, Pippa. When I as make up my mind what I want in my life I just go around 'till I get it. We can live a good life in America. You just think about that for as long as you like. I've got a lifetime. In all my years I've never asked a woman to marry me 'cept for now and I don't intend doing it again. The offer stands. Now we'll pour ourselves another glass of this champagne and drink to your 21st instead of our wedding as I'd hoped."

"You're not upset with me?"

"I've never been upset with you. Cheers. Happy birthday," and Chuck gave the band a pre-arranged signal.

"Cheers, Chuck."

"Smile," he said, "they're playing your tune and Gwen's waving at you."

"Why doesn't she come over?" said Pippa, weakly.

"I asked her not to," and he joined in the brief singing with Pippa thoroughly embarrassed.

"Now what are you going to eat?" he asked.

"Duck. Same as you… Thank you, Chuck. For the compliment… and I will think about it."

"That's my girl."

AT ELEVEN THIRTY, Pippa asked to be taken home to the Beaumont town flat and Lilly used her influence to find a taxi just as the air-raid siren sounded the warning.

"The warning's late," said Lilly, looking up as she heard aircraft overhead. "Those are German. Forget the taxi… Come on, driver," she said, shouting at him and pointing up and then at the entrance to the tube station. They were half way across the road when they heard the stick of bombs coming down. Chuck pulled them through the entrance and stumbled down the steps with the taxi driver close on their heels when the six bombs impacted in a line stretching from Park Lane to Hay Street. The last five hundred pound bomb in the stick cut through the building above Bretts without exploding and finally came through the ceiling directly above the packed dance floor where it exploded with all the venom of shattered steel. Bretts ceased to exist.

AT TEN-THIRTY in the morning after Bretts had been blown to pieces, Reggie swung the Bentley into the driveway that led up to Merry Hall on its well wooded hill with the lawns sweeping down through avenues and clumps of trees to the public road.

"Eleven years old and drives like a dream," said Reggie to Isabel sitting in the bucket seat next to him as he admired the long, sleek, barrel of the bonnet that swept away from the low windscreen. "Perfect day for a drive in the country. My, the girls are enjoying themselves," he said and waved at a particularly pretty girl who was arm-in-arm with a Merchant sailor as they strolled down the rolling lawn with a bright morning sun warming their backs and dispelling the first hints of winter that hovered in the late September air. "The plan seems to be working," he said as they flushed another couple from a garden seat almost surrounded by a red rhododendron bush. A peacock stretched one leg and surveyed the passing open car with disdain. "Are your mother and my mother coping?"

"Oh, yes. Georgina helps. She's become very good at organising things. There was a paper chase last week that kept twelve Bretts girls and thirty-seven assorted sailors, airmen and soldiers occupied for four hours. Georgina had them running all over the estate. One of the sailors tried to ride Lilliput, bareback. Poor man had a very swift run for his money. Said you shouldn't expect to find a racehorse looking at you over a hedge. He landed in the duck pond, thank goodness."

The gravel in front of the gothic entrance crunched under the motor car tyres and Reggie brought the tourer to a halt. The front door to Merry Hall was wide open as were most of the windows in the old house, sucking in the last days of a late summer before they were firmly shuttered for winter.

"Never changes," said Reggie looking up at the house. "I'm glad we drove down. It's amazing how resilient the body can be after rest and good food. The C.O.'s report said my brakes failed which is true in a way. They've posted me to Boscombe Down. Bomber station… Well, there's no point sitting here all day. Everyone seems to be busy."

"You bring in the bags," said Isabel. "I'll have Doris Breed run you a good breakfast."

"That's my girl… Tell her I'm hungry… and a quart of fresh milk."

"You're looking a lot better, Reggie."

"Thanks… And thanks for looking after me. Mother must always see her sons as being in the pink."

"You were well overdue for leave."

"Damn it. I forgot to mention that to the Luftwaffe."

"Any news of Gunter?"

"Not a word since a note through Switzerland that was mostly business. He'll come through. The Freebooters are a group of born survivors. Pity he isn't on our side. We can do with an extra pilot."

"Where do you want breakfast?" she said, looking back.

"In the morning room. Full of sun. A nice bit of sun and no-one shooting at me."

"Good morning Mr Reggie, I didn't hear the car."

"Morning, Pavy. You keeping well?"

"As well as can be expected. You are taking a little leave, sir?"

"Yes. Ten days. How about a glass of sherry before breakfast? Would that be very wicked?"

"With a sweet biscuit, sir?"

"Make it two."

"I'll bring it to the morning room, I believe you said."

After breakfast, Reggie took the path through the woods, the old oak leaves falling constantly as a prelude to autumn's climax. He looked up at the old trees and searched the hiding places he had known from childhood. "Must be dead," he said out loud. "Must have been thirty years old. Good life for a bird," he said again to the woods but he was wrong as the old owl had climbed out of the hollow elm tree ten minutes before to warm his old bones in the sun and from behind a gnarled bow of the biggest oak in the woods, he watched Reggie meander off down towards the river and then shut his big eyes to enjoy the sun's warmth that much more. Instead of carrying on down to the river, Reggie turned off towards the Thirty Acre and smiled to himself when he came out of the trees. 'At least that doesn't change,' he said to himself looking at Bert Brigley's cows cluttering up his runway. Even the spotted brown cow was in its place under the oak tree surrounded by cow pats. Reggie strolled out across the field, his hands clasped behind his back, drawn towards the cow shed down in the left corner of the Thirty Acre. Reaching the door, he pushed up the wooden bar and swung wide both the doors. The odd shoot of grass inside was yellow white. Sunless. The red tail section of Mathilda was caught by the noon sun, angled by the forerun to winter. Slowly his eyes became accustomed to the gloom and the smell of earth was stronger as he ducked under the biplane's lower wing and stood up next to the stubby nose with its wooden propeller and cold eyelets for exhausts. The cowling was rusting in one small patch and Reggie scratched at the intrusion.

"We had some good times, old buddy," he said, patting the cowling affectionately. "Shit, we had some good times," but he wasn't referring to Mathilda but to Tony Venturas. "Why the hell did you let them get you? We still had a lot of living to do together... Come on, Beaumont. Snap out of it. He's dead. Fucking dead and you can't be deader than dead," and he ducked quickly out of the shed and swung the doors back and let the wooden bar fall into its place and the spotted brown cow looked up, jaw going round and round and soft, liquid eyes watching the human master. Hunchbacked, Reggie crossed the field and found the path by instinct and sat himself down on the old tree trunk to take solace from the river. The willow, its summer leaves tired, dripped into the river and hid a speckle back, its fins working hard to keep station with the flow. With effort, and slowly, Reggie cleared his mind of the past and took a clear and calculated look into the future. He took his mind past the war and began to construct the kind of world his business would face and what he could do now to make it easier. 'Capital. That's going to be the short commodity. So much to replace, hands for the work but a shortage of money and Percy Hudson not around to lend it to me so easily. It took me years to build that kind of lending trust. I'll bring Billy into the business, his father's legacy to him anyway.' Reggie thought back, on the complex flotation of Beaumont Ltd which had gone so smoothly in expert hands. She wouldn't take money, just his pension. He'd tried that one. The only way to say thank you was through the son... Mining, that was the key to the capital he would need for Gunter until the strong flow of money began again from insurance... Property, there was something they would always need. Housing. Factories. He would tell Chuck to buy and mortgage. If a bomb hit them a grateful government would pay them back... America. Immediately the war was over he would go to America with Chuck and work that one out. The real growth would be in America. Their factories would be intact and ready to supply a ravaged Europe. Diamonds. He would have to find a way of selling his own polished stones in America and stop the commission he paid to De Beers... Or was that sensible? The Central Selling Organisation owned by De Beers let out a steady flow of rough stones, to the cutters. The market was controlled...

Farming. He would look at farming in Africa. Despite the war, modern medicine was building up the human race and they all had to be fed. Gunter's tractor... That would be a winner. Maybe better to give the peasants a better way than try to do it himself. The Beaumonts would come out stronger after the war. China trade. There were nearly a billion Chinese. Tug would be busy. Sharply, he looked up at the sky and his hands began to shake. 'The C.O. was right. It's the bloody Dexedrine. Take it more and more to keep awake and you have withdrawal symptoms. Two weeks will get the stuff out of my system and I'll be alright. I'd bloody better be. I'll have every German night fighter on my tail.'

Having watched carefully he caught the glint of sun on metal and then from high up above he heard the distinct sound of machine gun fire and a German aircraft exploded and a gap appeared in the bomber formation, the blast of the bombs going off having damaged planes on either side and they were falling back, turning in a wide curve back to Germany. One of the Hurricanes detached itself and shot them down. Amazed, Reggie realised the formation was not properly protected by fighters. The Germans didn't have enough to protect the laggard. The air battle flew over his head and two hours later, when Bert Brigley came looking for his cows, he looked across at the fighter pilot fast asleep, his head rested in the crook of the old tree. He left him there, hoping his dreams were good.

When Reggie woke it was with a stiff neck but the shakes had gone from his hands and he held them out in front of himself approvingly. Pulling himself up, he made his way slowly through the woods, savouring the solitude and remembering the happiness that the grounds had given him during his childhood. Coming up the path round the tennis court, the net still draped between the posts, the winding handle fallen off into a thick tuft of overgrown grass, he saw the army truck parked on the gravel next to the Bentley. 'More to Merry Hall to regain their sanity,' and he picked a dandelion, put the stem idly in his mouth and tasted the white goo before spitting it out. Bending his legs he made the bank up to the gravel when an army major came out of the shadow of the big front door towards him.

"GEOFFREY," shouted Reggie and began to run towards his younger brother.

"We thought we lost you," he said pumping the outstretched hand.

"Usual bloody army cock-up. So this is how the boys in blue fight their battles. Take off a couple of weeks, I hear... What's the real reason, Reggie?"

"Grounded. I parked my Spit on its nose in a hedge. Fell asleep coming in to land. Bent the bloody propeller. Nothing else. C.O. happened to be looking out of his window."

"You look alright."

"Amazing what two days sleep can do... You look as if you could do with some of it yourself. Where've you been since Dunkirk?"

"France. François sends his regards."

"He's in South Africa," said Reggie emphasising the first word and laughing.

"He's not, Reggie. We recruited him to lead a section of the French underground. He has some weird friends... Just the type we needed. They think he's some kind of Robin Hood."

"Simone?"

"Yes. She's part of it. She was the bait to winkle him out of South Africa."

"He should have stopped playing ducks and drakes years ago and married her."

"Easier said than done. Can you see her as mistress of the chateau?"

"You never know," he said leading Geoffrey into the house.

"How's your influence with the post office?"

"Haven't tried it recently."

"One of my lieutenants has a fiancée in Rhodesia. She was also told he went missing four months ago. Can Carl get her a message? They can't raise the farm where she works."

"I'll try. How did you get back?"

"Submarine. There were ten of us left. I lost two. Jim Forrester and Dusty Miller are staying here for a couple of days. They're sleeping. I've billeted the men in the village as close to the local pub as possible. We're off to North Africa at the end of next week."

"There's something building up there?" said Reggie picking up the phone and giving the operator his office number. "I'll wait thank you. Very urgent... I'm sure they are... She says they're all bloody urgent mate," he said winking at Geoffrey. "Thank you. Hello. Thelma? No, let me speak first. I want you to phone our contact and have Carl put on the line to Merry Hall. And it is military business. Usual thing. Sorting out the army. What they'd do without an Air Force... Having a rest love... C.O. sent me packing. If he hears I've even phoned the office he'll cut my balls off... Now what's your news... WHAT... Oh, shit... How many... Poor bastards... Right on the dance floor... thank goodness for Chuck... Yes... Ring me back when you have a list of the names from the A.R.P... Yes, Thelma, I know about François... He told you about Simone...? Shit, I wish I could be in ten places at once... I'll be Okay, Thelma... Oh, and we've found Geoffrey. Bugger's just pitched up at Merry Hall, large as life.

"He's standing right next to me... Keep holding the fort, Thelma... I will..." And he put the receiver back onto its cradle.

"She sends her love, Geoffrey. That's a good girl... Bretts. The Germans landed a five hundred pound bomb on the dance floor last night and blew the place to smithereens. Chuck, Pippa and Lilly had just gone out... Don't say anything yet but they think Gwen was one of the victims. And Bertie Featherstone. Migroyd had left early."

"How many dead?"

"Thirty-seven. Most of them unidentifiable."

"Take it easy, Reggie," he had noticed his brother's hands shaking.

"What can we do?"

"Fight them the way we know."

"We're going to win the war, aren't we?" said Reggie.

"Sure we are. No question."

"I heard Lady Hensbrook saying to mother how glad she was only having daughters. And one of them's first to go."

"Is there any doubt?"

"Not much. She was on the dance floor. Poor kid hadn't even turned twenty. Thelma said that since they got her out of her tweeds she was a raving beauty... At least Tug and his family are out of this war."

"Don't be too sure. It's almost certain the Japs are going to try their luck."

"That's all we need."

"How's the war? Really?"

"It's been close. Too close but I think we've turned the tide this month. The Germans are also running out of pilots. You can't just make pilots, you have to train them. And Gerry isn't going to invade without air supremacy. If he tries without we'll clobber him in the Channel. It's one thing to get an army off the beaches under the guns of the Royal Navy. Another to land it with Bomber and Fighter Command breathing down your neck."

"Let's have a drink," said Geoffrey.

"Why not?"

"No reason."

"A good stiff scotch or two… That's the phone. Pour the drinks… Hello Ashtead 101… Hello, Carl, you old bugger… How's the mining magnate…? I'm fine… Can you do me a favour. A Lieutenant Miller was posted missing. Part of Geoffrey's unit… That's the point, they're fine. I want you to get a message through to a Megan Strong, the… What…? You know her… Where…? Well, give her the message yourself. We'd better cut. I don't abuse the lines. Keep the money flowing… Cheers," and he put down the receiver.

"How do you like this one? Your lieutenant's fiancée is staying at Timber Lane."

"With Carl?"

"He wasn't specific."

"Ouch," said Geoffrey.

"You'd better just tell Dusty that she's got the message. She's probably just a house guest."

"With that predator?"

"He's my partner."

"I'm very fond of you, Carl, François and Gunter but I wouldn't trust any of you with my wife, let alone my fiancée."

"Oh, come off it, brother, we're not that bad."

"Not that good either."

ISABEL'S first male target was deliberately picked in front of Reggie on the last night of his leave when the family resumed their habit of including four of their recuperating male guests to join them for dinner. Lady Hensbrook was not present but the rest of the family kept the death of a family member hidden from the outsiders. Geoffrey had sailed with his unit for Cairo two days earlier, taking the long route around the Cape to avoid German land-based air attacks. Without his C.O.'s knowledge, Reggie had been up to London on four occasions to do what he could for the victims of the bombing, particularly the girls with dependent children. He had arranged for three orphans to be sent to South Africa and had set up a financial trust for any other orphans of the London bombing. Carl had found a smallholding outside of Johannesburg and had employed staff to care for the children. By the time Reggie's last night at Merry Hall came round he was sleeping without pills and had shaken off the side effects of Dexedrine. His squadron at Tangmere had been taken over by Terrence Pike and the C.O. had put Reggie up for a D.S.O. The bombing of London had intensified. Being a friend of Reggie's, Angus Montel had been automatically put on the invitation list having not been able to take his leave at home on account of owing his father eleven thousand pounds sterling. The amount had plagued Angus and his father for some time. Angus had brought with him his friend Freddy Gore who flew with him in the Fleet Air Arm. Both of them were excited as they had heard that morning they were being posted to an aircraft carrier at the end of their current leave. Angus saw the picture from the word go and raving, as he told himself, no morals whatsoever, he was prepared to make his play, Reggie's sister-in-law or not. If it wasn't him it would be someone else and as it happened, the someone else was Freddy Gore as Isabel had decided that Angus was just a little too smooth and anyway she wanted a better challenge to show Reggie before he went back to war. To brighten the evening and remove the cloud of war that had settled over his mother, Reggie had brought up two bottles of red wine from the family cellar and Isabel had drunk three glasses with her rabbit stew and was holding out her glass for a fourth.

"Will you excuse me," said Lady Beaumont and the men got up as she left the room, to telephone her husband in the London family flat, something she tried to do every night if she could obtain the connection and the wires weren't down. Georgina had pushed a piece of rabbit around on her plate for ten minutes having lost her appetite.

"Excuse me," she said, "the children," and the men got up again as she left the room with the field left to Isabel with only Reggie to be her witness.

After her fourth glass of wine, and watching the performance with an element of awe, and judging by the expressions on Freddy Gore's face, Reggie wondered if she was having him off under the table. Angus having apparently lost his chance made an excuse about needing an early night and made his way off to keep his rendezvous with the blonde girl with the big tits. Reggie watched his friend leave the table and hoped that Angus's stamina was good enough to keep pace with Wanda.

"Lovely girl," he said softly so only Angus could hear and then he winked and was gratified to see the faintest of blushes rise in Angus's cheeks.

"You don't mind old boy?"

"What the lady wants the lady gets," he whispered and turned back to the remaining guests.

"I always keep my promises," said Isabel looking straight at Reggie.

"If you'll excuse me, I think I'll catch some sleep as well," but his eyes told Isabel there were some things he preferred not to know about. 'There's always a rotten one in every family,' he said to himself as he left the room and went to say goodnight to his mother.

6

CAIRO JUNE 1941

"Good of you to come, old boy," said Colonel Sir Thomas Beaumont, pulling back the wicker chair from where it stood on the outside veranda of Shepheard's Hotel in Cairo and sitting down at the low table. "Drink, old boy?"

"Tea, thank you, sir," replied Lieutenant Colonel Gerald Escort who had got up when the colonel with the red staff tabs had approached his table.

"Tea?" queried Sir Thomas. "Damn it, it's past eleven o'clock. Have a B 'n S myself… Waiter…! Waiter…! Ah, thank you, boy. Bring me a brandy and soda. Make it a large one… and a dish of tea for this officer."

"Bit early for you, eh Escort?"

"I don't drink."

"Admirable. Picked up the habit in India. Claret. A lot of claret. Look at this place," he said sweeping his hand round the vast veranda. "Babylon, towers of Babel. Never think there was a war on." They waited in silence for the waiter to return. "You gave it up?"

"What, sir?"

"Drink."

"Yes."

"Admirable… Ah, thank you waiter. Put that down here… Don't pour it. Always pour my own soda. Too much soda makes the damn brandy soapy. Thank you," said Sir Thomas taking the chit and the pen. "Just put the tea on the table… You can pour the damn stuff, can't you, Escort?"

"I think so, sir. Took a little practice."

"Right," said Sir Thomas, giving back the signed chit and the pen. "Chin, chin."

"Your good health."

"And yours old boy. Have you heard of my department?"

"Yes. I checked up."

"Tea alright?"

"Bloody terrible," and Sir Thomas smiled at him with quizzical sympathy. "There's going to be a big shindig. Balloon goes up tonight. Biggest artillery cannonade in history. Montgomery's reserve."

"Should you be telling me?"

"Not much the Germans can do about it now, but that's by the by… My job is to analyse the other side's management, so to speak, and find its flaws. Find anything we can exploit. Give our generals a psychological advantage. I have studied one man for three months and I can't find any flaws. In my opinion he's the best general on either side and generals of that calibre can win wars. Provided Hitler lets this man have a free hand a British victory is by no means certain. We have to take him out. I want you to attack his headquarters."

"Who's?" asked Gerald who was enviously watching the level of brandy and soda drop, only half listening to the portly old gentleman pontificating in his well-cut uniform that went some way towards hiding his paunch.

"Rommel," said Sir Thomas, putting down his empty glass and signalling the waiter for a refill.

"I couldn't get anywhere near him," said Gerald.

"You did it against the Turks in the last war."

"That was different. We were dressed as Arabs. We fought as Arabs. I can't see an Arab on a camel riding up to Rommel's headquarters."

"But you might if you were dressed as a German."

"That's against the Geneva Convention. If they catch you they shoot you."

"It would shorten the war. Save thousands of lives. His job is to kill Englishmen and I don't see why the generals should be exempt from an attack on their person. By whatever means. If we could drop a bomb on his caravan we would do it right away. Fact is he moves the bloody thing around. The R.A.F. have tried four times and merely blown a lot of holes in the sand. Good Lord," he said interrupting himself and getting up from the table. "That's old Bill Sykes. Haven't seen him since I was in Puna, 1898. Before the Boer War. Excuse me a minute," and he got up and crossed to another table beside a pillar and heartily shook hands with an equally portly gentleman who was dressed as a brigadier. Gerald watched smiling ruefully at how they could remember each other after over forty years. He felt his greying moustache and took a distasteful sip of his tea as the second large brandy was put down on the glass-topped table by the waiter. The waiter stood back waiting with the chit and the pen.

"Not stay hotel," said Gerald having no wish to let the man know he could speak a rusty Arabic. The waiter smiled and they both watched Sir Thomas who had broken off the hand shaking and was moving between the tables on his way back.

"Damn embarrassing," he said, sitting down and pouring the other half of his soda carafe into his brandy. "Wasn't Sykes at all. Could have sworn. Where was I?"

"Suggesting I kill General Rommel," said Gerald a little sarcastically.

"Don't get me wrong, Escort. I'm deadly serious. I tried to get my son to do it but the army have his unit fully occupied. You know, Geoffrey, I believe?"

"One of his officers was engaged to my daughter. I gather it's off."

"I'm sorry to hear that," said Sir Thomas looking straight at the man for the first time. "Our problem has been to find someone like Geoffrey who can navigate to within half a mile in the desert."

"Aren't I a little old for solo commando raids."

"You'll have six men. You are fit?"

"Yes… Since I stopped drinking."

"How long ago was that?"

"Four months. Who are the six men?"

"Regular army commandos?"

"Commanded by a colonial?"

"This is wartime."

"When do you want me to try?"

"Tonight."

"Don't be damn silly. Rommel must be hundreds of miles away."

"He is. The R.A.F. will fly you in. We know the position of his H.Q. from radio intersections. Once the big battle starts, we don't think he'll move. If you knock him out, the German battle plan will be in disarray."

"How do we get out?"

"In the confusion. The same way you get to him. The artillery noise will be deafening and though the guns can't reach the caravans, the noise can."

"You really think it's possible?"

"What I don't think is that Rommel or any of his staff would imagine a British officer crazy enough to try and shoot him at his own desk. The surprise. Heat of battle. They'll all have a lot more on their minds. It's bloody dangerous, Escort, but it can be done. The six men have been trained for the attack. All they need is someone to get them there. Take them in."

"A bloody tourist guide?"

"Something like that."

AT 2.00 AM on the 14 June 1941, when Reggie Beaumont was returning from his forty-sixth Pathfinder operation over Germany, his elder brother Henry cowered in a shallow trench, scared shitless. The British bombardment had commenced twenty minutes earlier and the constant wave of fear had emptied his bowels and he had been powerless to do anything about it. He dreaded the moment when he would have to force himself off his hands and knees and lead his men through the German minefield that the bombardment was meant to destroy. Gripping his service revolver, he desperately tried to overcome his fear but he could feel the shit trickling out of his baggy shorts and seeping into the desert. He thanked his God that the night was pitch dark and moonless and the smells of battle were stronger than the shit oozing from his airtex underpants. There was one thing that 2nd Lieutenant Henry Beaumont feared greater than fear and that was ridicule.

From the moment he had forced himself to volunteer for the army, from the moment in fact when as a boy he had been unable to climb down from one of the elm trees and the gardener's boy had had to get him down, a ten-year-old that looked more like thirteen, the fear had grown in him and was now so monstrous he wished he could die. Anything from fast bowlers at cricket to flying in Reggie's dreadful aeroplane had caused him the same panic and the need to empty his bowels. And warfare, finally, had opened them and this was the fourth occasion and his men were about to find out and there was nowhere for him to go to hide his shame. Around him, his platoon crouched in the desert waiting for the German artillery to fire on them or the whistle to go that would make them get up and follow the mine-clearing sappers as the fire from the British twenty-five pounders crept further forward with military discipline. The battle of El Alamein had begun.

TWENTY MILES AWAY, with the horizon flashing fire from the guns, Geoffrey Beaumont led his L.R.U. of fifteen armoured cars out of the wadi where they had been hiding for two days behind the German lines. As they came over the dune, long and smooth in the starlit darkness, they split away and followed an individual course. Each car commander had his head out of the turret and was navigating by the stars like a sailor. There was no radio control and the cars shrunk back to commander, driver and gunner.

"Keep her as straight as you can," said Geoffrey.

"They're makin' a lot of fuckin' noise, sir."

"Making a lot of noise, Private Kemp."

"Beggin' your pardon, sir."

"Drive, Wilf," said Corporal Harry Sparrow. "Don't even try and observe."

"I can hear, can't I? What I want to know is how the fuck we find our way back to that wadi?"

"The major will get us back," said Harry.

'I hope so,' thought Geoffrey, wondering how many in his L.R.U. would see the beginning of another day.

As GEOFFREY'S armoured car moved across the Libyan Desert towards its target, Lieutenant-Colonel Gerald Escort let go and fell out into space following the six men who had tumbled out of the Wellington bomber in front of him. Gerald counted up to three and pulled his ripcord bringing out the canopy above and jerking him back violently from his fall. Below, drifting at different heights, were six parachutes of black silk carrying six sergeants of the British commando force, their only cover a German forage cap that they would wear on their way in to the target. The sound of bombardment had drowned out the engine noise and Gerald was hopeful they couldn't be seen against the blackness of the night sky. Below and well to his left was the miles of gun flashing, British and German. From three miles behind the German lines the noise was painful to his ears. Bringing up his knees he watched and waited to hit the desert and roll with his fall. Without warning he hit and rolled. Unbuckling his harness, he left the parachute and took up the sterling light machine gun from the pack where it was strapped over grenades and ammunition pouches. They had dropped into a hollow and by the time he looked around for some of his men, he was disorientated and had to read the stars to find out where he wanted to go. To Gerald Escort it was home, the desert of his twenties and the bush of Africa. As he got ready and waited for his men to assemble, he was as comfortable as if he was paddling down the Zambezi at the height of the rains.

"Where the fuck are we?" said a Scots voice. "A couple of minutes ago it was all spread out. All we had to do was go in, laddies, and knock him off. Now, I'm as blind as a bat."

"Everyone to me," called Gerald. "Any injuries?" and he made a roll call in the dark. Within five minutes of leaving the belly of the aircraft they were away in marching order.

'What a way to spend your forty-eighth birthday,' Gerald thought and then concentrated on the task ahead of him.

SOMEONE BLEW a whistle and Henry saw his men get up around him and move forward. He watched, gripping the butt of his revolver, attached by a lanyard to his breast pocket.

"You alright, sir?" said his sergeant and Henry forced himself up to his knees.

"Carry on, sergeant."

"Very good, sir."

"Get the men in behind that tank. There'll be German infantry coming the other way."

"We'll be alright, sir?"

"No question of it, sergeant," said Henry getting up to his full height and taking off his tin hat to show his men that no-one was shooting at them. "Right men. Let's go and get Rommel," and he was pleased to hear a faint laugh under the cacophony of sound created by the guns. As he'd got up, he'd rolled slightly and wiped off the side of his leg and hoped that what was left would stick to his pants. Now they were running forward, bent double, behind the tank and Henry could clearly see the head and shoulders of the British tank commander against the flashes of the German artillery.

BY THREE-THIRTY IN THE MORNING, the tank, gun and infantry battle raged on a twenty mile in front in a state of noise, smoke and bewilderment. Henry had stumbled around, chased by the stench of his own shit but he had done the right thing even though he hadn't seen a German that he recognised.

GEOFFREY HAD REACHED to within striking distance of his target and stopped.

GERALD HAD GOT within sight of the German headquarters without detection. In the bad light and urgent confusion, they had constantly been taken for Germans. 'We're going to get him,' thought Gerald as the excitement of the hunt built up in him. 'If we can get in, in the confusion, we can get out in it.'

AT THREE FORTY-FIVE Geoffrey detonated the German ammunition dump and there were eleven simultaneous attacks behind German lines, three of the armoured car crews having been despatched by the Germans before they could reach their targets.

AT THE PRE-ARRANGED time of three-fifty, Gerald Escort wrenched open the door to

General Rommel's field caravan and burst inside blazing away with his sterling, spraying the empty command room.

"I don't believe it," he said out loud. "The right bloody place but the bugger's not here," and he gave a short command for the six commandos to disperse as he backed down the steps of the caravan, this time wearing his distinctive British Army hat. If he was going to kill a man in cold blood he was going to do it in proper uniform with the word Rhodesian underneath the crowns and pip on each shoulder. Two guards shot him dead at the same time but four of his sergeants got back through to the advancing British lines. In the final count, Gerald Escort had achieved absolutely nothing.

THE RENDEZVOUS AT the wadi was a long and painful procession for Geoffrey as the trickle of returning vehicles went on for a long time and finally dried up when the battle rolled past them with Rommel in full retreat and the British 8th Army in hot pursuit. It was ten-thirty in the morning and the crew including Jim Robertson and Stew Philpott had failed to return.

"Never own 'is fuckin' boozer after all," said Wilf Kemp chewing an unlit cigarette.

"Maybe he's captured," said Harry Sparrow but Geoffrey, knowing what had happened shook his head and turned away. He knew he was lucky to have only lost four vehicles and he knew his superiors would count the havoc they created behind enemy lines to be well worth the losses. As wars go it was fair exchange.

AT NINE-THIRTY IN THE MORNING, Henry Beaumont stumbled into the remains of Rommel's headquarters which had been abandoned in a hurry with many signs of self-destruction. In the continuing confusion, Henry mustered his platoon outside the general's own caravan and went inside himself. He was the first British officer in the Battle of El Alamein to take a bath that day and when he emerged from the caravan, he had washed his shorts and underpants as well as his battledress and the stench of stale shit had been washed out into the desert sand and Henry could face the day. One at a time, starting with his sergeant, Henry had his platoon take a bath. The only thing Henry had not understood were the bullet marks around the compartment used by the general as his office. If had stooped down outside and looked under the caravan he would have been surprised to see the body of a British Lieutenant-Colonel that had been pushed there by the retreating Germans. The dirty water from the men's baths had washed over him.

SEVEN DAYS later on the 21 June 1941, while François Deauville was blowing up a German supply train on the outskirts of Paris, Sir Thomas Beaumont answered a knock at the door to his suite on the third floor to Shepheard's Hotel in Cairo.

"Come in," he commanded loudly and the door was pushed open.

"Oh, come in, old boy," he said looking up. "Want a drink?"

"What's that?" asked the colonel commanding the commandos.

"B and S."

"That'll do."

"Pour your own soda?"

"Please… Damn bad luck."

"Yes… Chin-chin… Damn bad luck," said Sir Thomas.

"Read the report?"

"Right there on the table."

"Ah! That's the one. Cheers, old boy," said the colonel.

"Bloody fine victory."

"We needed it. Morale. Back home. In a way you were his C.O. Writing to his family?"

"Not actually, old boy. Young subaltern in my son's outfit. Knows the family. I'll get him up. Show him the report."

"Bit confidential."

"He'll understand."

"Good show, your son."

"Good show… What's the problem?"

"There wasn't a more senior officer who saw him do it. Those four sergeants aren't enough. You can try."

"Maybe it'll be enough," said Sir Thomas. "To be recommended, I mean."

"Not many officers get recommended for a V.C… Right in the bloody trailer. The fortunes of war."

". . . or misfortunes of war. That report is pretty strong… You know he dyed his hair to look younger?"

"I didn't. Forty-seven. Bit old."

"Forty-eight, actually. It was his birthday."

"Bloody bad luck. You were right. Got them in. The senior sergeant told me Escort was as confident as walking down Piccadilly. In the dunes. Couldn't see a bloody thing. Sky and sand. Escort told them it was something called bush sense… No bushes around there. Born in the open spaces. Geoffrey, my son, said he learnt a lot coming down Africa. Did Cairo to Cape overland before the war."

"Jolly fine show."

"Yes it was. He met Escort in Rhodesia."

"Some of the colonials are damn fine soldiers."

"He was a regular. Four of them got out, anyway," said Sir Thomas.

"Mind if I have another, old boy?"

"Help yourself… I've some contacts at war office. Couple at the palace. I'm going to get him that Victoria Cross."

"Family will appreciate it… When are you going back to London?"

"Couple of weeks."

"Cheers, old boy."

"Cheers."

"Thought old Featherstone was running your outfit," said the colonel.

"Was. Killed in the bombing."

"Damn bad luck."

"Damn bad luck."

"You'll sign the recommendation as the sergeants' C.O. Put a bit in about their integrity."

"Damn brave man."

THE SAME AFTERNOON, Dusty Miller, spruced up and ready, asked the lift man for the third floor and saw the cage rise through the levels until it jangled to a halt and he was out in the corridor on the maroon-coloured carpet. Geoffrey had told him where to go. The door was ajar.

"Come in Mr Miller," said Sir Thomas putting his reading glasses back on the table. "Can I get you a drink?"

"Not for me, sir."

"Come and sit down. Good show last week."

"Thank you, sir."

"It's about Colonel Escort."

"What about him, sir?"

"He's dead. Didn't my boy tell you?"

"No. I'm sorry."

"You were engaged to his daughter?"

"I still intend to marry her, sir."

"Good. Well, what I want you to do is write to his daughter. For me. In a way I was his C.O. Responsible anyway. Here, you'd better read this report. You can take your time. Confidential, of course."

"Of course, sir," said Dusty and began to read the report of the four surviving sergeants who had attacked the field H.Q. of General Rommel. It took him five minutes to finish.

"That was suicide," he said, the indignation finally boiling over.

"Four got out."

"A bloody miracle, beg your pardon, sir."

"I'm putting in for a V.C."

"He came so close."

"Would have altered the war. Brave man. It was a privilege for either of us to have known him."

"I'll write the old man."

"The who?"

"Father. Gerald's father. Farms tobacco up in the Umvukwes. They'll want to know on the farm. Meg's on her own now... Seems they all die on Meg. Husband, son, mother and now her father... Must have been off booze."

"He was."

"Right in the bloody trailer."

"Yes."

"YOU'D BETTER SIT DOWN, GEOFFREY."

"I'd rather stand."

"You are losing your temper."

"Possibly."

"It is not military etiquette for a major to abuse a colonel. Or for a son to abuse his father."

"But it was suicide. The man was old. Why didn't you send me? I've been trained for that kind of thing?"

"They wouldn't let me. Said you were too valuable. Escort could do the job. Damn it, he fought with Lawrence against the Turks."

"So damn what? So that was it. He was expendable but I wasn't?"

"Something like that."

"Can't afford to lose too many Sandhurst men, old boy," he mimicked. "So send in the colonials."

"You could just as easily have been killed."

"No, father. When I plan an operation I want to be sure of getting my men home."

"Are you accusing me of deliberately killing that man?"

"Well, you did."

"SIT DOWN, Geoffrey, and that is an order. You will retract that statement."

"It's true," said Geoffrey, remaining standing.

"Let's get one thing absolutely clear. War. War, damn bloody war killed Colonel Gerald Escort. Not me. Not Rommel. Not even the poor sod who shot him. WAR. The most puerile, stupid, wasteful and totally bloody useless thing the human race invented but continue to use with twenty year monotony. And they don't damn well learn. You say I killed him. No, not me. The human system. You are the soldier, Geoffrey, not me. I'm a farmer. A Beaumont farmer and we survive. And I'll do anything to shorten this stupid, bloody war… What do you think is going to happen in ten years' time, probably five? Your brother Reggie will be trading with the Germans like his long lost brothers. He'll even be planning it now whilst he's trying to kill them and he's certainly done his fair share of that. And he's right to trade. People just want to live. Get on with their own lives at whatever level. They do not want war. Do I make it plain? The system wants war. The system manipulates war. Yes, you were right, Major Beaumont was more valuable to the system than Colonel Escort. They want you for the next round."

"So if you are so damned anti-war, why did you send him in?"

"To shorten the miserable war. Rommel's good. Montgomery may have won this time but there are going to be a lot of dead bodies before Rommel is forced out of North Africa. I have three sons fighting and God only knows what those Japs are going to do and then Tug will be in it as well. You've already lost a sister in-law. And let me tell you something, Geoffrey. When people are dead they are very dead. You don't get practice shots at that one. If Gerald Escort had killed Rommel it would have shortened this war and given me a better chance of having some sons alive at the end of it… And there was another reason."

"To kill him. Damn it, father, HE HAD NO CHANCE."

"But we did. We had the chance of killing Rommel."

"So it was a suicide mission?"

"I still thought he might get out in the confusion. Four did."

"That's not the way it's played."

"Oh, I like that. So you play war?"

"There are rules."

"Bully for the rules."

"We just don't fight wars that way."

Father and son glared at each other and then Sir Thomas sat down in his chair and tried to marshal his argument. Geoffrey had burst in on him soon after Dusty had left. He hadn't been prepared.

"You said there was another reason," said Geoffrey.

"Yes… I had to find a man who could do the job and be less on my conscience."

"Charming."

"Don't be rude."

"I'm sorry, dad. Take that one right back. I know you mean well. I just don't understand."

"He was a very unhappy man. Drank a lot. Wife died. The doctors told me his liver was grossly enlarged. If he had survived the war he would have gone back to that house at Mazoe and drunk himself to death. Would have embarrassed himself, lost his daughter's respect. He's been off whisky for four months and was fully in command of his actions. I watched him. Downstairs. Deliberately drank in front of him. The poor man watched every inch of the brandy down the glass. I'm trying to tell myself I gave him a better way to die but I'm not succeeding. Maybe it would have been better if it had been you... And Geoffrey he damned nearly succeeded. Please, son, don't blame me. Blame the bloody war. This one or any other stupid damn war. We have armies to prevent war not make them."

"Maybe I've been a soldier too long."

"Now will you have that drink?"

"Thanks, dad."

"That's better. God, do I worry about you boys. And it's worse just watching your mother."

Geoffrey went to the cocktail cabinet, poured his father a brandy and soda and himself a straight whisky.

"I owe you an apology, dad."

"You're my son. I know how you feel."

"Get him that damn V.C. It might make a little sense."

"I'm doing my best."

"They might remember him longer with a Victoria Cross."

THE THIEF CLIMBED the fire escape at the back of his block of flats and began to feel for the inside catch to his small, trapdoor bathroom window. It was two hours before dawn and black, moon-fringed clouds, scudded across the November sky. His hands were stiff with the bitter Paris cold and he cursed the delay until he slithered head first into the small room and silently pulled himself down by his hands until he was able to crawl down into the empty bath. Swiftly he removed his black beret with the almost detached pom-pom and with the old black polo-necked sweater and old rubber-soled shoes, opened the trap under the bath and threw them, smelling, into the cavity under the taps. By feel again, he carefully closed the plumber's trap and turned on the hot water tap in the basin and washed his face thoroughly. Finally, he took the red-silk, Chinese dressing-gown from behind the bathroom door and shivering from the winter cold, slipped it on and turned on the light, immediately checking that nothing was untoward. He put the black plug in the bath and turned on both taps, smiling hopefully at the steam. Testing the water temperature, he slipped off the rest of his clothes and got into the bath, wallowing in the heat. A big, white bath towel, left by a lady friend, was used to rub him down and after cologne on his face and some baby powder around his crotch, the silk, gown Reggie had brought back for him from Singapore was slipped back on and he turned the key in the door and François Deauville stepped out into the warmth of his centrally heated, luxury flat on the Rue de Honours and strode across to the frantic scratching coming from the other side of the kitchen door. Fifi leapt straight into his arms and in a frantic array of pent up movement, licked him all over the face.

"Are they feeding you alright my darling? Yes, daddy's home. Did you miss daddy? Alright. Let's look in the fridge and see what the maid has left for you. Stop it, Fifi. How can I open the fridge with all this licking…? There… Now look at that… What a lucky dog… Little bits of cooked liver for you and a chunk of cheese for me."

Four minutes later, the dog snuggled into the crook of his neck, François fell asleep for the first time in forty-eight hours.

ON THE OTHER side of Paris, in the attic room on the Left Bank, Simone woke in the old double bed and stretched out for him to find an empty bed. Smiling to herself, she knew he would be back before dawn and again wondered to herself when he was going to permit her to go operational. The Thief was using his small army sparingly and there had to be a reason. Totally trusting, she went back to sleep and only woke again with the dawn.

A week later, and still sleeping in the empty bed, she was terrified for him.

"It is The Thief," said one of the nine in the sewers, laconically. "He comes and then he goes again. It is his style. It is why the Germans cannot catch him after a raid. He disappears. Each time you worry for nothing. He'll be back."

AT TEN O'CLOCK THAT MORNING, and dressed like any other wealthy Frenchman despite the occupation, François opened the door to his expensive offices in the Paris business centre and was greeted by his new secretary with a long face and the glint of terror in her eyes. Taking off his heavy overcoat with the black fur lining that spilled over the collar, François hung it up with the fur cap he had worn against the weather and refused to be alarmed. Catching him by the arm, she pointed to the heavy oak door to his office.

"There's a German in there. German officer. Came earlier in the week. Didn't know what to say. Said you'd be back today from Marseilles. He just marched in there and closed the door as if he owned the place. The other staff are just keeping to their offices… How was Marseilles?"

"Very good. We are beginning to do good business in occupied Europe. The Italians and Germans. Insurance is always needed."

"There was a terrible explosion at the German barracks."

"Was there? I haven't read today's papers."

"The Germans are taking reprisals."

"What reprisals?" asked François, walking towards his door.

"They are going to shoot ten Frenchmen. They say the explosion was caused by the Marquis. It is terrible."

"Maybe the Marquis will take reprisals on the Germans," he said softly, bracing himself to open the door and face the consequence.

"Maybe," said his secretary, miserably. "I hate this war."

"Don't we all," and he turned the knob and pushed open the door to his office.

The German officer stood up as the door opened and with a broad smile turned to the door.

"Morning, François," said Gunter in English and saw the expression of instant joy reciprocated on his friend's face.

"Gunter," said François and moved across to him, got him in a bear hug and kissed him on both cheeks like any good Frenchman. "You son of a gun. What are you doing in Paris?"

"Leave. Two weeks. But they won't let us out of uniform. My apologies. Your secretary…"

"Come in, Miss Bontoux," said François to his secretary in French who had witnessed the exchange. "We are not always at war with the Germans. Beaumont Ltd is owned by four friends. One of them is a German, Herr von Ribbeck here."

"I didn't know," said Miss Bontoux, closing the door almost rudely.

"It's the uniform," said Gunter.

"Yes… Don't like it much myself."

"How are you? How was South Africa?"

"Good. All is well."

"Why did you come back?"

"Are you asking as a friend or a German officer?"

"As a friend, François."

"I had business to attend."

"Be careful. There are Germans I do not like."

"Me neither. Why do you spend your leave in Paris? How is Birgitt?"

"This is the reason. For all intents and purposes our marriage does not exist."

"I'm sorry."

"No more than I. Can you stop all calls and visits for the morning?"

"Of course."

"Good. Apart from being damn good to see you, we have so many business problems to discuss that can't be done in letters out of Switzerland. This war. Can't go on forever and if the Americans join the Allies after our North African defeats… Please don't… I know. Then Germany will not win the war. Our primary task, all of us, is to stay alive. That is why I say to you, be careful. I want live partners at the end, not dead heroes."

THAT EVENING, outside Cologne, Birgitt von Ribbeck was delighted her husband was spending his leave in Paris and even more delighted that her father, Baron von Essen was away from the schloss in the Ruhr on business. Four new girls had arrived from the bombing of Berlin, having been driven from their homes by the R.A.F. and one of them was particularly pretty with short blonde hair and firm young breasts. Her mouth, always slightly open, had attracted Birgitt and given her a flush of excitement which returned whenever she thought of the girl. Apart from the staff, she was in sole control of the schloss and the sixteen refugees that Birgitt had been happy to welcome into her father's house. Standing on the second-storey landing, she looked out of the darkened house across the wintry landscape towards Cologne where the R.A.F. had just dropped a series of flares for the bombers to aim for shortly. She would wait for the bombs to start falling ten miles away before she made her move and then afterwards, like so many of the others, the girl would be too ashamed to tell her friends or family and Birgitt would be able to have her whenever she wanted. The girl was fifteen. She had looked it up in her dossier that had arrived with German efficiency in an envelope with the girl and her suitcase. Almost impatiently, Birgitt waited for the inevitable Lancasters to drone out of the West on their four engines.

Five minutes later the first wave of bombers came over the target and unloaded their cargoes amidst bursting ack-ack shells and probing searchlights and then came the steady crump of high explosives and Birgitt took the stairs to the third storey and the individual rooms she had allocated to the guests in her care. Birgitt had deliberately put the girl at the end of the west wing's corridor, nearest the bombing and now hurried down the thick carpet runner by instinct, every light in the schloss having been extinguished. Taking a match out of the box she had kept expectantly, she flared it briefly and confirmed the name she herself had written on the door-card and silently let herself into the room.

"It's alright, it's Mrs von Ribbeck. Are you frightened by the bombing? I came to see if you are alright. The planes are far away and the schloss is very dark," and this brought her to the window where she drew the curtains tightly and came back to sit on the girl's bed and stroke the silken strands of young hair and then to gently smooth the girl's brow, backwards and forwards, backwards and forwards, and then down to the ear, nestling under the hair, small and smooth and warm at the lobe and Birgitt wanted to suck it in her mouth but knew she must wait and went on stroking security into the girl forever so slightly increasing the range of her hand increasing the pressure until finally she was kneading the girl's neck. Her breathing had quickened against the crashing violence ten miles away.

"Don't be frightened" crooned Birgitt. "I'll look after you," and she bent down and very lightly touched her lips to the mouth she knew was slightly open and with the movement slipped her hand down onto the night-gowned shoulder of the girl and gently but firmly pushed the strap off the girl's shoulder.

"Are you very frightened?" she asked.

"Yes," came a small voice out of the dark.

"Shall I get into bed with you?"

"I don't mind," and Birgitt dropping her heavy winter dressing gown onto the floor, slid under the sheets and blankets, her long, exquisitely beautiful body completely naked and took the girl into her arms and brought her round with a firm hand on her bottom and pulled her gently towards the very wet patch between her legs.

"What are you doing," murmured the girl.

"Looking after you," and she pulled up the girl's nightdress and pushed one of her long legs in between the girl's as she pulled the nightdress over her head and brought her mouth down onto the girl's so she couldn't make a noise. Finally, Birgitt had the girl's legs wide open and she was on top of her, pushing herself rhythmically at the soft down between the girl's legs until she climaxed wetly. After a few moments she cuddled the girl, sucking her nipples, and the sweet roundness of her ears and ten minutes later the girl began to respond and Birgitt brought her to her climax expertly with the barest touch of her fingers.

When the girl was asleep she got up, put on her dressing gown, drew the curtains slightly to look out across at the distant burning towns that had now been left by the R.A.F. to the fire engines and let herself out into the corridor.

"A perfect natural," she said out loud when she'd closed the door and then she hurried back to her own room wondering how many young girls the bombing would send into her arms.

A WEEK LATER, at the end of November 1941, when the Japanese were preparing to invade Malaya and bomb the American installations at Pearl Harbour, Reggie Beaumont took off from R.A.F. Boscombe Down in his Mosquito Pathfinder and headed out for Cologne. It was his seventy-first operation over Germany and his tunic carried the ribbons of a D.S.O. and a D.F.C. The D.F.C. was old and faded, but the D.S.O. had not succumbed to washing. Climbing to maximum height his navigator shot the stars and they headed on accurately to their target.

As THE MOSQUITO headed out in level flight on its direct flight to Cologne, Gunter arrived at the schloss for the final day of his leave to find the great house in total darkness and his wife nowhere to be found. Picking up a decanter of French brandy on the way he headed for his favourite smoking room where he poked the fire into life and added more logs, blowing on the fire till the logs caught alight and then piling on wood until the blaze was warm enough for him to take off his uniform jacket and sit in the comfortable armchair in front of the fire with his snifter of brandy gently held in both hands. The old clock on the wooden mantelpiece above the fire, wound itself up with energy and spent a long time telling the silent house that midnight had come. An hour and three quarters later, when the brandy decanter was one third empty, Gunter's well trained ear picked up the sound of an unfamiliar engine and involuntarily looked up at the ceiling.

"Pathfinder. Poor bastards. Not again," and went on drinking and watching the fire and listening to the build-up of the R.A.F. raid. Upstairs, unknown to him, his wife was seducing a second fifteen-year-old that week, a rather large, heavy breasted girl that had come in from Stuttgart that morning. The girl was proving much easier than the blonde and responded immediately even going down and sucking Birgitt till she came in the girl's face. The girl had done it before and liked it and insisted Birgitt give her the same treatment and had climbed up in the bed and wiped herself over the older woman's face until Birgitt thrust her long tongue into the big cavity and made her climax, her anguished shouts of ardour fortunately drowned by the R.A.F. bombers. The girl climaxed three times the same way before being satisfied and when Birgitt got out of her bed she was fast asleep, one large breast lolling hopefully which Birgitt tucked in gently before completing her routine back to her own room on the second floor.

REGGIE HAD ELECTED to circle the bombing and allow his navigator to photograph the bomb explosions to ascertain how many were falling inside the ring thrown down by the Pathfinders. It was a chance piece of flak that hit one of his engines. The engine caught fire immediately and began flowing down the wing of the wooden Mosquito coming straight at the cockpit.

"We'll have to get out," said Reggie by now an expert at bailing out of damaged aircraft and he dipped the undamaged wing and slapped his navigator on the back before watching him climb out of the aircraft. Reggie fought to hold a steady course with the fire raging next to him, the heat pushing at him through the perspex.

"Pathfinder D for Donald, T for Tango, A for Apple. Bailing out. Burning. Navigator gone. Over and out," and Reggie clawed his way out of his seat and finally dropped into the cold blackness.

GUNTER SLEPT in front of the dying embers with only an inch of brandy in the decanter. He was happily quite drunk and snored loudly, the old noise in the old, dark room with its low, smoke-blackened oak beams that had held up the house for centuries. By then the bombing raid was over and the dying were being rushed to hospitals and the dead being pulled out of the rubble and taken to the city's mortuaries at a slower speed. High into the night stood the spire of Cologne Cathedral, still standing in the rubble as a reminder to Birgitt, if she had looked, that she was married to a man.

REGGIE CAME down in a pine forest and crashed through onto a wet floor of old pine cones that crunched with his unexpected arrival. Propping himself against a tree, he waited for morning. This time the local populace would not be so accommodating. He hoped his navigator had landed safely and cursed his luck. Taking a piece of chocolate from his iron rations pack he began to chew and grow excruciatingly cold. Looking around the darkened wood he wondered where the hell he had landed. In the morning he would get his bearings and head for the schloss. At least he could be expected to go in the bag and not be ripped apart by angry civilians.

AT TEN O'CLOCK the following morning, when the Japanese fleet was leaving Japan in preparation for its sneak attack on Pearl Harbour and the American Pacific fleet, Reggie Beaumont knocked on the front door of the schloss and asked for Baron von Essen in his bad German and was greeted by a look of total monster-horror by the old butler whose name defeated Reggie as hard as he looked for it in the recess of his brain. In full R.A.F. flying kit but without his parachute and proper hat, covered in scratches from his descent through the pine trees, caked with mud and blood all over his face and wet hair plastered over his ears, he looked far worse than he felt which was now only mildly cold after his battle over field and hedgerow in his pursuit of the elusive schloss that sat proudly on top of its hill but wouldn't come any closer. The man finally retreated and left Reggie at the open front door, his flying boots dripping water onto the ancient stone step. Reggie waited politely for a few moments and then realised how ridiculous it would seem and stepped into the house he had last visited at the time of Gunter and Birgitt's wedding. Birgitt finally found him wandering around in the vast hallway that was colder than the country outside.

"Good morning, Birgitt," he said in English. "I'm jolly glad to find you at home. I must look a mess. Sorry. Reggie Beaumont. I came to your wedding. So did my brother Henry," he added when he saw that he wasn't getting through to her.

"Reggie Beaumont," he repeated giving a belated smile. "You know, Gunter's partner."

"What on earth are you doing in Germany like that?" as if his appearance altered the fact. Reggie pointed upwards and began to feel acute discomfort.

"You were part of last night's raid?"

"Yes."

"And you've come here?"

"It's the only house I know in the neighbourhood," he said, again realising how ridiculous he sounded. "We have to give ourselves up to somebody… That's what I'm doing… Is your father at home?"

"No," said Birgitt. "I'm alone."

"Not completely," said Gunter in English having been called by the butler.

"I arrived late last night. On leave. You'd better come in and have a drink. Are you badly hurt?"

"Scratched."

"You look terrible."

"Haven't seen a mirror."

"Look over there."

"Ah… I see what you mean. No wonder I frightened your man."

"What are you doing here?" asked Birgitt icily, in German.

"Visiting my wife. You weren't at home. The servants said you were staying with your father. Good idea. The house is too close to the town. Even the R.A.F. miss their targets," he said acidly in English having still a clear picture of the previous night's devastation.

"This is a pretty kettle of fish," said Reggie brightly.

"You're lucky," said Gunter.

"Why?"

"Your war is finished."

"Not at all. If you could lend me…"

"Don't be bloody silly, Reggie. We'll have a brandy. There's some in the decanter. Birgitt can order some breakfast. Then I'll call the police."

"What for? I can walk to France."

"Reggie, I want live partners after this stupid bloody war. I told that to François last week. Silly bastard's got himself involved in the French underground."

"How do you know?"

"I know François. You don't think he'd come all the way back from South Africa to run a lousy wartime reinsurance company."

"That was the idea?"

"My foot, Reggie… Don't worry. I understand the prisoner-of-war camps are fairly healthy. And please, Reggie, don't try and do anything silly. When it comes to a physical fight you know damn well I always win."

"Not always," said Reggie following him. "I can remember a couple of occasions at Oxford."

"I was drunk both times. How's business your end?"

"Not bad… Yours?"

"Not bad."

"Bloody stupid?"

"Yes. Be over one day. How are the others?"

"Gwen was killed… Isabel's sister."

"I'm sorry."

"Your family?"

"Still alive… So far… Remember, officially from now on you are under arrest."

"I'll try and remember it."

"I'll try and work something on food parcels."

"Better not."

"No… Maybe not."

"Are the Gestapo as bad as they sound?"

"Worse, Reggie. A bloody sight worse."

WHILE REGGIE WAS BEING TAKEN AWAY by two belligerent country policemen, on the other side of the world, Adam Beaumont aged seven and his sister Tammany aged six were holding hands as if their lives depended on it which in some ways they did. The *S.S. Oranje* was slowly pulling away from the quay and the streamers they held tightly in their free hands, connected to their parents were pulling up from the Singapore docks. A band was playing *'Heart of Oak'* as if nothing was happening to the British Empire and the crew were lining the upper decks of the liner in white tropical uniform, immaculately pressed. Behind the children stood Linda and Sally who were waving to their new employers. Adam's jaw was moving visibly as he struggled to control the flood of tears that was waiting behind his eyes. Tammany junior was not so successful and her little round cheeks were vehicles for a steady stream of salty tears that eventually dripped onto the well-scrubbed deck. When the coloured streamer in her hand finally snapped she howled out loud and the flood gates opened for Adam, and Sally, remembering her earlier months as a children's nurse, put her hands on the children's shoulders and tried to give them some comfort.

On shore, Tug and Tammany, holding hands, bravely waved their children off to the supposedly safer waters of Australia and silently wished the ship a safe voyage to Fremantle. They stood on the quay for a long time, unable to talk. They both knew a way of life had come to an end.

As THE *S.S. Oranje* sailed south through the Java Sea, Captain, recently promoted from Lieutenant, Horoshini embarked on a troopship in Yokohama Bay with his destination Singapore. Only this time he was not going to buy guns from Ping-Lai Ho and Perry Marshbank but use the copies that had been mass produced in a large factory just outside Tokyo. Being a sadist, he was looking forward to his war and all its personal pleasures. The fact that none of his senior or junior officers liked him worried him not a jot. He, Horoshini, was the true Samurai.

FORTY-EIGHT MILES OUTSIDE PARIS, The Thief pointed his shielded torch at the night sky and flashed three longs and a short. The bonfire at the end of the field was burning well. They could hear the Lysander and then they could see its shape coming into land and bumping its way over the grass towards the flashing torch. The Thief hugged Simone for a long moment and, bent over for imaginary protection, broke away from the clump of trees and ran towards the taxiing British Army aircraft, the pom-pom still holding on to his beret by a thread. The pilot pulled him hurriedly into the plane and gunned the engine. By the time they were airborne and heading at tree level for England, the bonfire was already out and Simone and Danielle were headed deep into the woods where their bicycles were hidden and where they would wait until morning before peddling back into Paris. The extra bicycle would stay in the bracken waiting for The Thief's return.

THAT MORNING, when the girls were ten miles on their return, the French offices of Beaumont Ltd were visited by two Germans in uniform and this time Miss Bontoux had no doubt about their hostility. They wanted to know the name of the German officer seen entering and leaving the office and who he was talking to for so long. The information they gleaned made them satisfied.

BY THE TIME the girls had reached Paris that afternoon, Lady Beaumont was opening a cable from the Air Ministry that violently shook her hands. Pavy, full of discretion, moved away with the silver salver that had held the brown envelope.

"Not Reggie," she said out loud. "Not my Reggie," and then she read the cable and burst into tears with relief.

THAT NIGHT at two in the morning, Chuck Everly tossed and turned but couldn't get himself off to sleep. All around him the sounds of sleeping, restless humanity echoed down the badly lit tunnel. One family, sleeping on the normally electrified line, was quietly playing 'I Spy' but there wasn't much to spy in the semi-darkness and the smoke from the wicks of the hurricane lamps. "Can't sleep luv?" asked the shop girl lying next to him on the south-bound platform of the Bakerloo line.

"No."

"Want to talk? Can't sleep neither."

"Sure."

"Reserve job?"

"I'm an American."

"Got any gum, chum?" and she laughed. Chuck couldn't see her face, the light coming from behind.

"Are we all like that?" he asked.

"Don't know, luv. Never met a Yank before… Not been 'ere long?"

"Since early 1940."

"Blimey. Right through it. Thought you was new. Why can't you sleep?"

"Too many friends in uniform."

"I've got a brother. Lot older. Been a private for ten years. Drives an armoured car or something. Can't write proper so we don't hear much. Pal of 'is got made an officer. Caw. How 'bout that? Bleedin' officer and 'e started with our Wilf. Wilf probably drives the rations to the N.A.A.F.I.

"Told me dad once some cock and bull story 'bout jumping out of aeroplanes. Always was a one. Never believe nothing, that's me. What you do?"

"You'd think it a 'cock 'n bull story'. Is that how you say it?"

"Course I wouldn't. You're an American. No, you can't act in cowboy films, not in England. Can you ride a horse?"

"Sure."

"Go on. You're avin' me on? True as bob?"

"True as bob," said Chuck beginning to enjoy himself despite being tired and unable to stop his brain from churning around so he could get some sleep. "Next thing you'll tell me you's a millionaire."

"I am."

"That's not difficult. My dad told us all Americans are millionaires. Said 'e tried to emigrate when 'e was a nipper but they didn't want no chimney sweeps in America. Pity, else I'd 'ave been American."

"You might not have been anything if he hadn't met your mother."

"That's a fact? Caw. Never thought of that… You's right… No mother, no me. No," she said, after a while. "Don't be daft. I'd 'ave 'ad another mum, that's all… How'd you make all that money?"

"Insurance broking. Gold mines. Diamond fields. Rubber plantations," and Chuck stopped realising how stupid it must sound coming from a stranger wrapped in two blankets and lying on the platform of an underground railway station.

"Go on," she said excitedly. "What else you got?"

"A few tin mines… In Malaya."

"And them gold and diamonds?"

"South Africa and Bechuanaland."

"Where's that?"

"Southern Africa."

"You been to all these places?"

"No. I. run head office."

"You the boss?"

"With my partners."

"Got a plush office, I'll bet?"

"Used to have."

"Now you was cock 'n bulling me. All those things and no office for the what you call it, head office. Sounds fishy to me."

"Not really," said Chuck quietly. "The Germans bombed 51 King William Street to the ground at ten-thirty this evening. It's why I can't sleep."

"That's lucky. Office workers go 'ome at six."

"Charlie was there."

"Who's Charlie?"

"Our caretaker. On his own. Must be terrible to die all alone. I don't even know who to write to. Reggie knows. He's my partner but the Germans have got him in Stalag 17."

"What's that?"

"Prisoner-of-war camp… Maybe Thelma will know. Poor old, Charlie. Must have had family somewhere."

"I'm sorry… You ain't bullshittin', is you?"

"No, love, I'm not… And thanks… I feel better talking. Get a bit lonely myself."

"Not married?"

"No."

"There's the answer. Find a nice girl and marry her."

"Found her but she doesn't want to marry me."

"And you a millionaire:"

"Doesn't work all the time."

"She must be daft, stark ravin' bleedin' daft."

THE DOCTOR CLOSED the door quietly on Sir Thomas Beaumont and left him to his memories and very little else. The private room was bright, full of sunlight, life and the sounds of Cairo from out there through the open window where the cars honked horns and then from many directions, from the tops of all the mosques, the singing began, facing Mecca, their God, their immortality.

'Or was there one?' he thought, and lay back on the white pillows, puffed up as they should be for a colonel and a baronet of ancient lineage. Or am I just another baronet to be ticked off to tally the final count?' The counterpane was a light cotton and moulded the box covering the wound in his leg, keeping the weight away as if that would do any good. So he thought back and remembered his life and the smiles came back, many of them, and he used up some of the hours of his future before turning back to look again at his death. Six months. Maybe a year. Maybe more. A small lump in his leg. Football at school. He remembered the kick. Put him out of the school team for a month. Now it was going to kill him. So he looked hard and saw the reality. He was going to die anyway, now he was just going to die a little sooner than he had thought. Sixty-six years. He'd told the War Office he was fifty-nine. A life here after? Or was this just the conceit of man who could not accept the loss or his individual existence. What do I believe, he thought and didn't know. Was his immortality through the line of his children? Was he reproduced by his sons? Was he a reproduction, a reincarnation perhaps of old Sir Henri de Beaumont and a line of blood that went back to the caves and beyond? He had so little knowledge. What did he really know? He had been born. He had lived. Now he was going to die. The in-between so little. Had he made the best of it? Had he enjoyed his life? Had he been happy? He thought of the last question again and again and dredged from his own life the memories that added up to his personal balance sheet. Yes, that was the important factor. To be happy. If not delirious then just content. The rest was worthless. Money. Position. Power. Nothing without content and with Alice he had had his plenty of contentment, happiness too and so he brought himself to the present. The line was secure. Four sons of his. Three grandsons and surely more to come. Reggie'd secured the money. Lucky to have one son who knew how to make the stuff and loved the family and all it meant as much as he.

"Can I get you anything?" asked a pretty nurse bustling into his room to smile and puff his pillows.

"Another twenty years," he said and then he was sorry for the compassion he saw in the young girl's eyes.

"We all have to die, Sir Thomas. Even me. But you will live to be a hundred. Doctors are very often wrong. I know. I work with them."

"Thank you."

"My pleasure," and she left the room.

'What are the problems?' he thought. 'Family problems? The war would go and come again. That part did not matter… A nice girl,' he thought but not for Henry. Reggie? Maybe. But did it matter in the final count. Were his wife's and Lady Hensbrook's worries worth doing anything about? There had been more than one illicit affair at Merry Hall in the past and certainly Isabel was not the last of a long line of adulteresses. He'd been unfaithful himself so how could he throw stones? And if anyone had had a good marriage it was he and Alice. Isabel's sin was the lack of her discretion. Hurting other people. Causing pain to others. We all have our failings, he thought, and there is nothing we can do about them. She would be Lady Beaumont when he died. Then she would have to behave… Maybe… Alice would miss him. Be lonely too for so many future years. There was family but not the quiet content they enjoyed so much together. He was glad he had taken her to India. Poor old Bertie. Maybe that was better. Bertie hadn't had to lie in a hospital bed and think about his death. You are getting maudlin, he thought and stretched up for the bell that hung from the ceiling and pressed the small button and waited for the nurse.

"Yes, Sir Thomas?" she said as brightly as ever.

"Bring me a B and S, if you know what that is," he said, a twinkle in his eye.

"Brandy and soda."

"Splendid… And make it a large one, nurse."

"I will go out to the hotel myself."

"Smuggle it in. That's my girl… What's your name?"

"Mary."

"That's a nice name, Mary."

"Thank you."

"You're just lucky I'm not a few years younger," and he smiled and she smiled back and for the moment death went out of the window and Sir Thomas tapped his fingers lightly on the cover and began to think of all the ends he must tie up, the things that he had not yet said to his sons that he would tell them before he died. That would be his legacy. The benefit of his life and experiences. What else could a man leave behind?

PING-LAI HO, dressed as a barefoot coolie, followed his guide through the thick Malayan jungle 110 miles north of Kuala Lumpur. They were two miles from the Thai border. Above them, the foliage was so thick that only an accessional beam of sun light reached down to the narrow pathway that his guide was continually hacking a path through with a sharp, curved knife that he wielded with effortless ease.

"Can't people follow us?" he asked.

"You not get home if you turn round now. Only my people can move through the jungle."

"How much further?"

"Not far."

"You said that yesterday."

"It wasn't far, yesterday. Just takes long time to get to."

'Comedian,' thought Ping-Lai Ho, fingering the revolver strapped to his money belt under his filthy clothes.

Ping-Lai Ho, having shut up his house in Singapore, had faded back into the

Chinese peasant population and was fast losing the girth that gave the lie to his new role in life. He was well satisfied with himself and calculated that even the last major portion of his wealth, outside of the house itself, was on its way to Australia. The fact that his paintings and oriental carpets, his old china, were on their way to Australia pleased him and he was confident that Linda and Sally would store them for him so that he could bring them back when the country had returned to normal. It wasn't only the millions that counted but the time he had spent on his collection. The moment orders for the guns ceased he knew the Japs had what they wanted and a full-scale invasion of the East and its islands was on its way. He trusted Captain Horoshini as far as Captain Horoshini trusted Ping-Lai Ho, which wasn't far. For all intents and purposes, Ping-Lai Ho had ceased to exist and his former Japanese client would be unable to conclude other than that he had perished in their invasion, the one Ping-Lai Ho and Edward Gray knew to be on the way, something the British Governor and army refused to admit, sitting back smugly behind their long, naval guns in Singapore, all of which faced out to sea.

The man in front signalled him to stop and he came out of his thoughts into the sweating heat of the jungle unaware that a leech had got up his trouser leg and was sucking blood from his ball-bag. Slowly they crept on through and into the sudden clearing and piercing power of sunlight.

"Morning, old boy," said Perry Marshbank that Ping-Lai Ho's seared eyes couldn't see.

"How did you know it was me?" said Ping-Lai Ho, annoyed.

"Arrogance, my dear boy, is always apparent. Come in out of the sun," he said and then told the guide in Malay where he should go for food and his reward. Perry had a lot of them working for him and looked after them well. Perry always knew when he needed people. Inside the long hut, built off the ground on stilts, the air-conditioning hummed, powered by a diesel generator that Perry had installed himself and paid large sums of money for fuel supplies to be brought into his hideout through the jungle.

"Can't make heroin without power," he explained, taking a cold beer out of a refrigerator and pouring it into a tall glass for Ping-Lai Ho.

"Your most excellent health," said Perry and lifted his own glass.

"Thank you."

"To our first jungle factory."

"To as many more as we need," said Ping-Lai Ho and began to let the ice-cold beer run down his gullet into his belly.

"That's good," he said, sighing with satisfaction.

"Tough journey?"

"Not a way I'd choose to travel."

"It's why it's safe. No-one. British. Japs. No-one can find us. And if they got anywhere near we'd be gone with everything of value before they arrived."

"Perfect."

"Now we can settle down to making real money, partner."

"How good is the quality?"

"What a bloody stupid question."

"Sorry, old boy," said Ping-Lai Ho imitating and then lifting his glass to finish his beer. "Another?"

"Why not. There's nothing else to do for recreation."

"No girls?"

"You touch one of the locals and we are finished."

"Like that?"

"Yes."

WHILE PING-LAI HO sipped his second ice-cold beer, Edward Gray studied the map of Borneo and Malaya spread out on his desk and estimated that even with a successful Japanese invasion he would be in control of seventy percent of the territory. The enemy would control the cities, the villages and the railway lines for some of the time but they could never conquer the jungle without the people's consent. He looked out over Kuching Harbour, past the limp Union Jack on its white flagpole and then turned to Tug Beaumont who was seated in a comfortable armchair drinking a Stenga, a scotch with lots of water and ice.

"The children will enjoy the voyage," he said to Tug.

"Probably. Their mother isn't."

"How's she adapting to village life?"

"Badly. Misses the kids."

"Brave girl to volunteer."

"You didn't give her much choice."

"She's a very good radio operator."

"She did well at school. Now, when do you want me to leave?"

"Tomorrow morning. You'll be based about one hundred miles north-east of Kuala Lumpur. On the Thai border. What's in that wooden crate?"

"Paints. Canvasses. Brushes... You said I'd have a lot of time on my hands."

"Splendid... They're lowering the flag. Time to go into dinner."

"Guerrilla warfare?" said Tug.

"Impossible to defeat and difficult to live with."

"No sign of Perry Marshbank?" asked Tug.

"Disappeared into thin air... Refused to help us. Ping-Lai Ho's gone as well. House boarded up. Heard all his paintings are on the *S.S. Oranje*. Someone must have been paid off."

"I wonder what they're up to?"

"They won't get a bloody trading licence after all this lot."

"Don't be too sure. It's amazing what a lot of money can do. You think Tammany will be alright blended in with her family?"

"Yes... She wouldn't have enjoyed Australia."

"There's still a lot of prejudice."

"White Australia policy, number one. Even if I'd wanted to I couldn't have got her in."

"How are you enjoying being a bachelor?" asked Tug.

"Very peaceful. I'm very fond of Rebecca in some ways but no-one can say she's peaceful. Women never seem to stop talking."

"Not Tammany," said Tug getting up and watching the soldier fold the Union Jack and take it off under his arm, swinging his one arm professionally. "We can sit for hours not saying a word."

"You're damn lucky... There's wine with the meal."

"WELL, OF COURSE," said Mrs Gray to the captain, leaning slightly nearer at the dinner table. "They'll never overrun Singapore. Quarter of a million troops in Malaya. British troops."

"I hope you're right."

"I had a letter the other day from Lady Hensbrook. Lord Hensbrook's wife. Charming woman. We correspond regularly, you'll understand. She says there's no chance of the Japanese even invading and she should know."

"I hope she does," said the captain, putting a piece of rare steak in his mouth and chewing diligently.

"Isn't Lord Hensbrook dead?" asked Linda who had heard it from Adam.

"Oh no. House of Lords. No less. Well, it won't be long now. Dear Edward. My husband you know," and the captain quickly fed another piece of steak into his mouth. "They'll make him a baron when all this nonsense is finished. Lord and Lady Gray of Kuching... We have influence, you see," and she looked around the silent captain's table for confirmation that they understood.

"The children," said Sally Bollas, pushing back her plate. "Will you excuse me for a moment, captain? The children are a little unsettled away from their mother."

"Children, Miss Bollas?" asked Mrs Gray, arching her eyebrows.

"My charges. You know their grandmother, Lady Beaumont?"

"Of course, of course."

"You must ask Adam about Lord Hensbrook. Lady Hensbrook now lives at Merry Hall."

"Does she?"

"I believe so... With her daughters."

"How interesting."

"I thought you would find it so."

"COME IN, Mr Deauville. Please sit down. Did you have an enjoyable flight?"

"Yes, thank you, major," said François and took his seat round the conference table in a building he had been brought to opposite the Admiralty in Whitehall. "Major Beaumont regrets he is unable to be here. He is in Egypt, I believe."

It was ten-thirty in the morning and François was tired, having neither eaten nor slept since peddling out of Paris.

"The reprisals, Mr Deauville. We cannot allow the Germans to kill French civilians. Morale. We have decided to suspend sabotage attacks until you are more organised... There is more than one army contemplating invasion and with our resounding victories in North Africa we intend to invade Europe with or without our American friends. We have recently shown that the German Army can be beaten. When we invade Europe, it is then that we want your resistance to rise up and stab the Germans in the back. In this way the French people will have a major hand in liberating their country."

"What do we do?"

"Train. Build up arms. Send back information for the R.A.F. to target. Get our downed pilots back to England. Keep up the spirit of the French. Build up an underground army that can sabotage the German line of supplies at a time when he can least afford interruptions."

"There will be reprisals."

"Not for long. When we invade it will be done from strength. Do you know a man called Jean-Pierre Agier?"

"He is married to my mother. My father was…"

"We thought as much. Earlier this morning the offices of Beaumont Ltd were visited by the Gestapo. Your secretary talked her heart out. Quite sensibly. We think they have connected François Deauville with The Thief and you must therefore remain underground when you return to France."

"What has this to do with my stepfather?"

"He is collaborating with the Germans. When the fabric of your life is built on lies you are vulnerable. The Germans had him marked out before they crossed the Maginot Line. Did you know he deserted from the French Army during the last war? That he was a corporal, acting sergeant?"

"I checked up. He was commissioned from the ranks."

"No. A mess orderly."

"He made my mother laugh. She hadn't been…"

"Quite. The point is your stepfather would totally consolidate his position with your mother if you were to die. Your own estate would revert to your mother. We have a copy of your father's will."

François remained silent.

"You do understand?" said the major.

"What do you want me to do?"

"Kill him… Not you personally… The resistance movement before he kills a lot of loyal Frenchmen."

"It will break my mother's heart."

And this time it was the major who remained silent.

MEGAN STRONG HELD the unopened letter she had been given by Mafutha and taken it down to the bottom of the garden by the river and the stone seat that sat beside the water. Looking back, still not opening the envelope that was sticky with her fingerprints, she could see the double storey of Timber Lane and the balustrade that guarded the blue waters of the swimming pool: Between the trees, that is, tall, some flowering, a few hung with morning-glory creeper and one was clung to by a bougainvillaea that had crept right up to the top and flowered thirty feet above the well cut grass and the flowers, and the two gardeners cutting to keep it right and humming with the insects… Procrastinating. She knew what it was. The bad handwriting was unmistakable. Did it really matter if Carl didn't marry her? They had fun, lots of it. She'd never had so much fun and she was crying, leaning forward over the water and seeing her teardrops pitch down to the slowly moving water and were gone. She'd lost them all now, so what the hell did it matter, she told herself. To start again and feel something? It wasn't worth it. No, she was glad she had given up her job to live with Carl. Who the hell cared what the neighbours thought. She opened Dusty's letter… Her father was dead. She didn't have to be told again.

"Major von Ribbeck," said a soft voice as he was boarding the train in Paris at the end of his leave.

"Yes," he said stepping back onto the platform and facing the two German officers in black trench coats.

"I'm due back at the aerodrome."

"It doesn't matter." And one on each side with strong hands at either elbow he was led off away from the train and out of the railway station and into the back of a car that left the curb immediately the two back doors closed with Gunter in the middle.

"What do you want?"

"Why does a German officer have English, American, French and Danish partners? Have you been hedging your bets, Mr von Ribbeck? Don't answer we know. But did you know that your good friend and partner, Mr Deauville is also The Thief? No. How could you? He was only your partner for eleven years and you recently spent six hours with him in his office. What were you doing? Carving up the spoils? Or more likely passing to the Americans your system for synthetic rubber. When do you start your manufacture in America, Mr von Ribbeck? Before or after we have defeated the Allies? Very considerate of you to hand over your English partner and personal friend. If it was not for your father-in-law, the good Baron von Essen, we would have you shot as a spy. As it is, you will be sent to a detention camp."

"I can explain," said Gunter.

"You can't."

"I certainly can."

"Is anything I have said untrue?"

"Yes. I would never assist the Allied war effort by enabling them to manufacture my synthetic rubber."

"You are only interested in money, Mr von Ribbeck. There were many business men like you. Milking the German people. Too much personal profit."

"My father-in-law is an industrialist."

"But he co-operates. A loyal supporter of the party. Why have you never become a member of the Nazi party, Mr von Ribbeck?"

"Major von Ribbeck."

"Mr von Ribbeck. You lost your rank and decorations earlier this morning. It is my personal opinion that you will probably lose your life as well."

TWO WEEKS after Gunter was roughly pushed into a concentration camp to fester with his already festering inmates, the Japanese Navy attacked Pearl Harbour with Naval Strike Aircraft, and the Japanese Army landed at three points on the Malayan coast. Without waiting for further instructions from London, Edward Gray left his post in Kuching and crossed to Singapore from whence he moved inland across the causeway into the jungle and prepared to lead the guerrilla army against the Japanese, whether they succeeded in beating the British Army or not. A deputy took over the hoisting and lowering, morning and night, of the Union Jack on its white flagpole outside his office overlooking Kuching Harbour.

THE FOLLOWING MORNING at eight o'clock, Chuck Everly was standing outside the American Embassy in Sloane Square waiting for the doors to open with a crowd of fellow Americans all of whom were equally incensed by the Japanese sneak attack and all of whom were clamouring to offer their services to Uncle Sam. By lunchtime the Americans were in the war against Japan and Germany and Chuck had been refused entry into the American Air Force on account of his age.

"I tell you," shouted Chuck. "I was flying aeroplanes when you were still in junior school."

"That is just the point, buster. I was in junior school a long time ago and aeroplanes have changed. Why don't you try the Tank Corps? They haven't changed their tanks for a good few years."

"Who do I see?"

"Get yourself back to America first, buster… How old did you say you were?"

"Twenty-nine."

"Well lose some of that fat before you use that story again. Now get the hell out of here. I got a lot of young guys out there wanting to be pilots."

"Thanks for your help."

"Thanks for nothing… Tanks. They even take guys wearing glasses in tanks."

"How do I get a passage to the U.S.?"

"How the hell do I know, Charlie?"

"Chuck. Chuck Everly. Beaumont Ltd. Union Mining and Exploration."

"Hey… Wait a minute… Are you the big guy at the mining house?"

"Yes."

"Well why the hell didn't you say so, buster. Now sit down and I'll get you some coffee."

"Air Force?" said Chuck hopefully.

"No… But I've got a buddy in Washington in the cavalry. Mix that with your financial clout and you're in."

"Well, that's something anyway."

"We'll get you on a military transport."

"Aircraft?"

"Sure. Like I said."

"When?"

"You can go this afternoon, as a matter of fact."

"Good. That's my luggage," Chuck said pointing to his grip.

"Travelling light."

"Sure. Apart from twenty thousand dollars in travellers cheques. American Express."

"Twenty thousand dollars? I'd call that travelling heavy."

7

JULY 1942

*A*t the end of July 1942, sometime after the Japanese had chased the British out of Singapore and America out of the Philippines, MacArthur vowing he'd get back again, Sir Thomas and Lady Beaumont walked through the woods hand in hand in the summer evening enjoying the sound of pigeons in the big trees and the crackle of warm bracken, browned by the sun and bent with the summer.

"That one," said Sir Thomas, tapping a gnarled oak tree with his walking stick, "was around when Sir Henri took up this land. Must be a thousand years old."

"Do they really grow that old?" said Lady Beaumont, despite having been told a hundred times.

"If you cut it down, you can count the rings. Thousand years. Probably more. Knights in armour have rested their horses under that old fellow."

"Do you want to rest?"

"Good spot... Commune with my ancestors. Give me a hand, Alice, this damn leg's as stiff as a post," and he managed to get down to sit on the thick green moss growing in profusion among the great roots, only half in the earth, that radiated from the massive trunk and fed the bows and foliage of the oak, spreading high and wide above the squire and his wife.

"We'll have to think again about getting me up. There'll be a way."

"I love this walk," said Lady Beaumont. "We've done it so many times over so many years. Without this war everything would be so very beautiful. It's the pain of worry."

"I know," said Sir Thomas patting his wife's hand. "Tug's alright. No news is good news. A lot of them went into the jungle. He'll be there, right as rain. He knew what was happening or why did he have the children sent to Australia?"

"It's not knowing."

"Stop worrying."

"I can't. The moment I stop worrying about one of them I think about another.

And Thomas, what are we going to do about Isabel? Can't you talk to her? A perfect disgrace. And all those girl friends of Reggie's that invite themselves down to Merry Hall. I just wonder."

"It stops the sailors worrying. The Merchant Navy are having a bad time in the North Sea. They need company, Alice. Reggie knew that, that's why he gave them open invitations. For far too many or those boys it will be the last bit of female company they'll have. Isabel…? What can we do? An old man of sixty-seven says to her she's looking after some or those boys too well and she'll say there's a war on. It's probably happening all over England. Look at these Americans coming into the island without their wives or girlfriends."

"But this is family."

"It is always somebody's family. Henry is married to Isabel. They have a daughter. Bringing the whole thing out in the open will create more of a problem. And please remember one thing, Alice, we have no proof."

"Thomas! Just the way she looks at them. There's absolutely no doubt in my mind. Georgina is sick with worry and her mother is beside herself."

"It's the war," said Sir Thomas.

"We blame everything on the war. What if she were to fall pregnant with Henry hundreds of miles away for months on end. And don't say we'll cross that bridge when we get to it because it's here right now."

"She doesn't care what we think. When you don't care what happens it is very easy to be wicked."

"The servants are talking."

"All servants talk, facts or no facts… That Beau's going to be quite a fellow," he said to change the subject. "Seven years old and he's playing football for the under nine's. Takes after his father. Mark my words, that boy's going to be an athlete."

"Lorna is very shy. Like her mother."

"Georgina isn't shy."

"Well," said Lady Beaumont, laughing. "She certainly isn't an extravert. I'm so glad she's had another baby. That girl was born to be a mother. The children adore her."

"Yes, Geoffrey was lucky."

"So unusual to find such opposites in one family."

"Is it? Our four are very different."

"But they behave themselves… Karen…? I think Geoffrey should have called the baby after my mother."

"Fanny is a word that has two meanings these days, my dear."

"Oh, Thomas! How can you say such things? They've all got dirty minds, that's what's the matter."

"They want to cut off my leg."

"What did you say, Thomas?"

"My leg. They want to cut it off. The surgeon thinks it could stop the cancer from spreading."

"Oh, Thomas, how terrible."

"Can't get around much as it is."

"When?"

"Next week. At the Cottage Hospital."

"Couldn't you go to London?"

"The London hospitals are full of war casualties. They don't have room for old men."

"But you can pull some strings."

"The young ones deserve the better treatment. And from what I've heard it won't do much good anyway. Might give me a couple more years. My real ambition now is to reach the three score years and ten. We've had a good life. Nothing to regret. I'm glad now I left the Indian Civil Service. Merry Hall's been good to us. A wonderful old home to bring up children, even if they do fall out of trees like Raoul, yesterday. It would have been nice to grow very old beside you in front of the fire, or rocking our chairs in the conservatory and shouting our words. But that's the part of life we can't have and we must thank whoever made us for the years of peace, the pleasures of our life… You remember our trip to India?"

"Of course, Thomas," but she was unable to say anymore.

"You've been a good wife to me, Alice. A good mother." She squeezed his hand as her eyes and throat were full.

"When we've beaten the Germans and the Japs, and all the boys are home again, we're going to throw the biggest victory ball of the century… Reggie can finance it… He'll like the idea… That's why it's called Merry Hall. They'd better get on and win it… The Americans will make the difference… That's it, the biggest victory ball the old Hall has ever seen… They'll talk about it all their lives."

"We're not exactly winning the war, Thomas."

"Don't be silly, of course we'll win. The British always win in the end. Geoffrey will be a full colonel if not a brigadier. That boy's going right to the top in the army. Henry will come back with a mass of decorations and Tug will come out of the jungle as if nothing had happened. Even Isabel will behave herself… Who's that coming down the path? Didn't bring my glasses."

"Bert Brigley."

"We'll, that's something… Evening Bert… Can't get up, bloody leg. How's your boy?"

"Not a scratch, Sir Thomas."

"Same as ours… Lilly?"

"Working hard… Quite the business lady… She and Thelma are running the business or so's they say… Keeps her mind off Tony… Any news from Mr Reggie?"

"The Red Cross send us letters once in a while," said Lady Beaumont.

"All he says is he's alive and well," said Sir Thomas.

"That's the only kind of news my Martha wants to hear. . . Them Land Girls work well. Strong as men some of 'em. We'll be lifting them potatoes in the Thirty Acre tomorrow. Take us a week. There's money in them potatoes… Just got to keep the leather jackets out of 'em."

"How's Martha?" asked Lady Beaumont, trying to get up.

"Well, my lady. Can I help? Not getting younger, none of us," said Bert Brigley giving Lady Beaumont an old gnarled hand.

"Thank you, Bert."

"My pleasure, my lady."

"One on each side," she said.

"Up you come, sir."

"That's it… Once I'm vertical… It'll be easier without the leg, Alice. Didn't you see how it got in the way? Give me that stick, Bert… Thank you… Strong enough, eh… Right, now. Take it slowly and we'll walk down to the cottage and say hello to Martha. Haven't had a cup of Martha's tea for almost a week," and they all laughed and began slowly walking away down the acorn-strewn path, mulched with many leaves and soft to walk upon. The old owl watched them go from the hole in the elm tree, three old people helping each other.

AT THE TIME Sir Thomas Beaumont sat down beside Bert Brigley's honeysuckle and rose creepers with a cup of tea, and Tug Beaumont put the last touches to his sixth canvas in his jungle hideout, The Thief dipped into the pot in front of him and began to feed contentedly without using knife, fork or spoon. To the amusement of the others in the forest, The Thief ate as slowly as possible, savouring each mouthful and finally scooping up the gravy and barley in a cupped hand and dribbling some of it down his bearded chin and onto his filthy shirt front that had been washed so many times it was a dirty grey with a large gash at the belly button.

The man sitting on the grass in the middle of the glade was in his early fifties with an elegant dash of grey at his temples and in his military moustache, only half of which could be seen above the old piece of smelly cloth that Simone had used to wash the dishes and which now acted as a gag. The man was unable to utter a sound. He was bound hand and foot and most of the circulation to his hands and feet had stopped and the only true, live part of him was his eyes.

"Excellent, Simone, my darling. When times are hard we must catch and eat rabbit more often," and the others laughed, lounging back on the soft grass, still patterned by the shadow of French oaks that were sun drenched at the upper branches.

"Have you heard of The Thief?" asked François casually and saw the instant signs of recognition. "My instructions are to kill you. Do you have anything to say…? Better take off his gag, someone, and loosen those ropes or he'll just die on his own… Maybe we should just leave him here. Unfortunately I can't… You are a traitor to France. Twice in fact… You collaborate with the Germans. Entertain them at the chateau."

"They will catch you," snarled Jean-Pierre as the rag came out of his mouth.

"Possibly… but I doubt it… they have been trying for a long time… You don't deny what I said?"

"They will have missed me by now."

"Probably. Possibly. Maybe they think you've gone for a long shit. Because that is what you will tell them when you return. Oh, yes you are going back," said François returning to his normal accent for the first time. "But you are going to behave yourself and, in your role as collaborator, you will tell us everything they know. You will be an informer's informer, if you see what I mean. But you must be very careful. If the Germans catch you they will shoot you and if you betray your country just one more time I will cut off your balls and let you bleed to death… Do you see, Jean-Pierre?"

"Who are you?" said Jean-Pierre, knowing perfectly well.

"Don't you recognise your own stepson?" and Simone looked up in surprise along with the others. "It is a pity for me that you are married to my mother as otherwise I would personally cut out your balls with a blunt knife," and François lunged forward and grabbed them tight and squeezed as hard as he was able and

Jean-Pierre screamed in agony. "Take him back," he said to the others and then to his step- father, "We will contact you when we are ready... And remember. You went for a long shit."

TOWARDS THE END of February 1943, when Henry Beaumont was home on leave, Sir Thomas sat in a comfortable chair in front of a blazing log fire and massaged the stump of his left leg wishing he could scratch the toes which had ended in the incinerator of the Cottage Hospital. The den was the only warm room in the house as the others were too big for the meagre supplies of fuel and Sir Thomas refused to cut down timber. He got up painfully, balanced on his one good leg and managed to fit the crutches under his armpits and swing his good leg forward to the display cabinet. After a few minutes of careful study he decided the balm of his butterflies was doing him no good and he manoeuvred himself back into his chair before answering the knock at his door.

"Hello, son," he said when the door opened. "How are your horses?"

"I'll win the Derby yet," said Henry.

"Any man with a firm purpose always wins."

"Can I pour you a brandy?"

"Neat. No soda. Too damn cold. Prefer Egypt this time of the year."

"Does it hurt, dad?"

"A bit... Damn thing itches... Funny. You'd think when you cut off the damn thing it would stop itching. You going to do some shooting?"

"When it stops raining."

"Thank goodness Reggie put a new roof on the Hall."

"Let's hope Gerry doesn't knock it off again. Those doodle bugs don't differentiate between urban and rural areas. Just drop when the fuel runs out. Hell of a mess... Cheers."

"Chin-chin. Bring up that chair and poke the fire... How've you found the army?"

"So so."

"Not for you?"

"Not for me... I survive. Put on the right face. That kind of thing."

"We're all scared, Henry... I was."

"The secret is not to show it."

"That's the secret."

"Rosalyn's grown," said Henry.

"Soon they're grown up. She'll be five on the 23 March."

"She's not my daughter, you know?" he said, suddenly.

"What was that?"

"I wanted an heir as much as you did... Nothing seemed to happen. The depot doc, friend of mine. Ran some tests. Usual thing."

"How long have you known?" asked his father quietly.

"A year."

"Have you spoken to Isabel?"

"Does it matter...? Nothing can be changed. I don't know what I would have done if Rosalyn was a boy... As it is... Leave it. I can live with it. In many ways better to have a child that thinks you're their father than not to have one at all. Reggie's kids can inherit. He'll be potent."

"If he marries."

"There's Tug and Adam," said Henry.

"We'd better make sure that marriage was done properly. Right papers. Lot of fuss, otherwise. Have to be after the war. Remember that Henry, when you are the baronet. Don't want arguments in the family. That kind of thing could easily destroy the Hall."

"Do you think she will calm down in later years?"

"Who?"

"Isabel."

Sir Thomas sat back, his brandy on his belly, contemplating the fire before he spoke.

"They usually do, son," he said. "I've seen marriages start that way and end up very well. There are a lot of different years to be lived... Death duties won't hurt you," he said, changing the subject. "Reggie took care of that. I spoke to Chuck Everly when he was down in '41 after I came back from Egypt. Insured in America. Premiums up to date, that kind of thing. Everly's in the army. The last Pippa heard he was in North Africa. With de Gaulle's Free French. Americans support. She'd better make up her mind. There must be a lot of eligible girls in America. I like him. Honest. Enjoys himself."

"She doesn't want to leave England."

"In this life, you go where your husband takes you."

"Sometimes," said Henry, getting up. "Re-fill?"

"Thanks, my boy. Lucky to have a cellar. Best type of air raid shelter. Direct hit on that and the family's really pickled, what," and he laughed... Yes... Well... Pour me another... You can put some soda in it this time. Fire's damn hot since you gave it a poke... Do you know old Bert Brigley's turning seventy next week?"

"I didn't."

"Lucky he kept that Aga cooker. Cheapest way to warm a room."

"You think Tug got into the jungle?" asked Henry, sipping his drink.

"Of course he did, my boy."

"Shouldn't we have heard?"

"The jungle is a damn long way from Merry Hall. Cheers."

"Cheers."

"Try and enjoy your leave."

"It's not so easy when you know you've got to get back again."

"That bad?"

"Don't want to let the side down."

"You won't. Beaumonts don't let down the side."

"I hope not."

"Remember son. Everyone's just as scared as you, including the Germans. Now, tell me what you are going to do with the old Hall once this war is over. Bring up that chair. Sit down. We haven't had a good talk for many a year. Tell me what you're thinking son. Two heads can be better than one and you aren't going to have this one much longer," and he tried a bad laugh.

"Actually, I've lots of plans. Apart from the stud, that is," and he pulled the chair round and sat facing the fire with his father, his legs spread out, brandy in two hands, a long, stolid man with a grin on his face for the first time since coming home on leave. "The army leaves you plenty of spare time. Even in wartime. You sit around worrying, waiting to do the bit of fighting when they tell you... Oxford was good for a classical education but it didn't teach me much about farming. In the past we've relied upon paid staff and the tenant farmers, the old traditional methods... They're not good enough, dad. The Americans are mass producing food like they are aeroplanes and tanks. Scientific farming, they call it. Unless we modernise at Merry Hall, the land will cost us more than it's producing and in a few years we'll be selling off parcels of land to make ends meet. That's not my idea of being the next baronet. I want to do what you did. Take over something and hand it over to the next generation better than it started. It's the only way we can justify inheriting wealth. Land must be used to the maximum and if it isn't it should be handed over to someone else who will work it properly. First of all the estate is broken up into too many little fields and fifteen percent of our arable land is taken up with hedgerows and ditches."

"Drainage," said his father having given his son his full attention.

"There are modern ways of draining land. From underneath. You can grow crops, better crops on top and still drain properly from underneath. Of course it takes capital and I had a word with Reggie before he was a P.O.W. and he agrees with me and will put up the guarantee I need at the bank. Old Simmons doesn't mind lending if he knows Reggie will pay up if we default which we won't... Modern piggeries. We are just outside of London and transport costs are less... Trout in the River Mole. No-one's tried that before but it might just work if we clean the river and make it flow faster. Friend in the army has trout streams in Scotland... More game birds from better breeding methods. I have two books on that one. The Hall itself must be re-wired and the plumbing changed. Central heating. We can't afford wasted fuel and a log fire is the most wasteful way of heating a room. Most of the heat goes up the chimney.

"Tax. We must minimise tax. Reggie had a man called Bennett who's now in my unit. There are many expenses of the Hall that can be written off against farm and stud income. We'll get Bennett down here for a week's holiday. Give him some shooting... Experts. We need experts in every field. As I see it, there will no longer be gentlemen farmers and profitable farms will only be run as a business. Most important of all, I want to go to America. Everly's family are farmers. Not big themselves but they know big wheat farmers in Wisconsin, wherever that is in America. I want to go and see. Pick their brains. I want Merry Hall to make the largest profit per acre of any farm in Surrey and it can be done. The one thing I don't want to do is turn it into a show house for weekend trippers like Bedford is contemplating. Beaumonts have always lived at Merry Hall. They invite their friends. They don't charge people. Now if having paying guests isn't being common then I don't know what is. Then we come to the tenant farmers. They must be educated to the new farming methods and given the capital to modernise. Lionel Bennett suggests each of them form a private company to run the business of farming and we take up a part of their shares in exchange for capital. We also charge them a management fee for advice and accounting services. Bennett says if you don't know what you are making when you are making it there isn't much point in trying. Provided we increase the wealth of the tenants they'll be happy and they'll certainly be paying a lot less tax."

"Does Reggie know about this?"

"He's got his own business to run. I told him a bit. Bennett and I have spent hours talking in the desert. Smart man. Had the youngest C.A. in England, so Reggie told me."

"I won't have to worry about Merry Hall," said Sir Thomas gazing deep into the dancing flames and seeing himself as a young man with enthusiasm, energy and the will to change.

"No, dad. You won't… I just want this war over. It's so frustrating knowing what to do finally, and not being able."

"You'll have plenty of time, son… I wonder how Bert Brigley will take to it," he said, chuckling.

"He won't. But I spoke to Terry and he sees it my way. With the Brigleys in agreement the other tenants will follow. Lilly thinks it's a first-class idea. Lionel spoke to her… And everyone is going to need food after the war. We won't have any dollars to import the stuff from America."

"When did you talk to Bert's son?"

"In the desert. There were a lot of us in the Western Desert. They've made him a full corporal. Proud as a peacock of his two stripes. Wish I had him in my platoon even though there's nothing wrong with my own corporals," and his eye fixed on the pith hat his father had brought back with him form the North West Frontier, the one with the bullet hole in the top.

AT THE TIME Henry got up from the fire to pour his father a third brandy and soda, Captain Horoshini of the Japanese Imperial Army sat in a cane chair with his tubby legs apart and his knees showing below his army shorts. He was thoroughly enjoying himself and had been doing so for seven hours, meals and drinks brought to him as he wanted. He decided he would see this one out before he slept as his enjoyment was excruciatingly beautiful, his sadism more powerful than any woman or any pleasure he had known in the past. The person in front of him had once been a beautiful woman, had been only seven hours earlier, but she would never be very much again even if he stopped his treatment immediately. Resting his cold beer on his round little paunch he relaxed back in his cane chair but still kept his small, oriental eyes on the girl tied to the chair by one of the soldiers who stood behind, waiting his turn, the enjoyment for him more sexual than sadistic. Under his dirty jungle pants he still had a hard on but he knew from past experience that the Captain would only allow them to go on hitting the girl, admittedly wherever they liked and he had liked the big, brown breasts, and would not allow them the pleasure of rape, despite her total nakedness.

"Come along, Mrs Beaumont," said Horoshini in good but accented, sing-song English, caressing each word, "we know who you are. We know you speak English even as well as Captain Horoshini of the Japanese Army. We know you are Mr Tug Beaumont's wife and what we want to know is where he is and how you will take us to him or better, how you can bring him to us… How are your children, Mrs Beaumont? Have you heard from them? Australia is such a nice place to send them while you work for the British. Why did you work for them? We are both Orientals. We must hate the British. You must help us drive them further from the East. Speak to me Mrs Beaumont or I will ask that nice man behind you to hit you very hard and if then you say nothing we will kill you. But oh so very slowly. We will put a young bamboo shoot under your chair and water its growth up into your sexual parts and from there it will gently grow and break into your intestines and when it has grown enough it will kill you… But best of all, I will watch. The pain, they say, is so excruciating that you will scream and scream but it is never bad enough to make you faint. And Mrs Beaumont, I want to watch you really scream but before that you will tell me all about your radio and the whereabouts of your husband and Mr Gray. And you will want to tell me as you will want to die a lot quicker than I will let you, Mrs Beaumont."

FIVE MONTHS LATER, on the 3 August 1943, the British began to win the war against the Japanese in Burma and the guerrillas left behind in the Malayan jungle became active and the Japanese found that it was easier to conquer but impossible to subdue an unwilling enemy. There was too much jungle and too few Japanese.

At the time twenty-seven coolies left the jungle factory over a space of three hours for the coast, carrying with them a ton of the purest heroin, three miles away Tug Beaumont was seated at a long table in his jungle clearing with his fellow British officers. Two Malays sat with them and one Chinese who would translate should it become necessary. At the head of the trellis table sat Colonel Edward Gray. Everyone was in uniform and the British turnout was immaculate despite the damp jungle that rotted leather and curled the soles from army boots. The seats around the bottom of the table were empty. Some of the British officers had walked for a month for the meeting and if the Japanese had been able to find and penetrate the clearing they would have snuffed out the resistance movement in one blow and given them a much needed boost in the eyes of the local population. But even the three miles between the British and the very comfortable Perry Marshbank and Ping-Lai Ho was as far as the moon if you had to walk.

Tug looked up from his doodling, having drawn on his notepad the sweeping lines of *Windsong* under full sail, to see a group of scruffy Chinese and Malays being led in by an emaciated man in his early fifties who was wearing the floppy black shirt and baggy trousers of a Chinese peasant. As he walked over the baked clearing in his bare feet, Tug noticed the callouses and that half a big toe was missing. The man was walking with a swinging gait to compensate. There were fifteen in his party and the communists took their seats without saying a word, the man with the missing toe opposite the somewhat distant Colonel Gray. There was a glass and a full jug of water in front of each person with a notepad and two pencils properly sharpened. All British military conferences were handled in the same way. Above them stretched a camouflage netting, partly propped on bamboo poles that covered parts of the clearing. Over most of the huts and the netting grew the taller trees of the jungle that had been left when clearing the scrub. After a moment, Tug realised the man at the other end of the table was watching him with undisguised amusement and to Tug's surprise the face looking at him became vaguely familiar but it was only when the man began to talk in perfect English that he recognised the voice of Kim-Wok Ho and a brilliant smile creased Tug's face. Two hours later the British had agreed to arm the communist guerrillas against the Japanese and the well-ordered cadres that had been built up through labour movements in the rubber plantations would be brought into the war. Gray had shrugged to himself.

'If the Russian Communists can be armed by Roosevelt and Churchill who am I to stop a few guns to the Malayan Communists.'

"THEY'RE VERY GOOD," said Kim-Wok Ho with a glass of warm whisky in his hand as he walked round Tug's room after the conference looking at the paintings.

"There's nothing else to do here," said Tug. "For the last eighteen months we've been laying a foundation... Are you really a communist?"

"Yes. My father, you remember?"

"Was he alive?"

"Still is. Can't walk. They carry him around. Very well respected."

"And your brother?"

"Very well respected... What happened to my housekeeper?"

"Linda?" said Tug smiling.

"That was her name."

"At the moment she is in Australia, Melbourne. Living in a place called South Yarra with my children and her friend Sally. The girl who was your cousin's housekeeper."

"I know the one."

"Why didn't you let her know?" asked Tug.

"Who?" asked Kim-Wok Ho unwilling to admit that Linda was anything more to him than a housekeeper.

"Linda. When you didn't return she moved in with her friend Sally."

"The bastard," said Kim-Wok Ho.

"Who?" asked Tug innocently as if he didn't know.

"Ping-Lai Ho. He'd been after her ever since she came into my house."

"Was she a very good cook then?" asked Tug, thoroughly enjoying his friend's discomfort.

"You knew?"

"Singapore is too small for secrets. She counted you dead. The offer must have been good... Have another drink."

"Thank you. I haven't lost the taste."

"Why communism?"

"It took me months to find my father. Months afterwards to train with the peasants and then long months of walking and sometimes riding back to Singapore. Making the contacts. Building an infrastructure that will one day run Malaya. If the communists finally beat the nationalists in China that is. In that time I saw the real poverty of China. The total lack of any chance for their lives. The exploitation that had gone back over tens of thousands of years and enjoyed by my family for most of them. My father said it. The people deserve a chance. I think he says it because he thinks Mao will win. We have an old Chinese saying, 'When the wind blows, the reeds must bend.' You see, when the wind stops the ones who have bent, stand up again... My family wish to stand up again."

"Very sensible... An expedient communist."

"Expediency is often good business which is what we will be talking about when this war is over."

"Talk to Reggie... I'm leaving the East," said Tug.

"You've heard?" asked Kim-Wok Ho.

"Yes… Our information system is very good. We heard three weeks after that bastard killed her."

"Would you like your revenge?"

"What do you mean?"

"Let us go and kill him. There are junks sailing to Sarawak the Japanese know nothing about. Those boats nave been sailing the waters for centuries. No-one takes any notice. Let's you and I test this new alliance. It will be good for morale."

"We'll need twenty men. His camp has over a hundred soldiers."

"You've thought of it?"

"What else. Do you know how he killed her?"

"I've heard. Keep your hatred calm. Thirty men. Half of each."

"Do you think communism will help the peasants?"

"It definitely can't do them any harm. Your system gives any man a chance, however small. A man can dream of riches and he can find them if he has the guts. The warlords are worse than feudal Europe. Most of them have no interest in their peasants. Let Mao give it a chance. Nothing else has worked. The Middle Kingdom is too big for democracy. Too many people calling themselves Chinese. They must have discipline but not of a dictator."

"Isn't Stalin a dictator?"

"He has abused communism."

"Are not all systems abused if there isn't a system of checks? The Lords checked the British monarch and now the Commons checks the Lords and the people can chuck out the Commons."

"Your system has grown up over hundreds of years. You respect authority because it is rarely abused. Your policemen don't even carry guns. Very civil."

"There won't be any trading, in a communist China."

"There will always be trading. There will always be a profit. It will just be done a different way. A better way, I hope… What are you going to do after the war?"

"Paint. Go back to England. And you?"

"Take up my life again. Go back to business."

"But you're a communist:"

"I'll talk to Reggie about it," he said smiling. "I see a fine future."

"You haven't changed."

ON THE 6 JUNE 1944, by which time Perry Marshbank had run six tons of pure heroin into the United States and he and Ping-Lai Ho were looking forward to their return to Singapore when the Japs were forced to leave, the Americans, British and Canadian forces invaded Europe.

Inland, on the Leatherhead by-pass, Lorna, Beau, Raoul and Rosalyn aged ten, nine, eight and six waved enthusiastically at the armada of tanks and trucks and gun carriers that streamed past their vantage point close to the roundabout above Lorna's school. All the schools had been given the day off to watch.

Montgomery was leading the British back into Europe and Patton the Americans. Above the R.A.F. and American Air Forces hurled continual bombing raids across the English Channel, almost unchallenged by the Luftwaffe. In one of the transport aircraft the father of three of the children sat on his parachute on the floor of the stripped down Douglas Dakota along with the rest of a handpicked team from his L.R.U. They were the only troops not destined for the Normandy beaches or the immediate area behind.

"We're a long way from the Congo River," said Geoffrey Beaumont, "but this one won't be any worse."

"Do you think it will take as long, sir?" asked Wilf.

"A few months. Then we'll go back to peace time soldiering."

"Can't bloody wait," said Harry Sparrow putting a well chewed piece of American gum from one side of his face to the other.

"Hope them bleedin' Frogs is waitin'," said Wilf. "Can't use all these bleedin' guns ourselves even if we was to take on the whole German Army."

"They'll be there," said Dusty.

"We'll blow up every bleedin' supply line the Germans bleedin' thought of with the help of them Frogs."

"That's the idea," said Geoffrey politely trying not to smile at Wilf's simplicity. 'A bit more to it than that,' he said to himself, hoping that François would be there to meet him when he dropped out of the sky and not a German Panzer Division.

As the Dakota crossed the French coast a wave of British landing craft were approaching the coast of Normandy and Henry Beaumont was sitting up front against the closed door with the cold sea slapping violently on the other side as they pushed on through the swell. His full concentration was given to controlling his bowels and he ignored two of his men being violently sick into the bottom of the boat.

Chuck Everly's tank-landing craft was standing off from Omaha Beach and trying to get into its proper place to follow the waves of landing craft heading for the beach from the great fleet whose guns were pounding the German land positions with a constant arcing of shells that shrieked over Chuck's head as he looked up from the open turret of his tank.

"Nothing can live through that lot," he said to no-one in particular as the noise was too great for conversation.

Carl Priesler heard the news of the invasion on the eight o'clock news and delayed his departure for the newly constructed office in Fox Street by five minutes.

"Looks like the end of the war," he told Mafutha as he got into the back seat.

"Is that good or bad, baas?" asked Mafutha.

"Depends on which side you are," said Carl, waving to Megan who had come to the door to see him off to work.

Alice, Lady Beaumont, took her invalid husband's hand and squeezed it tight so that her fingernails cut into the palm of his hand.

"They'll be alright," said Sir Thomas. "I told you Tug was alright and you didn't believe me. This is the beginning of the end. I've never seen so many aircraft."

WITHIN THREE MINUTES of landing in the field behind the chateau, Geoffrey and Dusty linked up with the French Resistance and the worth of four years nurturing flowered across France behind the stretch of Normandy coast. At first the Germans thought they were being attacked on a second front. Simone, Danielle and François carried machine guns openly for the first time since joining the Resistance. The pent-up frustrations were being broken loose all round Geoffrey as he organised sabotage attacks across a ten-mile front, moving every hour on foot to confuse his position. Dusty was convinced he was thoroughly enjoying himself.

CHUCK'S TANK rolled off into the surf and trundled up to the beach traversing the one big gun and firing at will. To give himself a better view for command Chuck had his head out of the turret and used his field glasses to search out targets his gunners couldn't see from below.

"Seems like these guys don't like us," he observed and was pleased to get a dry chuckle back from his crew. "Next stop Berlin."

"THE LAST TIME we did this it was the other way round," said Henry referring to his ancestors' arrival in England on the beaches at Hastings. He was feeling totally confident. The ramp in front of him was winding down, ready to show him the enemy beaches and his pants were as dry as his mouth.

"I'll go first, sergeant."

"Very well, sir."

Using a sub-machine gun as his personal weapon, Henry led his platoon out into the surf between two markers put up especially by the Germans and as a result took a burst of heavy machine gunfire that stitched his chest and dropped him into the surf.

8

JULY 1946

*B*y three-thirty in the afternoon on the 29 July 1946, the old owl was thoroughly irritated. From early morning, cars had been passing along the road on the other side of the wood on their way up to Merry Hall. Two of them had backfired. Having been cheated of sleep he looked out of the hole in the elm tree and up at the top of the tallest oak. With considerable effort he fell out and slowly flapped his great wings up to the topmost perch. Blinking rapidly in the unaccustomed sunlight he looked around to see what was happening. The tall clusters of Queen Anne chimneys rose from different levels of the Hall over among the trees. Ducking a bit, the owl made out in the distance a row of white clothed tables running the length of the terrace.

A small sports car rushed down the narrow country lane making a lot of noise. The car changed gears and started up the driveway. From the tennis court came the 'tonk' of a mixed doubles and a 'good shot, Geoffrey' and shortly after a 'I can't, I can't' and 'never thought she'd get to that one.'

Opening his wings to stretch himself, the owl embraced the countryside and its Hall and then folded them back again with a ruffle and cocked an ear at the couple he could see getting out of the sports car. The girl had a beautiful laugh as she disappeared among the oaks, hand in hand with the man.

"ISN'T THAT AN OWL," said Angus Montel, coming out onto the veranda, pinging the strings of his tennis racket on his knee.

"Can't be," said Reggie unscrewing the clamp from the tennis racket. "They don't come out during the day."

"That's an owl, old boy."

"Where?"

"On top of that oak tree. There he goes."

"Good lord. Never seen that before in daylight… Geoffrey's taking a long time," said Reggie.

"The American's good," said Angus. "We'll have to put in a tennis court."

"Where?" asked Reggie.

"Bought a house in Sussex. Used to belong to the family. The old pater's tickled pink. Not often the family can afford to buy back what they've lost. First time for fifty years."

"Much ground?"

"Five hundred."

"Farm them?"

"Not really. Bit of shooting. That kind of thing."

"Not staying in the Fleet Air Arm?"

"Not anymore, old boy. No need."

"Of course," said Reggie. "Pippa's better than Georgina. Did you see that shot…? Big house?"

"Paid back the old pater. Tickled him pink. Took to Linda immediately didn't he, darling."

"Immediately."

"You look jolly good in tennis gear, old girl," said her husband as he put his hand under her elbow to lead her down to the lawn and the tennis court where the mixed doubles had ended in British victory.

"Nearly got us," said Geoffrey.

"Is he really coming?" said Linda to Reggie.

"He'll arrive. Flew in from Hong Kong last week. Plenty of business to talk about on Monday. Do you prefer the backhand or forehand court?" he said turning to a well- groomed Sally Bollas whose long legs even Reggie found distracting.

"My backhand's awful."

"Settled then… How did they beat you, Chuck?"

"Geoffrey's fit."

"Shows what happens when you stay in the army," said Geoffrey.

"I'd prefer to get fat again," said Tug.

"All to their taste," said Geoffrey walking past holding his wife's hand. "The balls are on court. I'll put money on the Air Force."

"Navy," said Angus confidently. "Linda is far too good."

"We'll see," said Sally, thoroughly enjoying herself.

CARL PRIESLER HAD PUT on weight with his prosperity and it did not suit him well. The big, strong frame of his days at Oxford with Reggie, Gunter and François had turned to rolls of fat and his chin oozed down past his neck as he watched Mafutha take round a tray of glasses for lemonade with a tall, cut-crystal jug, pouring the ice-filled liquid as expertly as Pavy. The fez was on top of his black, tight-curled hair but the leopard skins, brought over specially, had been left for later.

"Born to it," said Carl.

"What?" asked Chuck lowering himself into a deckchair.

"Mafutha… Marvellous butler. Very regal. Royal blood. Zulu."

"Really?"

"Absolutely. Grandfather's mother's brother was an uncle of Shaka."

"Who's he?"

"Warrior king... Wiped them all out," he said frowning as Megan walked away from the lawn and down the path. Deliberately he pulled his gaze away and continued to study the length of Sally Bollas's legs. "Bloody marvellous."

"No chance, there," said Chuck, following his gate. "Looking for a title. Very rich lady."

"Didn't want to marry her... Gunter definitely not coming?"

"Reggie's upset," said Chuck.

"Probably right. Someone might be rude."

"He's sick... That camp was a horror. He wants to forget the war. Said no-one won. Told Reggie no-one had anything to celebrate and Reggie got annoyed. Said we all had something to celebrate. The fact we came through alive. Gunter's coming Stateside for treatment. Take him up the mountains. Get him away... Maybe you should get him out to Africa. Safari or something. Fresh air. Sunshine. Just the thing to get that smell out of his nose. Can't get it out of mine and I just visited the place."

"Where's his wife?"

"At her father's schloss. On her own."

"Divorce?"

"No... They wanted to charge her. Interfering with minors. Bad business. The baron got the authorities to leave her in the schloss provided she is alone with male servants. No-one visits. Birgitt's terrified of going to jail. She thinks not divorcing Gunter will help make them drop charges... Gunter's just cut her out of his mind... She'll go daft in that great house on her own. Some kind of punishment."

"How'd they find out?"

"Seven sets of parents laid charges."

"What about their daughters' reputations?"

"That was the baron's argument. Maybe the daughters enjoyed it. Wily old bastard. Richer after the war despite losing and with the Marshall Plan he'll make a fortune."

"Gunter won't be poor," said Carl.

"Neither will we. That patent's worth a fortune. Had two of the rubber companies trying to buy it. Want to sit on it. Who wants cheap tyres if you're selling expensive ones?"

"I'll have him over to my game farm," said Carl. "Banks of the Sable River. Lowveld. Beautiful. We'll get our minds back to being young and enjoying ourselves. Maybe lose some weight. How did you lose so much, Chuck?"

"Joined the U.S. Army."

"I missed all that."

"You missed nothing, buddy."

"It's very good," said Lilly.

"Thank you," said Tug, not turning round.

"Mathilda's still in the shed," said Lilly.

"Are the memories bad?"

"No. Very good. I had the best of him. While we were married he was mine... That island was beautiful."

"Is Reggie going ahead?"

"No. Without Tony it wouldn't work. A woman can't run a casino and professional managers can't be trusted. Reggie's putting up a small house for the likes of you and me… I like the fox."

"Must have a focal point. He lives here. Seen him a few times. What are you going to do?"

"Live. Help run the business with Thelma. And you?"

"Penzance. Cornwall. Fisherman's cottage. Paint all day and sleep all night."

"The children?"

"My mother. Takes her mind off my father. He's sinking fast. Won't last the week. Got to his seventy years and doesn't feel cheated… Adam will go to prep school. Weekly boarder. Same with Tammany. Merry Hall's a wonderful place to grow up in. You know that."

"Yes."

"How do you like their accents?"

"Fair dinkum."

"They were in Australia for four years. They want to go back. Friends."

"They'll make more. They have each other. She's as pretty as her mother, Tug. I was looking at your portrait of her in the old hall."

"She never told the bastard a thing. I was going to kill him the same way but couldn't stoop to his level. Shot him along with a couple of corporals who'd helped. It's amazing how many people tell you things when you're holding a gun."

"Is there a grave?"

"No. They just threw her in the river."

"Will you marry again?"

"I need a lot of time on my own."

"What will you live on?"

"I bought paintings. Kept them in the basement of 51 King William Street. Don't you remember the Gauguins in Reggie's office?"

"Yes."

"They belonged to me. I've sold two. Enough to put Adam and Tammany through school. Reggie said he'd pay but he can't pay for everything. Now that he's going to inherit the Hall and the baronetcy, he'll need all his money."

"He's going to make it pay. Dad told me. Reggie will have Merry Hall making a perfectly good return on capital once he's finished with Henry's ideas. Lionel Bennett's coming in as an advisor."

"Come and visit me when I'm settled, Lilly," said Tug.

"I'd like that. I'll bring the children."

"On your own."

"We'll both have to think a long time about that one."

"Maybe, maybe not… Do you think the fox has the right kind of cunning in his look?"

On their way to the river, Megan waved as they passed Tug and Lilly, Megan taking two steps for every one of Dusty's who still found it difficult not to take the regulation step. He also found it uncomfortable wearing civilian clothes but Geoffrey had told him that uniforms were not permitted at Merry Hall and he had gone off to a recommended tailor and had himself run up the requisite blazer with the regimental badge and a very smart, dark suit. They came to the river and sat on the trunk of a tree watching the water flow past. There were six of Bert Brigley's cows on the other side of the water that looked up but continued to chew.

"Corporal Kemp doesn't like being a corporal," he said for something better to say.

"Doesn't he?"

"No."

The silence continued as the humans watched the cows. A kingfisher, bright in all its colours, dived down at the minnows from a bush on the river bank.

"I've resigned my commission."

"You were doing well," said Megan.

"I went to Rhodesia House in the Strand and put my name down."

"What for?" said Megan, knowing perfectly well.

"A crown land farm. Ex-servicemen. Seven and sixpence an acre payable five years later, provided you have some cash and the knowledge to grow tobacco. My gratuity will help and once I'm a farm manager there'll be bonuses. The man at Rhodesia House said the bonus can be as much as five thousand pounds… Three thousand acres. More than this whole estate. Big enough to build a house and see nobody's chimney smoke. But you know that… Near Umvukwes. It's to coincide with the centenary of Cecil Rhodes. The Centenary Block. Haven't you heard? Once they've shot the game out and got rid of the tsetse fly it'll grow the best crops in Africa. Many rivers. Sweet water. Rolling hills, they say it's just right for tobacco. Light sand-veld whatever that is. Officially the block opens in '53 but they'll let us on sooner and I'll need a few years to get the experience… Why are you crying, Meg?"

"You sounded like Martin. That was all he ever wanted. A farm so big he couldn't see another man's chimney smoke."

"I got that feeling for space first in the Congo. Do you have it?"

"Yes."

"Did you want that farm?"

"Yes."

"Why not have it with me?"

"What about Carl?"

"What about him? Do you want to marry him?"

"Not anymore."

"We'll be poor."

"Grandfather will help."

"Why don't we get married in that church you can see from Merry Hall? The Beaumonts built it. I owe a lot to Geoffrey Beaumont."

"Whatever you want."

"You will?"

"If you still want me?"

"We'll have lots of children."

"Maybe a couple."

"Have the biggest farm in Africa."

"Maybe 5,000 acres."

"Found a dynasty in Africa."

"I hoped you weren't dead. I was so lonely. Dad away. Poor dad. They didn't even give him a medal."

"To be recommended for a Victoria Cross is a great honour."

"What a waste of a life."

"We must give him grandchildren. Replace his life with others."

"I like that Dusty."

CARL PRIESLER WATCHED them come back, arm in arm.

"You win some, you lose some," he said.

"What are you saying?" asked Chuck.

"Priesler's back in the bachelor business," and he nodded at Dusty and Megan.

"Oh."

"Now, I'd really better lose some weight. What do you think I should give them for a wedding present?"

"Wish them a good life. Excuse me, there's Pippa. She wanted to change out of her tennis dress."

"Go for it, buddy. You seem to have a lot more sense than me," but Chuck didn't hear as he was on his way up the steps to the veranda where Pippa was talking to her mother.

"Do you want any help with the arrangements?" asked Chuck when he joined them.

"I think we are organised," said Lady Hensbrook. "One hundred guests for supper and another two hundred afterwards. I do hope that band arrives."

"Stop worrying, mother," said Pippa, "of course they will, won't they Chuck?"

"Sure they will. Even if I have to use Reggie's new plane to go fetch them."

"You were in tanks?" said Lady Hensbrook.

"Aeroplanes before that, ma'am."

"Well, I never. A man full of surprises," and Chuck was about to open his mouth when Pippa gently shook her head and smiled. Surreptitiously she took his hand.

"WELL," said Lady Hensbrook, surveying the main kitchen. "I have never seen so much food. Not even before the war."

"Mrs Breed has excelled herself," agreed Lady Beaumont leading her into the large pantry with the stone topped tables running for fifty feet either side of the low ceilinged room.

"Bless my soul. More food."

"Ah, the oysters," said Lady Beaumont, taking off the top of a three-foot carrel that was crammed with unopened oysters driven up that morning from Cornwall. "The only reason I come down here is not to check up on Mrs Breed but to make myself thoroughly hungry."

"Look at those lobsters," said Lady Hensbrook.

"Better go and check the place settings in order of precedence, I've had to put Lord Gray next to you and his wife opposite you on Reggie's left. Then comes Lord Migroyd and I."

"Dreadful creature. The woman, I mean. Migroyd's alright, bit pompous... How can they possibly have made Gray a baron?"

"Labour government," said Lady Beaumont, "but Tug says he did an excellent job."

"I don't mind him so much," said Lady Hensbrook, "but he should have been more careful when he chose his wife. Do we have plenty of wine, Alice? I shall need it."

"Pavy is tasting the bottles."

"How many?"

"A hundred I believe."

"Poor man. He'll be as drunk as a Lord."

"Tastes and spits. Rather vulgar."

"Thank goodness. Better have Pavy keep my glass filled. I shall consider it duty, Alice."

"The children can have the chicken. Children like chicken. Mrs Breed has made armfuls of jelly. I was convinced Raoul would topple out of that fir tree."

"Small boys bounce," said Lady Hensbrook. "Rosalyn doesn't miss her mother."

"Best thing to go. Family can't afford scandal… Sorry, my dear."

"Men are blind when they want to be."

"Reggie was very generous. Good allowance. Flat in Mayfair. I think he gave her a good talking to… Anyway, we haven't seen her for three months and the Hall is returning to normal. l just know the servants were talking behind my back. Thomas hopes she finds someone to marry. Old age is not so pleasant alone."

"We have the children."

"And the Hall. We were just lucky to have so many children. Even if we do lose some of them… Everything looks perfect," she said as she took a last look round the kitchen.

"AH, BILLY," said Reggie, having trounced the Navy at tennis. "How are you enjoying Beaumonts?"

"Fine, sir. I had no idea how diversified you had become. Did you win your game?"

"No problem. Lord Angus was more interested in my partners' legs than the ball."

"I heard he's just married."

"Doesn't stop him looking. How is your mother?"

"Lonely. Otherwise well. I've built a new *Wavedancer* but she won't come out. What can I do, Mr Beaumont?"

"Be kind. She's lucky to have you… I wrote down my plan for you. Miss King will give you a copy on Monday. A year in London and then out to America with Mr Everly. When it comes to selling, marketing they call it, they are years ahead of us. They have treated business as a science… Then Australia. We must have a strong company in Sydney. After that Hong Kong. Mr Ho has joined us as a full partner and will be running the Far East interests but he wants to centre in Hong Kong. Nearer mainland China. He has contacts. If the communists win as he expects, they will still have to trade with the capitalists. Your next stop will be Johannesburg to understand the true source of our wealth. Gold, diamonds. Mr Priesler will introduce you to the Mining Camp. Finally, France and Germany. The Marshall Plan is throwing billions of dollars into the rebuilding of Europe. A growth centre. Business must boom. After that I want you to return to the U.S.A. and take an M.B.A. at Harvard."

"How long will this all take?"

"Five years. How did your mother find the investiture?"

"The King spoke to her for a whole minute."

"I'm glad they gave him the George Cross."

"WHO IS SHE?" asked Simone in the banquet room.

"Tug's wife," said François answering her in French.

"Is she here?"

"No."

"She is very beautiful. Who did the painting?"

"Tug. You can see his signature in the right hand corner."

"I know many painters in Paris. None this good. Where is she?"

"Killed by the Japanese."

"Why did they kill someone so beautiful?"

"I don't know my little one. Why do they kill anyone? Why did we?"

"Because we had to."

"Maybe."

"Who are all these old people?"

"The ancestors. The Beaumonts have lived here for almost nine hundred years."

"This room is so big. Can you imagine the rent?"

"Yes," smiled François.

"Who is the baronet?"

"Sir Thomas. He's upstairs… Dying."

"How sad. Is he very old?"

"He wouldn't say so."

"He won't be at the party?"

"No. But he'll hear it all. They've moved him to one of the front rooms overlooking the terrace."

"How terrible to hear your own party and not be able to join in. Oh, are they giving us a room to ourselves or will we have to share it with other people. I don't mind but it would be nice to be on our own," she giggled.

"We have our own. Right at the top."

"An attic?" she asked excitedly.

"Something like that. It looks out over the woods and fields."

"Oh, isn't that lovely?"

"Yes… Like you… Will you marry me?"

"That is sudden."

"Not really."

"And who are you going to be when we marry?"

"Who do you prefer?"

"Oh, The Thief. Definitely. You can make all the money you want playing the violin and if we ask Danielle I'm sure she'll let us have the attic to ourselves. And in the summer we can go down to our forest and you can catch rabbits and I'll make the rabbit stews just how you like them. I'll always remember to put barley in it and lots of carrots… This place is very old. Can't you smell it?"

"Yes. Don't you want to live in a chateau? Have money. Lots more fine dresses. Have our children go to the best schools. Servants. Big parties like this one. Never to have to worry about rent or where your next meal is coming from?"

"No. I met The Thief not François Deauville. It came as a great shock to find you weren't a thief. Our lives will be much more fun on the Left Bank even if the painters aren't as good as Tug. Anyway, our children will enjoy it a lot more."

"Couldn't you bring up children in this house?"

"Don't be silly. It's far too big. I'd never find them. How can you live in a family that is always getting lost?"

"You must be serious."

"Oh, but I am. I bet these people don't know where half the rooms are. How many rooms are there anyway?"

"I don't know."

"There you are… How did that man get fat?"

"Which one?"

"The one watching tennis. He waved to you?"

"Didn't you recognise him?"

"With all that fat and belly it would be difficult to recognise anyone."

"Carl. Carl the painter. The one Danielle always talks about."

"What about him?"

"He waved to me on the lawn."

"Don't be silly, I'd have seen him."

"The fat man is Carl. He's also my partner."

"How awful… You mean that nice man became like that?"

"Yes."

"That settles it. He'd better come and live in the attic for six months."

"I can't let down my partners."

"You can either let them down or me. All I hear about rich people frightens me to death. None of our friends are fat. Terribly uncomfortable. Rabbit stews without barley. That would fix him. Has he got a wife?"

"No."

"Well, I must say, that doesn't surprise me. Don't tell Danielle. Break her heart. She's never fallen for anyone like the painter before or after and a lot of men have tried. Where does he live?"

"In Africa."

"Well, that is something. She won't have much chance of meeting him there. Who else is your partner?"

"There's a German and a Chinaman you haven't met."

"A German!"

"He was imprisoned by the Gestapo."

"Is he Jewish?"

"No."

"Why then?"

"Because he was my friend. My partner."

"I don't like Germans."

"Most of them are like you or me."

"Then why were we fighting."

"They don't know either."

"Well then, that's plain silly."

"Yes. It is."

"Can we go, now?"

"Do you want to see the room?"

"No. Let's go home. Paris. Danielle. All our friends. They'll be so excited."

"We must stay for the party," said François. "These are also my friends. Good friends. You will also find them good when you know them. What about Geoffrey?"

"He is a good man. Very brave."

"And Captain Miller?"

"Dusty is brave."

"So, may not the others be the same? Am I so different as François Deauville?"

"No… Not really… Not when we are on our own."

"Couldn't you get used to François Deauville?"

"I could try, I suppose."

"I'll try not to change. And we can make rabbit stew in the forest."

"Won't the owner mind, now the war is over?"

"I don't think so. I'll ask him?"

"Do you know the owner?"

"Very well."

"Who is he then?"

"Me. The big chateau when you come out on the old road is where I was born. Where we'll live when we are not in Paris."

"Are you very rich?" asked Simone in awe, putting her hand up to her mouth.

"Yes. Very rich. But it won't make the slightest difference."

"How rich is very rich?"

"I told you before but you said no-one could earn ten million francs a month. But that was a long time ago. Since then it's all grown a bit."

"Now I don't know what to believe."

"Will you believe I want to marry you?"

"My mother was a prostitute."

"So what?"

"Do you know? The old seaman would have liked you. Yes, he would."

"I'm glad."

"If he hadn't I wouldn't marry you," and she laughed and took him by the hand glancing sideways at the full length portrait of Tammany as she led him out into the sun.

"WHO ON EARTH IS THAT ARRIVING?" said Lady Hensbrook turning her attention away from the men's singles between Reggie and Geoffrey.

"He'll never make a good communist," chuckled Tug as he followed her gaze and saw his friend being let out of a Rolls-Royce in all his glory of electric blue and huge red dragons, his drooping moustache now grown to a comfortable six inches on either side of his face. Tug waved as he got up and Kim-Wok Ho raised both of his arms, flourishing the whole pattern of dragons. Lady Beaumont watched her son's beaming smile, the first she had seen since he had arrived back from Australia with the children.

"Mr Kim-Wok Ho, Lady Hensbrook," said Tug.

"You do have unusual friends, Tug."

"Yes. But he's not really so unusual when you get to know him. Will you excuse me?"

"My goodness," said Lady Beaumont watching Kim-Wok Ho. "He's even got Pavy bowing and scraping all over the place."

"He has that way with him," said Tug, walking up the lawn.

"FIREWORKS!" said Linda watching the rockets burst over Merry Hall as the church clock struck midnight five hours later.

"Very civilised," said Kim-Wok Ho.

"A lovely ballroom."

"Yes."

"So many people," said Linda.

"I need fresh air."

"Not as hot as Singapore."

"No. Where's Reggie going?" asked Linda.

"A beautiful girl walked out earlier. She's standing alone under the oak tree."

"I wonder who she is?"

"A beautiful girl… Congratulations."

"Thank you."

"It couldn't all have been my money?" said Kim-Wok Ho.

"No. Some… And thank you."

"Ping-Lai Ho?"

"Yes."

"His paintings?"

"Sold very well in America."

"I'll bet they did," chuckled Kim-Wok Ho. "He'll be as mad as a snake."

"He is a snake," said Linda.

"Do you want to go inside?"

"You must find yourself a Chinese wife. Have children," she said taking his arm.

"You sound like my father," said Kim-Wok Ho looking up from the lawn at the floodlit house full of people and happiness.

ENJOYED BEND WITH THE WIND?

~

If you enjoyed reading my book, *Bend with the Wind*, and have a moment to spare, I would really appreciate a short review at your favorite online retailer. Your help in spreading the word is gratefully received.

PRINCIPAL CHARACTERS

The Beaumonts

Sir Philimore — Sir Thomas's cousin

Sir Thomas — descendant of Sir Henri Beaumont and heir to Sir Philimore Beaumont

Lady Alice — wife of Sir Henri Beaumont

Henry — eldest son of Sir Thomas Beaumont

Reggie — second eldest son of Sir Thomas Beaumont

Tug — third eldest son of Sir Thomas Beaumont

Geoffrey — youngest son of Sir Thomas Beaumont

Beau, Lorna and Raul — Geoffrey's children

Pavy — Butler to the Beaumont family

Doris Breed — Cook to the Beaumont family

Claud — Lady Alice's brother

John — Claud's son

The de La Rivières

Baron Hensbrook — family friend of the Beaumont's

Georgina — youngest daughter of Baron Hensbrook

Isabel — third daughter seventh Baron Hensbrook wife to Henry Beaumont

Gwenneth — youngest daughter of Baron Hensbrook

Philippa — youngest daughter of Baron Hensbrook

The Brigleys

Bert — tenant farmer on the Merry Hall Estate

Martha — wife of Bert Brigley

Lilly — daughter of Bert and Martha Brigley

Terry — son of Bert and Martha Brigley

Reggie Beaumont's Friends and Associates
Thelma King — Reggie's secretary
"The Freebooters" François Deauville, Gunter von Ribbeck and Carl Priesler — business partners of Reggie
Lord Migroyd — a business associate and chairman of Union Mining
Tony Venturas — a Lebanese owner of Bretts nightclub and business partner
Sally Bollas — Hostess at Bretts nightclub and friend of Lilly Brigley
Lionel Bennett — Reggie's accountant
Percy Hudson — Reggie's bank manager
Billie Hudson — Percy Hudson's son
Koos van der Walt — Manager of Union Mining
Chuck Everly — American business associate of Reggie's
Penny and Claire — Hostesses at Bretts

Geoffrey Beaumont's Long Range Unit
Dusty Miller
Captain Jim Forrester
Private Wilf Kemp, Corporal Harry Sparrow, Private Stew Philpott

The Singaporean Set
Perry Marshbank — Tug's best friend and District Commissioner for Rejong district of Sarawak
Edward Gray — First Officer of Kuching
Rebecca Gray — Edward Gray's wife
Kim Wok-Ho — Very rich Chinese business man; Reggie's friend and business partner
Ping-Lai Ho — Kim Wok-Ho's cousin
Linda — Kim-Wok Ho's English housekeeper
Lieutenant Lord Angus Montel — Sunderland pilot and son of the Duke of Surrey
Freddy Gore — Friend of Angus Montel

The Rhodesians
Major Gerald Escort — Liaison officer for the Southern Rhodesian army
Megan Strong — Gerald Escort's daughter

Minor Characters
Birgitt — wife of Gunter
Bertie Featherstone — friend of Sir Thomas from India days
Rajah Brooke — Charles Vyner Brooke, the third and last White Rajah of Sarawak
Jean-Pierre Agier — Francois's stepfather

GLOSSARY

∼

Bosch — Also spelt Boche, a derisive term used by the French meaning 'the Germans'

Chotapeg — A half-sized drink especially of whiskey or whiskey and soda

CIF — Cost, Insurance and Freight

Copper Belt — An area in Northern Rhodesia now Zambia

LRU — Long Range Unit

Marshall Plan — The Marshall Plan was an American initiative to aid Europe, in economic support to help rebuild European economies after the end of World War II.

NAAFI — An organisation created by the British government in 1921 to run recreational establishments needed by the British Armed Forces

UME — Union Mining and Exploration

Printed in Great Britain
by Amazon